Ladies of England Novelist.

THE

PRIDE OF THE VILLAGE;

OR, THE

FARMER'S DAUGHTERS.

BY HANNAH MARIA JONES,

AUTHORESS OF "THE GIPSEY MOTHER," "EMILY MORELAND," &c., &c., &c.

"YOUNG LADIES OF ENGLAND" OFFICE, 145, FLEET STREET.

THE PRIDE OF THE VILLAGE;

OR,

THE FARMER'S DAUGHTERS.

CHAPTER I.

"She had a form ; but I might talk till night,

*   *   *   *   *

Ere I had told its beauties !—It was slight,
Even as yon willow, and like its soft stem,
Fell into thousand motions, and all lovely !
But for her cheek—look on those streaks of rose,
Tinting the white clouds o'er us !"

ANON.

IT was at the close of a fine day in June, one thousand eight hundred and
————, that a carriage and four, with outriders and postilions in handsome
liveries—with all indeed that could betoken the possessor a person of rank
affluence—drove up to the door of the principal inn in the small town of
T————, in Gloucestershire. It had been, as we have already said, a fine
day ; but it was more, it was the evening of the Sabbath—that blessed
interval of rest, for the toil-worn artisan—of enjoyment, for those who find

their best pleasure in the exercise of their duties—and of peace and quietude to all.

The religious observances of the day had closed; and while the elder folks were gathered together, to enjoy the beauties of the setting sun, and breathe the cool fragrance of the evening breeze in the porches of their doors, or at their casements, garlanded with honey suckles and jasmines, the younger were collected in small groups, either at the garden gates, or on the green which ornamented the centre of the village.

The arrival of such a gay equipage in this sequestered spot, of course, superseded every other topic of conversation, and engrossed the attention of every eye and ear among the simple villagers. The young men quitted their fair partners, to approach the objects of their curiosity; and the girls gathering closer together, by turns gave utterance to their conjectures, or their admiration of the splendid carriage, the bright bays, or the showy liveries of the attendants.

"There is only one gentleman in it," said a young man, approaching a knot of girls, who looked anxiously to him for information, "and he looks so yellow, and sickly, and discontented, and spoke so ill-temperedly to his servant, that in spite of all his riches and finery, I felt I did not envy him."

"Not envy him, William Mansel;" exclaimed a beautiful girl, who had stood hitherto silent; "not envy him!" she repeated with animation; ": heavens, how can you talk so foolishly! "

William Mansel coloured with vexation.

"It may be foolish in your eyes, Miss Woodford; but I say it again—it riches and distinction could be purchased, by my exchanging with that unhappy-looking man, I would sooner remain what I am—a plain farmer's son."

Maria Woodford, however, heard not, or attended not, to his reply to her exclamation, for she at that moment discovered that the envied possessor of the elegant equipage, having entered the best parlour at the inn, was now busily employed in scrutinising, with the help of his eye-glass, the different groups who were assembled in front of it; and totally regardless of William's angry surprise at her inattention, the conscious beauty immediately drew aside from her companions, so conspicuously to display her elegant figure, and with an affected air of negligence, which strongly contrasted with the undisguised rustic curiosity of her mates who still stood staring at the carriage, from which the horses were now unharnessing; she contrived to approach near enough to the window of the room, to give its inhabitant a full view of a face which she was conscious could not be beheld without admiration.

"Where are you going, Maria?" demanded a mild, pale, gentle-looking girl, who hastily followed her; "have you forgotten that we promised to be home at nine; and that William Mansel and his brother are waiting to ———"

"You may go with them, if you like, Grace; but I am not in such a hurry, and if William does not choose to stay my time, I can find somebody, I dare say, to see me home," said Maria, casting another glance at the window; and observing, with inward exultation, that the person whom her fancy had invested with, at least, the rank of a nobleman, if not of royalty itself, had now raised the sash, and was leaning eagerly forward to catch, as she flattered herself, a nearer view of her unrivalled attractions.

"How can you be so captious and unjust, Maria?" returned her sister; "William, I am sure, would do anything to please you; and only a few minutes ago you were yourself anxious to go home."

"I have altered my mind, then," said Maria petulantly; "but I wish you would not teaze me so, Grace. I don't hinder you from going home, if you want to go;" and without waiting for, or seeming to expect an answer, she threw herself, in a studied attitude, on the rude wooden bench which surrounded a large walnut-tree, exactly opposite to the window which now engrossed all her thoughts, and drawing her glove off from one of the whitest and most beautifully-formed hands that nature ever moulded, she began playing with a dog, which was fawning upon her.

For a moment Grace regarded her with surprise, and in silence; but, by degrees, the motives of her sister's at first inexplicable conduct were revealed, by the furtive glances which the latter from time to time threw towards the inn-window; and, uttering a deep sigh, Grace walked away, to endeavour to soften to William Mansel Maria's refusal to accede to his wishes.

"You need not try to disguise it, Grace," said the impetuous youth, his manly cheek crimsoning with vexation, at his own disapointment and shame, at the versatile conduct of the capricious beauty,. who held his senses in a bondage which his reason contemned. "I know your kind heart, Grace, induces you to make excuses for your sister; but this is not the first time that I have seen her so led away by her love for show and finery that——"

"Hush, hush, William, I will not hear *you* condemn her," interrupted Grace, placing her slender hand on his lips. "Come with me," she continued, drawing him playfully along, " and try whether she will not yield to your persuasions."

William did but half resist the gentle force with which she seconded this request, though he replied, in a tone of despondency——

"No, no, Grace; I know very well she will not listen to me until her present fit of vanity and ambition is over." And they were already close behind the tree, which concealed the fair object of their solicitude, when William suddenly started, and uttered an exclamation, which made Grace let go his arm in horror—while she eagerly demanded what was the matter.

William did not reply, but her eye followed his fixed indignant glance, until it rested on the countenance of the stranger, who was now seated by the side of Maria; and while his admiring looks were fixed with rapture on her lovely face, the confidence of his tone, and the easy familiarity of his attitude seemed to feel that he was conferring an honour on the village beauty by thus singling her out as the object of his attention.

"By heavens! I won't bear this!" exclaimed William, "if he is the first peer in the land;" and without attending to Grace's frightened exclamation, he darted forward to Maria's side.

"It is quite time for you to return home, Miss Woodford; he observed, in a voice trembling with emotion, and seizing at the same time her hand with no gentle grasp.

"You need not be so rough, William," said the half-terrified, half-indignant maiden, hastily releasing her hand, but at the same time rising from her seat, as if to show her readiness to obey him.

"Your brother, I presume, fair lady," whispered the stranger, throwing at the same time a scrutinizing glance of observation over the athletic form, and manly features of the young rustic, who, bold and determined as he felt himself in this cause, nevertheless shrank with somewhat of confusion from the cool supercilious look of his opponent.

"No, sir," replied Maria, "he is not my brother, nor indeed any relation to me."

"Indeed," returned the stranger, who detected immediately in her reply a lurking desire to be rid of the intruder; "may, then, I inquire by what right this young man claims——"

"It cannot concern you, sir to know," interrupted William, in an angry tone; "but Miss Woodford is well aware that her father expects me to see her home."

"Perhaps, young man, Miss Woodford's father would be equally satisfied to see her under the protection of any other friend," returned the stranger coolly, "or are you alone considered worthy of such a valuable trust?"

"Oh, no, indeed," observed Maria, whose dread of William's anger was fast evaporating, on finding that the stranger was inclined to become her champion; "my father does, indeed, regard him as a neighbour's son, but my mother——"

"Do not say a word of your mother, Maria; it is your mother's folly that has made you what you are, but I have done with you." And without bestowing another look on her, he vaulted over the low fence which divided the green on one side from a narrow secluded lane, and disappeared in a moment.

"Dear Maria, what have you done to William?" exclaimed Grace, who had timidly stood aloof during the preceding altercation. "Will he not come back to see us home," continued the anxious girl, gazing in the direction he had taken.

"Do not be alarmed, dear," said the stranger, "I will myself see you home."

"You, sir," exclaimed Grace, looking earnestly at him; "oh dear, no, I should be very sorry to trouble you to walk three miles, for you don't look as if——"

Maria gave her an impatient pull by the arm, which prevented the conclusion of her speech.

"Three miles," repeated the gentleman, "good heavens! surely you do not intend to walk so far to-night?"

"We have no choice," said Maria, faintly, "though, indeed, it is a terrible long walk."

"Dear me, I am excessive sorry," said the gentleman, looking about as if in search of an alternative; "my horses, too, are unfortunately quite knocked up, or I would have had the felicity of offering you a conveyance."

"Oh, it is of no consequence, sir; I beg you will not think of it," said Maria, whose beautiful blue eyes sparkled even at the bare idea that there existed a possibility of her entering that elegant carriage, which the grooms were now busily washing.

The stranger caught the expression of those brilliant orbs, as they dwelt with regret on the equipage.

"If I could prevail on you to prolong your stay for an hour or two," he commenced; but Grace decidedly interrupted him.

"No, sir, not for five minutes!" she observed, in a firm tone. "We have already lingered too long;" and drawing her sister's arm through hers, she slightly curtsied to the stranger, and turned away.

"You must not leave me thus," said the stranger, interposing, "though my unlucky stars prevented my having the honour I covet to-night, you must, at least, allow one of my servants to attend you home, and grant me permission to wait on you to-morrow."

It was in vain that Grace impatiently declined the proffered attendance. Maria was completely fascinated at the idea of being attended by one of the dashing servants, whom his master called from his lounge at the door of the inn, to receive his commands, and having reiterated his intention of calling on the following day, the stranger kissed his hand with an air of gallantry, and retired.

"How delighted mamma will be to see us come home with a livery servant behind us," whispered Maria, as they came in sight of the heavy turreted chimneys of Westwood Farm.

"And how sorry my father will be to find that you have affronted William Mansel," said Grace, with a deep sigh; "and his brother Belgrave too, I know he was quite alarmed at William's hastily going off, for he ran after him, without———"

"Yes, that is what vexes you, I know, Grace," observed Maria, with a significant sneer, "you are mighty sorry for William—but you are thinking, all the while, of Belgrave."

Grace's pale cheek crimsoned, as she looked round to see whether the servant (who had followed them at a sauntering pace, which seemed to say he was not much delighted with his commission) was near enough to hear them, and then in a loud voice, replied, "that is a very unkind observation, Maria; but you cannot mean that I should be so foolish, so presumptuous, as to think of Belgrave Mansel, except as a friend and the brother of———"

"Presumptuous!" repeated Maria, "I wish, Grace, you had a little of my spirit, and then you would learn to set a higher value on yourself, and not suffer such people as the Mansels———"

"Hollo, what is all this about, girls?" exclaimed a plain, farmer-looking man, who at that moment jumped over the style from an adjoining field. "Where have you left the boys? Where's my friend Will, and Old Sober-Sides, his brother? and who's that Johnny Lick-platter following you? I hope he's not had the impudence to be making love to either of my little cherubs, because if he has, I can tell 'un———"

"No, no, dear father, you quite mistake," interrupted Maria, hastily; "he has been sent by his master to see us home."

"See thee home, child! why what has become of thy own eyes, since thee went to church this morning, that thee couldn'st find thee own way? Grace, my child, what is the meaning of this?" he added, in a graver tone, "who is this man's master, and———

"I have the honour, sir to serve Sir William Fitz-Geffrey, and at his desire attended these young ladies home," said the servant, stepping foward with an air of consequence, which seemed assumed to daunt the farmer.

"Likely, likely," replied the latter; "but though I'm obliged to you and your master for your civility, I can't understand how it came to be wanted, seeing they had two honest lads to take care of them, that would have beat half a dozenof such like chaps as you."

The lacquey tossed his head with an air of infinite contempt at this speech, and his anger was not lessened, when in reply to something Maria whispered in his ear, the farmer replied—

"Half-a-crown! I'd see him hanged first. Why, child, I do not give more than that to a good honest fellow for a day's hard work, and it's likely I'll throw it away upon the likes of him, that is come up here may be only as a spy, for some rake of a master."

"Oh, no, indeed, father, the poor gentleman is no rake," observed the ingenuous Grace, "for he is quite old and ugly, and looks as if he was dying with the yellow jaundice like poor old Betty Thomas."

"Aye, indeed—well, I'm sorry to hear that," said the kind-hearted Woodford; "I would be loth to wrong any man, much more one that's afflicted as you say he is; so come in, my man, and have a cup of ale, and you can give my service to your master, and tell him I'm thankful for his good intentions, but they were quite needless, for my girls here could come every inch of their way from T—— blindfolded; and as to anybody's harming them, I believe there's little fear of anybody that knows Roger Woodford offering harm to anything, living or dead, that belongs to him.

The servant started back a few paces, at sight of the tremendous fist which the farmer clenched and advanced within a few inches of his (the man's) nose, to enforce his last observation. But the good-humoured smile with which farmer clapped him on the shoulder, observing—

"Don't be frightened, lad, I'm not going to do thee any harm," had the desired effect of re-assuring him; and he followed his now friendly conductor into the kitchen, while the two girls entered the house by another door, to communicate to their mother the result of their evening's adventure.

The peevish reproof which Mrs. Woodford was about to utter at her daughters' long stay, was converted into instant pleasurable surprise, when Maria, on entering the parlour, where the lady of the house kept her state, exclaimed—

"Oh, Mamma! such an adventure!—all your predictions have been likely to come to pass this evening—for I have been very near coming home in a carriage!—and with the owner of it too! such a polite, gallant, man!—and oh, so different from the awkward, country clowns that we have been used to!"

Mrs. Woodford's curiosity and earnestness to hear this adventure, was not exceeded by her daughter's pleasure in relating it; but when she learned, that the servant who had attended them was actually then in the kitchen, and being regaled by the hospitable farmer, she hastened out of the room, as fast as an infirmity, which compelled her to use crutches, would let her, at once to satisfy her curiosity, by learning all she could of this important stranger, of his man—to prevent the husband, whom she despised, from exposing, as she said, his ignorance—and to impress the servant with what, she thought, he could not fail speedily to discover; namely, that she was herself infinitely her husband's superior, and one whom it would be no disgrace even to his master to associate with.

"What is the matter with you Grace?" said Maria, turning from the glass, before which she had been, evidently well pleased with the reflection it presented, standing some minutes after her mother had left.

Grace turned away to the window to hide the tears that were stealing silently down her cheeks.

"Why do you not speak to me, dear Grace?" and Maria, who was really affectionately attached to her sister, threw her white arms around her neck.

The gentle girl strained her passionately to her bosom; but, unable to utter a word, could only reply by a still more copious flood of tears.

"Nay; now, Grace, you are foolish—what have I done to call for all this? Granting I am, as I know you think I am, a little vain and fond of admiration—and suppose I did feel a little proud of being selected by this noble and elegant stranger still———"

"Elegant!" repeated Grace, recovering her speech, and staring at her sister with unfeigned surprise; "surely you cannot seriously call that man elegant!—But that is not what I am thinking of," she continued; "I do not fear *his* influence: for I am sure if you see him again you will confess that———"

"Well, well—never mind what he is;" Maria impatiently interrupted, "you must confess that his carriage, and horses, and servants, in short, everything about him bespeaks the man of taste and fashion."

"It may be so," said Grace with ingenuousness; "but I confes, Maria, I know nothing of taste or fashion, nor do I wish to know more, if this man is a specimen. We were so happy before he came among us this evening," she observed, the tears again streaming down her cheeks, "and now see how different! Instead of sitting down to our comfortable supper with William, and—and—and—his brother, they are wandering about, miserable and unhappy, for Belgrave cannot be happy, I know very well, if William ———"

"For heaven's sake, Grace, don't teaze me any more about William; if he chose to be unreasonable and take airs upon himself, I do not see why I should fret myself to death." And again Maria returned to the contemplation of her beautiful face and form in the mirror.

"My dear child, my own girl," said Mrs. Woodford, re-entering the room, "I am now indeed happy; Sir Walter Fitz-Geffrey, I understand, from his servant, is a man of immense fortune, a bachelor, and I have reason to believe, determined to marry. He is coming here to-morrow, and if I judge rightly, it will be my Maria's own fault, indeed, if she does not fulfil all her mother's predictions. Yes, yes, I have always felt convinced that I should live to see my child restored to that rank, which her mother's girlish imprudence deprived her of. What is that girl sobbing about?" she added, suddenly breaking into the harsh tone which appeared so natural to her, when she addressed her youngest daughter.

"Grace is hurt and vexed, because I have offended William Mansel, mamma," said Maria, in a deprecating tone.

"William Mansel," repeated her mother, in a tone of contempt, "but you are father's own child, Grace," she continued, "and I find that it is impossible that I can instil into you any proper pride; your ideas are like his, low and grovelling. Heaven help me if I had no one but you to depend upon. I should be compelled, I am well aware, to moulder out the remainder of my days, as I have been compelled to do the last twenty years of my life, in obscurity. Ah! I have paid dearly for the romance and folly of my young days, but I am thankful I have still one hope left, one dutiful child who will avoid the rock on which her mother's peace was wrecked—an unhappy ill-assorted marriage."

"But surely, dear mother, you would not call a marriage with William Mansel an ill-assorted marriage!" said Grace, timidly, "he has had an education far superior to—to———"

"To your father, I suppose you mean, miss! really you are a very dutiful young lady."

"I did not mean my father!" faltered Grace.

"Who did you mean, then?—not your sister! You could not mean her, after the money that has been spent upon her; but it is not worth my while to ask questions of such a dolt, who does not know her own meaning. So go about your business, and make your father's porridge, for he has been waiting for it this hour, because nobody can make it like his darling; there's a pair of you, indeed, you and your father."

The contempt with which the latter words were pronounced, might have induced a spirit of reply in any other but Grace's well-schooled bosom—but she had been too long accustomed to such taunts, and, by patient and just reflection, too well convinced of their worthlessness and insignificance, to regard them in any other light than as mere empty wind. With a smile, therefore, which said, as plain as looks could say, that she was perfectly content to bear the imputation of being her father's own child, she hastened to the kitchen, leaving her mother to her private conference with *her*

Mrs. Woodford was used, with emphasis, to style the beautiful

Maria, who certainly, if personal charms would have formed any plea to excuse a mother's partiality, possessed a most abundant share.

Maria Woodford was at this period in her nineteenth year, but the clear transparency of her complexion, the delicacy of her exquisitely moulded form, and the profusion of light auburn ringlets which shaded her fair face, and hung over her ivory shoulder, in thick glossy curls, gave her the appearance of almost infantine beauty. Taught, by incessant lessons, from her earliest years, by her weak and partial mother, to consider the preservation of the charms which nature had so liberally bestowed as the most important object of her life, no frown had ever wrinkled the fair open forehead; nor aught but smiles, which parted her rosy lips to display the pearly treasures within, had been allowed to disturb for a moment the perfect regularity of her faultless features. The sole subject of her mother's thoughts by day, the sole object of her dreams by night, Maria's beauty had hitherto been the talisman which had secured the indulgence of every wish, and which the fond foolish mother firmly believed was to purchase for her hereafter all she conceived was necessary to secure her perfect happiness—rank and riches.

CHAPTER II.

" Whose imp art thou, with dimpled cheek,
And curly pate, and merry eye?
* * * * *
* * * * *
What boots it, who, with sweet caresses,
First called thee his—or squire, or hind?"

JOANNA BAILLIE.

ROGER WOODFORD was the son of a small farmer in Cardiganshire, and in his youth was remarkable for a handsome active person, great good-humour, and a most insuperable love of mischief; for which of these qualities he was, at the age of fourteen, taken into the service of his father's landlord, a gentleman whose pedigree was much longer than his rent-roll, it would perhaps, now be impossible to say; but such is the fact, that from idling about the hedges, looking for birds' nests scraping on an old broken fiddle, and cutting grotesque figures in wood with his knife—which, in spite of his father's threats, and his mother's scoldings, occupied three-fourths of his time, and left him with ragged elbows, bare feet, and brimless hat—he was, at once, translated to the squire's kitchen, and his goodly person clothed in a showy livery, which had only one fault, that of having been made for a full-grown man, and, therefore, being twice as long and twice as wide as it need have been had it been suited to his fair proportions.

Roger, however, found that the dignity of being clothed in green and gold, and of wearing good boots every day, and a smart hat, with a gold band, on particular occasions, was not to be purchased without some sacrifices. The harmonious sounds of his fiddle were exchanged for the grating of the knife-board; his knife, and the materals upon which he exercised his taste, were unceremoniously thrown behind the fire by the female who shared with him the domestic duties; and his out-of-door recreations or pursuits were exchanged for three or four hours' hard labour every day, when the weather permitted, in the garden, which supplied all Squire Jenkins' household with vegetables.

Roger's long-indulged habits stoutly rebelled, at first, against these impositions; but he looked at the glossy green coat, and surveyed his own rosy and now well-washed face in the little looking-glass which ornamented his toilette, and then he thought of the kickings, and cuffings, and the hunger which had too often been the reward of his idle habits at home. The urbanity, too, with which he was now treated by those who formerly bestowed only epithets of reproach, and prognostications of an evil ending to such a bad beginning, operated as an inducement to persevere in his newly-adopted calling; and, in a few months, no one could have recognized, in the smart alert footman of Squire Jenkins, the ragged idle vagabond who had been the disgrace of his family, the torment of all cats, dogs, and old women in the village, and the predestined to an evil end by many whom he had never injured or offended.

The family of Squire Jenkins consisted only of his wife, a quiet weak woman, without an idea beyond the narrow circle of her own domestic occupations; and one daughter, who, unlike her mother, voted her home, and all connected with it, an insufferable bore, studied novels for rules of action and modes of behaviour, cultivated a fine head of hair and a good complexion, and flattered herself with making imaginary conquests of the heroes who, twice a-week, passed, on the Cardigan heavy coach, the little summer-house on the wall of her father's garden, where she never failed, "wind and weather permitting," to be seated in the most approved attitude of her favourite heroines.

Numerous were the slaughters her charms perpetrated at this fatal spot; but, alas! though she looked, and sighed, and languished, the heavy coach rolled on, and carried with it the victims of her charms—leaving her only the slender satisfaction of feeling that she had made an indelible impression, though cruel fate forbade her to hear the soft confessions which she read in the looks of the flying heroes.

At the time of Roger Woodford's entrance into her father's service, Winifred Wilhelmina Jenkins was almost out of her teens; and consequently could boast of several years' experience over the awkward footboy, whose blushing cheeks and stammering diffidence she beheld with ineffable disdain, and whose good-humoured attempts to conciliate her favour she repaid by the most arbitrary and unreasonable exertions. Time rolled on heavily, and yet too quickly for Winifred; for the suitors that she sighed for came not, and the glass told her that the attractions she so prided herself upon did not improve with her years, while certain defects, which she had been used to flatter herself would weigh but as a trifle against the beautiful hair, and eyes, and complexion, became still more prominent and even to herself wearisome. Of these, the chief was, that nature or some mischance had, in the formation of her petite person, made one leg considerably shorter than the other, and thus rendered her unable to support herself without the extraneous assistance of a stick, which though fashioned into a most pastoral resemblance of a shepherdess' crook, was at best but an awkward appendage. The inactive life, too, which this misfortune had induced her to lead, had considerably increased a natural disposition to a warp in her shape; and this became at last so striking that it was no unusual observation of those who unfortunately came under the lash of her displeasure, to observe that Miss Winny was as crooked in her temper as in her shape.

Of all the little household at Jenkins Hall, there was only one who never by any provocation (and yet there were not a few on her part), was irritated into a momentary forgetfulness of that pity which her unfortunate defects had created in his bosom: that kind-hearted, thoughtful being was Roger Woodford.

"The poor body didn't make herself," he was accustomed to observe;

" and, if she was cross and cantankerous, we could none of us tell what we might be if we were so afflicted."

Such were his answers to the females, who sometimes roused him to the defence of his unfortunate mistress by their unfeeling sneers at her personal deformities; but to those of his own sex who had dared to raise their ribald wit at her expense Roger had recourse to a much shorter mode of argument, and many were the battles by which he silenced those ungenerous sarcasms, and obliged his opponents to acknowledge their error.

It was impossible in such a place as Llan——, that these transactions should be buried in oblivion without reaching the ears of those so deeply interested in them. Winifred was grateful; and, in addition to more substantial proofs of her acknowledgment of his services, Roger received many kind words and gentle looks from her who had been hitherto nought to him but a capricious tyrant.

Kind-hearted and good-tempered as Roger Woodford really was, he had never succeeded in attaching to himself the regard of a single human being. His mother, whom his wayward and profitless youth had alienated from him, had died just as he began to redeem his character in the eyes of those who had sagaciously predicted that "Ro. Woodford," as he was familiarly called, would never come to good. Sisters he had none; his brothers were all "out in the world," and had no time or love to spare for the young vagabond, whose idleness and mischief had often been the subject of their angry animadversions; his father had married again, and got a second family; and, in short, "Ro." was alone in the world, till his sympathy in the misfortunes of his mistress, aided a little by his increasing good looks, and a certain despairing consciousness in her mind that she was not likely to create now any interest in a more gentle and high-born bosom, created a tie between them which hourly strengthened.

Roger was no longer the despised footboy whom she delighted to humble and mortify—he was the gallant, handsome youth whom she wished she had the power to raise to a station suitable to his merit; while Roger, on his side, felt the warmest gratitude to her for every little mark of kindness and favour, without being at all conscious how he had excited feelings so different in her bosom to those she had formerly displayed.

It was at this critical juncture that Mrs. Jenkins suddenly departed this life, an event which the Squire mourned by a more than usual application to the barrel of strong ale which was tapped on the occasion.

Winifred had no one to confide in—no one to soothe her sorrows, but the tender-hearted, sympathetic Roger. He dried her tears as fast as they started, listened to her plaintive lamentations for the loss of the tender parent, whom she had treated as a cypher while living, had conveyed all her messages with punctilious exactness to the mantua-maker who made her mourning, and, finally, was the first person admitted to see how well it became her.

"Yes—you do look very nice in it, dear Miss Winny," he naively observed; "but you look better still when your nose don't look so red; but that's all along of crying so much, I suspect."

One of Winny's sharpest reprimands was rising to Winny's lips, at this mal-apropos observation, but Roger fortunately, though not designedly, diverted its course, and sent her thoughts into a very different channel by exclaiming—

" Oh, Miss Winny, I forgot to tell you what a bit of news I heard at Mrs. Stitchwell's, the mantua-maker's! Who'd have thought it? Miss Peggy Lewis is run away with her father's journeyman to get married at Bristol or somewhere; and they say they can't get married there, because they are not of age; and they'd no money to go to Scotland or some other foreign part, where they say a blacksmith would marry them, because they haven't money enough to take them there; so they be coming back like two fools, they say, without getting married at all."

"Fools, indeed!" said Winny, tossing her head; "such creatures as them pretending to elope and imitate people of consequence!"

From this period Winny's thoughts, let them set out from whatever quarter of the globe they might, invariably veered to and settled in the north. She read over and over every novel in which that grand piece of machinery—an elopement—is described; pondered on the dress it would be most proper to wear on such an occasion; contrived, by consulting a book of roads, to trace all the stages to Gretna, and calculate, within a pound or two, what would be the expense; fancied the colour of the suit of clothes for which Roger should exchange his livery; made him four fine shirts, with her own lily hands, in private; and then, after giving him two days to decipher the hints she gave him of her intentions, and finding him as stupid, as he said, and *ramfoozled* as ever, she hid her blushes on his shoulder, and fairly told her dear Roger, that she had determined to reward his constancy and affection by becoming his wife.

Never was astonishment greater than that which Roger displayed at this avowal; which he, however, after the first brief moment of unconcealable surprise, had sufficient tact not wholly to reject, though he felt convinced, in his own mind, that it was utterly impossible he could ever profit by the tender attachment. But this lukewarm expression of gratitude and kindness was not what the gentle Winifred deserved, or was contented with; and with considerable sharpness of accent, and a deep blush of resentment, she observed, that she feared she had quite mistaken his feelings towards her, and that after all he cared nothing about her.

"Nay, nay, Miss Winny, don't say that," replied the simple youth; "I be sure I do always take your part against everybody, and I'd go to t'other end of the world to do you any service; but as for marrying, you see, Miss, why I be but a poor sarvant boy, and how should I be able to keep a wife specially one that's been used to live like a lady all her life!"

Miss Winny murmured something about being happy with her dear Roge in the meanest hut that poverty could inhabit, could she be assured that he loved her; and proceeded, with "due emphasis and discretion," to repeat several rhapsodies on the subject of love and a cottage, which, however were far less intelligible or consonant to Roger's mind than the welcome conclusion of her harangue, which informed him that, by her grandmother's will, she was entitled to two thousand pounds on her wedding-day, which would enable the man of her choice to enter into life with a reasonable prospect of establishing himself and family.

Winifred again hid her blushes as she pronounced the last word, but Roger did not observe her delicate embarrassment; she had opened a new prospect to him, and his mental vision was fully occupied in contemplating it in all its details.

Two thousand pounds! could it be possible that he could ever be destined to become the happy possessor of such an incalculable sum! He might at once, even with a less sum than that, attain the very summit of his ambition!—he might stock a good farm, ride his own galloway, and attend markets and fairs with the proudest of them all!

Winifred stole a sly glance at his countenance, which was lighted up with these thoughts; and, choosing to interpret in the way most pleasant to her feelings, she attributed the grin which distended his features to his complacence, from the reflection of the favour and honour she had bestowed upon him; but it cost her some trouble to elicit from her rustic swain some expression of that rapture which, she flattered herself, he felt.

By degrees, however, Roger began really to consider that which she was so anxious to impress on his mind—that she was to be the means of his felicity, and, therefore, ought to be regarded with due consideration and gratitude. And though as far, perhaps, as any human creature could be from possessing either cunning or hypocrisy, he succeeded to admiration in his new vocation of lover, Winifred kindly attributing all his backwardness and embarrassment to the overpowering effect of her charms, and his sense of her excessive condescension in bestowing them upon him; and Roger retired to muse in secret on the glorious prospect of being his own master, and the proprietor of a farm, which was to surpass those of all his neighbours, under his careful management.

Though totally unable to comprehend the motives of such an arrangement, Miss Winifred being of full age to bestow herself and her fortune where she chose, without any possibility of her father's intervention, Roger yielded implicitly the direction of the affair into her hands; and within a week of *her* first declaration of her love, the fair damsel was lifted by her grateful swain into the post-chaise, which, at her suggestion, he had in readiness, at the back gate of her father's demesne.

So little of secrecy had there been in this arrangement, that half the population of the village were assembled to see the happy pair off; and probably Squire Jenkins himself was the last person in Llan——who became acquainted with the fact that Miss Winifred and her man Roger were on the road to Gretna Green.

The effect upon him was awful; the breakfast table was instantly kicked to the other side of the room, and, for nearly a quarter of an hour, he refused to listen even to the suggestion of his housekeeper, that he had better have a mug of ale and a toast in it, to keep the wind out of his stomach, and not go to kill himself by fretting after an ungrateful child, that would have reason to rue the day she left such a father.

Nature, however, requires due refreshment in spite of grief, and Squire Jenkins at length yielded. A second potation lessened considerably his irritation of spirits, without, however, diminishing his anger against Winny and her companion; and he began seriously to reflect on the means of revenge.

"She must have the money that old fool left her," he observed, as he walked over to the public-house, where he usually found consolation and advice in all his difficulties; "but she shall never touch another farthing of my money."

The buxom landlady received him with sarcastic expressions of condolence and affected surprise that such a pattern of prudence as Miss Winifred should so far have forfeited her character; but there was one who neither disguised her pleasure nor hesitated to point out the most proper mode in which the squire could show his resentment towards his disobedient daughter.

Peggy Evans, the blooming damsel alluded to, the sole heiress of the virtues, the beauty, and the wealth (the latter was questionable) of the widow Evans, the hostess of the Jolly Farmer, had long fixed her ambitious hopes on becoming Squire Jenkins' lady; and, in pursuit of this object, she had lost sight, it was believed, of that prudence which the world would have considered absolutely necessary to its attainment. Scandal, indeed, had long joined the names of the squire and Peggy in many unseemly anecdotes; her female acquaintances had, in consequence, all withdrawn their countenance from the offending fair one, and she was destined to suffer many annoying jokes and inuendoes from the male sex, whom pleasure or business brought within the hospitable walls of the Jolly Farmer; but hitherto her indignant remonstrances, her tears, and her threats of going away altogether, and getting a *sarvice* in *Lonnon*, had all been thrown away upon the squire; he had an uniform obstacle to oppose to all her importunities—"Winifred." He had promised Winifred's mother that he would never bring another wife home to be mistress over her child, and he wouldn't break his word to the dead; no, not if the Queen of England and Wales was to offer to have him.

This impediment was now removed; Winifred was gone, and Peggy failed not to take advantage of the opportunity to press her own claims, her wrongs and sufferings, from having trusted to his deluding flatteries. Her mother joined in demanding that he should now do justice to her daughter, and punish the disobedience of his own. A second, and a third, and a fourth jug of ale enforced their arguments, and the squire was at length induced to yield a reluctant assent to their importunities, and give Peggy a promise, in black and white, to make her his wife whenever she chose to demand the performance of the ceremony.

Before Roger and his bride returned from their northern expedition, which had been no ways distinguished from similar affairs, except by the excessive regret of the bridegroom that so many good *gooden* guineas had passed out of his possession to pay the extortionate demands of inn-keepers, postilions, and their numerous adjuncts on the road, Peggy, by the aid of a regular license, and a regular clergyman (and not by a sham marriage, by a dirty blacksmith, as she tauntingly observed), was duly installed the mistress of Jenkin Hall, and Winifred and her bridegroom, when they presented themselves according to usage for the forgiveness and blessing of papa, found that there was another and much more inexorable relative to conciliate. Peggy, now Mrs. Jenkins, had long burned with desire to retaliate upon Winifred the insulting remarks which she had been compelled hitherto silently to put up with; but that which weighed far heavier upon Roger than all the taunts and arrogance of his new mother-in-law, was the information which had reached him, that his beloved bride had made a small mistake in stating the amount of her independent fortune, and that she should have said hundreds instead of thousands, in specifying its amount.

"Well, well, never cry about it, Winny," said the good-humoured lad, as they turned away from the inhospitable door, which they were plainly told was never again to unclose its hinges to them. "Two hundred pounds is better than nothing to begin with, and though I can't hope to keep you like a lady, yet I'll work as hard for you as any chap in the country, to make you comfortable."

Winny, however, was not of a disposition to be made comfortable by such means, she had been woefully disappointed by her father's imprudent, as she called it, marriage; for she had flattered herself, from his long-tried partiality for her, that she should induce him to make up the deficiency in her fortune, and place her husband at once in a farm which would satisfy his ambition, and enable her to enjoy those comforts which she had been accustomed to. The disappointment of these hopes did not increase her amiability, and poor Roger soon had sufficient reason to repent the hasty step, by which he had tied himself to one every way so utterly unqualified to be a meet helpmate for him.

Year after year, Roger toiled on with unwearied toil and patience, cultivating the little farm, which, by the aid of his wife's two hundred pounds, and his own character for honesty and industry, he had been enabled to enter upon. Contrary to his own, or any one else's expectations, Mrs. Woodford had presented him with several children, and though to his sorrow they all died soon after their birth, the expenses attendant on these events kept him constantly poor, and his wife constantly complaining in secret her hard fate, and repenting the *unguarded moment* when she had listened to Roger's solicitations, and united her fate to his.

The birth of two girls, successively, who seemed more likely to live than the boys, whom he had one after the other seen deposited in their native earth, awakened new feelings and new solicitudes in the farmer's honest bosom, and kindled new regrets in his repining discontented wife.

The eldest of these children, Maria, was distinguished from her birth for the rare personal beauty we have in the first chapter of this history vainly attempted to give some faint idea of, and as she grew up, seemed equally endowed with those graces of mind and disposition, without which, the most perfect beauty must soon cease to please or to interest. Grace the second daughter was, on the contrary, remarkable for nothing but the gentleness and docility of her temper, and her warm affection towards her parents, and indeed, everybody to whom she could attach herself.

It was not surprising, though it was to be regretted, that each parent selected a favourite; Mrs. Woodford beheld, with a rapture she never attempted to conceal, the budding charms which she confidently predicted were to secure to her the fortune and splendour which was denied to her unfortunate mother; while Roger beheld in his little darling Grace, the child who was to sooth and comfort his old age, and reward him for the days of toil, and nights of anxiety, which were now deprived of more than half their bitterness by her endearments.

Accustomed, from the first momment that she was capable of observation, to hear every tongue loud in commendation of Maria's beauty, the gentle Grace never for a moment suspected that she herself possessed the slightest personal claims to be admired; yet Grace, though far from a striking beauty, would have been called any where but by her sister's side, a very pretty girl. Her clear hazel eyes sparkled with sensibility and intelligence, her crimson lips expressed the sweetness of her disposition, and her pale but clear compexion, and slender yet agile form, were in strict consonance with the delicacy yet strength of her mind. Beholding her sister with the fondest affection, not a a spark of envy ever disgraced that pure and spotless mind, and though she sometimes sighed at the petulant comparisons which her mother was too apt to indulge in, between her and her more favoured sister, it was not that she wished Maria less beautiful but that she regretted that she too did not possess that recommendation to a mother's love.

Naturally well-disposed and affectionate, even her mother's injudicious fondness and admiration could not corrupt Maria's heart; and though she sometimes presumed upon her influence over her mother, and was occasionally a little too exacting in the homage she demanded from her sister, it would be unjust to say that, Maria Woodford was other than a pleasing amiable girl, up to the age of twelve years, when a circumstance happened which made a considerable alteration in the situation and prospects of the family at Rose Farm, which was the name of Mr. Woodford's habitation.

This was the sudden death of squire Jenkins (the father of Roger Woodford's *amiable* spouse), who, having resisted all his consort Peggy's hints, inuendoes, and persuasions respecting the final division of his property, had only just time allotted to him, at the last moment, to signify that Winny was to share with his children by the second marriage.

The amount of this portion, which, after much delay, conjecture, and dispute, was paid into Roger's hands, somewhat exceeded the sum with which Winny had in the days of her maidenhood dazzled the eyes of the honest rustic; and Mrs. Woodford did not forget to dwell upon the circumstance with no small exultation, that after all she had kept her word in bestowing on him a fortune.

Poor Roger, however, soon found that though his anxiety for his girls' future provision was thus removed, and the necessity for his own indefatigable labour lessened, his real comforts were not much increased by this accession of fortune. Mrs. Woodford was no longer content with the inglorious obscurity in which she had lingered out the years of her marriage, she was determined to " enjoy life, and do as other people did;" and her poor husband had soon the mortification of seeing his house crowded with all the idle, the dissipated, or ill-natured people of the neighbourhood, who came to laugh at Mrs. Woodford, and devour the good things with which she repaid their condescension.

The farmer bore this invasion on his domestic peace, and his moderate income for a little while, with his accustomed good humour; but he soon discovered that these very friendly people were not content with laughing at his wife, but that his own rusticity and want of information on all topics, except those which related to his farm, made him a constant butt to his visitors, and he determined at once to put a stop to this species of entertainment at least.

"From this day, Winny, henceforward," he observed, in a decided tone, " the parlour is yours and the kitchen is mine; you may make yourself as great a fool as you like, but I won't be made so any more."

Mrs. Woodford scolded, remonstrated, and persuaded, but all in vain; no entreaties could ever induce the farmer to put his foot within the parlour, or, as Mrs. Woodford chose to call it, the drawing-room; and after many awkward and ineffectual attempts to disguise the cause of his absence, she was at length compelled to avow to all her visitors, that Mr. Woodford's eccentricities induced him to prefer the company of his servants to more polished and suitable society.

Mrs. Woodford and her favourite daughter now, therefore, reigned uncontrolled in their peculiar domain; the latter, dressed in the most preposterous style, was the admiration and delight of her mother's visitors; while Grace, seated close to her father's elbow, by the kitchen fireside, during the winter, beguiled the hours with her chat to him while she plied her needle, or fixed the attention, and called forth the admiration of the homely circle, by reading to them aloud such books as suited their capacity, and possessed sufficient interest to rouse their dormant faculties. While in the summer, her evenings were spent delightfully in accompanying her father to view the progress of his different crops, count the increase of his flocks, and watch their sportive frolics, or sitting by his side with her voice mocking the carolling of the birds, or excite his smiles by relating such tales of wonder or of interest, as her very limited acquaintance with books had enabled her to recollect for his entertainment.

It had seemed so perfectly natural for Grace to follow her father, that it scarcely excited a remark from Mrs. Woodford, until her attention was called repeatedly to the subject by inquiries after her youngest daughter, which she was puzzled how to reply to, and which determined her, to use her own expression, to turn over a new leaf with Miss Grace, and not suffer her to lose her time, and her (mamma), by learning her father's low ways and vulgar habits.

This was an accusation which Grace, young as she was, felt was most unjust towards her simple good-meaning parent. He was illiterate, un-versed in the ways of the world, and unapt in acquiring its manners, but in the true sense of the words he was refined and polite; far, far more so than many of her mother's cringing, simpering, scandalising acquaintances.

Mrs. Woodford was thunderstruck at the eloquent and spirited defence which Grace—the hitherto meek, gentle Grace—gave utterance to, on hearing the charge against her father; but she was still more astonished, when in reply to her (Mrs. Woodford's) injunctions that she should henceforth take her tea, &c., in the drawing-room, Grace, bursting into tears, observed—

"If my father orders me, mamma, to leave him, I will come, but ——"

"But what, Miss? will you dare to oppose me? I say you shall come, let your father say or do whatever he may."

Mr. Woodford at this moment made his appearance, and it was impossible to conceal from him the cause of the contention.

He, poor man, looked at Grace with tears in his eyes, as his vain and termagant wife expatiated on the flagrant act of disobedience, of which her daughter had been guilty.

"And so you would rob me of my comfort, Winny;" he observed, "and what for, to make her—no, to try to make her, for she is too good to be spoiled, even by you—— ——."

Grace slipped out of the room, to avoid hearing the contention which she knew would follow; but when, at length, she ventured to return to the scene of combat, she found, to her great satisfaction, that her father had prevailed, and that he was waiting for her to make his tea.

She soon learned, however, on what terms this victory had been purchased.

Mr. Woodford had hitherto, by a certain decision of character, which, though he seemed not to think it worth while to exercise it on ordinary occasions, stood him often in good stead on extraordinary ones, always retained the entire dominion in money matters, limiting, with scrupulous exactness, his own, his household, and last, but not least, his wife's expenses.

The increase of fortune which had fallen to his share, had, of course, induced him considerably to extend this scale, but it was still very inadequate to Mrs. Woodford's wishes, and it was only by agreeing to add considerably to her allowance, and enable her to carry into effect the darling wish of her heart, of sending Maria for a year to a fashionable boarding-school, at Bath, that he was enabled to secure to himself the society of his dear Grace without fear of interruption.

"Your poor sister will be quite ruined, now, Grace;" he observed, in a tone of compassion, "for the little good that's left in her will be all lost, when she gets away from you and me,"

Grace hoped not, but she mourned sincerely at the loss of her sister, whom she fondly loved, in spite of all that their injudicious parents did to weaken their affection towards each other.

More than half the time of Maria's limited residence at Lansdowne Establishment for Young Ladies, Mrs. Woodford passed in a hot, confined, unwholesome, and extravagantly dear lodgings in the city of Bath, for the ostensible purpose of recruiting her health, by means of the waters for which that place is famous; but in reality, that she might be nearer to her darling daughter, and contemplate with ecstacy her rapid improvement, both in personal charms, and the superficial graces and accomplishments which this expensive sojourn was to bestow.

THE PRIDE OF THE VILLAGE;

OR,

THE FARMER'S DAUGHTERS.

CHAPTER III.

Those eyes, those full and fixed eyes,
  They cannot beam, nor glow with fire,
Or herald as the wishes rise,
  The thoughts the spirit would respire ;
But passionless themselves, they wake
  In us that feeling's tender strife.

ANON.

Maria was indeed apt enough to profit by the instruction she received, and sedulous to make the most of the opportunity afforded her; and when, at the end of the twelve months, she returned with her mother to Rose Farm, even the old

2

farmer was astonished, and entrapped into admiration of her various accomplishments, and the improvement of her person.

Grace was in raptures with her beautiful sister ; and for some days she was unwearied in listening to her, as she rattled over the keys of the pianoforte, which the indulgent mother had provided for her—or watched her, in the graceful steps of various dances she had studied—or listened, with smiling surprise, to the stammering uncouth sounds which Maria designated French or Italian.

In a very short time, however, Maria tired of exhibiting what Grace could not appreciate; and Grace began to wonder whether such acquisitions as these were worth the sacrifice of time and money which had been expended to secure them. She could not, with all her partiality for her sister, avoid seeing that the latter was far from improved in many other respects ; she had a higher opinion of herself, and a kind of contempt for every one else, which rendered her often much less amiable than she was wont to be, and she had acquired a love of show and parade, which even went beyond her mother's devotion to the same object, aud rendered the latter restless and uneasy, from being unable to keep up with her daughter's wants and wishes.

"The girl is ruined—utterly ruined !"—the old man would exclaim, in a tone of lamentation, " and I have foolishly thrown away sixty pounds, to make her unfit for anything but to be looked at."

"We shall see, Mr. Woodford," replied his wife ; who, at her daughter's request, had dismissed the old-fashioned method of addressing her husband by his christian name. "Have a little patience, and you'll will find your money has not been thrown away, but spent wisely, to make her fit for her station—Maria is born to be a lady."

The period which Mrs. Woodford had so anxiously anticipated, which was to make her favourite daughter's fortune, seemed to have at length arrived, for on the morning following the event which we narrated in the first chapter, Sir Walter Fitz-Geffrey arrived at the farm so early, that nothing but the impatience of love could have excused the want of proper etiquette.

Sir Walter, however, much to Mrs. Woodford's disappointment, gave a very different motive for his early visit.

He was about to quit Llan——, he said, immediately ; and he had taken advantage of the brief interval, while his carriage underwent some slight repair, to——

Mrs. Woodford looked eagerly for the finishing of the sentence, but Sir Walter seemed to have forgotten that it was necessary to the completion of his apology ; and with a look of surprise, which his hostess interpreted into pleasure, but which any one else would have called sarcasm, was taking a minute survey of all that constituted the furniture and embellishments of the room into which he had been introduced.

Mrs. Woodford was longing to tell him that all the ornaments and gewgaws, over which his eyes wandered, were the offspring of her daughter's taste, but there was a something in Sir Walter's look and manner which repressed all her attempts to be at ease with him ; and she felt heartily glad, for her own sake, when Maria, in all the blaze of beauty, displayed to the utmost advantage by an elegant and studied dishabille, entered the room, and at once fixed his eyes and thoughts.

Hour after hour passed away, and Sir Walter still lingered in the *drawing-room* of Rose Farm. He seemed, indeed, totally to have forgotten the contemplated continuance of his journey, and in the pauses of his conversation with Maria, contrived to throw in so many inquiries and observations to her mother, evidently all tending to the same effect—namely, the possibility of his establishing himself for a short time in the vicinity of Llan——, that it required not even the aid of Mrs. Woodford's sanguine fancy, to enable her to discover that her visitor had found there an attraction which he could not resolve to quit.

"I will tell you candidly, madam," he observed, addressing Mrs. Woodford, at length, "that I have no fixed residence in England; the best part of my life has been passed in India, and I am now about to settle in my native country; but I am not yet decided in what part of it, nor am I indeed in any hurry, until I have completed my tour of observation. From what I have seen in this neighbourhood, however," and he fixed his eyes expressively on Maria's face, "I should certainly give it a preference, if it were possible for me to find a suitable residence."

Mrs. Woodford was in raptures at this avowal; but the satisfaction was damped by the circumstance, that there was not, within her knowledge, any place vacant, or for sale, that could suit her visitor.

Jenkin Hall, indeed, the *seat* of her late father, could the widow be prevailed on to give it up—

"Your father, did you say, madam?" said the stranger, looking earnestly at the speaker, "I thought—I understood that the late Mr. Jenkins had left only the two—I beg your pardon, are you really the daughter of the late Mr. Jenkins?"

"I am his eldest daughter, sir," replied the matron, drawing herself up with an air of consequence, yet with extreme surprise, at the stranger's earnestness of manner, and his evident acquaintance with the name of her father.

"Is it possible?" replied Sir Walter, in a musing tone. "You are surprised," he observed, after a few moments' silence, during which he had appeared to be hesitating, whether he should communicate the cause of his particular inquiries. Another glance at Maria seemed to decide the question.

"Have you never heard your father speak of a relative—a half-brother who quitted England at an early age, and was afterwards a stranger to his family?"

"Oh, yes, poor Watty Geffrey; I have heard him talk of him many a time, and wondered what become of him."

"It is in my power, then, Mrs. Woodford, to solve that mystery," said the stranger; "I am the son of Walter Geffrey, and consequently your cousin."

All Mrs. Woodford's golden dreams seemed to vanish in a moment at this explanation. Walter Geffrey, she had often heard, had quitted his home with a single guinea in his pocket, and with habits which indicated anything but a probability that he would be likely to turn that possession to any advantage. He had been, indeed, always spoken of by his relations as a profligate spendthrift, who would never do any good for himself, or anybody else; and various as had been the tales that had been circulated, and the predictions that had been uttered, as to Watty's probable fate, not one had been to the effect that he had improved his condition. It had even been rumoured that he had figured in the catalogue of criminals which periodically appear in the London newspapers; and though Squire Jenkins was silent on the subject, and tried to discourage all such reports, by not seeming to understand them, it was impossible to stop entirely the busy tongues that propagated Walter's disgraceful exit from his native land.

Accustomed, therefore, to suppress, in her genealogical reminiscences, of which she was very fond, all mention of Walter, as one whose very existence it was desirable to forget, Mrs. Woodford was some minutes before she could reconcile her visitor's declaration of his consanguinity with the visions of rank, and splendour, and riches inexhaustible, which had been dazzling her eyes, and heating her brain, from the moment Maria had in glowing terms described the carriage and liveries, and the stately look and steps of the stranger, and last, but not least, the evident effect her own charms had had upon him.

By degrees, however, Mrs. Woodford became convinced of, and reconciled to, the fact, that the supposed illustrious stranger was, in reality, the son and heir of her despised kinsman; who had been induced, by curiosity, and perhaps some better feeling, to visit the birthplace of his father, and make some distant inquiries into the condition of his family.

He had been, it appeared, to Jenkin Hall, previous to his arrival at the inn where Maria first beheld him; but the result of the interview with the widow and daughters of his deceased relative was so little satisfactory either to his pride or his feelings, that he had not thought fit to make known to them the motives of his inquiries, and would have quitted for ever in disgust the village of Llan——, had not the bright eyes of Maria Woodford convinced him that it contained something worth looking at a second time.

Thoroughly satisfied, at length, of the fact that the despised Walter Geffrey had, in reality, died the possessor of an immense fortune, and that his son and heir, her present visitor, added to its possession a title which was likely to sink all recollection of the stigma which, even yet, in the memory of those who could recall his dwelling among them, attached to the name of his progenitor, Mrs. Woodford became more than ever sanguine of her daughter's elevation to the station in life in which she conceived her so fitted to shine in; while Maria, relieved of a great part of that awe and embarrassment which, in spite of her fashionable education, she could not entirely shake off in the presence of one whom she believed so much her superior in birth and rank, became infinitely more amiable and interesting as she became more natural.

"But you have another daughter, Mrs. Woodford," said Sir Walter; when, after two or three hours' chat, and incessant display, on the part of the anxious matron, of her favourite's charms and accomplishments, a pause at last occurred, which seemed to demand a new subject. "You must make me aquainted with all your family," he contined.

"Oh, yes, Grace; where is Grace, my dear, do you know?" replied Mrs. Woodford, addressing Maria.

"You should have had a third daughter, madam, to complete the circle of the three Graces, since it appears you possess two," said her newly discovered relative.

Maria bestowed on him one of her sweetest smiles; and then, in answer to her mother's inquiry, replied, that she had not seen her sister since she arose, but she supposed she was, as usual, out with her father, in the grounds.

"Your father!" repeated sir Walter. "Good heavens!—how unaccountable! I had actually taken it for granted, that you were a widow, Mrs. Woodford!—but I am very happy that——"

Mrs. Woodford uttered a sigh so audible, and turned up her eyes to the ceiling, as a substitute for the Heaven to which she appeared to be appealing, with a look so expressive, that Sir Walter involuntarily suspended his congratulation, and remained silent, in evident expectation of receiving an explanation of these mysterious indications.

"It is very hard, cousin," said Mrs. Woodford, laying a great emphasis, "to be obliged to speak of the follies of one's youth; but the fact is, when I married, I was very young and giddy, and——"

"I understand you, madam; spare yourself any farther pain; I am, indeed, truly sorry that Mr. Woodford should have proved unworthy of such an inestimable blessing, but————."

Insensible as Maria generally appeared to her father's really good qualities—whether it was a sudden qualm of conscience, that whispered to her, at this moment, that it was wrong to suffer her new-found relative to imbibe such an unfavourable idea of the poor man, or that she thought his observation more ironical than sincere, could not with certainty be ascertained; but so it was, that a deeper blush than usual suffused her fair cheek; and hastily rising, before Sir Walter could finish the sentence she observed—

"Grace will be so glad, mamma; shall I go and look for her?" and without waiting a reply, she glided gracefully from the room.

"Is she not a sweet girl, Sir Walter?" said the doting mother, before the door was well closed upon the darling of her heart.

Sir Walter warmly assented to her praise.

"Ah! she's all my comfort, cousin," continued Mrs. Woodford; "if it was not for her, I should hate my very existence!"

"Is Mr. Woodford, then, so very————?" Sir Walter looked the rest of the inquiry, which, even with all Mrs. Woodford's evident desire to be communicative, he could scarcely venture to make.

"Oh! my dear Sir Walter!" and again she lifted her eyes, with that expressive look of such intense misery. "Such a brute!—I *may* say it to you, what I try to conceal from all the world—but never was a woman such a martyr!"

"Good heaven! then those crutches————!" and Sir Walter again supplied the pause by an expressive look.

Mrs. Woodford was, for a moment, lost in unutterable amazement. What could the man mean by his indelicate allusion to what *she* called her supporters!—for she had long been compelled to relinquish her pastoral crook for these vulgar and unromantic assistants.

"I hope he could never so far forget the delicacy due to a female, as to————"

It seemed a besetting sin in Sir Walter to leave his sentences to be concluded according to the construction his hearers might put on the first part of them; and Mrs. Woodford, accordingly, interpreting this in the light most obvious to her imagination, with a still deeper sigh, and more intense intonation of misery, exclaimed—

"Delicacy! Sir Walter. Alas!————! but you will see him, and then you will judge what must be the wretchedness I endure from such a connection!"

It was a subject on which Sir Walter felt it impossible to offer any of the usual topics of consolation; and a long pause ensued, during which Mrs. Woodford had recourse to her handkerchief, to hide the tears she did (not) shed, at being thus compelled to expose the delinquency of one she had sworn to love, honour, and obey.

"But, your daughter! Grace, I think, you called her; how comes it, my dear Mrs. Woodford, that she should be the voluntary companion of such a being?" observed Sir Walter, suddenly.

"Ah! there is another of my afflictions, cousin! The girl is the very counterpart of her father!—she has no soul—no sensibility—no fine feeling! She is never so happy as when she is with him! and is equally low, and grovelling, and brutish, if I may so express myself, as him!"

"Good Lord! how one may be deceived!" said Sir Walter, as if speaking to himself. "I thought, last night, she looked singularly modest, gentle, and engaging! and she is so delicate and pretty, too!"

"Pretty! Sir Walter!" screamed Mrs. Woodford; "you cannot, sure, be serious! Grace pretty!——a poor, pale, lifeless thing!—and so awkward and uninformed, too! Oh, no; you cannot mean it!—you surely could not have looked at her by the side of my Maria!"

"It was precisely there that I did look at her, madam; and though, certainly, she has no pretensions to vie with her beautiful sister, who is, without any exception, the most faultless female form and face I ever beheld——"

"I knew you would think so. Oh! I am sure you could not be blind to the striking difference!" interrupted Mrs. Woodford. "Yes; Maria is beautiful!—but as to Grace——"

"The name, indeed, seems somewhat misapplied," murmured Sir Walter observing, at this moment, the bashful hesitating girl endeavouring to avoid his earnest glance, by shrinking behind her sister, as they entered the room together.

"Where have you been, all this morning, miss?" inquired the mother, in a sharp tone: with your father, I suppose; tearing the clothes off your back and scorching yourself with the sun, till you look more like a haymaker than a young lady."

"I have been haymaking, mamma," replied Grace, in a deprecating tone; "father is so afraid that the rain will come on before——"

"There, Sir Walter, hear now; is not this enough to drive a woman of feeling and refinement mad?" interrupted Mrs. Woodford: "but this is the way I am constantly insulted by Mr. Woodford: and if I was to say a word he would tell me, with all the impudence in the world, that haymaking was a better occupation for his daughters than sitting strumming at a piano, or daubing sheets of paper with things that are not a bit like what they're intended for, and if they were, would never be half so much worth looking at as the real things themselves. I assure you that's exactly what he said once, when I showed him a beautiful landscape that Maria had just finished."

Sir Walter smiled; but whether it was at her observation, or Grace's futile attempt to hide a large rent in the skirt of her plain white frock, it was impossible to decide; certain it is, that Grace believed he was laughing at her. But even while she thus decided that it was herself who excited his risibility, the conviction rather removed than strengthened the prejudice which she had been inclined to foster against her new acquaintance; and she replied by a look of arch intelligence, which at once decided the latter in her favour.

"And so you prefer hay-making to music, my little cousin," observed Sir Walter, getting between her and her mother, so as to afford her an opportunity of screening the fractured dress from the observation of the latter, by twisting it behind her, and then sitting upon it.

"No, sir, not to music, but I do not know anything about the piano, and if I can help my father sometimes, I think," said Grace, "that——"

"You think, miss!" interrupted her mother; "yes, you always think exactly as that low-minded vulgar man, who encourages you in all your disgraceful hoydenish tricks, chooses to direct you to think—you are both the torment of my life."

Grace's eyes were cast down in deep confusion, and Sir Walter beheld with interest the pearly tears trembling beneath their long dark fringes; while a deep blush crimsoned her cheek, and rendered still more conspicuous the paleness which succeeded it.

Sir Walter murmured something, which was in reality inaudible, but which Mrs. Woodford interpreted from his looks to be intended to solicit indulgence for the culprit.

"And pray, where is your father?" continued the amiable wife; "is he aware that there is a gentleman here who wishes to see him?"

"No, mamma, he is helping to turn the hay, and"——

"I should like to walk down to the hay-field, madam, if you have no objection," interrupted Sir Walter; "it is a scene which I shall, I am sure, enjoy; and Grace will introduce me to her father—will you not?" and he turned and took her hand, with a look and a smile, so unlike the cold haughty air which had prejudiced her against him the preceding evening, that Grace instantly forgot it all, and accorded her consent with a readiness that called forth a new censure from her mother.

"You are very forward all at once, miss;" observed the latter in an under tone of vexation, "but you will please to stop till your sister is ready to accompany you."

Grace drew back, and Sir Walter, after an indignant look at the partial and unjust mother, turned to the object of her reprehension, with a view of consoling her, by his attentions, for the undeserved rebuke.

To his surprise, however, Grace's countenance betrayed not the least symptom of confusion or resentment.

"Is the girl insensible?" he thought, to himself, "or has she been so well schooled that she can conceal those feelings which must arise in every human being at oppression?"

Before he could well utter a sentence, Grace darted off evidently in obedience to a signal from her mother.

"Is she gone?" he exclaimed, in a tone of disappointment, looking after her.

"Only to fetch her sister's bonnet and veil," returned Mrs. Woodford; "the sun is too hot for her to venture without them."

Sir Walter walked to the window, to conceal the disgust and impatience he could not suppress, and Grace in a few minutes re-entered with the bonnet and veil, and with the most busy solicitude assisted to array her sister.

"You had better take your parasol too, Maria, the sun is quite scorching!" and away she flew again in search of the latter article.

"Now, Sir, we are quite ready, if you please."

Sir Walter turned hastily round at the sweet accents of her voice.

"But you go with us, do you not?" he demanded, observing that she made no preparation for the walk herself.

"Oh, yes, certainly; that is, if mamma does not want me," she added, looking timidly at her mother.

Mrs. Woodford was acute enough to have discovered, by this time, that it would not be politic to let Sir Walter see so clearly her bias towards her favourite. It was evident, already, that he was disposed to view Grace with considerable interest, and that it would increase it by letting her appear in his eyes oppressed and injured, she could have little doubt, after the recent specimen she had seen of his disposition; with a graciousness of manner, totally unknown, hitherto, and now quite incomprehensible to Grace, she replied—

"No, my dear, I do not wish to detain you from what I know will give you pleasure."

For a moment, Grace stood as if bewildered.

It could not possibly be her whom her mother addressed, but she looked at her, and she could no longer doubt, for Mrs. Woodford, conscious her visitor's eyes were upon her, actually relaxed her features into a look of kindness suitable to her words.

Grace's pale cheeks flushed with surprise and pleasure, the big tears started to her eyes, and darting hastily towards her, she threw herself upon her mother's neck.

"What does the foolish girl mean?" exclaimed the latter; Sir Walter looked at Grace for an instant with visible emotion, and then led Maria from the room.

"Pray let us have no more of this fine feeling," said Mrs. Woodford, the moment he was out of sight, repulsing the affectionate girl; "look how you have rumpled my lace frill."

Grace retreated, her countenance expressing the deepest disappointment; but as she quitted the room, her mother called her back.

"Do not let me see any of your artful tricks to get in favour with Sir Walter, miss;" she observed, "for I assure you, if I see any attempts to put yourself before your sister, I will at once put a stop to it, and make you bitterly repent it, and so now you may go as soon as you please."

Instead of bounding away as was her usual habit, when released from her mother's presence, Grace walked leisurely and reflectively along, meditating on the words the latter had just uttered, nor did she see, until she was close to them that Sir Walter and Maria were waiting for her a few yards from the house.

The keen eye of the baronet rested inquisitively on her countenance, but her mother's insinuation and threat were fresh on her mind, and, without noticing him, she placed herself by her sister's side.

"Dear me, Grace, how thoughtless you are, to suppose I can walk so; it is quite smothering me;" said Maria, hastily pushing her from her, before they had walked many yards.

"I beg your pardon;" returned Grace, submissively, and immediately falling back a few paces.

"Will you take my other arm?" said Sir Walter, looking over his shoulder at her.

Grace was about to accept the offer so frankly and cordially made; she was beginning to feel an interest in Sir Walter's favour, whom she no longer thought either so proud or so ugly as he had at first sight appeared; but again she recollected her mother's caution, and with a coldness of manner totally foreign to her own nature, she refused it.

Sir Walter looked disappointed, but Maria at this moment contrived to centre his thoughts and attentions on herself; a frog leaped across her path and with the prettiest shriek imaginable, she clung to his arm in a seeming agony of terror.

Sir Walter, entreating her not to be alarmed, raised his stick to demolish the poor unoffending reptile; but Grace, dexterously springing forward, caught it up, observing,

"It is a pity to kill such a harmless creature, merely because it is not handsome in our eyes—there, it is gone now," and she placed it on a tuft of grass at some distance.

"I bow beneath your correction, Miss Grace," said Sir Walter, in a tone half-earnest, half-jocular; "you have given me a very proper lesson."

Grace blushed, and disclaimed all intention of lecturing; and then, as if fearful of having said, or being likely to say, too much she observed that she would run on and tell her father they were coming; and without a reply she darted off at full speed, and was out of sight in a moment.

"That is certainly a very singular girl!" said Sir Walter, looking after her, and speaking as if unconscious that any one was near him.

"She is very wild," said Maria; "but then she is very kind and good-natured."

"I am very glad to hear you say so," returned Sir Walter, looking earnestly at her, and thinking at that moment that she looked even handsomer than when he first beheld her: "I mean," he added, seeing Maria look surprised at the warmth of his manner—"I mean that I am glad to find my opinion of your sister correct; for I fancied from the first moment I beheld her that her countenance was indicative of the qualities you ascribe to her."

They were now within sight of the haymakers, among whom they soon distinguished Grace and her father, both busily employed, and apparently totally forgetful of the honour intended in the proposed introduction of Sir Walter."

"I declare it's just like my father," observed Maria, in a tone of vexation; "now he pretends not to see us, and will make us come up quite to the end of the field before he will speak to us."

Sir Walter made no reply, but his keen eye was diligently scanning the still fine form and open ingenuous countenance of the farmer, who, in his large coarse hat of wheaten straw, and stripped to his shirt-sleeves was diligently aiding the labours of his men.

"How are you—how are you, sir?" he exclaimed, in a good-humoured tone, as Sir Walter, with Maria hanging on his arm, approached him. "You'll excuse my not standing to talk; but you know the old saying—'Make hay while the sun shines;' and I doubt if it will shine much longer; it has been threatening to rain ever since daylight this morning, and the glass is at rain, too."

"You might leave off for a few minutes, however, papa," said Maria in a reproachful tone, having quitted Sir Walter's arm on purpose to utter this remonstrance. "This gentleman is a near relation of mamma's; and a very rich one, too," she added, in a lower key.

"So much the better for him, child; but rich as he is, I doubt if he'd be willing to pay me for the hay that will be spoiled if we don't get it in before the rain; so get thee in, my good girl, and don't stand idling about, in the way of those that will work."

"Mamma will be fine and angry when she knows that the gentleman has seen you and Grace both at work, like two common haymakers," said Maria, still trying to carry her point.

"I tell thee what it is, Maria," replied the farmer, elevating his voice to an unusual pitch of anger; "it would far better become both your mother and you to lay aside all your frippery, and come and lend a helping hand, than—— ; but, there, go along with you, what's the use of talking to such helpless souls? Take the gentleman with you, and make yourself comfortable in your own way, for I suppose he's like yourselves, all outside, and good for nothing in the world but to eat and drink, and make other people work for them."

During this short dialogue Sir Walter had contrived to approach Grace, though she evidently wished to avoid him, and kept her attention diligently fixed on her work, while he addressed some commonplace compliments to her, which were apparently intended to ascertain whether she was as insensible to flattery as she appeared to be.

"For goodness' sake, Grace, do leave off; and go in with me," said Maria, approaching her; "mamma will be vexed to death, if she knows that you are labouring here, blistering your hands, and scorching yourself till you will be as brown as a gipsy."

"No, indeed, you are mistaken," replied Grace, with *naiveté*; "for my mother knew I came out this morning on purpose to help, and she told me "——

Maria contrived to draw Sir Walter's attention away before her sister could finish the sentence; and Grace, without seeming further to notice them, continued her employment.

Sir Walter continued to watch both her and her father, in silence; he saw the smile of encouragement with which the latter, from time to time, turned to his daughter, and the still more lovely smile of filial affection with which she repaid him.

"It is impossible that man can be the wretch his wife describes him—his own countenance is a contradiction to her assertions; but the smile of that sweet girl speaks volumes! What would I give to have one such directed to me! and how insipid do those which dimple that lovely face appear! he reflected, looking earnestly at the beautiful girl who was walking by his side.

Maria, however, at this moment, as if divining the object of his reflections, began to speak in extenuation of what she styled her father's eccentricities, which, she said, made him appear what he really was not, rude and uncivil. Her sister, too, she said, "from her great attachment to her father, had adopted many of his strange habits and thoughts; but "——

"There is no need to attempt any vindication of your sister, my dear Miss Woodford; I am charmed with her; her every action is the result of pure nature and innocence—in my eyes a charm superior to all the brilliancy of accomplishments, or the refinements of what is called taste."

That is not very polite, however, thought Maria; who, though she had been, in reality, influenced by her naturally good heart, in endeavouring to set her father and sister off to the best advantage, had, at the same time, not lost sight of the opportunity, as she imagined, of displaying her own superiority.

Could she, at that moment, have read Sir Walter's heart, she would have been still less pleased; for she would have seen that, far from being inclined to admit her superiority over her sister, he actually considered her as greatly inferior, and was glad when her truly amiable and affectionate manner of speaking of her father and sister restored her, in some manner, to a place in his esteem.

CHAPTER IV.

Though many a mouth be diligent to praise thee—
Though Beauty pine until that she hath won thee—
Though Worship, wheresoe'er thou goest, delays thee—
Though Fate and Fortune emulate to raise thee;—
Yet, all the thronging honours that surround thee
Shall not avail thee, since that Care hath found thee.
                                        ANON.

The person whom accident had thus introduced to the family at Rose Farm, and who seemed destined to become of infinite importance to more than one member of it, was, as he had announced himself, the only son, and heir to the estates and honours, of the some-time despised and till now nearly-forgotten Walter Geffrey.

The tale which had been circulated of Walter's misdeeds, and consequent expatriation, had not been wholly without foundation, but the circumstances had been somewhat misrepresented; for Walter, instead of having been sent out of his native land by way of punishment for detected crimes, had himself voluntarily quitted England; and it was not until he had been gone some weeks, that it was discovered he had carried off with him a considerable sum of money, the property of his best friend and benefactor.

From this period Walter was never heard of in England among his former connections, but among a very different class, as the faithful, the diligent, the indefatigable Geffrey was well known and appreciated. The ill-gotten wealth with which he had fled from his native country had contrary to the universally received maxim, thriven in his hands, until, at the end of ten years from his departure, it had increased to an immense sum, a sum beyond any which, in his most sanguine days of youth, Geffrey had ever dreamt of possessing.

There was a time in which to determine to make a fortune in India was sufficient to insure it—that is to say, a man had only to lay aside conscience, to resolve to let no opportunity pass him that could produce money, and the opportunities were never wanting. Those times have now passed away, but those were the times in which Walter Geffrey landed in India.

But though fortune thus favoured him with her brightest smiles, Walter was an unhappy man: when were the guilty otherwise? Amid the silks, and spices, and gems, and all the other luxuries that a princely fortune could command, the Welchman sighed for the green vales, the cool breezes, but most of all, and the most vainly, for the fresh untainted feelings which he had once enjoyed in his native principality. There was a blue-eyed fair-haired maiden too, once the sharer of those pure and innocent feelings, and afterwards the companion, if not the participator, in less blameless scenes, who still haunted his memory, rendering his days cheerless, and his nights feverish and restless. Where among all the friends which wealth had purchased him, could he find one like Margaret? Her, whose never-tiring love had borne with all his wanderings and vagaries, had submitted to poverty, disgrace, and destitution, and had attended him with never-fading constancy, through every reverse, even to the last minute, when under pretence of providing a place for her expected confinement, he had quitted her, and abandoned her and her unborn infant to their fate.

Margaret had been the daughter of an humble tradesman in the village where Walter was born; she had been the companion of his childhood, had shared with him the simple education of the village school, and like him had been pre-eminent among their compeers for personal beauty. Walter and Margaret were by universal acclamation decidedly destined for each other; even in their childhood Walter was taught to call her his little wife, and as they grew up, he would, though never expressly declared her lover, have considered his rights invaded had any one dared to single Margaret out by any particular attentions.

But the time too soon arrived when these artless feelings became vitiated, and Walter was taught to look upon the simple village maiden with very different thoughts and desires to those which had hitherto actuated him. A residence of a few months at Bristol, for the purpose of learning navigation, it being intended that he should take the command of a vessel, of which an uncle was the owner, introduced the hitherto uncorrupted village lad to society, which, masking their vices under the specious appearances of jollity, frankness, and generosity, were in reality the most dangerous and destructive he could have encountered.

Walter at first mingled with fear and trembling in the midnight orgies of these youthful libertines, but gradually he became hardened and callous to the scenes of vice and infamy to which he was introduced, and he returned to Llan—— a corrupted heartless libertine.

Margaret was the only one who did not quickly perceive the alteration. How slow is love to believe evil of its object! But proof thickened upon proof, and as the only way of saving his child from the consequences of her passionate devotion to the unworthy object of her love—her first, her maiden love—honest David Meredith, her father, determined on removing her from within the sphere of his attractions.

So secretly were his intentions put in practice that even Margaret did not suspect them, and she was already some miles advanced on her journey to London with her father, before she was aware that they were going further than Cardigan, to which place she had several times before made excursions with her mother, whom she had lately lost.

She was, however, fairly seated on the London coach before the discovery was made, and as much as she felt disposed to resent this clandestine proceeding, and deny its necessity, she was compelled to smother her feelings, for there were four strangers seated in the coach with her, and she could not of course discuss the subject of her wrongs before them.

In safety after a long and wearisome journey, the anxious father and his daughter reached London, and then in the hackney coach, which he had by the recommendation of one of his fellow-passengers, taken to convey them to the house of a sister, whom he had not seen since she had eighteen years before come down to Llan ——, on purpose to answer at the baptismal font, for Margaret, who was named after her, did honest David enter into discussion of the feelings which had prompted him to this step.

"I knew, Margaret, it was no use to talk against him, or to tell you what I knew about him, while he was there close by, to contradict me, and persuade you out of your senses as he has done before; and to leave you to be ruined by him, without trying to save you, is what I couldn't do; but now that you can listen to me, and that you see what a deal of expense and trouble it has cost me, and that you must see how hard put to it I shall be to manage at home without you, you'll lay it to heart, and think that I can have no meaning but only for your good."

Margaret, amid the showers of tears, which now burst forth with the more violence, for having been long suppressed by decorum, now protested that she never doubted that her father had been actuated by the kindest motives, but indeed, and indeed—and again the fresh tears burst forth—he was mistaken in Walter. Walter was indeed wild and thoughtless, and she couldn't say but that it was wrong for him to be idling away his time so much at the ale-house, but then how many she could name who had been as thoughtless and prodigal as him in their youth but had turned from their bad ways as soon as they were married and settled in the world, and why shouldn't he do so too, that was so good-hearted and so fondly attached to her, she would have added, but that natural timidity kept her silent on that point.

"I tell thee what it is, Marget," rejoined the anxious father, after listening somewhat impatiently yet attentively to her defence of her lover; "I tell thee plainly, that if I thought he really intended to marry thee I'd never have stepped between him and thee, to cross your love, because I know that a sensible girl like you might have done a good deal towards breaking him of his faults, but he never did intend it, Marget, he intended nothing but to bring you to ruin, and bring disgrace on my grey hairs, and now I tell you, Marget, what I *do* know he has said about marrying, because I heard him with my own ears, though he did not know I heard it."

David Meredith proceeded to relate a ribald conversation, which he had accidentally overheard between Walter and a profligate companion, who had recently come over from Bristol, to shoot with the former for a few days; and Margaret, however inclined to defend her lover, could not suppress the blush of indignation and shame at the sentiments which had issued from the lips of him whom she had considered all purity and truth.

"He did not *name* thee, my girl," continued the father, "or old as I am, I should have rushed on him, but it was well for him, and perhaps for me too, that he didn't, though I couldn't help guessing who he meant, when he talked of the girl who had very nearly drawn him in to make a tool of himself, but who he was determined now to have upon easier terms. He said, too, that he had at last resolved to sell the little property his father had left him, and then he meant to have a month or two's sport in Bristol, among his friends, and should in all likelihood be able to bring the girl he spoke of over with him."

Margaret hid her face in silent shame and confusion while her father proceeded to relate, with somewhat too triumphant a tone, his secret determination and plans to outwit the villain who thus coolly meditated his daughter's destruction; but the coach now entered Barbican, to which his sister's letters directed Meredith, and the coachman, stopping to inquire what number they wanted to go to, reminded the weeping girl that she would, in a few moments, be in the presence of a relative, who would, perhaps, be less indulgent to her weakness than her father, who had never, even when most provoked by her perseverance in error, uttered a reproach, or seemed to consider her other than as an object of compassion.

"Does my aunt know all this, father?" she inquired, hastily drying up er tears.

"Your aunt?—no, child, how should she?" he returned, "it is more than a twelvemonth since she answered my last letter, but I told her then not to be surprised if some day or other she was to see a fine, tall young woman, answering to the name of Margaret Meredith, come to see her aunt and godmother; God knows how little I thought then that I should ever come to London with you, and on such an errand too."

"Now, my dear father, promise not to tell my aunt a word of what has brought us up, but say that I've a mind to see how I like London, and if I find it agree with me, I mean to go to service (you know that she once offered to get me a place, if I had a mind to it), and I will promise you that I will drop all thoughts of Walter."

"I do, I do promise you," returned the father hastily, as the coach drew up to the door of a mean-looking grocer's shop over the door of which, the name of Jackson, in large letters, convinced honest David that he had found his destined haven.

"Well, here I am, Peggy, at last, in my old days, come to pay you a visit, and see how you get on," exclaimed Meredith, to a large, redfaced slatternly woman, who advanced from the little parlour behind the shop to meet them.

"Mercy upon me, if it isn't David!" screamed the lady, having stared at him a moment, in silent surprise. "Laws! Mr. Jackson, if here isn't my brother come to see us!" and she turned to a little, pale, sharp-faced, mean, old man, who had risen from his dinner, and now came out at her exclamation.

"Dearee me!—well to be sure!—who'd ha' thought it!" said Mr. Jackson, still keeping his station at the end of the counter, so as to block up the entrance to the room. "And so you've come up to London, Mr. Meredith; business, I suppose, of course;" and he peeped under his lady's arm, with a look of curiosity, at Margaret, who stood behind her father.

"Why, no, not altogether; I can't say I've much business in London; said Meredith, pulling off his hat, and wiping his forehead, to conceal a something like perplexity how to reply to this question.

"Dearee me! it must be expensive travelling so far; and it's very expensive, too, living in London—*lodgins* are very dear, 'specially hereabouts, in the City."

"Well, and so that's one of your daughters, I suppose?" said Mrs. Jackson, leaning across the counter, on which she rested her fat arms, and looking Margaret full in the face.

"One! Peggy; you can't, surely, have forgot that I never had but one, and that she was the child that you stood godmother to, and that was named after you!" replied Meredith, who began to be rather indignant at a reception so different from what he had anticipated.

"Oh!—ah!—yes! I recollect; and by-the-bye, miss, you were a very great fool, I can tell you, for refusing my kind offer to get you a place; you'll never have such another, I can tell you—twenty pound a year, beside *parquisites*, and with a real lady, though she was black, and she'd ha' taken you upon my character, and that's what you won't find everybody willing to do, I can assure you. But pray, now, if I may be so bould as to ax, what *has* brought you and Marget up to town, brother, so all in a hurry, as one may say?"

"Why, just what you've been talking of, Sister Peggy: Margaret wants to see how she should like London; and if it will agree with her, she is thinking of getting a place; not that there's any occasion for her going to service, because, thank God, I'm well enough to do in the world, and would be very well pleased to keep her at home, like a lady, but she would like to see a little of the world before she settles for good, and as I've no occasion to grudge myself a little pleasure for once, I've been expensive enough to come up with her."

"Well, but walk in—do walk in, Mr. Meredith," said Jackson, whose mind being relieved of the fear which had seized him, that his wife's relative had been unfortunate in business, or that some other sinister event had occasioned his coming to trouble him, was now inclined to be somewhat more generous. "Do walk in, young woman; that is, if you can find room to sit down in our little bit of a place; you see, we citizens are so heavily burthened with rent and taxes, that we are obliged to crimp ourselves up for room; our house is all let, but just this little bit of a parlour and the shop."

"And where in the world do you contrive to sleep, and to cook, and to———?"

"Here—all here in this little place, Mr. Meredith; that *sofy* that you're setting on is our bed," said Jackson, busying himself in hastily clearing the little round table, and cramming the remnants of the dinner into a cupboard behind the door.

Meredith looked at his daughter in silent dismay. How different was all this to the hearty welcome he had anticipated—the hospitality which he believed it impossible they could refuse!

Margaret, on her part, felt even more hurt and mortified than he did, from the consciousness that her folly or weakness had been the cause of exposing her father to this humiliation; but she tried to revive his drooping spirits by whispering, when Mr. Jackson attended his lady's summons to assist her in serving two or three customers, who had all come in of a lump, as she expressed it—

"Never mind, father, keep up your spirits; while we have the means of paying for what we want, we need not be downhearted in London, or anywhere else."

"No, certainly, Marget; but to think of the geese, and the turkeys, and the hares, and the flitches of bacon, that I've sent up, year after year, for now near twenty years, to Peggy and her husband; and for them never even to say, 'Have you had your dinner, David? when I've just come off such a long journey."

"I suppose you have had your dinner, brother," said Mrs. Jackson, as if she possessed the power of interpreting the dismal look which she had seen, through the glass of the door, Meredith cast towards the cupboard.

"Why, no, I can't say I have; and that's the truth," replied the plain-spoken Welchman.

"Laws! I'm sorry for that;" she replied; "but, however, we'll have an early cup of tea, to make up for it, for there's no fire to cook a steak or a chop."

Poor Meredith's countenance, which had assumed a somewhat brisker look at her question, again sunk.

"If I knew which way to go, and was sure I could find my way back," he observed, turning to his daughter, "I'd go and see if I couldn't find something to eat."

"Oh! there's a nice cook-shop t'other side of the way, brother, without going out of sight; and their joints are just now nice and hot," observed Mrs. Jackson; "and while you and your daughter are gone, I'll set the place to rights, and then we can have a comfortable cup of tea, and a bit of talk about old times; I want to hear how all my old sweethearts get on, but I must not ask before Jackson, for he's dreadful jealous."

This, which was accompanied by a most significant wink at Margaret, completed the unfavourable impression the latter had already received of her aunt; and she felt at that moment, as if she could have been willing to have abjured, in the most solemn manner, all further correspondence with Walter, could she have prevailed on her father to take her back with him, rather than submit to be left even for a day under the dominion and control of such a woman as Mrs. Jackson.

The cook-shop was found, David satisfied his hunger and thirst, and then becoming infinitely more bold and independent, by finding, as he said, "how easy it was to get anything in London, with money;" he determined to show his resentment of his sister's and brother-in-law's shabby behaviour on his return.

Matters, however, had taken a very different turn to what he had expected; when he again entered the little parlour, the fire was burning brightly, the kettle was singing merrily, and the best china arranged on the tea-table, seemed to indicate at least a wish to make the travellers comfortable; but David soon discovered, that all this magnificence was not on their account, but that Mrs. Jackson expected a lady to take tea with her, who had called during their absence, and promised to return in time for the social meal.

"We shall be two too many, I'm thinking," said David, taking up his hat, and reaching his thick oaken cudgel, from the corner in which he had deposited it; "so we'll go and see if we can't get some tea where we got our dinner."

"Laws, don't be foolish, brother!" said Mrs. Jackson, "do you think I don't know what I'm about, or that I should have asked anybody to tea if I hadn't had some meaning in it?" No, no, trust me, that's not the way to get on in London; but, however, I'll tell you at once, that it is Mrs. Dollas son, the fashionable dressmaker, in Crutched Friars, that's a coming; she always buys her tea and sugar of us, and a very good customer she is, especially for the four shilling Bohea for her 'prentices and workwomen. Now, struck me all at once, as she was giving her orders, that it might be a ,od chance for Margaret, if she could get into the dress-making line—for :s to places of service—laws bless you! she might wait for months and months before she'd meet with anything better than a place of all work! especially as she is good-looking, which I assure you is no recommendation to most ladies, as I know to my sorrow—by sad experience, when

I first came up to London; for many and many's the time I was sent away with, 'you don't suit me young woman;' when all they'd got to object against me was, I was too good-looking."

David opened his eyes wide at this assertion, which, at any other time, he would have taken some pains to prove was utterly unfounded, his sister having at no period of her life been remarkable for personal charms. He was now, however, too anxious and intent on seeing Margaret comfortably and respectably settled, to enter upon any other subject, and therefore proceeded to ask a variety of questions respecting Mrs. Dollasson, all which were answered by his sister, by the highest eulogiums upon her house, her management, her business, and in short, all connected with the establishment in Crutched Friars.

"She will live like a queen," said Mrs. Jackson, in conclusion; "and of a Sunday, when it's her turn to come out, she can go with us in the fine weather to Chalk Farm, and Copenhagen House, and Highbury Barn, for we always (Jackson and I) takes our pleasure like gentlefolks of a Sunday; and why shouldn't we, seeing we work hard, and live hard all the week, and have neither chick nor child to provide for? And by the bye, brother David," she added, lowering her voice to a whisper; "I may tell you, between ourselves, that if Margaret behaves well, and is dutiful, and modest, and industrious, and contrives to get on Jackson's blind side, that go when he will, he hasn't got a relation in the world, being as one may say, a chance child brought up by the parish, and no disgrace to him, that he's made his way in the world without the help of kith or kin."

"Mrs. Jackson, do pray come and attend upon the customers," said the old man, putting his sharp withered face within side the glass door; "here's a whole shop-full waiting, and you know it's people's tea-time, and they are all in a hurry to be served."

Mrs. Jackson bustled out, to attend her *cara sposa's* summons, and Meredith, turning to his daughter, demanded what she thought of her aunt's proposal.

"I am content with anything you approve, father," she replied, in a tone of humility; "but with your leave, we will first see this lady before we decide."

"Yes, and if you are not perfectly satisfied with her, Margaret, I would sooner run all risks, and trust to your own good sense, and take you back with me, than——"

"Oh! no, no, you are too good, too kind," interrupted Margaret, bursting into tears; "oh! no, I would rather—I would submit to anything rather than run the risk of giving you uneasiness again."

"God bless you, my child, you will live, I trust, to thank me for what, I am afraid, seems harsh and cruel on my part, but——"

"This is my brother and his daughter, madam," said Mrs. Jackson, throwing open the door to its widest extent, and introducing a thin, genteel-looking well-dressed woman. "This is the lady, brother—Mrs. Dollasson—that I was talking to you about; and I am sure, if you can agree about terms, it will be quite a blessing for my niece to get into such a respectable house, where she'll be treated as one of the family."

"I shall not be very exorbitant as to terms, Mrs. Jackson, for I like the young lady's appearance, and I am very apt to decide at first sight."

Margaret's spirits revived at the apparent frankness and cordiality of this address, which a few minutes' conversation seemed to increase. Her father too, was well-pleased at the attention which Mrs. Dollasson showed him, so unlike the cool indifference with which he had been received by his sister and her husband; and the tea passed over much more comfortably and sociably than Margaret had anticipated.

THE PRIDE OF THE VILLAGE;

OR,

THE FARMER'S DAUGHTERS.

CHAPTER V.

'Twas sad to gaze upon a brow so fair,
And see it traced with such a tale of woe;
To think that one so young and beautiful
Was wasting to the grave,

ANON.

MRS. DOLLASSON'S terms, however, though she herself declared them most moderate, and protested that the strong liking she had taken for Miss Margaret only had induced her to have such a small sum, as she had never taken so little with any of her other young ladies, were far above what David could either afford or was prepared for; but serious as the sum was

3

to him, and greatly as it would straiten him to part with it, the affectionate father resolved to overlook all difficulties, in order to place his child in a comfortable situation; and before they parted, the bargain was concluded—half the money paid down, and security given for the remainder.

It was with a heavy heart Margaret witnessed all this; she was fully aware how little able her father was to afford such heavy expense, and she felt grieved and ashamed that her weakness and folly should cost him so dearly.

Relieved of the fear which seemed to have possessed them, that David and his daughter were come to be a trouble and expense to them, Mr. and Mrs. Jackson were now very sociable, and willing to give that which most people are very liberal of—advice; and the honest Welchman, though at first inclined to be sulky and resentful, at length yielded in consideration of their promised attention to Margaret, who it was agreed by her new mistress was to spend every Sunday with them, when she was not otherwise engaged.

"Where can she be otherwise engaged?" inquired the anxious father; "seeing she hasn't got a friend or relation in London, but her aunt here."

"Oh! but my dear sir, you forget that she is going to join a family of six or seven young people," said Mrs. Dollasson; "and it can't be expected but they will sometimes have engagements that aunts and uncles can have nothing to do with."

David looked grave; there was a levity in the manner even more than in the matter of this speech, which he did not think altogether becoming in one who held such a responsible station, as to have the management of five or six young women. But Margaret's earnest assurance that she should enter into no gaieties, which her aunt's presence did not sanction, somewhat re-assured him; and when on the following day he accompanied her to Mrs. Dollasson's house, and beheld the grave countenances, the silent and orderly manners, and the indefatigable attention to their employment, which characterised the young people to whom his daughter was introduced, all fear or suspicion was banished from his mind, and he quitted London, under the comfortable conviction that he had succeeded effectually in his plan of detaching her from Walter Geffrey, and had likewise placed her in a fair way of acquiring a respectable living.

It was with a heavy heart poor Margaret beheld her father depart, and her sorrow was not lightened by discovering that it excited in the greater part of her companions only sarcasm and ridicule. The poor girl, indeed, soon found that her plain rustic appearance, her unsophisticated manners, and the peculiarities of her dialect, were all food for ridicule to the young ladies, and she had been only a few hours among them, before she discovered that unless she could gain courage to retaliate and defend herself her situation would be very far from enviable, even should there be nothing to render it irksome but the taunts and jests of her companions.

Margaret, however, soon found that there were many other causes to regret having so suddenly decided on becoming Mrs. Dollasson's inmate. It had been specified to her father, in making the arrangement, that she would be required to work only ten hours a day, and the rest of her time would be at her own disposal. But she soon found that Mrs. Dollasson's agreements were all made to bend to the pressure of business; the ten were extended to twelve, fourteen, and even on extraordinary occasions, poor Margaret sometimes numbered eighteen hours at the weary work-table; nay, upon a public mourning taking place within the first month of her apprenticeship, Margaret was compelled not only to sacrifice two nights' rest, but the whole of Sunday, that day which she had been taught to hold so sacred, was to her extreme horror, passed in the same occupation as the rest of the week.

Accustomed to constant exercise, to pure air, and plenty of wholesome food, Margaret's health and strength rapidly declined; she had exchanged the green fields for the heated unwholesome atmosphere of a small dark room, which was scarcely large enough to allow a person to pass round the table, at which were generally seated from twelve to twenty females, and this room, too, was at night, when they did go to rest, the bed-room of the six apprentices. It was no wonder, therefore, that Margaret lost her colour and her appetite, or that she turned with disgust from the coarse unsavoury diet, which was so slovenly served up to her and her companions. She was indeed wretched, and Mrs. Dollassons's exorbitant requisitions, seemed to increase every day, while the flimsy wash of good humour and consideration for the novice which she had at first worn was new completely thrown aside, and she appeared what she really was, a mean mercenary tyrant, who considered her young pupils, as she called them, only as so many slaves, from whose labours she was to make the greatest possible profit.

Margaret's first two or three Sundays had been passed, as it had been agreed upon, with her aunt and husband, to whom she had taken care to render herself welcome, by presents more than commensurate with the expense of her entertainment; but their habits, their associates, and the places which they frequented on these occasions were so little to her taste that she could derive no satisfaction from what, under other circumstances, would have been most welcome—a change of scene. Mrs. Jackson, too, on her part, became tired of her niece, whose scruples about going to tea-gardens instead of church, and reservedness to the male sex, whom they met with there, did not at all assimilate. Margaret, indeed, saw many things in the conduct and character of her aunt that appeared revolting and inconsistent with the character of a respectable tradesman's wife, and Mrs. Jackson, at length out of all patience, as she said, at such squeamishness, in a girl like her, absolutely quarrelled with her niece, and gave her to understand, that her company on Sundays would henceforth be dispensed with.

The next two Sundays were, much to Margaret's discontent, devoted to Mrs Dollasson's business; but on the third she was again at liberty. But where to go? She could go to church, to be sure, as she always did; but church would not last all day, and she was given to understand by her companions, that there was no dinner or tea provided on this day; and that the servant would consider it a great intrusion, if any of the apprentices returned home before the set hour, ten o'clock at night, which was, indeed, by most of them, extended to eleven or twelve: Mrs. Dollasson herself always going out of town on Saturday night, and returning on Monday morning.

"But what shall I do to-day?" said Margaret, to the young girl who was her bedfellow; "I cannot walk about the streets till that hour, and I am determined I will not go to my aunt's."

"It is a hard thing, indeed," said Charlotte (her companion), "certainly, to have no friends in town; and I can't offer to take you home with me, because my mother is so particular. But I'll tell you what I'll do, if you like, I'll meet you after dinner, and we'll have a nice long walk together to my aunt's at Walworth, for she will be glad to see anybody I choose to bring with me.'

Margaret did not object to this plan. She was, indeed, beginning to feel very desolate; and the thought of having some one to attach herself to, and some plan for passing what else would have appeared a tremendously long and cheerless day, was grateful to her.

She failed not at the appointed place and time, but no Charlotte came; and to add to her mortification the sky began to darken, a few drops of rain fell, and there was every indication that it would set in for a regular wet evening.

The place of appointment was Blackfriars-bridge; and Margaret, who had with some difficulty found her way thither, and who had, with the exception of the time she had sat in church, been on her feet, without any refreshment, since she had left her home in the morning, began to contemplate with dismay the prospect of being wet through, and was hurrying off, in order to seek some shelter, when she was suddenly stopped by hearing Charlotte's voice, calling to her, from the window of a hackney-coach, which the next moment drew up to the side of the pavement.

"Oh! you poor forlorn-looking thing, I suppose you thought I had entirely forgot you; but come along, and sit here by me—there, make room—squeeze close. She won't take up too much room, for she's like me, lost all her fat since she came to Dolly's (the name by which they usually called their lady mistress when not present)." In the midst of this rattle Margaret seated herself, without any reflection but that of pleasure at the unexpected relief, or without knowing with whom, beside her friend Charlotte, she was in company; but now that she was comfortably settled, and the coach off the stones, she found time to look at her companions. There were Charlotte's two sisters, one elder and one younger than herself, whom she (Margaret) had casually seen, when they called at Mrs. Dollason's upon the former; a young man, whom she had also seen, and understood to be engaged to Charlotte's sister; and last of all, one, of whom the first glance took her breath away, and made her heart beat so that it almost burst from her side —he was so like, so very like, Walter. Yet it could not be him—she ventured to look again; but she could scarcely discover the features of this person, for the rain was now pouring down; he had drawn up the glass, and was sitting back in the corner, so that she could scarcely distinguish his features—yet the size, the look! She longed to hear him speak—to hear some one address him by his name—and at last she was gratified.

"What are you thinking of, Walter?" said the other young man, slapping him familiarly on the shoulder. Margaret uttered a faint scream, and the attention of all was immediately turned on her, except apparently that of him who was most interested.

A feigned excuse satisfied her companions; and Margaret, now as much piqued at his evident indifference as she had been surprised and alarmed at this strange rencontre, struggled hard to regain her calmness, and convince him that she was as little anxious as he could possibly be to renew their former acquaintance.

They arrived at their place of destination, which Margaret naturally supposed was the aunt's of whom Charlotte had spoken; but she soon discovered that she was mistaken. The young man who was addressed as Mr. Harrison gaily welcomed them to bachelor's fare. The girls began to examine and quiz, as they called it, the apartments and accommodations; and Margaret soon discovered, to her infinite mortification, that she was actually a visitor to the very person whom she had come to London to avoid—the apartments they were in being shared between him and his friend Harrison. After abundance of laughing, joking, and ridiculing the bachelor's establishment, by Charlotte Edwards and her sisters, the whole party sat down to tea. Margaret had manœuvred to place herself as far as possible from Walter, who seemed equally desirous of forgetting their former connection; and all was mirth and jollity among the rest of the party. The young men had provided a very substantial tea for their visitors; but poor Margaret, who but a short time before was thinking, almost with tears, of the comfortable dinner which on that day never failed to grace her father's table, and contrasting it with the penny bun, which was all that formed her cheerless meal, could now scarcely contrive to swallow a bit of the dainties that were offered to her.

"Do not be foolish," said Charlotte, helping her to a hugh slice of cake; "we all know very well that you've had no dinner; and indeed it was that consideration that made us come so far out of the way, to take you up. For, as I told Jemima, says I, 'The poor girl will be starved before night, for I know she has lent all the little money she brought with her, to one and the other. I owe her some—more's the pity; but she's a good little soul, she never asks for it.'"

"Probably, because she knows it would be of no use," said one of the sisters; but really, seriously, Charlotte, it is a shame—you are always over head and ears in debt."

During this speech, which had crimsoned Margaret's cheeks with vexation, Walter had arisen to assist the eldest of the Edwards, who was making tea; and as Margaret raised her eyes, they encountered his fixed upon her with a look of such tender pity that the tears involuntarily rushed down her cheeks, and she was constrained precipitately to rise from the table, and retreat to the window.

"I wonder you have not a little more thought, Charlotte," observed the eldest sister, in a loud whisper;" see how you have mortified your friend—it isn't every one who like's their affairs to be exposed so in company.

"It is Welch pride," observed Charlotte, laughing; "she can't bear it to be told, that she walked about for a dinner."

"Welch!" said Mr. Harrison, repeating the word in an inquiring tone.

"Oh, dear! I declare I quite forget that you are both Taffys," returned Charlotte, laughing. "Lord, I ought to have formally introduced Miss Margaret Ap Evans to Mr. Walter Ap———: what is it?"

"How can you be so thoughtless and nonsensical, Charlotte?" said the sister, again interfering; while Mr. Harrison, approaching Margaret said—

"I was not, till now, aware that I was in company with a countrywoman; may I ask what part of Wales you come from?"

"Cardinganshire, sir," said Margaret, in a low voice, and with great confusion.

"Ha! indeed! I say, friend Walter, come here, here's news for you!"

"No news at all," said Walter, without seeming at all confused. "I was quite aware, the moment the young lady spoke, what part she came from;" and then, evidently anxious only to avert the impending discovery, he contrived, by upsetting his tea cup over Jemima's muslin frock, to withdraw their attention entirely from Margaret, who was now, more than ever, determined to preserve the distance between them, and never to acknowledge she had known him, unless he betrayed the secret himself.

The tea was finished, amidst laughing and romping between the Edwards and Mr. Harrison, Walter occasionally joining them, or suggesting some subject for their mirth, though it was evident he did not really participate in it, and only forced himself to join to escape their observation.

Margaret, too artless and unpractised to assume what she did not feel, was the only silent one of the party: and Charlotte, evidently without the slightest suspicion or any particular cause for her reserve, from time to time rallied her on her serious looks, observing that she should give a good account of her to Dolly.

"And, pray, who is Dolly?" said Walter, with pretended indifference ; "is she a person of so much importance that her influence extends even here ?"

"Oh, yes," returned Charlotte, "poor Margaret is sadly afraid of Dolly. For my own part, I do not care a farthing for her, and she knows it, and hates me, accordingly ; but as to Margaret, she never hears Dolly's voice, without trembling and turning pale."

Walter turned a look of pity and sorrow on Margaret; their eyes again met—they were not so quickly withdrawn as before. Margaret began to think that she was mistaken in believing him to be indifferent to her; but at the very moment that she made this observation, she recollected her promise to her father—she remembered, too, what the latter had told her of Walter's designs on her, and she was again plunged into an agony of sorrow and fear.

The time appointed for their return approached ; and Walter quitted the room for a short time, previously observing that he would return in time to accompany them home.

"Well, I never was so much deceived in all my life, as in your friend, George," observed Eliza Edwards, the young woman to whom Mr. Harrison was paying his addresses. "I thought, when first I was in his company, he was one of the pleasantest young men I ever met with ; but he seems, to-day, quite contrary—as stupid and dull——"

"And so malicious, too," interrupted Jemima ; "I know he threw the tea over my frock on purpose ; and if I'd been a man I would have knocked him down."

"And Mr. Harrison kindly intends him for my beau, too," said Charlotte ; "and introduced him, I believe, on purpose ; was it not so ?"

"I plead guilty," replied Harrison ; "but, really, I do not know what has so metamorphosed him. Had I supposed he would have been so dull, and deficient in gallantry—— yet, nevertheless, I must do him justice—the whole of the arrangements which you have praised so much, were made by him, and at his expense."

"Oh, the man's well enough, and handsome enough ; and I should like him well enough," replied Charlotte, "if he was not so silent ; but, really, it would be quite awful to have a beau that does not open his mouth above once in half an hour—but, perhaps (and she burst into a laugh) he can talk better in Welsh, than in English—we will try him when he comes back—Margaret shall have a talk with him in her own language ; look, how she blushes at the thoughts of it," she added, laughing.

Margaret did indeed blush, though Charlotte little suspected why ; but the return of the object of their discussion put an end to the conversation, and they departed.

The rain had cleared away, and the evening was altogether favourable for their long walk ; but Margaret shrank back, trembling and confused, when she found that Eliza and Jemima Edwards having each taken an arm of Mr. Harrison, Charlotte and herself were committed to the care of Walter.

Charlotte, without any reserve, immediately took the arm that was proffered her ; but Margaret, affecting not to see a similar offer to her, continued to walk by his side, until laughingly rebuked for her prudery by her gay female companion.

"Do, for goodness sake, child, take Mr. Geffrey's arm," she concluded ; "or else, when we get into the Blackfriars-road, we shall be separated, and then I shall have to pay the crier to find you, for I am sure you would never find your way home."

The arm was again held out; and Margaret, as lightly as possible, passed her own trembling one through it.

For the first half hour not a word passed between her and her companion, to whom, however, Charlotte chattered incessantly; but it was impossible for Margaret to dissemble her agitation, when the giddy girl, at length, reverted to the circumstance of his being a countryman of her silent companion.

"It is a tie between us, which, I fear, your companion is not pleased to allow," said Walter. "Miss Margaret seems by no means anxious to speak of the place of her birth: she has, probably found attractions in London which have induced her to forget it altogether."

"Indeed I have not," said Margaret, spontaneously, "Indeed, I wish, sincerely wish, I were there, now, and should never see London again."

"You are disappointed, then, in your expectations of London," he remarked.

"Not exactly so," replied Margaret; "because I had formed no expectations on the subject."

"Ha! indeed!—may I presume to ask what induced you to leave home, and come up here?"

Margaret was silent—she felt she was treading on dangerous ground; for if she acknowledged that she was brought to the metropolis, without any consultation of her will or wishes, it would lead to farther explanation, and thus ——. Oh, no; it was better, far better, to remain thus, than run the risk of renewing the connection which her father had taken so much pains to break.

Walter did not repeat the question—he did not even show a wish to continue the subject, but immediately addressed some trifling remark to Charlotte, who, not having felt too well pleased at the commencement of a conversation which threatened to shut her out altogether, immediately commenced her usual strain of badinage, and thus dismissed the subject altogether.

They reached the end of the street leading to Mrs. Dollasson's without another word having passed between Margaret and Walter; and she was about to withdraw her arm from his, preparatory to their parting, when he contrived suddenly to direct Charlotte's attention in another quarter, and then thrust a letter into Margaret's hand, who was so entirely surprised by the unexpected action, that she had not recollection to refuse it, and almost involuntarily concealed it from her companion.

They parted—Walter uttering a profusion of unmeaning nonsense to Charlotte, and comprising all his adieus to Margaret in one expressive look and tender pressure of the hand; and the latter retired, agitated with a thousand contending emotions.

It was impossible for her to elude the observation of her companions, who were now all assembled together, and all eager to talk of where they had been, what they had seen, whom they had met, and a hundred other topics, equally uninteresting to Margaret, whose thoughts were all concentrated in one object—the letter which she was compelled to let remain unread till the morning. Her attention, however, was soon withdrawn, even from this important object, by hearing Charlotte in a conversation, which was carried on, in an under tone, between her and a young female who slept in the adjoining bed—in which Walter was described as having fallen violently in love with her (Charlotte), and having solicited her to go with him to America, whither he proposed to go very shortly.

"I have not quite made up my mind that I shan't accept his offer," she continued, "for I'm sick of this life; there's another week of slavery to begin, for we are to be up at five, Dolly told me, before she went, to commence the wedding-dresses."

"Well, then, do let us go to sleep, and don't talk any more," rejoined her friend: "it is past twelve now, so we shall not have too much sleep."

Margaret, however, in vain, tried to profit by the silence that ensued.

Could it be possible that Walter had indeed renounced her, and so soon transferred his affections to such a giddy, volatile, thoughtless girl as Charlotte, and was he really going to leave England for ever? The letter, probably, was to bid her adieu, to tell her he had seen her for the last time; Margaret's tears wetted her pillow at this thought, and yet, had she not voluntarily renounced him, sworn—no, not absolutely sworn to her father, but promised, irrevocably promised, that she would never renew the connexion, which had given him so much uneasiness; but then to think that such a girl as Charlotte should banish her from his affections; she quite hated Charlotte, and she shrank away from her to the farther side of the bed, as though the poor girl's touch was infectious.

Charlotte was, by this time, in a happy state of unconsciousness, forgetful of the morrow's evils, which she had so pathetically deprecated, and dreaming over again the transactions of the day, for more than once she murmured words which her companion interpreted, as relating to what had passed between her and Walter; but poor Margaret in vain attempted to lose the remembance of her sorrows in repose, and the clock had chimed two before even a momentary forgetfulness stole over her. Now, however, she had forgotten Walter—the letter which was pressed under her pillow—Charlotte's presumption—her own mortifications, all were sliding into indistinctness, but they were succeeded by feelings of extreme horror; the room was suffocating, the sound as of roaring waves was in her ears, and she laboured for breath, as though she had been plunged beneath. In another moment she threw off, with a violent effort, the burthen that seemed to press her down, she started up and gazed wildly around; she was no longer asleep, it was not a dream, the sound—the smell was that of fire, and with wild screams, she roused her young companions from their slumbers to the horrid certainty that the house was in flames.

For a moment, all was wild and aimless dismay. "The staircase is on fire —we are lost!" was the general cry. Margaret flew to the windows, but the height rendered all hopes of escape that way impracticable, and her companions now hung from them, shrieking to the crowd, who were already gathered in the street beneath.

At this moment, a ladder, which had been secured to the scaffolding of a house, which was under repair, at a short distance, was hastily raised to the window, and a man actively ascended and implored them to lose no time.

"Margaret! Margaret! trust yourself to me!" exclaimed the well-known voice of Walter, who had distinguished her, though she shrank back as he approached the window. Margaret, however, did not forget, in the midst of the horror and confusion, that she was not clothed, and while the rest of the girls crowded to their only chance of escape, with an impetuosity that threatened danger to themselves as well as their companion, Margaret was hastily throwing on such articles of dress as came first to hand.

Her companions were now all safe in the street, and Margaret, in reply to Walter's agonised exclamations and entreaties, had replied, as she advanced towards him—

"I am here, Walter;" when the fire suddenly burst forth with such intense fury from the windows of the first floor, that not only was her descent rendered quite impracticable, but Walter was obliged to save himself from immediate destruction, by leaping into the window of the apartment in which he had so fatally lingered.

"We are both lost now!" said Walter, straining her in his arms with desperation.

The flame, which was now entering the windows, shone upon a door which was exactly opposite, but which was nailed up.

"Where does that lead to?" and Walter, without waiting for a reply, sprang towards it, and with a few blows, aided by his feet, forced it inwards. The instantaneous change of atmosphere, rather than their sight, told them they were in the open air, and Margaret now recollected that she had been told the door led to the leads over the roof of an adjoining building, on which they had been accustomed to keep flowers, but that the door had been nailed up by Mrs. Dollasson, who declared that they neglected their work to attend to their garden.

Walter paused a moment to reconnoitre their situation, which at first sight did not seem much bettered by the change, for there appeared no means of descent, and though, by going to the extremity of the leads, they were now pretty well out of the reach of the smoke and flames, which were ascending in immense volumes, yet they could scarcely hope that the building on which they stood would escape the conflagration; and to make their situation known to those who might have aided them seemed impossible, for they were now in the rear of the other houses, the inhabitants of which had all fled at the first alarm into the street.

Walter gazed round him in despair, and traversed the flat roof hastily in every direction, to discover if it afforded no means of escape.

"We are saved, Margaret!—we are saved!" he exclaimed, as his foot at length struck against what proved to be the wire projection of a small skylight. To wrench up the wire and demolish the glass was but the work of a moment; and then he hastily slung himself through the aperture to discover whether the height would allow of his lowering Margaret without any other assistance. Fortunately he found a footing: and, in a few moments, Margaret was safe in his arms. But here a new difficulty arose: they were in a large apartment, which Walter rightly conjectured was used as a warehouse; but the sudden change from the blaze of light to comparative darkness, and the heat of the place, which was closely shut up, so bewildered him, that for a long time he searched in vain for any means of egress.

"I shall be stifled, dear Walter! let us go back into the open air, at all hazards!" said Margaret, clinging still closer to her protector.

Walter did not reply, but he redoubled his frantic haste to find the door, which must of necessity, open to a staircase. Before it was found and opened, Margaret lay an insensible weight in his arms. He carried her down, forced open another and another door, and then found himself in an open quiet court, leading in a street, so far removed from the scene of tumult that not a person seemed to have been disturbed by it.

The cool night air, and some water which a neighbouring pump opportunely supplied, soon brought Margaret to herself; and, in an agony of gratitude and affection, she threw her arms around the neck of her preserver.

Walter, however, though his first impression was that of joy at her and his own escape, did not lose sight of the advantages which her present helpless situation afforded him.

" Where can I take you to, Margaret ?" he demanded ; " there is no place here which can afford you an asylum."

Margaret was bewildered. In the exultation of having escaped such a dreadful fate she had forgotten that this calamity had rendered her house-less and desolate, with scarcely covering to shield her from the elements. Her aunt—it was the only place she could look to for shelter; yet she doubted, sadly doubted, the kindness of her reception ; and, for the first time, fully aware of the misery of her situation, she burst into tears.

"Do not be thus distressed, dear Margaret," said her wily lover; " I did but ask you if there is any person or place you would wish me to con-duct you to ; but if you will trust yourself to my guidance, I will take you to a kind, good old creature. Though her place is but homely,———"

" Oh ! take me anywhere, Walter, I shall be safe and happy with you !" exclaimed Margaret, warmly.

Walter pressed her still more closely to his bosom ; and Margaret forgot her recent danger, her father's anxieties and warnings—all, in short, but that Walter still loved and had risked his life for her.

She accompanied him to the place he had spoken of, was received with the most officious welcome, and——— but why follow minutely this record of woman's weakness and man's perfidy ! Margaret was henceforth acknow-ledged as the wife of her seducer; and his promise to give a legal right to that title, from week to week, and month to month, quieted her scruples. She had written to her father, immediately after the fire, detailing her provi-dential escape, and the means by which it had been effected, and leaving it to him to say what was to be her destiny ! But this letter Walter had pru-dently consigned to the flames, after having first perused it.

From day to day the unhappy girl looked and waited for the com-munication which, she flattered herself she was irrevocably deter-mined to abide by, but it came not; and she was at length compelled re-luctantly to yield her belief to Walter's assertions that her father had re-nounced her.

" So bitter," said the latter, " is the old man's hatred of me, that it is my belief he would rather you should have perished in the flames than that I should have been the happy means of saving you."

Margaret wept long and bitterly at this alienation from her only parent ; but Walter was passionately devoted to her : and his love, and gratifications and indulgences which that affection procured for her, soon lessened the intensity of her regret, and banished, except in private, the tears from her eyes, as the name of her father was henceforth banished from her tongue.

Walter's passion, however, like all which have no better foundation, soon began to cool; and Margaret had, too, the additional misery of dis-covering that his extravagance was rapidly exhausting his means of support.

All her imprudence, her ingratitude, and want of affection to her father, now stared her in the face. She had never heard anything of the old man since the eventful night of the fire, for he had never answered the letter she had written to assure him that she was safe. During the many hours of solitary and painful reflections which were now her lot to endure, the wish and hope of being reconciled to the kind and affectionate parent was evermore uppermost in her mind. As the wife of Walter, however he might condemn the imprudence which had made her so, she felt that she would dare present herself to her father ; but without that title, she dared not ; and it became anew a motive with her to urge on Walter the fulfilment of his often-repeated promises. At first he procrastinated, and promised again ;

but at length the theme became disagreeable to him—he tried to put her off by treating the engagement itself with levity.

"How can a few words, muttered over us by a parson, make us more one than we are, Peggy?" he observed, with a laughing air.

"No," returned Margaret; but it is the solemn contract that we make between ourselves, in the sight of———"

"Pshaw!—well, come, we'll make the contract as solemn as you please—come, here is your prayer-book; I will read my part of the ceremony—yours, I dare say, you have got by heart, long ago."

Margaret burst into tears at this unfeeling sneer; and Walter, after making a slight attempt to dry them, by declaring that he meant nothing by his raillery, quitted her, declaring that he was quite tired of melancholy looks.

Again and again was the subject renewed between them; and Margaret, at length, ventured to acknowledge, that her wish to be reconciled to her father was her chief motive for urging him to what he had so often promised.

"Your father, Margaret," he replied, assuming a look of deep concern; "if that is the only cause of your anxiety, I am sorry to say that it is too late for you ever to fulfil your wish; I have been unwilling to give you pain, but the truth must be told—your father has been dead these two months past."

Margaret now believed her cup of sorrow full; but she had as yet tasted but slightly of its bitters; she was doomed to drain it to the dregs. By degrees she learned the particulars of her father's death. The melancholy news of the fire, and the supposed loss of his daughter, had abruptly met his eye in a public newspaper. Her efforts to save herself, her frantic screams for assistance, and the daring attempt of a young man to save her, who had shared her horrid fate, were all detailed with heart-rending accuracy, and the poor old father sank under the unexpected blow. His business was henceforth neglected—the world was a blank to him—his whole thoughts were absorbed in the dreadful catastrophe, which was ever present in all its horrid circumstances, and after a short struggle he sank silently into the grave.

By what strange fatality her letter to him had been prevented reaching its destination Margaret could not learn—it was, indeed, now useless to inquire; but she mourned for her father as only those can mourn who feel the consciousness of having by their misconduct hastened that catastrophe, which they would, when too late, have given worlds to have retarded

Margaret, however, soon learned that the indulgence of her grief was not likely to recall the wayward heart of Walter, who detested, as he said, all sighing and sobbing, especially when it could do no manner of good, as was the case in the present instance; and she, therefore, exerted all her fortitude to conceal the grief that rankled at her heart. But she soon had fresh and infinitely more bitter cause to regret the hour when she had listened to the insinuations of passion, in opposition to those of reason and filial affection.

She was hourly expecting to become a mother, when Walter, who had for some time casually absented himself, upon frivolous pretences, from her sometimes for two or three days, and once or twice for even a whole week, suddenly disappeared altogether.

They were considerably in arrears, not only for rent, but to all the trades-people in the neighbourhood, who, deceived by Margaret's innocent and modest appearance, had readily credited the account Walter chose to give of himself, and her; and the unhappy girl's first supposition, was that he had absented himself to avoid these creditors, who were beginning to grow importunate. He had, indeed, more than once hinted to her, that without some unexpected stroke of good fortune, he should never be able to discharge those debts, and that the only alternative he saw, was to get out of the way, and though it had never occurred to her as possible that he would take this step without advising her of it, yet she was now for a long time willing to believe that this was the only motive of his absence, and that he would send for her whenever he considered it safe to do so, without betraying the place of refuge.

By degrees, however, the fatal truth became apparent; Margaret was deserted, and in addition to the misery of finding herself thus left destitute at the very time when she most required assistance and protection, was added the galling sting of contempt and reproach, from those who considered her as accessory to the imposition which had been practised on them by her seducer. It was in vain that Margaret tried to induce their pity, by candidly revealing her own history. There could be no pity for one, who, far from being able to pay the debt which had been contracted, as they insisted, if not by her, for her use, was absolutely in danger of wanting common necessaries. Her landlady, the mother of a large family, had no notion of pitying such creatures, and insisted that her husband should compel the unfortunate lodger to quit her apartments without delay.

Margaret could oppose only tears to this peremptory mandate, and on a cold rainy day in November, she sallied forth to procure another lodging.

Her beautiful face, her evident melancholy, and the unequivocal prospect of soon becoming a mother which her appearance betrayed, were sufficient reasons for the contempt and rudeness which she experienced from some, the suspicion and rejection of all to whom she applied, and hopeless and sinking with fatigue, she returned to be told there was no longer a home there for her.

"Not for this night, for this night only!" she frantically exclaimed; "surely you cannot turn me from your door at this hour, and such a night, too; you have daughters of your own, and——"

"Yes, ma'am; I have daughters, and it's just because I'm determined they shan't have a bad example before their eyes, and shall see what wickedness and disobedience of parents brings people to, that I won't let you in; no, not for another hour!" said the self-complacent lady, through the window of the parlour, which she had opened to answer her unhappy lodger, as if fearful that the latter should force her way if the front door was opened.

Margaret could not reply to this, it was too true; and in despair she wrung her hands, and turned from the inhospitable door.

The few articles she had left (for stern necessity had compelled her to part with all but those that were indispensable to personal comfort), including those for her expected infant, were all left in her bedroom; but even these were denied her by the inexorable woman, who seemed determined to make the unfortunate girl experience, in its utmost degree, the consequences of guilt.

That night and the next day the unhappy Margaret traversed the streets of London, unknowing whither she went—regardless of the observation her appearance, from time to time, attracted—repulsing even with fierceness the repeated attempts which were made to address her—and conscious only of one wish, and one purpose—to find Walter Geffrey, to let him see the wretchedness to which he had reduced her, and then to die at his feet.

The second evening closed in; she had tasted no food since early in the day before, and all the rest she had taken from her weary walk was upon the steps of doors from which she had usually been driven in a short time, either by the insolence of curiosity, or the impertinence of levity:

The rain had at first fallen so heavily, that it had drenched her to the skin; but had now ceased, and the chill wind seemed to indicate frost.

Suddenly the preternatural strength which had sustained, seemed to desert her; she felt her limbs tremble, and become unable to bear her further; her head then became confused, her sight obscured, and after vainly grasping at all around to save her, she fell with violence on the pavement.

When Margaret recovered to perfect recollection of the past, and consciousness of the present, she was the inhabitant of a parish workhouse, and by her side lay the infant to whom she had given birth in the pangs of insensibility. Many days had elapsed since she had been found perishing in the street, and conveyed to her present asylum, but she had remained in a state of torpid unconsciousness of her situation, until the birth of her boy roused her once more to misery.

It was a beautiful child, and even amongst those whom poverty and wretchedness had rendered selfish, both the mother and her boy excited universal observation and attention. The tale Margaret had to tell was one, however, too common in that miserable abode to excite more than common sympathy, and from that Margaret turned away; the wound had stricken too deep, and even her child's innocent smiles failed to banish for one moment the look of settled despair from her countenance, or the deep-seated conviction from her mind that she was dying.

Weeks, however, passed on, and Margaret still lingered in a world of woe; but though her homely companions tried to cheer her by speaking of her youth and her good looks, and by relating instances of good fortune and after prosperity which had befallen many who had possessed half her advantages, she still shook her head, and pressed her child closer to her bosom, from the conviction that ere long that bosom would be cold even to its innocent endearments.

The hour of final separation from that sole remaining tie at length arrived; Margaret was pronounced past recovery, and her child was taken from her, to receive nourishment from another nurse.

"This is the last—the last!" murmured Margaret, hiding her face with her attenuated hands, as if to shut henceforth all view of that world which was now a blank to her. She had beheld her child for the last time; and there remained not now an object which could induce her to unclose her eyes again. She was mistaken. A voice, which even at that awful moment thrilled through her heart, sounded in her ears. She looked up, and beheld Walter gazing upon her with looks of deep agony and commiseration.

"Margaret, forgive me!—forgive me!" he wildly exclaimed, "not willingly did I quit you; but——"

Margaret heard not the conclusion of the sentence.

"My child—your child, Walter," she frantically exclaimed; "promise me —swear that you will never desert it."

"I do swear, solemnly swear, Margaret, be my fate what it may, that child shall share it."

The woman to whom the child had been entrusted at this moment re-entered the room. The information had reached her that the father of the boy had at last made his appearance, and partly from curiosity, partly with the hope of receiving a present from him, she now made her appearance at the side of the bed with the infant in her arms.

With almost supernatural strength, the dying mother raised herself on her pillow, and taking the child in her arms imprinted one long kiss upon its lips, and then placing it in Walter's arms:

"So may you prosper as you keep your oath!" she uttered in a hollow voice, and raising her hands and eyes to heaven.

Walter bent his head over the child to conceal the tears that trickled down his cheeks and fell upon its unconscious face, and when he again raised his eyes those which had gazed upon him with such intensity were closed for ever. Margaret was dead!

Profligate, unprincipled, and abandoned as he was, Walter still felt deeply, at the time, the melancholy fate of the poor girl who had so fatally proved her deep devotion to him. He had, too, been less blameable in his desertion of her than he appeared; for the real fact was, he had not voluntarily deserted her, but had been placed in a situation which he dared not communicate to her, fearful of the effect it would have upon her. He had, in reality, been in prison—had been charged with a capital crime—and by what even to himself seemed little short of a miracle, had escaped condemnation.

"It would kill Margaret if she knew it," was his constant reflection, while yet in uncertainty of his fate, "and she had better, therefore, think anything than know the truth."

When, however, he found himself once more at liberty, his first thought turned to her, of whose affection he was too firmly convinced to doubt for a moment his being able to make his peace by a feigned tale, accounting for his absence without betraying the truth; but Margaret was gone, and left no clue by which he could trace her.

It was only now that Walter knew the real worth of her he had lost Shunned even by his former dissipated companions, who, though they had without hesitation shared in the profits of his crime, felt it necessary for their own safety to avoid all public association with him, his heart softened by his recent danger, Walter might now have returned to the right path had Margaret been at hand to strengthen his half-formed resolves, and give form to his shadowy plans for the future; but long and vain was his search, for he had been deceived into the belief that she had voluntarily quitted her home, unable to endure longer the anguish and uncertainty of his absence.

By one of those accidents, as they are termed, which frequently surprise even the most unthinking and unreflecting, into the conviction that

> "There's a divinity that shapes our ends,
> Rough-hew them how we will,"

he was led to the very place which had given a last asylum to the unhappy Margaret, and a birth-place to her child—but it was too late. The bright spot in Walter's life was darkened for ever by her death, and from henceforth the only trace that remained of her gentle influence was, that he still adhered to her child. Amid all the various fluctuations of a life of adventure, unrestrained by any consideration but that of personal security, from the time he quitted England, the young Walter was his constant companion, and though often a sufferer from the uncertain temper, the alternate fits of violence and depression, which, especially towards its close, marked the unhappy tenor of Walter Geffrey's life, the son of his early love, of the lost and lamented Margaret, ever held more influence over him than any one besides. While yet struggling for fortune, he had married, and thereby attained not only considerable wealth, but had been placed on the first step of that eminence which he had after succeeded in climbing to its topmost height, but though a large family had been the result of this union, none of his children had ever seemed to hold that place in his heart which Walter did, and he had beheld them drop off, one by one, with little emotion, for Walter was yet spared, and to Walter at length devolved all that wealth, the accumulation of which had long swallowed up every feeling and sensation, regard for his son—the son of Margaret—alone excepted.

The effects of this exclusive partiality could not be expected to operate very favourably on the character of the young Walter. He was not naturally bad inclined, for he possessed much of the better parts of his mother's character; he was generous, kind-hearted, and affectionate, but a long course of unlimited indulgence in all his desires, the flattery and servile submissiveness of all who wished to pay their court, not only to the father, but to the future heir of his fortunes, and the luxurious and immoral habits of life in which he had been bred, had all contributed to deaden and obscure the natural disposition of Walter Fitz-Geffrey, as he was by his father's express desire named.

Retaining not the slightest recollection of the land of his birth, Fitz-Geffrey felt no wish, even when the slight restraint which his father's existence had created was removed, to re-visit England, of which his father had never spoken but in terms of contempt and hatred; but the pleasures which wealth enabled him to enjoy in the sultry climate of India at length palled upon his taste, and were rendered joyless by the loss of health, and at the age of forty the very rich East Indian Walter Fitz-Geffrey, landed in that which was literally to him a new world.

For some months the pleasures and novelties of London held him captive. His spirits returned, his mind was interested, and he fancied that his bodily health was equally renovated. His wealth and name secured him all outward respect and attention, and for a time he thought himself completely happy.

A fit of sickness dissipated this illusion; it was true money could command obsequious attendance, the most eminent physicians crowded his chamber, and a host of menials were ready to obey the slightest indication of his wishes; but still he sighed for that which money could not command, for the sympathising tear, the anxious look, the kind inquiry, and indefatigable attention of affection. A disappointment in early life had disposed him to look with suspicion on females in general. A girl, who had come out to India, with the (then common) view of gaining a rich husband, had fascinated him by her beauty, and the superficial accomplishments which, as usual in such cases, constituted all her dowry. She had listened with complacency to his addresses—she had condescended to accept the most costly presents from him; but at the moment he was about to make a formal proposal for her hand she suddenly married a man older than his father, whom she had only known a few days, and who possessed no other claim to her favour than being reported to be the richest man in the presidency.

It was the recollection of this mortification and disappointment, which had, however, at the time piqued his pride much more than his affections, that rendered Fitz-Geffrey so cynical and incredulous respecting females, that he had arrived at the good old bachelor-like age of forty, without having found one on whom he could repose the confidence of a heart, which yet yearned to share its now solitary feelings with some gentle partner.

At the period of the sickness of which we have before spoken, in the crowded solitude and noisy quietness of a fashionable hotel, this want and wish returned upon him with tenfold violence. It was then that his mind reverted to the enthusiasm with which his father, in moments of unusual excitement, had been accustomed to speak of his deceased Margaret.

"And she, to whom he ascribed every virtue under heaven—she, the mother whom I so unhappily lost, before I could know her worth, was a simple country girl," he exclaimed. "Oh, yes, it is there, amidst the beings uncontaminated by art and fashion, that I must seek for a heart which can attach itself to mine."

A circumstance which this illness also brought forward, contributed to strengthen this impression. A host of papers which, since his father's death, had lain neglected and unexamined, were accidentally thrown under his observation, and among them he discovered the whole correspondence of his father's early life; and among much to pain and to surprise him, there was also much which interested, and made him anxious to put in practice a plan he had formed, of visiting the place of his parent's birth, and endeavouring there to find if there still existed any remnants of the families with whom he could claim kindred.

It was in pursuance of this intention, that he entered the village of Llan——, as we have in our first chapter recorded. His father's letters had without difficulty enabled him to trace the scene of the latter's youthful existence; but he had been so disgusted by his reception from the widow of Squire Jenkins and her daughters, that he had left them without discovering who he was, or the motives of his inquiry.

Of his mother's family he in vain attempted to trace any remnant. There were few who even remembered the person he attempted to describe, and he was about to quit the place for ever, when an accident which compelled him to return to the inn in the village, and to remain there for the night, unexpectedly introduced him to one whose personal beauty exceeded all that he had ever yet beheld, and who he eventually discovered had a still farther claim upon his interest, as being the descendant of one of those to whom his father acknowledged not only affinity, but great and continued obligations, which the latter had never, it appeared, either had the opportunity or had wanted the inclination to repay.

And so it always is, and no doubt always will be in life—upon the smallest and most trivial events the destiny of nations or the fate of individuals will often hang, and we could, had we space, narrate countless anecdotes of the inscrutable ways of Providence in this respect.

> For want of a nail the shoe was lost,
> For want of a shoe the horse was lost,
> For want of a horse the man was lost,
> For want of the man a kingdom was lost.

The above lines,—old as the hills no doubt,—more fully express our meaning than page upon page of anecdote could do.

So it was with Fitz-Geffrey, had he not stopped at the village inn all night, he would not have seen one who was destined to exercise so great an influence on his after life—whether for good or evil the course of our story will show. But we find that we have been digressing from that story sadly; trusting that our readers will excuse us, however, we now resume the thread of our narrative.

THE PRIDE OF THE VILLAGE;

OR,

THE FARMER'S DAUGHTERS.

CHAPTER VI.

"They loved for years with growing tenderness,
They had but one pure prayer to waft above,
One heart, one hope, one dream, and that was love."
—Anon.

THE morning visit to Rose Farm of the strange gentleman who owned the beautiful carriage and horses, that had dashed through the village on Sunday evening formed the sole topic of conversation among the various groups that were again collected, though more scattered, and less under restraint, than when in the bravery of their Sabbath attire, they had paraded the green on the preceding evening.

4

"They do say," said one pretty demure-looking damsel, "that the London stranger is going to marry Maria outright, and that she will ride in her carriage to church next Sunday, for they won't be ask'd in church, like we do, but they will have a licence from London, to marry them quite a different way."

"Yes, if he ever does marry her, it will be in a different way, I fancy," said another, tossing her head with an air of incredulity and contempt; "but as mother says, these fine gentlemen are none of them so fond of marrying girls that have nothing but their face for their fortunes."

"And after all," added a third, who was far from possessing any great stock of personal charms, "after all, I don't see what Maria Woodford has so particular to boast of; I've heard her called, forsooth, 'The Pride of the Village ———'"

"And so she is the Pride of the Village, you little envious puss," interrupted an old man, who was leaning over the half door of his cottage, and listening unobserved to their conversation; "she is properly called the Pride of our Village; but if what you say is true, Sally," addressing the first speaker, who was his own daughter, "she'll be likely to become London Pride soon;" and the old man chuckled with satisfaction at his own conceit.

"But are you sure it is Maria?" said a youth who stood near them, and who had not seemed before to join in the conversation.

"Sure, why you do not think any man that had got eyes could look at Grace Woodford, when her sister was by," impetuously interrupted another. "Oh! yes, I know," he continued, observing symptoms of dissent from this remark, in the other's looks, "I know very well that you think that there is not such another girl in the world as Grace; but I say that she's not to be mentioned in the same day with Maria, in regard of good looks."

"'Pretty is that pretty does,' our old dame says," observed another girl, "and I'm sure, as to sweet temper, and kind-heartedness, and ——· but who are these coming at such a rate? Well, I declare then, it is all true, for here is Maria Woodford herself, and Mrs. Woodford, too, along with the gentleman himself in the fine carriage, and they're not a going to stop here either! where can they be going?"

It was indeed Maria Woodford, who, with triumph fluttering in her little heart, and scarcely concealed in her countenance, under a pretended indifference, was seated between her mother and Fitz-Geffrey; who, at once, diverted at her little airs of coquetry, and still enthusiastically admiring her beauty, was willing enough to be the object of it.

The discovery that there was a house and grounds to be let, at a few miles' distance from Llan——, which Mrs. Woodford thought might, with some improvements and alterations, be made a fit residence for her cousin, had been the basis of this excursion, which now gave additional food for gossip and scandal to those who thus saw themselves thrown at an immeasurable distance from their late companion, who even now seemed scarcely to recognise those who, regardless of all but the gratification of their curiosity, had approached the carriage during the brief moments it had stopped at the door of the village inn; the owner having, or pretending to have, some orders to give to his valet, who came to the door to receive them.

"How she held up her head, and how proud her mother looked!" said one of the girls, who had been particularly free in her remarks.

"Yes, the old woman considers it a made match," returned another, "but there's many a slip 'tween the cup and the lip, and after all, perhaps——"

"I'll never believe they're married, till I see them go to church," interfered the plain girl, who had been before so sceptical on the same subject; "for I've heard my mother say many times, there isn't such a slippery deceitful set in the world as them Londoners."

"But this is not a Londoner, Jenny Williams," said a tall old woman, who, leaning on her stick, had, unobserved by any of them, approached to listen to their remarks; "and more than that, he's one of our townspeople—that is to say, his father and mother were—and well do I remember them—as handsome a couple as ever the sun shone upon; aye, and modest and well-spoken *she* was, there was no such giggling, ill-behaved minxes in my young days, as there is now, making their jeers at old people."

"I didn't jeer at you, I am sure, Alice," said the girl, to whom, by her looks, this reproof was particularly addressed; "I was only laughing at Belgrave Mansel, to see how eager he looked, to hear what you were saying, though ——"

"Belgrave, how are ye, my lad?" interrupted Alice, her wrinkled countenance unbending into almost a smile at the sight of her favourite; "ah!" she continued, "I'm afraid it's ill news for thee, boy, that Grace has found a rich relation, for, of course, he's as much Grace's cousin as he is her sister's; there's no saying, indeed, how much nearer he may be to both yet, for he arn't so near of kin that he can't marry them."

"What! both of them, Alice?" said a roguish-looking young man, who stood behind her; "why that's more than the king can do, or anybody but the Pope of Rome, or the grand Turk—he may have two wives, they say."

"I know nothing about that, Tommy Lewis," replied the old woman, very seriously; "but goodness forbid I should be such a heathen as to think that anybody could marry two wives in England; all I meant to say was, that if this Walter Geffrey, or Fitz-Geffrey, for it seems h's got another name tacked on to his father's——"

"Aye; that means that he is the son of father, Alice. Fitz means son," observed a fat, rotund, important personage, who, in addition to his trade of village shoemaker, exercised the responsible and dignified calling of parish-clerk, and was renowned among the rustics for his wonderful erudition:—

> And still they gazed, and still the wonder grew,
> That one small head could carry all he knew.

"The son of his father," repeated Alice, a sneer of contempt curling her thin lips; "I suppose there's no need to be a conjuror to tell that a man must be the son of his father—but some people must always pretend to be wiser than others;" and without vouchsafing another look at the idle group who were awaiting the remainder of her communication, the old woman hobbled off towards her own cottage, as fast as her infirmities would allow.

"It's no use, now, to ask her a single question, for she wouldn't answer, if it was to please the queen herself, when once she's got into her tantrums," observed one of the girls; "but I should like to have heard who this great relation was that nobody ever before knew anything about.

"Oh, he's sprung up like a mushroom, all at once, in a night," said the would-be wit who has been before mentioned; "or perhaps some kind fairy has made him a carriage out of a pumpkin, and horses of mice, like Cinderella's that we used to read of. Poor Maria! how foolish she would look if they were all to be suddenly changed back to their old shapes, and she, perhaps, left in a bog."

"Don't talk such nonsense, Thomas Lewis," replied the girl who had before spoken; "it's not lucky to jest with the good people; they don't like to be called fairies," she added, in a lower voice, as if fearful the objects of her superstitious fear should be within hearing.

"Nonsense Jenny? I'm sure I would'nt think it nonsense, if they would make a gentleman of me, and let me go courting in style, like——"

"There's a great many Geffreys in the church-book," interrupted the parish-clerk, who had been apparently deeply reflecting on this abstruse subject; "and I will look whether there is any register of the marriage of any of them with the Jenkinses; for it must be of the mother's side, if there's any relationship; for as to the father's everybody knows that Woodford sprang from nobody."

"That's about as wise as his discovering that a man's the son of his father," whispered Tom Lewis. "I wish old Alice had been here to hear him; she would fight tooth and nail for any of the Woodfords."

"We should have heard all about the stranger," said another speaker, "if Powell hadn't have interfered, and affronted the old woman; for she knows every family roundabouts for years and years back, and can tell you all about what's happened to them long before you and I was born: but there's Belgrave Mansell gone after her; and if anybody can get her into a good humour he will—for she's mighty civil always to him, and so we shall be likely to hear all about this Fitz-Geffery, when he comes back."

"It's a fine evening, dame," said Belgrave, as he paced by the side of the old woman towards her cottage. "I'm thinking of going to the monthly market at Aber——, next Monday; is there anything I can bring for you on my return?"

"No, lad," replied the old woman, her countenance relaxing from the frown of severity; "I have not half used the snuff you brought me last time, and there's little else there that I care for. Yes—I tell you what you may do, if you will, for me; you may call on old Honor Meredith, in the back lane, and tell her that after all these years, there's news of Walter Geffrey; and that a son of his, poor Margaret's, is here, and a very well-spoken man, and well to-do in the world, though no more like Walter or Margaret than I am like the Queen of England, God bless her."

"Honor Meredith," repeated Belgrave, taking out his pocket-book, and there, among sundry other memorandums for his own private and peculiar guidance at the approaching market, carefully inserting the name and residence of the ancient dame whom he was to visit.

"And do you think there is any likelihood, Alice, of this gentleman marrying either of Farmer Woodford's daughters?" he ventured at length to ask.

"You may make your mind easy, so far as regards Grace," said the old woman; "for though riches, and a coach, and grandeur, might tempt most, they will never make her false-hearted."

"But do you think, then, that he is likely to make her an offer?" demanded Belgrave, with ill-dissembled terror.

"Who?—Grace? No, you foolish boy; there's very few, besides you and me, and one or two more, that ar'n't so dazzled by Maria's fine face and showy looks, that they can see nothing particular in Grace. Now, I do say, and maintain, that Grace is the prettiest, when you come to know her, and look much at her sweet face. God bless her! that pillow she made herself for me, but the other day; the down she gathered herself from her own nurslings, and the tick she spun herself, and paid for the weaving out of her own little pocket-money; and 'There, dame,' says she, as she shook it, and put it under my head, when I was laid up with the rheumatiz;

, there now, I hope your poor head won't ache so bad any more, and you'll have pleasanter dreams of a night.' Ah! poor dear; she little knows how many things, after living eighty-odd years in a bad world, will rise up to make one have uncomfortable dreams, but if I do not sleep sound, it's not her fault."

"No; nor your own either, I'm sure, good Alice; old age will have its infirmities."

"And youth its errors to make them even more painful," said Alice with an air of solemn reflection.

Belgrave looked grave and concerned; it was seldom he had seen the old woman so deeply affected, and he had good sense sufficient to let her feelings take their own course, without offering any attempts by commonplace observations to console her.

"Then you think it quite improbable that this Mr. Fitz-Geffrey—I think you called him, should have any liking," and he hesitated before he used the words, "for Grace."

"I think, and am sure, that he has no such thoughts! and, moreover, that the mother would sooner see Grace dead and buried than that she should step over her darling's head. And besides all that I am sure, as I said before, that Grace is true-hearted, and would rather die than deceive you; and I am sure, too, that all the money in the world would never buy a kind look from Grace if her heart did not go with it."

"Then Fitz-Geffrey is not a person likely————, I had only a slight glance at him, but I thought there was nothing in his appearance that ————"

"Nothing that is likely to stand against a fine, handsome, young man, under twenty; you need not blush, lad, but Grace has eyes to choose, and Fitz-Geffrey is double thy age, and sunburnt and sickly to boot—but there's another cause for uneasiness to you, Belgrave;" she added, after a few moment's pause, "which you seem to have overlooked."

"What is that?" he exclaimed, starting.

"Why; that if this Fitz-Geffery marries Maria Woodford, her proud, upstart mother will be so lifted up that she will never consent to Grace's marrying anything beneath the rank of a gentleman, and Grace is such a dutiful child that I am afraid————"

Belgrave sighed deeply.

"I don't know that I can be worse off than I am now, Alice," he observed; "for Mrs. Woodford always treats me with as much contempt as if I were somebody not worthy to be looked at, much less spoken to: and though the worthy farmer always makes me welcome if I go there, yet he will not give me encouragement to think of Grace, because he says it's no use to think of it, his wife will not agree; and then he says, too, that Grace is too young, and so many other objections, that I am quite in despair," and the poor youth sighed heavily.

"Well! and what does Grace herself say?" demanded Alice, looking earnestly in his face.

"Oh, she does not say anything but that we are both young enough to wait, and that there is no knowing what good fortune may happen to alter her mother's resolution. I sometimes think, indeed," he added, with an appearance of resentment, "that Grace, after all, cares nothing about me, for she seems so happy and contented to remain as she is."

"She's quite right," returned Alice; "why should a girl of seventeen— and she's not more, if so much—be in such a terrible hurry to alter her situation? Besides, after all, Belgrave, you must confess that your prospects, at present, don't offer much to tempt a girl like Grace; you have a pretty little farm, to be sure, between you and your brother, but if he should get a wife and family, as is likely, seeing he is some years older than you——"

"I don't know that there's any more prospect of his getting married than of my doing so," interrupted Belgrave hastily, "perhaps not so much, for he's fixed his mind on one that he's never likely to have."

"What, Maria! oh, that will wear off, trust me; a young man like him will have too much sense to pine away his life, fretting after a girl that despises him; but, however, as I said before, if he should marry, or you should marry, the farm won't keep two families."

"Then the other must turn out and do something else," replied Belgrave, coolly; "and, indeed, I've got thoughts myself of giving up my share of it, when I come of age, if Grace doesn't alter her determination, and listen to my proposals."

"And what would you do then, you foolish boy?" demanded Alice, imperatively.

"Do! he repeated, petulantly, "why, go for a soldier, or a sailor or beg, or starve, or anything, for I'm sure I shouldn't care what became of me;" and without waiting her reply, the youth walked hastily away.

"Poor lad," said Alice, as she watched him from her cottage window, bounding along the path they had come together, as though he wished, by the celerity of his motion, to drive away the heavy thoughts that oppressed him. "Poor lad, it would be a pity, indeed, such a kind heart should be driven to despair; but who knows? It is not the best or the kindest that are the most prosperous."

"No; or else good Alice would be better off than she is," said a soft voice from the further end of the apartment, and in a moment the slender and agile form of Grace Woodford glided from behind the curtain, which half concealed the old dame's bed.

"Mercy on us, child! how came you there?" demanded the old woman, starting; "how could you frighten me so?"

"I hope I have not frightened you very much," said Grace, looking earnestly at her, "but, indeed, I thought you knew all the while that I was there; I thought you saw me as you were coming in when I ran behind the curtain, or I should not have remained there, though I particularly wished to avoid being seen by Belgrave."

"And why so, dear?" demanded Alice.

Grace looked down for a minute, as if at a loss what answer to give.

"I don't know," she at length observed, raising her eyes to the old woman's; "I don't know, after what I heard Belgrave tell you, and which I should not have listened to but that it was no secret, but only what he has said twenty times or more to me since my mother first told me she did not approve of my being so much with him. I don't know, I say, why I should scruple to tell you that I am very unhappy, not so much on my account either, as my sister's, because I am sure she would have been so happy with William Mansell, who you know dame, is such a good young man, and who loves her so dearly he would lay down his life for her, and they are so suited to each other, and now I am afraid——"

"That she will marry this stranger, Fitz-Geffrey, I know you think," said Alice, as the gentle girl paused.

"It is not exactly that," said Grace, "it would not, perhaps, be altogether so bad if she married him; but the truth is, I do not believe, at least my father says, he does not believe, that the man has any such foolish thoughts as of marrying a girl young enough to be his daughter: and then how it will make us all look, and what will they say, when Maria has driven away

William, and my mother has forbidden Belgrave the house, and after all the stranger has no thought of a wife?"

"And leaves Maria in the lurch," said Alice, smiling at the innocent girl's mode of stating her uneasiness; "but why did this render you particularly anxious to avoid Belgrave?" continued the old woman.

"Why, because in the first place, he would see that I am uneasy, and I couldn't bear to tell him the true reason, that I am afraid my mother and sister are making themselves————"

"A laughing-stock," said Alice, with bitterness, seeing her hesitate. "No, you are too dutiful and affectionate to say that, though you are well aware that it is so; but you know, child, I always speak the honest truth, and if your mother herself were to come in my way, I should tell her candidly my opinion."

"And that's just what I want to say to you Alice," returned Grace; "my mother is bent upon giving what she calls a *fête champetre*, in honour of this Sir Walter Fitz-Geffrey, whom she calls her cousin."

"He is a sort of a cousin, certainly," muttered Alice, "but go on, child."

"Well, you know my mother knows very little about such things; but she says you must know all about them, because when there was one given at the Old Priory, that's all in ruins now, you ————"

"Yes, I was there," interrupted Alice, with vehemence; "I see it all now, as fresh as it was then, before my eyes, and yet it is all faded into air; the very walls are crumbling into dust, the young and the gay. and the beautiful, are all in their graves; and I, that was then s o young, as gay, aye, and as beautiful, or the tongues of all around me lied, I am, what! look at me, the poor, decrepid, despised ————"

"No, no, Alice, not despised," interrupted the half-frightened Grace, "I am sure there is not anybody that knows you that can despise you; on the contrary, everybody says that there is not a person in the whole village who knows so much as you, or turns their knowlege to a better account. Does not everybody ask your advice in difficulties, even my mother acknowledges that ————"

"Aye, they all fear me, that is the truth, child, and you know it," replied Alice; "all but you and Belgrave, and one or two more, who know me better, and have too much sense to believe such nonsense as that any human being can have communication with the powers of darkness, at least that they can, through their means ————; but I forgot, my dear, what was it you were saying about that ————"

"Why, that my mother is bent upon giving some entertainment, to introduce our new-found relation, as she calls him, to the neighbourhood; and that she thinks, she says, with your advice. and a description of what you remember of that which took place at the Priory, she could manage something like it, only on a lesser scale. But for goodness sake, dear dame, do persuade her out of it, if you can, for in the first place I know it will make my father miserable, and that he cannot afford the expense; and in the second, it will only make my mother disliked by people that can't do the like, and sneered at by those who can surpass her. I have seen too much of that already"—and she sighed.

"She shall have no assistance from me to make a fool of herself," said the old woman, who had listened attentively to her young companion; *she* vie with *that* fête! As well might the little brook that runs by my door vie with the noble river whose waves wash the ruined walls on which my last look at night, and my first in the morning, is bestowed. Yes; there it stands," continued the old woman, in a tone of enthusiasm, pointing te the hill, on the side of which stood the remains of the noble building. "There it stands, all that is left to remind this generation of the noble and high-born, who have all passed away, or are scattered in foreign lands, and Alice, only Alice, of all who beheld and shared their glory, is left to weep over its ruins." The old woman passed her hand across her brow, as if to recall her thoughts, and then hastily drying her eyes with her apron, said, resuming her usual tone, " Trust me, Grace, I will do all in my power to assist you, and I hope I shall be able to convince your mother that it would be folly for her to attempt such a thing, and now, good night, my child, it is time you were on your way home, if you go alone, as I suppose you will."

Grace waited not a second intimation, for she recollected that it was necessary she should be home before her mother and sister returned, in order to conceal her visit to Alice, and hastily returning the old woman's farewell, she ran off with the speed of a fawn across the fields, to the farm.

CHAPTER VII.

I tell of festivals, and fairs, and plays,
Of merriment and mirth—
And then comes death, and shuts out all the scene.

—ANON.

IN spite of all Alice's warnings and disapprobation, in spite of Mr. Woodford's declaration that his farm had been a losing concern for the last three years, and that, therefore, he had no money to spare for such foolish extravagance, in spite of the difficulty of getting music, of constructing tents for refreshments, the uncertainty of getting company to attend, in short, in spite of every possible obstacle to such an entertainment, and the folly and incongruity of attempting it in her station in life, Mrs. Woodford astonished the good people of Llan——, and the neighbourhood, in which was included a circle of at least ten miles, by announcing her intention of giving a *fête champetre*, in the grounds of Rose Farm, in celebration of the return of Sir Walter Fitz-Geffrey, her near relative, to his native land.

Never was surprise more extravagantly and ludicrously expressed than in the countenance and ejaculations of the hero of this festival, when he discovered the solution of a mystery which he had felt very little curiosity to penetrate, though much had been said and done, which perhaps under other circumstances would have excited some desire to unravel; but Sir Walter had been busily employed for the last fortnight in arranging for his future residence in the neighbourhood of Llan——, and the obstacles which had arisen, and the circumstances which had come to his knowledge, during his negotiations, had sufficiently occupied him, to the exclusion, almost altogether, of Mrs. Woodford and her mysteries. When, however, the neatly-written card was put into his hand, which announced her intended *fête*, and in which he beheld his own name figuring as the hero, nothing could exceed his consternation and surprise, and after giving vent to it in all the most approved forms of oath, exclamation, adjuration, and execration, he hastily caught up his broad-brimmed, Indian straw hat and set off for Rose Farm to expostulate with the lady, and explain to her more positively than ever what he had more than once before very strongly descanted upon—namely, his wish to live unnoticed and in privacy. He was sick of the gay world and its fancied enjoyments, he said, and he now meant to try whether he could not find the happiness he sought in rural life, unrestrained by empty parade and ceremony.

Mrs. Woodford had heard all this, it was true, but it had made no impression upon her mind. How could it be possible, she thought, that a man with five thousand a year, and that she had reason to believe was the very lowest estimate of Sir Walter's fortune—how could it be possible, she argued, for him to live private? and even if he was so inclined she was sure Maria would not agree to it. No, she must have a house in London, to be sure, like other ladies, and she must go to the watering-places in the season, and give routs, and balls, and card-parties, and concerts.

"But, ma', suppose he should insist upon living all the year in the country, as he seems now to propose," said Maria, after one of these conversations.

"Nonsense, *he* insist, indeed! what, when you were determined otherwise! You must manage him very badly indeed if you suffer a husband to *insist* upon anything contrary to your inclinations."

"Ah! but every husband is not like my father," returned Maria; "look at poor Mrs. Pritchard and John Price's wife; they neither of them——"

"Pray, Maria, let me beg you do not mention such people to me," interrupted her mother. "Mrs. Pritchard, indeed, a poor, ignorant woman, that never was five miles from her home, and worships her husband as if he was a monarch; but there, let us hear no more of them; I hope a daughter of mine will know better than to follow the example of such people as those."

"My dear, good madam," said Sir Walter Fitz Geffrey, entering the room abruptly, "excuse me if I intrude, but I am come most anxiously to solicit you not to put yourself to the unnecessary expense and trouble which this card indicates. Consider, my dear Mrs. Woodford, how contrary this will be to the plan which I have marked out for myself, of enjoying my days in quiet and solitude; here we shall have all the gaping, idle people, for miles round, coming to eat and drink, and discussing birth, life, parentage, and education, and talk of me as some monster——"

"Oh dear, no, you are quite mistaken; indeed, Sir Walter, you will find everybody treat you with great respect; I have asked none but quite the genteelest people, I assure you; not a single trades-person will be admitted, unless they like to mix with the crowd that will be in the field, where the fat sheep will be roasted."

"Master says, ma'am, he'll see you hanged before you shall have one of the sheep to spoil in any sich manner," said a great coarse country servant, who, to the horror of Mrs. Woodford, now popped up her head from behind the sofa, having been down on her knees engaged in searching for some coral beads, a string of which Maria had broken and scattered on the ground.

"Get up, do, and go about your business," said her offended mistress; "your master is like you, an ignorant, unfeeling wretch."

The girl rose, muttering that it would be a good thing if some people were a little more like her master, who never called people out of their names for no reason in the world but telling the truth, and Sir Walter resumed his eloquent exposition of his numerous reasons for disliking this public festival.

All, however, that he could advance was overruled by Mrs. Woodford; and Sir Walter, hopeless of making any impression upon her, was at length compelled apparently to yield, resolving, however, in his own mind that he would make some urgent necessity to be, on the memorable occasion, at least twenty miles from the scene of action.

For nearly a week before the appointed time every person over whom Mrs. Woodford could enforce any jurisdiction, or whose services she could by dint of bribes and promises command, was engaged in making the preparations which were eventually to excite the envy and admiration of all the beauty and fashion in and around Llan——; and the whole house and household were thrown from morning till night into the most admirable disorder. The kitchen utensils and furniture were all transferred to an outhouse, in order that it might be transmogrified into a supper-room, and the beds, and all the paraphernalia of the bedrooms, were hoisted up to the garrets, which had long been delivered over to the sole dominion of the rats.

"But I thought it was to be all out of doors?" said the disconsolate Woodford, as he beheld the devastation extending to every habitable part of the house.

"Yes, but we must have card-rooms and retiring-rooms in-doors, Mr. Woodford! what would become of us if a heavy shower of rain was to come on? I should die with shame, if we were not prepared to entertain our friends within doors."

In the midst of all these preparations poor Mr. Woodford was seized with an excruciating fit of the gout; and Grace, to whom alone this appeared of any serious consequence, and who was alone left to attend to him, had the misery and mortification of seeing him stretched on a bed on the floor of a dark dirty garret, surrounded with lumber of every description, and suffering not only the torment of his disorder, but the annoyance of incessant knocking and hammering in the rooms beneath; the lumbering up and down stairs of the awkward farm servants, and the shrill voice of Mrs. Woodford exalted above all other sounds, either in giving directions which could not be comprehended by her inexperienced ministers, or in raving at the mischief occasioned by their too literal obedience to her command. Occasionally this was varied by the crash of glass or earthenware, a signal which was sure to increase to a hubbub resembling nothing on earth, the poor invalid observed, " but the uproar at the building of the Tower of Babel;" and when to all this was added, the reflection of the sum of money which this foolish woman was thus wasting, and which the farmer had never perhaps been less able to spare, it may be conceived that his situation was none of the most pleasant.

Amidst all this disorder, and confusion, and toil, and labour, for a few hours' ostentation, Grace alone kept on " the even tenor of her way," although her mild temper was sometimes a little ruffled at the annoyances to which her father was subjected, and at the difficulties which frequently impeded his having the little comforts his situation demanded; but in spite of her mother's impatient and unfeeling observations, Grace still devoted her whole time and attention to the sick bed, and resolutely refused to take any part in the preparations, unless it could be done there.

"You will be ready enough though, I dare say, Miss," observed Mrs. Woodford; "to take your share in the pleasure, though you won't assist in preparing for it."

"Indeed, you are mistaken, mother," replied Grace, mildly; " for unless my father is a great deal better indeed, I shall not leave his bed-side."

"Ah! he will contrive, I dare say, to be better on purpose to indulge his darling," remarked the mother, who had scarcely condescended to bestow a glance once a day on the invalid.

"I wish I could contrive it so well," observed the farmer, " both for your sake and my own, Grace. But it would be very unreasonable of me to expect that you should remain altogether in this dark dismal place, when they are all merry and dancing downstairs."

"Indeed, my dear father, I don't think I should be a bit merry, if I were to be among them," replied Grace; "for there will be nobody there that I like or care for."

"Will not Belgrave be there then?" said her father, looking up with surprise.

"Oh, no, my mother has not asked any of our friends, they are not genteel enough," replied Grace, with something of sarcasm in her tone and look, unusual to her.

"So then I shall have made enemies of all my neighbours, for the pleasure of—— do ask your mother to come here, child! I must talk to her a little about this."

Grace had seldom or never seen her father so excited, and apparently so determined, and, with some apprehension, she hastened to tell her mother that her presence was required in the sick room.

"What in the world can the man want with me now, interrupting me just as I am so busy?" said Mrs. Woodford, who was just in high glee, super-intending and directing two of her men, who were putting up a large mirror with brackets, which after a long negociation, and by the aid of a consider-able order for wines and spirits, she had succeeded in transferring from the ball-room of the monthly assembly, at the King's Arms, Llan——, to her own drawing room. "There, Thomas, just drive another large nail there, and that will support it on this side."

Thomas did as he was desired, but Thomas's eyes were at that moment fixed on Grace, whose countenance he thought betrayed unusual uneasiness —a confused idea of his master's death, his own loss of a good place—the transformation of all these kickshaws, as he called them, into funeral solem-nities, and he forgot what he was about, the hammer descended with all force his brawny arm could give it, but it was about an inch too much to the right, and the magnificent mirror was shattered into a thousand pieces.

Screams of affright, vexation, and dismay, broke from Mrs. Woodford and her daughter Maria, who were contemplating with great complacency the dazzling and brilliant effect, which this addition to the usual furniture of the drawing-room would produce, and poor Grace, calculating the addi-tional expense this accident would occasion to her father, stood still in silent affright.

"I couldn't help it, mistress, if I had been sure to be hung for it," said Thomas, in answer to the torrent of reproaches and maledictions which were now levelled at his head. "Summut comed over me, like, that master was a dying just then, and it set my hand a trembling, you see."

Grace flew out of the room, to avoid the storm, which she saw would now change its direction, for to her ill-timed appearance Mrs. Woodford now at-tributed this irretrievable disaster; but what was the poor girl's consternation and dismay, to find her father in a state that seemed likely to verify Thomas's prediction!

He had got out of bed, as Grace supposed, at the alarm of her mother's and sister's outcries; and had, in the confusion of the moment, and the dim light which struggled through the cobwebbed windows, mistaken his way, and fallen down the trap staircase which led from the attics to the second landing-place.

Grace's screams, loud and frantic as they were, were for some moments unheard amidst the din of words that still raged in the drawing-room ; but at length they pierced the ears of some of those who were not immediately concerned in the affray, the noise of which had drawn together every living creature within reach of it, and one of them exclaiming—

"I do believe Thomas is right—master is dying—for nothing else could make Miss Grace scream so," flew out of the room, and was quickly followed by the whole household; the mother and daughter being left alone, to pick up and weep over the glittering fragments of the fragile evidence of their folly.

"Oh, it's no use, my dear," said Mrs. Woodford, still totally inattentive to what was passing without; "its no use to try to do anything with the pieces —it's totally demolished; and it's too late now———"

"Oh, no, it won't be too late, Miss Grace says, if the doctor will come directly ; but there isn't a horse left—Jem has got Captain, to fetch ———"

"What is the wench talking about?" said Mrs. Woodford, looking up at the speaker, who stood staring at her mistress with wild affright; "Who ever heard of a doctor for looking-glasses?"

"Oh, no, ma'am, it's my master—my poor master—and Miss Grace says if he don't have help———"

"Do, child, go and see what all this fuss is about," said the affectionate wife. "I declare, I think everybody's in a conspiracy to torment me. Ten pounds, I shouldn't wonder, I have to pay for this stupid clodpole's awkwardness; and, even then I shan't be able to hush it up; all the world will know of it—for they can't possibly get another in time for the month's assembly, on Thursday."

"Mamma—dear mamma—pray come directly."

It was Maria's voice that thus implored, and Mrs. Woodford hastily deposited the fragments of the mirror on one of the chairs, to attend to the call.

"What can be the matter?" she exclaimed, as she ascended the stairs slowly ; a matter always of difficult to her, from her infirmities, but now rendered doubly so, from their being up to the second story encumbered with pans and pails, and brooms and mops, and all the necessaries of a thorough scouring.

"What can the stupid wretches mean by bringing that supper-table up here?" she exclaimed, as her eye glanced, in passing one of the room doors at the arrangements which were here well-nigh completed. "Sally, Thomas, some of you come and take it down again. I declare I need have eyes all over the house, and then I can't have anything right ; and these flowers, too, they've been brought up here and forgot, and they'll all be dead before tomorrow night, for want of water."

"He can't live till to-morrow night, ma'am ; it's a thing unpossable," said Sally, who now appeared at her elbow ; "and as to water, it won't do no good, no more nor nothing, for the rattles are in his throat."

Mrs. Woodford was now really roused from the infatuating dream which had rendered her blind and deaf to every thing of real danger.

"Good God! it can't be serious. You are trying to frighten me to death, I think, between you :" and unable to proceed farther, she tottered to a chair, and seated herself, just in time from falling.

"Oh, will nobody go for Dr. Richards?" exclaimed Maria, rushing down the stairs, regardless of her mother. "My father—my poor father—is dying ! —and in such a place, too !"

"Help me up-stairs, Sally ; let me see what all this is about. You are all out of your senses, I think," said Mrs. Woodford, whose recollection had somewhat returned at the last observation, which seemed to convey a censure on herself, and that from her favourite ally and coadjutor.

"You had better not go up, indeed, ma'am, you can't do no good," said Sally crying; "and you'll only disturb the poor dear creature. Miss Grace wouldn't let me come nigh the bed, because my noise, she said, disturbed him."

Mrs. Woodford was now indeed frightened, but still willing to believe that they were exaggerating the danger, she persisted in climbing the remaining stairs; but when she reached the top, what a scene presented itself—her husband was lying in the agonies of death, on the bed which had been dragged out of an inner room to receive him, as soon as his men had carried him up. By his side, Grace was kneeling, her whole thoughts absorbed in the silent prayer, which—with upraised eyes and hands and lips scarcely moving, and as white as her death-like cheeks—she was uttering.

The servants, lately so noisy, and busy, and clamorous, were huddled together in a corner, divided between the terror which kept them motionless and their wish to assuage the sufferings of him who had been more their friend and companion than their master; but not one stirred to assist Mrs. Woodford, as with extreme difficulty, she succeeded in getting on her feet from the staircase.

"He is in a fit," she observed, trying to speak with composure; "and you all staring, instead of trying anything to bring him to. Grace, where is your smelling bottle? Maria bring me a glass of water. Can none of you have sense enough to know what's proper in such cases?"

The dying man evidently heard and comprehended these noisy exclamations: he opened his eyes, and looked sternly at her for a moment, as if to reproach her insensibility; and then, as if suddenly recollecting himself, his countenance regained its placidity, and he stretched out his hand to her, as in the act of bidding her farewell for ever.

"How are you now, Mr. Woodford, better?" said the lady, in an inquiring tone, which was, however, evidently rendered tremulous from affright, though she still struggled to conceal her conviction of that which not one besides herself could doubt—that he was dying.

Poor Woodford looked wistfully in her face for some moments; he was desirous, it appeared, of saying something to her at that impressive moment, but his speech was gone, his eyes wandered from her to Maria, and his hand was withdrawn from his wife's, to be placed in hers. She drew closer to him, and his lips were pressed tenderly for a moment on her forehead while a look of pity and parental fondness, lighted the rigid muscles which were fast stiffening into death.

"My father, my poor father!" broke from Maria, with passionate sorrow. Grace was still—still motionless—but her eyes were now bent on her father in all the agony of speechless grief.

"My child! my child!" burst from the father's lips. They were his last words—it was his last effort which strained the ever-dutiful affectionate Grace to his bosom.

CHAPTER VIII.

"Sir, I am a true labourer; I earn that I eat—get that I wear—owe no man hate —envy no man's happiness.—SHAKESPEARE.

GREAT was the consternation and surprise which reigned in the village of

Llan—— when the solemn intelligence of Farmer Woodford's sudden death superseded the almost hourly reports which had been carried from house to house, and commented upon in every shop, from that of the village apothecary, Doctor Richards, as he was gratuitously called, to the humblest huckster's that could boast of her two or three daily customers, of the extravagant and, as most styled them, crack-brained doings at Rose Farm, which ancient homely dwelling was, according to the old women's phrase, turned topsy-turvy and quite out at windows.

Not a single messenger could arrive from the farm at Llan——, if it were only to purchase a few nails, or some ounces of pins, or threads to fasten up the drapery, but he was instantly seized upon, and compelled to run the gauntlet through a whole host of merciless jesters and inquisitors, who, many of them feeling highly offended and aggrieved at the exclusive nature of Mrs. Woodford's intended fête, were disposed to indulge, with the utmost bitterness, their wicked wit at her expense. One declared that he heard that the pigs had all been turned out, and their sties occupied by card tables, and that the animals had, in revenge, broke into the supper-room, and feasted themselves upon the confectionery and sweetmeats, and littered upon the damask tablecloth ; another demanded if it was true that the whole family slept higgedly-piggedly in the mangers, and that the old lady had been seriously hurt by falling from her elevated bed-place. Innumerable, indeed, were the homely jokes which were levelled at the lady of Rose Farm and her coadjutors ; and a whole group of these would-be wits were collected around the door of Alice's cottage, whose sarcasms, now doubly envenomed, by the slight with which her advice had been treated by Mrs. Woodford, gave point and zest to the harmless jokes of the others, when a messenger was descried coming at the fullest speed, to which he could urge his horse down the hill, from the farm.

"Here comes another," said one of the men. "What's in the wind now ? the fellow will surely break his neck, and then she will have murder to answer for."

"That's nobody from the farm, I'll swear," remarked another. That's Belgrave Mansel, I know, and he dosen't go near the farm now, since the great man came there."

"No, he went by this morning early, I saw him," said another ; "and he told me he was going to look at a couple of plough horses, over the hill, at old Dobson's."

"What in the world can make him ride at such a mad rate down that steep, dangerous hill ?" added the first speaker. "If I didn't know that there's no getting him to drink at all, I should swear he was drunk. Old Dobson keeps famous strong ale."

"I shouldn't wonder but he is," said another, "for the young fellow has seemed quite beside himself for the last few days ; he was going to knock me down last night because I asked him how they were getting on at the farm, and whether they had found another rich relation for Grace."

"It would have served you right if he had ; but look, something must be the matter, he has rode up straight to Dr. Richards.'"

"The doctor's not at home, I know," observed one of the party ; "but I'll go over and hear what it is all about ;" and one by one the whole gossip deserted their post at Alice's door, and crossed by various paths the green, to the neat little house of the apothecary, at the door of which yet lingered Belgrave Mansel, making earnest and impatient inquiries of Mrs. Richards, and seeing undetermined from her intelligence how to act.

"What's amiss, Mr. Mansel," said the boldest of the village gossips, who was ahead of his companions, having taken, without any ceremony, the shortest cut to his object.

"I cannot tell you, myself; but I overtook one of the men from Rose Farm, running for his life, all their horses being out, to fetch Dr. Richards. Mr. Woodford, I understand, had met with some serious accident; the man said he was dying, but I hope——"

"It's just what I expected," burst from half-a-dozen voices at once; "poor man, I guessed that woman would be the means of sending him out of the world at last, and Dr. Richards, too, to be out of the way just when he's wanted;" and without waiting to hear Mrs. Richards' explanations, or consider how they could make themselves useful in going in search of him, they separated to spread the intelligence they had received, in all the exaggerated shapes their imagination suggested, either in their own families, or at their various places of resort.

In less than a quarter of an hour, Dr. Richards, by Belgrave Mansel's provident care, mounted on a fresh horse, was off to Rose Farm; where, however, his services came, as we have shown, too late; and long before that time, the news, not only of Mr. Woodford's death, but that of nearly the whole family, who were, it was asserted, buried in the ruins of the house, which Mrs. Woodford had, by some of her contrivances, undermined and pulled down upon them, was in the mouths of all the village, and nearly all the idle and curious of its population were pouring forth into the road and fields towards Rose Farm, to behold the supposed devastation.

"There's sad news from the farm, sir," said Sir Walter Fitz-Geffrey's servant, entering uncalled his master's presence, just as the latter was making up his mind to elope from the scene of mortification and folly, which he saw awaited him on the morrow.

"The fête's all at an end, I hope;" replied Sir Walter, starting up with unusual alacrity.

"Yes, indeed, sir, one if not both the young ladies killed, and the poor old gentleman dying when they came away, so——"

"How! what—good heavens, what do you mean, Wilson?" and Sir Walter actually overcame his usual apathy and inertness, so far as to start upon his feet.

"Too true, indeed, sir," said Wilson. "I was quite horrified when I heard the young man, who had almost by a miracle escaped, telling the landlady below about it."

"Where is the man? send him to me—stay—no; I'll go to him;" and Sir Walter, with more alacrity than he had shown for years, actually preceded his man down stairs, and without any ceremony, into the bar parlour of the astonished landlady.

"This is a very shocking affair, sir, a very shocking affair," said the latter. "Poor Mr. Woodford—Miss Grace——"

"Where is the man?" demanded the breathless Sir Walter, interrupting her.

"Oh! he's gone, sir," replied the said lady, by no means pleased at his unceremonious cutting short of her lamentation. "For my part," she continued, "I never busies myself about nobody's business, and so I did not keep him asking a thousand questions, but sent him off to see if he couldn't be of no use at home; but here's Mr. Mansel, sir, going by if you like to call him, he can tell you all about it."

Sir Walter waited not a second intimation, but hastily stepping to the door, in one of his most authoritative tones he called to Belgrave, who was leading his horse towards the stables of the inn.

"Did you speak to me, sir?" said the young man, turning round at the second salutation and fixing his dark eye with a look of haughty surprise on the countenance of the stranger.

Sir Walter involuntarily shrank back.

"I beg your pardon, sir," he observed in an altered tone; "but I am told you can inform me of the particulars of this dreadful affair."

"I cannot, indeed, sir," replied Belgrave, still slowly proceeding on his way, as if in imitation of Sir Walter dropping the haughty look and tone he had assumed. "I know nothing myself, except that I was requested to send Dr. Richards to Mr. Woodford's assistance."

"Mr. Woodford!" repeated Sir Walter; but Belgrave was gone without waiting to reply, and the disappointed baronet returned into the house.

"That is a very strange young man," he observed, seeming to forget in the unexpected check his personal consequence and assumption had received from the important subject of his inquiries.

In a few minutes, however, he recollected himself, and rang to desire that the horses might be put to the carriage as quickly as possible.

Before this operation was completed another version of the affairs at Rose Farm reached the servant, and Sir Walter heard with considerable emotion that Mr. Woodford's death was too certain, and that it was believed one of his daughters was dying.

There was no one in the way when Sir Walter Fitz-Geffrey arrived at the farm, to receive him, or to answer his anxious questions, but a boy, who, seemingly quite stupefied, was sitting on the gate of the farmyard, adjoining the house.

"I be sure I know nothing about it, only they do say master be dead, but I havn't seen him," he observed, in reply.

Sir Walter walked into the house, the strange desertion of which harmonised very little with the gaudy preparations for festivity, which were so ostentatiously displayed.

The sound of loud lamentations above stairs, directed him to where the family, as he supposed, were collected, and without ceremony he ascended the stairs.

"And then to think after all the expense and trouble I've been at, and just got everything so beautifully arranged!" she exclaimed. "Never could anything have happened so unlucky."

Sir Walter hesitated a moment whether he should advance or go back, but one of the maid servants, to whom this lamentation, it appeared, was addressed, at this moment caught sight of him at the door of the room, and in a loud whisper, announced to her mistress that "the gentleman" was there.

"What! who! where!" said Mrs. Woodford, rising in a hurry. "Oh, Sir Walter, my dear cousin, such a misfortune, I shall never recover it— oh, oh," and she threw herself back on the chair and drew her smelling-bottle and handkerchief from her pocket.

"I hope the calamity is not so great as has been represented," said Sir Walter. "Your daughters——"

"Oh! Maria is quite overcome; I am afraid she will never get the better of it. Dear creature, she is so delicate, so very delicate, that," and Mrs. Woodford would have proceeded still further with her exemplification but that she was interrupted with the baronet's anxious inquiry for Grace.

"Grace!" she repeated, looking surprised; "Grace is, really, I don't know, I don't remember; but Dr. Richards is with Maria, she has been in hysterics ever since, and the doctor insisted on my leaving the room for fear she should make me as bad as herself."

THE PRIDE OF THE VILLAGE;

OR,

THE FARMER'S DAUGHTERS.

CHAPTER IX.

" 'Tis not alone my inky cloak, good mother,
Nor customary suits of solemn black,
Nor windy suspiration of forc'd breath,
No, nor the fruitful river in the eye,
Nor the dejected 'haviour of the visage:
*   *   *   *   *   *
But I have that within which passeth show."
—SHAKESPEARE.

SIR WALTER was now satisfied that the fatal event, whatever might have caused it, was confined to Mr. Woodford alone, and, shocked and surprise

5

as he was, his acquaintance with Mr. Woodford had been too recent and too slight to make his death a subject of any very great importance in his sight; still he could not but be struck with the way in which it was borne by the widow. Not a single word of regret for the loss of her husband, no expression of sorrow for the neglect with which she had treated him, or the injustice she had ever displayed to his plain honest worth, broke from her lips; her lamentations were all selfish; how she was to manage with such a charge left entirely upon her hands; the trouble that would accrue to her from the unsettled, loose manner in which his affairs were kept, mingled with her lamentations for the useless expense and trouble she had been at, her regret at the disappointment it would be to the company she had invited, and her fears that there would not be time sufficient to give them all notice of the melancholy event, before the hour appointed for the entertainment, which had thus been so unfortunately put a stop to.

Sir Walter heard her with evident impatience.

"My good madam," he at length observed; "all these are but secondary considerations—the loss of a good man——"

"Oh dear, my head! my head!" exclaimed the lady, who thought it proper to create a diversion in her favour, perceiving very clearly the drift of Sir Walter's observations, and possessing just sense enough to know that she deserved them, though she did not read his sentiments in time to adopt a different course.

Dr. Richards at this moment entered, Maria was somewhat recovered, he said, and he was come to see if he could be of any service to her (Mrs. Woodford).

"I am glad, however," he continued, "to find that you bear it so well; grieving for the dead, to be sure, is a folly; but still, this is such a sudden blow, and so unexpected, everybody thought poor Woodford likely to live to a good old age, and that he would bury you; but there, a creaking door hangs long upon its hinges, they say. And, by-the-bye, sir, that is a bit of comfort for you, for you don't look one of the heartiest in the world, and yet you see you've outlived the farmer, with all his strength, and health, and good looks. By-the-bye, Mrs. Woodford, where's my poor little favourite, Grace? She feels this, I'll be bound, worse than any body."

"I've not seen her since—since—" Mrs. Woodford thought proper to sob so loudly and thickly, as to stifle her words, and render them quite unintelligible, and the doctor rejoined,

"Not since you left the room, you mean, I suppose; then, I should not be at all surprised—— good gracious, Mrs. Woodford, it was really very thoughtless of you not to make some inquiry after the poor thing; but I'll go this minute; and you've all left her, too," he added, looking round at the servants, as he hobbled to the door.

Scarcely conscious of what he was doing, Sir Walter followed the kind-hearted old man up stairs to the attic; but it was not till he had stood some moments, and heard the faint low voice of Grace respond to the doctor's earnest remonstrance to her, not to remain in this dismal place, that his eyes became so far reconciled to the glimmering light, as to ascertain what were the objects around him.

Shocked as it was, he remained as it were rivetted to the spot, as he gazed upon the calm face of the corpse, the expression of which, far from denoting a painful death, seemed that of the most perfect serenity; but his eyes were soon withdrawn from that object, to fix upon the countenance of Grace, who seeming totally heedless and unconscious of the presence of any one, sat upon the ground, by the side of the bed, her eyes fixed upon the face of him who could no longer return her looks of love, her cheeks and lips scarcely less rigid and colourless than those on which she gazed, and her whole appearance and attitude betokening the most intense abstraction of sorrow.

To the doctor's earnest demand, "Grace, child, why do you stay here? why don't you come down stairs?" she only replied,

"Oh! no, no, I cannot leave him;" and then resumed her silent and tearless gaze.

"This is worse for her, a great deal, than if she cried and took on like her sister," said the doctor, in a confidential whisper to Sir Walter, who made no reply, seeming totally absorbed in contemplating the interesting sight before him.

"Grace, my dear, you must consent to leave him, you can do no good now, my child, for your father is past all human help," said the doctor, gently attempting to raise her from the ground.

"I know it! I know it!" she murmured, in a hurried tone, "but still I cannot bear to leave him in this wretched place. Oh! Dr. Richards, and you, too, sir," she exclaimed, clasping her hands, "do, pray, beg of my mother that his chamber may be made ready for him. Oh! had he been in his own bed——"

"Grace, Grace, recollect yourself, child, you are talking wildly," interrupted the doctor, evidently alarmed at her manner; "consider, my dear," he continued, "that all places now are alike to those poor cold remains.

"It may be so, sir," she replied mildly; "but it does not look respectful, or kind, to leave him here alone. I am not afraid—it will do me more good to remain here by his side, than to go down stairs; but pray do not let me detain you here, only as I know you have great interest with my mother, sir," she added, "you might, perhaps, persuade her to have my poor father removed to his own bed——"

"I will willingly obey your request," said Sir Walter, who was now convinced that her mind was quite collected, though her face betrayed such fearful emotion. The doctor, however, was by no means so well convinced, and after observing in a low tone, to Sir Walter, that the removal must be deferred until the corpse was coffined, he added,

"It will never do leave this poor child here alone."

All his persuasions, however, together with Sir Walter's, failed in accomplishing their wishes.

"I do not like to appear obstinate," observed the gentle girl; but I must stay."

"Then I will stay with you," observed Sir Walter, "until either some one more proper and fitted to be your companion in this melancholy duty, can be found; or you are released by the object of your care being consigned to his last habitation.

"Very strange—very odd resolution, indeed," said the doctor, half-audibly, "if it was Miss Maria, indeed, that was to be his companion, I shouldn't wonder, for love makes even the chamber of death pleasant—but as it is, I'm quite surprised. He'll be heartily tired, by-the-bye, I'm thinking if he has to sit up all night with her. What will Miss Maria say to this I wonder? And by-the-bye, that reminds me I ought to see her again before I go."

"Very strange singular man, this admirer of your's, Miss Maria;" he observed, as he entered the little closet, into which, in pursuance of the general movement, that young lady's bed had been thrust, and on which she was now laid.

Maria's bright eyes glanced a look of keen inquiry through her tears.

"It's a proof, however, of his great respect for you no doubt," continued the gossiping old man, "though he is so very attentive and affectionate to your sister." An explanation was now eagerly demanded, and readily given ; and Maria in her surprise and animadversions on this strange conduct in Sir Walter, seemed totally to have forgotten the melancholy cause which had elicited such a proof of interest from one whose general manners had appeared so apathetic that she had more than once, although not gifted with any very excessive sensibilities herself, been struck with the idea that he possessed no feeling at all.

"Does mamma know that he is up stairs ?" she demanded, after expressing in unison with the doctor her surprise.

"Yes, she knows he left the room with me to go up stairs," returned the latter.

"I think I am much better, I will go down with you," said Maria, jumping off the bed with very little appearance of her late indisposition ; "or, perhaps, it would be more proper that I should go up stairs to poor Grace, for though the sight will almost kill me, I know," and she burst into fresh tears, "yet I should not like to be thought disrespectful to my poor father."

"Nobody can consider you so, because your nerves are not strong enough to bear the sight of death;" replied the doctor, who scandal-loving and gossiping as he was, was yet at the bottom, kind and good-hearted. "As my patient," he added, "I must take upon myself to forbid your exposing yourself to the danger of renewing your late attack. But come, we will go down and talk the matter over with your mother, who is in the drawing-room."

Leaning upon the doctor's arm, Maria appeared before her mother, who with evident surprise and alarm, instantly inquired for Sir Walter.

The doctor with his usual—or more even than his usual—interjections of "very odd," "by-the-bye," and "quite singular," now contrived to make her understand the very extraordinay conduct of the baronet ; and Mrs. Woodford appeared to coincide in opinion with him, that it was very odd, for she sat for some moments completely silent from astonishment.

"I must not suffer this !" she at length exclaimed, as if recollecting herself ; it is quite wicked of Grace to give way so to her grief. Sally, do you go to her, and tell her I desire she will come instantly to me. And d'ye hear, ask Sir Walter to walk into the little supper-room, and I'll come to him there, that's the most to rights of any place. We must set about clearing all away, by-and-bye," and she looked around her with a disconsolate air.

Sally made a sign to her fellow-servant to come with her, the doctor followed them, and Mrs. Woodford, thus left to the free expression of her sentiments, turned quickly to Maria.

"Did you ever hear anything so ridiculous, Maria, as Sir Walter's behaviour ? But I don't know how it is, from the very first moment he saw her, I've always suspected that he thought more of that girl than I liked. Oh ! she's an artful young hussey, but she's not going to do with me as she's done with her foolish fond father, I can assure her ; she will find that she has got somebody else to deal with her now, whom she won't be able to blind with all her art."

"Grace artful ! she, the most candid the most open-hearted, generous being that ever existed !" such were Maria's mental exclamations, as with astonishment, she heard this charge brought against her sister ; but though her heart thus did justice to the injured Grace, her tongue uttered not a word in vindication, for she was too much occupied in settling her looks before the expected meeting with Sir Walter, as she stood before the mirror.

"Beauty, they say, looks most beautiful in tears," she thought to herself; "but tears, I am sure, do not become me, for my face looks all blotched and blowzy, and my nose so frightfully red, I should scarcely know myself."

Her observations were scarcely finished, before Grace's trembling form and death-like features glided into the room.

"Do you want me, mother?" she demanded, without raising her eyes, and seeming by a great effort to command her voice to speak with tolerable firmness.

"Yes, miss, I do want you," replied her mother, sharply; "You can do no good upstairs, and I insist upon it you keep away from that room. I don't like so much pretence and affectation, I can tell you; everything that's proper will be done, without the interference of a girl like you, and so let me hear no more of your obstinacy—but stay here, and try to be of some service to me."

Grace listened to her in silence, she did not attempt to remonstrate, nor was there anything in the expression of her countenance, which could denote that she felt the injustice of her mother's observations. She tried to give utterance to some request (when her mother had concluded), looked earnestly at Maria, as if to implore her interference in her favour and then stood still, as if awaiting the further orders of her imperious parent.

"Where is Sir Walter, pray?" demanded the latter.

"He is—he is—" Grace in vain attempted to articulate another word— the efforts she had made to subdue the expression of her grief, rendered it now but the more overwhelming, and she fell fainting on the ground, at her mother's feet."

The screams of Maria brought Sir Walter and the doctor both to the room.

"I was right in my opinion," observed the former; "it would have been better to have let her have her own course." And, without paying the slightest attention to any one else, he raised the insensible girl in his arms, and continued to support her until the doctor's remedies recalled her to life.

During the time that Grace remained insensible all her mother's significant looks and hints seemed lost upon Maria, who really loved her sister as much, or perhaps more, than she did any earthly thing except herself, and was, consequently, alarmed at seeing her in such a state; but now, when Grace was sufficiently recovered to speak, and even make an effort to withdraw herself from Sir Walter's protecting arms, Maria began, as well as her mother, to feel that it was not quite pleasant to see her (Grace) so exclusively the object of the baronet's attention. He appeared, in fact, to have totally forgotten that there was any one else present who had a claim upon his sympathy; and both his looks and expressions towards Grace were those of undissembled tenderness and compassion.

"She had better lie down for an hour or two," observed Mrs. Woodford looking significantly at the doctor, who understood the hint to second her suggestion.

"You cannot walk alone, dearest Grace, we will assist you," said Sir Walter, as the poor girl made an effort to rise and obey her mother's affectedly-tender injunction to go to bed and try what an hour or two's sleep would do towards recovering her.

The doctor turned an irrepressible look of astonishment upon Mrs. Woodford at this undisguised expression of tenderness on the part of the baronet and the latter, catching his look, seemed at once to recollect the impression which it was likely would be made, and withdrew to make room for Maria, who had offered to assist her.

"Poor child!" he observed; "it is a sad shock to her young mind to lose so suddenly one to whom she was so tenderly attached."

"Yes, poor thing," said Mrs. Woodford, catching eagerly at his words; "she is indeed but a child, and one cannot expect that she will have much command over her feelings; but Maria was always remarkable for her fortitude, though she is, like me, the victim of excessive sensibility."

Sir Walter looked earnestly in her face as she uttered these words. A sarcastic smile for an instant played upon his features, and he seemed to be on the point of giving utterance to some sentiment in conformity with that expression, but he suppressed it whatever it might be, and proceeded to ask some explanation of the cause which had produced this fatal event.

The return of Maria and the doctor, who declared the patient likely to sleep, she having taken a composing draught, interrupted the long and, in some points, interesting conversation which had ensued between Sir Walter and the widow; and having promised to see them again early on the morrow, the baronet left them.

––––––––

The remains of the honest farmer were committed to the earth in due time, amid the lamentations and regrets of all who had sense or feeling enough to estimate his worth; but there were none who felt, with the exception of Grace, more truly sorry for his loss than Belgrave Mansel.

In the arrangements for the funeral Mrs. Woodford had suffered great mortification from being unable to procure the attendance of more than one or two of the neighbouring gentry. They had all been willieg enough to accept the invitation to eat, and drink, and laugh at the expense of the foolish woman, but they all fled hastily at the sound of the mourning; and she was thus compelled to include in the list of those who were requested to attend poor Woodford to the grave, several who would have been left out of the formal list, and among them were the two brothers, William and Belgrave Mansel.

More than once since the occasion which had called it forth had the marked haughtiness of manner, and the keen flashes of Belgrave Mansel's eye, recurred to Sir Walter Fitz-Geffrey's recollection, and he had wished that an opportunity would occur to bring the young man again within his reach that he might learn whether he possessed in reality those superior qualifications which his look and manner denoted.

At the funeral of Mr. Woodford this wish was gratified, and he found himself seated by the side of Belgrave, whom he instantly recognized, though his downcast eye and his look of deep sorrow had very materially changed the expression of his countenance.

Sir Walter's interest in him, however, suffered no diminution by this proof of his feeling and sensibility, and laying aside that reserve and commanding tone which were calculated little to impress strangers in his favour, the baronet contrived to draw the young farmer into a conversation, in which he fully confirmed the impression of the former in his behalf.

Sir Walter, however, soon learned a secret, which was, in fact, only a secret to him, the whole village being perfectly aware, that Belgrave Mansel was deeply in love with Grace Woodford.

Sir Walter was in deep conversation with Belgrave when the sisters entered the room together, and he marked with surprise the sudden embarrassment—the look of earnest inquiry, succeeded by an expression of extreme anguish—which distinguished his companion, as his eyes rested on Grace's pale face. Yet, in the conversation which had been thus abruptly terminated, Belgrave had spoken more of Maria than of her sister; and, except when Sir Walter had himself mentioned Grace's extraordinary attachment to her father, and her consequent grief for his loss, the name of the latter had never been mentioned.

"Yes; she knew his value, and she regrets him accordingly," he had said; "Mrs. Woodford has done her best to spoil Maria, though she has not succeeded, for her heart is too good to be entirely spoiled; but Grace has been her father's favourite; and, therefore, I will not say that her mother has disliked her, for I think it impossible that a mother can dislike her child; but certain it is, Mrs. Woodford has troubled herself very little about her, and it has been all the better for her."

Though firmly convinced of the truth of his observation respecting Belgrave's attachment to Grace, Sir Walter was by no means equally satisfied that Grace felt a reciprocal affection: he even thought that he could discover that she rather shunned than sought any communication with the young man, who, on his part, he saw, wisely refrained from addressing, either to her or her sister any of the awkward commonplace topics of condolement, and appearances of friendship, by which the other part of the company sought to diminish the grief of the family. Grace, indeed, was wholly absorbed in that grief which, in her mother and sister, was divided by other feelings. It was scarcely in nature that Mrs. Woodford should not mourn for the chosen husband of her youth, and the indulgent partner who, during all the years of her marriage life, had quietly yielded to all her whims and extravagances, even sometimes to a blameable degree, as had been the case in the last instance, which had proved so fatal to him: but whatever emotions of natural sorrow and regret were kindled in her bosom, they were stifled by her excessive vanity and love of parade and show, which even at this solemn moment, and on an occasion which ought to have humbled her pride to the dust, broke out with most offensive intrusiveness.

The very widow's garb in which she was clothed was so fantastically modelled, so carried to excess, that she looked rather like the mourner in some theatrical pageant than the bereaved wife of an honest English yeoman; and the studied display of her white cambric handkerchief, the very attitude in which she sat, and the modulated tones in which she replied to the rough kindness of the farmers who attended to pay the last mark of respect to their companion, all seemed rather the mockery than the reality of grief.

Never, perhaps, had Maria looked more transcendently beautiful than she now appeared in her mourning dress, which, however, was too much like her mother's, evidently calculated for display, to be quite accordant with the profound grief which her countenance so feelingly expressed. But Sir Walter, as he gazed on her fair face and faultless form, felt that what was detestable in her mother was at least excusable in her; and though he would have felt better satisfied had she, like her sister, appeared with a plainness that evinced she had indeed "that within which passeth show," he felt she might be pardoned the long transparent black veil, which was now thrown gracefully aside, and again drawn, with equal grace, forward, to conceal her face, the jet earrings, bracelets, and combs, which served to display the dazzling whiteness of her skin, and even the furtive glance, which stole from amidst her tears, as if seeking in the countenances of those around her, the effect her beauty created.

With Grace it was very different: the only effort she made was to suppress the outward expression of the grief which nothing could conceal and nothing heighten.   The world—all that surrounded her—seemed but as the faint and far-off visions of a dream: she heard the voices that spoke to her from time to time, and she saw the looks that were turned upon her of pity and compassion, but her own thoughts and looks were centred in one object —the coffin which contained her best, and almost her only friend; and when it was at last removed for ever from her sight, she felt as if all that she had lived for—her sole thought, care, and occupation—was gone; and she sat silent and stupefied with grief, a spectator of her mother and sister's tears and loud lamentations, which lasted until the funeral procession had entirely disappeared.

"Come here, my love, that frock does not altogether please me;" observed Mrs. Woodford, after a few minutes' pause, during which her tears had been dried, and her white handkerchief laid aside.   "It is scarcely low enough to show the fall of your shoulders—we must have an alteration;" and she turned and examined the object of her maternal care, round and round three or four times.   "You certainly do look charmingly in black, Maria, and so you need not fret at being obliged to wear it, though I own I expected that your next new things would have been your wedding clothes : but all in good time—I could see Sir Walter thought black set you off to great advantage, for his eyes were never off you : as to Grace"—and she turned and looked scrutinisingly at the sorrowful girl—"Grace looks absolutely like a ghost; I am sure she will have reason to be glad as well as me when she gets out of mourning."

"I shall never be out of mourning," sighed Grace to herself: but had she said it aloud there would have been no one inclined to answer her; for Maria and her mother were both busily engaged in discussing how long it would be necessary to wear "very deep," and by what gradations it would be genteel and fashionable to leave off their suits of sables.

"It would not be proper for a wedding to take place in less than three months," observed Mrs. Woodford; "but if Sir Walter should press it, I certainly should not object then; and then, you know, you will be obliged at once to leave off your mourning."

A slight flush crossed Grace's pale cheek : it was an irrepressible evidence that she heard and condemned this impatient anticipation of the moment when even the shows of grief might, in her mother's opinion, be decently dispensed with.

"You need not look so contemptuous, Miss Grace," continued the latter, whose eyes happened, at that moment, to be fixed on the features which were seldom so honoured; "we are quite aware of what you are feeding your vanity with; but, you may rely upon it, you are greatly mistaken, if you suppose Sir Walter has any other idéas or intentions towards you than as a mere child.   I know you flatter yourself differently; but he has opened his mind to me; and I can tell you for your comfort, that your sister will be Lady Fitz-Geffrey."

"I am glad to hear it, I am sure," said Grace, with an air of absence and deep despondence mingled, and without attempting to utter a word in vindication of herself.

In real truth, Grace was totally unconscious of the charge brought against her.   She had been so accustomed to hear nothing addressed to her from her mother but the language of reproof, that it became a matter of course to expect it; and often it had happened, as in the present instance, that, in spite of her wish to behave with proper respect, and receive her mother's corrections with due deference, Grace had listened, without being able to comprehend, when her mother had done speaking, what it was that had occasioned her observations; or, as she would, when in a sportive mood, observe to her father, " what in the world it had all been about."

" Glad; yes, I dare say you are glad, because you have sense enough and know your own interest well enough, to see that such a connexion will be of importance to you; but you would have been much better pleased, I fancy, if your artifices had succeeded, and you could have supplanted your sister, and got the title and fortune yourself."

" Me, mother ! " said Grace, lifting her eyes with extreme astonishment to her mother's face; " surely surely," she added, in a tone of touching remonstrance, " you cannot seriously mean to make such a charge against me, and at such a time as this, too; and Maria, do you, too, believe me ———"

" No, no; I do not believe any such thing, dear Grace; and I have always told my mother that I was sure she was mistaken," returned Maria, with considerable emotion. " No; I am sure I know your heart too well, Grace, to believe that you would purchase wealth and rank at my expense."

" You did me justice, then, Maria," returned Grace with spirit; " and henceforth I hope my mother will know me better. I have now no other friend—no other protector!" and she burst into a flood of tears.

" You need not have so cruelly reminded me of my loss, miss," said her mother again drawing out her handkerchief; " but you are determined, I see, that I shall not, even in the prospect of your sister's good fortune, forget for a moment the heavy misfortune that has befallen me."

Grace replied not to this really cruel and unjust remark; for her thoughts were again devoted to the memory of her kind and indulgent father, and to him were now given those tears which had first been drawn from her by the strange, perverse misconstruction her mother had chosen to put upon her.

" And now I've got something else to say to you, Grace," said Mrs. Woodford, " before these people come back, and that is, that I utterly forbid any communication between you and Belgrave Mansell. I saw his anxiety to get near and speak to you while he was here, and I was very glad to observe that you shunned him; I hope, indeed, that you are quite convinced that you will have a right to look above such folks as the Mansells; but, however, I think it right to tell you at once my ideas and resolutions on the subject."

Grace was silent; she felt keenly the cruelty, the indelicacy, and the impropriety of such observations at such a moment; yet her heart refused to allow her to temporise, by appearing to be convinced by her mother's words, and she, therefore, declined altogether answering her. Fortunately at this moment an accident by which Maria broke the clasp of one of her bracelets, attracted and absorbed Mrs. Woodford's sole attention, and put an end to all discussion on the subject; and before the mischief could be repaired, and all that had been put out of order restored to its pristine state, the train of mourners were seen " wending their slow way" back to the house.

CHAPTER X.

" Self-pois'd, in awkward state,
The lavish widow sate."

—ANON.

TIME, the great physician and healer of all wounds, performed a more than usually quick cure with Mrs. Woodford and Maria; for, in less than three weeks, all traces, except their mourning habiliments, were banished of the loss they had sustained.

The widow seemed, indeed, to have gained a fresh accession of youth and strength, and of that too which she far less needed—vanity; and, though forbidden by custom from throwing off the garb of sorrow, or even from making any very striking or material alteration in its form, it was plain that she wore it only in conformity to that custom, and that she looked forward with impatience to the time when she should exchange it for a dress more suited to the frivolity of her disposition.

But far different was the case with poor Grace, whose looks, instead of improving, seemed to become every day more and more melancholy and desponding.

It was not, indeed, merely the loss of her father's kindness and affectionate indulgence that Grace found cause to deplore but that that loss brought also upon her, with tenfold bitterness, the infliction of her mother's vile temper.

Absorbed in the anticipation of her favourite's greatness, and planning a thousand schemes to make it more speedy and certain, Mrs. Woodford had no time or inclination to attend to petty household cares, or even to exercise her former vigilant superintendence over her servants. All was left to Grace; and Grace, with a load of misery, past, present, and future, pressing on her mind, and suffering under the bodily ill health which a mind diseased is sure to create, was little fit or capable of fulfilling all that was expected of her.

There was, too, another source of trouble, which Grace's inexperience had never till now suspected, and which, therefore, fell heavier upon her; the fact was, that poor Woodford's affairs had been, for some time past, anything but flourishing; but the respect with which he was beheld by all with whom he had any dealings, and the opinion which they had of his integrity, had prevented his being inconvenienced by any very urgent demands for money. Now, however, the case was greatly altered; for, although there was property considerably more than adequate to discharge all demands, it was in hands which could not be trusted, and, consequently, the creditors became most pressing as soon as decency would allow.

It was in vain, however, their frequent appeals were made to Mrs. Woodford; she was blind and deaf to everything but the idea of keeping up appearances, as she conceived it necessary to do for her daughter's welfare, and therefore continued launching into extravagances, which would, at any other time, have been improper and inconsistent with her situation, but which were now doubly so, as increasing tenfold her embarrassments.

For some time the prospect of Maria's marriage, which Mrs. Woodford never failed broadly to hint at as an event which would make a great alteration in the situation of her family, soothed the fears of those who beheld the finances, which should have been applied to the liquidation of their claims, speedily disappearing, without attempting to provide other resources, for Mrs. Woodford now totally neglected all those means by which she had formerly contributed towards her household expenses, as totally beneath her attention. She had no longer the first turkey poults, the finest ducks, and the sweetest butter to send to market, productions for which Rose Farm had long been famed, but which were now in vain sought for by the gentry around, who heard with no little surprise that the farm no longer produced more dainties than were wanted for the family's own consumption. Grace, indeed, for a short time, struggled indefatigably to keep up the usual supply; but her labours in that way were soon stopped; for her mother had so many ways to employ her, that it was impossible she could attend to all; and the discouragement and obstacles she met with on every hand, added to her own ill health, obliged her at last to let things take their own course.

In the mean time, Sir Walter Fitz-Geffrey had established himself in his habitation, which he had christened Belle Retraite, and had drawn from London a whole host of useless servants, whose manners and habits threatened to create complete revolution in the simple and rustic village of Llan ———. But all this time, though Mrs. Woodford talked incessantly of his approaching marriage, and though she had persuaded Maria to look upon herself as the intended bride, not a word had been said on the subject by the person most concerned—Sir Walter himself.

That he greatly admired her there could not be a doubt, for he had repeatedly declared, he had never seen any female whose personal charms could be compared with those of Miss Woodford. He had made her, too, several elegant and expensive presents, but equally had her mother and Grace been sharers of his bounty, and equally when they were present did they share his attentions; but Grace was not often to be seen, for her mother's employments and her own inclinations united to keep her absent whenever Sir Walter favoured them with his society.

But even Maria with all her vanity, and the natural propensity to believe as true what she wished, could not be deceived for ever; and Grace's observant and affectionate disposition soon detected in her sister symptoms of uneasiness and despondency which were totally unusual.

"Why do you sigh so, dear Maria?" inquired the gentle girl, as she was assisting her sister to undress after an excursion which the latter had been taking with her mother to Belle Retraite. "I hope you have no cause to sigh," she added with emphasis.

"Indeed!" returned Maria, somewhat pettishly, "You seem to think then, Grace, that nobody but yourself has any feeling."

"Oh, no, indeed, that was not what I meant," returned Grace warmly; "but only that you have seemed to return hitherto in such good spirits, and to be so well satisfied with ———"

"I am not satisfied then at all, Grace, and so I will tell you the truth," interrupted Maria hastily; "and, indeed, I am very much afraid that I have been made a fool of all this time, and that Sir Walter has no more idea of marrying me than you."

"Well, but did he not settle it all with your mother," observed Grace—"he must be very dishonourable if ———."

"Aye if," said Maria; "but the fact is, Grace, mamma is very sanguine and so apt to run away with a notion when she gets it in her head."

Grace was surprised, nay more, she was sorry, for she had been now so accustomed to look forward to her sister's marriage as an event that was to put an end to a thousand difficulties and mortifications, that she had learned to consider it rather as desirable than otherwise; although at the same time, she could never look at Sir Walter, without wondering how her sister could bear to think of him as a husband, especially when, as was often the case, the natural repulsiveness of his stern features was heightened by his having received some irritation, either from his servants or from the work-people, who either could not, or would not, keep pace with his impatience.

"I have for some time past thought," resumed Maria, finding her sister continued silent; "that mamma had flattered herself and me into a fool's paradise, but I am more than ever convinced of it this evening."

"And why so, dear, Maria?" demanded Grace.

"I will tell you; he was talking of India as usual—I'm sure I'm quite sick of it, for he talks of nothing else from morning till night; but that's not what I was going to say—he was talking of marriages in India, how certain a handsome woman was to get a rich husband; so I said jokingly, 'I wonder if I was to go, whether I should be lucky enough to get a fortune;' and he answered so quickly, and with such earnestness, 'Upon my word, Maria, I do not think you could do a wiser thing, for with such a face and person as yours you would only have to make your own selection.'

"'And are you really serious Sir Walter?' said mamma 'And would you recommend my daughter to such a step?'

"He looked rather confused. 'Not recommend it certainly,' he observed; 'Because I should be very sorry, in the first place, to lose Maria and in the second, it is not exactly what I should wish to recommend to one whom I esteem; but when she spoke of the probabilities of her success, I was tempted to speak warmly, because I felt there could not be a doubt on the subject.'

"Ma' will have it," continued Maria, in a tone of pique and vexation; "that he did but say all this to try me and hear what I should say to the proposal."

"And what did you say?" demanded Grace, with anxiety.

"Oh! why, ma' says, it was impossible I could have answered better if I had studied for a month, for I told him 'I should be very sorry to think so meanly of myself, as to suppose I need travel so many thousand miles in search of a husband."

"And what was his reply to that?" asked Grace, "it was a fair opportunity I think for him to have declared his intentions."

"Why so I've thought since," replied Maria, in a disconsolate tone; "but however, he did not take advantage of that, but only said, with one of his ugly formal bows, that he was quite of my opinion."

"Well, but dear Maria, after all, you do not like him, that is plain, by the contemptuous tone in which you just now spoke of his formality; how then is it possible that you can regret————."

"Regret!" interrupted Maria, sharply. "I suspect you would regret too, if you had fancied you should speedily become the mistress of a fine fortune, and house, and carriages, and to be raised above every body, and then to find————" she burst into a flood of tears, unable to conclude the sentence,

"But my dear, dear Maria," said the compassionating Grace; "these are all very fine things no doubt, though I must confess, I cannot see the pleasure of being raised above one's companions and friends—but allowing that it can be a satisfaction, and that it is very pleasant to have plenty of money and all the rest, yet you would soon get so used to it that it would cease to be a pleasure; and then only consider how wretched it would be to feel that you were tied for life to a man you could not like, and who would perhaps, when the novelty was over, fancy he had done you a great honour and favour in making you his wife, as I am sure I should expect Sir Walter would, for though he has certainly some good qualities, and I believe would often do better then he does, only that he does not know how, because he has been so spoiled by having nobody about him to tell him the truth; yet you certainly must acknowledge that he is outrageously proud—and then only consider how different your dispositions are—he is fond of quiet and retirement, and you like company and visiting—and then your ages so unequal—he cannot be less than fifty."

"He says he is only forty-two, but if he was eighty-two I should care nothing about it," interrupted Maria angrily; "as ma says, mutual love is all very well where there is money on both sides, but as I have none, I would be content to let the love be all on his side; but what is the use of talking? I see plainly that I have been made a fool of, and so I shall tell mamma to-morrow morning, and so pray don't teaze me with any more of your arguments."

"I am sure I would not marry him if he were the king himself," she sighed to herself. "And how Maria can think of it—poor William, she has quite forgotten him; but he spoke true, when he said she never could have had any affection for him, though she pretended it. I am sure I do not believe that I ever gave Belgrave reason to think I liked him better than anybody else, and yet I could not make him so unhappy if I were to gain all the riches in the world by it."

"There is a letter that was given me for you, Miss Grace," said one of the female servants, who had just returned from an errand in the village, a day or two after this conversation.

"A letter for me, Sally!" she replied in astonishment. "Who could want to write to me, or what could they———"

"You had better open it and then you will see," returned Sally, with a significant smile. "I don't know that I have done right to bring it, but the poor young man looked so melancholy, and spoke so very civil, that I had not the heart to refuse him, though I suppose I should get in fine disgrace with missus if she knew it."

"You had better give it back again, then to—to the person," said Grace with extreme confusion; "I am sure, Sally, if it is not right for you to bring it, it cannot be right for me to read it without my mother's knowledge."

"Oh! I didn't say it wasn't right, I am sure Miss Grace," returned the girl, "only since this great gentleman is come among us, missus is so altered, there's no knowing how to please her. And, indeed, to tell you the truth miss, I'm sick of trying, for nothin's done right now, and I'm sure to be twitted that the London maids at Sir Walter's would be ashamed of this, and ashamed of t'other, and then she———"

"I am very sorry, Sally," said Grace, mildly interrupting her; "but I really cannot take this letter. Pray, do you take it and put it by, and then when you go to Llan—— again you can give it to him again, and tell him ———"

"Oh! indeed, miss, I can't do no such thing," said Sally vehemently; "why, I should expect the poor young man would drop down stone dead before me, or go and make away with himself, or some dreadful thing or another, if I was to treat him with such unfeelingness; besides," she added, after a moment's pause, "there'll be one of his boys coming up to-night, and I've promised to meet him at the stile in the Five Acres, to give him your answer, for he made sure you would send him an answer."

"Well, then, you can give the boy this," said Grace, trying to force the letter into her hand.

"No, Miss Grace; I'm sorry to say no to you, but I won't, without you'll put it up in another bit of paper, and write a few words on the inside, just to let him know that I kept my word to him, and that it's your obstinacy that wouldn't read the letter, though what harm there could be in reading a few words, and from one, too, that's as kind and true-hearted as ever anybody was in the world."

"Well, I will comply with your request, Sally; I will enclose the letter,'" observed Grace, after a few moments' recollection, "and that will, perhaps. be the best way, too, as it will prevent his ever troubling you again.'

"Well, if ever in my life, I ever heard such foolishness," said Sally, as Grace hastened out of the room, to find the necessary materials for enclosing the letter. "If she didn't like him, it would be a different thing; but I know she does, she never hears his name mentioned without colouring and trembling, and as to him, poor young man ——"

Grace's re-entrance interrupted her soliloquy,

"There, Sally," she observed, "you shall see what I have written, in order to put a stop to what will end in bringing you into trouble, as well as me."

"I can't very well read such small-hand, Miss Grace," said the self-sufficient damsel, "so you must please to read it for me."

Grace commenced—"Dear Belgrave." "Oh! you do call him dear Belgrave," observed Sally in a tone of delight; "well, I am glad of that, because that will show him that you don't disrespect him."

"Disrespect him!" repeated Grace, "no, indeed, Sally, and more than that, I have told him here that it gives me as much pain to send back his letter, as it will him to receive it, but that——"

"Do, pray, Miss Grace, read all of it, I'm sure it's enough to make the tears come in one's eyes to hear you."

Grace again proceeded with the letter.

"Dear Belgrave,—

"I assure you it gives me quite as much, if not more, pain to send back your letter, as it will you to receive it; but as I am convinced I should be doing wrong to read it without my mother's knowledge, and as I dare not show it to her, for fear of bringing poor Sally into trouble, whose good nature led her to do what she must know, as well as you and me, cannot be right—that is, to disobey and deceive her mistress, I thought this the best mode I could adopt; at the same time, I beg you to believe that the greatest pleasure I could have in this world, now, would be to see you once more on the same terms that you formerly were at Rose Farm, and to that purpose, I pray night and morning, that my mother's heart may be softened towards you. God bless you, dear Belgrave, and believe me ever, your faithful friend,
                                                    "GRACE WOODFORD."

"The Lord send it, say I, and that I may live to be your servant when you are Mrs. Mansel, and manage the dairy for you at the Rocks as Mr. Belgrave once promised, when you were both children together, and little dreamed that anything would divide you."

Grace blushed deeply, for well did she recollect the time Sally alluded to; but the blush was quickly succeeded by a deep and heartfelt sigh, for the recollection brought with it the image of her kind indulgent father, smiling at Belgrave's sportiveness, and then, as if prophetically shaking his head, and observing,

"Ah! lad, I wish thy plans may all go on as smooth and easily as thou canst lay them; but who knows what time may bring forth, and how many troubles may be hanging over thy head, and thy little wife's, as thou callest her?"

"It is a pretty letter she has written, a very pretty one, said Sally, when Grace had departed; "and who knows," she continued, "whether, if she had read this, whether she could have said anything to convince him better that her love for him hasn't cooled—but he won't think so. How rejoiced he will be when he sees this beautiful handwriting," she continued, looking at the letter with its enclosure; "but then how disappointed he will be when he opens it and finds his own there. I declare I shall be quite ashamed to look him in the face—and then Miss Grace needn't have said to much about my deceiving my missus—I don't know who would scruple to deceive such a scolding, niggling, on-reasonable creater. But laws a mercy, it's no use; I suppose I must give this to him, for she won't listen to none of my persuasion."

"Whatever shall I do?" Miss Grace, observed Sally, about two hours after this conversation. "It's past eight now, and I promised to meet Mr. Mansel's boy at a quarter after, and missus, just as if she suspected me, has ordered me to go up and help her sew the new fringe on the drawing-room curtains. Whatever is to be done about this letter?" and Sally drew it from her pocket, and looked at it with an air of perplexity. "It won't do for me to trust anybody with the secret," she resumed, looking earnestly at Grace.

"Oh, no, no!" exclaimed the latter. "For goodness' sake—but he will go away, Sally, when he finds you do not keep your appointment?"

"Yes, he will go away, certainly," returned Sally gravely; "but I can't answer for the consequences, Miss Grace, if Mr. Belgrave should think that you treated him with such scorn, that you would not even notice his letter. You don't know as much as I do, Miss Grace," she continued with great solemnity, "or else you'd think it a very serious affair to drive a young man to——"

"But how am I to help it now, Sally?" demanded Grace impatiently. "If you could tell me what is to be done——"

"Why, what can be easier, Miss Grace," interrupted the wily Sally; "than for you, just to step as far as the Five Acres yourself, and give the lad the letter; it's only for you just to say, Sally was busy, Jem, and could not come, so I promised to give this to you; and he won't be a bit the wiser, because he doesn't know but it's all from Miss Maria, because he used to fetch her letters to Mr. William."

Grace was astonished, for though she knew that her sister had continued to encourage William Mansell's attentions, long after her mother had forbidden her to think of him as husband, and indeed, up to the very hour when Sir Walter Fitz-Geffrey's arrival had given such a different turn to her thought; she (Grace) knew not, nor had ever suspected, that there had been any clandestine correspondence between her sister and William Mansell, though she knew that the latter was quite romantic enough, and quite ardent enough, in his attachment to the subject of his affection, to render it probable.

"Well, but Sally," she commenced, as her thoughts returned to what more immediately concerned herself,

"Oh! Miss Grace," I cannot stop another minute to answer you," said Sally, hastily thrusting the letter into her hands. "If you don't go you may as well keep the letter as me, for I can't go; hark there's missus calling me now. Coming, Ma'am!" and without giving Grace time to utter another word, she ran out of the room.

For some time after her departure, Grace remained hesitating and trying to decide which would be the best—to go and deliver the letter, or leave it to chance; but the recollection of Sally's indiscreet warning of the danger that might attend Belgrave's believing himself treated with contempt dwelt on her memory; and at length she resolved to go to the Five Acres, as the field was called, which Sally had made the place of appointment, and which was distant about half a mile from the house.

"I will caution the boy never to come on a similar errand," she thought to herself, as she proceeded with hasty step in the direction Sally had pointed out; "and yet," she continued, "I cannot blame him, poor fellow, for obeying his master."

The stile which had been named as the place of rendezvous was situated at the bottom of a steep descent, and the path that led to it wound through a thicket, so that no place could be more calculated to a secret meeting. Grace, however, had nearly reached the stile before she ascertained that the person she expected was already waiting for her; but when she had advanced a few paces nearer, she stopped short in an uncertainty, which the next instant removed, for Belgrave himself sprang from the stile to meet her.

"This is, indeed, kind—this is more than I dared hope for, Grace," he exclaimed passionately. "Oh, Grace, how I have longed to see you, at least to speak to you, for I have seen you more than once—I saw you at church, last Sunday, Grace, and you looked so ill, and so melancholy. Oh, how altered you are, my dear, dear Grace; and I am altered, too; and all is altered around us; but you have, at last, listened to my earnest prayer; I know you have, or I should not have seen you here. Nay, Grace; I will not listen to you, if, as your look says, you mean to deny——"

"Belgrave, you must, you shall hear me," interrupted Grace, at last making her voice heard. "I knew not that you were here; I have been trepanned, I suspect purposely, into this improper meeting."

"Trepanned, Grace!" repeated Belgrave, his fine face crimsoning with emotion; "that is a strange word to apply to me, nor am I conscious of having in any way deserved it."

"I did not mean to apply it to you, Belgrave; but tell me, was not Sally aware that you would be here?" said Grace.

"Certainly she was; and you expected to see me here did you not?" replied Belgrave.

"No; a messenger from you, I was led to believe, awaited here my answer to your letter," she replied, producing at the same time the enclosure,

"And you have brought it yourself! Heaven bless you for that, my own Grace," returned her lover, taking it from her.

The grave and deeply sorrowful expression of Grace's expressive eye at this moment struck him most forcibly; and Belgrave, pausing as he was about to tear open the enevelope, exclaimed—

"Grace, what can I anticipate from that mournful look but unhappiness to us both? Tell me, is it so? or rather delay the fatal news, and let me still enjoy the only moments of happiness that I have known for——; how long is it? to me it seems years of misery."

"It is five months since, I was going to say, that unlucky night, which brought Sir Walter Fitz-Geffrey down here, Belgrave," returned Grace; "for certainly that was the first commencement of our unhappiness—every thing is changed since that event."

"Except ourselves, Grace; and we, I trust, are still unchanged: for myself, I can answer that I have never ceased, night and day, to think of you; but you, Grace, amidst so many enjoyments——"

"Enjoyments!" repeated Grace, in a melancholy tone; "indeed, indeed you wrong me, Belgrave; I have had nothing but sorrow, and affliction, and mortification—too bitter mortification," she added, as her thoughts reverted to circumstances, with which, she rightly judged, Belgrave could not be wholly unacquainted.

"I know partly what you allude to, dearest Grace," he returned, "though I thought it possible those circumstances might not yet have reached you; but now, Grace, that I find you are aware of the situation in which your poor mother is placed, let me urge it as another and more forcible reason to those I have stated in my letter——"

THE PRIDE OF THE VILLAGE;

OR,

THE FARMER'S DAUGHTERS.

CHAPTER XI.

A hope so much divine,
May trials well endure.

"Stop, Belgrave, let me at once set you right on that head," said Grace. "I have not read one word of your letter; you will see that I have not opened it, for you have it there in your hand enclosed in a few lines in my writing, in which I explain my reasons and feelings on the subject. Belgrave, I will be candid with you; I dared not trust myself to read what you had written, because I know my own weakness: the same motive now

6

induces me to bid you farewell. I dare not, I must not, listen to you; but I will unite my prayers with yours that the time may speedily arrive, when, under my mother's sanction, I may both listen to you, and say to you all that my heart would dictate. Heaven bless you, Belgrave; and if we never are to meet again on earth, this life is but a short pilgrimage, and we shall at last be united in heaven."

She tried, as she concluded the last sentence, to extricate her hand from Belgrave's firm grasp; but the latter felt his power, and he, with gentle force, drew her back to him.

"Listen to me, Grace; if not for my sake or for your own, at least for your mother's, listen to me," he exclaimed. "Grace, you are aware, in part, I know, from your own observation, of the unfortunate circumstances —I say in part, because I do not think you do know exactly how your mother is situated."

"I know that there are several heavy debts," returned Grace, "for which my mother is pressed, and which she cannot at present discharge."

"You are aware of some, dearest Grace," replied Belgrave; "but are you aware that the heaviest one is due to my uncle Meredith, for which she has never been pressed, but which I am sorry to say——"

"Why should you hesitate, Belgrave? Your uncle, of course, expects to be paid as well as any other creditor, and——"

"Do not look thus coldly, Grace; would to heaven it were in my power to prevent your ever hearing that odious word, creditor; but——"

"But you are afraid, Belgrave, that the wife and children of his late bosom friend will feel too soon the power which Mr. Meredith holds as their creditor," said Grace, coldly.

"Grace, Grace, do not drive me mad by speaking and looking thus," exclaimed the impetuous youth; "but," he added, after a short pause, and with increased animation, "I will force you to hear the whole truth, and to do me, and my uncle, too, justice. Grace, at a time when I was happy in what I thought a certainty, that I should become the son of him I respected as a father, I accidentally learned that he was greatly embarrassed by the loss he had sustained by the failure of the C—— Bank, the depression of the markets, and some other causes which I need not explain to you—he was in want, in fact, of four hundred pounds, and without it, he ingenuously confessed to me, that he saw no prospect of retrieving himself. I had not the money myself, Grace, but I knew my uncle Meredith had; and to him I instantly went, and stated the case, which your father, though on terms, as you know, of the greatest friendship with my uncle, had concealed from him, because he was in the habit of speaking very freely his opinion of a part of your family; in short, Grace, he knew that your——"

"Say nothing of my mother, Belgrave," interrupted Grace, with a deep sigh; "it would not be becoming of me, I am sure, to listen to anything disrespectful of my mother."

"And I would be the last in the world, I am sure, Grace, to wish to speak disrespectfully of her. I wish I could respect her; I wish she would act so as to make everybody respect her; but—— Well, I will say no more on that subject, only that it was the same feeling on your father's part that prevented his at once applying to Mr. Meredith, who, he knew, would not fail to blame him for not exercising his proper right, and curtailing all unnecessary expenses. However, for my sake and for yours, Grace—for you know how partial he has ever been to you, and how he has always from your childhood looked upon you as destined to——"

"Do not say any more on that subject, Belgrave," interrupted Grace, with emotion; "we must not think of that now."

"Not think of it, Grace!—not think of it!" repeated Belgrave impatiently; "I can think of nothing else—I do not think of anything else from morning till night; and can you then so coolly say, 'We must not think——'"

"Belgrave, I must leave you," again interrupted Grace, "if you give way to such violence; I meant only that the present is not the time when we can, with any propriety——"

"Propriety! how I hate that formal word!" exclaimed Belgrave. "Nay, Grace, do not look so angrily at me; it is the first time I ever saw you frown at me, except once when I brought you a linnet's nest with the young ones; and then what a lecture you gave me on cruelty and thoughtlessness, and how imperiously you ordered me to take the nest back and place it exactly where I found it; do you remember that time, Grace? and how——"

"Yes, yes; I remember it all," said Grace blushing and smiling; "but you must remember now that I am very anxious to hear the conclusion of the affair with Mr. Meredith."

"Ah! I wish to heaven it was concluded!" sighed Belgrave; "but, however, my uncle lent the money, observing that he had no hopes of its being paid during his life-time, and that, therefore, he should consider it as a part of what he meant to give me when you and I should be married. I was of course very willing to agree to this; but I begged my uncle would not hurt your father's feelings by seeming to have any doubt of his ability to pay as he proposed—at the end of twelve months—and accordingly my uncle took his bond for that time. Had your poor father lived, Grace, that bond would never have been put in force; or had your mother behaved with common —— well, well, I will only say, then, that had she shown any disposition to regard her husband's friends as her's, my uncle would not only have forborne to press for his lawful demand, but he would have exerted himself to the utmost to assist her in arranging matters with others who are less liberal than himself; but when he sees himself and his counsels spurned at and treated with contempt, and above all, when he finds, Grace, that I am made wretched and miserable, and that you are even forbidden to speak to me—I will say nothing about poor William, because, you know, my uncle was always opposed to his thinking of Maria, who he always prophesied, would turn out as extravagant and——there, you are angry again; but how can I help speaking, Grace, when I see my poor brother looking the image of despair, and find myself little better, though I still place confidence in you, and constantly defend you against those who predict that you will be corrupted at last, and brought to look upon me with as much contempt as Maria looks upon poor William."

"You only do me justice, then, Belgrave," observed Grace; "for I should hate myself, if I could ever forget——the friends of my father, she added, after a short pause: but tell me, Belgrave, does Mr. Meredith think so meanly of me?—does he, too, join with those who believe I shall be corrupted?"

"My uncle, you know, Grace, is very passionate and very obstinate when he takes anything in his head, and he fancied that on Sunday you purposely took Sir Walter's other arm, when you came out of the pew to avoid speaking to——"

"Good Heavens! I did not even see your uncle, Belgrave. I knew that you and William were in your pew, but I had received a long lecture from my mother, before we went to church, about stopping behind her, the Sunday before, to speak to all my friends, as I'd been used to do in my poor father's lifetime, and she had mortified me to the utmost before Sir Walter, by telling me that it was in reality only you that I stayed behind to see."

"And why should you be mortified at that, Grace?" exclaimed Belgrave, indignantly; "are you, then, ashamed that he should think——oh, Grace! in the face of the whole world, I should be proud to call you mine! and yet, before that upstart, base-born, proud, contemptible——"

"Belgrave, I cannot waste my time in listening to your violence," said Grace, calmly. "You must know that I am situated very differently to you: a man may feel no hesitation in avowing his regard for a female, whom he believes worthy of it; but for a young woman——"

"You are right, Grace; and I am sorry that I gave way for a moment to passion," interrupted Belgrave: "but you forgive me, do you not, Grace? say that you forgive me, and you shall see I will not offend again."

"On that condition, then," said Grace, half yielding and half retreating from the embrace with which he considered it necessary to seal his penitence: "but pray go on; your uncle Meredith then is angry with me, as well as the rest of the family."

"I cannot deny, Grace, that he believes the dazzling prospect of your sister's intended marriage, and the style of luxury and extravagance in which you have been living has had its effect, and that you have been, at length, brought to despise your former friends, and look forward, as well as Maria, to a splendid fortune. It has been hitherto in vain, all I could say on the subject," continued Belgrave: "but he has agreed at least to defer his intended violent proceeding until after this interview, or at least your answer to my letter; and, then, unless you unequivocally agree to become my wife whenever he should think proper, no power on earth, he declared, should prevent his enforcing his rights; for then he should be convinced that his suspicions were right, and that you, to use his own expression, was as bad as the rest, and meant to turn out a fine lady, and jilt me after all."

"And could my old friend Mr. Meredith wish me, then to act in open rebellion against my only remaining parent?" said Grace, reproachfully; "he who has always such high notions of the duty a child owes to its parents, and who used to praise me so much for never disputing my mother's commands, even when he considered them unreasonable, and he threatens, then, ruin to my mother and her family, if I refuse to yield to his conditions, without consulting her."

"It is even so, Grace," returned Belgrave, in a melancholy tone.

"And would you wish, Belgrave, to owe your wife to her fears?—to gain my consent by compulsion, and not by inclination?"

"Certainly not, dearest Grace," said Belgrave, looking rather confused, "but I have always believed—I have flattered myself—"

"No, you have not flattered yourself, Belgrave, for I acknowledge all that you wish me to acknowledge;" and she sank her voice almost to a whisper, and averted her blushing face; "but I cannot consent, dear Belgrave, even to save my mother, at the expense of acting in direct opposition to her commands. She has forbidden me to listen to any proposals from you, by which, of course, I understand that—nay, listen to me with calmness, as I have listened to you, Belgrave. I promised her that I would never form any connection without her consent; but I did not promise what I knew to be impossible, that I would cease to think of you as—as the chosen of my dear, dear father. But now, Belgrave, I will tell you how we will act, to prevent all reproaches, either on my mother's part, or from our own consciences; you shall go with me to her, tell her all that has passed between us, and all that is threatened, and I think—I hope—"

Grace faltered, unable to conclude the sentence, and thereby proving—

what was, in fact, the case—that, even with all the consequences that must stare her in the face, Mrs. Woodford would still remain inexorable.

"I am afraid, Grace, that this will never succeed," observed Belgrave, after a few moments' pause, during which he appeared to have been weighing in his mind the probable consequences of the appeal Grace reccommended : "your mother is evidently blind—infatuated to her own course; and if she should insult me——"

"You will bear it patiently, for my sake, Belgrave," said Grace, imploringly ; "nay, if you cannot bridle that impetuous temper, Belgrave," she added, gravely, observing his impatient gesture, "even on a subject of so much importance to us both—when our future happiness, perhaps, will depend on your bearing, for a short time, with that most empty and worthless of all injuries—a woman's tongue—

"That gives not half so great a blow to the ear
As will a chestnut in a farmer's fire.'

Come, there is your own Shakspeare to persuade you patiently to listen," she added, with one of her sweetest smiles; "and will you not promise ——— "

"I will promise anything you wish or require; Grace, you are an angel !" he replied with ecstacy : "but oh, Grace, if she should still continue obstinate—if she should refuse to hear me,——— "

"If she does," said Grace, "but, no, no (checking herself), she must hear you, Belgrave ; and I have strong reason to think that you could never have chosen a better time than the present to induce her to listen to reason."

Belgrave suffered himself to be persuaded. What was there, indeed, which Grace could not have persuaded him to essay ? And with her arm through his, in all the confidence of youthful innocence, and the ardent hope inspired by a confidence of the justice and rectitude of their intentions, they took their way to the farm.

CHAPTER XII.

"Since my tenth sun gave summer to my sight,
Thou wert my life, the essence of my thoughts—
Loved ere I knew the name of love."

BYRON.

MRS. WOODFORD was engaged with Maria in an earnest conversation, the subject of which appeared very unsatisfactory to both of them, when a sudden turn was given to both their thoughts by the appearance of Grace, whom Maria first pointed out to her mother's observation by an expression of surprise.

"Who is it ?" demanded Mrs. Woodford, eagerly, raising herself to look through the window, from which Maria had discovered her sister's approach with her forbidden companion.

"What can be the meaning of it ?" said Maria, without appearing to notice her mother's question ; "Grace, I am sure, would never bring *him* here without some strong reason."

"I care not what *her* reason may be," returned Mrs. Woodford, angrily "but this I know, that I shall certainly affront Mr. Belgrave, if he presumes to force himself here ; and as to Grace, I will take care she shall have no more excursions to meet him—it is no more than I have suspected for some time past, for all her pretensions to the contrary."

"Then, I am sure you have wronged her," said Maria, warmly, "for Grace is incapable of deception."

Mrs. Woodford paid no attention to this sisterly vindication, for she was mustering all her forces to daunt at once the persevering young man, as she would have styled him; and when Belgrave followed Grace into the room, the look with which he was received was quite enough to convince him that, in spite of all that Grace had confided to him respecting her mother and sister's apprehended disappointment from Sir Walter, they had neither of them lowered their pretensions, or were disposed to regard him with any more favour than they had lately shown towards him.

"I am really quite at a loss to think what can have brought you here, Mr. Mansell," said Mrs. Woodford, drawing herself up with what she intended to be a very majestic look; "and still more surprised," she continued, "that if you have any business with me, as I suppose you have, for I can't suppose it's mere pleasure that's led you to come so abruptly——"

"I have business, Mrs. Woodford, which, I trust, will account for and excuse the abruptness of my visit," interrupted Belgrave, gravely.

"Well, then, Sir, pray let me know it at once; for, though your company may be vastly agreeable to some people," and she looked reproachfully at Grace, "I can assure you my daughter's time and mine is too valuable to be thrown away."

"I do not wish to trespass on your daughter's time, madam," returned Belgrave, who appeared no way disconcerted by this ungracious reception; "and, indeed," he continued, "if you will allow me a few minutes' conversation with you alone I shall be able, perhaps, to convince you that——"

"Maria, my love, will you go to your own room for a few minutes," said Mrs. Woodford; "and you, Miss Grace, I dare say, can find something to employ you a little more usefully than picking rosebuds to pieces, and strewing them on the carpet: you need not stop to pick them up now, madam, there will be time enough for that when Mr. Mansell is gone."

Grace flew out of the room with burning cheeks and tearful eyes, at the severity of her mother's manner, and her sarcastic observation upon an act which had been the result of her (Grace's) extreme confusion and vexation at her mother's rudeness.

"Where are you going to, Grace? Come here; I want you to tell me —for, of course, you know—what does all this mean, and what has brought Belgrave Mansell here, now," said Maria, who had lingered at the foot of the stairs till Grace came out.

"I cannot tell you, now, dear Maria; you will hear it all from my mother, presently," replied the agitated girl; and without waiting for any further remark from her sister, she flew out into the garden, and down to the arbour, which had been her father's favourite seat, and where she could give unnoticed vent to the tears which she could no longer suppress.

Of her mother's consent to Belgrave's proposal she entertained scarcely a hope, for well she knew that the disposition of the latter would lead her to reject with scorn any attempt to control her; but it was not her own unhappiness—the disappointment of those hopes which her father had not only permitted, but encouraged, though he had with propriety considered her too young to enter into any absolute engagement—nor was it even for Belgrave, though she doubted not the sincerity of his affection for her, that her tears flowed; she mourned for the ruin and disgrace that she foresaw awaited her mother, if the latter still continued in her present infatuated course, and for the mortification which must befall her sister, at being compelled to give up her present high-flown hopes.

What, indeed, would become of either of them, should Meredith persist in enforcing his claim, and she too much feared he would?

"And I could save them from all this, Belgrave says," she repeated to herself; "for if I become his wife, his uncle will give up the security in his hands."

Grace reflected again and again, whether she would not be almost better fulfilling her duty by accepting her lover's offer, even in direct opposition to her mother's wishes, than, by obeying her, to leave the latter exposed to all the evils which he had so forcibly depicted; but the consciousness that in the former case she should be following the dictates of her own inclinations rendered her doubtful, and at length induced her firmly to decide that she would implicitly obey her mother, let the consequences be what they might.

"It is not your place, my child, to argue whether your mother is right or wrong, but to obey her in silence," had been the answer with which her father uniformly met her complaints, whenever she had been tempted, by the unreasonableness of her mother's despotism, to murmur. "You may find obedience painful," he would say, "but you would find the effects of disobedience far more so, and more lasting; so now dry your tears, and go and do what your mother has desired you, and then you and I shall be quite comfortable together."

The lesson thus kindly inculcated on the one hand, and strictly enforced on the other, had had its due effect; and Grace had learned so strictly to subdue her own feelings and opinions, when they were in opposition to her mother's, that not even a look betrayed her dissent. And should she now, in the most important action of her life, renounce all control, and act in direct contradiction to her dear father's maxims, and the conduct which under his auspices she had so diligently pursued? No; it would not, it could not be right: and again Grace mentally repeated her determination, rigidly to abide by her mother's decision.

The shades of evening had veiled all around her in obscurity, ere Grace had so effectually subdued the traces of her recent agitation as to venture to return to the house.

Candles were already lighted in the sitting-room, and the timid girl cast an anxious glance through the unclosed windows, as she hesitated whether she should enter, or wait till she was sent for to supper.

Belgrave was gone, and that was sufficient to assure her that his suit had been unsuccessful, had she indulged any hope to the contrary; but it was a source of some consolation to her to see that Sir Walter Fitz-Geffrey was seated on the same sofa with her mother; and that he appeared in very earnest conversation with her.

"After all, perhaps," she softly ejaculated as she crept up stairs to her own room, "after all it may be Maria was wrong in thinking he slighted her, and he has come thus unexpectedly to explain his intentions. Thank God; if there is no hope for Belgrave and me, she will be happy, and my mother will be rescued from all difficulties; for Sir Walter is rich, and generous, and, of course——"

Her thoughts were suddenly interrupted by discovering, at this moment, that Maria, whose absence from the parlour she had not noticed during the cursory survey she had taken of it, was sitting in an apparently disconsolate mood in the window of the bedroom.

"Have you been here ever since, Maria?" she demanded, in a tone of surprise. "Do you know who is downstairs with my mother, and that Belgrave"—with some difficulty she pronounced the name—"is gone."

"Yes, I know it all very well," returned Maria, somewhat petulantly. Grace was silenced. It was seldom that Maria, spoiled and perverted as her disposition had been by her mother's injudicious indulgence and flattery, ever betrayed any petulance or unkindness towards her sister; and, convinced that something unusual must have occurred to occasion it in the present instance, Grace sat quietly down by her in the window-seat, to await the communication which she felt no doubt her sister would make when her fit of pettishness had subsided.

As she had expected, Maria's silence did not last long.

"You are a strange girl, Grace," she observed, in an altered tone; "I cannot suppose it possible that you can have learnt the result of my mother's conversation with Belgrave, and yet you do not express any curiosity or anxiety on the subject. Is it that you are insensible? or perhaps you and he have made up your minds to act without her consent."

"Neither, I assure you, dear Maria," said Grace, with earnestness; "I have determined to be entirely guided by my mother's decision; and if it is against Belgrave,———" her voice faltered, and she remained silent.

"It is against him, then, Grace, I am sorry to say," rejoined Maria, in one of her kindliest tones. "I had not time to learn all the particulars, for Sir Walter made his appearance just as my mother was beginning to tell me, and I ran away to my room again, because, to tell you the truth, Grace, mamma has come to the resolution of putting the plain question to Sir Walter, whenever he chooses next to visit us; and his coming to-night so unexpected, seemed too good an opportunity to be lost. If we should both be doomed to disappointment to-night, Grace,———"

"We must try to console each other," said Grace, softly passing her arm round her sister's waist, and leaning her head on her shoulder.

Maria burst into tears; and Grace, who had before with difficulty suppressed hers, now wept in concert.

They were still in this position, when Sally came to say that her mistress wanted Miss Maria.

"Is Sir Walter going to stay to supper, Sally?" demanded Maria, taking the candle from her, and beginning hastily to arrange her hair at the glass.

"Laws bless you; no, miss, he's gone," replied the girl; and missus seems all in such a quandary like."

"Did my mother ask for me, Sally?" inquired Grace anxiously.

"No, miss. Yes; that is, she asked where you was; and when I said I believed you was down in the bowry as I thought you was, for I didn't see you come in, she said, 'Let her stay there, then, I don't want her yet-a-while; but fetch Miss Maria directly.'"

Maria, during this explanation, had hurried out of the room; and Grace, with a deep sigh, re-seating herself, observed, "That will do, Sally, I won't detain you any longer."

Sally, however, still lingered; and, under pretence of putting the carpet straight, contrived to shut the door.

"I hope you aint angry with me, Miss Grace," she observed, coming close, "but poor Mr. Belgrave is in the garden; he saw me as I was going across to the dairy, for it seems he's been loitering about the house ever since missus ordered him to go out, and never darken her doors again."

"Did my mother say so?" exclaimed Grace hastily; but, recollecting herself, she added, "my mother has a right, Sally, to say what she pleases.

But what do you mean by saying that Mr. Mansell is in the garden ? Surely you have not been so imprudent——"

"I couldn't help it, miss, for the life of me. When he begged so hard to know where you were, and for me to ask you to see him for a minute, I couldn't help telling him you was in the garden ; and so, he know'd the way to get over the old wall, as he used to do when my poor master——oh, miss, how little did anybody think then——but do, for pity's sake, just step down to the bowry and speak to the poor young man, for he'll be quite beside himself when he finds that you aint there."

"I will not go into the garden to-night, Sally," replied Grace firmly ; "and I advise you, for your own sake, to go and persuade Belgrave to leave the place at once. Tell him from me that it is utterly useless for him to remain, for that without my mother's permission I will not see him."

Sally hesitated ; she looked as if she would have remonstrated against this decision ; but Grace turned from her with a look and manner so determined, that, muttering to herself something about hard hearts and cruelty, the girl quitted the room and Grace, relieved from her observation, gave way without control to the feelings that swelled almost to suffocation in her bosom.

From this transient indulgence, however, she was quickly roused by a loud scream from the parlour ; and in an instant she rushed down the stairs, and was at the side of her sister, who was screaming and struggling with her mother, in a fit of of hysterical passion.

"Let me go—I will go—I will not stay to see it—to be mocked and laughed at ! I will die first ! Let me go—I would rather beg my bread than stay here to be insulted and trampled upon !" were her frantic exclamations, as she attempted to force herself from her mother's grasp, and that of the terrified Grace, who was assisting to hold her.

"My dear, dear Maria have patience, do listen to reason ;" exclaimed the alarmed mother—"you know, well, if it depended on me, that your welfare would be the first consideration ; but ——"

"Yes ; you have proved it," interrupted Maria, with vehemence ; "if you had cared half as much for me as you have always pretended, you would not have listened for a moment to such an insulting proposal, you would have ordered him to quit the house, as you did poor Belgrave Mansell. And you, too, deceitful as you are," she added, turning to Grace , "I do not wonder, now, that you were so calm and resigned to your mother's pleasure. You knew very well that a better offer would be made you, and your pretended hopes, too, that I should not be doomed to disappointment when you were aware all the time that nothing but the bitterest——" She burst into a flood of passionate tears, and Grace, whose surprise and affright had hitherto kept her silent, now turned to her mother to demand of her an explanation of her sister's mysterious expressions.

"Ah ! you may well look surprised, Grace," said the latter, "for I don't believe you did know anything of it ; indeed, I'm sure you didn't, for it is not probable that, if you had been aware of Sir Walter's preference of you, you would have been so foolish as to let Belgrave Mansell try to force me into giving my consent to——. However, there is one consolation, at least —that I shall triumph over him and his insolent, mean-spirited uncle. Sir Walter has promised me to settle his demand himself, personally, to-morrow, and then they will see that all their hopes are at an end. I only wish that I had seen Sir Walter first, for then I should have been able to silence that insolent young man at once."

Grace had listened thus far with looks of fixed and incredulous amazement; but before her mother had concluded the last sentence, or Maria, who had raised herself, with marks of the strongest indignation, from the sofa on which she had thrown herself, could utter a word in reply, the poor girl sank down, fainting with agitation.

Mrs. Woodford's attention, was wholly fixed by Maria, whose vehement reproaches were now all directed against Grace, whom she accused of sacrificing her without pity or remorse to her own interest.

"What would you have me do, Maria?" exclaimed the weak and doting mother. You are aware how I am situated, and that I have added to my embarrassments, in the hope that Sir Walter intended——and when I found that his heart was fixed on Grace, and knew that though it might be for the time a disappointment to you, yet that it would be the means of introducing you into company, and that as the sister of Lady——"

"That I will never be!" screamed Maria, with frantic violence; "no, I will die first!" and again she threw herself down.

"What can I do—what is to be done?" ejaculated Mrs. Woodford, in a tone of despair, turning round at the moment, to consult the countenance of Grace; but her surprise drew from her a loud exclamation, as she beheld the fixed and ghastly look of the latter, who had sunk into a *fauteuil*, and remained there motionless, and apparently senseless, though in reality, she both heard and saw what was passing around her.

"There, Maria; see what your violence has done," exclaimed Mrs. Woodford; "you are very unjust, I must say, to reproach Grace, who cannot be at all answerable for——"

"Grace, dear Grace, speak to me—for mercy's sake, speak to me!" exclaimed Maria, alarmed at the fixed and death-like expression of her sister's countenance. "Oh! Grace, forgive me if I have said anything to hurt you; but I have been so led away, and made believe that——but I will try to bear all quietly and with patience if you will speak to me."

Grace made an effort to raise herself, and to reply to her sister's passionate adjuration, but it seemed as if the vital current had been frozen within her by what she had heard, and with a deep sigh she fell into Maria's arms, which were now tenderly opened to embrace her.

Many hours had elapsed before Grace became fully conscious of all that had passed, and capable of seriously reflecting upon it; and the first use she made of her returning reason was to persuade her mother to retire to rest, and to leave her alone with her sister, who was still shedding torrents of tears, not, however, she professed, for her own disappointment, but for the effect which her unjust reproaches had had upon her dear sister.

"You are mistaken, Maria," said Grace calmly; "it was not your reproaches that so affected me. I am, indeed, hurt and sorry that you could, for a moment, suspect me of having acted with deliberate cruelty and artifice towards you, but I knew that truth would prevail, and that you would soon see that I did not deserve your unkindness; but it was the knowledge, Maria, that it was in my power to save my mother in two different ways, and that —— Maria, you will feel how much you have wronged me when you hear me swear, solemnly swear ——"

"Grace, do not make any rash oaths," interrupted Maria, hastily; "I can believe anything everything you say, for I know you are sincere and candid."

"Then you will believe me, when I say that no consideration on earth shall induce me to marry Sir Walter Fitz-Geffrey. I will obey my mother to the utmost, even if she forbids me to look at Belgrave; but I can never, will never, falsify my own conscience, or deceive Sir Walter, by swearing to love and honour him, when my whole heart is given to Belgrave."

Maria seemed thunderstruck, the idea that Grace could possibly refuse so splendid an offer seemed never till this moment to have occurred to her mind; but she knew that her sister, gentle and meek as she was in temper, was nevertheless firm and determined in purpose; and a dawn of hope seemed again to shine upon her as Grace reiterated her resolution decidedly to reject the baronet's offer.

It was a matter of no small surprise to the high-minded Grace to find that her sister, mortified and offended as she was, at the declaration of Sir Walter's sentiments, seemed inclined to forget all his offences, and study only the most likely way of drawing his attention to herself; and that she seemed so fully certain of accomplishing her purpose, when once he should be convinced of the hopelessness of his suit with Grace, that the latter could not forbear giving her a slight hint that it might be possible he would feel too much offended at his views being thwarted in the first instance to think of transferring his attentions, at least at present.

" But will it not be possible for you, Grace, to give him a gentle hint that there is a person to whom his addresses would be more welcome than to you. He would easily guess, and ———"

Grace turned away; she was vexed and hurt at her sister's want of self-respect, and the mercenary spirit which dictated all her observations, and guided all her actions—but she remained silent; and Maria having exhausted all her stock of conjectures, and surmises, and hints, at length buried them all in a profound sleep, a luxury which poor Grace invoked in vain.

CHAPTER XIII.

" All things that were ordained festival,
Turn from their office to black funeral."

—SHAKSPEARE.

ANXIOUS as Grace felt to terminate at once all doubt or misconception' either on the part of Sir Walter, or of her sister, who still seemed at times scarcely to believe it possible that any one could reject such an opportunity of becoming rich and distinguished—the shock she had sustained rendered her too seriously indisposed to be able to leave her bed on the following morning, and fearful of provoking a contest with her mother, who, she was well aware, would oppose with all her power the determination of her daughter, Grace imposed upon Maria a strict silence as to her intention.

Maria, in fact, though perfectly convinced of her sister's blamelessness in the affair, was not so favourably disposed towards her mother, whom she accused of being lukewarm in her (Maria's) cause, and careless of every one's happiness or interest, so that her own was secured. She therefore rather enjoyed than lamented the utter extinction of her hopes, which threatened her mother; and to prevent the latter's questioning her on the subject of her conversation with Grace—and being led, perhaps, to suspect the truth, she affected to be also so unwell as to be unable to leave her chamber, and took care, whenever her mother entered, to be always close to Grace's bedside, and thus prevent the subject nearest all their hearts, from being made the subject of discussion.

" Thank heaven!" exclaimed Mrs. Woodford, suddenly entering, towards the evening, "I shall be freed from Mr Meredith and his family for ever, before I sleep, for Sir Walter has just gone off to pay the old wretch, and force him to give up the bond."

A pang shot through Grace's heart—her fate then was decided for ever, for never could she hope, that her mother would grant her free and unconstrained consent to an union with those whom it was plain she beheld with more than common hatred. But there was another, a still deeper source of pain to poor Grace, in this information. She was aware that Sir Walter had not been wholly influenced by generosity, in taking upon himself to settle the account with Meredith; and it seemed to her as if she was accessory to a fraud upon him, in suffering him to pay so large a sum, under the delusive idea that she was favourable to his wishes.

"Oh, how glad I am now, that I did not suffer myself to be frightened by that artful young Mansell," continued the mother with exultation; "but something told me that I should get over my difficulties, and be able to laugh at their malice: but come, Grace, you are looking a great deal better and Sir Walter is very anxious to see and talk to you; so do try and get up there's a good girl, and let him see that you are grateful for his kindness What is the foolish girl crying for? Surely you can have no cause for tears. Your poor sister, indeed————"

Maria returned to her station by the bedside, which she had quitted for a moment, and her considerate mother suddenly stopped.

"You look uncommonly well in that dress, Maria," she observed; "if you come down to tea with your sister, I would advise you not to change it."

"What does it matter what I wear now?" returned Maria, in a disconsolate tone.

Mrs. Woodford sighed: it was evident, indeed that she deeply lamented the injustice done to her favourite; but she also felt in its full force all the advantages that she believed would arise from Grace's advancement, and was therefore willing to overlook the affront offered to her sister's superior charms.

Before the time at which Sir Walter was expected to return to tea, bringing with him Mrs. Woodford's release from the hated Meredith, Grace leaning on her sister's arm, entered the room where Mrs. Woodford was seated in more than even her usual state, expecting her visitor.

"Good heavens, Grace! what could have induced you to make such a fright of yourself!" she observed, surveying her from head to foot; "why your eyes are absolutely swelled out of your head, and not a curl in your hair either, and that insignificant, childish-looking, white frock, too! but it cannot be helped now—Sir Walter will be here, I dare say, in a few minutes, and it will look more respectful and attentive to find you here, so sit down—not there, with your back to the window—take that chair.

Grace complied with this instruction, though she would fain have placed herself where the expression of her countenance could not have been so conspicuous, especially as her mother, from time to time, continued to survey her with a scrutinizing glance; though the fact was, that Mrs. Woodford, far from penetrating into the thoughts that were passing in her daughter's mind, never suspected that the latter could dare to entertain an idea of acting in opposition to her wishes, and was only thus observant of her, because she thought she had never seen her to so little advantage, and was fearful that Sir Walter might think so too.

A long half hour passed away, Mrs. Woodford fidgetted, and looked at her watch every five minutes, and Grace herself wished that he would come, that the disagreeable task might be ended; but another half hour crept tediously away, and still he came not.

"What can have happened?" exclaimed Mrs. Woodford, apprehensively; "he surely could not have so little sense as to listen to anything that old wretch could say to him!"

A ray of hope shot into Grace's mind; she had more than once had occasion to remark, that Sir Walter, though hasty and repulsive in his manners, was ever liberal, generous, and delicate in his sentiments. It might have been that old Meredith had, in his usual plain, and straightforward way, related to the baronet the story of his nephew's wrongs, which he so bitterly resented, and Sir Walter might generously have resolved to relinquish his suit, and become the friend of Belgrave and herself.

These, and other equally romantic, and, perhaps, improbable and unfounded conjectures, fully occupied Grace's thoughts for the next half-hour; her eyes beamed with hope and expectation, a bright and beautiful blush suffused her pale cheek, and no longer sunk in hopeless languor, her voice betrayed that some new hope had arisen in her bosom, from the circumstance which now excited her mother's fears.

"I do not believe he will come at all," said Maria, rising, and unclosing the curtains which had been drawn when the candles were brought in. "There is no moon, and you know how cowardly he is about riding in the dark. If he had had the carriage, it would have been a different thing; but I would lay any wager that when he left old Meredith's, the thought struck him that it was nearer to Belle Retraite than to Rose Farm, and that it would be better for him to go home, while there was daylight, than to come over here, and have to ride back in the dark."

"It may be so," replied Mrs. Woodford, "but it is not very considerate of him, I must say; he knew how anxious I was to hear how it was settled, and I told him besides that I knew Grace would be ready to meet him at the tea-table."

The long tedious evening at length terminated; and Grace, divided between hope and fear, and forming to herself a thousand fanciful conjectures as to the cause of the baronet's delay, retired with her sister to rest.

Maria's spirits had risen in proportion as her mother's had become fluctuating and eventually depressed, and she indulged, during the time that her sister and she were undressing, in a hundred playful jokes upon Sir Walter's impatience and alacrity as a lover.

"And yet," thought Grace, with astonishment, "she would consent, even now, to accept this man, whom she so laughs at and ridicules."

"Good night, Grace," said Maria, "mind you wake me at daybreak, if you are awake first, that we may get up to receive the impatient lover, who will be sure to be here as soon as he can see the path."

"Go to sleep, do," said the now smiling Grace, "you will not let me rest."

Exactly at daybreak, Grace roused her sleeping sister.

"Maria, listen; there is somebody at the gate," she observed. "What can it mean? it is scarcely three o'clock; and, by the dogs' barking so, it is some stranger."

"There, I told you so," said Maria, laughing, before she was well awake; "I knew he would be here with the light."

"Nonsense, do listen; there it is again: who can it possibly be?"

Maria raised herself in the bed, and seriously listened.

"It is Sir Walter's valet," she observed; "I can hear his broken English, persuading the dogs to be quiet; after all, I am afraid this is no laughing matter: something must have happened."

In another moment she was at her mother's bedside, who had also been awakened by the unusual alarm, and now, by repeated ringing the bell at her bed's head, succeeded in rousing, not only one, but all the servants.

Maria had, in the meantime, partly dressed herself; and regardless of appearance, she was at the gate, and questioning the valet as soon as the servants.

His master had not been home all night, he said; and knowing how regular they were at Rose Farm, he (Dupré) had become alarmed, and had come off with Baily, the butler, in search of him.

Maria could only explain that Sir Walter had left the farm early in the evening, with the avowed intention of returning to tea, but that he had not done so; and she was in the midst of an attempt to make the two men, who appeared, either from fright or some other cause, in a state of stupefaction, comprehend which road they must take to the Elms, Mr. Meredith's residence, when she observed a person lean forward from behind a large walnut tree, which stood exactly opposite the lawn-gate, as if anxious to learn what she was saying.

The first ray of the rising sun fell full on the spot on which this person stood; and while it prevented his seeing that he was observed, it afforded a full and correct view of his features, and Maria, with a surprise she could not conceal, recognized Belgrave Mansell.

"Who was that, Sally?—did you not see him?" said Maria, turning to the latter, who stood by her side; "what in the world could Belgrave want here at this time of the morning!"

"Belgrave! Laws, miss, was it young Mr. Belgrave Mansell? I'm sure I never suspected it was him, though I see'd somebody start off down the lane. Yes, I declare it is him, for there he goes, as fast as ever he can, up the hill.

"He could have told us whether Sir Walter had been at his uncle's, most likely, if he had stayed," said Maria; "but no matter, you had better, Dupré, go on at once to the Elms, it is not above four miles."

"Four miles! oh, Sacre Dieu! how vill I valk four mile, and I have valked one, two, and tree already? I sall drop on de way."

"I'm sure I can't walk four mile farther: and the Welsh miles are such plaguey long ones, too, you could make two English ones out of them," said the butler, who had seated himself on a stone, outside the lawn-gate, and was very leisurely awaiting the result of Dupré's conference with Maria.

It was plain, indeed, that neither of these trusty servants was in a fit condition to prosecute the search after their absent master—they were both, in fact, intoxicated, and had found it a task of no ordinary difficulty to reach so far as Rose Farm, for their shoes were covered with clay, as if they had wandered far out of the turnpike road, and Dupré's clothes betrayed that he had more than once measured his length on the ground, for the clay and grass still adhered to them in several places.

"You had better remain here, then," said Maria, "and I will send one of our men on horseback to Mr. Meredith's, to inquire."

The two worthy domestics most willingly agreed to this proposal; they were admitted to the kitchen—one of Mrs. Woodford's lads was in a few moments mounted, and clattering along the road leading to the Elms—and Maria returned to communicate to her mother, who with Grace's assistance had now risen, the alarming intelligence, of which the servants had been the bearers.

"Merciful goodness! if any accident has really happened to him, and if he should not have paid Meredith, what will become of us all!" said Mrs. Woodford.

Grace turned away; how could her mother, at such a moment, indulge a selfish thought? even she herself, little cause as she had to regard or be anxious for Sir Walter's safety, would have given all she possessed to be assured that he was living, and yet her mother could thus think only of him as connected with her own interest.

Leaning on Sally, who being strongest, was generally her mistress's assistant, Mrs. Woodford went down to the kitchen, to question the men further, though it was scarcely within the limits of possibility that they could give her any clue to their master's mysterious disappearance.

Maria and Grace were now left together, and the former, looking steadily in her sister's face, said—

"Grace, will you answer me one question, honestly and sincerely; did you see Belgrave Mansell, last night, after his interview with my mother? or, had you any reason to expect to see him, either last night or this morning?"

"I did not see him, Maria," replied Grace, turning pale; "but, —— " she hesitated; and then, recollecting the probable consequences to the thoughtless and ignorant, but well-meaning Sally, should she betray the deep interest the latter took in Belgrave's cause, she checked herself from making the disclosure she intended, of her knowledge that Belgrave had remained about the premises for some time after his supposed departure, and added, "but why did you ask me if I had seen him, Maria? had you any reason for thinking—— "

"It is a most strange circumstance, Grace; but while I was talking to Dupré, I saw Belgrave steal along the sweet-briar hedge, and place himself behind the walnut tree, evidently to listen to what I was saying."

"Are you sure it was him?" demanded Grace, who, herself entertaining no doubt on the subject, was most willing to acknowledge that conviction.

"I am certain," returned Maria; "and indeed, to remove all doubts on the subject, our old Nero, who had been barking at Dupré and the other man, suddenly ceased at sight of Belgrave, and ran off frisking and fawning as if to welcome his favourite."

"It is strange," replied Grace, becoming still more confused.

"And you really had no expectation of seeing him, then?" said Maria, still looking at her with incredulity.

Grace again replied in the negative; but it was evident to her sister, though not possessing any very extraordinary powers of penetration, that there was some concealment, some equivocation very unlike Grace's usual candour in these replies, and she was about to renew her inquiries when both her and Grace's attention was withdrawn by hearing loud exclamations from the party who were assembled in the kitchen, and, convinced that something extraordinary had occurred to cause it, both sisters ran hastily down stairs.

Occupied but by one subject, Grace felt considerable relief on reaching the scene of earnest consultation at finding that Belgrave was not there, her mind having misgiven her, either that he had been discovered and brought forward by some of the servants, or that he had himself become impatient of concealment, and had come boldly forward in spite of her mother's interdiction; and, in either case, she was well aware that the consequences would be to her most painful; but her self-gratulation was soon forgotten, and every other feeling absorbed in horror, when she at length comprehended what had been the source of the unusual clamour she had heard.

Sir Walter's horse had been discovered by one of the boys belonging to the farm, grazing in a bye-lane turning out of the road by which he must have come from Meredith's.

That some fatal accident had befallen the baronet there could no longer exist a doubt ; but Grace's heart thrilled with unspeakable horror when she heard one of the farm servants declare, after a minute inspection of the horse, that there could not be a doubt that its unfortunate rider had been murdered.

"Look at the reins," he observed, "they have been cut right across to make him let go. Yes, yes, there has been foul play, that's for certain."

The whole household were now roused and afoot to make search for the body of the unfortunate Sir Walter ; while one of his own men, appearing suddenly to have overcome the stupidity of inebriation which had till then kept him, as it were, confined to his chair, departed to give information of the violence that had been, as it was supposed, committed, to the parish authorities at Llan——, a course which had been suggested by Mrs. Woodford, as the most proper that could be adopted.

An hour's anxious suspense ensued with those who were unable to join in the search ; and various and vague as the conjectures were which the recent circumstances gave rise to, Grace took no part in them, nor gave, indeed, any indication that she comprehended them, until the name of Belgrave Mansell, uttered in a low tone by Maria, suddenly struck on her ear.

What could her mother's exclamation of horror mean, as she repeated loudly that name ?

"Belgrave Mansell, at this time of the morning—trying to conceal himself, too : it looks black, very black," continued Mrs. Woodford. "But are you sure, Maria, that it was him ? Recollect how serious may be the consequences should you be called upon to prove that he was lurking about the lanes at this unseasonable hour—so far, too, from his own home, and out of the road to any other place than this, where he is expressly forbidden to come."

"Good heavens ! you cannot, surely, snspect that Belgrave has had any concern in this affair !" observed Maria, looking aghast at the inference her mother had drawn from her communication, although her whispering earnestness and the mysterious comment of her looks were certainly calculated to give birth to suspicion, even in minds less prone to it or willing to indulge it than her mother's.

"I should be sorry to say half that I suspect," returned the latter, with a glance at Grace, who, pale and breathless with indignation, was yet so far able to govern her feelings as not to give utterance to a single word. "I should be very sorry, indeed," repeated Mrs. Woodford, "to say what I suspect ; but should it prove that poor Sir Walter has been made away with, I would not stand in Belgrave Mansell's shoes for —— nay, Miss Grace, you need not turn your head so scornfully away, for—"

"Oh, dear mamma, do not say anything to poor Grace now," interrupted Maria. "I am sure I am heartily sorry that I mentioned what I had seen ; I shouldn't have done it, if I could have thought that it would have been the means of bringing suspicion on Belgrave, who, I am certain, is the last in the world that would commit a cruel or a base action."

Grace grasped the hand which Maria had, at the commencement of this vindication, placed in hers—as if to entreat pardon for having been the primary cause of her suffering so much pain—and burst into tears.

"Ah you may keep those tears, Grace, for another occasion," sharply observed her mother ; "for should it turn out, as there is but too much reason to fear that Sir Walter is no more, and should he not have settled that affair with old Meredith, you will have good reason to cry."

THE PRIDE OF THE VILLAGE;

OR,

THE FARMER'S DAUGHTERS.

CHAPTER XIV.

"He is a great observer, and he looks
Quite through the deeds of men.
—SHAKESPEARE.

"LORD, mamma, do not frighten one so—surely we are not so badly off as that," exclaimed Maria, forgetting in a moment all her sympathy with Grace, her anxiety to exonerate Belgrave, and in fact, every thing but the prospect of personal inconvenience.

"I speak nothing but the truth, Maria," returned the mother; "and

7

though you did not believe me, and accused me of injustice and indifference to you, when I told you it was absolutely impossible for me to resent Sir Walter's conduct, or refused my consent to his having your sister instead of you———"

"I am sure I never wished you to do any such thing," interposed Maria, tossing her head with great indignation.

Mrs. Woodford rejoined with equal anger, that she was not in the habit of uttering what was not true; and Grace, taking advantage of their being engrossed by their angry feelings and mutual reproaches, so unusual between them, escaped from the room, and sought in the garden her favourite retreat, that she might give free and unnoticed vent to the bitters tears which she had with difficulty restrained in the presence of her mother.

That Belgrave stood in any danger, or that there existed the slightest reason to suppose that suspicion could attach to him, never for a moment entered her mind. She was herself perfectly convinced of the innocence of his purpose, in lurking, as her mother had significantly expressed it, at such unseasonable hours; and she never for an instant, conceived it possible that any one else could attach to him the idea of guilt; but she bewailed, with the deepest sorrow, the cruel and unjust prejudice which had thus influenced her mother to attempt to throw the shade of guilt on one of whose innocence she believed it impossible she could doubt.

For nearly two hours she remained undisturbed in the arbour; the whole of the male servants and one of the female were still absent; and Grace, from her elevated seat, which commanded every path for upwards of a mile from time to time threw an anxious and shuddering glance around, at times from their long delay, hoping that their fearful conjectures were unfounded, and again dreading to see them in their utmost horror confirmed.

One by one, however, they all dropped in, without having gained any additional light on the subject, except to confirm Mrs. Woodford's worst fears on one point; that, indeed, on which she felt the most intense anxiety;—Sir Walter had never reached Meredith's; and the latter at once declared his incredulity that it had ever been the baronet's intention to discharge the debt.

The idea of his having been murdered, the old man treated as equally improbable.

"Who should know that he had such a sum of money about him, or where to waylay him? and as to any strangers casually meeting and making an attack upon him, was it probable, in that secluded and unfrequented part of the country, and in a bye road, leading nowhere but to two or three farms? Old Bill Francis, the well-known horse stealer, was dead, and his two sons transported; and since they were gone, such a thing as a robbery, beyond that of a hen-roosts or a few turnips or apples, had not been known. No, no, thank God, such things might be common in the outlandish parts that the baronet came from, but they had no thieves or murderers about this part of the country."

Such was the substance of what, with much more circumlocution, Owen, Mrs. Woodford's principal farm servant, repeated to his mistress.

"But for all that," observed Owen, "and though old William Meredith's a long-headed man, and one as isn't apt to be much out in what he says, yet I do verily believe that there's been foul play, and I shan't believe no otherwise till I see Sir Walter himself alive, which I shall never see, it's my firm belief."

"Well, but Owen, what can have become of the body, if he is dead?" observed Maria, who was the only one sufficiently collected to make a remark upon his communication.

" That is a thing unpossible for me to say, miss ; but, upon the little bridge that crosses the brook, there was marks in the clay, as if there'd been a scuffle, of two or three feet ; and down on the bank, the weeds were all torn, and the earth kicked away, as if somebody had been pushed down and clung there for life. We tried to see if we could make out anything in the water, but it's so deep there, and the rains have made it so thick and muddy, that we couldn't make nothing of it."

" Bah ! it is not probable that they vould take him so long vay as dat. Non, non ; he is not dere, mon pauvre maitre," said Dupré, Sir Walter's servant who had been Owen's companion in this search.

" So far ! how far, master Frenchman ?" vociferated Owen, with surprise ; " How should you know where the bloody deed was done."

" Non, non ; certainement, I not know ; I know nothing about it, Monsieur Ovan ; bote the horse was not find by the bridge," said Dupré very eagerly.

" By the bridge ! no, it wasn't likely, I should think ; the poor beast would hardly stay there all night ; of course he wandered on without knowing where. If he had been any of our own horses, they'd have found their way home at once ; and then we should have known, in some reasonable time, that summut was amiss, and gone out at once ; but the poor creature knew nothing but that he had lost his master, and so fell to grazing the first fresh piece of grass he met with."

" And Meredith, then denies having seen Sir Walter ?" said Mrs. Woodford, at length recovering the power of speech which seemed to have totally failed her, till now, from the moment Owen had imparted in his rough way, this astonishing intelligence, which much as she feared, she yet hoped to have found untrue.

" He has never set eyes on him," repeated Owen. " Indeed, I knew that before I saw Master Meredith : for as soon as ever I knocked up Lewis, his bailiff, he told me that his master was ill of the gout, and that not a soul had been near him all the day, not even his nevy, Belgrave Mansell, who was used to come up every evening after they had done work at the Woodhouse" (the name of Mansell's farm).

" No, no," said Mrs. Woodford, with a malignant glance at Grace ; " Mr. Mansell was differently employed, I can answer for it, than wasting his time upon a sick uncle."

Maria uttered a remonstrance, in a low tone, to her mother ; and Owen, who evidently misunderstood his mistress's motives, or was totally unconscious of what she meant to insinuate, replied, in a voice modulated in tones of pity, and stealing at the same time a look at Grace, whose cheeks now glowed with the fever of indignation—

" Yes, ma'am ; as I told Lewis, Mr. Belgrave couldn't be there and here too ; and I know'd I see him here, and bid him good night, though he didn't answer, and seemed to be——"

" And did Meredith say anything of——did he mention anything of his intentions towards me, Owen ?" interrupted Mrs. Woodford. " You know what I mean, for I believe he has taken pretty good care that everybody should know it," she added, in an angry tone.

" He didn't say anything particular, ma'am ; nothing more than he's said afore, and that you have heard," replied Owen, looking down on the ground, with an air of confusion.

Mrs. Woodford's eyes sparkled with rage ; and she was on the point of breaking into a torrent of invectives against the old man, but again she was withheld by a low remonstrance from Maria, who truly suggested to her violent mother that it would be far more prudent to conciliate than exasperate one who had her so completely at his mercy.

"It may be that I shall have him at mine?" she observed, in the same tone, in reply. "He may be glad to purchase the safety of his favourite nephew, and dearly will I make him pay for my silence." "And would you then, really, would you dare insinuate, that Belgrave is really guilty of this crime?"

It was Grace's expressive eyes that conveyed this question—her lips were silent; for she dared not unclose them lest all those hard lessons of dutiful submission, which she had with such infinite pains attained, should vanish before the excess of the present provocation.

All Owen's stock of information was now exhausted, and unable, as he said, to devise any means of ascertaining the truth, he was very willing to obey his mistress's commands, to get his breakfast with the other servants; and Dupré, after expressing in a variety of what he considered intelligible and appropriate terms, his sorrow and despair, departed for Belle Retraite, to communicate, as he observed to the rest of the household, the *tristes nouvelles* of the loss of the best of masters.

"Mounseer seems to have quite made up his mind that it's no use to make any further search," observed Owen, after the Frenchman had quitted the kitchen; "but for my part, had it been my poor master that had been so unaccountably made away with I would never have eat nor drunk, nor laid down in a bed until I knew what was become of him. However, its no business of mine, I've done all I could;" and Owen whose naturally good feelings were in this case considerably blunted by the the dislike with which he viewed Sir Walter in the first place, as being a proud, upstart foreigner, as he was generally considered, and in the second, as having been, though indeed indirectly, yet no less certainly, the cause of his late good master's (Mr. Woodford's) death, and all the sorrow that had consequently fallen upon the family, very composedly seated himself at the breakfast table with the rest of his fellows.

NEVER had the secluded and peaceful village of Llan——, in the memory of its oldest inhabitants, been thrown into such consternation as by the intelligence which was conveyed to them in all its horrors by Bailey, Sir Walter's servant, of the dreadful event that had taken place.

For days all their avocations were suspended and young and old, rich and poor, alike directed their efforts to discover the remains of the murdered man—for no longer did any doubt remain of the commission of the horrid crime—and to detect in what manner and by whose hands the crime had been committed.

Amid these fruitless though well-directed efforts, and the discussions to which they gave rise, it was some time before any one but those interested in his welfare made the discovery that Belgrave Mansell was absent.

Where could he be!—he who was ever the most active in coming in the assistance of his neighbours, whose head ever the quickest to devise, whose arm the readiest to assist! William, his brother, it was known, had been for some weeks unable to quit his home, having accidentally wounded his foot with a scythe, while mowing; Meredith, his uncle, was confined to his chamber, with the gout; but where was Belgrave?

The inquiry was answered by his servants, of whom alone it could be asked, in a manner that only increased the general surprise, and made the matter more mysterious. Their master had quitted the farm the very night of the supposed murder, he had remained out all night, and had returned home only a few hours before the news of Sir Walter's mishap had reached them. Before, however, that news had arrived, Belgrave, having taken with him only a change of clothes and some other trifles, had departed on foot, whither they knew not; but from his brother's lamentations and expressions of deep regret, they understood he (Belgrave) was not likely speedily to return to the Woodhouse, or Llan——

'Twas strange! 'twas passing strange!—so thought, and said, and looked every one who heard this account: yet it was long before the thoughts, which, in spite of their firm conviction of Belgrave's worth, his benevolence, his singular humanity, and kindness of heart, would and did intrude into more than one bosom, found utterance, so unlikely, so impossible did it appear, that he could in any way be connected with such a crime; but when at length the hint, the surmise, the conjecture as to what could possibly occasion one so favourably situated, so universally liked, and so warmly attached, not only to his relatives, but to one likely, even in the estimation of the sober and the sedate, to be of much more consequence, in the eyes of an ardent susceptible youth, than his nearest relatives—when against these ties was weighed all that his warmest friends could adduce as probable motives for his abrupt departure, it was allowed on all hands, that there must be something of infinitely greater importance to induce him to desert his home thus abruptly.

That, however, which his friends and companions, which even those least prejudiced in his favour among the inhabitants of Llan—— hesitated to say, and scarcely dared to think, was soon openly proclaimed by one, who had no feelings of prejudice or partiality, either to prompt or to restrain him from speaking boldly his opinion.

Despairing of success from common means, and aware of the superior tact of the officers of justice in the metropolis, in tracking the perpetrators of crime, some of the neighbours of the late Sir Walter had, with laudable anxiety to to quiet the panic which this unprecedented affair had created, sent to London for the assistance of an experienced officer; and he it was who having, in reply to his numerous questions, learned that one person of their little community had disappeared as suddenly and mysteriously as Sir Walter himself, though evidently not by force, hesitated not a moment to affix to the fugitive the brand of a murderer.

A thousand circumstances seemed now to break forth to confirm this assertion. Belgrave had been heard to express, in strong terms, dislike of Sir Walter; he had, more than once, spoken of him, with acrimony, as a heartless, ostentatious, selfish wretch, whom he despised even more than he hated, and it was well known that he attributed to him (Sir Walter) all the misfortunes that had befallen the family at Rose Farm, and his own and his brother's consequent disappointment.

So said now those who professed to have been in his confidence! But the London officer paid little attention to these, the reasons by which they considered themselves justified in believing, or trying to believe, Belgrave Mansell guilty. In his eyes, the money of which Sir Walter was known to have been the bearer, seemed a much more tempting and decisive motive than any feelings of paltry animosity, and to prove that Belgrave knew of his having it at the time in his possession seemed, in his mind, all that was necessary to warrant his fixing openly on the former the stigma, and proceed at once to the necessary means for his apprehension.

For this purpose, and without giving time to any one to apprize the family of his vocation, or the purpose of his visit, he took with him the first person who presented himself as guide, and proceeded without further ceremony to Rose Farm.

The entreaties and representations of her favourite daughter, who had her own private motives, besides the ostensible ones which she offered to her mother for wishing to conciliate, rather than aggravate, the breach between the Mansell family and her own, had hitherto prevailed with Mrs. Woodford to keep silence on the subject of Belgrave's mysterious appearance on that eventful morning. Mr. Meredith, doubly occupied by his own painful disorder and his nephew's unaccountable elopement, had scarcely had time to think of her, and seemed, at all events, to have postponed *sine die* his hostile intentions; and Maria, with some little trouble, and with the exercise of much more perseverance and ingenuity than she usually evinced, had succeeded in extorting from her mother a promise to forbear giving utterance to aught that could irritate the old man or prejudice his nephew, unless provoked to it by any indications of the renewal of hostilities on the part of the former. But though thus debarred from the satisfaction of giving vent to the malignant spirit which seemed to gain greater force in proportion as her difficulties and embarrassments increased, Mrs. Woodford could not, even by Maria's interpositions and entreaties, be restrained from breathing in Grace's ears perpetually her conviction, not only of Belgrave's having been the assassin of Sir Walter, but her firm belief that he would yet, without her intervention, be detected and discovered.

Conscious that it was in her power, with Sally's evidence to confute all that her mother so confidently asserted of Belgrave's having departed from Rose Farm before Sir Walter, purposely to waylay him, and that the same means would, as she believed, fully explain his mysterious appearance, he having, no doubt, lingered the livelong night, in the hope and determination to profit by the agency of his partisan, Sally, to induce her again to meet him, Grace, though she could not listen to her mother without horror, yet learned to conceal that horror, and to bear, without replying, the merciless taunts by which Mrs. Woodford strove to vent the

overflowing of her bitter disappointment and revenge, the consequences of her own folly, upon her innocent and unoffending child. But there was yet a bitter draught reserved for poor Grace to swallow, and her stock of patience and fortitude was rendered all necessary to enable her not to sink under it, when she at length learned from Sally that Belgrave Mansell had quitted his home, and was now a wanderer, no one knew why or where.

Resolute not again to put herself in the power of this ignorant but well-meaning girl by sharing with her any secret, Grace heard the stunning news without uttering a single comment, or, indeed, otherwise than as her death-like paleness and gasping for breath betrayed her, without giving any indication of feeling more than a common and natural surprise at such an event. "And does my mother, does Maria know this, Sally?" she demanded, foreseeing in a moment the additional persecution which this circumstance would subject her to from her.

Sally had not herself told them; but she dare say they had by this time heard it, for the men in the kitchen could talk of nothing else.

Grace was silent; she was mentally praying for strength to bear the affliction that had fallen to her lot.

"Could I have been the only sufferer! could I alone have borne all! —but that he, once so gay, so prosperous, so happy—and for me, only for me, he would still be so! Oh, Belgrave! Belgrave! can I hope that I shall ever be able to requite you for this sacrifice!"

"You be wanting in the parlour, miss," exclaimed Sally, who had left her alone, now putting her head again withinside the room door. "There's a strange gentleman with missus; and John Price, that showed him the way here, do say that he's come all the way from London, about poor Sir Walter."

"And did my mother send for me?" demanded Grace, who at that moment, overcome with a thousand harassing thoughts, and still struggling with the sorrowful surprise she had received, would fain have declined the introduction to a stranger, and been content to hear the particulars of his errand, at second hand.

"Yes, miss! and when Miss Maria wanted to come to fetch you, he told her to sit still, and let the young woman go, just as if he had been master of the house, or Sir Walter himself, that used to speak so proudly, poor man."

The stranger fixed his keen eye on her pale, expressive face, as she entered the room; and, after a moment's scrutiny, requested her to be seated, pointing at the same time to the chair next himself.

"You, of course, are acquainted with a young man, named Belgrave Mansell?" he observed, again looking into her face, as if he would there read every secret of her soul.

The blood mounted to her very brow, at the unexpected question; but it rested there but for a moment, was succeeded by even a more death like paleness, before she had well answered it.

"When did you last see him?" he resumed; "recollect yourself, if you please, and be particular as to the hour and place, for it is of great consequence that I should know, even to a minute."

Grace replied, not without some indication of offended delicacy at his rude, abrupt address, that she had not seen him since she had left him, in the room they were now sitting in, with her mother.

A variety of questions followed; and Grace, who at length began to see with horror to what end this all tended, though she did not suspect who or what the important person who thus required an account, as it seemed, almost of her very thoughts as they regarded the absent Belgrave, at once took the resolution of explaining at all risks all that she knew or believed to be the cause of his having been seen by her sister at such a strange hour.

The man listened to her with attention and interest, though there was an expression in his eye, as he bent it earnestly on her fair face, while in faltering accents she related Belgrave's avowed attachment to her and his despair at her mother's decision, which would have greatly embarrassed her had not her mind been so deeply engrossed by the perilous situation in which, to her horror, she found Belgrave was likely to be placed by, as she supposed, her mother, as to be insensible to everything but the earnest desire to make his innocence as apparent to every one else as it was to herself.

"I must see this young woman, that your daughter speaks of as the go-between her and this young man," said the stranger, abruptly, turning to Mrs. Woodford, who had with difficulty restrained, in obedience to his authoritative signals, from loudly expressing her surprise and displeasure at this discovery.

The bright crimson again flushed Grace's cheeks, and her usually dove-like eyes for a moment darted lightning at this coarse and insolent observation; but Sally now entered the room, in obedience to the bell, and all other feelings were absorbed in indignation and surprise, at hearing her, *in toto*, deny knowing anything about Mr. Mansell, or having been made, as Grace had represented, the medium of communication between him and herself—on the contrary, she had never seen him, she declared, since he came out of the parlour from her mistress, and left the house.

Confident, however, and determined as Sally appeared to adhere to this account, which, it was evident, was not the impulse of the moment, but had been previously, for some reason, preconcerted in her own mind, it was impossible she could deceive the keen and practised officer, or induce him, for a moment, to weigh her vehement and outrageous assertions against Grace's plain unvarnished tale.

"Stop a moment, if you please," he observed, as Grace, with undisguised astonishment, was about to address her—"stop, and let me tell Mrs. Molly, or Sally, or—what's your name, girl? come, no prevarication speak out."

Sally looked with terror at the memorandum-book, in which he had been, from time to time, apparently making notes of what he heard, and replied "Sarah Dears."

"And a very pretty dear you seem to be," he observed, having demanded how she spelt it, and entered it accordingly in his book. And let me tell you, Miss Sarah Dears," he continued, "that I am convinced nay, that I know that all you have been saying is, in plain words, a lie; and that you are running a fair chance, by your falsehood, of being sent to Cardigan gaol, and tried, for an accomplice with your friend, Mr. Mansell, for murder."

"Oh, Lord! is poor Mr. Belgrave there! Oh, sure, in the name of goodness, they can never do anything to him, who is as innocent as the child unborn!" exclaimed Sally, the tears rushing into her eyes, and clasping her red hard hands together in undissembled grief.

"Upon my word, this young man seems to have been a lucky fellow among the ladies," observed the stranger, in a tone of levity, which sounded more harsh and repulsive, in Grace's ear, than even the very loudest tones of assumed authority. "Like mistress, like maid; it seems," he continued, "all anxious to screen land save him: but I tell you once again, girl, and once for all, that if you do not tell me the exact truth, you'll be sent ——"

Sally hesitated a moment; she looked at Mrs. Woodford, who turned disdainfully away, and then she glanced at Grace, who sat with clasped hands and eyes fearfully fixed on the face of the man who thus cruelly sported with her feelings, and profaned the name of Belgrave Mansell.

"It's no use denying it then," said Sally, seeming suddenly to gather courage; "if missus turns me away there's other places to be got, and so I'll tell the truth. I did see Mr. Belgrave Mansell afterwards, and he gave me half a crown to try and persuade Miss Grace to come out to speak with him; but I couldn't, though he waited and waited about behind the great barn all the evening, and for what I know, the whole night, for he said he would never go home to sleep again."

"The great barn! whereabouts does that lie? Is it in the road which Sir Walter must have gone through?" demanded the stranger of Mrs. Woodford.

"The latter rose, with Maria's assistance, and from the window pointed out the situation of the great barn, which was at the extremity of the cattle fold adjoining the house.

"And that narrow path passing the end of it," she observed, "and then crossing the field till it is lost in the wood, Sir Walter went along."

"And you had told this young man that Sir Walter was expected by you, and that he would have a large sum of money about him to——"

"Yes, to pay his uncle," rejoined Mrs. Woodford, eagerly.

"Oh, it's all plain, as plain as a pikestaff," observed the man of authority, closing his memorandum-book. "Your constables and magistrates, and the rest of 'em here in the country, must be precious thickheads not to see how everything hangs together; he would be found guilty in any court of justice in England; I defy the cutest counsel at the Old Bailey to save him.'

"It's a wicked lie," said Sally, suddenly gathering courage, as the man was about to quit the room. "As to Old Bailey, he's much more likely to have done it than Master Belgrave; a nasty drunken, blaspheming wretch, that instead of searching every ditch and hedge, and tearing up the very ground, as he ought to do, to find his poor master's bones, and give 'em Christen's berrying, is set down at Mother Morgan's, at the Hen and Chicken's, guzzling from morn till night."

"Who is the girl talking about?" said the officer having turned back to listen attentively to her harangue—does she mean to charge anybody ——"

"I means no such thing," interrupted Sally; "only when you talked of Old Bailey not saving Master Belgrave ——"

Mrs. Woodford, who was somewhat more enlightened than the poor simple girl on this subject, now interfered to explain to the officer the latter's misapprehension, observing, that the Old Bailey she alluded to was a drunken servant of Sir Walter's, whose singular apathy, and adherence to the seat he usually occupied at the public-house, when not only his own fellow-servants, but the whole village were out searching for the murdered remains of his master, had exited remarks not very much to his advantage.

"I must see this Old Bailey," said the officer, making an entry of the name in his note-book. "Was he an acquaintance, do you think, or had he any intercourse with this young Mansell?"

"He an acquaintance of Belgrave!" interrupted Sally, before Mrs. Woodford could utter a word, or Grace raise her drooping head, to glance at him the contempt and surprise which had entered her mind at the thought of Belgrave Mansell's being classed, even in a stranger's idea, as an associate and companion with Sir Walter's drunken butler. "He have any 'course with him!" repeated the now bold and voluble Sally; "why, he would scorn him as the dust beneath his feet. Go along, man; you don't know anything about Master Belgrave, or you'd know that he could hold up his head with the proudest, aye, and be as proud as any of 'em, though he was never so to poor people, but as gentle and humble———. Don't cry, Miss Grace," she continued, while her own tears burst into a loud blubber,—"don't cry, we shall live to see him triumph over all his enemies."

The officer quitted the room, seemingly impatient that he had delayed so long as to listen to what conveyed no fact that he could lay hold of to his mind—nothing, as he expressed it, available; and before the next morning, by dint of his activity, and goading the usually supine inhabitants of Llan———, it had been agreed upon to print and publish handbills, descriptive of the supposed murderer offering a reward for the discovery of Sir Walter, dead or alive, and a still greater reward for the apprehension of the person who was supposed to have been the perpetrator of the act.

What were Grace's feelings of indignation, of mortification, of horror, and of contempt, when on the following day her mother put into her hand one of those public traducers of the fame of him whom she herself knew—she did not believe, she was certain, as of her own existence, that Belgrave Mansell was guiltless.

"You have brought pretty disgrace on yourself and your family miss," she observed, in a taunting tone; "for the tale of your secret meetings and his haunting the house at all hours of the night, has been repeated by that Londoner in the public meeting of all the neighbouring gentlemen and tradesmen."

"They know me, and they know him," said Grace firmly, but mildly, "and I fear not that they will misconstrue my motives."

Confidently, however, as Grace reckoned upon being able not only to prove Belgrave's innocence, but to acquit herself of all blame, Mrs. Woodford thought otherwise. She was, not indeed, inclined to believe the former guilty, and in fact she, now that the suspicion had been raised, began to consider it unjust and unfounded—she even wondered to herself how she could for a moment, have admitted it into her mind; and probably, but for her habitual opposition to Grace, she would at once, have avowed her belief that it was utterly impossible that Belgrave Mansell could have committed such a crime. But it was enough that Grace warmly espoused a cause to induce her to take the opposite side of the question; and she could not, or would not, now depart from it.

"I insist upon it, that you do not put yourself forward in this affair, Grace," she observed; "if you are not aware of the consequences, I am, of your name being brought forward in such a manner."

"I must speak the truth, even if death were the consequence," said Grace firmly.

"Wait till you are called on then," replied Mrs. Woodford, "I insist, and remember I expect to be obeyed."

CHAPTER XV.

> "The spirit that I have seen
> May be a devil, and the devil hath power
> To assume a pleasing shape."
> —SHAKESPEARE.

THE means which were adopted to discover the retreat of Belgrave Mansell proved as utterly inefficient as the search, which was continued many days, for the murdered remains of his supposed victim; and at length the zeal even of the most interested began to relax, and the subject to die away, except in the minds of those to whom Belgrave was personally dear, or who had their private reasons to mourn the loss of Sir Walter Fitz-Geffrey. Among the former there was, perhaps, not one to whom it afforded such incessant food for regret and grief as Grace Woodford; and, in the latter class, it may be questioned if any one more sincerely mourned for the event which had brought Sir Walter to an untimely end than her mother.

Mrs. Woodford had, indeed, for some time buoyed herself up with a hope, that there being, as far as she knew, no other person who could establish a relationship to the deceased, she, however remote her claim, would have been enabled to prove herself the heir of property, which would have amply compensated for all her difficulties and sufferings; but after giving way to the most violent and indecorous ebullitions of joy at the prospect, which was first pointed out to her by a casual observation of Maria, that she wondered who would have all Sir Walter's money if he had not made a will, she was doomed to find her hopes end in disappointment, it appearing utterly impossible for her to adduce any proof of Sir Walter being the person whom she represented him to be, the son of her father's half-brother.

It was true she had called him her cousin, and he had tacitly admitted her claim : but to no one had he ever spoke of her as a relation, to no one but herself had he even revealed who he was, or from whence he came; and so distant and remote appeared her chance of establishing what she asserted, that she soon ceased, amid the pressure of more immediate affairs, to speak even of the probability of her becoming the heiress.

It was late in the autumn when the events recorded in the preceding pages agitated the inhabitants of Llan——. The winter of 18— set in uncommonly early, and with unusual rigour; and the prospect around Rose Farm, in the beginning of December, was as dreary and cheerless as that of the inhabitants within: all Mrs. Woodford's dreams of opulence, and rank and splendour had faded away, and she beheld nothing but poverty and obscurity awaiting her and her daughters.

To Maria the prospect, which could no longer, even by her indulgent mother, be hidden from her, was dreadful; and Grace, with heart-felt pain, was compelled to listen to her repinings and murmurs, as well as her mother's. It was in vain she tried to cheer them both, by assuming spirits which she could not feel, and endeavouring to suggest hopes which her own reason told her could never be realised—both were alike hopeless and despondent; and Grace, though in their presence and for their sakes she concealed it, in reality, suffered more, infinitely more, than either.

In a few weeks they would be turned out of the home in which she had spent her happy childhood—for happy it had been, thanks to the disposition with which Heaven had endowed her, and which had made her capable of enjoying to the utmost all that was pleasurable in her lot, and passing lightly over that which would to many have embittered it. In a few weeks they would be necessitated to seek a home among strangers, for her mother had decided that she would not remain in her altered circumstances at Llan——, or in the neighbourhood.

"No;" she observed, "they shall never have the satisfaction of insulting my poverty, under the pretence of pity; I know well that it would be a pleasure to half of them to see me humbling myself to live on the scanty means that will be left me—but I will go where they shall never have the satisfaction of seeing it, or hearing of it, if I can prevent it."

Grieved as Grace was at this declaration, and unjust as she considered it to many who she was convinced would, from their respect for her father's memory, have been not only willing, but anxious to assist the widow and children of their former friend, Grace dared not offer the slightest observation, for so deeply had the natural violence of her mother's temper been increased by her late mortification and difficulties, that the slightest opposition never failed to draw down the most bitter reproaches. To Maria, however, Grace was less reserved, and she did not scruple to lament to her her mother's resolution.

"And what should we remain here for?" returned Maria," with quickness. "When all is sold, and the debts paid, my mother does not expect that there will be more than two, or at the most three hundred pounds left, and what would that do for us in Llan————"

"What can it do in a strange place?" said Grace. "Here where we are known, indeed, everybody would be happy to assist our honest endeavours, and we might————"

"Set up for semptresses, I suppose, and bore our eyes out of our heads to earn a shilling a-piece a day," interrupted Maria, angrily; or perhaps you would prefer going to work in the fields; I recollect you used to be very fond of hay-making when Belgrave was your companion and ————. Nay, Grace, do not cry, I did not mean to hurt your feelings; but now, only tell me yourself, what can we possibly do in Llan————?"

"What can we do anywhere else that we cannot do better here?" said Grace, drying up the tears which her sister's mal-a-propos remark had occasioned; "we cannot sit down idle and live upon————"

"We shall see—we shall see," interrupted Maria, again growing impatient;

"but as to remaining here, I am quite of mamma's opinion—any place is preferable to this."

" And where, may I ask ?" said Grace, after a few moments' pause, "does my mother intend to go, for of course she has some place in view ?"

" I will tell you, if you will promise not to breathe it to any living creature," returned her sister; "for mamma is determined to puzzle them all, and leave them without giving a single hint where she is going to."

" And she will turn her back, then, upon the place where she was born, and lived all her life, and not keep up any correspondence, or give an opportunity————"

" It is just what she intends," said Maria, hastily; "and how can you wonder at it, when all things are considered ?"

" But there are some here who deserve different treatment," replied Grace. " Mr. Meredith, for instance, who, harsh as he appeared at first, would, you know, have given up his claim, if he could have brought the creditor to any compromise ; and then, there is," she hesitated for several moments, and then added : "William Mansell, I am sure, Maria, that should he recover his health, and the shock that———— ;" her voice trembled, and she was unable to finish the sentence.

" I will own to you, Grace," said Maria, after some minutes had passed, during which both sisters had apparently been absorbed in melancholy retrospection. " I will own to you, that I have had my thoughts about William—and as I told mamma it would be foolish to run out of the way of a good offer ; but she will have it that William is too much under his uncle's domination, and that the old man, though his heart failed him when he came to the push, and he couldn't resolved to ruin the children of his old friend ; yet she is sure, she says, that he hates the very name of her and of me, and would never consent to William's having me ; and, after all, Grace, I'm not sure that I could make up my mind now to be a farmer's wife.

" And what, then, can you now hope to be ?" thought Grace ; but she suppressed the words which sprang to her lips, and merely ejaculated—" Poor William ! "

" Well—but I have not answered your question yet, about where we are going to settle," resumed Maria, pretending not to have heard her sister's ejaculation, which certainly must have been understood as a reproof to her levity and inconstancy. " Nor have you promised me," she continued ; but, however, I know I can trust you, even without a promise—and so I may as well tell you at once that we are going, first of all, to Bristol, and perhaps to Bath ; at any rate, if we don't settle in Bath, we shall be near enough to go there very often."

" And what should we do there ?" demanded Grace, astonished more than ever at her sister's thoughtlessness.

" Oh, I don't know," replied Maria, looking rather confused, as if conscious of the reproof of her sister's question conveyed ; but there is no knowing, as mamma says, what may happen—there are plenty of great and rich folks at Bath.

" And will the great and rich folks have any sympathy with us humble and poor ones, Maria ?" said Grace, looking at her with affectionate regret. " Or will our being placed among those favoured by fortune alleviate our misfortune ? Besides Bath, I have heard, is a most extravagantly dear place, and surely that cannot be a recommendation to those ————"

" Goodness, Grace, how you preach !" interrupted Maria, assuming a laugh. "I am sure if mamma was to hear you, it would be almost enough to frighten her out of her intention."

"I should be sorry to assume any influence over my mother," said Grace, sighing at the consciousness of how little cause she had for that sorrow; "but you, Maria, who really do possess power with her might ———"

"Certainly not use it to persuade her against her projected journey, which I am as much set upon as she can possibly be," said Maria hastily; "desperate cases require desperate remedies, dear Grace," she added after a few moments' silence, "and that may perhaps plead my poor mother's excuse for what I dare say to sober, sedate people will look like madness; but mind, Grace, I have your promise that you would not say a word to any one."

"I will not," said Grace, "you may depend upon it. It would, indeed," she added in a melancholy tone, "be little pleasure to me to repeat that which I am sure all who are her real friends must condemn."

Satisfied with what she had learned, or rather too much dissatisfied to wish to renew the subject, nothing further passed on the subject of their intended removal for several days, when Grace heard, with an emotion she could scarcely conceal, that her mother had made up her mind to leave at the end of the following week, having determined not to await the coming festivities of Christmas.

It was to the free and social intercourse, which this season never fails to bring about among neighbours in the country, that Grace had looked forward with hope as affording the last chance that her mother might be induced to rescind her intention of quitting It was more than possible that William and Maria might be brought together during these merry-makings, and Grace could not help prognosticating the happiest results could William be brought once more to offer, and Maria to receive, his vows; but these hopes were all at once given to the wind by Mrs. Woodford's determination, and in despair Grace sought Maria to learn from her own lips whether this arrangement met with her approbation.

"Certainly, Grace," replied her sister, "It is my wish to go. Why should I stay? You cannot suppose that we could *now* mingle in the company we did last year—circumstances are greatly altered since then."

"They are indeed," returned Grace, with a deep sigh; "but I do not believe that there is one of our former friends who would not be happy *now* to have us of their party."

"I have no doubt of it, either," returned Maria, with a supercilious smile; but I am really surprised, Grace, that you, above all people, can look forward with any sort of pleasure to Christmas, considering that——"

"I know what you would say," interrupted Grace, bursting into tears; "but it is not the mirth, or the feasting of Christmas I could wish to mingle in, Maria, but I was in hopes that it might bring us once more among friends from whom we have been too long separated. It might restore my mother to the society she has so strangely learned to despise, and which has learned to despise her. How different would have been our situation now, Maria, if my mother had been on good terms with people—but you know, you must know, that——"

"I neither know nor care anything about it," said Maria disdainfully; "all I know is that in another fortnight we shall be beyond the reach of their love or their hatred."

"Lord! miss, there is strange news," exclaimed Sally, bursting into the room, and interrupting them in their conversation; "Who do you think is down stairs talking to missus?"

Grace, whose thoughts could only revert to one person, as the object of so much interest, sank faint and trembling into a chair; and Sally, who saw the expectations she had raised, and felt the folly of prolonging a hope which she knew was fallacious, instantly added "Oh, dear, no, Miss Grace, it isn't him—I wish to goodness it was; but it is one as near as can be, for it is Mr. William Mansell himself, and he asked to see you, as soon as missus came into the parlour, for I helped her there; and while I stayed a little settling the chairs I heard him with my own ears ask if he might not be 'permitted' (that was the word) to see Grace."

"And did my mother refuse?" demanded Grace, eagerly; "surely she could not be so unkind."

"No; she did not altogether refuse," replied Sally, "because I heard her say, 'Have you any particular business with Grace, sir?' and then I was obliged to come out of the room."

Grace hesitated for a moment. "It may be, perhaps, the last time I may see him," she at last observed; and—without heeding some remark of Maria's, who was hastily making some alterations in her dress, evidently expecting to be called down, and wishing, in spite of the disdain she had so recently expressed for William's situation in life, still to appear as much to advantage as possible in his eyes—she hastened to the parlour as quickly as her trembling legs would bear her there.

William was standing with his back to the door when she glided into the room, and she heard him, in a tone of indignation, exclaim—

"And does Grace, then, dare to harbour a suspicion of my brother's innocence?"

"No! oh, no, William," she eagerly exclaimed, stepping forward; "I know his innocence. Oh that he was but here to vindicate himself! none would, I am sure, not one would dare to look in his face, and——"

"Silence, miss, this is not at all becoming of you, I assure you," interrupted Mrs. Woodford. "But as I told you before, Mr. Mansell, I am willing to think the best of your brother; but, you must allow that things have a very suspicious look, and, until they are cleared, I cannot think that you or anyone else can blame me for saying that I do not choose my daughter to have any correspondence with Mr. Belgrave Mansell."

"There is no fear of it, ma'am," replied William, in a tone that showed how deeply he felt her insinuation; "for, unfortunately, Belgrave has given us no clue to his present situation; but I thought, perhaps foolishly, I acknowledge, that it would be a satisfaction to Grace to hear that I have received a letter from him, and that he is well in health."

"It is a satisfaction, indeed, to hear that," said Grace warmly; "but tell me, William, does he not give any hopes of his return or any account of——"

"You shall read the letter yourself, Grace," said William, his fine countenance brightening at discovering that Grace, in spite of her mother's frowns and coldness, still retained all the warmth and kindliness of her natural character. "Oh, Grace," he continued, if he could but know that you were so anxious for his welfare! but he thinks you indifferent—thinks, indeed, that——"

"It is of very little consequence to Grace Woodford, what Mr. Belgrave Mansell thinks of her," interrupted Mrs. Woodford; "and I am really surprised, Mr. Mansell, that you should take such advantage of my easiness in letting you see her as to give her a letter, before my very eyes, from one whom it is her duty to forget."

"But whom I never can forget," said Grace, her eyes beaming with animation—"whom I always must remember as the companion of my childhood, my kind instructor, and the favourite and trusted friend of my poor father. But here is the letter, dear mother; I wish not to read it if you consider it improper; I am satisfied to hear that Belgrave is well, and does not forget his friends; I hope," and her voice faltered, "he is happier than some of them."

Mrs. Woodford took the letter thus frankly offered : but her chief curiosity seemed to be directed to the outside, and she appeared to have totally forgotten everything else in her anxiety to decipher the post-mark.

" You may spare yourself all trouble, Mrs. Woodford," observed William, looking at her with visible indignation; " the letter is dated from Portsmouth, and that is the mark on the letter."

" Oh, I thought you said just now that you were in ignorance of your brother's situation," returned Mrs. Woodford, " and I thought it might be some gratification to be able to ascertain what part of the world he was in."

" I spoke the truth," observed William, coolly taking the letter from her and putting it in his pocket, " since he had quitted that place before the letter was put in the post, having left it, as I learned from a note in which it was enclosed, in the care of a person there, to be forwarded a week after his departure."

" It is pretty clear, however," said Mrs. Woodford, with malicious emphasis, " that Mr. Belgrave is aware that a search has been made for him, and that it is necessary for him to keep out of the way."

" On the contrary, I am certain," replied William, " as certain as that I am in existence, that if he had the slightest suspicion of what has taken place, and the stigma that has been attempted to be affixed to his name, not one hour would elapse before he would be on his way hither."

" It is a pity, then, but that he should know it," returned Mrs. Woodford, with a sneer, " both for his friends' sake and his own, if he can, as you seem to think he can. so clearly establish his own innocence."

" *If*, Mrs. Woodford !" repeated William, indignantly; " can you, after reading that letter, even if you could before hesitate, entertain a doubt ?"

" I see nothing in that letter which would be received in a court of law as evidence in his favour," said Mrs. Woodford, in a tone which shewed she considered her observation excessively shrewd and clever. " If, indeed, she continued, in the same tone of self-approval, " we are to take what people say in their own defence for Gospel truth, I fancy we should very seldom find people guilty. As to what Belgrave says of his despair, and his being unable to bear to behold Grace the wife of Sir Walter, it is all very fine and romantic, and certainly no one could write on the subject better than he does; but, as I have said before, I am afraid his word would weigh very little against facts."

" And what facts are there that can warrant your attempting to brand my brother as a murderer, Mrs. Woodford ?" said William, losing the little remains of coolness which he had hitherto preserved. " Were it, indeed, any one else but yourself who had uttered half so much as you have done——nay, Grace, you need not look so imploringly at me; for your sake I have done; only this I will add, that for the future, I trust your mother will be more cautious of giving utterance to her suspicions, when I tell you that there is the strongest reason to believe, after all that there has been no murder committed."

" God be thanked," said Grace, devoutly clasping her hands. " Oh, how I have prayed, night and day, that some convincing—some evidence that could not be contradicted or doubted, would arise to establish that which I have never, no, never for a moment, doubted—his utter innocence of a crime which is so foreign to his kind nature, which he would shrink from with as much horror as I would myself; but tell me, dear William, where or how is it proved that———"

"Nothing has, as yet, been proved, Grace," returned William, regardless of the incredulous sneer that played on Mrs. Woodford's features; "but I will tell you what has occurred to throw a doubt upon the supposed murder, if, indeed, there had not been before quite enough to make all reasonable, unprejudiced persons doubt, in the utter disappearance of the body."

"That was sufficiently accounted for, I should think," interrupted Mrs. Woodford, with eagerness, "when there was such undeniable evidence that my poor dear cousin, Sir Walter, had been thrown into the river: we all well know that there are so many deep holes that it is impossible to get at or fathom———"

"I acknowledge all that, madam; but you seem not to be aware that the suspicious appearances to which you affix so much importance have since been perfectly explained by the discovery that a considerable quantity of smuggled goods have been recently landed at the spot you speak of, and that one of the gang, who is now in prison, acknowledges that on the night of the supposed murder he was stationed on the bridge to watch that his companions were not interrupted while they landed a cargo from their boat."

"Perhaps, then," said Mrs. Woodford, beginning to feel how odious and cruel she must appear, in still determinately shutting her eyes to all evidence in favour of Belgrave, "perhaps it was by some of that very gang that poor Sir Walter———"

"Sir Walter is not dead," said William, coolly; "not if the word of a man, who has no partialities or prejudices to influence him, can be taken."

"Not dead!—Sir Walter not dead!" screamed Mrs. Woodford; "what then can account for his disappearance, and at such a moment, too?"

"That it is impossible for me to say," replied William; "but this I know, that Mr. Tyson, the butler at Mr. Vaughan's, who had seen Sir Walter several times before the family went to Bath, was sent over here by his master purposely to depose to the fact that he had seen and spoken to Sir Walter in the street, at Bristol, the very day that the handbills were published, which described him as murdered, and of which, of course, Tyson was not then aware."

"Bath! Bristol! do you hear that, Maria?" exclaimed Mrs. Woodford to her daughter, who, at that moment, entered the room. "Sir Walter, after all, is alive and well, at Bath or Bristol."

"I did not say that," observed William; "on the contrary, Mr. Tyson said that he remarked Sir Walter looked dreadfully ill, and walked, with difficulty, with the aid of a stick."

"Well, but what did he say?" demanded Mrs. Woodford eagerly; did he give no reason, no account of his mysterious ———"

"I have already said that Mr. Tyson was not aware of the circumstances that had transpired; he thought, naturally, from Sir Walter's appearance, that he had come to the Hot Wells, near which he met him, on the banks of the river, in consequence of ill health."

"But did he say nothing at all?" persisted Mrs. Woodford; "surely it was natural he himself should make some observation, if it was indeed him, and Tyson was not mistaken in taking some other person for him."

"I can prove to you that was not the case," replied William; "for upon his touching his hat to him, Sir Walter came close up to him, and looking him earnestly in the face, said—

THE PRIDE OF THE VILLAGE;

OR,

THE FARMER'S DAUGHTERS.

CHAPTER XVI.

True—but there still is something given to guess
Which a shrewd gleaner and quick eye would catch at—
A whisper or a murmur——

—Byron.

"'Do you know me, friend?" Are you the person ——? I do not remember to have seen you before;' to which Tyson replied, 'No, Sir Walter, I could not expect you would remember; but I hope you are not offended at the liberty I took, for somehow I felt so happy to see any body from my native place.'

8

" ' And where, then, is your native place?' said Sir Walter, looking surprised. Tyson immediately replied 'Llan——;' and Sir Walter, he says, started as if he had been stung with a snake.' 'And you did not expect then to meet me here?' he said, after a moment's thought, during which Tyson said he looked into his face, as if he would read his very heart. 'I never in my life saw such a pair of eyes,' he said to me, yesterday, when he was repeating for the twentieth time, I believe, all that passed; 'they seemed like two burning coals of fire glowing in his head and his cheeks too, and lips so deadly-white.' Tyson, of course, assured him that he did not, adding that it was by mere accident that he was there himself, having come over from Bath with one of the ladies, who was going to try the waters of the Hot Wells.

" ' Well, my man,' said Sir Walter at last, in his proud way, " there is five shilings to drink my health; but I request you will not notice to any one, at present, that you have seen me here.'

" It struck Tyson at the moment that he took the money, that there was something curious in this request, and he said ' he would willingly have given the five shillings to have been able to ask Sir Walter after the family at Rose Farm;' but, as he said, 'Sir Walter was not a person whom, anybody could venture to make free with, especially a servant, whom, we all know, he considered as no better than a slave at any time; and so he thanked him civilly for the present, and walked away, little thinking, as he laughingly says, 'that he had been talking and taking money from the ghost of a murdered man.'

" Not considering himself bound, however, to keep Sir Walter's appearance a profound secret, he says, he should, in all probability, have mentioned it at home on his return, had any of the Llan—— servants been with him at Bristol; but there was only Miss Vaughan's lady's maid, who is a Frenchwoman, with her lady there, and of course he did not say anything to her.

" A whole month passed before he returned to the family at Bath, and then, to his utter surprise, he heard of the dreadful murder committed here," continued William; " and to his still greater consternation, one of the advertisements was put into his hand, from which he learned that all this had occurred long previously to his having met Sir Walter at Bristol.

" 'It must be all what the Londoners call a hoax,' was his first exclamation; ' for the man is no more dead than I am, for I have seen and talked to him long since that date, and have even now got the identical piece of money he gave me to drink his health, in my pocket.' It was a new, bright Spanish dollar, and Tyson, struck with the beauty of the coin, had determined to keep it, as a present to his litle god-daughter, when he should return to Llan——.

" Paragraph after paragraph relating to the dreadful murder, and narrating the suspicions that had arisen, and the measures that had been pursued were now, however, pointed out to him, in not only the county newspapers, but the London and others; and Tyson became, as he said, ' convinced that there was either some horrid conspiracy against my poor brother; or, that some strange misapprehension had arisen, which he could remove. And he, therefore, took the first opportunity of speaking to his master, and relating what had occurred.

" Mr. Vaughan was, of course, as much surprised as Tyson himself; he had read with astonishment the accounts in the papers, but had never for a moment, as he said, ' given credit to the supposition that one whom he had known so intimately as my brother;' for you know, Grace —," and William turned to the latter, who was listening with the deepest interest to this detail, "You know what a favourite Belgrave from his boyhood was with the family of the Vaughans, and how it has ever been said, though very improbably, that it was old Squire Vaughan's intention to marry him to one of the young ladies."

"Yes, yes, I do well know it, replied Grace, her cheeks glowing with a deep blush, as William's remark recalled to her mind how often she had in girlish frowardness, reproached Belgrave for his partiality to the family at Old Court, and insisted that there must be something more than mere friendship in his attachment to the society of two accomplished and beautiful females like the two Miss Vaughans.

William proceeded : "I have nothing more to relate. Mr. Vaughan of course felt the deepest anxiety, as every one who knew my brother and had a heart capable of valuing him"—he added looking with peculiar significance at Mrs. Woodford—"must, to restore him to society, and prove his entire innocence; and accordingly Tyson was sent over here without delay, to repeat, which he has done upon oath, what I have told you."

"Then he is, indeed, at last vindicated," said Grace, joyfully.

"In every bosom, but those who are predetermined to find him guilty," replied William.

"But why did you not tell me all this at your first coming, Mr. Mansell?" demanded Mrs. Woodford. "You must naturally suppose that it would be a great consolation to me to hear that my poor cousin, Sir Walter, was still living.

"I will tell you candidly, Mrs. Woodford, that I was desirous of seeing whether Belgrave's own candid reasons for absenting himself, would succeed in removing the prejudice which I understood you indulged against him."

"And he is in Bristol," said Mrs. Woodford, musing and evidently totally callous to the reproof which William's last observation conveyed. "It is curious, is it not, my dear; she continued, looking at Maria; a strange coincidence ; but of course, this information will confirm me more and more in my plans."

"It can make little difference to us, mamma," returned her daughter with an air of pique, "where Sir Walter can have chosen to hide himself, since it is plain he has no intention to favour us with his confidence ; and for my part, ' she continued, stealing a look at William, who was now deeply interested in some remark, which Grace in an under tone was making to him ; "for my part I can have no good opinion of a man, who, without any reason, as far as we can judge, but mere caprice, has chosen to leave his friends in ignorance of what had become of him, and involve innocent people in so much trouble."

William's attention had from the moment she began to speak, been withdrawn from Grace, and wholly fixed on her beautiful sister. It was some months since he had beheld that lovely form and features, for William had long been helpless and hopeless on a bed of sickness; but never had she appeared to him half so lovely, as when at this moment, unequivocally declaring her indifference to one, whom, until very lately, he had been taught to believe, from the moment of his introduction, was destined to carry off the fair prize, for whom so many had sighed in vain.

Maria was by nature a coquette, and her mother's instructions and evil counsels had made her a heartless and practised deceiver ; she saw instantly that she still retained all her former power over the heart of the sensitive and unsophisticated William, and in a few minutes more, in spite of her mother's frowns, and fidgets, and discouragements, her artless lover was once more at her side, and in spite of his former convictions and experience, inclined to believe that Maria really returned his affection, and that it would still be his happy lot to secure for his bride, the Pride of the Village, as Maria was emphatically called, by the admirers of her exquisite beauty.

In Maria's mind, however, no correspondent emotion was awakened : she was glad, indeed, to see William, and to renew the acquaintance between them which had been so long interrupted, and she was proud at reading in his eyes that she still retained her power over him : but beyond the entertainment of the moment she had neither wishes nor intentions, though as she acknowledged to Grace, when they retired for the night, she thought William wonderfully improved in person since she had seen him, and as to manners, really, she observed it was quite surprising to think, that under all his disadvantages, William appeared in her opinion, quite as gentleman-like and well-bred as ever Sir Walter did.

"And why should he not ?" demanded Grace. "By Sir Walter's own admission, he had not much to boast of over William, in point of education, and we are all aware that Sir Walter had never been in much society any more than William. Surely then, Maria," she continued, "you could not suppose that the mere possession of riches was to make such a decided difference." "If, indeed," she added with animation, "you were to ask my candid opinion between the two, I should say that William Mansell is, in reality, far superior to Sir Walter in manners as well as everything else, except money, because I have read that the surest proof of good sense and good breeding is, to be mindful of the feelings and wishes of others rather than your own."

The surprising information of which William had been the bearer, though it excited new hopes in the bosoms of Mrs. Woodford and Maria, and removed from Grace's heart a load of indescribable misery, was still far from entirely giving satisfaction to either of them. Sanguine as Mrs. Woodford still was that she should eventually secure the fortune of her "dear cousin" to her family, she could not but feel that Sir Walter's unaccountable desertion and subsequent total silence, even as to his existence, augured anything but favourably to her cause.

Some serious cause there must undoubtedly have been, to induce him thus to quit them at such an eventful moment. The moment of all others when he had decisively explained his views and intentions, and had every reason, from her (Mrs. Woodford's) ready acquiescence and confident anticipations that Grace would receive with equal pleasure and gratitude his declaration in her favour, to believe that everything was settled to his utmost satisfaction.

"There can be but one reasonable cause assigned for it," observed Mrs. Woodford to Maria, after considering and reconsidering and suggesting and rejecting a thousand not probable but possible causes for the baronet's departure. "He must have seen Belgrave Mansel lingering about the house, and having, as he acknowledged to me, suspected from something he had heard, that the young man had been a favoured lover in your poor foolish father's life-time, he was suddenly struck with a fit of jealousy, and so went off in a rage, determined to drop the connection altogether ; and, besides, who knows but that Belgrave and him might have met, and perhaps the artful young rascal may have said something—there's no knowing, indeed, what he might say to carry his purpose."

"Well, but if that was the case, Belgrave would have stayed, mamma, instead of going off too," observed Maria.

Mrs. Woodford was for a moment disconcerted in her suppositions by this remark, but it at length occurred to her, that it was very probable that Sir

Walter might conceal from his rival that his schemes had taken effect, and therefore Belgrave had quitted in despair.

The consequence of these suggestions and conjectures was that Grace became more than ever the object of her mother's aversion and spleen, and twenty times in the course of the day following William's visit, was the poor girl condemned to listen to reproach and insult as having, by her deception and intriguing with Belgrave, brought disgrace upon herself and misery upon her connections. On these occasions Maria, indeed, was her firm champion, venting on Sir Walter every epithet which folly, indecision, and imbecility could deserve; for Maria had neither forgotten nor forgiven the slight he had shown to her, in preferring her sister after suffering her so long to be the dupe of her own vanity in supposing that it must be to her his homage was directed. For the first time in her life Mrs. Woodford discovered that her views and those of her favourite were, though still tending to the same end, totally dissimilar as to the course each thought best to pursue. Believing, indeed, as she had been taught to believe, in the irresistible power of her own beauty, Maria conceived the loss of the Baronet as of no material consequence to herself, except delaying for a short time her acquisition of the wealth and rank which she imagined that beauty was certain of securing to her; while to Grace she knew that, however inconsistent with her own feelings, the breaking off the match under any circumstances except those which had seemed to involve the safety and honour of Belgrave Mansell, was a source of excessive satisfaction.

With all Maria's good nature and affection for her sister, it had indeed been a most galling subject to her, the prospect of that sister attaining without any trouble, or even wish on her part, that for which she (Maria) had sighed and languished, and dressed and exhibited her beautiful person in vain. That Grace would marry well, that was to say, that she would get a rich husband, had never appeared unlikely, for she could do justice to her sister's worth and attractions, meanly as her mother thought of them, but then Maria had always considered this desirable event as secondary to her own elevation. She was to form the great connection, and Grace was afterwards to profit by the advantages she would thus acquire. All this had been deranged at once by Sir Walter's declaration in favour of Grace, and Maria, with no small mortification and vexation, saw the unpretending little girl, whom she was to lift into consequence, now likely at one step to supersede her; much, therefore, as she had really felt shocked at the horrible circumstances which had appeared to attend Sir Walter's disappearance, there were moments when it was impossible for her to suppress, or to disguise her secret exultation that the match she had contemplated with so much bitterness was prevented, and she was therefore now decidedly opposed to any measure which might forward its renewal.

It was in vain that Mrs. Woodford again and again pointed out to her the advantages that must accrue to herself from her sister's forming so advantageous a connection, Maria was obstinately bent on owing her fortunes to herself alone, and therefore decidedly averse to taking any steps to renew the connection with Sir Walter.

"I will not go to Bristol, mamma," said the self-willed beauty, "until we are sure that the good-for-nothing wretch is not there. What, indeed, could we expect but to be again insulted by him; for he would certainly think and say, and so, indeed, would everybody else, that we had meanly followed him there; and for your own pride's sake, if for nothing else, I would never let him have the satisfaction of saying so."

The result of this and similar declarations on her part was that Mrs. Woodford was reluctantly induced to rescind her determination, and after a

long discussion it was finally settled between the thoughtless and imprudent mother and daughter, that Cheltenham, of which they had heard so
much from a young female, the daughter of a farmer, who had spent one season there, with a rich old maid, her relation, should be the scene of their
debut, and Maria's anticipated triumphs.

In the meantime, Maria, while thus finally arranging with her mother
their future plans, was once more successful in entangling poor William in
the toils from which he had once so desperately broken. It was true that
she did not actually tell him that she preferred him to all the world, and
that she would be content to renounce all her ambitious views for his
sake, and it was true that in confessed obedience to her mother, she referred
him to her, whenever he attempted to draw from her any promise
or acknowledgment; and it was equally true that Mrs. Woodford,
without any ceremony, decidedly told him that she had other views for her
daughter than to suffer her to tie herself to a life of toil and obscurity;
but still, when Maria met him with a sweet smile, listened to his impassioned whispers not only with patience, but with evident pleasure, and
finally encouraged him to believe that he was dear to her, by assuring him
with earnestness that she had never liked Sir Walter Fitz-Geffrey, and that
the world (the world of Llan———), had been quite mistaken in supposing
that she ever intended to marry him—when, too he reflected what her
situation was, and that she could, as he imagined, be no longer blinded by
vanity into believing that she could command rank and riches, and when in
addition to all this, he added his own now prosperous condition, the comforts and conveniences which he was enabled to command by a fit of unexpected generosity on the part of his uncle, who thought by the gift of a
few hundred pounds to his nephew, to compensate to him for the disappointment and shock which he (William) had suffered, he felt convinced that he
could have no reason to despair, not only of gaining Maria's consent, but
eventually conquering the scruples of the old woman, as he was accustomed,
somewhat disrespectfully it must be acknowledged, to call Mrs. Woodford.

It was some days before Grace, whose mind was painfully absorbed in
contemplation of and the attempt to unravel the strange mysteries of Sir
Walter's disappearance, and the effect it had had, discovered the cruel and
ungenerous game her sister was playing. Judging by her own heart, she at
first believed Maria had seen the folly of aspiring to that which fate had
never intended her for, that she at length did justice to William's merits
and his long attachment to her, and was determined to renounce her ambitious views, and settle at once into the humble domestic wife of a farmer;
but a very short time convinced her that Maria harboured no such intentions,
for the preparations for their departure from Llan——— conducted, as they
were, with all possible secresy, could not be concealed from her, though they
were successfully so from him who was so deeply interested in all their
movements.

"Surely, surely, Maria," she exclaimed; after witnessing the latter's at
least equivocal manner of receiving and replying to her ardent lover, who
had, in spite of Mrs. Woodford's discouraging coldness, passed every evening at Rose Farm, from his first or rather his re-introduction to it, "surely
you can never intend to keep poor William in the dark to the last moment,
and then leave him in utter despair."

"And how can I possibly help it, Grace," returned Maria, blushing at
the earnestness of her sister's reproof, "if he will deceive himself? I have
told him, and mamma herself has told him, that she will never consent to
our marriage, and of course I would not act in opposition to her; and
when he asked leave to visit us as a friend, and mamma did not object, I

certainly could not be expected to do so. It is not my wish to give him any uneasiness, if I could help it; but as to letting him know that we are going to quit Llan——, mamma says it would be the height of folly and imprudence."

" And you really can consent, really can make up your mind to leave him without even a word of explanation, or —— you cannot have any affection for him, Maria; it is impossible, or you could not have listened to his anticipations to-night, that all would yet end well and happily, without betraying yourself, and yet I saw you smile at him, and certainly not one word was uttered by you, that could give him a suspicion of the treachery that is about to be practised towards him."

" Treachery, Grace!" repeated Maria, angrily, yet, with a confusion that betrayed that she felt the term was not inapplicable. " I don't know that you or he either can have any right to accuse me of treachery: he has received a decided refusal from my mother, and I defy him to prove that I have ever uttered a word to lead him to think that I would act in opposition to her. Mamma considers it necessary to keep her intentions for the future a secret; and I am really surprised that you, above all persons, who have always prided yourself on being so dutiful and submissive, should now wish me ———— "

" I do not wish you, Maria," interrupted Grace, with warmth; " far would it be from my thought ever to wish you to act in opposition to your mother ; but I do say, do think, that whatever your words may have been to William, your manners, your looks, have been such as to warrant the hopes, which, I am sure, he entertains, and which you are now coolly preparing to blast for ever."

" Upon my word, Grace, you seem to be much better learned in the meaning of looks than I am, and you are quite romantic, too, in your expressions," said Maria ; " but, as mamma says, all these fine things about love are very pretty in novels, but they don't do in common life."

Grace felt abashed. She was conscious, indeed, that her warmth in William's cause had led her into using language which certainly did savour a little of romance, though she felt also that it did not misrepresent the case, and she did not therefore attempt to reply to her sister.

" I will tell you the real truth, Grace," observed Maria after some minutes' silence. " I do really prefer William to any one I have ever seen, and if he was a gentleman I would marry him directly ; but I am firmly convinced that love marriages, where people's circumstances are not equal to their wishes, are the greatest folly a woman can be guilty of. Look at mamma, for instance ; she married, you know, entirely for love ; and yet, you well know, nothing could be more unhappy than the life she led with my father. And just so," she continued, without appearing to notice Grace's agitation at the mention of her father thus disrespectfully, "just so would it be with with me and William. I could not make up my mind to lead a life of drudgery and obscurity, and what else can a farmer's wife expect or hope for ?"

" And what else can a farmer's daughter have a right to expect or hope for ?" said Grace, with seriousness.

Maria tossed her head scornfully. " I shall hope, and do hope, for something more," she replied ; and then, after contemplating for some moments with evident satisfaction her own features in the dressing-glass, before which she was standing, she added, with a smile ——

" You may think as humbly as you please, Grace, of the farmer's daughter, but I will never believe that I am destined to waste my life in obscurity.

"But why not, then deal candidly with William?" said Grace, who was not even yet discouraged from pleading warmly the cause of her friend.

"Because my mother has a motive for wishing me to be otherwise" she replied. "To tell you the truth, Grace, it has struck my mother that it would be very possible, through William's means, to get Mr. Meredith to give her a receipt for his debt : that is, I mean to give up the bond he holds ; and you know, that would be a great relief, because———" Grace did not wait to hear any further explanation.

"And can it be possible, Maria, that you can coolly, for a mercenary purpose, thus trifle with poor William's feelings ?" she interrupted, in a tone of reproach.

Maria, however, was totally insensible to her reproaches ; she was content, she said, to know that she could save her mother, and she concluded by observing———

"It is in your power, Grace, by telling him all this, to disappoint your mother's expectations ; perhaps you will think it your duty to do so but———"

"There is no occasion for any threats, Maria," returned Grace ; "I feel, if you do not, the impossibility of my representing either my mother or you, in the light which I must do, were I to betray your confidence. I shall keep your secret ; but I wish, I do wish," she added with emphasis, "that I had never heard it."

CHAPTER XVII.

"That such things were,
And were most dear to us."— SHAKESPEARE.

THE time at length arrived which Mrs. Woodford had fixed for her departure with her family, from Rose Farm. She had succeeded in cajoling William who had been led, by indirect insinuations, to believe that his success with her depended entirely on his uncle's giving this proof of the sincerity of his friendship towards the children of his deceased friend.

Mr. Meredith had, indeed, at first, stoutly protested that he never would consent to William's marrying one who had jilted him so soon as a richer match offered, and who now, as he said, only consented because, she had been disappointed in making that match, and feared she might not meet with another ; but Mr. Meredith's obstinacy was no match for his nephew's perseverance. He was anxious, too, to see the latter settled, fearing, as he observed, that he might take some mad-headed freak like his brother ; and, therefore, he yielded to purchase Mrs. Woodford's consent at her own price.

"And now dearest girl," said the sanguine youth as he gave the coveted bond into Maria's hand, "there exists, I trust, no further impediment to our immediate happiness, and to-morrow my uncle will ride over with me and settle with your mother.———"

"No, not to-morrow, William," interrupted Maria, breathless almost with shame, though rejoicing in the success of her efforts—" not to-morrow give me one day to—to prepare ; that is—no, your uncle must not come to-morrow, nor you either. I shall lay my commands on you for the last time—and she tried to assume a playful smile, to disguise her agitation and her real meaning ; "to-morrow you must stay at home and leave me to myself."

William remonstrated, grumbled, persuaded, and implored ; but all in vain. Maria was firm, or, as he said, obstinate; and he departed—to behold her no more. The next day was devoted to their remaining preparations; and at dark, Mrs. Woodford, Maria, and Grace, were driven to the next town, in the cart which had been used by Mr. Woodford to attend the markets in the neighbourhood and from that alighted only to enter the mail-coach, which at that hour, passed through towards London by the way of Bristol and Bath. So secretly had all been managed, that, with the exception of the boy who drove the cart, and his father, who had previously conveyed the luggage to the waggon, by which it was sent forward on the same road, not a single person was aware of their departure or destination, the only female servant who remained having, on the previous morning, upon some frivolous pretext been discharged, and the men sent out of the way.

The silence of the boy was effectually secured, by his being deaf and dumb, as well as scarcely possessing sufficient intelligence to comprehend anything except that he was to drive the horse till his mistress chose to stop, and then bring it home again; while that of his father was purchased by a handsome present, and a promise of remitting a further mark of favour should he keep the secret faithfully.

To the last moment, Grace, amidst a thousand contending and painful sensations, preserved more composure than either her mother or Maria, whose fears of disappointment in their scheme, and consequent exposure, became quite overpowering when the time for carrying it into effect arrived. But when they were, at length, seated in the vehicle which was to convey them for ever from Llan——, and she heard the smack of the coachman's whip, and found herself rolling along the road at a rate which would, in a short time, remove her from every scene she had known and loved, Grace's fortitude forsook her; and leaning back in the corner of the coach, she gave way to an hysterical burst of tears.

A whispered remonstrance from Maria, and a harsh exclamation of, "What is all this nonsense about? do you recollect where you are?" from her mother, were intended to remind the weeping girl that there was a stranger present, a gentleman who occupied the fourth corner of the mail, and who, after having at first seemed disposed to reply to Mrs. Woodford's apologies for the trouble she gave in entering the coach from her lameness, with some *brusquerie* changed his tone, when he beheld the fair faces of her two companions, though only imperfectly seen in the fading light, and became all politeness and attention, congratulating himself, as he said, in being so favoured as to have ladies for his companions, instead of being bored to death with brutes of men.

"Grace, recollect yourself; what will strangers think of you?" whispered Maria again, but Grace cared nothing for strangers, or for the whole world, except the identical little spot which she was fast leaving behind; and her sobs and tears redoubled, as Maria, who, having relinquished the attempt to silence her, exclaimed, in a a tone of exultation,

"Here's the milestone, mamma, I declare we are a mile from———— already. How pleasant it is to get on so fast."

"Did you never travel by the mail before?" inquired the stranger in a familiar tone.

"Never, Sir, indeed, I have never travelled at all," she added with *naiveté*.

"Is it possible; and have such charms been confined to this secluded spot of earth?" returned the gentleman.

"My daughter has never been from home before, sir, except when she went to boarding-school, and then she went in her father's own chaise, so that she knows nothing about travelling," said Mrs. Woodford who seemed by no means disposed to let the conversation drop.

The stranger appeared equally inclined to be upon good terms with his companions, and after another compliment to Maria, he observed, "That young lady who seems to regret her departure so much, of course, has not the happiness to call you mother, madam."

"She is my daughter, sir; but I am sorry to say, she has very little of the feelings of one, or she would not give way to this nonsensical grief, at leaving a place, which I am sure, has nothing to recommend it to people of any refinement;" returned Mrs. Woodford, dwelling with peculiar emphasis on the last word.

"But, perhaps it is not the place itself the young lady so much regrets," observed the stranger, significantly; "there are sometimes persons who ———"

"Oh, dear! no, sir—nothing of that kind, I assure you," interrupted Mrs. Woodford, pertly; "there is no person there, indeed," she added, with an air of consequence, "whom my daughters would consider worth bestowing a thought upon."

"Indeed, it is something singular for a lady so young, to regret so deeply, leaving the country to enter into gayer scenes, for I presume you are going to the metropolis, madam."

"No, sir; we stop at Bath, I have been recommended to try the waters there," and Mrs. Woodford's consequential tone became still more important, as she gave utterance to this falsehood.

Grace had in the meantime, succeeded in stifling the tears which had provoked this discussion, though it was impossible for her to banish the feelings which had given rise to them, or take any part in the conversation which ensued and in the course of which the stranger contrived to learn all he possibly could respecting them, their connexions, situation in life, and intended mode of living, all of which were, however, considerably embellished, and modified by Mrs. Woodford's usual habit of speaking of herself, and all that concerned herself.

With the same apparent thoughtless candour that prompted his questions, the stranger contrived to let them know that his visit was to Bath—he also was to stop in Bath—was of mere pleasure, that he was independent of all controul, and sufficiently at ease in his circumstances to indulge his inclinations.

Quite undesignedly too, as it appeared, he named several persons of rank, as his intimate friends, and Mrs. Woodford in return, talked of her cousin, Sir Walter, and her father, who was very near marrying Lord Loppington's daughter, which would have been sure to have gained him a seat in Parliament, but that the lady preferred her own cousin, and ran away with him.

"Do you know the Melverlys, of Cardiston Hall?" inquired the stranger, after listening patiently to her pompous and tiresome description of some festivities, which she, after all, could of course, only know by hearsay, since they had taken place at the marriage of her father and mother; but they served to show, as she was used to observe, that she was not sprung from the dirt, and that was the point aimed at with her new acquaintance, whose account of himself, as far as it went, was highly satisfactory to her.

"Do I know the Melverlys, she repeated; "yes, my father's estates and theirs joined, and many a romp I have had with Frederick and Henrietta Melverly, poor things; their father was a shocking rake, he used to spend all his time and money in London, and leave Lady Melverly and her children at the hall, with scarcely the necessaries of life; but he's dead now, and Frederic has got the title and a large fortune, which was left him by his mother's uncle, and they say he is as saving as his father was the contrary —but that he's got a son that is likely to tread in his grandfather's steps, and spend what his father saves."

" But they do not live at the hall," said the stranger; "how then can people in this remote part of the world pretend to know so much ?"

" I don't know, evil fame flies fast, they say ; but it is reported, I believe, that the family are coming down to live at the hall again ; they have been abroad for many years."

" Yes, it was there I knew them," said the stranger.

"Oh, but Henrietta is dead, is she not ?" demanded Mrs. Woodford.

" Lady Alston you mean, of course. Yes, she died in giving birth to a daughter."

" She was reckoned very handsome," observed Mrs. Woodford ; " I wonder is her daughter like her."

" I do not remember my——, that is Lady Alston," replied the stranger; " but Julia is the most beautiful creature——; at least people say she is, and certainly I once though myself that she could not be surpassed."

The stoppage of the coach for supper put an end for the present to the conversation which had become so interesting. The stranger, with great patience and attention, assisted Mrs. Woodford to alight, supported her into the house, and Grace, who had at first felt considerably annoyed by his levity, and the flippant freedom of his remarks, was now greatly reconciled to him for the humanity with which he attended to her mother's infirmities. She shrank, however, with great confusion from the scrutinising survey which he took of both sisters, as soon as they came in the full light of the supper-room, and pulling her large bonnet closer over her face, to conceal her swollen eyes, she quietly seated herself in the most unobtrusive corner she could find.

Not so Maria, under the pretext of heat and head-ache, her bonnet was pulled off the moment she entered the room, and her long and beautiful hair instantly fell over her shoulders in the most graceful confusion.

" Heavens ! I declare I had quite forgotten, I have no comb to fasten my hair," and she made an attempt to gather it up together.

" It would be a sin to hide such beautiful tresses, by torturing them into form," said the stranger, viewing her with evident admiration. " Let me entreat therefore, that you will not concern yourself about that which becomes you most admirably."

" Oh, but I must ! I can't sit in this manner ;" and Maria with a deal of well-acted confusion, gathered up her curls and replaced her bonnet.

The stranger's eyes seemed fascinated ; and Mrs. Woodford, with ill-concealed pleasure, beheld the tribute which he paid to her daughter's charms. From this moment, indeed, until the termination of their journey at the White Hart, in the Market-place, Bath, the stranger's every effort was directed to conciliate Maria and her mother.

Business of importance, he said, compelled him abruptly to leave them at the moment of their arrival; but he should live only in hopes of meeting them again, in the course of a few hours.

Mrs. Woodford was in high spirits, and loud in his praise, the moment he was gone, " so truly polite, well bred, and genteel," she observed.

" And so handsome too, mamma," chimed in Maria.

" There is no goodwill lost between you, my dear, for it plain he thinks you very handsome," returned her mother. " I wonder who he is ? something strikes me he will prove to belong to a great family. Did you observe how familiarly he talked of lords and ladies ? yet we must be careful Maria, for I have heard there are many impostors at Bath."

"Impostors!" returned Maria. "Surely no person with common understanding could be doubtful that this is a perfect gentleman."

"Well, well, we shall see him again, and have further opportunities of judging;" replied the mother, who fancied that in thus qualifying her praise of him, she was displaying necessary and prudent caution; and immediately launched out again.

"How fortunate it is for us that we came a day sooner than we intended, or we should have missed making this acquaintance, my dear, and we should have felt quite lonely for a time, even in this beautiful place, without some friend."

Maria cordially assented; she was in raptures with the place, and never tired of standing at the window of the room to which they had been introduced, to admire the dresses of the passers by, and wonder what could bring so many people out into the streets.

The number of carriages, too, excited her astonishment; and as she gazed at them with interest, fresh hopes that her mother's constant predictions, that she was born to ride in her carriage, arose in her bosom, and she sighed, only that she could not immediately realise the delightful prospect.

The day passed away in wondering, admiring, and consulting. All recollection of Llan—— seemed to have vanished from their minds, except poor Grace, whose thoughts were oftener employed in depicting the consternation and despair of poor William, and the condemnation which would attend their conduct from all his friends, than on present scenes.

"What a fright the girl has made of herself," observed Mrs. Woodford, when she at length found leisure to look at Grace. "I am sure if Sir Walter were to see you now, with your eyes swollen out of your head, and your cheeks as pale as death, and the tip of your nose as red as if it was a frosty morning, it would be enough to frighten him away again."

Grace almost started at the mention of Sir Walter; it had never till this moment occurred to her that it was possible that they might again meet him, whom she considered the origin of all her misfortunes—and if they did, and she should be compelled to listen to his odious proposals.

"Oh, no, there is no fear of it," said Maria, to whom she ventured, the first moment they were alone together, to whisper the terror her mother's words had inspired.

"I cannot think, how you, or my mother either, can for a moment think such a thing possible, for even if the story of his being alive is true, which I have great doubts of, since it has never been confirmed, except that Tyson, whom everybody knows is a great drunkard, and therefore likely to have told such a story without any foundation, or perhaps took somebody else for Sir Walter, whom he couldn't know much of; but even, I say, if he should be alive, it must be very plain, Grace, that he can have no affection for you, or he would, before this, have made some communication. No, no, depend on it, the poor man, was afraid of marriage, and did not know how to get out of the hobble he had got into, without running away, that is if he really is alive, which I very much doubt."

Grace, however, did not doubt it; she had never believed in his death even when every one around her was fully convinced of it, and she would not now, for a moment admit a doubt that he would one day make his appearance; though, that Maria might be right in her conjectures of the cause of his absence, she heartily prayed.

Many hours passed away, and their fellow-traveller, on whose coming both Mrs. Woodford and Maria, seemed to rely, as on that of a friend, did not make his appearance: and. too much fatigued, to bear up any longer, the whole party retired to rest, determined to lose no further time, but on the morrow proceed to establish themselves in apartments, and commence their career of pleasure.

"I wonder what they are doing now in Llan——?" was Maria's observation to her sister, as the latter assisted her to undress.

"I could give a shrewd guess," she continued, finding Grace not inclined to speak. "It is just nine o'clock; William, who has returned with Uncle Meredith two hours ago from Rose Farm, and has tired himself and the old man out with wondering and imagining what can have become of us, has taken his horse, left his uncle to go to bed if he likes, and ridden over to Llan——; and there, either at Watkins' the grocer's or Morgan's the ironmonger's he is in the middle of a whole crowd of them, telling his dismal tale, and listening to a hundred jeers, and jibes, and falsehoods, at our expense. Oh! I know them all well, the scandalising narrow-minded illiberal set, and know they will not scruple to say anything."

"They will have plenty of room to condemn, without saying any thing but the truth, now," said Grace, pointedly.

"In your opinion, you should say, Grace," returned her sister; "but I hope you will learn how to despise what such a set can say of us. The time will come, and I hope soon, when we shall be able to look down upon such people with contempt."

"That time will never come to me, Maria," observed Grace. "I can only contemn those whose motives are bad, and I never saw among the people you mention any want of good feeling or good principle. I wish we may find no worse among those we are now thrown ——"

"I wonder what old Alice Meredith will say," interrupted Maria, laughing, and appearing totally inattentive to her sister's observation. "Oh! how I do hate that old woman! But thank goodness, I shall never see her sharp scowling eyes scornfully surveying me from top to toe, and then breaking out into some impertinent remark.

"Alice was always very kind and good-natured to me," observed Grace; "and poor Belgrave"—it was the first time Belgrave's name had crossed her lips since they left home; and she suddenly paused, as a whole train of recollections, crowded into her mind.

"Aye, Belgrave and Alice were dear friends," said Maria, without noticing Grace's agitation; "but I have never told you what the old witch, as the boys call her, said to me only last Sunday, when you know I went to church without you. William was as usual walking by my side, and she put herself just in the pathway before us."

"So, she said, looking at me, 'Pride has been obliged to stoop, but it will stoop much lower yet.'

"'Do not be ill-natured, mother,' said William, colouring, but trying to speak in his usual free tone.

"'Mother!' she repeated. 'If I were your mother, boy, I would find you better employment, than to waste your time on that piece of painted earth, that heartless image.'

"William was now very angry," continued Maria, "and I was half-frightened, and glad to get away; so I left him to talk to her, and got off as fast as I could, not even stopping till I reached the stile, for I knew that half the envious snarling misses in Llan—— heard her, and were enjoying a laugh at my expense; though she gives it to all of them in their turn. William would not tell me what she said to him after I left them, but he looked very angry, and called her 'a troublesome meddling old dame;' adding, 'but we shall soon convince her, as well as others that envy my happiness, that they are out in their reckoning.' Poor fellow," she ejaculated, after a few moments' reflection; "I do not think I ever felt so sorry and ashamed of deceiving him as I did at that minute."

"Poor fellow, indeed," re-echoed Grace; and yet at that moment, for the first time, the thought suggested itself to her mind, that after all, it was perhaps a fortunate thing for William, that he had escaped marriage with one whom, in spite of all her sisterly affection, she feared, deserved but too well the epithet old Alice had bestowed, of—heartless.

The breakfast was over and no appearance of their expected visitor; and reluctantly the mother and daughter left the inn to seek for lodgings, leaving Grace with strict orders to detain him, if it were possible, should he come in their absence.

"Grace earnestly hoped he would not, but her hopes were not fulfilled, for they had scarcely left the inn, when he was shown into the room by the waiter.

The most friendly inquiries as to their health, accommodation, &c., &c., showed that the interest he had expressed for their welfare had suffered no diminution; the air of levity he had worn during the first hour of their acquaintance had totally disappeared; his manners were gentle, soothing, and respectful towards Grace, whom timidity and inexperience rendered awkward and confused at first, but whom he soon contrived to render quite at ease, with both herself and him, though she could not agree with him in thinking that Bath was such a delightful place, that she would soon forget all her regret at leaving the country.

Grace was still less inclined to believe this when in an hour or two after, at her mother's command, she followed the porter with their luggage to a lodging in ——— street, two small rooms and an attic; looking out, the dining-room on a dead wall opposite, at the distance of about twelve feet—the back bedroom into a small yard, around which were tailors' workshops—and the attic upon an interminable range of red tiles and chimney pots.

And this was to be their future residence, and for this they had left the range of a large substantial house, with nothing to intercept the pure breath of heaven from entering all the windows but clusters of eglantine and jasmine, or the delicious fruit of the vine.

Poor Grace looked disconsolately around her as the mistress of the house preceded her into the apartments, as she called them, apologizing at every step for their not being quite so nice as she could wish them, but the ladies that had them last had only left last night, and she had not had time to put everything to rights.

"All the cleaning and putting to rights in the world," thought Grace, as she gazed at the greased and stained sofa-cover and curtains, the dusty, discoloured carpet, and the fancy chairs, on which a patch here and there alone remained to tell that they had once been decorated with wreaths of flowers; "not all that hands could do could ever make this place and furniture look wholesome and comfortable."

The bedroom was even more repulsive. The counterpane looked as if it was years since it had been acquainted with the washing-tub, the hangings were of dingy drab moreen, loaded with dust, the dressing-glass was cracked, and everything looked slovenly, close, and unwholesome.

"There is another room at the top of the house, miss, with two beds; one, I suppose, for you, for the lady said that her youngest daughter would sleep there—and the other for the maid that I am to get for you. You will like perhaps to have some of the things carried up there out of the way?"

Grace acquiesced,—the top of the house seemed to promise, at least, more air and better light than the first floor ; and she followed the dirty-looking servant-girl who was called from her occupation in the kitchen to carry the lady's things up stairs.

The first view of the attic, however, convinced her that her expectations had overrated its attractions. It might once, indeed have been light and airy, but economy had closed up two of the windows, and the third was scarcely large enough to show the dismal obscurity of the room. Two mean-looking beds, with a scanty piece of white, or what had once been white, calico, as an apology for drapery, a ricketty deal table, and two ricketty chairs, completed the paraphernalia of the room which Grace was to consider hers.

"Did my mother see this room before she took the lodgings?" she inquired of the girl, who stood staring at her, after depositing the trunks and band-boxes, which she had assisted her to bring up.

"No, miss; the old lady was too lame to come up stairs; and, besides, the beds wasn't made, for master's 'prentices slept here, and deuced mad they'll be, when they come to know they're turned out of their beds, and must pig it in the workshop."

"Is there no other room I can have?" said Grace, whose horror at the appearance of this miserable place was increased by finding she was to be the successor of the tailor's apprentices in their wretched bed.

"Lauk, no miss," said the girl; "all the rest of the house is let, except the back parlour, where master and missus sleep, and the back kitchen, where we cooks for the lodgers, and where I sleep."

"Good Heavens!" Grace had never formed an idea that it was possible for human beings to exist thus cooped up, and to eat and drink, and cook and sleep, all in one kitchen. Poor Grace! what would she have given at this moment to have been an inhabitant of the meanest cottage in Llan——? for there they all had light and fresh air and room to be cleanly.

"The old lady said there was no occasion to be very partickler about your room, miss," said the girl, seeing that Grace still stood with dissatisfaction strongly painted on her countenance; "but if there's anything you want, sich as a washing-stand or a bit of carpet, to make you comfortable, why I'll try if I can get it from you of missus, or out of one of the t'other lodger's rooms. There's one as isn't werry good pay, for missus ain't seen the colour of his money this three weeks, so she won't be werry partickler what she takes out of his room. And now I think of it, there's a fender there will make this fireplace look quite comfortable, with a bit of chimbly-board, that missus 'll get Sam to knock up when he's done work in the shop; for he's the only one of our six boys—great hulking fellows, as missus calls em—that knows how to handle a hammer or drive in a nail."

"Not for me, I beg," said Grace, recalled from her melancholy thoughts by the maid's preparing to leave her, to commit the proposed spoliation on the lodger's room who was so unfortunate as not to have paid his lodgings. "I do not wish to have anybody put to inconvenience for me; this place will do very well as it is; at least, I will try to be contented with it."

"Laws, bless you, miss; there was a very nice lady, and her little girl—a real lady, they said, she was, in her own country—A Spanish woman she was, and had had houses, and lands, and servants, at her beck and call—and yet she was glad to put up with this room, nigh upon two years, and there was less furniture, too, in it than there is now; for missus, finding she was very unsartain pay, took out the best of the things, after she had been here six or seven months. Indeed, she wouldn't have let her stay at all, only that she taught our Miss Matilda, missus' daughter, French, and dancing, and music, and needlework, and so saved the expense of schooling.

But, poor thing, my heart often ached for her, after she took bad in the winter, and sometimes could hardly crawl out of bed to light her bit of fire, and get the child victuals; and often I used to run up, on the sly, when I'd a minute to spare, and do any little job for her; but, laws, I have got such a hard place—six single men, besides the first floor lodgers, and missus is such a dragon (in a low whisper)—that, between you and I, I couldn't do half what I would for the poor thing. She used to promise me, sometimes, that if she lived to go back to her own country, she would take me with her, and I should never work again: but there was no such luck for Becky, she went to the country where people never come back, poor creter."

"Died !" said Grace, raising her tearful eyes to the good-natured, begrimed face of the loquacious Becky.

"Yes, miss; in that werry bed, there," pointing to the meanest-looking one of the two.

"And the poor child ?" demanded Grace.

"Oh, God Almighty was pleased to take that first," returned the girl, "and so saved it from going to the workhouse; for it must have gone, if she'd have died first; and I should have fretted my life out to see it, for I was a parish orphan myself once, till they put me 'prentice to missus, and I knows what it is not to have a friend in the world to look arter you."

Grace slid the shilling with which she had intended to reward Becky's civility and evident wish to oblige, back again into her purse, and substituted half a crown.

"I'd rather miss, if you please, that you'd keep it," said Becky, retreating; if you likes to give me a cap, or an apern, or anything of that sort, I shall thank you kindly; but missus takes all my *wails*, she says she lays 'em out in clothes for me, but I've a hard matter to get a pair of shoes out of her once in a half year, let alone other things, which I never have, only what the lodgers are kind enough to give me. Oh, Gemini, if there isn't missus raving like a mad woman, I suppose she thought I'd gone down before, and has just missed me. How I shall catch it !" and Becky, without waiting for farther observation from Grace, clattered down stairs, leaving the latter standing alone in the middle of her desolate-looking room.

It was not of herself, however, that Grace thought, as she seated herself on one of the chairs, her eyes still dwelling on the shabby bedstead, the paltry patchwork counterpane, and the dingy-looking blankets to which Becky had pointed. It was of the delicately reared, perhaps nobly born female, who, amid strangers even to her language, and still more strangers to her feelings, had there watched over the death-bed of her child, the last remaining link between her and perhaps the husband of her love, the all that was left her to hope for and to cherish; and then, when that last blossom was blighted, laying herself down and patiently waiting God's own time when she would be permitted to follow it. And she was young too, and beautiful, and accomplished. How she must have shrunk with disgust from the people whose paltry spirits could induce them to insult her, even by depriving her of the wretched comforts such a place afforded ! How in the long dreary winters she passed here, deprived of every comfort, must she have looked back with sickness of heart, and longing for her own warm genial climate, its bright cloudless days, and splendid moonlight nights, while all around her was now cold, and gloom, and darkness !

"And shall I then murmur at being obliged to make this my resting-place ?" thought Grace. "No, let me learn patience and humility from her example, who had much less right than I to expect such a lot."

THE PRIDE OF THE VILLAGE;

OR,

THE FARMER'S DAUGHTERS.

CHAPTER XVIII.

" Oh, there are some
Can trifle in cold vanity will all
The warm soul's precious throbs—to whom it is
A triumph, that a fond and devoted heart
Is breaking for them."

—L. E. L.

FOR the first two or three days of their residence in Bath, Mrs. Woodford and Maria were delighted with all they beheld the weather was beautiful the streets were thronged with fashionables, and not unobserved or undich valued by either mother or daughter, was the notice and admiration wher the latter excited. Even Mrs. Woodford's infirmities were less felt, and less painful than ever, for she beheld many among the rich, the great, and

9

apparently even the gay, who might have been glad to exchange situations even with her; but the novelty faded, the admiration went no further than looks, or at most, an audible whisper, which always terminated with "Who are they?" and both mother and daughter began to feel it tiresome to be thus perpetually in a crowd, without recognizing a single face that they could claim the most distant acquaintance with, or who even seemed to take the slightest interest in them, except honouring them with a stare, and not unfrequently a smile of derision at the singular discrepancy which Mrs. Woodford's habiliments and person exhibited.

Maria's natural good taste and personal beauty rendered her appearance, though considerably far behind the reigning fashions, sufficiently becoming not to create ridicule; but it was not so with her mother, who was never satisfied unless she was loaded with finery, and whose petite and deformed person was thus rendered ten times more conspicuous, as she slowly paraded the promenades, or tottered to a seat amidst the smiles of most, and the pitying looks of others.

"We want somebody to introduce us properly, my dear," she observed, when, after a week's dull round they found themselves still in the same situation—still isolated amidst a crowd who were now become too familiarised with their appearance to bestow even a look of curiosity on the odd-looking little woman and the beautiful girl who had at first excited so much. It was true that Maria seldom met a glance from the gentlemen which did not express admiration; but it went no further than glances, for her demeanour was too modest to encourage levity, and even had that not been sufficient to repel assurance, she had always her mother at her side.

And where, all this time, was their stage-coach acquaintance? He had called, as was before mentioned, on the day following their arrival at the hotel, had chatted away nearly two hours with Grace, who had found him, as she told her sister, a very pleasant, kind-hearted young man, and had heard with very sincere satisfaction that he meant, with Mrs. Woodford's permission, to be a frequent visitor during his stay in Bath.

He had announced himself too, as Captain Frederick, a distant relative of Lord Melverly, and had, with apparent sincerity and candour, assured Grace that he should be most happy to render them any services which as strangers they might require. But more than all this, he had spoken in such terms of her sister, that Grace, in the innocence of her heart, believed him actuated by the best and purest principles.

Maria's beauty, he observed, in such a place as Bath could not fail to attract a number of admirers; but he hoped and trusted Mrs. Woodford would be extremely cautious in forming acquaintances, since, perhaps, in no place in the whole world were there collected so many reckless, heartless, profligates: men, indeed, of rank and fashion, but totally destitute of feeling and principle, and who would laugh at and triumph in the destruction and degradation of beauty and innocence.

"He has talked to me," said the artless Grace, in repeating their conversation to her mother and sister, "just as a kind brother, or long-tried friend would, and I am sure I felt as much at my ease with him as if I had known him for years, instead of only the day before yesterday."

In spite, however, of all these promises and professions, Captain Frederick, for one whole, long, and tedious week, never visited them in their new lodging. Several times, indeed, Maria in her promenades with her mother, had caught a distant view of him, but it was always in company with two ladies and a gentleman, and he had always appeared to be in such earnest conversation, that he could not see his stage-coach acquaintance.

Once, indeed, they had met face to face in one of the libraries to which they had subscribed, having learned from their landlady, that it was fashionable to do so, and Mrs. Woodford still retaining her old predilection for novel-reading; and then Captain Frederick, finding it impossible to shun them, had vouchsafed to bestow a distant bow, and a more familiar smile on them; but this had rather mortified than pleased either Maria or her mother; the ladies whom he accompanied were remarkably plainly dressed, and unassuming in their manners; the gentleman was absolutely a shabby-looking, old-fashioned fright, to use Maria's own terms in describing the party, and why he should think it necessary to look strange and take airs in such company, they (Maria and her mother) could not possibly imagine.

"I am sure," observed Maria, "he need not have been ashamed to own us, for all the ladies had on was not worth so much as my Leghorn bonnet. By-the-bye, mamma, did you see how the young lady turned away from the young man behind the counter, when he wanted her to look at the beautiful earrings that we are to raffle for to-morrow. I suppose she wanted to pretend to be above such things, but I rather suspect the truth is they are above her."

"I am sure her gingham gown never cost above a shilling a yard," replied Mrs. Woodford; and as to that great straw bonnet that hides her face, so that I declare I hardly know now whether she was a black or a white, it would be dear at seven shillings."

"And yet, mamma," said Grace, who had, on this occasion, for the first time been of their party; "from the manner of the shopman, as well as that of several persons whom I saw bow to her, I cannot help thinking that she is of some consequence; and as to her face, I caught a full view of it, when she turned suddenly round to give some money to that poor woman, who stood at the door with a poor sick child in her arms, and I thought I never saw such a sweet beautiful countenance in my life."

"Oh! you are a judge of beauty, I dare say," retorted Mrs. Woodford contemptuously; and by-the-bye, Miss Grace, it was very impertinent of you to step back and give that beggar woman something, but I suppose you thought it pretty to imitate your lady of consequence."

Grace did not reply, as she might with truth have done, that so far from imitating, she had been the first to notice the poor woman and unostentatiously, and as she imagined unobserved, had stolen back to slip a sixpence into her hand, with a gentle half-murmured wish that she had it in her power ——

"God in heaven prosper you, young lady, and grant that you may never know the want of it," had been the exclamation of the woman on receiving it, and the tone in which this benediction was uttered, whether true or false, had roused, it appeared, the feelings of the young lady, who had been the subject of Mrs. Woolford's disquisition, and she had, after glancing on Grace's blushing face a look of kindness and sympathy, turned back and added something to her gift, which had sent the poor woman away, evidently astonished and overwhelmed with pleasurable surprise.

More than once, in the course of the two or three following days, some ill-natured remark on the part of Mrs. Woodford, or expression of mortification on that of Maria, recalled to Grace what she would otherwise probably have forgotten—the meeting with Captain Frederick and his friends; and she was compelled to own that she had been hasty in forming so strong a predilection in his favour, for that, certainly, his conduct did not at all correspond with his very warm asseverations of friendship and respect for Mrs. Woodford and her family.

"It is not that I valued him a bit," said Mrs. Woodford, one evening, after having, as usual, made his extraordinary neglect of them the subject of a thousand animadversions ; "for, after all, what is he ? Some poor relation, no doubt, of the Melverly family, and as to his captaincy, we all know captain is a fine travelling title, and it's ten to one if he's more than an ensign or a lieutenant at most ; but even if he's a captain, he would be no great catch, for they can none of them manage to live on their pay, and can have very little to spare for a wife."

"And yet, mamma, Captain Barnet's lady, that was down at Llan—— all last summer, made a great dash," observed Maria ; "and wore very expensive dresses, you know."

"Yes ! but she had a private fortune, child, or she could not have done it. No, no, depend upon it, no woman could live upon her husband's pay as an officer ; and so, if Captain Frederick, as he calls himself, has nothing more, he's quite in the right of it not to think of marrying."

"And yet," thought Grace, "I would wager my life he does think of marrying, and has chosen his wife too, and that sweet beautiful young lady that hung so familiarly on his arm is destined to bear that title, or I am much mistaken."

Aware that such an observation would only draw from her mother some ill-natured remark, Grace, however firmly convinced in her mind of the fact, suppressed her thoughts, and she felt doubly glad that she had done so when, some days after, Captain Frederick, having first sent up his name, followed the maid-servant into the room, before Mrs. Woodford had time to say whether she chose to be visible to him or not.

A whole torrent of surprises, reproaches, insinuations, and affected resentment on the part of Maria and Mrs. Woodford was listened to with patience and pretended sorrow on the part of the gentleman ; but Grace, who was perfectly silent, though she had replied to his greeting with as much freedom and kindness as ever, read in his countenance that he was far better pleased with this reception than he would have been with a more quiet and indifferent one.

"I plead guilty," he at length observed with a smile, "to the charge of having designedly avoided you, but my motives were anything but disrespectful to you ; the fact is, my dear madame," addressing Mrs. Woodford, "the two ladies you have seen me with are my aunt and cousin, the gentleman I have the honour to call my uncle, and three more tiresome bores never existed. My aunt is a bigoted Methodist, and she has made as great a fool of her pretty little daughter as herself. Their whole and sole aim here is to make converts, and had I yielded to my own inclination and made you acquainted with each other, the consequence would have been that you would have been bored to death as I have been with their fanatic nonsense ; but, thank goodness, I am at last rid of them, they have gone off to Devonshire to-day, and the moment I was free I have hastened to you."

Maria did not seek to dive very deep into the truth of Captain Frederick's motives ; his present avowed devotion soon effaced all past mortifications : "he was henceforth wholly devoted to their service," he said, and as a proof of it, he had brought tickets of admission for the theatre for that very night, and requested to be allowed to escort them there.

Mrs. Woodford was in raptures ; at last, her Maria was in a fair way to be introduced to the world, and as she accepted his offer, she acknowledged that he had quite made the *amende honorable* for what she had prematurely considered his unpardonable neglect.

Much as Grace still inwardly grieved at the alteration which had taken place in her situation, unhappy and desponding as she felt, whenever—and in justice to her it must be said that whenever was nearly every moment of the day—that she thought of Belgrave, ashamed and distressed as she was, when she recalled to her mind the circumstances attendant on her mother's departure from Llan——, melancholy as these causes combined could and did make her, still Grace was but a girl, naturally lively and fond of pleasure, and as such it could not be surprising that she heard with an emotion of pleasurable surprise Captain Frederick's proposal to accompany them all to the theatre. She had never but once witnessed anything approaching to a theatrical representation, and that was, malgré ... deficiencies of scenery, machinery, dresses, and decorations, so interesting to her that she had often, when listening to Belgrave Mansell's description of the wonders he had beheld at the Bristol theatre, when he had accompanied his uncle there, and in faint imitation of which William himself and some other young men of the town had once got up in their barn the tragedy of "Douglas," Belgrave having himself enacted the part of Lady Randolph, and William Anna, because not a female was to be found who had confidence or talents to take a share in their diversion. Ever since that memorable evening, as has been beforesaid, Grace had indulged the wish to behold a theatrical representation, with all those advantages of which Belgrave had spoken, and her little heart bounded now at the thought, though the next moment her eyes filled with tears at the recollection that he who had so often described to her the splendour and illusions which had appeared to him so perfect was no longer near to behold it with her, and partake her pleasure.

To Maria it was an epoch which seemed to be of the utmost importance to her future life—alas! how little did she dream that, in reality, it would decide what the tenour of that life was to be!—and some hours were spent in dressing for this momentous appearance, which, in both Maria and Mrs. Woodford's estimation, was not of less consequence than that of a first-rate beauty in the court circle. During all this arduous task, in which Grace, not without many secret sighs at the meanness and frivolity which even filial duty could not blind her to in her mother, had been most actively and usefully employed, not one word had been said as to her (Grace's) own appearance; and when at length she timidly inquired whether she should now go and change her frock, Mrs. Woodford's look of astonishment, whether real or affected, at once bespoke what her words speedily confirmed, viz., that she had never for a moment thought of Grace, and that it was now too late to commence the task of dressing.

"It wants but five minutes of the time Captain Frederick appointed," she observed, "and, of course, we cannot keep him waiting. But, what in the world can you have been thinking of, Grace, to leave till this time —— but, no matter, you can go another night; this will not, of course, be the only time we shall visit the theatre. And, besides, I don't at all like trusting Jane (the servant their landlady had recommended them) to sit up alone for us; she looks stupid and sleepy, and if she was to fall asleep she might set fire to herself and the place; so it will be better you should stay at home, and then you can finish altering Maria's pelisse, in case she should want to wear it to-morrow.

Grace, perhaps, had never felt more keenly than at that moment the immeasurable distance which existed in her mother's heart between herself and her sister. She looked at the latter, for the thousandth time surveying herself in the mirror, smiling in anticipation of approaching pleasure, and triumphing in the consciousness of being at last enabled to display to the utmost advantage, that beauty which she had been taught to consider so inestimable. But Maria was too much absorbed to bestow even a thought on her (Grace's) disappointment; and when, at length, she did turn from the glass, and caught a glimpse of Grace's mournful features, conceiving only that it arose from the disappointment the latter felt at not being of the party she exclaimed——

"My dear Grace, how sorry I am, and this is the first time, too, that ever I saw you anxious about pleasure."

"I am not anxious now, Maria," returned Grace in a grave tone; "a few minutes ago, indeed, I acknowledged, I anticipated an evening's agreeable entertainment, but now——

She cast down her eyes and her voice faltered.

"Now, miss!" repeated Mrs. Woodford sharply; "and, pray, what has happened now, to make you think otherwise?"

"Nothing has happened, mamma," replied Grace with emotion; "but my feelings are changed, and I would not now go if it were in my power."

" I understand all this, perfectly well, Grace," observed Mrs. Woodford, after surveying her, for some moments, in silence; "it all arises from a mean jealousy of your sister: this is not the first time I have seen it; but let me advise you not to give way to it, for it can only serve to make you miserable."

Without waiting for a reply, she turned to Maria, and again commenced her survey of her, turning her round and round, to see that every plait of her dress was properly disposed, and nothing omitted which could heighten her beauty, and totally regardless of the feelings which swelled Grace's bosom almost to suffocation at this undeserved and cruel reproof.

Grace jealous of Maria's beauty!—she who had patiently employed three long hours in assisting her to set off that beauty to the greatest advantage, who had arranged and re-arranged her ringlets and her flowers, clasped her necklaces and bracelets, and brought forth her own little stock of ornaments for Maria to try whether there was any of them she liked better than her own, and had without a murmur submitted when the capricious beauty, after being once completely dressed, and as even, Mrs. Woodford allowed, never to greater advantage, had suddenly torn off the coronet of flowers, pulled the combs out of her hair, and shaking loose all the ringlets and bandeaux which, in compliance with her taste, Grace had formed, declared it was frightful altogether, and she would have it all done over again!

Even the partial mother had loudly exclaimed against her caprice, and declared it was a shameful waste of time and trouble; yet Grace had not only borne all with a smile, but had instantly commenced again combing, brushing, and forming, round her pliant fingers, the long glossy ringlets which had been thus deranged, without a single word of reproof, but, on the contrary, agreeing with her sister, that, although she looked well, still it was not exactly the most becoming style to her features.

"She would look well any how," said the doating mother, gazing, with a ook of approval, on her daughter's beautiful face.

"Yes," replied Grace; "and in my opinion, never so well as totally nadorned. Look, mamma, now at her; if it was but the fashion to wear the hair loose, hanging over the shoulders in such curls as these, would she not look better than ever?"

And she was accused of mean jealousy! Grace turned one look upon her sister; but Maria was again absorbed in the alteration of her sash, which she had now decided looked most graceful fastened at the side.

"Do, Grace, just tie it for me; nobody can tie a bow so well as you."

Grace laid down the work which she had taken up to hide the emotion which her mother's observation had created, and, without uttering a single word, obeyed her sister's request; and, at that moment, Captain Frederick was announced as awaiting them in the drawing-room.

"You need not come down, Grace," observed Mrs. Woodford hastily; " I will make a proper apology to him for your not going, though I don't suppose it will be any great disappointment to him, unless, indeed, he is inclined to be a second Sir Walter, and fancy you into a beauty.

"God bless you, Grace," said Maria, tripping good-humouredly back into the room, and affectionately kissing her cheek. " I wish you were going with us; but never mind, do not be low-spirited, it is only for one evening that your pleasure is delayed. Good gracious! is it possible that you take it so seriously at heart, Grace!" she continued, as she beheld the tears, which Grace could no longer prevent flowing down her cheeks " I am sure I would rather stay at home altogether, than that you should fret about it."

"And is it possible, Maria, that you too so grossly mistake me as to suppose that I envy you the pleasure you are going to enjoy? or that it would at all reconcile me to the loss of it that you should be deprived of it too? No, no; you ought to know me better, though my mother is determined to believe me so base and little-minded; and again she wept as she recurred to her mother's cruel observation.

" She does not believe you any such thing, Grace. How can you be so foolish as to fret at anything mamma says? You know it is only a bad habit she has got into of saying sarcastic things at everybody's expense."

" Except yours, Maria," said Grace, emphatically. "But, do not again mistake my meaning; I do not envy you that you are beloved by your mother, but I do lament that I have no portion of that love. But, do not let me detain you, dear Maria; this is no new theme of sorrow to me, and, unfortunately, there will be opportunities enough for me to speak of it, if, indeed, it would not be wiser and better to bury it in oblivion."

"I shall talk to mamma about her injustice," said Maria, thoughtfully, as if it had but just occurred to herself that Grace had a right to complain of the preference shown; and, repeating her affectionate good-bye, she hastened to join her mother and her companion, and, in a few minutes, Grace heard the coach which had been sent for drive from the door.

Never, perhaps, in her life, had Grace passed so dull and utterly comfortless an evening as this; the noise of rain beating heavily against the windows was only interrupted by the click of pattens on the pavement, and occasionally the heavy lumbering of a coach or cart, of which but few passed down the narrow, unfrequented street they inhabited. It was cold and chilly, too; but she could not have a fire, for her mother would have perhaps considered it useless luxury. The task of completing Maria's pelisse, which Mrs. Woodford had so unfeelingly extorted, prevented her for a moment beguiling her melancholy thoughts with a book, though a new novel of Miss Edgeworth's which Captain Frederick had recommended was temptingly placed on the table before her; but Grace soon forgot the novel, though she had glanced through the two or three first pages, and found in them a strong incentive to go on; and mechanically she continued for hours to ply her needle, for her thoughts were busy with past scenes, and the present were forgotten.

What soothing recollections throng,
Presenting many a mournful token,
That heart's remembrance to prolong,
Which then was blest, but now is broken.

The coach stopping at the door, gay voices speaking, and light footsteps ascending the stairs, aroused her from her dream; and before she could gather up her work or light the second candle, which in obedience to her mother's instructions, stood ready to be kindled on the table, Maria her face radiant with pleasure, and accompanied, not by Captain Frederick, but a stranger equally handsome, fashionable, and captivating entered the room.

"It is only my sister, Mr. Grant," said the former, as the stranger drew back and respectfully made room for Grace to pass with her bundle of work, into the next room.

"Do not run away, Grace," she continued, "mamma is coming up, and Captain Frederick, but she is rather slow. Do pray be seated," and she pointed to a chair, to the gentleman she called Mr. Grant, who was still standing gazing at Grace, whose usually pale cheek was now lighted up with a deep glow, at being thus surprised in a confusion and litter, as her mother would have termed it, and which would not have failed, she knew, to have called forth the severest reprehension of the latter.

"I cannot consent to sit down, if I am to be the means of disturbing your sister," said the stranger, still keeping his eyes fixed on Grace, who, having hastily thrown her work into the adjoining room, ran back to gather up her thread, silk, &c., from the table.

"Oh, no, Grace will sit down with us directly," returned Maria; "only mamma is a little particular, and she is afraid of being scolded for littering the drawing-room."

Mr. Grant threw a look round the room as he repeated,

"Scolded! heaven forbid that any one should think of scolding such a gentle timid being;" but Grace, though she saw the look, and felt her cheeks burn still more painfully at the derision it conveyed, of the elegant apartment, which was thus pompously designated, did not hear the accompanying words, for she had—somewhat alarmed at her mother's remaining so long in the cold passage below—run down to meet her.

Mrs. Woodford, however, was ascending the stairs, leaning on Jane, the new servant, and pausing at every step, to give her some directions, from which Grace learned that the two gentlemen intended staying to sup with them.

"Grace, do you go down and see that everything is sent up properly," she observed, the moment she beheld her anxious daughter.

"There is nothing, ma'am, but the bone of the leg of mutton left," said Jane, earnestly; "downstairs, and the pie you have locked up in your cupboard."

"You need not mind about supper, Grace," said Mrs. Woodford, without noticing her servant's pert observations; "only see that a clean table-cloth, and knives and forks, and every thing proper is put in the tray, the rest will be brought presently."

A loud knock at the door, now announced the arrival of Captain Frederick, and while Jane at her mistress's desire, ran down to let him in, the latter whispered to Grace.

"Our fortunes are made, Grace, Captain Frederick is desperately in love with your sister, and his cousin, Mr. Grant, who we met with to-night ———"

Captain Frederick ran hastily up the stairs, and prevented the conclusion of her communication, which, far from producing as she seemed to expect, a correspondent pleasure to that which danced in her own eyes, had only the effect of rendering Grace more confused, uneasy, and embarrassed.

"Surely—surely these men will penetrate my mother's intentions and we shall all become the subjects of their ridicule," she thought to herself, as she proceeded to the kitchen, to superintend the sleepy and more than half reluctant Jane, who, by no means relished the additional work of waiting upon the supper-table, after having, as she grumbled more than once, " been slaving like a horse at the wash tub all day."

" Missus told me, she kept very little company," she observed, " when she hired me—but this don't look like it, bringing home gentlemen to supper at this time o'night, to keep poor servants out of their beds ; and how it looks Miss Grace, to see Missus and Miss Maria stuck up, and over flowers, and lace, and ribbon, and you with nothing but that plain muslin frock ; I never see such a difference made between children in my life, and I wonder how you can bear it. I wonder what the gentlemen can think.

" I care nothing what any one thinks, Jane," replied Grace ; " I am perfectly contented——"

" Oh, no, miss ; don't say that, for as I was saying to the young man that lodges in the front attic——"

" I hope you do not make me the subject of your conversation, Jane, with the young man in the front attic ;" interrupted Grace, hastily ; " but come, carry the tray up, and lay the cloth, and I will remain here, and attend to the door, if the person comes with the supper, whatever it is."

Grace, however, was not a little surprised and confounded when, a few minutes after, in obedience to her promise, she answered the summons at the street door, and beheld no less than three persons loaded with every delicacy that could be procured at so short a notice, and learned that there was yet another to come with wine.

Could it be possible that her mother was so infatuated with her imaginary prospects for her daughter as to have thus expended in luxurious indulgence for two or three hours a sum which would have been sufficient, with economy, to have provided for her family for a month. There was, indeed, another thought came over her mind, as she gazed with wonder at the cold fowl, ham, lobsters, tongue, jellies, tarts, salad, &c., &c.—another thought which might account for the profusion and extravagance, but it was too degrading, and Grace devoutly prayed it might not be so.

All suspense, however, was soon at an end.

" Mercy ! Captain Frederick," exclaimed Mrs. Woodford, approaching the supper-table, having, during its preparation, affected to be totally indifferent to it, and wholly occupied in conversation with her visitors. " Mercy, what an extravagant man you are ! who would ever have thought of your ordering such a supper ? I thought, to be sure, you were only going to send in a lobster or something of that sort to make up with my cold leg of mutton, or I should have put a stop to it, I assure you ; why here's a supper fit for a prince."

" A prince might think himself honoured to partake of it in such society," returned Captain Frederick, looking at Maria significantly.

" Well, I am sure, you are polite," returned Mrs. Woodford, whose spirits seemed exhilarated beyond all prudence ; " but I really don't know how I shall ever make you amends, for putting you to so much trouble. Maria, my dear, you take this seat, and Captain Frederick will sit next to you ; Mr. Grant, will you honour me by taking this chair at my left hand."

Mr. Grant's eyes had, until this moment, been fixed on Grace's deeply glowing and expressive countenance ; he had marked the deep flush of vexation, and the start of surprise, which she could not control, at hearing her worst fears thus confirmed, and he seemed totally absorbed in endeavouring to penetrate the meaning of this emotion.

The mention of his name by Mrs. Woodford, recalled his recollection to what was passing, and he was about to seat himself in the chair she pointed to, when he saw that Grace was still standing, looking irresolutely at her mother, as if doubtful whether she was expected to sit down, or whether she was at liberty to withdraw.

"Miss Woodford, I beg your pardon," he observed eagerly; "you are not seated, pray ———"

"Oh, Grace will sit anywhere, Mr. Grant," said Mrs. Woodford, hastily; "pray do not give yourself any trouble about her; sit down where you are, child, and then you can make yourself useful, without incommoding anyone."

Grace complied with this mandate, though her eyes involuntarily filled with tears. What would the strangers think of her, to see so striking a distinction made between her and her sister? She dared not glance towards either of them, but in silence seated herself where her mother had indicated. The supper passed off very gaily, the gentlemen were both pleasant, well-educated men; but poor Grace felt more than once ready to sink with confusion as her quick eye detected the significant smile which was frequently interchanged between them at Mrs. Woodford's assumption and ignorant garrulity, especially on the subject of the play they had seen, and those she had witnessed in her youth in the country.

She thought nothing at all, she observed, of what they had seen to-night, the "School for Scandal" and the "Padlock." For her part, she liked nothing but deep tragedy, such as Shakespeare's "Douglas" and "Alexander the Great," for she would not give a pin to see a play where the people were only such as one could see every day in the streets, and walked about and talked just like one's-self; and as to singing, she liked nothing but Italian songs.

"Do you understand Italian, madame?" inquired Mr. Grant.

"Very little," she replied, with an affected toss of the head; "but my music master was an Italian, and after hearing him I could never bear English songs."

Grace's eyes were fixed more firmly than ever on the table-cloth. She felt, though she could not see, that their guests were laughing at her mother; and she felt too, most acutely, that her mother deserved to be laughed at.

The wine raised Mrs. Woodford's spirits still higher, and dissipated the slight bashfulness and constraint, which had prevented Maria's taking any very prominent part in the conversation, and Grace soon had reason to blush, as much for her sister's folly and flippancy, as she had previously done for her mother's. Grace, indeed, of the whole party, was the only one who remained totally unaltered, but she resolutely and positively declined to taste a second glass of wine; the first she took in obedience to her mother's command, who, seeing her hesitate, when Mr. Grant requested to have the pleasure of taking wine with her, abruptly desired her not to make a fool of herself, but to thank Mr. Grant for the honour he did her.

Not even her mother's commands could prevail on her the second time. She was in agonies at all she saw and all she heard, for Captain Frederick was now, in accents sufficiently audible to meet her attentive ear, from time to time, addressing the most ardent declarations of eternal love to Maria, while his friend took every opportunity, which her reserve would allow, of assuring her, Grace, how greatly he admired her; and there was something in the manner of both the gentlemen which to her sensitive mind conveyed anything but respect. Respect! how can they feel respect for the daughters of one who takes such infinite pains to convince them that she is undeserving of respect, thought Grace; but the next moment, she reproached herself for the idea, for she looked up, and beheld her mother's eyes fixed on Maria, with a look of the most doating fondness, and the recollection that after all it was her affection for her favourite child, and her hope of seeing her aggrandized, seemed sufficient to the kind-hearted Grace to excuse her every folly.

Hour after hour passed away, and the gentlemen's hilarity became still more unbridled, though even Mrs. Woodford had been at last so far awakened to the imprudence she had been guilty of as gradually to sink from the most unbounded familiarity and ease to comparative reserve and silence. Grace was still, as she had been from the beginning, distant, cold, and utterly impenetrable to all Mr. Grant's flattery and hyperbolical compliments; but Maria, unsuspicious, giddy, and innocent of any intentional evil, was still all liveliness, chat, and frivolity. Grace was upon thorns—more than once she ventured to hint that the morning was far advanced, and that they were unaccustomed to such late hours; but Captain Frederick replied by gaily singing,

> "What have we with time to do?
> Sons of Care, 'twas made for you."

And Maria so loudly applauded this sentiment, that Mrs. Woodford seemed to be unable to enforce what the uneasiness and gravity of her countenance betrayed her understanding suggested, that it was quite time to separate. The sun had long risen before the visitors could, as they said, tear themselves away, and Grace, miserable, dejected, anticipating evil, to which she could give neither shape nor make, retired to her gloomy chamber, without remaining to hear the remarks which Maria eagerly began on the subject of their evening's amusement and companions.

"Laws a mercy, Miss Grace, what be you just come to bed?" said Jane, raising her head to look at the latter, as she softly stole into the room hoping to retire without any remarks from their garrulous handmaiden, whose manner and observations were very little to her liking at any time, and had been on the preceding evening particularly offensive.

Jane had herself been dismissed to bed the moment she had cleared the supper-table, and her having had two or three hours' sleep, together with the brightness of the sunbeam, which for a few minutes at this early hour, found its way into the room, made it appear to her even later than it was.

"Well," she continued, turning herself about; "it's fine to be gentlefolks, for they can do any thing, and nobody must think no harm, much less speak it; but if it was poor folks who set up all night with strange men, and let 'em treat 'em with supper, and wine and that, Lord they'd be every thing that's bad, and their characters gone for ever; but I s'pose its all right, and I'm sure it's none of my business, if missus like it if she sets up every night, so as she don't keep me up, for I'm a very bad un at late hours."

Grace continued silent; she had no disposition to enter into any justification or explanation with this malicious and ignorant being, and having grumbled a little longer, and wondered what the landlady would say to such racketty doings, Jane again fell asleep.

Fatigued and wearied as she was, however, Grace found it impossible to follow her example.

What would be the end of the rash imprudent course her mother was pursuing? must it not end in ruin and disgrace? were questions that she perpetually asked herself. That Captain Frederick entertained one serious thought of making her sister his wife she had not a hope, for if he had would he not have been anxious to screen her, who would henceforth become so nearly allied to himself as Mrs. Woodford would be, should such an event take place? And on the contrary, how many times had she, Grace, detected him leading her on by sly and apparently deferential questions to expose her vanity and ignorance; even Maria, with all his warmth of admiration and passionate asseverations of love, had not escaped his propensity to ridi-cule, and more than once Grace's calm severe glance had disconcerted him, and convinced her by his confusion that there was no sincerity in his pro-fessions. But, allowing that he meant all her mother took it for granted he did mean, who was Captain Frederick? what did they know of his family, his character, or even his means to support her sister as her mother ex-pected?

And besides, said Grace to herself, when thus recalling every circum-stance to her mind—even granting that his fortune, his disposition, every thing could accord with my mother's wishes, he will not expect that in marrying my sister he is to marry all her family, and to be charged not only with a portionless wife, but a mother and sister little better than beggars, and even if he was willing, could I bear to live a mean dependent on such a man, or indeed any man? No, sooner would I earn my living by any means, however humble; and my poor mother too, miserable, in-deed, would be her situation, to be dependent on one, who even now, when it is his wish to conciliate and please her, cannot conceal that he despises her.

For long after Grace had laid her head on her pillow, did these and similar thoughts continue to keep her from repose; but tired nature at length asserted its power, and she slept soundly, till awakened by the sound of Jane's voice close to her ear.

"Laws, Miss Grace, do'ee get up and come down," she exclaimed; "for there be a country chap of a boy downstairs, has got a letter for missus, for I read the direction; but I can't get a word out of him good or bad, and in-deed, it is my opinion he cannot speak, or else he don't know no English, and he won't give the letter to me."

Grace was up and dressed in a few minutes, for she instantly recognized in the description of the body the son of the man who had been her mother's confidant in quitting the farm; and the expectation of learning some intelligence of the place and friends she feared she had beheld for the last time, speedily banished all feeling of fatigue from the revels of the preced-ing evening.

It was indeed "Dummy," as he was usually called among the country people, who awaited her appearance, and it might have been doubted whose countenance expressed the most joy, Grace's or his, when she descended the stairs, at the bottom of which he was waiting.

To every living being about the farm Grace had been endeared by the gentleness of her disposition, the sweetness of her manners, and the warmth of sensibility which made her constantly the friend and advocate of all who needed her services; but, perhaps, among them all, none had ever been so devotedly attached to her as the poor lad who now stood before her. and whose irremediable affliction had made him the object of her constant attention and care.

Poor Joe, indeed, could scarcely have explained, had the power been given him, why he followed, and worshipped, and watched the eyes of his divinity, to anticipate her meaning; for nature, contrary to her usual bene-ficence, which generally induces her, when there is a deficiency in one sense, to compensate for it, in some measure, by extraordinary acuteness in another, had scarcely bestowed a common measure of understanding on this her neglected child. But what he wanted in sense, he possessed in feeling; and of this he now gave a forcible testimony, by breaking into a loud blubber the moment he beheld Grace, and then capering round and round her, until her lifted finger, the check which he never disregarded, silenced him, and he stood stock-still, until Grace, by signs, inquired if he had not brought something for her.

Thus recalled to the consciousness of the purport of his errand, Joe drew from the crown of his hat a letter, which she with difficulty deciphered as addressed to her mother; and then squatting himself down on the ground at her feet, he seemed to be disposing himself to take a rest till he received her answer and his dismissal.

"You must take him down in the kitchen, and make him some breakfast, Jane," observed Grace, "while I go and awaken my mother, for this letter may be of importance."

"I am sure, miss, I can't never think of taking such a creter down-stairs where the landlord and his wife are at their breakfast," replied the flippant Jane. "If it was all to ourselves, it would be a different thing; but——"

" That is enough; I do not wish to incommode anybody; Joe shall go up stairs," said Grace; and without farther ceremony, she beckoned the urchin to follow her; and. grinning from ear to ear, and hastily slipping off his heavy-nailed shoes, he complied with the sign.

The task of getting her own breakfast, and of discussing with the land-lord and landlady the events of the preceding night, had so fully occupied Jane's mind, that nothing had as yet been removed from the table in the sitting-room; and Joe's eyes expressed more surprise than Grace had thought it possible he could feel, at the scene of disorder which the room presented.

" Even this poor fellow," thought Grace, is enabled to contrast in his mind the difference between this mode of living, and our quiet, orderly regular life at the farm."

Joe's objections, however, if any existed, were speedily put to rest by the glass of wine Grace poured out for him. His eyes sparkled, as he made signs to her that it was very good, and the accompaniment of some sweet cakes set him again capering, till Grace's well-known and obeyed signal rendered him once more tranquil; and she left him to carry the im-portant letter to her mother.

"What can the man be thinking of?" said Mrs. Woodford, when she raised her head from the pillow, and thoroughly comprehended who the messenger was who had been thus singularly chosen instead of the regular post. "Do open the letter, child; and let us see what the fool has found of so much importance to write about."

With trembling fingers, Grace obeyed her orders, for she anticipated that something must have happened of more than usual importance to warrant Owen's having despatched a special messenger.

The first part of the letter, however, was filled with insignificant details of the surprise which had been expressed by the inhabitants of Llan—— at discovering that the family at Rose Farm had "run away," and his own dexterous concealment of the part he had taken in the transaction, which, however, had not, it appeared, kept him clear of suspicion.

"After all," he continued, though I swore, through thick and thin, that I knew nothing in the world about you, nor where you was gone, nor how you got away, nor nothing else, nobody believes me, and so I'm like to pay pretty dear for what I got by the job, for nobody won't hear of taking me into their employ here, and old Mr. Meredith threatens that he'll take care my character shan't get me a place in the county of Wales without I tell the truth.   Poor Mr. William, his nephew, indeed, though he's gone quite distracted and melancholy, and has never looked to his farm, or seemed to care what become of himself ever since, says that he don't blame me for being faithful to my mistress; he wished everybody kept their promises, and he shouldn't be so wretched; and then he, sometimes, when he meets me, slips a shilling or so in my hand: but you, know, mistress, that will not provide for my family, and so I must be obligated to do the best I can for myself.   Now, the long and short of the matter is, that I've got the offer to go out, with Squire Shepherd, to America, and it's his footman that writes this letter to acquaint you of the same.   But the squire, though he's ready and willing to take out my wife and the young ones, because they'll be useful to him in the great farm that he's going to in America, yet he won't anyhow hear of paying for Joe, especially because none of the servants like to have him among them, and the lady's maid will have it that he knows more than he ought, because he contrived to tell something he saw of her to my wife.   Now, there's another reason why I can't think of taking Joe; and that is, that not being my wife's own child, they don't at all agree, and that makes me very uncomforatble at times."

"What is all this to me?" interrupted Mrs. Woodford, impatiently; "what have I to do with Joe?   Do, for goodness sake, child, pass all that over, and see what it is that he has sent about."

"I can see very little but what concerns Joe," replied Grace hesitatingly, after having cast her eye over the remainder of the letter, and evidently, by her change of colour, met with some intelligence not of the most agreeable nature.

"What can the wretch mean, then?" exclaimed her mother; "but read it on, in your own way, and perhaps, I shall be able to understand it in the end."

"Too soon, I am afraid," mentally ejaculated Grace, as she proceeded with the letter.

"Now, I've been thinking whatever I should do with the boy; for, though he's willing and able to work, and as strong as I am, pretty near, he's no manner of use to them as can't understand him, or make him understand them.   And, so it came into my head, that you must want a boy, to clean knives, and the young ladies' shoes, and other matters, as Joe was used to do here; and as he would do anything in the world to be near miss Grace, I have thought I couldn't do better than send him to you, which I do this day, September 18th, by the carrier, from here to Bristol, who has promised to get him sent safely to Bath, to where you directed me in your letter to write."

"Merciful goodness!" exclaimed Mrs. Woodford; "sure he never has had the impudence to——why don't you speak, girl?—is that poor fool——"

"The boy is in the other room," said Grace, in confusion.

"Go, then, instantly, and turn him out into the street!" stormed Mrs. Woodford.   "Do you think I am going to be quietly imposed upon, in this outrageous manner, by that artful, designing wretch?   Go, I say, and bundle him down stairs at once, or I'll send you with him."

"My dear mother, you cannot surely, wish me to send the poor creature away, without a place to go!" said Grace; "and without power, either, of making himself understood by anybody!   And I have not finished reading the letter, either," she continued, eagerly referring again to it, in hopes that her mother's passion would have time to cool and she would retract her unfeeling order.

" Do, mamma, let us hear what else he has got to say, before you fly out so," said Maria, peevishly ; and Grace proceeded——

"As to his clothes, as you'll most likely be for putting him on a bit of livery, as I know you like everything stylish ; and Joe, for all he's so afflicted, is a smart-looking, tidy lad————"

"That is Squire Shepherd's footman's own impertinence," interrupted Maria, angrily ; "Owen would not be such a fool as to call that stupid-ooking, awkward, crooked-legged lout a tidy lad : but I haven't forgot that fellow's impudence. When first Squire Shepherd brought him from London, and before his livery was made, he imposed upon me, one evening as a gentleman, a stranger in the town ; and I was walking with him, when William Mansell came up, and whispered to me——

" ' So, Miss Maria, you have certainly now made an exchange to your advantage ; and you will have more reason to be proud of your companion when he has got his splendid white coat, silver lace, and scarlet velvet breeches, that are making for him at Tailor Pritchard's. ' "

"Merciful goodness ! and you had really suffered the fellow to walk by your side !" said Mrs. Woodford, in a tone of affected horror, "Dear, dear, Maria, how mortifying ! But, how did you get rid of him ?"

" Why, I directly took hold of William's arm, and said——

" Dear William, I'm so glad you are come, for this man is quite trouble-some, and I did not know how to get rid of him. The footman did not seem at all abashed, though I knew he heard all William said about him ; but he wanted to be free and familiar with William : but you know what a proud look and manner both Belgrave and William Mansell could put on at times ; so that, as I've often heard you say, anybody that didn't know what they were would have taken them to be real gentlemen : so he put on one of his very proudest looks, and said——

" ' You will excuse my telling you very plainly, sir, that Miss Woodford is in the habit, occasionally, of sitting as a guest at Mr. Shepherd's table, and cannot, therefore, with any consistency, associate with one who will be sufficiently honoured by standing behind her chair.' "

"Well that was glorious !" exclaimed Mrs. Woodford. "Poor William ; he certainly had a fine spirit, if his fortune and quality had been equal to it. But what did the fellow say ?"

"Oh, he was at first very impudent," returned Maria, " and gave William to understand that he thought himself quite as good, if not better than any country looby ; but William turned upon him with such a fierce look, observing, 'We will take another opportunity of settling that mat-ter, where we shall not annoy females,' that he was glad to sneak off ; and I don't know how William settled the matter afterwards, but he never ventured to speak to me again. But I've no doubt, as this letter is his writing, that he has taken this opportunity to have a sly fling at us."

"And perhaps, after all, it is him who has put Owen up to this scheme of getting this poor wretch off his hands, or at least to annoy me, by pretend-ing to throw him on mine ; but I shall soon convince him I am not so easily imposed on, and poor Dummy shall be packed off back again, the moment I have had my breakfast, and can ascertain the cheapest conveyance, for I suppose I shall be put to the expense of sending him."

"I am afraid," observed Grace, who had at her leisure finished reading the letter during the preceding conversation; "I am afraid," she re-peated timidly, and keeping her eyes fixed on the letter, "that it will be too late."

"Too late !" repeated Mrs. Woodford. "What does the girl mean ?"

"I mean," returned Grace, "that according to this letter, Mr. Shepherd and his people left Llan———— the very day after this was written, and that as poor Joe has been somehow five days on his journey, his father and the rest of them have already sailed for America."

"And do you then think that I shall keep this helpless animal?" demanded Mrs. Woodford, in a rage.

"I cannot pretend to judge, dear mother, what you can or will do; but I will, with your permission, read the rest of the letter."

"Do, pray, do so then, without any further comments," said her mother.

Grace could have replied that she had not as yet ventured a single comment upon the extraordinary communication which she was compelled to make, but she was accustomed to submit in silence, and she proceeded—

"I have not, therefore, burthened him with any clothes, as he'd be very apt to lose them by the way; not being up to the tricks that are played upon travellers. I hope you won't be angry at my not having consulted you first about this affair, but one good turn deserves another; and I having stood your friend and helped you off, setting aside the money I made for you, that should have been paid to your creditors, by selling the barley and oats at Cardigan Market."

"What is that?" exclaimed Mrs. Woodford with pretended surprise. "Surely the fellow has not the impudence to insinuate————"

Grace averted her blushing cheek, which burnt with shame at this exposure, and proceeded in a faltering voice, but with an evident determination to get to the end of this mortifying epistle.

"Besides many other little things that I could put you in mind of, but which I shall say nothing about, if so be that you show gratitude by taking care of the boy: but as a friend has put it in my head that out of sight is often out of mind, that when I'm clear out of the way, you may forget your obligations, I have got this to say, that I've left a true and particular account of all transactions and affairs in which I have been engaged with you, together with your direction in Bath, in the hands of a person sealed up, and should you prove ungrateful, it will be directly put into the hands of Mr. Meredith, and I'm told for certain that there's enough to transport you, seeing that the property was downright and *bonâ fide*, as Dawkins, the lawyer says, Mr. Meredith's, at the very time you was selling it, and so drawing in a poor man like me to what might some day have proved my ruin, if I had not got out of the way of it, which I take to be a very unfriendly act, and one which a lady ought to be ashamed of; however, I trust you will make it up by kindness to the poor lad, and so I rest your faithful servant to command,   OWEN WILLIAMS."

"The wretch, the vile, artful, ungrateful wretch," broke forth Mrs. Woodford, as Grace concluded; "and to dare to insinuate that I was concerned in taking away the produce of the farm, which I knew nothing about, though he certainly brought me a part of the money, pretending it was out of pure respect to me and my children; but what is that postscript, Grace, that you have been so long looking at without attempting to read it out."

"Nothing that concerns Owen or you, mother," faltered Grace, crushing the letter together in her hand.

"Let me read it, Grace," said Maria, observing for the first time her sister's trembling lips, pale cheeks, and universal agitation.

Grace resigned the letter, and leaning back, so as to shroud her face behind the bed curtains, by the side of which she was sitting, listened in breathless silence to the words which her clouded eyes had been scarcely able to decipher, though they conveyed to her intelligence even more painful, if possible, than that which the previous sentences had conveyed.

THE PRIDE OF THE VILLAGE;

OR,

THE FARMER'S DAUGHTERS.

GRACE VINDICATES HER CHARACTER.

CHAPTER XIX.

> The world will think with worldlings, but my heart
> Has still been in my duties, which are many,
> But never difficult.   —BYRON.

MARIA then proceeded to finish the letter, which went on to say :—

" I am very sorry to inform Miss Grace that there's no news at all of **Mr.**
Belgrave, and, after all, it's thought by many people that he won't ever
show himself again, for it's come out at last that Tyson's story of having
seen Sir Walter in Bristol was all false, or at least there's great reason to
think so, for Tyson has been taken up for robbing his master, Squire
Vaughan, and it's got wispered about that it was Sir Walter's coachman,

10.

who, you know, is Tyson's brother-in-law, that was with Tyson in Bristol instead of Sir Walter himself. Everybody is greatly surprised, because Tyson bore such a good character for many years, but he was given to drink, and that accounts for it. However it may turn out, things seem blacker than ever against Belgrave Mansell, and so there's no likelihood of his coming back; but if I should meet with him in America, as many say that he's gone there, I shall certainly tell him how much Miss Grace fretted after him, though I hope Bath will drive him from her memory with a good rich husband."

"There is not much probability of that, I am afraid," observed Mrs. Woodford, in a tone of vexation, and without taking the slightest notice or interest in Grace's very apparent emotion. "Rich husbands are not so easily got," she continued, "by those who have got so little to recommend them. I was very foolish and short-sighted, by the bye, to tell Mr. Grant so positively that she was engaged, for if Sir Walter is dead———"

Grace could bear it no longer, and without uttering a word she darted out of the room and ran swiftly up stairs to her own miserable apartment, where she threw herself on the bed and stifled the hysterical sobs, which in spite of every effort, broke from her overcharged heart.

An hour passed away and she remained undisturbed, but the first burst of sorrow had subsided, and, as was usual to her, her thoughts had passed from all selfish regrets to the consideration of what was due to others; her poor, dumb, helpless, protégé—what had been her mother's conduct towards him? Harsh, she was afraid, and though poor Joe could not comprehend the expressions of her resentment, he was sufficiently versed in the expressions of the countenance to know whether his appearance excited good or evil feelings. He was accustomed, too, from his infancy, to fear Mrs. Woodford, whose stick had often, with rather more violence than was justifiable, attempted to correct the errors into which his deficiencies, rather than his faults, had led him.

Anxious to repair as far as possible her mother's unkindness to the poor lad, Grace, the moment she recollected the situation in which she had left him, arose, and having bathed her eyes in cold water and reajusted her dress, proceeded to the room which her mother chose to dignify by the name of drawing-room, but which was, *par necessité*, alternately breakfast, dining, and sitting-room, and in which, as she expected, she found Mrs. Woodford and Maria at the former meal; and, which sufficiently accounted for her having been left so long unmolested, at the breakfast table in complete deshabille, and with all the ease and familiarity of established friends, sat Captain Frederick and his friend, Mr. Grant.

Absorbed as she was in feelings and anxieties in which they had no concern, it could not escape Grace's quick observation, that the two visitors evinced strong symptoms that they had protracted their jollity even beyond the late hour that they had quitted them, and this was soon confirmed, for Mr. Grant, as he arose, and insisted on resigning his chair by her mother to her, observed,

"I am afraid, Miss Grace, that our intruding last night upon your regular hours has been a serious inconvenience to you, for you look even more gravely at me than I expected."

"Oh! Grace has received some news this morning that has not pleased her, poor girl," observed Mrs. Woodford, in a tone of affected kindness, "but she will get over it: it will, not I hope, break her heart."

"Heaven forbid!" exclaimed Mr. Grant, with emphasis.

Grace, for the first time, raised her eyes to his face; it was a look of contempt at the hyperbolical tone which she had several times on the previous evening felt so annoying; but she instantly withdrew them again, for his unsteady look and flushed cheeks, convinced her that he was far from being in a fit state to comprehend her rebuke.

"These naughty men have not been in bed all night, Grace," said Mrs. Woodford, in a playful tone; "and so I am trying whether a strong cup of coffee will not restore their senses."

Grace looked down and blushed still deeper than before, while Mr. Grant, seeming to feel the reproach her look conveyed, uttered a confused apology, which seemed intended rather to vindicate himself in Grace's eyes, than any other of the party, from having wilfully intruded himself.

"The fact is," he observed, "that I actually did not know, when we entered the house this morning—my friend Frederick having proposed to take me to some friends of his, who he knew would welcome us to their breakfast table—I actually did not know," he repeated, "that it was the same house I had been at last night, for having come and departed in a coach, I did not notice the place, or I should certainly have decidedly objected to intruding a second time, however anxious to cultivate so valuable an acquaintance."

Again Grace raised her eyes with a look of contemptuous reproof, but Mr. Grant's last words seemed to have been entirely addressed to Mrs. Woodford; or, at least, the bow with which he concluded was given to her, and simpering, bridling, and looking very gracious, she accepted it as a full and sufficient apology for what, indeed, it would have been easy for a stranger to see, she in her heart considered rather as an honour and a pleasure than as needing an excuse.

The breakfast passed over, and still Grace, anxious as she was, could find no opportunity of asking a single question of Maria, whom alone she dared question, as to the fate of poor Joe, but her uneasiness was at length most agreeably removed by her mother's desiring Jane, who was clearing the breakfast-table, to give the lad below some with her.

"It is a poor unfortunate boy," she observed, "the son of one of my tenants, who I have taken till I can get him into some institution for the deaf and dumb, who, I am told, can teach him to get his livelihood."

Though not a little damped by the falsehood and ostentation with which her mother chose to clothe this act of charity, Grace's pleasure at hearing this was so evident as to totally alter her look and manner, and Mrs. Woodford saw, with an exultation she could scarcely conceal, that scarcely were her eldest daughter's attractions more decidedly acknowledged by Captain Frederick than Grace's were by his friend.

"The girl certainly at times looks pretty," she observed to Maria, when at length their visitors departed; "but what the men can see in her to admire so much I cannot find out; however, if she can make a good match, it will be so much the better, and certainly this Mr. Grant seems greatly struck with her."

Thus concluded this singular breakfast party.

The acquaintance which had in Mrs. Woodford's estimate been so auspiciously commenced, continued to afford her unabated satisfaction for some weeks, during which Captain Frederick and his friend were constant visitors; but it did not escape Grace's observation, that with all their professions of respect and admiration, and although Captain Frederick declared openly that he considered every hour was a blank that was not passed with his lovely Maria, and Mr. Grant affected to lament with the utmost pathos her (Grace's) coldness to him, not one word was ever breathed by either of that which formed the end and aim of Mrs. Woodford's hopes and exertions —marriage. It was plain, too, that familiar and communicative as both of them were on every other subject, both the gentlemen st   ly avoided all mention of their family connection, and Grace more than once saw with an indignation she could scarcely conceal, that they shunned, as much as possible, all public attention to them, and even more than once had absolutely affected not to see them, when they had accidentally encountered them in company with their associates.

To Maria, Grace spoke openly of these portentous omens; to herself, the consequences were nothing, for she had no feeling towards Mr. Grant but that of utter indifference, and though she dared not in her mother's presence repel his attentions so decidedly as she would have done, she took care to make him feel that they were only suffered, and that she would have been far more content had he withdrawn them entirely; but with Maria the case was very different, for though vanity and ambition still, perhaps, had a large share in the pleasure with which she received Capt. Frederick's attentions, it was plain to her observant and affectionate sister that Maria felt towards her ardent lover a much greater degree of attachment than she had ever before bestowed on human being.

Young, handsome, and elegant, and apparently devoted to her, possessing, too, all those advantages which Maria had been assiduously taught to value beyond all others—birth, fortune, and fashion—it could not be supposed that she would remain indifferent to him; but Grace, who had hitherto believed her sister incapable of feeling any very passionate attachment, was at once grieved and surprised at discovering the unlimited dominion which he had acquired over her mind. Maria was indeed deaf and blind to every thing which could have tended to lower her lover in her esteem, and with a violence which astonished and alarmed Grace, she defended him on every occasion, when the latter would have pointed out to her how different was his conduct from his professions.

"If he really loved you, Maria," she observed, one day, when he had passed them in the public walks, in company with some ladies and gentlemen, and pretended not to see them. "If he really loved you, and intended to make you his wife, would he not be anxious to show you every mark of respect? Would he not seek opportunities to introduce you to his friends—to procure you respectable female society—to induce his own family to countenance you—and in short, to procure you every advantage that could make you of consequence in the eyes of the world; but instead of doing so, what is his conduct? He visits you at home, your obscure home, where none can observe his visits, and out of doors he shuns you, except at times and places where he knows it it is not likely he shall meet any of his friends, except indeed, a few gay young men like himself, and then, indeed, he seems proud of showing you off to——. Oh Maria, you can't know or think how unhappy and degraded I sometimes feel—"

"And what right have you to feel so, I wonder?" replied Maria angrily. "I am sure you've no occasion; for nobody thinks anything about you, I am sure, and so how can there be any degradation to you?"

"Not for myself, perhaps, if I was not your sister," replied Grace mildly; "I am quite conscious that I am too insignificant to be the subject of conversation, but disrespect towards you, Maria—."

"Oh! there is no disrespect in the case," interrupted Maria, in a confident tone. "The fact is, that Frederick is afraid of disobliging some of those ugly formal women that we sometimes meet him with; they are friends of his family, and might make mischief if they were to see him with me, and so he is obliged to be cautious."

"But if he marries you, Maria," said Grace, "his family must know it, and then, I should think, they would be much more seriously displeased."

"I shouldn't wonder if they were," returned Maria, in a tone of indifference; "but however, I care very little about it; I shall leave Frederick to fight it out as well as he can."

Grace was silenced; she felt indeed that it was useless for her to say anything on a subject on which it was plain her sister had made up her mind; but her uneasiness was by no means decreased by what the latter had said, nor did it lessen it to see that her mother remained totally blind to all that afforded her (Grace) food for many hours of painful reflection.

They had now been resident nearly six weeks in Bath, and Grace trembled as she heard her mother casually mention to Maria the sum she had already expended out of their little stock.

"But then you know, my dear" observed the thoughtless woman, "a great part of that has been paid for things to make you fit to appear with Captain Frederick, and you won't want but little more before your marriage."

Grace involuntarily sighed so deeply as to attract her mother's notice.

"What are you sighing for, Grace?" she demanded. "Are you afraid your turn won't come so soon as your sister's? because I am sure it will be your own fault, for it's very plain, though it's somewhat unaccountable to me, that Grant is every bit as much attached to you as Captain Frederick is to your sister."

"It may be so," said Grace, again sighing; "but I was not thinking of that indeed."

"And pray what might you be thinking of, if I may be so bold as to ask?" returned her mother, with an air of mock humility.

"Thinking," replied Grace, colouring and looking down in confusion.

"Yes, what did you think of that made you sigh so? I insist upon knowing," said Mrs. Woodford, growing angry.

"I was only thinking, mamma," said Grace tremulously; "that I hoped nothing would happen to disappoint your's and my sister's expectations."

"Well, there is no harm in that," said Mrs. Woodford in a kinder tone; "though I should, I ought to be vexed with you for being such a croaker, only that after your own disappointment I can hardly wonder at it." Grace looked up with surprise—"I mean, that Sir Walter's sudden disappearance, just at the moment when you had a right to flatter yourself that your fortune was made, is enough to make you doubtful and fearful; but it would be hard, indeed, to be a second time disappointed so cheer up, Grace, and put on your best looks, for your adorer will be here presently."

"And can it be possible, then, that my mother seriously expects that I should accept this man's offers, if he really were to make any?" said Grace, when Mrs. Woodford, at the conclusion of the last sentence, quitted the room.

"Certainly she does," replied Maria, looking earnestly at her sister; "and, indeed, Grace, I think she would have good reason to be surprised and offended, if you were to refuse such an offer, should it be made to you. I know, indeed, very well, that you never felt any disappointment about Sir Walter, nor can I blame you; for though I once thought of having him myself, I must confess he was not a man that a young girl could have been happy with. But Grant is quite different, for he's a very fine-looking young man, and gay and fashionable, and everything, I'm sure, that could be wished. But I know, Grace, what it is that makes you so indifferent to him; you are still fretting after Belgrave Mansell, though you ought to know that, even if his character was cleared, and he was to come back, and wish ever so much to have you, it would be quite impossible for mamma ever to give her consent; for of course Captain Frederick could never think of owning such a brother-in-law.

"Captain Frederick would have no occasion to feel himself disgraced by such a brother-in-law," returned Grace with quickness. "But, why should I dispute with you, Maria," she added, resuming her usual, mild, placid tone; "or why, even for a moment, feel angry at what is so unlikely ever to happen? No, no, Maria,; be assured there is not the smallest fear of Captain Frederick's ever being rendered uneasy on that account."

"I don't think there is myself," replied Maria, who evidently misunderstood her sister's last observation; "but still Grace I must say that I think you are very foolish to be constantly thinking of and fretting about that young man. You can't disguise it from me, though mamma does not see it, that your mind is always running upon what is past and gone. Frederick himself is always telling me that he is sure you have left a lover behind you in the country, and are always fretting after him; and though I deny it—as I can do, you know, with truth, because you certainly did not leave him behind you—yet I know he don't half believe me; and I'm often afraid, when Grant watches you so, and you sigh, and seem to forget where you are, and who is by, that he suspects you; and I would tell Frederick the real truth, and convince him that Grant has nothing in reality to be jealous of, only that it is mortifying to own even that one has had any connections with——"

"For heaven's sake, Maria, do let us dismiss this torturing subject!" exclaimed Grace, with a vehemence so unusual as to cause Maria to start. "You and I," she continued with emotion, "have such different views; you are so incapable of comprehending what I think and feel; you so misunderstand——pray pray, Maria," and she burst into a passion of tears, "let it be the last time that Belgrave Mansell's name is mentioned between us."

"I am sure, Grace, I am very willing to agree to that," returned Maria who was more than half frightened at her sister's unusual vehemence, "and this shall be the last time you shall hear it from me."

"But there is also another request I must make, Maria," said Grace, in a subdued tone; "and that is, that you do not by any misrepresentation to Captain Frederick encourage his friend to torment me with his hateful addresses."

"Hateful addresses, Grace. you cannot surely mean to ——"

"I mean," interrupted Grace, with impetuosity; "I mean what I say, he—the whole of mankind—are alike hateful to me in that light, in the light of a lover."

"And you will not have Mr. Grant, if he offers himself," said Maria.

"No, never, as I hope for mercy from Heaven," returned Grace, raising her hands with solemnity "No, Maria, here in your presence I solemnly swear, that neither entreaties nor force shall ever induce me to listen to either him or any——"

"Grace, what nonsense you are talking! are you mad?" interrupted Maria.

"Almost, I believe I am," said Grace, smiling with an expression so ghastly, as her lips quivered and her bosom heaved with tumultuous sobs, that Maria in alarm threw her arms round her neck, and strained her to her bosom.

"Grace, dear Grace, do not speak and look so! You frighten me, indeed you do; rouse yourself, there's a dear girl; I hear them coming upstairs, Frederick and Grant, and if they see you so——"

"Let me go, pray let me go!" exclaimed Grace, and before the expected visitors could reach the room-door, she darted out, and upstairs to her own room, where she could uninterruptedly give vent to her emotions.

A flood of tears soon calmed her agitation, and a few minutes' quiet reflection convinced her how weak she had been in suffering herself to be thus violently excited by observations which should rather have been met with pity and contempt; but, though she could thus calmly argue with herself, and blame her own weakness, she could not even now recall Maria's contemptuous expression towards Belgrave without feeling towards her anger and indignation such as she had seldom experienced.

"Heaven in its mercy grant," she ejaculated, "that Maria may never need the kindness and protection of him whom she now so much despises; and yet something seems to tell me that sad experience will teach her, some day, the real difference between those on whom she now places all her reliance, and him whom she now rejects with such scorn."

"Missus wants to know, Miss Grace, why you don't come down to tea; and there's Muster Grant looking as dull as a mute at a funeral because Miss Maria said you wasn't very well," said Jane, putting her head in at the door of the bedroom.

"I'm coming directly, Jane," replied Grace, pretending to be busy with her hair, in order to avoid the prying eyes of the waiting-maid.

Her voice, however, it appeared, betrayed her, for Jane, instead of going down stairs, entered the room.

"Can I do anything for you, miss?" she observed, and then discovering, or affecting to discover, that her eyes were red and swelled, she added, "Dear heart, Miss Grace, what in the world can you have to vex and fret you so, and such a fine young gentleman as Mr. Grant a dying, as I may say, for you?"

"I beg, Jane, you will not take the liberty to mention that person's name to me," replied Grace angrily.

"Well, to be sure, Miss Grace, I didn't think that I should offend you; but, howsomever, I'll keep my tongue within my teeth for the future, though I can tell you something."

"Nothing I wish to hear, probably, Jane," replied Grace coolly.

"May be not, miss," she returned very tartly; "howsomever, whether you do or not now, I'll take care I won't say not another word; if people likes to be ungrateful to people, and give them nothing but airs when they means to do them a bit o' kindness, why they may suffer for their pains, says I; but you'll think of what I says now, miss, or my name isn't Jane Dawson, when you finds it all out."

"Find what out, Jane?" demanded Grace, struck with her very emphatic look and manner; but Jane was already at the door, and without vouchsafing even another look she quitted the room.

Deeply as Grace's thoughts were occupied on more interesting subjects during the whole of that evening, she could not divest herself of the idea that Jane, ignorant, and pert, and self-sufficient as she was, had by some means become possessed of information of importance.

There was something so significant in every glance of Jane's eye, whenever she entered the sitting-room during the evening, and whenever she had occasion to speak to Grace, something so peculiar in her manner, that the thoughts, the fears, the hopes of the latter were all excited, and at length, unable to bear the suspense any longer, she took an opportunity of going down to the kitchen, under pretext of giving Joe directions as to waiting at table, bringing up the tray, &c., in all of which duties he was making wonderful progress under Grace's tuition, for from no one else would he receive instructions, displaying towards his kitchen companion, Jane, the greatest doggedness and ill-will, so much so, that Jane had repeatedly complained to her mistress that there was no living with " that disagreeable, contrary dummy " who just took a pride in making her as uncomfortable as ever he could.

On all these occasions, much to Jane's discomfiture, Grace was poor dummy's advocate ; and infinite were the pains she took to explain to the obstinate, self-conceited girl how easy it would be by a kind look and a little seeming attention to conciliate poor Joe's favour, and make him ready and willing to do all she required.

" How else is it, Jane," she would observe. " that the poor fellow is so anxious to comprehend me, and flies to perform anything that I point out to him ?"

Jane did not know ; certainly, it was very curious to see how he understood her (Grace) in a moment, when she herself had been perhaps an hour trying to hammer something or another into his stupid brains—and it was interesting, if not curious, to observe the devotion with which Joe did attend to every glance or movement of Grace ; and yet it was not altogether that he understood her better, or that she had a more perspicuous way of making him comprehend her, for the fact was that Jane. with all her coarseness, and ignorance, and conceit, contrived with considerable ingenuity to make him und-rstand her whenever she chose to take the trouble, and, as she frequently observed, she believed, even when she took no trouble at all, there were very few things passed that he did not in some measure comprehend and busy his head with.

On the occasion in question, Grace found her more than commonly loud in her abuse of the stupid fool, as she called him, whom she declared she could not get to do a single thing to help her, though she was drove about up stairs and down stairs, and almost to her wits' ends.

Grace looked at Joe, who was sitting, looking more than usually sullen, by the kitchen fire ; but the moment he caught her reproachful look he started up, and commenced busying himself, looking from time to time at Grace for direction. Jane, however, far from being pacified by these indications of his willingness to assist, was only more loud in her anger, declaring that it was " nothing but artfulness of him just to keep in with Miss Grace, because she indulged him, giving him everything that he coveted, just as if he was like another Christian."

It was in vain, Grace saw, to hope that in her present humour Jane would be induced to enter into any other subject than the one on which she was ever most fluent—her own wrongs and sufferings from being obliged to put up with such a disobliging, disagreeable brute ; and Grace having therefore concluded her errand into the kitchen, and tried to establish peace between them, was on the point of leaving the room, when Jane suddenly interrupted her.

" Stop a bit, if you please, Miss Grace, I've something to say to you. I did think," she continued, re-assuming those airs of importance, which made her at all times disagreeable even to Grace, who, with her usual propensity to believe the best of every one, was inclined often to give Jane credit for being much better at heart than her disagreeable manner made her appear. " I did think," she repeated ; " to say nothing about it, because you snapped me up so short this afternoon; but howsomever, I don't know how it is, but I can't help liking you, Miss Grace, nor more can anybody as I knows, for as that young man in the two pair, as is out of place, says to me "Mrs. Jane," says he, "for he always calls me Mrs. Jane, knowing I've lived in such respectable families—but, however, that's not what I was going to say. But pray Miss Grace, do you know anything of a tall, genteel, thin sort of a person, that rather oldish, and stoops in the shoulders?"

"I know no one in Bath, Jane; not a single person out of this house; and indeed, not all those in it, I believe," returned Grace : "but, why do you ask me?"

"I'll tell you, then miss. The young man in the two pair——"

"Oh, this eternal young man in the two pair!" thought Grace, who had noticed, ever since Jane had been in the house, that this nameless personage was, on every occasion, if Jane uttered more than a single sentence, brought in as an authority. Convinced, however, that any interruption at the present moment would have the effect of checking the desired communication, she remained silent, and Jenny proceeded in her own desultory way.

" Well, miss, you know, he's out o' place; and so, of course, he's upon the look-out, as you may say, and walking about a good deal, up one street and down another; because it's so lonesome, as he says, to be settin', doin' of nothing in his own little back room, that's as dark as a *dunjin*. Well, as I was a sayin', of course he looks about him, and takes more notice of every-thing than people as has got business on their hands, which I wish he had, poor young man, for he's a very quiet, civil-behaved person, and he's been out o' place more than six months, he says, all through his master's running away to France, with another gentleman's wife, without giving him a character. So, as I was a saying, miss, he was coming in, three or four nights ago, and he sees this gentleman, or whatever he is, standing right opposite our window, and lookin' up, as if he was a watchin' what was a goin' on in the drawing-room; for the shutters wasn't shut, 'cause missus think it looks more respectable to see the light shining through the red curtains, though she forgits how it shows all the moth-eaten holes, at the same time, and that they are so thin, that anybody at t'other side the way can a'most make out anything that's a doin' in the room : but, however, that's nothin to me, if so be as missus likes it, though——"

" Well, but did this stranger speak to the young man, your acquaintance, Jane?" interrupted Grace, who became too impatient at the girl's continued digression, to bear it any longer. She soon, however had cause to rue her impatience; for now a fresh subject to dilate upon was started by her incautious expression, and Jenny continued to protest and vow that the young man was no acquaintance of hers, and to assure Miss Grace that she never changed a word with him, "only in the way of civility, and giving him the time o' day, and sich like," until Grace, completely weary, was on the point of telling her that she must defer the rest of the story till another time, when Jane was fortunately brought back to the starting point again, by her own observation, that till the young man stopped to ask her whether she had ever noticed the person that was always watching about their house after dark, she had " never exchanged not six words at a time with him."

" Well, but how did the young man know," said Grace, " that he was watching us? It might be——"

" I'll tell you, miss, if you'll only just have patience to hear me out; and indeed Miss Grace," continued Jane, again flying off from the subject, " I'm surprised that you, that seem all patience in general, and will set and hear missus goin' on for half an hour at a time, ratin' you about nothin' at all and findin' fault where nobody else could find it, and never answer her not a word, but seems to listen to her so meek and mild, can't have patience to listen to me, but, the minute I begin to talk, off you are like a shot, though I'm sure I never wished you anythin' but good, and would do anything for you sooner than I would for my own sister, that's what I would."

"I'm sure I'm very much obliged to you, Jane, for your goodwill," returned Grace ; " but, if I am silent, and not inclined, sometimes to listen to you, it is that my spirits are often so low——"

"Ah, Miss Grace, that I know they are," interrupted Jane, emphatically ; " for often and often I hear you sigh, and see you shed tears, when nobody else notices it ; and sometimes I think that may be you've like me met with somebody as hasn't behaved as they ought to do ; not that I *vallys* any man enough now to cry and fret about him, though I used at first, when my cousin Timothy went to sea, just before his 'prenticeship was out, and when everybody thought we was a goin' to get married and settle ; but, however, that's neither here nor there, Miss Grace, only it makes me have a kind of feeling for any young woman, gentle or simple, that's been so *misfortunate* as to meet with a false-hearted young man."

" That has not been my case, I assure you, Jane," said Grace, finding Jane was not inclined to proceed without some definite reply from her ; " I have other and more serious causes for grief," she continued—" I have lost a kind affectionate father, and have left a once happy home—"

" Ah, that's just my case, too, miss," interrupted the sympathetic Jane ; " I am a horphan, as I may say, for I've got nobody but mother-in-law, as brought me up, and then turned me out into the world, though my father was well to do, and left hundreds and hundreds behind him ; but laws what was it I was saying ? Oh, about this here man that was watchin'. Well, the young man up stairs, watched him over and over, three or four nights, hankering about, and at last he determined to speak to him, and try and find out what it was he was after ; and so accordingly he did speak to him, and I don't know how he contrived it, but they went into the public-house down the street, and the gentleman treated him to a bottle of wine, and he might have had anything else he says, for asking, when the gentleman found out that he lived in the same house with you, Miss Grace, and could tell him all the goin's on and about the two gentlemen that comes courtin' here, for you know it's no use to deny it, miss, they can't mean nothin' else, because no gentleman that's like them, would come here, into such a poor little place as this is, if they had not some meaning in it, whether it is for good or for ill, as the strange gentleman said, time 'll show, but your mother must be mad to encourage—but I won't tell you half as he said about missus, or what he called her, though, as I said to the young man, it certainly is an unbecoming thing at her age ——"

" I cannot listen to any remarks disrespectful to my mother, Jane," interrupted Grace, mildly but firmly, " and I am now fully convinced of what I from the first suspected, that this strange man, whoever he may be, can have no friendly motives, or he would not have ——"

" Laws, how you do always stand up for your mother, Miss Grace ! I declare, if missus was an angel of light, you couldn't —— ; but its no business of mine : ' every one for their own, as their own,' as the saying is, though as to the gentleman's not being your friend, I can't believe that, because he spoke so well of you, and said you were too good for them you belonged to, and then he said he believed if ever a young woman could be trusted in the middle of temptation it would be you ; but then he said the way your mother was going on would be sure to bring her to ruin, and poverty would corrupt a saint, he said, and so it would, you know, Miss Grace, for hunger would break through stone walls. But, howsomever, he said, if anything happened particular, that is to say, if you was brought to any distress, there was a friend who would assist you, and he gave a card to the young man, and desired him to give it you; but then he bethought himself again, and said it would perhaps be of no use, for you would be too delicate to apply to a stranger, though in real earnest he was no stranger, but, said he, 'I've my reason for not making myself known at present, though if I could see the poor girl without any of her family being the wiser of it, it would be a good thing for her, and a satisfaction to me——.' But lauk, miss, there's missus rung twice, I declare, and dummy's carried up all the things for supper; we shall both be killed;" and Jane, without waiting any further remark, rushed up the stairs, leaving Grace lost in astonishment and conjecture as to who this mysterious stranger could be who had evinced so strong an interest in her welfare.

There was but one person whom she had ever known, who corresponded at all, she reflected, with Jane's description of this person. Could it be that Sir Walter Fitz-Geffrey was yet living, and yet considered it necessary to preserve his secrecy? Oh! if it were so, and she could see him, how would she implore him, as the greatest proof of his friendship for her, to come forward and rescue Belgrave from the imputation that now lay so heavy upon him.

"Surely! surely!" she exclaimed, "he would never refuse, whatever his motives for this strange conduct may be, he could not refuse to do any act of justice towards one who has never offended him, and even if he should be deaf to my entreaties, would not my testimony that I have seen and conversed with him, added to what has been brought forward, as to his being still in existence, be sufficient to set at rest for ever all those horrible suspicions?"

Anxious, however, as Grace was to hear more from the loquacious Jane, and thus be determined, whether she should or not seek an interview, for which the mysterious person had declared his anxiety, Grace was obliged to postpone, till they retired for the night, all farther questions on the subject, and then Jane was so full of complaints of the grievous wrongs she suffered from her mistress, in being kept up to all hours of the night (it was now morning, for it had struck one before Captain Frederick and his friend could, to use their own expressions, tear themselves away), her additional hard work, in having company to attend to every day, though, when she was hired, her missus said she kept very little, and an endless string of similar murmurings, that it was with infinite difficulty, and not without an exercise of patience and more ingenious manœuvring than she had ever in her life practised before, that she (Grace) at length brought her round to the subject—namely, the young man in the two pair and his interview with the gentleman, as she called him.

Great, however, was Grace's disappointment, when, after infinite circumlocutions and beating about the bush, she at length came to the final close of this mysterious affair by acknowledging that the young man in the two pair had drunk so much wine during the conversation as that he owned he could not very distinctly state the gentleman's final observations, but he had got some sort of a direction to somebody in his pocket, though what he was to do with it, or why it was given him, he could not now distinctly remember; indeed, he rather thought it was given him with a recommendation to apply there for a situation, especially as the gentleman had given him a guinea at the same time, which he fancied was to bear his expenses, for it was all the way to—to——

Here Jane's recollection failed, just at the precise point which was likely, in Grace's estimation, to throw light on the subject more than anything else she had related.

"How provoking !" exclaimed Grace aloud. "Do, pray, try and recollect Jane ; was it——"

"Laws, Miss Grace, how unreasonable you be !" interrupted the peevish and now sleepy handmaiden ; "if you had been half as many hours as I have upon the foot, up stairs and down stairs, and Jane here, and Jane there, and——"

The sentence died away unfinished. Jane was now really asleep, and Grace was condemned to suffer for the remainder of the time allotted to repose, all the misery and restlessness of conjecture, without end, and without the smallest chance of a satisfactory elucidation of the mystery that tormented her.

Full of expectation that she should be enabled, through the aid of Jane's acquaintance, "the young man in the two pair," to discover who it was that had professed so much interest in her, Grace anxiously waited, during the first part of the next day, for an opportunity of renewing the subject with the former ; but extreme indeed was her disappointment, when, having at length found the desired opportunity, Jane, in a tone of pique, replied—

"Indeed, miss, I've had no time to think of anything besides my work, for that's enough for any two people in the world ; and how your ma' can expect I can get through it I can't think. As to the young man in the two pair, he's took himself off this morning to a place he's got somewhere, all of a hurry, without hardly so much as saying good bye, though I'm sure I always behaved with all sort of civility to him : but there's nothing but ingratitude in this world, I think, and I've a'most made up my mind never to do a good turn to anybody again. Howsomever, I did ask him about what we was talking about last night, and he said he should most likely see the gentleman again in a day or two, and then he would call and tell you all about it ; and he gave me this card too, she continued, pulling one from her pocket, "and told me that was a direction he had just found in his dirty waistcoat-pocket, and so he supposed it was the same the gentleman had given him."

Grace eagerly examined the card, but the name on it was one totally unknown to her ; and completely disappointed, she remarked to Jane that it must be altogether a mistake, for she knew not that she had ever even heard the name of Dunbar before, and was certain she had never known any one of that name.

"Then he's most likely given me a wrong direction," observed Jane, with great *nonchalance ;* "but, however, if he does come, as he said he would, to treat Becky and me with something handsome, for our civil usage, I'll contrive you shall see him, Miss Grace, and then you can ask him what questions you like."

————

CHAPTER XIX.

"——By the roses of the spring,
By maidhood, honour, truth and everything,
I love thee so that————
Nor wit, nor reason, can my passion hide."
                                        SHAKESPEARE.

RASH, and weak, and shortsighted, as Mrs. Woodford had proved her-in every action since she had been left the uncontrolled mistress of her own actions, she could not remain for ever blind to the consequences which must speedily result from continuing in the course she had adopted.

Liberal and generous in money matters, even to extravagance, as Captain Frederick appeared, whenever he had an opportunity, still his constant visits, and those of his friend, added most materially to the heavy expenses which were rapidly exhausting the little stock of cash Mrs. Woodford had preserved from the wreck. Maria, too, reckoning with perfect confidence on having it speedily in her power to repay her mother for every sacrifice, was inordinate in her demands for every expensive and fashionable novelty in the way of dress or ornament that she beheld; and Grace, with the bitterest anxiety and alarm, beheld the hour rapidly approaching, which, she too truly anticipated, would at once dispel her mother's golden visions, and lead her to misery and despair.

By degrees the same feelings which had even from their first entrance into Bath, rendered her nights restless, and poisoned her enjoyment of any pleasure by day, seemed to be communicated to her mother and sister ; and Grace beheld with anguish the look of painful anxiety which clouded her mother's features even when she strove to appear most gay. Maria's usual thoughtless placidity was frequently exchanged for fretfulness and evident gloomy thought, which she in vain tried to conceal under a plea of slight indisposition; all were indeed alike unhappy, though each strove to conceal it from the other. With Captain Frederick, however, the attempt to appear at ease, as usual, seemed perfectly to succeed, for he was still as gay, as attentive, and as much devoted to Maria, as ever, though he evidently did not or would not notice Mrs. Woodford's hints which became every day more plain, and more frequent—that it was time he should declare decisively his intentions. It was in vain that she declaimed against protracted courtships, or related tales of those who in consequence of unnecessary delays in " speaking their minds," had experienced some fatal overthrow to their happiness. Captain Frederick coincided with her, declared she was perfectly right, condemned those as fools who trifled with happiness, when it was in their power to secure it, but never *appeared* to conceive anything she said as at all levelled at or applicable to himself.

There was but one way to bring him to a positive and speedy decision, Mrs. Woodford thought, when, after having successively parried one of her most direct attacks, the captain suddenly recollected, or pretended to recollect, an engagement which obliged him to leave his dear Maria for the rest of the evening.

" I will put an end to this suspense I am determined to-morrow," said Mrs. Woodford, for the first time giving audible vent to her anxiety.

The colour mantled over Maria's fair face and neck, as she looked with inquiring haste in her mother's face ; but the next moment dropping her eyes, she burst into tears, and hid her face on Grace's neck who was regarding her with the most intense anxiety.

" Don't cry, my dear child, pray don't," said the fond mother, while her own tears streamed copiously down her cheeks ; " I should break my heart, Maria," she continued, " if anything was to happen ; but no, I'm sure it will all turn out right, though I cannot comprehend why he is so backward in speaking of your marriage."

" I wish I had never, never come here—I wish I had never seen him," sobbed Maria ; " for I shall die if he deserts me now."

"Desert you, my dear child! what in the world could put such a thing in your head?" exclaimed Mrs. Woodford, in a tone of the most painful alarm. " Tell me," she continued ; " has he said anything to you, that——"

no, no," returned Maria; " but I have such fears and doubts come over me, whenever he is away from me."

" I will put an end to it all to-morrow," repeated Mrs. Woodford, again hastily; " and so do you be prepared, Maria, when you hear me tell him that we are going to leave Bath."

" I wish we had never seen it," sighed Maria again.

" And now, pray, Grace, tell me," resumed Mrs. Woodford, addressing the latter in a petulant tone, " what has passed between you and Mr. Grant, that he has kept away these three days ? I have thought twenty times of asking you about it; but my mind has been so distracted about your poor sister that it has gone out of my head."

" I know not that I have done anything to drive him away, mamma," said Grace, with considerable confusion.

" But I do know it, miss," returned Mrs. Woodford, with asperity; " and so I desire you to speak the truth. What was the conversation that passed between you, the last time he was here, while Maria and I were out with Captain Frederick ?"

Grace blushed and hesitated, but again her mother imperatively ordered her to speak; and she acknowledged that she had been led by his passionate declarations of love to her to reproach him at once with insincerity and to include in her charge, also, his friend Captain Frederick.

" Mercy on me !" exclaimed Mrs. Woodford. " And have you, then, with your pretended meekness and mildness, dared to say to him what I have been vainly trying, to gain courage——but, go on, what did he say in reply ?

" He appeared greatly astonished," returned Grace, " at my plain speaking ; for I told him, without hesitation, all I thought of both him and the captain. I told him," continued Grace, becoming every instant more agitated, " that I was convinced that both him and his friend imagined that they could impose upon two simple country girls, and make them believe anything they pleased ; but I assured him they were quite mistaken, for that I had all along seen their real characters and despised them, and——"

" And how dare you say all that?" interrupted Mrs. Woodford, in a violent passion.

" Because it was truth, mother" returned Grace, firmly, " and because —because," and she burst into tears; " he forced it from me, by daring to attempt to corrupt me—by daring to insult me—by——. Mother do not ask me any more," she continued, passionately ; " you cannot be angry with me for having refused to listen to the proposals of a libertine."

Mrs. Woodford looked confounded ! " Why did you not tell me all this before, Grace ? But I can scarcely think he meant any insult; young gay men will sometimes forget themselves, and express themselves with more freedom than——"

" No man who means honourably and honestly towards the woman he loves will attempt to degrade her in his own and in her own estimation," interrupted Grace with firmness.

" Upon my word, Grace, you seem to pride yourself greatly on your prudence and wisdom," returned Mrs. Woodford; " but after all, I do not think you had any right to be so very positive in your dismissal of a person of Mr. Grant's fortune and consideration without consulting me on the subject."

" Had it been the King of England," replied Grace with emphasis ; " I should have told the truth, that I despised him and his principles."

" And did you know nothing of all this, Maria?" demanded Mrs. Woodford, turning to the latter.

"Oh, yes, I knew it all," she returned in a desponding tone ; " but it is easy for Grace to talk and act so calmly, it is no sorrow to her to lose one whom she never liked, but I——" again she gave way to a flood of tears.

" You would, I trust, I am sure you would, my own dear sister," half whispered Grace; " be equally indignant, equally decided, should even the man you love avow such base principles as those which induced me to threaten Mr. Grant, should he ever come here again, that I would expose him, however painful to my own feelings, to my mother, my only protector," she added, with peculiar emphasis, and looking earnestly in her mother's face—" and in the presence too, of his friend who would then be obliged to avow himself—he has kept away ever since," she continued, " and Captain Frederick has not even appeared surprised that he has done so."

" Now that is false, Grace," said Maria, with vehemence ; " for Frederick has more than once said to me, he could not think what was the matter with Grant ; but that he could not get him out from his lodgings and that he seemed quite melancholy; and you know he told you, mamma, that Grant was ill, and yet he could not find out what was the matter with him."

" And yet," said Grace, calmly, " I would lay my life that he knows every thing that passed, and that he considered, as well as his friend, that it was the wisest plan to keep away.'

" There, again, how shamefully and cruelly do you judge, Grace !" exclaimed Maria.

" Rather say, Maria, how partially do you," returned Grace in a sorrowful tone ; " and yet I know in your heart, that you believe me right."

Maria's tears again flowed, and she remained silent.

" This is dreadful cruel of you, Grace," observed Mrs. Woodford, with a look and manner which confessed that while she uttered these words, she felt that they were unjust, and that in reality Grace merited praise for endeavouring to open her sister's eyes to the true character of the man who pretended to love her.

" I am cruel only to be kind," replied Grace with emotion, and passing her arm around her sister, who still continued to weep, she fervently observed,

" God grant, dear Maria, that it may prove I am wrong, for be assured with ten thousand times more pleasure shall I acknowledge myself wrong and unjust towards Captain Frederick than——"

" We shall know to-morrow," interrupted Mrs. Woodford, whose manner had unconsciously softened towards Grace, and who for the first time probably felt the injustice she had always done towards the latter. " To-morrow, Grace, I will bring him to the plain question, and if he proves what you prophesy——God forbid," she added, hastily shuddering at all the consequences that must ensue, should her proposed trial of his sincerity verify her fears and Grace's prediction.

The night was passed by Grace in restless anticipation, and gloomy foreboding of the distress her mother and sister would feel, at the final dispersion of those hopes which had so long rendered them insensible and reckless of the ruin impending over them. To descend at once from their fancied height of rank and riches, to renounce wholly and for ever their dreams of wealth and splendour, and determine henceforth to rely on their own industry and exertions, was the only safe course now left them, but alas ! Grace feared that even this fearful disappointment of their first project would fail to awaken them to their error, and she dreaded that they would expose themselves to still further humiliation and mortification before they would relinquish the darling idea so long cherished.

Maria's heavy eyes and pallid cheek, when they met at the breakfast table, betrayed that she had not passed a more tranquil night than her sister, and Mrs. Woodford, was evidently in an agony of suspense and impatience to put her project in execution.

"The voice of Captain Frederick gaily singing a French air, which he had the preceding night taken pains to teach Maria, at length warned them of his approach.

"Sit still both of you till I give you the signal to go," said Mrs. Woodford, as he *sans ceremonie* opened the door.

A faint blush rose on Maria's cheek, after uttering his familar "*bon jour* to all and every one," he as usual advanced to make more particular inquiries of her; but instead of replying with her accustomed cheerfulness and alacrity, she turned her eyes away, and bowed with a distant air, as he hoped she had enjoyed good repose.

"What is the matter?" he exclaimed looking from one to the other. and observing the same look of gloom and constraint on the conntenances of all. "What can have possibly happened to occasion this change, my good friends?"

"Nothing very particular," returned Mrs. Woodford, assuming a tone of indifference; "only the girls are fretting because I have made up my mind to leave Bath at the end of the week."

"Leave Bath!" re-echoed Captain Frederick in astonishment. "Surely you cannot be serious, dear madam?"

"Perfectly serious, sir, I assure you," she replied; "Why should I not? I came here only on account of my health, and as I do not find it at all bettered, the sooner I try some other place, the more likely it is to be of advantage."

"And whither then do you propose to go?" inquired the Captain, after a a few moments' thoughtful silence, during which his eyes had glanced from one to another, as if desirous of finding there an explanation of the mystery of this sudden resolve.

"I have not resolved yet where I shall go," said Mrs. Woodford: "perhaps," she added, with a consequential air, "I shall travel some time before I settle again, I don't know that I mayn't take it in my head to go abroad, it would perhaps be the best thing I could do for the girls to give them a polish."

Grace felt her cheek colour, and she caught a hasty glance at their visitor, who, while he tried to assume a look of sorrow and dismay, evidently struggled to conceal a smile at her (Mrs. Woodford's) mock importance.

"This is unexpected, indeed," he at length observed, "and it is the more singular, as I came to announce, that I have this morning received a letter, which obliges me to go to London, and thus put off for two or three weeks, an event, which I had joyfully anticipated would take place much sooner," and he looked at Maria with tender significance.

Mrs. Woodford's countenance underwent an instantaneous change, its previous gloom and dissatisfaction disappeared, and she darted at Grace a look of triumph, which did not escape her wily visitor.

"Well, that is curious," she exclaimed, "that we should both be going to leave at the same time; but you, I suppose, will return, Captain Frederick."

"Not if you quit the place, certainly, my dear madam," he replied "Bath will loses every attraction to me, when it loses you."

THE PRIDE OF THE VILLAGE;

OR,

THE FARMER'S DAUGHTERS.

JANE GIVES NOTICE TO LEAVE.

CHAPTER, XX.

"I do not like thee, Doctor Fell,
The reason why I cannot tell,
But I don't like thee Doctor Fell.

ANON

"You are very polite, sir" said Mrs. Woodford, who evidently anxiously expected a farther and more direct elucidation of the Captain's views and intentions.

11

"Polite, my dear Mrs. Woodford," he repeated, in a tone of regret; "what can induce you to use such a cold formal word to me, after suffering me to hope that you regarded me with such different feelings? I had hoped, indeed," he continued, after a few moments' pause, during which, Mrs. Woodford seemed studying how best to draw from him that explicit avowal she so longed to hear. "I had hoped that all unnecessary ceremony and reserve were banished from our intercourse, but I see something has happened to prejudice me in your opinion. I have some secret enemy—some one who takes advantage of my being compelled, by family circumstances, to postpone for a short time, the avowal of my dearest wishes and intentions, to misrepresent and calumniate me. Yes, yes, I see it all," he continued with warmth; "and I am so wretchedly tied down and hampered at the present moment by family arrangements that I cannot at once, as I would do, dispel all misconstructions and suspicions by at once explaining candidly my wishes; but you, Maria," he continued, affectionately taking her hand, "you, I trust, do not doubt me, you can confide in my honour."

"Yes," returned Maria, her beautiful face lighted up with a smile of perfect confidence and exultation; "I do, and will confide in you, Frederick; I have never doubted you myself, though I have been made miserable and wretched by the suspicions of those who are always thinking themselves wiser and more prudent than others."

The look which she significantly directed to Grace at the conclusion of this speech could leave no doubt on the mind of her lover as to whom it was that he was indebted for the catechizing he had undergone, and Grace timidly shrank from the sarcastic expression with which he fixed his eyes upon her as he observed he hoped the time was not far distant when he should have to congratulate himself on being allied to one so eminently distinguished for prudence.

It was impossible to mistake the sneering tone in which the last word was pronounced, and Grace, roused by the implication it conveyed, summoned all her courage, and looking him steadfastly in the face, observed—

"I have heard nothing this morning, Captain Frederick, that could change my opinion as to the prudence you sneer at."

"Grace, hold your tongue, instantly," interrupted Mrs. Woodford, with extreme anger. "How dare you take such impertinent airs?—upon my word, Captain Frederick," she continued, "I am quite ashamed of this bold girl; but the fact is that I never had anything to do with her bringing up; she was her father's pet, and she's just like him, rude and abrupt, and so opinionated, always fancying himself in the right, and I in the wrong, though, poor man, he knew so little——"

Grace could bear it no longer—she cared nothing for her mother's harsh and undeserved reproof of herself, but she could not stay to hear the memory of the best of parents profaned by her mother's unjust and unfeeling remarks, and, without uttering another word, she flew from the room.

It was not until she was summoned to dinner that she again met her mother and sister; but the interval appeared to have been passed much to their satisfaction, for both were in high spirits, though they gave no explanation of what had passed to occasion so material an alteration.

"I have promised Captain Frederick to be friends with you, Miss Grace," observed Mrs. Woodford; and so I shall say nothing about your behaviour this morning."

"I am indebted to Captain Frederick, then, mamma, for a favour which I have vainly striven all my life to deserve," replied Grace, with difficulty suppressing the tears which filled her eyes.

"What do you mean, miss?" demanded her mother sharply. "Do you mean to insinuate that I have ever acted otherwise than friendly and as a mother should do towards you? Have not I always studied your interest, even quite as much as Maria's, who never did anything in her life that was undutiful and disobedient?"

"And what have I ever done, dear mother, to deserve to be called so?" said Grace earnestly.

"What? everything," replied her mother; "but I won't quarrel with you; I promised Frederick I won't, and I'll keep my word."

Grace with difficulty repressed the reply which rose to her lips; her spirit seemed at length thoroughly roused against her mother's injustice; she was indignant, too, at the influence which the latter unhesitatingly avowed Captain Frederick had again resumed over her, and she remained for some time gloomily absorbed in thought, and inattentive to the chit-chat that was passing between her companions, until Maria turning to her observed,

"Well, I will trust to Grace's decision, for, after all, she has the best taste, and he always praises my appearance most when she has dressed me. Which do you think I look best in, Grace, the peach-coloured crape, or my green gros-de-naples?"

"I like you in the green best," said Grace, in a tone which betrayed that she had paid little attention to the subject in dispute.

"And yet I look so very pale to-day," continued Maria, rising and looking at herself in the glass; "and green always makes me look paler. I think I had better wear the crape."

"Where are you going, then?" demanded Grace, for the first time comprehending that some engagement to which she was not a party had been made during her absence.

"I am going to a concert with Captain Frederick," replied Maria, in a tone of joyous exultation.

"Yes, and your sister is to be introduced there to some ladies, near relations of his," added Mrs. Woodford, in the same tone; "and so now I hope all your wise suspicions and observations will be at rest, Madam Prudence."

"I shall be most happy to have them set at rest," returned Grace, sighing; "but you are going too, mamma, are you not?" she added timidly, but with evident earnestness.

"No, I am not going, indeed, Grace," replied Mrs. Woodford, in a composed tone; "it is a private concert," she added, after a moment's pause, "and Captain Frederick cannot procure a ticket for more than one lady and himself."

Grace was answered; it was impossible for her to suggest a doubt that all was not exactly as Mrs. Woodford was determined to believe it, yet she listened, with an incredulity she could not conquer, to the remarks and suggestions and anticipations, to which her mother and sister gave utterance respecting the valuable female acquaintance that this evening was to introduce them to.

The green, the peach-colour, every dress, and every ornament she possessed, were successively tried on before Maria could make up her mind to what she should wear, and appear to most advantage, and do honour to Captain Frederick's choice, for as his affianced bride she felt convinced that she would be introduced on that important evening, and her toilette was scarcely concluded before her attentive conductor arrived.

Contrary to his usual custom on such important occasions, not a word of compliment escaped his lips, as he hurriedly glanced over her dress.

" We shall be late, my dear," he observed, hastily throwing her shawl over her shoulders, and then uttering a hurried " good-bye," he led her without another word to the coach which was waiting for them.

" They are a beautiful couple," said Mrs. Woodford, with exultation, retiring from the windows, from which she had watched them get into the coach ; " and handsome and elegant as he is, Frederick will have no reason to be ashamed of his partner to-night, even though the first people in Bath will be there, he says."

Grace made no reply, a vague sensation of fear and uneasiness had taken possession of her mind ; she longed for the evening to be over, for Maria to come back, and to hear whether her reception had answered her expectations ; but the very anxiety she felt served but to make the time seem longer and more tiresome.

Mrs. Woodford was little inclined to talk ; her mind was, indeed, fully occupied by the imagined certainty, now, of her hopes being all realised. Captain Frederick had, indeed, insinuated that there were obstacles which prevented his fully avowing himself; but, at the same time, he had greeted her ears with the welcome information that this private fortune was quite sufficient to enable him to provide handsomely for his intended bride, even should his family object, and that he was determined that no consideration on earth should separate him from his beloved, adored Maria.

" He is going to London, to-morrow, on purpose to try to get his father's consent," she observed, when, at length Grace ventured to ask whether Captain Frederick had relinquished his intention of leaving Bath. " From what I can learn, there's a lady of title and great fortune in the way, that his friends might have long wished him to marry, so that he's obliged to act cautiously ; but one thing is certain, that before the end of another month your sister will be his wife, whether his family like it or not."

" It will be very unpleasant, though, for Maria to be upon such terms with her husband's family," said Grace, who tried to persuade herself that she had been wrong in suspecting Captain Frederick of dishonourable intentions, and that all was really as he had made her mother believe.

" Oh, they will soon come to, no doubt, when they find it can't be helped," returned the sanguine mother.

Grace remained silent ; she was thinking that she could not so easily as her mother had done, reconcile herself to being thus, as it were, thrust into a family. But Mrs. Woodford did not observe her, for she was now fully occupied in planning the particulars of the marriage ; the white feathers, white and silver favours, and numerous etceteras, all passed in review, and were dilated upon with unceasing volubility and satisfaction, until, having at length wearied herself out, she sank back on the sofa, and fell asleep.

One o'clock, two, three passed ; and then Grace, no longer able to endure the uneasiness she felt, ventured to awake her mother.

" Maria is not come home yet, mamma," she observed.

" Well, and is that your only reason for waking me out of the soundest sleep and the pleasantest dream I have had many a night ?" returned her mother peevishly.

" It is past three," said Grace, by way of excuse.

" Three ! bless me, how the time flies ! But they will not be long, now, I dare say," and Mrs. Woedford after two or three yawns, again composed herself to sleep.

Grace was now again left to her own painful reflections ; another hour dragged slowly and tediously away, and then a coach was heard rattling swiftly over the stones.

" Thank God !" exclaimed Grace, who had been watching through the window, though it was still too dark for her accurately to distinguish objects.

Mrs. Woodford awoke with the exclamation.

" Are they come ?" she inquired, beginning to adjust her cap, which had half fallen off.

" Yes," said Grace, in a half doubtful tone ; for it now struck her that the coach was coming in a different direction from that which they had gone.

Mrs. Woodford was now quite roused, and she looked surprised, at the agitation which Grace's countenance and attitude betrayed, as she stood in the middle of the room, listening to the sound of the carriage, which she was too soon convinced had passed the house, and stopped two doors off.

" What is the matter with the girl ? what have you taken in your head, Grace ?" demanded the former ; " there can be no fear of any accident, for they had not above three times the length of this street to come home," she continued ; " but, I shall give Frederick a scolding for keeping her out so late, though, as it's the last night for a week or so, it's hardly to be wondered at.

Grace did not reply ; she dared not give utterance to the fear that had taken possession of her mind ; and again she returned to her post at the window.

" This is very strange," observed Mrs. Woodford, after another interval of silence ; " Grace, do you recollect where it was he said the concert was to be ?"

" Oh, no, I never heard any place named," returned Grace ; " if I did but know," she hastily added, " I would find my way there at all risks, and put an end to this suspense."

" What suspense ? what is it you are afraid of?" demanded Mrs. Woodford, with an eagerness that spoke too plainly, that she herself was far from being so completely at her ease, as she had hitherto appeared.

" I know not what I fear," replied Grace ; " and yet——Oh, how I do wish she had never gone," she added, passionately clasping her hands.

" Heavens ! why do you frighten me so, Grace ?" ejaculated Mrs. Woodford, seeming at once to comprehend the fears that were floating in Grace's mind ; " He cannot, surely he cannot———Oh, no, he would not have been so wicked as to deceive me."

" I hope he has not ; Oh, how fervently do I pray that he has not," said Grace, tremulously ; " Hark, there is five striking, and it is getting quite light. Oh, if I did but know which way to go."

" What would be the use ?" returned Mrs. Woodford, petulantly, and evidently still struggling with her fears ; " If she is coming back," she continued, after a moment's pause : " your going after her can do no good, and if she is not———but I cannot, will not think it, she could not be such a wretch as to have deserted her mother."

Unwilling, however, as she was to believe the fatal truth, it soon became too palpable to be doubted, and Grace had soon to struggle with her own overwhelming grief, that she might endeavour to support her wretched mother, who was now in an agony of terror and self-reproach, at her wilful blindness to the artful machinations of the man whom she loaded with every epithet that rage and despair could suggest.

One hope, and only one remained, and to that she still continued for some time to cling with pertinacity. He had hinted, that in case of his father's refusal, he would instantly, but secretly, make Maria his wife, and the moment prudence would allow, openly avow his marriage. It might be, that he had suddenly determined to put it out of the power of fate to disappoint him by marrying her first; and still in spite of common sense, she indulged the fond idea that he would speedily return and present her darling child to her as his bride.

The day however wore very nearly to the close, without the slightest intelligence of the fugitive; and totally unable to bear the tortures of fear and self-condemnation any longer, Mrs. Woodford, after a paroxysm of despair and rage, which Grace tried in vain to calm, was seized with strong convulsion and continued for many hours in imminent danger of her life.

It was impossible to conceal from the house the event which had occasioned her mother's illness; and Grace, while she felt grateful for their well-meant efforts to serve her, was nevertheless mortified and pained to excess, at the freedom of their remarks and censures, both on her mother's folly and imprudence, and the irretrievable ruin and disgrace her sister had brought upon herself.

"I have never believed any good could come of it," observed the landlady, as she assisted Grace to undress the wretched mother, who exhausted by the violent sufferings she had undergone, had at last become totally unconscious of what was passing around her; "I said to my husband," continued the former, "the very first time I saw Captain Frederick, as he called himself, in the house, that he came on no good errand, no, nor his sly quiet friend either; but you had a little more prudence, miss, than your sister, it seems, for Jane tells me you wouldn't have anything to say to him and———"

"Oh how I wish I could see Mr. Grant," interrupted Grace; "he might perhaps, if he were to behold the misery his unprincipled companion has brought upon us, give some clue as to where he has conveyed her."

Mrs. Stevens shook her head.

"I'm afraid, miss, they are all birds of a feather, and will stick by one another hard and fast; however, if it will be any easement to your mind, my husband shall try and find him out, and see if he can learn anything of him about this Captain Frederick, if that's his name, though, to tell you the truth, I've my doubts of it."

Grace anxiously inquired her reason for this assertion.

"Why, then, I'll tell you, miss. No longer ago than yesterday there was a customer of my husband's, a gay young gentleman, and one that we've taken a deal of money of; and so he was waiting in the parlour for my husband to come in, and who should come flying up to the door, in his usual harum scarum kind of way, but this Captain Frederick. And so, Sir George looked over the blind, and says he, 'What does Lord—Lord'—I can't for the life of me, now, think of the name; but, however, it was a Lord something—'does he patronise Stevens?' 'No, Sir George,' says I; "it's not Stevens that gentleman comes to see, but he's a visitor to my first floor lodgers. But, he's not a lord; his name's Frederick, Captain Frederick.' And so then he laughed; and he said, 'Indeed! may I ask who your first floor lodgers are?' and when I told him an old lady and her two daughters, he laughed again. And then he asked whether the girls, meaning you and your sister, were handsome, and a whole load more questions, till, at last, I was half affronted, for I thought he was reflecting upon the credit of my house; and so I told him, that, in my opinion, the ladies were more respectable than their visitor, whether he was a captain or a lord; and I was quite sure so, if he was imposing upon them in a false character. And so then he wanted to draw in his horns, and say that it was very likely he was mistaken: he could not boast of any acquaintance with the gentleman, and dare say his name after all, was Frederick.

"'Perhaps it's Lord Frederick" says I, looking at him full in the face. 'Very likely it may be,' said he growing very grand all at once, and snapping me up very short. So, I was just going to beg his pardon, if I'd affronted him, when Stevens came in, and I left them together."

"This is another proof of deliberate deception," thought the agonised Grace, who could no longer indulge a hope that her unfortunate sister had not fallen a prey to the designs of a villain. Again, however, she recurred to the faint prospect which an interview with Grant might realise and at her earnest request, Mr. Stevens, who was a good-natured, civil man, and seemed deeply interested for her, departed in search of Grant, to whose residence he had got a clue, by knowing the livery stables at which his horses were put up.

The composing medicine, which had been administered to Mrs. Woodford by the medical gentleman whom Mrs. Stevens had recommended Grace to send for, had the happy effect of throwing her into a comparatively calm and tranquil sleep; and Grace, relieved from the immediate terror of her dissolution, had now more time and opportunity to reflect on the situation in which her unhappy mother was placed by this overthrow of all her hopes.

"I am a ruined, miserable wretch, if she is not his wife, Grace. I have not ten pounds in the world; and what is to become of us, if she has indeed deserted me!" had been her despairing exclammation, when first the fatal truth had flashed upon her mind; and Grace, as she now sat by her bedside and contemplated her pale worn, cheeks and feeble frame, shuddered at the thought, that poverty and want would in all probability embitter the remaining days of her frail existence, and add pangs to those of mortified ambition and disappointed maternal affection.

From these and a long train of similar reflections, she was roused by Mrs. Stevens' appearance at the chamber door. She beckoned her out; and Grace, having whispered a charge to Jane, not to leave the bedside till her return, followed her conductress anxiously down stairs.

"My husband is come back, miss," said the important landlady; "he's met with no luck, but he'll tell you all himself."

From Mr. Stevens, Grace heard, after listening with ill-disguised impatience to the good man's exhortation to her not to fret, and to recollect that she was her mother's only stay and support, and therefore it would not to do for her to let herself be cast down, that he had succeed in finding Mr. Grant's residence, and had learned that he had quitted it for London three days since.

"I was determined, however," continued Mr. Stevens, "that I wouldn't come back with half an errand, so I asked the servant maid that answered the door whether his friend, Captain Frederick, was gone too."

"'Captain Frederick,' says she; 'I don't know no such a person; there was nobody of that name come here to see him, I'm sure.'

"I mean the gentleman that used to ride a roan horse and his servant a grey, you must know him, I'm sure."

"'Oh, that was Lord Frederick Melverly,' she replied; 'but he's not a captain.'

"'May be not,' said I, "but I didn't rightly know; but is he gone, my dear?'

"'Why, I can't hardly tell,' says she, 'whether he's gone for good or not; but his valet was here this morning, and he said his master was off, and he did not know whether he was coming back or not, but he was to stay at the hotel till farther orders.'

"This was just what I wanted," continued Mr. Stevens, so I got out of her which hotel it was and the valet's name, and away I went, without stopping a moment."

"The young man is a very decent, well-behaved sort of person, considering whose servant he is; and so when I had told him that I had a little business with his master, and should be glad to know when I could see him, or how I could write to him, he told me at once that he knew no more where his master was gone than I did, but he rather suspected he should hear shortly, as Lord Frederick had only taken one change of linen with him."

"It was a sudden journey, then, I suppose, said I, is his lordship used to such frolics?"

"He shook his head. 'It's not for one in my station to make observations on what gentlemen do,' he said; 'but I can't but say I'm sorry to see my lord so harum scarum, and 'specially when he's got the sweetest, kindest, beautifullest lady on earth; there arnt the fellow of Lady Frederick Melverly in England,' says he.'"

"Married!" ejaculated Grace, faintly.

"Aye, that's just what I said, miss," resumed Stevens. "'Married! says I; "Lord bless me, I'd no thought Lord Frederick was a married man."

"'Nobody'd think so, indeed, to look at his goings on; but he's been married only a twelvemonth, and my young lady doats on him. I call her my young lady, because I was brought up in her father's family, and my mother nursed her, God bless her sweet face.'"

"Then I'll tell you what it is," says I; "as you're Lady Frederick's friend, and not one that would encourage your master in his bad ways, I'll just tell you the business I come about, and perhaps it may lie in your way to do us some service; and I'm sure it will be doing him good, as well as your lady, and the poor young creature that he's taken away from her friends if a stop could be put at once to his journey.' So then, Miss Grace, I up and told him all about his coming here, pretending to be honourable, and how the old lady, your mother, had been foolish enough to swallow all he fed her with, and what the upshot of it had been; and then he told me that he had long suspected that his master was after no good, for that he had sent his lady and her mother off to Brighton, and made some excuse for staying behind. I could make out,' continued Stevens, 'that the family had put this young man as a bit of a spy upon his master; but though he didn't approve of his doings, he said he thought it was no use to be tittle-tattling everything he heard and saw. But he wished now he'd wrote and told the old lady there was something amiss; but, however, he said he'd promise me that the minute he did hear from his master, he'd let me know all he could.

"Married!" repeated Grace, to whose ear every other sentence that Stevens had uttered had been without meaning, so completely had that dreadful intelligence absorbed her every thought.

Maria was then, indeed, irretrievably ruined; for it was not in the power of her heartless seducer to repair the wrong he had committed, even if it were possible that he had the inclination.

Unconsciously almost to herself, Grace had, up to this moment, felt a lingering hope that Frederick, as she had used to call him, might even yet be induced to do her sister justice. But this faint ray of hope had now vanished; and in the deepest agony, Grace wrung her hands, as she repeated the fatal word which had at once pointed out to her the certainty of her poor Maria's infamy and degradation.

CHAPTER XXI.

"My poverty, but not my will, consents."—SHAKESPEARE.

A MONTH, a miserable month of grief, and regret, and suspense, passed away, without a single word of positive intelligence having reached the unhappy relatives of the lost Maria.

Slowly, and by almost imperceptible degrees, Mrs. Woodford's health mended, and she became able to quit the chamber, in which, from the moment she entered it, Grace had been day and night her constant, never-tiring companion.

It was in vain that Mrs. Stevens remonstrated with her on her thus sacrificing herself to one who felt neither affection nor gratitude to her in return, but received her most devoted attendance as only a matter of course, and repaid her most affectionate assiduity with petulant murmurings, and the most incessant lamentations for the loss of one who seemed totally to have forgotten that there was such a person as her mother in existence.

At Grace's earnest request, Mrs. Stevens had carefully kept secret their discovery of the real situation in life of the *soi-disant* Captain Frederick; and the former frequently, with the bitterest anguish, was compelled to listen to the fond mother's anticipations of even yet beholding her " child " the bride of the supposed Frederick. Other cares and anxieties, however, soon superseded all that Mrs. Woodford felt upon her favourite's account. The small sum of money which she was in possession of at the commencement of her illness, was nearly exhausted in the necessary expenses of a sick chamber ; and Grace heard with terror her mother's despairing anticipations.

" Yes, the ungrateful wretch has brought me to want, as well as shame," she would exclaim ; " the money that should have been saved to support myself in the decline of life, has all been wasted upon her, and I shall be left to die of want."

" No, no, do not say so, dear mother ; I am young, and strong, and active, and willing to work, and though————" Grace burst into tears at her mother's angry and contemptuous look.

" And do you think then that I would consent to live upon your earnings ?" she replied ; " and if I would, pray, what is it that you flatter yourself you could get a living at—hay-making, or weeding, or something of that sort, I suppose ; but you would find working in the fields a very different sort of thing, I can tell you, to what playing at it was, in your father's lifetime. No, no, Grace ; it's all very fine to talk of working for your living ————"

" I did not mean, of course, that I could earn a living at such labour as that," observed Grace, mildly ; " but even that," and she turned away to hide the tears that were swelling in her eyes, " would be preferable to seeing you want."

" Well, well, you are a good girl, Grace," returned the mother, somewhat softened ; " but we must try to find some better way of getting a living. Oh, how I wish we could find out whether Sir Walter is really living, and where he is, there would still be a chance that————"

" My dear, dear mother, never think of Sir Walter. Do not let us ever trust to chances again," interrupted Grace, who could not conceal her impatience at her mother's continuing to indulge her visionary schemes of aggrandisement. " There is a most excellent living to be got here," she continued with liveliness, " by possessing taste and ingenuity ; and you know both you and Maria have always allowed that I possess some ; I am sure I could make far prettier, and more tasty caps, and bonnets, and spencers, and pelisses than any we have seen in that milliner's window, that we pass round the corner; and, yet she can afford to keep a footman, and employs, Jane told me, who once lived with her, some twenty or thirty young people to work for her."

"And, pray, how would you make your wonderful taste and ingenuity known?" inquired Mrs. Woodford, in a contemptuuos tone; "you have not got a shop, or connections, or friends."

"No; but a shop might be had, or at least a handsome front parlour, and Jane says Mrs. Somerford, the milliner, only had a parlonr, and then I could make up some showy things "————

"And, pray, where's the money to come from for this fine scheme, and I have not a guinea left, and owe more than that to the doctor."

Grace did not dare reply what was in her thoughts, that they possessed many, many superfluous articles, which, if sold, would produce the necessary money. Her own share was, indeed, comparatively small; but she knew nearly fifty pounds had been expended upon Maria's finery since their arrival at Bath, and surely now there could be no use in keeping what was utterly useless, and must, every time she looked at it, remind her (Mrs. Woodford) of the folly and vanity of her expectations.

"And they must be parted with," sighed Grace, who saw that the scheme she had so sanguinely planned in her own mind would all fall to the ground from the want of her mother's concurrence. "Yes, poverty will compel her to part even with these treasured relics, and then it will be only to prolong the miserable day of utter want, without affording the means of trying to extricate ourselves."

As she had predicted, Mrs. Woodford acted; the dresses, the trinkets, all the mementos of her ungrateful daughter, were preserved as something too sacred to be touched till every other means of raising money were totally exhausted. The silver spoons, teapot, candlesticks, &c., &c., which she had, to Grace's infinite regret and shame, brought away from Llan—— were the first sacrifices, Mrs. Stevens, who was given to understand by Mrs. Woodford that her embarrassment was only temporary, having agreed to take them as security for rent due, and in addition advanced her a few pounds; but week after week passed on, the remittances she had pretended to expect did not arrive, and Mrs. Stevens began very plainly to hint that the rent was fast mounting up, and that Mrs. Woodford had already had more than it was prudent to advance on such old-fashioned plate, which wouldn't fetch a farthing more than its weight as old silver. Jane, too, was evidently fidgetty, as she expressed it, about her quarter's wages; she wanted shoes and a new dark gown for afternoons, and she dinned her wants so often in Grace's ears, that the latter was compelled to purchase her silence by presents from her own little wardrobe, which, without paying the debt, were worth more than it came to.

Incessant had been Grace's prayers to her mother to discharge at once this useless incumbrance to their sinking state.

"What will Stevens think? what will everbody think?" was her reply. "They will know directly wh are ruined. If I could get rid of that boy. indeed, and that vile, deceitful man, too, promised to use his interest to get him into some asylum. Oh! that ever I should trust such a false, vile, base villain————" and then a string of epithets and invectives would follow, which totally banished the subject in question, and again Jane and the poor dumb boy, who were now felt as burthensome, were forgotten.

Convinced that it was useless to hope that her mother ever would be brought to a reasonable view of her situation, or be persuaded to take reasonable measures to obviate the wretched state towards which she was fast sinking, Grace at length determined upon taking at least one decisive step by acquainting Jane of the little probability there was of her being paid her wages if she remained, and prevailing on her, not only to discharge herself, but to assist her (Grace) in secretly procuring the means of paying her what was due.

"Laws of mercy on me, Miss Grace, you make my hair stand on end to think that you should be brought to work for to pay me my wages, and my missus keeping up her consequence and——; but there, I won't say another word about her, only that yon are over and over too good to belong to such a——"

"And will you then, Jane, interrupted Grace mildly: "will you speak to Mrs. Somerford about your going back to her, as she said she wanted you, and that will be a good excuse to my mother for leaving her; and then, if Mrs. Somerford can give me work, she can pay you for it, and that will set all right between us."

"I delare I can't help crying to think of it," and Jane burst out into a loud sob; "but, howsomever, I'll go to my old missus this very arternoon, and if so be that she's perwided with a maid, I'll be bound it won't be so many days afore she can recommend me to some of her customers; and I know, too, that if I tell her about you, miss, she'll find you work, for she's a real good-hearted woman, only so passionate, which was the cause of my leaving, for I am very passionate myself, and won't be put out by nobody, and that Charlotte which lived housemaid with her——"

"Yes; she behaved very ill to you, Jane," interrupted Grace, who had heard the story of Jane's wrongs from Charlotte at least ten times; "but now I'll go to my mother, for fear she should want me."

"She is a nice, dear young lady," ejaculated Jane, looking after her. "only she's so fidgety she can't never listen to one."

Grace, however, listened with patience and undisguised pleasure to all Jane's long rigmarole story when she returned in the evening from Mrs. Somerford's, having asked leave of Mrs. Woodford to step out for a quarter of an hour, a permission she extended to nearly three hours, to her mistress's great annoyance.

"I am really surprised, Mrs. Jane, at the liberties you take," observed the latter, when Jane at length entered to know if missus wanted anything for her supper; "but I assure you, if you think to take advantage of me because I have not paid your paltry wages you are mistaken."

"I don't want to take any advantages, I'm sure, madame," replied Jane pertly; "and as to my wages, I shall never ask you for them; "but I've got another place, and shall be obliged to you to spare me as soon as ever it's convenient, because I hope you won't stand in a poor servant's light of getting a good place and good wages."

"This is very sudden," observed Mrs. Woodford, in whose mind there was an evident struggle between her wounded pride and her hope of getting rid of Jane, not only without her wages, but without being humiliated by acknowledging that she could no longer afford to keep her.

"Oh, no, it's nothicg sudden, ma'am, only my old missus has often wished me back again since I left her, and so, as she's without a servant, I thought I couldn't do otherwise than offer myself, and if you please I'd be glad to go as soon as convenient."

"Oh, you may go as soon as you like, but it is not convenient at present for me to settle with you," replied Mrs. Woodford.

"Oh, never mind that, ma'm, I arn't particular about the money, for my old missus will advance me enough to buy shoes and that, and a new dark gownd to wear of arternoons."

Grace stole out of the room, leaving Jane to settle with her mother when she was to go, and in a short time she was followed by the latter. '

"I've settled it all, miss; I'm to go to-morrow night. And Mrs. Somerford says she's got plenty of work for you, if you're capable, as I told her you was; but how you're to do it without missus finding it out passes me."

"Leave that to me, Jane," returned Grace, who felt at this moment as if a heavy burthen had been removed from her heart, by this annunciation.

"But you'll be obliged to call on Mrs. Somerford, miss, for she must talk to you, and indeed, she's mighty curious to see a young lady as has got such honest principles as to go to work to pay a poor servant their wages, she says there aren't many such to be met with, now-a-days."

Grace did not much approve of appearing as an object of curiosity to the milliner, but Jane assured her that Mrs. Somerford could not give out her work without proper directions; and it was concluded that Grace should attend her future employer's commands the morning after Jane had entered upon her service.

For the first time since she had entered Bath Grace retired to her bed with the happy anticipation of possessing the means of at least warding off the extreme destitution which she had so often contemplated as the inevitable result of her mother's thoughtless and improvident conduct.

"Of course, if I continue to give satisfaction," she reflected, Mrs. Somerford will not refuse me employment, after my debt to Jane is paid; my mother will by degrees become reconciled to my working; we must remove into less expensive lodgings and we shall be———oh, no, no, never, never, shall I be able to say happy again, while Maria——." A burst of grief interrupted her sanguine enumeration of the comforts that would spring from her humble but zealous exertions, and it was some time before she could again return to the tranquil contemplation of her plans for the future.

On the morning appointed, Grace readily found an excuse for going out for half an hour, for they had now no servant to fetch in what was necessary.

The disposal secretly. through the means of Jane, of her coral earrings, necklace, and other ornaments, which the latter had found a purchaser for in one of Mrs. Somerford's *young ladies*, at a tolerably fair price, compared to what they had cost, had provided Grace with the means of going to market.

Mrs. Woodford expressed no surprise when with a large shawl thrown over her shoulders, and a coarse straw bonnet, which she had carefully preserved, as having been the gift of her poor father, who had brought it himself from Bristol, to keep his pretty Grace from burning herself, and freckling her face in the sun—not that he thought freckles or a tanned skin any disadvantage to her, but that they afforded Mrs. Woodford an everlasting subject for finding fault, and scolding both him and his favourite—she presented herself at her bed-side, and inquired what she should purchase for dinner.

"Whatever you like, Grace," was the reply, in a tone half petulant, half dejected. "It's no use to ask me," she continued, her usual peevishness surmounting even the little natural feeling which had been for a moment excited by beholding the child, whom she had taken so much pains to spoil and alienate from her, thus cheerfully setting her the example of sacrificing pride and vanity at the shrine of independence. "You have chosen to act without consulting me, in getting the means to play the market-woman," she added, turning coldly away, " and it's only mocking at me to pretend to ask me for orders."

" My dear, dear mother, how can you so cruelly misinterpret my motives ?" exclaimed Grace.

" There, again, you've returned to your old custom of *mothering* me upon every occasion, though you know how I hate the word. Your sister never called me mother in her life, though your low-minded father was always ridiculing her for obeying me, and calling me"——

Grace had glided out of the room, without waiting for the conclusion of this censure upon her father, whose memory was too justly dear to her to allow of her listening with composure to aught that could reflect upon him ; and before Mrs. Woodford had finished upon the comparative gentility of her daughters, the gentle and really dutiful girl was standing, with glowing cheeks, and throbbing heart, waiting with her basket in her hand, at the counter of Mrs. Somerford : while the latter was assiduously endeavouring to satisfy the capricious taste of an elderly over-dressed lady, who was examining, and trying on, and rejecting, with expressions of affected contempt, all the showy silk bonnets the milliner offered to her.

" They're all *ojus*, I declare, Somerford," said the fat old lady, in a discontented tone. " But really, since I've been to France, I hate everything English. There is'nt a bit of taste in one of your women; all they make is somehow so frumpish and dowdy. I wish to goodness you'd get a French woman to manage your business for you, it would be pounds in your pocket."

" I'm sure, madam, I'm very sorry we can't give you satisfaction," said Mrs. Somerford, in an an humble tone ; " but, I expect a young woman, that's highly recommended for taste, to join my establishment in a day or two, and perhaps she'll be able to please you better."

" Well, then, I won't have any of these frightful things ; I'll wait till I see what she can do ; but she must be decidedly Frenchified, or she won't do, I can tell you. Wait, I think I'll make that French white, with the blonde lace round the edge, serve me for a day or two ; for it's quite impossible to go to the rooms in this thing ;" and she threw aside a handsome pale blue one which she appeared, from its freshness, to have scarcely worn.

" This is the best, though one of the most troublesome customers I have got, Miss Woodford," said the milliner, who had seen Jane's greeting to the latter as she entered the shop, and readily guessed that she beheld, in the pretty, unpretending girl before her, the new workwoman of whose taste her maid had spoken so highly. " If you can manage to please Mrs. Spriggs," she continued, " I can promise you employment ; for, it's as much as one person can do to work for her, she's so whimsical, and so fond of change : but come in, and we will have a little talk together. Jane talked of nothing else but you, ever since she came back ; and I assure you, she has made all my young ladies quite envious of you."

Grace felt that it was not any great subject for exultation, to be the object of envy on account of her capabilities to manufacture handsome bonnets, or tasty caps ; but she silently followed Mrs. Somerford into a room, where about a dozen young women were working, and she humbly and patiently submitted to the chatty milliner's directions as to the disposal of the silk, and lace, and ribbons, and flowers, and all the numerous etceteras, which were entrusted to her.

" It's not at all in my way, you see, Miss Woodford, to give such work out of the house ; and I did not intend to employ you except in dress-making, where, of course, I should know what you were about.   But I wish, if possible, to please Mrs. Spriggs, who is an uncommon good customer ; and so, perhaps, as you're a new hand, and will follow your own taste, you may have a chance of hitting her fancy ; but you must be very quick, and let me have two or three caps and a couple of bonnets as soon as possible, for it's ten to one she'll be here to-morrow again, teazing me again."

Grace promised attention, and the exertion of all the abilities she possessed ; but she almost trembled at the task she was undertaking when she saw the neat and delicate articles which the young women around her were fabricating, and heard that none of them could give satisfaction to the difficult Mrs. Spriggs.

"I'll put them up in a bandbox for you, my dear, for you cannot crush them into that basket," said Mrs. Somerford, who was evidently disposed to be very kind to her timid little workwoman ; "you won't mind carrying them home, I suppose?" Grace gulped down the small remains of pride, which made her feel somewhat humiliated, at the thought of appearing in the street with the emblem of her new vocation. Her mother had so often descanted on the impropriety and meanness of being seen even with a small parcel, that Grace had imbibed the idea, though contrary to her usual good sense, and she now felt ready to sink as she beheld the immense large bandbox which Mrs. Somerford fetched out and began to pack the materials in.

A long whisper from Jane, who had been watching Grace's countenance, however, put a stop to Mrs. Somerford's proceedings.

"You are right, that will be best," she observed. "Never mind, Miss Woodford, Jenny will bring the things home for you, as it is such a large box ; because, as she says, if your mother was to happen to see you, it would betray you at once, though, indeed, I can't think what sort of a mother she can be to make this necessary."

Grace looked her grateful thanks to Jenny for having thus contrived to spare her the anticipated mortification, and departed, having promised to use her utmost ability and expedition to please the difficult Mrs. Spriggs.

In a few hours Grace, having easily obtained her mother's permission to retire early to her room, was assiduously at work at her new employment, to which she devoted nearly the whole of the night. The next day and the next night were passed in the same manner, and on the morning following, before her mother had risen, or it was likely she should meet many people in the street, Grace proceeded with the fruits of her assiduity to the miliner's.

"Beautiful !—charming !—tasty, indeed !—were the epithets with which every single article was received by Mrs. Somerford as Grace drew them out, one by one, and timidly held them up for approval. "Look here ladies," continued the milliner ; "here's patterns for you ! I wonder when any of you will show me anything like these ; but there's one thing to be said, to be sure ; none of you have been in Paris, as Miss Woodford has."

Grace was about to disavow her having enjoyed this opportunity of improving her taste ; but a significant look and a sly pull at her frock explained to her that Mrs. Somerford had her motives for this assertion, and that it was no mistake on her part. She was not a little mortified, however, at the manner in which her profluctions were received by the young women to whom Mrs. Somerford's observations were addressed. Contemptuous tosses of the head, half-suppressed titters, and significant looks at one another, accompanied the display which their mistress made of the taste of her new workwoman; and Grace felt heartily rejoiced when the latter obsevred—

"Well, now, Miss Woodford, if you will come into the parlour, and we will have a little talk about terms, and so forth, while I get my breakfast."

The "terms, and so forth," as the milliner had phrased it, proved sadly beneath even Grace's moderate expectations; but then, she had drawn her inferences from the extravaant prices which she had seen given for similar articles, and her knowledge of the comparatively trifling value of the materials.

Such as they were, however, Grace was compelled to submit; for Mrs. Somerford assured her they were higher than she gave to any other of her women.

"But, as I mean to tell Mrs. Spriggs they're made by a French milliner," she observed, "I think I shall succeed in pleasing her; and so I can afford to pay you something more on that account."

"It will be a long time," thought Grace, as she walked slowly home; "a long time, indeed, before I have even paid Jane her four pounds at this rate; and how shall I, in the meantime, contrive to keep my mother from finding me out? And how, too, is she to be supported in the meantime? And when I am free to work entirely for her, and she, as she must do, consents that I shall devote all my time to it, how shall I ever be able to make sufficient to satisfy her wants, much more her wishes?"

These reflections were most dispiriting, and, added to the effects of her extreme fatigue, broken rest, and the recollections which in the long hours of silence and solitude had perpetually forced themselves upon her, made her look the image of melancholy and dejection as she walked into their usual sitting room, where to her utter surprise she found her mother already seated at the breakfast table, which she had, with the assistance of Joe, who now took the most active part in the household business, set ready before she ventured out.

"Upon my word, you seem to act quite independent, Miss Grace, going out and coming in just as you please," observed Mrs. Woodford, but, at this moment raising her eyes to the face of her daughter, she absolutely started.

"Good gracious, child!" she exclaimed, "where have you been, and what have you been about, for you look so deadly pale——"

"I am very well," interrupted Grace, beginning to take off her bonnet, and turning away to conceal her tears; "indeed, I felt so unwell that——"

"Well, well, if that was your reason for going out, that is enough; but now do make me a bit of toast, for I couldn't fancy Joe's making it."

Grace proceeded with alacrity to do as she desired; but, whether from the heat of the fire or the agitation she suffered, she had scarcely began her task before her head grew giddy, her sight failed, and, making an effort to rise, she fell senseless on the hearth-rug.

Mrs. Woodford's cries soon brought nearly every one in the house into the room, and Grace, when she recovered herself, found herself supported by Mrs. Stevens, the landlady, her good-natured husband holding a glass of water to her lips, and every one deeply interested in her recovery.

It required, indeed, absolute force to repress poor Joe's violent demstrations of joy at beholding her once more open her eyes; and the first thing that Grace became perfectly conscious of was Becky's vain, yet forcible atempts to turn the poor dumb boy out of the room, and his violent resistance.

"What is the matter? let him be, Becky; he will go if I desire him," said

Grace, looking around her, and then lifting her finger to Joe, who instantly omprehended her, and relinquished his opposition to Becky.

"I cannot think what is the matter with the girl, remarked Mrs. Woodford, who had recovered from the terror which at first seized her, she having believed actually that Grace was dead when she beheld her extended lifeless at her feet. "She used to be strong and healthy," she continued, "and now she——"

"It needn't be much wondered at, I think," observed Mrs. Stephens, bluntly; "the poor thing is killing herself as fast as she can, waiting upon you all day, and working for you all night. Ah, it's no use, Miss Grace, if you look at me ever so, I must speak my mind, and I do say that it's a shame you should be so imposed upon."

"What is the meaning of this, Grace ? What is Mrs. what's-her-name talking about?" demanded Mrs. Woodford, turning with an air of offended dignity from Mrs. Stevens's determined look.

"Oh, it's of no use to ask her, poor thing, for she'll tell you nothing about it," interrupted the officious landlady; but if she don't there's plenty that will. Ask my husband there, or ask either of them two gentlemen that live in my front two-pair, and that's just gone up-stairs when they see the poor girl wasn't dead. Just ask any of them, I say, and they'll tell what they think of your keeping up your consequence, and living in these apartments at a guinea a week, and wanting as much attendance as a duchess, and your poor daughter sitting up, night after night, when she ought to be at rest, working her fingers to the bone to keep you up in your grandeur; but it won't do, Pride must have a fall, as the old saying is, and it may as well come sooner as later; and so, Mrs. Woodford, I beg you'll look out for a place that will suit you, for I shall want these rooms for an old lodger of mine that is coming next week to Bath."

Mrs. Woodford looked thunderstruck.

"This is really quite incomprehensible to me," she observed, still striving to keep up her consequence. "Do you mean then, my good woman, to say that you will turn me out of my lodgings?"

"It's better for me to turn you out of your lodgings than be turned myself out of my house," replied Mrs. Stevens; "and that I must be if I don't pay my rent, and, I fancy, if I depend on you it will be a long time first. Good woman, indeed! I think you might condescend to give me my proper name, and not good woman me, as if you were talking to your inferiors."

"Come, come, this isn't a time to be scolding and pecking at one another," interrupted Mr. Stevens, good-humouredly. "She didn't call you out of your name, I hope, when she called you a good woman; and, as to turning out, why I should be sorry to behave so sharply, or put anybody to a *non plush*; and so——"

"And so just go down stairs, and mind your shop-board and your 'prentices," interrupted Mrs. Stevens, angrily; "I shan't do or say anything but what my conscience tells me is right, and you know what you said yourself this morning when you saw this poor girl stealing out of the house before her mother was up to carry home the work that she's been poring her eyes out at for these three nights."

"What work? what does the woman mean, Grace?" demanded Mrs. Woodford, in a violent passion.

Grace in vain tried to give utterance to a word, so completely was she overcome with the fear that her mother would attribute to her well-meant exertions all the mortifications she had received, and was likely still to receive, from Mrs. Stevens.

THE PRIDE OF THE VILLAGE;

OR,

THE FARMER'S DAUGHTERS.

GRACE AND MR. LOVELL.

CHAPTER XXII.

" He has been rash from his youth upwards,
Yet tempered by redeeming nobleness."—BYRON.

The explanation, which she was unable to give, was soon, however, and without any qualifications, given by the landlady ; and Mrs. Woodlord, had the mortification, not only of hearing Grace's honest, and upright principle commended in opposition to her own conduct, but of also hearing told, over and over again, that no one respected or pitied, or would even endure her were it not for the sake of the poor girl, whcm she had treated with so much coldness and contumely.

12

over again that no one respected or pitied, or would even endure her, were it not for the sake of the poor girl, whom she had always treated with so much coldness and contumely.

She was told, too, again and again—for Mrs. Stevens was determined, as she said, not to mince matters—that the sooner she gave up her present apartments and paid the month's rent that was due the more agreeable it would be to her landlady; and, to complete the measure of her mortification, the latter wound up the whole by observing that as, of course, the cheapest lodgings now would be the best, and she respected Grace so much, that she didn't like to turn them out, she thought the best thing they could do would be to make up their minds to have the two attics, which she would make comfortable for them, and only charge seven shillings a week, and the boy could sleep with their 'prentices; or, if they liked to have one room on the second-floor at the same price, she could accommodate them that way; but one thing was certain, they must without delay give up their present apartments.

With infinite difficulty Grace succeeded in persuading her mother to check the torrent of indignation that was ready to burst forth at the indignity which she conceived was offered to her in these propositions; but Mrs. Stevens, satisfied with having had the opportunity of saying, at last, without reserve, all that had been for the last week or two rankling in her mind, was by no means in a hurry to press for a decided answer, and therefore readily yielded to Grace's suggestion that she should give her, Mrs. Woodford, a few hours to consider what she should determine on.

It was some time after they had been left alone together before Mrs. Woodford thoroughly comprehended all that Grace had to tell her in explanation of Mrs. Stevens' assertion; but even her stubborn heart relented when she heard that her daughter had actually submitted to the mortification of engaging herself as a workwoman, and devoted to the completion of her task the time that ought to have been given to rest.

Grace's pleasure at finding that her mother did not feel angry with her was, however, greatly damped by the latter's indignant resolution to remove instantly from the house in which she had been so insulted.

"We will go this very morning and look out for other lodgings, Grace," she observed; "and so try and eat some breakfast, for you will look so pale——; why do you sigh and look in that manner, Grace? Surely you would not wish me to humble myself so as to take their wretched attics?"

"My dear mother, do not be angry with me for saying that I do not see that you can do better. There are only two shillings left of the last trifle which I raised, and how can we afford to remove, even if we should get rooms as cheap, and then there is the fortnight due, which, of course, if we remove——"

"I see how it is," interrupted Mrs. Woodford, in a tone of ming ledpetulance and despondency. "I see it is all settled, so I may as well give myself up at once. Well, it matters not, I suppose, where I spend the short remnant of my days, and so you may do just as you like, I shall not interfere again."

"Do not say so, my dear mother," said Grace, with affectionate earnestness; "would to heaven it were in my power to secure you every comfort that your heart could wish, but——"

"I know it, I know it, child, you cannot do more! but its hard, very hard, after such prospects as I've had, to submit ——Oh! if your sister—if Maria could see——"

"That is another reason why I think it best to remain here, mother," said Grace, timidly; "should any information arrive we should be moved to another——"

"You are right," interrupted Mrs. Woodford, with an eagerness that showed how much more deeply she was interested when Maria was concerned than when even her own comfort and almost existence were at stake." "You are quite right," she repeated, "and besides, it will show her what misery she has brought upon me, and prove how cruel it was of her to desert me in such a manner."

Grace was silent, she was thinking at that moment how probable it was that Maria, with more real truth than justice, was upbraiding her mother as the cause of all that had befallen her.

"She cannot, I know she cannot, be happy," thought Grace, whose mind was still totally absorbed in the subject which her mother had thus brought so strongly to her mind. "No, even though she may now be enjoying all the luxuries and pleasures that wealth can purchase; still, I am well convinced that her heart would not let her be happy, and if the time should come, as unfortunately it too surely will come, that the villain who has robbed her of her fair fame should become tired of her and desert her—oh! what then would her reflections be?"

"Do you hear me, Grace? This is the second time I have told you to go at once to Mrs. Stevens, and tell her I shall accept her offer of the two attics for the present; and tell her, too, that I hope she will make them as decent as she can."

Grace departed on her errand, well satisfied; and Mrs. Stevens, who had probably anticipated much more difficulty in getting possession of her *splendid* first-floor for her old lodger, who was such good pay, very readily promised to make Mrs. Woodford's new apartments as comfortable for her as she possibly could.

It was not without abundance of tears, ejaculations, and expressions of contempt, despondency, and useless regret, that Mrs. Woodford on the following morning, was installed the inhabitant of a three-pair-of-stairs apartment, as Mrs. Stevens was accustomed to designate what, in more homely language, would have been called the garrets.

Grace had laboured indefatigably all day, and, with the assistance of what little time and pains Becky could subtract from her numerous calls and occupations below, she had made the room as neat and nice as cleanliness, and a great deal of taste in the disposal of a few prints, which Mrs. Stevens had given her to hide the hole in the lath and plaister wall, which there was no time now to fill up, could do; three or four pots of geraniums had been transplanted by Becky from the back kitchen window, because she had heard Miss Grace say how fond she was of flowers; an old thin muslin frock of Grace's had been hastily disposed into a window curtain, and altogether the room was much more neat and comfortable than from the general scale of Mrs. Stevens' accommodation Mrs. Woodford could have had a right to expect. But still it was a garret; and the poor mortified victim of vanity and pride, after having with difficulty suppressed her feelings in the presence of her landladly, who very ceremoniously waited to give her possession of her new apartments, no sooner found herself alone with Grace than she gave way to a paroxysm of despair and lamentation, which in a moment dissipated all the innocent pleasure and pride which her daughter had felt in thus rendering the place comfortable for her.

"My dear mother, we shall be very quiet and snug here, indeed; and this room is so very warm in the winter, and my bed is close to the head of yours, and here is a door opens, so that I can come in a moment if you want me ; and I have got saucepans, and everything we want; in my room, and Mrs. Stevens is going to put a stove in there, and then I can cook and all, as comfortable as if it was a kitchen."

Grace would have run on for some time longer, in enumeration of the various advantages which attend their change of rooms, but her mother impatiently interrupted her.

"It is all very fine, I dare say, Grace, and it may suit you very well, but if I stay here three months I shall stay till am a corpse."

All Grace's smiles vanished in a moment, and she burst into tears.

"Besides," continued Mrs. Woodford in the same tone of despondency, and without appearing at all to notice the effect her observation had upon her daughter—"besides, now we have got up here, how are we to live? Not a hope can remain of any fortunate chance happening to extricate us from our difficulties ; and as to what you say about your working, I question if you would be able to earn more than would pay the rent, and much more keep us both, and that boy too."

"Grace's tears redoubled ; it was true that it would not be possible with her utmost exertions, and she felt painfully convinced of the truth of what her mother had uttered ; but still it was not a time for that mother, who had with difficulty, and almost as it were, by force, been brought to submit to this curtailment of her expenses, to utter these discouragements to the poor girl who was willing to sacrifice everything for her comfort.

Grace, indeed, was soon most painfully convinced that no efforts which lay within her power to make could satisfy her mother or even induce her for a moment to repress her selfish repinings and lamentations.

Removed from all restraint respecting the work, Grace now was, except when attending on her mother, constantly employed in manufacturing caps, bonnets, &c., the decidedly French taste which Mrs. Spriggs discovered in her first productions having given that lady such ample satisfaction that she had not only given Mrs. Somerford a large order, but recommended several ladies, who, if not equally fantastic, were equally desirous of being set off to the best advantage.

Long, however, before Grace had worked out the debt to Jane, every means that she could command of raising a shilling to provide necessaries for their subsistence was exhausted, and Grace was compelled, as she was making the tea for her mother at night, to tell her that she did not know how to provide breakfast in the morning.

"What is to be done then?" demanded Mrs. Woodford.

"I do not know, my dear mother," observed the dejected girl. "After this week, I trust, Mrs. Somerford will have to pay me, instead of Jane, and——"

"I wish I was dead and out of your way." sighed Mrs. Woodford, with her usual peevishness.

Grace answered only by tears ; she could not, indeed, command her voice to speak.

"That boy shall go about his business to-morrow, I am determined ; it's of no use attempting to keep him, when we are likely to starve ourselves," said Mrs. Woodford, who seemed to seek some object on which to vent her spleen, and whose eye at that moment chanced to rest upon Joe, who, on his knees was, with his breath blowing up the embers of the fire, to make the kettle boil, bellows not being among the necessaries allotted to the three pair of stairs.

"And yet it takes but little to keep him, and he is so useful," said Grace imploringly. "Indeed, my dear mother, if you consider how often I should be obliged to leave my work, and how little it would agree with delicate satins and gauzes, and all the rest of the articles I must handle, that I should have to light fires, and clean hearths, do numerous other little jobs that poor Joe does so willingly——"

"But, will this handiness and willingness enable you to find him in bread and butter?" interrupted Mrs. Woodford, impatiently. "To-morrow morning, for instance, he will, I dare say, get up and save you all trouble; but he will look for his meal afterwards."

"And I shall during the time he is so employed, have earned much more than would provide that meal," said Grace, with more spirit than she usually showed. "But, my dear mother, do not think that I wish to act in opposition to you. Let me prevail only on you not to turn the poor boy into the street, until we have made an effort to secure him a shelter. If you were to write to the parish officers of Llan——, they must take him."

"I write to them!" exclaimed Mrs. Woodford, in a rage; "would you have me then, expose myself to their impudence, and ridicule, and ——? but, this is always your kindness and consideration for me—my feelings are never to be consulted."

Grace knew that to reply to this unjust remark would only be to draw upon herself a torrent of equally unfounded but not less galling reproaches, and she, therefore, contrived to turn her mother's attention from the subject of immediate discussion by observing that Mrs. Stevens, she had no doubt, would be glad to purchase her (Grace's) green silk shawl, she having more than once remarked that it was remarkably neat and handsome.

"I shall then, you know, my dear mother, have my pelisse, and my old white shawl, and that is plenty."

"Mrs. Woodford made no reply, and Grace, concluding the matter thus settled, proceeded cheerfully to her evening's work, resolving not to speak to Mrs. Stevens until her mother should have gone to bed, and thus be spared the mortification, should the latter refuse, in which case, she (Grace) had resolved upon applying to Mrs. Somerford to lend her a few shillings.

During the whole evening Mrs. Woodford continued in the sullens; but Grace still persevered in trying to restore her to good humour, by describing to her the various characters whom she met with at Mrs. Somerford's, who, from being at best, only a second, or indeed even a third-rate milliner, was rapidly rising into fashion and reputation, from the belief that had been raised that the newest and most approved articles in her show-room were manufactured by a foreigner of rank, who was obliged thus to assist in maintaining her family, in consequence of her husband having lost his estate in the recent political dissensions.

Mrs. Woodford, however, would not condescend to join in the harmless laugh which Grace indulged at the expense of her employers; and wearied, at length, with her useless efforts, Grace herself, sank into silence and melancholy reflection, mechanically almost still plying her needle and scissors, and, from time to time, pausing to examine the success of her disposition of a flower, a bow or a feather.

"And now, pray, how much do you reckon you have earned to-day?" said Mrs. Woodford, when Grace, having finished all her present stock was gathering carefully together the remnants.

"I shall be allowed about three shillings I expect," returned Grace, timidly; "but I could do more, you know, mother, if I had it to do; it is yet quite early—only nine o'clock."

" And this Mrs. Somerford, I suppose, reckoning moderately, will get a couple of guineas profit, according to the usual prices, resumed her mother.

" Yes; but, then, she has, she says, great expenses, and great losses ——"

" I wish you would allow me to finish what I was saying, Grace," said Mrs. Woodford, peevishly. " I don't see," she continued, " why you should be wasting your time and abilities for such paltry pay. Now, if you could get a room fit for a show-room, and make up some cheap materials in the same taste as these, and have some cards printed, and make it known that you were the person employed by Mrs. Somerford, there is not a doubt but that you would succeed in getting all who now employ her on your account.

" It is very possible," returned Grace, whose cheeks glowed with indignant shame at a proposal which seemed the very climax of baseness and treachery.

" Well, and what then, need hinder you from trying this scheme, Grace? I have still the means left of raising ten or twelve pounds, and that would be sufficient to begin with, because you could, no doubt, get credit in the same manner as she does; and then too there would be a chance of something turning up in our favour, whereas, while we are prisoned up here there can be no hope. Yes, it will be the only way," she resumed after some moments' further reflection; " and so I would, at once, have you ask Mrs. Somerford's advice as to the best method of disposing of Maria's clothes and trinkets, which ought to fetch a great deal more than the sum necessary. I did think," she continued, " that nothing in the world should prevail on me to touch them; but, it is plain she is well enough off not to care for them; and if she isn't, she don't deserve that I should have so much care for her, a wicked, ungrateful girl, never even to write a word to let me know that she is safe, or that she cares about what becomes of one who has sacrificed everything for her. Yes, yes, they shall all go. There, Grace, there are the keys of the trunks; don't let me see them, for I should break my heart. Make Joe take them into your room, and then you can do the best you can; only, if you could borrow the money, leaving them as a security, I should be much better satisfied than selling them outright."

" My dear mother, I will not attempt to deceive you," said Grace, in a faltering voice, and without making a step towards taking the keys. " I cannot," she continued, " bring myself to think of acting with such treachery towards Mrs. Somerford, who has ever behaved towards me with the greatest kindness and consideration. How could I ever look at her customers in the face, and tell them I was the person who, having through her, gained some reputation, and answered some other purposes, now turned ungratefully round, and endeavoured to rise upon the ruin of her benefactress? Oh, no, dear mother; let me still be content with the moderate gains ——"

" This is all very fine and very romantic, Miss Grace," interrupted her mother, with vehemence; but you will please to recollect, that I am to starve, as well as you, upon what you are pleased to call your moderate gains; but which, when you come to live upon them, you will soon feel anything but moderate."

" I would sooner submit to live on bread and water than be guilty of such base ingratitude," observed Grace, warmly.

" Very well, madam, then live on bread and water, or how you like, for I will never submit to sit down patiently, and barely exist on your wages, as you are mean enough to call them; and now mark me," she continued, with increasing passion: " from this day I will not eat a bit or sup at your expense; you may provide for yourself, and your *protégé* there (looking at Joe, who, with extreme solicitude, was watching the changes of Grace's expressive countenance, without being able to comprehend what it was that agitated her), but I will rather die than accept a morsel purchased by your earnings.''

It was in vain that Grace remonstrated against this determination; in vain she endeavoured calmly and coolly to bring her mother to reflect upon and acknowledge that the course she had pointed out could not be followed without subjecting her (Grace) to the imputation of the grossest dishonesty and ingratitude. Mrs. Woodford was obstinately bent on viewing only the advantages it offered, and the certainty, as she believed, of being at once placed in comparative comfort; and what, indeed, weighed still more on her weak mind, the certainty of being released from her present obscurity, and being once more, though at a distance, enabled to mingle in, and take interest in the gay and fashionable world, of which she had all her life sighed to become a part.

Keen and cutting as were her reproaches to Grace for her undutiful conduct, in thus setting herself up in opposition to her will, the latter bore them with unshaken firmness, her heart. Her conscience, told her that she was right; and mild, and meek, and bending as was her temper, she was resolutely firm in maintaining her principles.

Wearied at length with her own vehemence, Mrs Woodford retired sullenly to her bed, and Grace, soon after, stole softly down stairs to make the proposal to her landlady respecting the shawl which she knew the latter had greatly coveted.

"It's really a shame, my dear, to see you stripping yourself in this manner day after day, and that selfish mother of yours keeping her runaway daughter's things and her own locked up, as if she expected her to walk back and be just as good as ever, and that they could begin to flaunt away again at the same rate they did before; and I declare, Miss Grace, I positively hate to take your clothes away from you one after another, only I know you would not get so much for them anywhere else?''

Grace, had she known a little more of the world than she did, might possibly have been inclined to dispute this last assertion, for Mrs. Stephens, with all her real and exaggerated feeling for Gace, had never failed to take every advantage of the offers made her of becoming the purchaser of such articles as Grace could, or rather was determined to, spare, and had done so with no small exultation and little thought of the mortification it was natural a pretty, attractive glri might naturally be supposed to feel at parting with all the ornaments which are imagined by most—however falsely—to be necessary to the most beautiful. Without one thought of all this, we say, Mrs. Stevens had weekly seen added to her wardrobe, at a trifling expense, articles of which she could never have hoped to be the possessor; and yet Mrs. Stevens certainly felt towards Grace considerably more than was her wont towards any of the human race, herself and her husband being the only persons whom she had for many years thought worth caring about, except as to what she could make out of them.

The green silk shawl was delivered to its new possessor, and Grace, placing the fifteen shillings, about a third of its value, in her purse, which her liberal landlady had given her for it, was quitting the room, with a heart comparatively at ease, at being thus enabled to keep off want a little longer, and a step rendered more than usually light and elastic, by her having so easily got through her mortifying task, when she was intercepted in a door-way by a gentleman who was entering, apparently in a violent hurry.

"I beg your pardon, pray do not let me drive you away," he observed, gazing at Grace, with evident admiration. "I thought," he continued, still standing so that Grace could not pass him without rudeness, "I thought Stevens had been here—at least, I understood so from your damsel who did not warn me that you had company."

"Oh, it's only Miss Woodford, my lodger's daughter, Sir George," said Mrs. Stevens, curtseying to her husband's customer. "Do pray, please to walk in, sir; Stevens will be here in a minute."

"I cannot consent to cross the threshold unless that young lady be seated again, and look as cheerful as she did when I caught a glimpse of her face, instead of looking thus coldly and angrily at me, for disturbing her pleasant chit-chat with you," said Sir George.

"You are mistaken, indeed, sir," observed Grace, with reserve; "I was leaving the room when you came to the door."

"Will you tell me, then," said Sir George, advancing into the room, but still standing so that she could not pass him; "will you tell me what was the pleasant thought that excited the sweet smile on those beautiful lips which I beheld, and of which I have been so unfortunate as wholly to banish the appearance?"

"I really cannot tell you, sir, what was the subject of my thoughts at that moment," returned Grace, blushing still deeper at the intense gaze with which he beheld her.

"Then will you give Mrs. Stevens leave to tell me what you were talking about?" he resumed, still persevering in his opposition to her leaving the room, though her look and manner plainly evinced how disagreeable to her the detention was.

"No; certainly not! decidedly not!" said Grace hastily. "Mrs. Stevens and I were merely talking together on business, and such business as was not likely to interest a perfect stranger; and now, sir, I hope you will allow me to pass you, my mother will miss me."

"Business!" repeated Sir George, still gazing earnestly in her blushing face. "I know but one business a lovely girl can have a right to think of: their trade, profession, occupation, should be love, only love. Come, tell me now," and he attempted familiarly to take her hand; "tell me, do not I guess right? Were not you boasting to Mrs. Stevens of the conquests those beautiful eyes have made, or anticipating the triumphs that are to come?" Grace turned away with vexation and contempt at this flippancy.

"She won't answer me; then I know I'm right; was it so, Mrs. Stevens?" and he looked at the smiling complacent landlady for an answer.

"No, indeed, Sir George, you're quite wrong, sir, begging your pardon for telling you so, for Miss Woodford and I were upon quite another sort of an affair than love matters, I do assure you."

"It was dress then. Oh, yes, I have guessed it now," as his eye glanced at the handsome green silk shawl which Mrs. Stevens was assiduously folding. "Oh, yes," he repeated, "I see now; Miss Woodford was in imagination triumphing in the additional attraction her beauty is to derive from this pretty attractive shawl, so like herself, neat, handsome, and unassuming."

"Ah, you're quite wrong, again, Sir George," simpered Mrs. Stevens, taking the shawl which he had opened, in affected admiration, and again beginning to fold it. "Quite wrong, indeed, sir, and I'm afraid you're a very bad guesser of ladies' thoughts, for I have reason, good reason, to know that Miss Grace could not have been thinking of any such thing, because the shawl happens to be mine."

"Grace what a lovely name, and how appropriate!" said Sir George without appearing to bestow the slightest attention on what Mrs. Stevens had uttered. "Nay, do not look so distressed at my simple observation," he continued, again attempting to take her hand, which Grace again eluded; "I would not for the whole world offend you," he continued; but I am a plain-spoken fellow, apt, whether right or wrong, to utter whatever comes into my head, and really, I am at this moment more seriously inclined to fall seriously in love, than ever I was in my life. Now, pray do not frown upon me, for I shall be miserable if you leave me in displeasure. Do you plead my cause, Mrs. Stevens, with your fair friend."

"Oh, I'm sure, Sir George, if you can't prevail," said Mrs. Stevens, "it isn't likely I should; but indeed, Miss Woodford, I must say, you are a little too *particler*, you needn't keep trying to get away in such a hurry, because I'm quite sure Sir George is too much of a gentleman to say anything that's *un*proper for you to hear."

"But I'm really anxious to go upstairs to my mother," said Grace, who was by no means of opinion that Mrs. Stevens was an adequate judge of propriety.

"Well, then, I will not run the risk of incurring your displeasure, by persisting in detaining you," observed Sir George, "only promise that you will see me at some favourable opportunity."

"I cannot make any engagements, indeed, sir," returned Grace, with increased vexation.

Mr. Stevens, at this moment made his appearance, and Grace, taking advantage of the baronet's turning round to speak to him, slipped past, and ran hastily up to her own room; not a little chagrined at the chance which had thus exposed her to the importunities of one whom she considered as bolder and more presuming than any person she had ever met with.

CHAPTER XXIII.

'Tis the mind that makes the body rich;
And as the sun breaks through the darkest clouds,
So honour peereth in the meanest habit.

SHAKESPEARE.

THOUGH determined to meet with firmness all her mother's solicitations and even to resist her commands, when she felt them to be contrary to what her conscience told her was just and right, Grace was by no means prepared to contend with the mode Mrs. Woodford adopted of endeavouring to force her into compliance.

At the usual time, she carried the breakfast she had prepared to her mother's bed-side, but vain were all her efforts to prevail on her to taste it.

"You may take it away," she said, in a sullen tone; "when I want anything, I shall find means to get it, but I am not going to be dependent on your petty earnings."

Grace's heart was almost broken; but vain were all her tears, her prayers and supplications—her mother was deaf to them; and she sat down to her work at which she had been employed from the first glimpse of day-light, without having herself broken her fast.

It was long past noon before Mrs. Woodford left her bed; and then, without condescending to explain where she was going, and sternly repulsing Grace's offered assistance, she commenced dressing herself.

Grace still continued working, though her tears almost blinded her, but her mother's intentions were soon clear to her, when she saw her putting into her pocket the small box which contained all her own ornaments, as well as those which had been Maria's.

"Had you not better let Joe go with you, dear mother?" demanded Grace; "I am sure it is dangerous for you to venture alone."

"I do not care anything about it," returned the mother; he may come or not, just as you choose, but I don't know how much use such a poor being can be."

Grace, however, felt satisfied that a stout, active, and attentive lad, even though he did not possess all his senses was likely to prove of considerable service to one so little qualified for walking as her mother; and she therefore persisted in recommending that Joe should go, and took infinite pains in explaining to the poor lad, that she expected he would take care of his mistress, and bring her safe home.

It was with considerable pain, however, that even under the protection of her escort, who seemed more intelligent than usual in comprehending what he had to perform, Grace beheld her mother leave the house. She could form no idea whither she intended going, or how long she would be absent; and, in the anxiety occasioned by her absence, all other sources of vexation were for the moment forgotten.

Minutes seemed lengthened to hours, and yet Grace could not get on at all with her work. It was impossible for her to reach across the parapet, so as to see into the street, or she would certainly have passed the whole time, even from her mother's first setting out, in watching for her return; but, as that was not to be done, she was compelled to sit still, and listen with intense anxiety to every sound, in hopes that it would announce the arrival of her mother.

At length a step ascended the stairs—it was too quick and light to be either of the persons she expected; and her heart beat quick with a thousand indefinite alarms, as she replied to the gentle rap by an invitation to enter.

It was Becky, Mrs. Stevens's maid; and Becky's eyes were sparkling with pleasure, as she put into Grace's hand a parcel directed to Miss Grace Woodford.

"Who can it be from?" said Grace, looking at it, over and over again, without offering to open it. "Who brought it, Becky?"

"A young man, miss; a porter, or shopman, or something of that sort. But laws, Miss Grace, do open it; there's something handsome in it, I'll be bound, by the feel of it."

"I suspect you know what is in it, by your manner, Becky," said Grace, who still hesitated. "Do tell me, my good girl, all you know about it."

"Well, then, miss, I'll tell you really and truly. But, oh, gemini, don't you say a word to missus."

"I won't, indeed, Becky; I give you my word I will not," replied Grace, impatiently.

"Well, then, when the young man gave it to me I carried it into the parlour to missus; and so, says she: 'I'd bet sixpence that I know what this is, without opening it; but I should like to see it before it goes upstairs." And so, without any more words, and afore master could hinder, she snaps the string, and what should there be but the most beautifullest shawl that ever eyes was set on."

"'I just guessed it,' says she. 'Well, I've often heard that the loss of one is sometimes the gain of two; and so I am sure the loss of Miss Grace's paltry shawl has gained her such a one as any lady in Bath might be proud to wear.'

"'Paltry!' says master, looking at your shawl, which was hung over the chair back, because missus expects her intimate friend, Mrs. Carter, to call to-day, and she loves dearly to make her mad, because poor Mrs. Carter has got such a many children, she can't afford much finery. 'Yes, I say, paltry compared to this, Mr. Stevens,' says missus; for this is a real Ingee one, and that's only Spitalfields.'

"'It's a pity you looked at it, to put you out o' conceit o, yours, said master, again.

"Oh, I'm not out o' conceit,' says missus; 'but it's a fine thing to be a young girl, and have a pretty face.'"

"'Well, well,' said master, in a funny way, 'you cant't expect to be young and pretty all your life, and you had your day once, my dear; so tie up the shawl again, and send it to its right owner, for she's not only young and pretty enough, but good enough, to deserve anything.' And so," continued Becky, "she tied it up again, and told me to say nothing about it, but contrive and wait till you opened it, and hear what you said about it."

"I will not open it at all, Becky," said Grace firmly; "take it back again to Mrs. Stevens, and tell her I am convinced there is some mistake, it cannot be for me."

"Oh, gemini," exclaimed Becky "she'll know then, that I have told you what's in the parcel: you must just open it, if it's only to save me."

"You may open it then; I will have nothing to do with it," said Grace, coolly resuming her work.

Becky waited not a second bidding; the string was broken, and she unfolded a really splendid and valuable shawl.

"They did't care for money that paid for this, miss," said Becky, looking very sly, as she diplayed it to Grace.

"Very likely not," replied Grace, in a tone of indifference.

"I must see how you would look in it, Miss Grace," said Becky, and without waiting for an answer, threw it over Grace's shoulders.

At this moment the sound of Mrs. Woodford's crutches on the stairs gave warning of her approach; and Grace, hastily throwing off the shawl, flew, without bestowing another thought on it, to assist her mother.

Mrs. Woodford's countenance betokened weariness, disappointment, and discontentment; and she replied only to Grace's solicitude by lamenting that she had suffered herself to be persuaded against her own judgment to take a lodging that made it a toil for her to go out.

Becky was still standing with the beautiful shawl in her hand, and Mrs. Woodford instantly inquired whom it belonged to.

"It has been brought here by mistake," said Grace, colouring deeply.

"By mistake?" returned Mrs. Woodford.

"Yes, ma'am, so Miss Grace says, though it was directed plain enough to her; for even I could read it, that am no scholar."

The paper in which it was wrapped up was now handed to Mrs. Woodford by the officious Becky; and with an amazement that banished all her studied reserve and determined resentment of Grace's obstinacy, as she termed it, she demanded of the latter if she conld give an explanation of the mystery.

Grace was silent, but her silence, and the confusion evident in her looks betrayed that she knew more than she was willing to allow.

"What does all this mean, Grace," demanded Mrs. Woodford, with more curiosity, however, than resentment in her manner. "I insist upon knowing whom this comes from. Are you, too, going to serve me as your sister has done—carry on a clandestine affair without——"

"I have no clandestine——I really do not know," stammered Grace, and then, suddenly recollecting herself, she added, "If you will send for Mrs. Stevens upstairs, mamma, perhaps she can explain it, and you can return the shawl to her, for I never, I assure you, had a thought of keeping it."

"Not keeping it!" said Mrs. Woodford, grasping it, as if she already beheld the splendid piece of finery vanishing. "Not keep it! then, I am sure, you would be mad. Why, do you know what such a shawl as this would cost?"

"Its value is nothing to the purpose, dear mother," returned Grace." I am sure you would not consider it proper that I should accept a present from a stranger."

"A stranger!" repeated Mrs. Woodford; "how do I know that it comes from a stranger? I should be very doubtful that any stranger would think of sending you such a beautiful thing as this; if it had been Maria, indeed——"

"Laws, ma'am, I can't have no patience to hear you talk so," interrupted Becky, with great pertness, "when everybody as ever I heard speak about the young ladies says that Miss Grace is quite as pretty as her sister, only that she don't set herself off so much, and thinks less of herself."

"Everybody knows nothing about it, then, Becky," said Mrs. Woodford, half smiling at the girl's warmth in defence of her favourite's beauty. "But do, my good girl, go and send your mistress upstairs, that I may hear whether she knows anything about this."

"I don't believe she'll come, though," muttered Becky, as she left the room, and after an impatient interval of half an hour Mrs. Woodford began to suspect that the girl had been right in her conjecture.

"Mrs. Stevens thinks it beneath her consequence, I suppose, to wait on her lodgers in the garrets," said the former, with vexation. "But, however, it's of little matter; for if I judge right as to where that shawl comes from it won't be long before we are out of our wretched apartments."

Amazement was pictured in Grace's countenance as she looked up from her work, over which she had been sedulously employed, hoping yet dreading to see Mrs. Stevens, and hear what her conjectures would be as to this unlooked-for present, which she herself, without hesitation ascribed to the young gay baronet, the Sir George, whom she had beheld the night previous, and to whom she had no doubt Mrs. Stevens had imprudently related what had been the errand which had brought her (Grace) into the power part of the house.

"Who, then, do you imagine to have sent it, dear mother?" she demanded.

"There is but one person in the world that I think likely," returned her mother; "and I should not be at all surprised if we were soon to see Sir Walter himself follow it. I have had a suspicion for some time that——"

"It is not from Sir Walter it comes, dear mother, of that you may be certain," interrupted Grace, with earnestness; "and now, if you will not think me vain and bold (and her cheek glowed with a still deeper crimson while she spoke), I will tell you all I know and suspect about it, and you will then, I am sure, join with me in thinking it highly proper that I should return the shawl to Mrs. Stevens, and insist upon her delivering it to the right owner."

Suppressing as much as she could the warmth of his flattery to her, Grace

then related her accidental interview with Sir George, whose other name she was still unacquainted with; but while she did so, she was hurt to see that her mother's looks, far from expressing any resentment, seemed to kindle with hope and pleasure; and, though she affected to commend Grace's prudence and reserve, it was evidently not that she thought these qualifications likely to repress the ardour of the baronet, but that they enhanced her daughter's qualities in his eyes.

"We must keep the shawl, Grace," she observed, carefully folding it up," "till we hear something farther from this gentleman. I am very glad now Mrs. Stevens did not come up, for I should be very sorry to put anything in the power of such a low woman as she is; and, mind, there is no occasion to take any further notice about it. I am very sorry you opened it before Becky, to give them an opportunity of talking; but if there's any more said about it to you, tell them you are aware it comes from a friend who has been in India, and that you expect every day to see him.

Grace's looks betrayed the distress she felt at this determined falsehood, and as she conceived highly improper determination on the part of her mother to retain the shawl. She tried to think that her mother was certainly the most competent judge of what was proper, and that she herself was wrong in thus perpetually opposing the dictates of her own heart and feeling to those of one whom she ought to submit to and obey; but it would not do: Grace's heart was naturally too upright, her power of reasoning to correct, to allow her to shield herself under this, and even the natural vanity of her sex, from which she was not entirely free, could not afford the slightest gratification, though her mother, after gazing in silence at her for some minutes, observed—

"Well, really, Grace, I must confess you certainly do look better, and that simple style of dressing your hair is certainly more becoming than when Maria used to do it into so many bows and curls. You have grown taller and fuller in figure, too, since we came here."

"It is a wonder, too," replied Grace with a sigh; "for constant care and late hours, and application to work, and a comparatively close, confined air, would not, one would think, be likely to improve any one's appearance."

"It don't signify, however," returned Mrs. Woodford; "but you certainly don't look the same girl you did; this shawl will become you delightfully, and just suit with your white bonnet and veil," and again she unfolded the splendid present and threw it over Grace's shoulders, who shrank from it as if it had been the web of some poisonous spider, which contaminated her by the touch.

"Get up, and look at yourself in the glass, girl," said her mother, giving her a playful push; "I declare you sit poring over that work till you lose all your life and spirits. I wonder, by-the-bye, whether Mrs. Stevens told this generous man that you were working at millinery for a subsistence?"

"And of what consequence would it be if she did?" said Grace, looking up with surprise at the tone in which her mother made the observation.

"A great deal of consequence, Grace," replied Mrs. Woodford; for young men of birth and fortune, though they might think nothing of marrying a girl without a farthing of money, would hesitate at having a wife who has been obliged to work for her living."

"And can my mother really be weak enough," thought Grace, "after so recent an instance of the effects of her folly, as still to flatter herself that her ruined fortunes are to be repaired by her daughter's marriage?"

She did not venture, however, to utter this reflection, but still sat wait-
ng with impatience for her mother's turning away her gaze from the shawl,
that she might throw it off.

"I never saw such a girl," observed the latter, after some moments'
silence. "I declare I do not believe you have even taken your eyes off
your work to look at your pretty present. But do, for goodness sake,
bundle all the trumpery into the box, and let the caps and turbans have
a holiday. Joe has got a fowl in his basket, and we will have a nice dinner,
and then we will get out ; or what say you to the theatre ? Grace, we have
been in these horrid dungeons of rooms six weeks, and never had an hour's
pleasure. I declare it is enough to make one downright melancholy. Come,
put up the trash, do ; all work and no play makes Jack a dull boy, you
know."

"I must finish this turban, dear mother," said Grace, through whose
heart her mother's unusual and unlooked-for pleasantry shot like a bolt of
ice ; for she beheld in it the forerunner to a renewal of all the preposterous
folly which had marked her conduct during their intercourse with Captain
Frederick. "I must finish this turban," she repeated, "for it is for a
lady whose daughter is to be married to-morrow morning, and I cannot disappoint her."

"You shall make me just such a one when you are married to Sir
George What's his name Grace," returned her mother. "How curious it
will be, after all, if you should be a lady of title ! I always thought poor
Maria was born to honour, but she has cut herself entirely out of it now."

Grace's long-repressed feelings now resisted all farther attempts at concealment, and she burst into an hysterical flood of tears, which effectually
hindered her proceeding with her work.

"It's no use to fret, child," said her mother, in a sorrowful tone, "she
has nobody to blame but herself ; for if she had acted with common sense
all would have been right, and she would have been his wife, instead of
————"

Grace hastily started from her seat, threw the obnoxious shawl off her
shoulders, and darted into her own room, where she gave way for some
minutes without interruption to the feelings which her mother's thoughtless
folly had occasioned.

The entrance of Jane, who came from Mrs. Somerford to hasten her
completion of the task entrusted to her, roused the afflicted girl from the
fit of utter despondency into which she had fallen ; but she tried in vain
to conceal from her humble friend the traces of her tears and recent
agitation.

"Deary me," exclaimed Jenny, "I thought to see you in such tip-top
sperrits, to be sure," observed Jenny ; for Becky whispered to me in the
passage as how you'd get a new lover, quite a grand, first-rate man, and
how he had sent you a shawl fit for a *Ingee* princess."

"Oh, that odious shawl—how I am tormented about it !" exclaimed Grace,
angrily ; "and as to anything else, Jane, I wish you would talk to Becky
a little about giving such license to her observations. I neither have nor
will have anything to say to the man she speaks of, and as to his present, it
is so hateful to me that I would rather see it thrown into the fire than ever
put it on."

"I will sartinly tell Mrs. Becky not to be so free with her tongue,
miss, as you wish it," said Jane, who felt her consequence raised some
degrees higher by Grace's observation. "I wonder, for my part, that a
hignorant gal like her should dare to meddle and make with her betters ;
and besides, as I said, I should think both you, Miss Grace, and my old

missus had quite enough of the deceit and treachery of gentlemen, after that fine Captain Frederick and his companion, Mr. Grant. And there, I've found out, arter all, that he was no cappen at all, but a lord, a deceitful wretch; and there's his lady, and her mother, and his little girl, all come down here arter him; and the poor lady's been in fits, they say, night and day, ever since, the day before yesterday, at finding out what a false-hearted wretch he is; for there was a letter from him to Mr. Grant laying at his lodgins', and so she opened it, because she knew her husband's writing, and there was all about Miss Maria in it, and then she found out everything, and how he's living at France, or some outlandish place, with your sister, more shame for her and passing her off for his wife. But as my missus, Missus Somerford says, ' it won't last, for he'll soon get tired of her, and then she'll be thrown a one side like an old shoe, and as little thought of too.' Now dont cry, Miss Grace, because everybody knows that it's none of your fault; and if ever anybody set another a good example, you did; for as I said to my missus 'Look how different Miss Grace behaved to Mr. Grant, and how she keeps him at a distance', but, as missus says, "The world won't believe it because it's uncommon, indeed, for a young girl like her to have so much prudence, especially when she's got a mother that encourages ——' Why there, now, Miss Grace, you're always angry when I begins to talk about your mother; but truth's truth, and I do say it that poor Miss Maria got nobody to blame but her mother, let her come to what she will."

Grace had been in agonies during this well-meant but torturing speech and she now, by a violent effort, suppressed all reply, and attempted to turn Jane's thoughts solely to the errand on which she had been sent by her mistress, observing, that she would be certain to finish the various articles entrusted to her, in time for the lady for whom they were intended.

"Ah, that's another pretty piece of work, all through the same affair,' said Jane, " and that's the way I come to know all I've been telling you, for Miss Molyneux, the young lady that's going to be married, is cousin and own sister like to Lady What's-her-name, Cappen Frederick's as he called himself's lady; and she's so cast down about her cousin's suffering and the cappen—Lord Frederick, I should say, for he is Lord Frederick something—that her maid, Miss Molyneux's maid, I mean, told my missus, this morning, she shouldn't at all wonder if it should be the means of putting off the wedding. So there, now, nobody knows what may happen, and perhaps, they may never come together; for as Mrs. Clarke, Miss Molyneux's maid, says her lady declared, this morning, it was enough to frighten any young woman from trusting her happiness to a man, and she thought those that *kep* single had mostly the best chance to be happy; and indeed Miss Grace, that's partly my opinion, for the men are certainly the most deceitfulest, false-swearingest, lying set in the world; I am sure I have reason to say so," and Jane's apron raised to her eyes evinced that, whatever were her fancied reasons, they had made impression deep enough to draw tears. "Howsomever, Miss Grace," she continued resuming her usual tone, " as my missus says, you mustn't be behind your time, because, whether they're married or not, the things must be paid for; and, besides, it would be comical enough, as she said, if you was to throw a hindrance in their way."

' "I say, Miss Grace," continued Jenny, in a confidential, whispering tone, 'how surprised Miss Molyneux would be, if she was to know who made her white satin hat and her mamma's turban. Missus says she wouldn't have it known for fifty pounds, and it wouldn't be very pleasant for you,

Miss Grace, neither, though, gracious knows, you are in no fault, and that everybody knows that knows you."

"What has that pert, prating creature been saying to you, Grace?" demanded Mrs. Woodford, when the latter, with determined effort, returned to the front room to resume her work.

Grace replied that she had come to request her to hasten with her work, and Mrs. Woodford, muttering an impatient observation, that she hoped the time was not far distant when they might dispense with her and her errands, too, sat down to await Grace's finishing it.

"They will fetch it, I hope, Grace; surely you are not going to lug that great band-box along the street," exclaimed her mother, hastily, when, having examined the articles her daughter had finished, and pronounced them elegant, beautiful, and soforth, she beheld the latter drawing down her large straw bonnet over her face, and wrapping herself up in a thick, large cloak, which totally concealed her person.

"I have trespassed too much on Mrs. Somerford's patience, already," replied Grace; "and besides" she continued, trying to smile, "my mistress has promised to make me a handsome present, if I please her and her customers, this time, and I must not lose sight of my interest."

Even this, now failed to reconcile Mrs. Woodford to the idea of her daughter being seen in the street with such an incumbrance.

"What would this gentleman, Sir George, think, if ———"

Grace flew out of the room without waiting for another word, for the last observation aroused a feeling so utterly at variance with duty, affection, or even common respect towards her mother, that she dared not hazard a reply.

"This is better than I ever hoped," said Mrs. Somerford, when Grace entered the shop; "I was sadly afraid from Jenny's account of you, that you would not be able to finish your work; and she, like a foolish creature as she is, didn't take the way to make you better with news; but come, let us see what you have done for me this time."

As usual, Grace had succeeded in giving satisfaction, and Mrs. Somerford, after examining and admiring what she had brought home, observed,

"Well my dear, Jenny tells me, that you had a present sent you, of a handsome shawl, and I think that blue silk bonnet which you made for the lady who was gone before it was finished, will suit you better than that thing," looking at the one she had on; "to wear with it, so I shall make you a present of it."

"I thank you, ma'am; I have several bonnets, but I chose this as better suited to my situation; but I am equally obliged to your kind intention," returned Grace, whose heart recoiled from accepting the proffered present on such terms.

"You really are a strange girl," said Mrs. Somerford, looking earnestly at her; "but I suppose you must have your own way. Well, then, as I wish to encourage you, I'll tell you what I'll do. I'll give you the money the bonnet cost, allowing you for the making, and you may lay it out as you like."

Grace accepted with readiness the offered compromise. It was the first money she had received of her earnings, and it seemed to her that, far from being humiliated by taking it, she beheld it with more pleasure than she had ever attached to the possession of a much larger sum.

"And so Jenny told you all about Miss Molyneux and poor Lady Frederick," observed the complacent milliner, turning about the turban on her hand, and seeming to have as little idea that she was torturing Grace's

THE PRIDE OF THE VILLAGE;

OR,

THE FARMER'S DAUGHTERS.

MR. LOVELL, IN THE SICK ROOM.

CHAPTER XXIII.—(CONTINUED.)

feelings than if she had addressed her speech to the wooden block on which
she now placed the object of her admiration.

"Yes, madam," replied Grace; "but if you have no further orders now,
will you excuse me, for I want to get home as soon as possible."

"Dear me, you *are* in a great hurry," said Mrs. Somerford. "I wanted
to have a bit of chat with you about this business; but, however I
must put it off, I suppose, till another time. I think, indeed, that it
would be but right for your mother to do something in this affair,
and, as I told Mrs. Clarke, Miss Molyneux's maid, if she had the feelings

of a mother for her child, or any compassion at all for poor Lady Frederick, who's made so miserable, she'll never rest till she gets your sister back again from him, and then, may be, he'll return to his wife and child as he ought to do.

" Will you oblige me, ma'am, by endeavouring to get, through the means of this Mrs. Clarke, a direction to Captain or Lord Frederick ——"

" Lord Frederick Melverley, my dear; that's his name," returned the talkative milliner. " But really, I don't see well how I can interfere in this business: you see, it behoves me to be very cautious having any hand in such an affair; because if it should be found out that I had any connection or dealings with——

" But, my dear madame," interrupted Grace, somewhat impatiently, " there can be nothing in your simply getting an address; that cannot connect you——"

" I beg your pardon, miss, it would be connecting me," said Mrs. Somerford, in a tone that showed she was highly offended at the liberty Grace had taken with her; " and, indeed, you must excuse me," she added, " if I beg that you will be very cautious, whatever you do, not to mention my name."

Completely disappointed in her hope of gaining, through Mrs. Somerford, the means of making an attempt to withdraw her sister from her disgraceful situation, and agitated and unhappy at the latter's unqualified condemnation of the wretched girl, whom she seemed to hold in utter abborrence, and to consider in this instance as the only guilty party, though, at the same time, she acknowledged that Lord Frederick was notoriously a rake and a libertine, and that this was not the first occurrence that had made him the object of censure, or his lady of pity. With her mind totally occupied by these and similar reflections, Grace proceeded towards her home, unconscious of the observations that were made or the eyes that were gazing upon her; but at the moment her hand was raised to the knocker, it was suddenly arrested by a firm though gentle grasp, and turning with astonishment to ascertain the cause of this interrpution, she beheld, to her no small annoyance, the gentleman whose obtrusive attention in the parlour of her landlord had so much annoyed her.

Her first impulse was to dart away from him, without listening for a moment to the rhapsody which his looks told her he was about to give utterance to; but the next minute, the shawl, and all its mortifying attendances rushed into her mind, and she suddenly stopped, and looked earnestly in his face, as if waiting the first word he should utter, that she might put an end to all intercourse between them by the most marked and determined refusal of his present, and an equally determined assurance that she was resolved, both now and for the future, to decline all his favours, and, in fact, to use the common phrase, have nothing at all to say to him.

Contrary, however, to her expectations, Sir George's address to her was far more distant and respectful than it had been when they had met before, and the first word he uttered, was an apology for his freedom in preventing her knocking at the door.

" But I was anxious," he continued, " to seize the opportunity that fortune has so kindly thrown in my way, of assuring Wiss Woodford that I am heartily ashamed of the freedom of my manner towards her on a recent occasion."

All Grace's intended plan was completely disconcerted by this address. She had prepared herself to meet with, and decidedly repulse, the same kind of familiar and almost impertinent freedom of manner that this man had before assumed; and her first look had been that of indignation, as she recoiled, and hastily withdrew her arm from his grasp; but she was by no means prepared for the look of humility or the tone of deference which she now beheld, and in a confused tone she murmured that there was no necessity for any apologies.

"For, indeed," she countinued, trying to assume a more confident tone and manner, "I did not think the matter, sir, worth my remembrance; and possibly, but for one circumstance, I should have forgotten it altogether."

"May I take the liberty to inquire what that happy circustance is to which I am indebted for Miss Woodford's remembrance?" inquired the baronet, with apparent mortification.

"The question is quite needless. I am sure," replied Grace, who began, from his seeming artlessness of manner, almost to doubt whether she was right in attributing to him the present she had received. "You must be aware sir," she continued, looking gravely, but diffidently in his face, "that I could not be a moment in doubt as to whom I received——" she paused suddenly, for the thought at that moment struck her ——

"Good Heavens! if it should not be he who sent it, will he not have a right to accuse me of the grossest vanity? or will he not, perhaps, put a much worse construction on it!"

"I really do not comprehend you," said Sir George, finding she did not proceed. "You have received what?—nothing, I should imagine, that can have had the happy effect of bringing such an insignificant individual as myself to your remembrance?"

"I must be mistaken," thought Grace, "and yet —— Pardon me, sir if I take the liberty of asking you to answer me frankly one question," she resumed, suddenly, resolved to run all hazard. "Did you, or did you not, send a—a parcel, addressed to me, this morning?"

"Since you put me so closely to the test, I cannot deny it," replied Sir George. "I was struck with admiration—more than admiration—I might better say veneration, of the virtue and feeling which——"

"Pray sir, do not say any more—it is very painful to me, and Mrs. Stevens has acted most imprudently and unkindly——"

"Oh, no, I am sure her motives were kind," interrupted Sir George, eagerly; "and it was kindness both to you and to me," for it sobered me at once, and made me see what a despicable fellow I must appear in your eyes. But you pardon me; I am sure you will, for Mrs. Stevens told me you were the most gentle, indulgent——"

"I have nothing to pardon, sir, indeed," said the blushing girl. "But I have one favour to request—nay, I must more than request—I must command it—and that is, that you allow me to return your present. I am sure, sir," she continued, looking down, and becoming still more confused, "your own heart, your own understanding, must tell you, on sober reflection, that it would be the height of impropriety for me to accept a present under such circumstances.

"There is nothing else that you could ask that I would not instantly comply with," said Sir George; "but on that I must be inflexible; besides, only for a moment consider, how I could submit to such a mortification, for, of course, as you publicly received it, for I have seen Mrs. Stevens, and heard the whole history from her mouth, you would, I dare say, undoubtedly wish that your refusal of it should be equally public."

"Certainly I should!" said Grace quickly; "but after what you have just said, sir, I see it is useless for me to indulge a hope that you are capable of acting with the generosity I thought you were."

"What is it you would wish me to do, dearest Miss Woodford? I swear, to obtain your good opinion I would do anything—make any sacrifice!" he exclaimed, with great warmth. "Tell me," he continued, after a few moments' pause, during which he had been ardently gazing on her speaking countenance, "explain to me how you would wish me to act to satisfy your delicacy, and, if possible, I will do it."

"It is too late now to do all that I wished," she replied in a disconsolate tone," for my mother by this time probably knows——" she paused suddenly, recollecting that if she proceeded she must expose her mother to his contempt; "but there is one thing at least in your power, sir," she added, after a moment's reflection, "and that is that you will henceforth consider me as a total stranger. Circumstances," she added, "may compel me to retain the shawl; but be assured that it is, on my part, with the most painful reluctance I do so, and that I shall hate and despise you if you persist——" again she paused, conscious that she was expressing herself with too much warmth, and pained and agitated beyond measure at the strange and equivocal situation in which she felt she was placed by her mother's folly.

"I confess I am at a loss what to understand by all this," said Sir George, in a tone that evinced some resentment; "surely Miss Woodford cannot suspect that I had any improper motives—she does not mean to charge me——"

"Oh! no, no," exclaimed Grace; "I do not suspect. I do not mean to say anything that can reflect dishonour on you; but you are a stranger, sir, to me, and I am, unhappily, placed in such circumstances——Sir," she continued, looking him in the face, "you are a man of the world, and must comprehend my feelings. If you are a man of sense and feeling you will respect them, and let this be our last interview," and, without waiting for his answer, she ran into the house, the door having been, during her last observation, opened by Mrs. Stevens herself, who had, from the parlour window, beheld this long conference, and whose curiosity was greatly excited to know the subject, or at least to hear what turn it was likely to take.

"What in the world is the matter, Grace?" demanded her mother of the panting, breathless girl, who had run up the three pairs of stairs as if she had been closely pursued.

"Nothing is the matter; only I have been a long while, and I—I was afraid——"

"That is a story, Grace; that couldn't make you look so confused, and your cheeks burn, and your eyes——I know something has happened, and I insist on knowing what it is!"

"Well, then, dear mother, I have met the gentleman—the person who sent that——" looking at the shawl, which was ostentatiously spread out on a chair, Mrs. Woodford apparently taking as much pleasure in contemplating its beauties, as Grace felt pain at the manner in which it had been acquired.

"Well, and what did he say?—what did you say?" inquired her mother, anxiously. "Dear me, I wish I could have been aware, I would have contrived to have gone with you; but did he express any wish to see *me?* He cannot come up here, to be sure; I should die with vexation, and yet——Dear me, what a litter the place is in!" and she, by signs, directed Joe to clear away sundry shreds, &c., which Grace, in her haste to carry home her task, had left strewn about.

He is not coming up, mother; I——"

"You did not affront him, I hope, miss," and Mrs. Woodford's voice resumed the sharp tone to which Grace's ear was so familiarised.

"I did not," replied Grace; but, my dear mother, surely, surely, after such proofs as we have had of the folly and misery of trusting to the professions of men in a sphere of life——"

"You are really very prudent, Miss Grace—wonderfully prudent," said her mother, in a tone of vexation; "but I think it would have better become a girl of your age to have consulted your mother as to how you should act. I ought certainly to have seen this man. It is by no means proper you should accept a present without my sanction; but tell me, Grace—tell me truly," and her voice again softened; what did he say to you? in fact tell me all that passed, and then I can be a better judge."

Grace repeated as nearly as she could the conversation between her and Sir George.

"Oh! then you left him talking to Mrs. Stevens. I shouldn't wonder, after all, then——"

The sentence was not finished, but Mrs. Woodford's rising and adjusting her cap at the glass sufficiently explained what her hopes were, and, after a quarter of an hour's anxious expectation on her part, and fear on that of Grace, Becky suddenly entered, with a face of importance.

"Missus wants to speak to you, Miss Grace, if you please."

"Your mistress!" repeated Mrs. Woodford; "are you sure, Becky, it is your mistress? Is she alone?"

"Yes, ma'm, quite sure," said Becky with confidence.

"Well, then, I really think Mrs. Stevens might take the trouble of coming herself, instead of sending for my daughter down stairs," observed Mrs. Woodford with an air of offended consequence. "Tell your mistress," she continued, "that I do not at all approve of there being any secrets between my daughter and any one, and that if she has anything to say to Miss Grace I shall thank her to say it before me."

Hour after hour elapsed, and Mrs. Stevens did not make her appearance. Grace, restored to comparative tranquillity by the hope that Sir George would interpret her mother's message (for she was convinced, in spite of Becky's confident denial, that he was at the bottom of her errand) as a proof of her decided disapproval of his attempts, and that she should hear no more of him.

"Yet how mean, how mercenary he must think me to keep his present," thought Grace, as she looked at the shawl, which still hung conspicuously before her; "I will never wear it, however, for I should drop with confusion if he was ever to see me with it on."

In less than ten minutes after she had made this reflection, and as if actually able to decipher her thoughts, Mrs. Woodford declared her intention, if the morrow proved fine, of going out.

"It would look very ungrateful, Grace," she observed, "if I did not try to see and thank this generous man; and I shall, of course, have a good opportunity of doing so, if we should meet him, and you have the shawl on."

"Oh! no, dear mother, pray do not think of it!" exclaimed Grace; "endeavour to see him first, and then, if you think there would be no impropriety——"

"Well, well, we will talk about it to-morrow," replied Mrs. Woodford; "you could not suppose, Grace, that I would wish you to do anything improper."

Satisfied, or compelled to appear satisfied, with having gained even this concession, Grace let the subject drop, earnestly, however, praying inwardly that her mother might alter her determination before the morning, or that something might arise to prevent its execution.

Before the morning dawned, Grace, with benumbed fingers, and a heavy heart, was again seated at her little work-table; but her thoughts now were less of herself and the difficulties of her own situation than of her unfortunate sister. She had dreamed that she beheld Maria, pale, dejected, and heart-stricken, reproaching her for having forgotten and abandoned her to die in a foreign land; and the impression was so forcible that she could not shake it off, the altered figure seemed still to stand before her, and she was compelled repeatedly to lay aside her work lest her quick-falling tears should stain the delicate materials she was employed on.

The entrance of Joe, who came as usual to kindle the fire and make the necessary preparations for breakfast, aroused her from this dream of imaginary sorrows. The boy proceeded with his usual alacrity to the performance of his task; but, contrary to her usual custom, Mrs. Woodford neither spoke, nor by any movement testified that she was aware Grace was in the room.

"My mother sleeps soundly," thought Grace; "what a happiness it is that she reflects so little on the past, and indulges in such sanguine dreams for the future!"

The breakfast was made, and Grace, with the tea and toast in her hand, gently withdrew the bed-curtain; but what was her horror, her consternation, her despair, when she beheld the countenance of her mother distorted with the pangs of death, her eyes open and fixed on vacancy, the cold dew standing on her forehead, and a slight heaving of her chest alone, bespeaking that her life was not totally extinct.

Grace's loud cries for help soon brought around her a crowd of assistants, and among them was one grave elderly man, who immediately administered comfort to the terrified girl by declaring her mother was only in a fit.

"I will bleed her: bring warm water, towels, basins," he observed. Grace's distracted exclamations were in a moment hushed, and before any one else had withdrawn their looks or attention from the frightful object before them Grace was at his side with the necessaries he required.

It was long, however, before the appearance of even a drop of blood followed the incision. Grace scarcely breathed, and the significant looks of those who stood around the bed, the shake of the head, and the half-audible whisper, proved that none of them placed much confidence in the skill of the person who had thus promptly exercised it, or, at least, that they considered the patient beyond its reach.

"Run, some of you, and fetch the box off my bedroom table!" he exclaimed. Grace was the first to fly, but in a moment she recollected that she did not know whither to go.

"Move, can't you, you stupid dolt," he repeated, and away ran Becky, to whom this elegant appellation was addressed.

Before, however, she returned the blood began to flow freely from the incision he had made, both in the patient's arms and temples, her breathing became more perceptible, she turned her eyes from side to side, and at length fixed them on Grace, with returning consciousness.

Grace sank on her knees with an ardent ejaculation to Providence for having restored her only remaining parent to her.

"And you, sir, oh! how shall I ever be able to thank you sufficiently—to repay you——"

"Psha! psha! my good girl, do not talk," replied the rough, unpolished man whom she addressed. "The poor woman is not out of danger yet. It will be time enough to talk of payment when she's well again."

Grace was silenced. There was something peculiarly repulsive in the tone and look of the surgeon, for such she naturally supposed him to be, and grateful as she felt for his valuable services, she shrank from the piercing glance of his fiery grey eye, as he bent on her face.

By degrees, Mrs. Woodford's countenance assumed a less ghastly appearance; she gazed around her, as if conscious that something unusual had happened to her, but speech seemed denied her, and repeated groans gave indication that she was suffering extreme pain.

Grace hung with intense anxiety on every look and then sought to read in the countenance of the doctor, who was holding her wrist, and counting from time to time, by his watch, her pulse, what was his opinion. But all there was fixed and immovable; it was a stern, hard-featured, and repulsive countennace and betrayed neither anxiety nor sympathy with her feelings.

"You may go," he at length observed, very abruptly, to those who still lingered round the bed; "this young woman is quite sufficient to attend her mother now, and so many people in a close room like this do no good."

"Hadn't I better stay sir?" said Mrs. Stevens, who was the last that lingered. "If anything should happen——"

"I shall call you if I want you, good woman; do go about your business."

Mrs. Stevens obeyed, in a manner that showed she was accustomed to his harsh and commanding manner; and Grace found herself alone with this stern unpolished man, who still kept his post.

A full quarter of an hour elapsed in total silence, or at least only broken by Mrs. Woodford's occasional low wailing, or sometimes an inarticulate attempt at speech. Grace had remained fixed in the position she had been in, on her knees at the opposite side of the bed; once only after she had been left alone with her singular companion, once only her eyes had wandered from her mother's face to his, and then she had hastily withdrawn them, for his eyes were fixed with a sneer that she could not mistake on the elegant shawl which her mother had forbidden her on the previous night to remove.

Grace felt her cheeks glow with mingled anger and confusion; but this feeling was soon after forgotten, when, rising from his station at the bedside, he observed—

"She will do now; I shall leave her to your care, while I go out and get some medicine."

Grace's thankfulness, sincere and heartfelt as it was, for his timely assisance, was now only expressed by the lowly bending of her head, for she feared to utter a word, lest she should again provoke a harsh reply; and without further remark he quitted the room.

In a few moments, Mrs. Stevens glided in.

"So, Miss Grace, your mother is likely to get round again," she whispered. "Well, what a mercy it was that Mr. Lovell was at home, and came up so readily: and who'd have thought that he knew so much about doctoring? I'm sure, I almost laughed when he said he must bleed her, for I thought none but regular doctors could bleed; but when he pulled out his lancet box, I began to think——"

"Is he not a surgeon, then?" demanded Grace.

"Lord bless you, no; it is my first-floor lodger, that took your rooms. He's always here three or four months in the year; but I never saw so much of him as I've done this morning, for he never speaks to nobody a word more than do this, or don't do that, and even when I or Becky—

but I *generally* goes myself, for fear she should affront him with some of her foolishness—goes to put his breakfast on the table, or lay his cloth for dinner, he always walks away into his bedroom, and stays till we goes out. And I don't sometimes see him for weeks together, for he never goes out like other people in the day, but early in the morning, before a soul's stirring, and he's abed by nine o'clock : and as to what he eats and drinks, he lays down the money, and writes on a bit of paper what I'm to get, and little enough it is, and yet I know he's as rich as a Jew, for I've seen him leave his iron box open in his bedroom while I've been making his bed, and it was chock-full of gold : how he gets rid of it I can't think ; and yet I've seen it emptied and filled and emptied again, before he's left me. Stevens often laughs, and says he's a conjuror, and can make it fill and empty when he pleases : howsomever, he's a good lodger, and pays me well, and troubles his head with nobody, so it's nothing to us what he is. But I think he's somebody that's had great troubles in his time, for I often hear him walking about, out of one room into another, half the night, over my head : and then he sighs, j·ist as if his heart was breaking. But, laws, I must run, for he'll be coming up again, and I s'pose I should get my nose snapped off,

if he was to catch me here, after sending me off."

Grace's fear, if it might be so called, of this mysterious stranger was not at all abated by this account of him from her garrulous landlady : and when he returned with the medicine, which was in a few moments after the departure of the latter, her trepidation was so evident, that, as he took the wine glass from her hand, which he had desired her to reach, he raised his eyes, with a look of inquiry, to her face.

"You are very nervous, young woman," he observed, "is it the recent fright, or are you subject to those fits of trembling? If you are, you ought to take care of yourself, and get into better air than this."

"I wish I could," sighed Grace ; " and, indeed, if my poor mother gets over this attack, I shall try and persuade her——"

"How do you feel, my good woman ?" interrupted Mr. Lovell, addressing Mrs. Woodford, and without seeming to attend at all to Grace's reply to his question.

The sufferer was now evidently quite restored to consciousness ; but Grace recoiled, shuddering at the strange inarticulate sounds by which she attempted to reply.

"It will be some time before she recovers her speech," said Mr. Lovell, pouring out the medicine, but it will most likely return by degrees. You will attend to the directions, young woman" pointing to the bottle : " I suppose you can read them."

A blush of mortification crossed Grace's pale cheek, as she replied in the affirmative, but her strange companion did not seem to notice it.

"I shall come up again, by-and-bye," he observed, as he abruptly quitted the room, after seeing his patient swallow the medicine.

For more than an hour Grace remained fixed at her mother's bedside, alternately rejoicing at the gradual restoration that became visible in the latter's countenance, or weeping at the pain and mortification she seemed to feel at being unable to give distinct utterance to her thoughts and wishes,

"Laws bless me Miss Grace you have certainly worked a miracle upon my lodger," said Mrs. Stevens, bustling into the room, with a basket in one hand, and a bottle in the other ; " he has sent this," uncovering the basket, and showing a couple of fine chickens, some tea, sugar, sago, and a variety of other articles necessary in a sick chamber. "The chickens are for you, and the wine, too, the best old port. I assure you he told me to spare no expense, but let everything be of the best quality, and come to him, if anything else is wanted; and he told me to tell you not to be afraid or sparing for yourself, for if you did not take care of yourself you could not do your duty by your mother. Ah, Miss Grace, I was longing to tell him that you had always done your duty, and more than your duty; but he won't bear speaking to, and the minute I opened my mouth he stopped it with ———

"'There, there, go about your business, I want no talking to.' Oh, he's a strange man; but I always thought he'd a kind heart, ever since I once saw him fly downstairs one frosty day, to pick up a poor blind beggar that had slipped on a slide some wicked boys had made, just under the window. I don't know what he gave the poor man, but he went away blessing and thanking him; and I saw him give another man half-a-crown to lead the poor fellow to his home: but there, what's money to him, and he's got such a load, and spends so little?"

Grace's surprise was only equalled by the gratitude she felt for the very seasonable benevolence of the stranger; her thoughts, indeed, during the last half hour, had been of the most melancholy complexion, for she felt that it would be impossible to continue her work, and to attend to her mother, in her present helpless state; at least, she feared it would not be possible for her to earn sufficient to supply her mother's necessities, and bestow that attention on her which her state demanded.

"Come, now, Miss Grace, don't cry," continued Mrs. Stevens; "it ought to cheer your heart up, and see how good God is to raise you up such a friend; and perhaps this may be the luckiest day of your life, for such people as Mr. Lovell, when once they do take to a person, are more apt to stick by them than your every day sort of folks, that are always talking of what they will do, and promising what they never mean to perform."

"I am sure, I am indeed sincerely thankful to him," said Grace, "how indeed, could I feel otherwise than grateful, since, but for his assistance, in all probability, my mother would now have been ———"

"Ah, it's most likely, indeed," said Mrs. Stevens, interrupting her; but I can't help saying, Miss Grace, though I know it will make you angry, that there's very few children would have less cause to fret after a mother ———."

"Hush, hush," exclaimed Grace, impatiently, in a wisper; my mother comprehends all that is said."

"So much the better," replied Mrs. Stevens, "for now or never's the time that she ought to begin to feel how shameful her conduct has been to you; but there, I won't distress you; for as Mr. Lovell says, you look ill, very ill."

"'My good woman,' says he—he always calls me good woman: and sometimes it makes me so pettish I'm ready to fly in his face, and tell him I don't like to be spoke to in that unproper manner and that I've got a name, if he'd be pleased to call me by it; but then he pays so handsome, and I don't think he means any harm by it. But what was I saying? oh—'that girl upstairs will have a fit of illness, if she don't take care of herself; there's money, get what I've set down there, and tell her to take care of herself, she won't be able, else, to do her duty.' Duty, indeed, thought I."

"Well, I suppose you'll see him yourself, by-and-bye, and then, you know, you can thank him, but, recollect, he won't stand many words."

In spite of every care and attention, Mrs. Woodford remained for many days in a state lingering between life and death; and when, at length, all immediate apprehensions of the latter event were removed, and she began to show symptoms of returning strength and perfect consciousness, Grace was shocked by discovering, from the observations of her indefatigable and skilful attendant, Mr. Lovell, that the distortion of her features, and the impediment which prevented her distinct utterance, were likely to continue lasting mementoes of the severe attack of the unfortunate patient had suffered.

CHAPTER XXIV.

Her form is like a form of light—
But all the woman dims her eye
With tears that dare to look to heaven
And griefs that mount—and are forgiven!—
Deep in her warm and holy heart,
Are thoughts that play a mortal part;
And her young worship wafts above
The breathings of an *earthly* love!
Of *earth*—yet not a love that flings
One clog upon the spirit's wings;
Or, like a shadow, dimly lies
Upon her pure heart's sacrifice.

T. K. HERVY.

During these melancholy days Grace's attention had been unremitting, and Mr. Lovell, though still maintaining the same harsh abruptness of manner whenever he had occasion to speak to her, yet proved by his observations to Mrs. Stevens that he was not unobservant of that filial affection which rendered her so insensible to fatigue, so utterly neglectful of her own comfort, or even her health.

"Can you not get some one to relieve that poor girl upstairs from constantly watching at her mother's bedside?" inquired he of the landlady. "I will defray the expenses," he added, "but you need not say anything about that. Get some trustworthy woman if you can, and say it's by my orders."

Grace was at first inclined to demur, when in consequence of these instructions, Mrs. Stevens introduced an elderly woman, whom she represented as an expert and careful nurse; but Mrs. Stevens's remark that it would appear very ungrateful to Mr. Lovell to refuse his offered assistance, silenced her opposition, and Mrs. Carr, as she was called, entered upon her office, to which, indeed, she seemed, by the quietness yet intelligence of her look and manner, well adapted.

"You will go to bed to-night," said Mr. Lovell, as he turned away from the bedside of his patient.

Grace made no reply; she was unwilling, it might be said she was afraid, to offer any opposition to her singular visitant, whose piercing eye dwelt on her changeful countenance with a look of deep interest, though he tried to veil it by knitting his brows and compressing his lips together, thus adding harshness to a set of features which were naturally stern and repellent, though not exactly unhandsome.

"You are very kind, sir, and I am deeply grateful," faltered Grace.

"Prove it! prove it, then, by obeying me! I like actions, and not words."

Grace bowed her head in silent acquiescence, and he hurried from her to give some directions to the new comer.

"Mind," he observed, as he quitted the room, turning to Grace and holding up his finger as if to enforce his words, "till eight o'clock to-morrow morning you give up the care of your mother."

"What a strange gentleman!" exclaimed the nurse. "But it is not the first time I have seen him, though he does not know me again; indeed, I don't think he ever looked me in the face, either then or now, though he attended morning and evening for nearly a month the person I was with."

"Yet Mrs. Stevens says he is not a physician," observed Grace.

"He is the best of physicians," replied the nurse, smiling, "for he cures all his patients without a fee; at least, I know he not only attended them without any, but he paid all the young man's expenses besides."

"Heaven will repay him," said Grace, fervently; "and yet, though I feel so grateful to him when he is absent, I cannot but confess that his manners make me fear, rather than love him, when he is present."

"At all events, you must not make him angry by disobeying him," replied the nurse; "for I will answer for it the first thing he will ask to-morrow is, how you passed the night, and I'll defy anybody to deceive him; besides, you may safely trust your mother to my care, for I will not leave her for a moment."

Thus reassured, Grace did, for the first time since her mother's seizure, retire to her own bed; where sleep soon buried all her cares in deep oblivion.

It was not till after the hour that Mr. Lovell had named for her rising that Grace awoke, and then, hurrying on her clothes, she hastened to the bedside of the invalid, who she found, to her great satisfaction, had passed a very quiet night.

"It is well for you you were a-bed, Miss," observed the nurse, smiling, "and well for me that I was not napping on my post; for the old gentleman stole up here in his flannel gown this morning at daybreak, and after taking a look at your mother he asked me where you were, and I said, 'A-bed in the next room;' and away he went, looking quite satisfied. I'm sure if he was your own father he could not feel more for you.'

"I only wish he would speak a little milder," thought Grace, "and I am sure I should love him almost as well as if he were ever so nearly related; but now, in spite of his kindness, I tremble whenever I his voice, or see his keen eye fixed on me."

From Mrs. Carr, the nurse, Grace learnt, during the time they sat over their breakfast, the particulars of that act of benevolence which she had before alluded to as having been the means of her first introduction to Mr. Lovell. A young man from some distant part of the country, she said, had been suddenly seized with the brain fever. He was a total stranger in Bath, and the people of the house where he had lodged a few days were in such consternation at the thoughts of his dying, and their having to bury him, that they were about to send him to the workhouse. Mr. Lovell, who had entered the shop, a small turner's, to buy some trifling article, overheard the conversation on the subject between the man of the house and one of his neighbours, who was advising him not to delay a moment in getting rid of one who might prove a burden to him.

Mr. Lovell, it appeared, requested to see the poor young man, who, it was said, could not live. He thought differently, however, and undertook to cure him, or at all events, to defray every expense attendant on his remaining in his lodging, and being properly looked to.

"And well did he keep his promise," continued Mrs. Carr; "for night and morning, and sometimes three times a day, he was at the poor young man's bedside, and handsomely, too, he paid me and everybody, and when the young man got well and could give some account of himself—he, that is Mr. Lovell, put aside all that roughness that arn't natural to him, though he keeps it up so: however, poor Belgrave, as he called himself, though that wasn't his right name, seeing his linen was all marked "B.M." Laws a mercy, miss, what is the matter? how you started, and you are as pale as a ghost: what could I have said——"

Grace held up her finger in token of silence.

"We will talk of this another time," she hastily whispered seeing her mother's attention was excited by the woman's exclamations of surprise.

Eagerly and anxiously did Grace wait for an opportunity of renewing the subject of the nurse's former patient; but it was impossible to conceal from her (Mrs. Carr), that she had especial motives for requiring a description of his features, the colour of his hair, his height, &c.

"Good gracious!" exclaimed the nurse, looking earnestly at her, "your name is Grace; yes, yes, I understand it all well enough now; it was you that he used to talk about, and fancy was at his bedside. Laws bless me, little did I think that I should ever see the Grace that I was used to say must have been very *ungracious* to have driven such a fine young man to despair; but excuse me, miss, I knew nothing about you then, and all I could make out from his ravings—and he was quite raving at times— was that he had been very cruelly treated, and that his Grace was lost to him for ever."

With mingled pain and pleasure, Grace listened to a detail which revived in her heart recollections that the pressure of care and misfortune had for some time stifled, though not extinguished: she was never tired of hearing the nurse repeat expressions, which convinced her that Belgrave still retained, in all its fervour, his youthful affection for the companion of his childhood, and though she heard with tears of heartfelt anguish the recital of his sufferings, and the narrow escape which he had from the grave, yet they were mingled with the rapturous tears of gratitude and hope.

"And so this man, who will scarcely suffer me to speak to him, and who never looks at me without seeming to despise and contemn me—to him do I owe the preservation of my mother, and of one almost as dear—'"—were Grace's reflections as Mr. Lovell entered the room.

His stern eye, as usual, took a hasty glance at her countenance, and was, as usual, as hastily withdrawn; and Grace's warm emotions, which a moment before would have urged her to throw herself at his feet, and try to give utterance to her fervent gratitude, were again all chilled by the expression of that look.

From this time his visits became less frequent. Mrs. Woodford recovered as far as it was likely that she would ever recover, and Grace, who felt humiliated and grieved at being the constant object of his bounty to a man who treated her with so much apparent contumely, summoned courage to say to him that there was no longer any occasion for the nurse to remain in attendance.

"And when she is gone, sir," continued Grace, faltering, and not daring to raise her eyes to his, "I shall be able, I trust, to supply by my own exertions all our wants. I am conscious that we have been a serious, very serious burthen——"

"There, please to say nothing more about that, young woman," he interrupted. "But have the goodness to tell me how you propose to support

"There must be some peculiar reason which could induce Mr. Lovell thus to lay aside his usual reserve, and curb that impatience which scarcely allowed him to listen, even when it was necessary, much less to such circumlocution as Mrs. Stevens's discourse displayed. Was it not possible that he, as well as Mrs. Carr, was in possession of the secret cause of his former *protége's* distress? Oh, yes, it must be so; and Mrs. Stevens in her loquacity had given him the clue by which he had discovered her."

"Such were the thoughts which occasioned those changes which Mrs. Stevens attributed to a very different cause.

"You needn t be afraid, Miss Grace, that I said a word to hurt your feelings, she observed; "and, indeed, if I could have avoided mentioning your sister altogether I would; but he's such a man, if you drop but half a word, he catches hold of it, and then he questions and cross-questions you, so that there's no help for it, you must tell the whole truth; But, laws, what a fright I was in, when I mentioned about the captain's never coming back with your sister, and how we found it out, after all, that he was no captain, but a lord.

"He'd sit all this time, with his dinner that I'd cooked so nicely, and brought up so smoking hot, getting as cold as ice before him and never touched; but when I mentioned his name—Lord Frederick, I mean—he gave his plate a push that sent the dish with the chicken and the sauce-boat to the other end of the table, spilt all the gravy, and, oh, such a mess, but he never took a bit of notice, but walked up and down the room, muttering to himself, and, I won't be sure, but I think I heard him swear.

"Won't you be pleased to take some dinner, sir?" said I, when I had wiped it all up, and put it tidy again; 'No!'" says he, as sharp as if I'd asked him to take poison.

"I know his way, so I wouldn't say another word, but began to clear the table; but just as I'd put all the things in the tray, he turned sharply round ———"

"'Don't go yet, Mrs. Stevens,' says he, 'this poor girl upstairs, then, is really quite destitute of friends, and nothing to depend upon but her industry?'

"I told him he might depend upon it, all was correct that I told him, and then he became quite mild again, and seemed to take such a pleasure in listening to what I said in your praise, that really I don't know where it will end; to be sure, he's rather elderly for you, Miss Grace, but then better be an old man's darling than a young man's slave, as the saying is. Well, after all, I should be glad to see you rich and happy, and ———"

"For mercy's sake, do not talk so, Mrs. Stevens," whispered Grace, who saw that her mother, though she was unable to take any part in the conversation, was yet attentively listening; and saw also that her eyes betrayed more pleasure and satisfaction than had beamed in them since the commencement of her illness: "such preposterous hopes and expectations," continued Grace, raising her voice, "have been the bane of my happiness; but you, I am sure, have too much sense to mean anything more than a joke, at my expense."

The unexpected entrance of the very person of whom they were speaking, prevented Mrs. Stevens' reply; Mr. Lovell stopped for a moment, as if disconcerted at the presence of the latter; but his habitual commanding manner was in a moment resumed, and he desired her to go downstairs, as he had something to say to "Grace."

It was the first time that Grace had ever been addressed by any softer title than "young woman," or "girl," and she felt the blood rush into her face, as Mrs. Stevens, in passing her, smiled expressively at his unusual familiarity.

"Sit down, sit down here, Grace," said the old man, drawing a chair close to the one he had taken himself.

Grace obeyed, trembling, however, in expectation of the scene that was to ensue.

"I'm very sorry," continued Mr. Lovell, "that I hurt your feelings so much this morning about that shawl; but I will tell you candidly, that I happened to be in the shop where it was purchased a short time after, and overheard the jokes and observations which were made upon Sir George's generosity in making such a present to a girl who one of the shopmen declared was nothing but a milliner's workwomen, he having repeatedly seen her bring home her work when he went there with parcels, and being rather struck with her as a pretty girl, had asked some questions, and thus learnt her name and address.

"The man laid the parcel dowe close to me, and I thus saw that it was directed to the very house I lived in. I need not now explain why I felt particularly interested in Sir George's actions."

"I determined, however, to watch his proceedings;——but all this is of no consequence to you, Grace, now; all I wish to tell you is, that I am convinced I have wronged you, and now I'm going to make a proposal to you. What is the matter with the girl?—why do you start and shrink away?—surely you do not suppose that I am going to propose anything improper."

"Oh, no, sir;" and Grace glanced timidly towards her mother, who, propped in her easy chair, sat silently regarding them, and evidently listening with high-fraught expectations.

"Well, then, I will tell you at once what I propose. The price which he gave for that shawl was fifteen guineas. You may well look surprised, for it is not worth above half the money. But that is not the point;" and he drew out his purse. "I will give you the cost price for it, if you will allow me in your name to return it."

Grace was about eagerly to reply that she should be most happy to be rid of it, but that she could not think of taking the money, when she recollected the necessity of consulting her mother on the subject.

Mr. Lovell's quick eye saw instantly the direction of her's.

"You are right," he said, "it is your mother I ought to have said this to. Are you satisfied, woman, with my offer?"

Mrs. Woodford nodded assent, and he threw the purse into her lap.

"Oh, no, mother, dear mother—do not, pray do not think——"

Mr. Lovell interrupted Grace, whose distress was strongly painted both in her face and the accents of her voice, at this proof of her mother's mercenary disposition.

"Be quiet, foolish girl," he observed, in a tone of kindness; "this is all fair, it is a matter of bargain between your mother and me; and she is perfectly right, having made up her mind to keep it, not to part with it to gratify my whims, without its full worth."

Grace turned away to conceal the tears of bitter mortification which streamed down her cheeks.

Mr. Lovell took her hand.

"Grace," he said, "do not grieve; I understand all your feelings and appreciate them; look upon me, henceforth, as your friend, as your father."

He left the room, hastily, as if afraid of saying too much; and Grace felt her spirits revive, at the expression with which he uttered the last words.

THE PRIDE OF THE VILLAGE;

OR,

THE FARMER'S DAUGHTERS.

GRACE PARTING WITH JOE.

CHAPTER XXIII.—(Continued.)

"Thank Heaven!" she mentally ejaculated. "I have, then, one real, one disinterested friend, on whom I dare rely with confidence."

Mrs. Woodford's eyes were still fixed on the money of which she had thus unexpectedly become the possessor, but the next moment she raised them to Grace.

"You have not given the shawl," she observed in her inarticulate accents.

Grace flew to the place where it was deposited, and then, without a moment's pause, down stairs to Mr. Lovell's sitting room, and without reflecting what she was about, opened the door.

14

" Who are you?—what do you want?" exclaimed the old man in his harshest, most repulsive tone, as he started from his seat at the table, on which he was leaning, with his face hidden by his hands.

Grace uttered a faltering apology, as she presented the shawl.

" Is it you, my child?" he replied, immediately softening. "Excuse me I was totally lost in recollections of the past—recollections which you have forced upon me."

" I should be sorry," said Grace, timidly, " if I should be the means of giving pain where I am soo deeply indebted."

" No, no; you are not indebted to me," he hastily replied, " what is the value of paltry coin? Between you and me, Grace, I have greatly wronged you—I have done you great injustice; but you are amply revenged by the pangs which you have, this night, excited in my bosom—pangs that I have long stifled. I had a daughter, once, Grace, young and innocent as——no, she was not innocent, or she could not have deceived a father; but I thought her so, and when——there, go along, child, this is all folly. What is this?" and he took the parcel from her.

" Oh, I recollect. Yes, yes, I will take care that it shall be returned, and returned so that you shall not again be troubled with that libertine. There, now go, my child, I cannot talk to you."

Grace reluctantly left him; she was shocked at the agony which his looks betrayed he had suffered, and would willingly have tried to divert him from dwelling on those melancholy thoughts, which, as he said he had so long stifled, and which had now, perhaps, on that account, broken out with redoubled force; but his manner was, even now, too decisive for her to dispute, even for a moment, his commands, and she slowly returned to her mother.

" Mr. Lovell's respects to you, Miss Grace, and will be glad, if you will come down and make his breakfast for him, at eight, to-morrow morning," said Mrs. Stevens, opening the door of Grace's bedroom, just as she was retiring for the night.

" The poor old gentleman seems quite ill, to-night," she added, and no wonder, for he has not taken a morsel of food to-day; he seems to have something on his mind, but I daresay you'll hear all about it, to-morrow. Lord, Miss Woodford, what a lucky thing, after all, your mother's being taken ill so suddenly may prove to you! It's plain the old gentleman has quite taken to you, and he hasn't, I do believe, a relation in the world. If you play your cards well, who knows what may happen?"

" I have no cards to play, Mrs. Stevens," replied Grace, who felt hurt and offended at the expression she had used. "Depend upon it, Mr. Lovell is one with whom——"

" Laws, bless me, Miss Grace, you do take one up so sharp. All I meant was, that if you contrived to keep the good opinion he's got of you there's no knowing but that you might come in for a good fortune, after all, and I'm sure, there's nobody in the world would be more glad to see it than me; for, as I said to Sir George, last night——by the bye, Miss Grace, you can't think how anxious and concerned Sir George has been, ever since he heard of your mother's dangerous illness. He wanted to send a physician; but I was afraid it would affront Mr. Lovell, and so I put him off that we had got one that you placed great confidence in."

" Well, then he wanted to give me money to pay necessary expenses; but I told him there was no occasion for it at present, and I knew you would be angry, if I took it without consulting you."

" You were very right, perfectly right," said Grace. "Dear Mrs.

Stevens, you cannot think how much obliged I feel to you ; and now excuse my giving you advice, but I am sure the less encouragement you give to Sir George to come here the better, for Mr. Lovell has a very bad opinion of him."

"Well, I declare I thought so," observed Mrs. Stevens ; "for, when I was telling him all about the shawl—which, by-the-bye, I can't think how he knew anything about ; but he did, and so I was obliged to tell him the rights of it."

"It was most fortunate that you did so," observed Grace, "for he knew all, except my reluctance to keep it."

"Well, I declare I thought as much," returned Mrs. Stevens, "and so I took care that he should know that; for, indeed, Miss Grace, though I really don't believe Sir George means anything but what's honourable and respectful, yet still, after what has happened in your family, you can't, as I said to him yesterday, when urging me to persuade you to see him—you can't I say, be too cautious ; and as I told him—

"'Miss Woodford says, she will think all the better of you for not intruding upon her while she is in trouble, and so you must wait patiently until the old lady is well enough to be left. But you can't think what a trouble I have had to persuade him ; and how he has watched and waited, backwards and forwards, here, two or three times a day, with first one excuse and then another. I really do think, if ever a man was sincerely in love, he is. Laws, he used to be such a gay, rattling gentleman, and now he's as dull and demure as a souse."

To all this Grace made no reply.

"Mr. Lovell will put an end to it all to-morrow," she thought to herself, "and, therefore, it is useless for me to enter upon the subject at all."

Precisely at the appointed hour, Grace, having first given her mother her breakfast, entered Mr. Lovell's apartment.

He was already risen, and busily engaged writing; but he laid it aside the moment he saw her, and returned her salutation with kind courtesy.

"It is long since I have had this pleasure, Grace," he observed, as he took his seat at the breakfast table, "and it will perhaps, be long before I shall again, for I am going to quit you. Yes, I have been soberly considering the subject, all night; and I have came to the resolution of setting out for Paris, at daybreak, to-morrow."

"To Paris !" repeated Grace, in surprise.

"Yes, Grace. I will not conceal from you what my errand there is ; it is to snatch, from the arms of a villain, the unhappy girl whom it is your misfortune to call sister ; and if I find her worthy of you, if her heart is not contaminated, to restore her to you. Do not thank ; me, Grace I have a deeper interest in this affair than you can guess. I have for some days meditated this; but it was not until yesterday that I learned the whole truth—learned that the unhappy girl was, in reality, more an object of pity than condemnation."

Grace's eloquent eyes thanked him through her tears.

"If you had but known my poor Maria," she faltered ; "she was so innocent, so unsuspicious."

"And so imprudent," said Mr. Lovell, shaking his head. "Well, well," he added, "I do not wish to give you pain; and perhaps I have no right to blame her, for a defect of understanding seems inherited; for, what but a want of common sense can have influenced that mother of yours? Do not look vexed, child ; I would not wish to think worse of your mother than that she is a fool. I cannot think better of her ; for none but one devoid of understanding, or one devoid of principle—in short, the most depraved of human beings—could act as she has done. I do not blame you, my poor girl, for wishing to think well of your mother, but whatever you may think and believe of her intentions, do not let your kind feelings blind you to the utter folly, the madness of her measures. But I need not say all this to you ; for you have already proved, by your conduct, that you have both sense to discriminate, and firmness to act up to your own sense of what is right and proper ; and now to business. In the first place, you will, perhaps, want money, while I am gone. Now, do not begin to object and protest, as I see you are preparing to do. I do not want to overwhelm you with obligations, and I respect the spirit which makes you shrink from them : but you will, perhaps, find your work less lasting or productive than at present, or your mother may be attacked with a relapse of her disorder ; in either case, you will want, perhaps, more than you can at present command ; and if so, there is an order to pay you at sight, ten pounds, so that you can use it or let it alone as you find necessary ; only premising this, that I shall consider it a proof of your want of confidence in me, if you do not freely resort to it in case of necessity. In the second place, with respect to that poor boy, I have just been writing to a person, who, I know, has interest to get him into the Asylum, in London, for the Deaf and Dumb ; so that I expect, before I return, that burden will be taken off your hands, and the poor lad put into a course of instruction which will enable him to maintain himself, or at least be useful in some way. If my friend succeeds, he will send a person down to take charge of him and convey him to the appointed place, so that you need have no uneasiness on that head."

Mr. Lovell now proceeded to give her some directions as to the management of her mother, all of which Grace listened attentively to, and promised faithfully to abide by.

"Now then," he observed, "I have nothing to add. Oh, yes, there is one thing here ; here is a direction to a poor family, whose hovel I accidentally entered, in one of my walks. I have allowed them five shillings a week, ever since ; and as I do not think them careful and prudent enough to trust them with the money, in advance, you must be my treasurer, and continue to pay them the allowance every Monday. Here are three guineas ; and before those are gone——"

Oh, long before that, I hope and pray," exclaimed Grace—"long before that I shall see you again."

"I hope so, child," he returned, turning away to conceal a starting tear, but life is uncertain, and I never part with one I love without reflecting how many chances there are that I shall never behold them again. God bless you, Grace. I shall not see you again before I go ;" and, without waiting for her reply, he walked into his bedroom, and closed the door after him.

Before the sun had risen Grace heard the chaise roll from the door, which conveyed her new friend on his important journey, and earnest and fervent were her prayers that his mission might be successful.

Never since the hour when she had become assured thar her sister had indeed deserted them had she felt so happy—her mother would be restored to health—Maria would forget the follies which had led her from the paths of happiness and virtue—they should unite their efforts to make their home comfortable, and prevent their mother feeling any privations. Oh yes, she knew—she felt they should all be happier than they had ever been since they quitted Llan———Belgrave would return, and——but no, Maria—poor

Maria —that path was for ever closed upon her. Yet still—still they should be happy; and Grace continued to conjure up visions of happiness until they were all buried in sleep.

A long and loud groan awoke her from a dream, which had, in part, embodied all her waking thoughts, and without a moment's pause she flew to her mother's beside to behold her in the last agonies of death.

Oh, how frantically did Grace now call on him, who was far removed beyond the reach of her prayers, to save her mother.

Mr. Lovell's skill, his prompt attendance, had before rescued her mother from apparent death, and if he were but here now!

Alas! vain were all Grace's regrets, and equally vain the assistance that was as quickly as possible afforded to the sufferer: she was now beyond the reach of mortal help. A second attack of her disorder had proved fatal, and in less than half an hour from the time she had been roused by her groans, Grace beheld her mother a lifeless corpse!

CHAPTER XXV.

"E'en while the mourner's eye is wet
With nature's tears for nature's woe,
There is a balm—a solace yet
For all that wrongs or wounds below;
My griefs remain, but thine are o'er!
My loss thy endless gain shall be!
I weep but thou canst mourn no more!
I still am bound, but thou art free."

DALE.

IT was not as one that "sorrows without hope" that Grace mourned the death of her mother. There were many reasons why she would indeed acknowledge that it was a merciful dispensation which had removed her from a scene which could henceforward be only one of endless trouble and discontent. Disappointed in every hope, foiled in every scheme on which she had set her weak and vain heart, condemned to linger on an only half-existence, in poverty and obscurity, to Mrs. Woodford, life could offer few charms, while to those who were compelled to behold her sufferings, and consequent regrets, she must have been, indeed, a constant source of melancholy and disquiet. But, though Grace acknowledged that it was better that she was taken from "the evil to come," still she could not but feel with bitter agony the forcible rending of that sacred tie which bound her to her only remaining parent—could not but mourn, with almost hopeless regret, that she was now totally alone in the world, without one heart to feel, beyond the common sympathy of strangers, for her loss.

"And Maria, too—poor Maria!—oh, how will she deplore the fond mother who so idolized her! how will she lament that she was not here to receive her last sigh, and be assured of her forgiveness!" she exclaimed as she lent over the pale features, which were now by the hand of death restored to their usual fair proportions.

The dreadful distortion of her once handsome features, which had rendered Mrs. Woodford for the last few weeks of her life a painful spectacle to look upon—an awful memento of the weakness of vanity—had all vanished; and Grace, as she contemplated the calm, tranquil countenance which seemed almost to smile, as if pitying the fate of those who were still condemned to struggle in the troublesome world which she had quitted for ever, gradually felt that extreme despair, that utter hopelessness which had at first rendered her insensible of everything but the magnitude of her loss, subside; and though, for her own sake, she mourned that she was left desolate and alone, for her mother's she ceased to regret that the scene of trouble and suffering was over.

Tears, however—bitter tears, forced their way, and for a time disturbed that calmness which had succeeded the first intense burst of sorrow, when Mrs. Stevens, who had been busily engaged with two or three others, in performing those offices towards the deceased which custom renders necessary, put into her hands her mother's pockets, which she (Mrs. Stevens) had taken from the pillows on which she died.

"You had better see what there is in them, Miss Woodford, before I put them with the other things to be washed." Scarcely reflecting what she was doing, but mechanically obeying this direction, Grace drew forth the contents.

"Lord bless me! whatever could your poor mother keep that money for, and you so short as you have been! even parting with your clothes to find her necessaries!" exclaimed the landlady, looking with surprise at the gold which rolled on the table. "Surely," she continued, "she must have felt that she had not long to live, and so have hoarded this up to pay for a decent funeral."

Grace did not think it necessary to explain how her mother had become possessed of this sum, but it recalled to her mind forcibly how her eyes had sparkled with pleasure—almost childish pleasure—as she, with feeble hand, counted it over, and deposited it where it was now found.

"Alas! it was not then of death that she thought," reflected Grace, "though she concealed from me to what purpose that sum was to be appropriated; and he, who, with such indulgence for human frailty and weakness, placed that money in her hand, even he little anticipated the purpose to which it would be appropriated."

The sight of this—the necessary means to procure what Mrs. Stevens had so emphatically styled a decent funeral—secured that good lady's most indefatigable services, and saved poor Grace from repulsive details, which break in with seemingly heartless coldness upon the sanctity of sorrow.

Mrs. Stevens took it all upon herself. She had a cousin, or uncle, or something, who was an undertaker, and he would do everything in the best and genteelest style, at the lowest possible prices, and Stevens and her would follow, with her (Grace) that proper respect might be shown to the dear departed.

Grace felt grateful for everything, but she requested she might be left as much alone as possible, till the time appointed for the ceremony.

"I shall get more fortitude and resolution by myself," she observed; but Mrs. Stevens could not believe that—she was sure it was enough to drive her quite melancholy, for a young creature like her to be shut up hour after hour in that manner with a corpse; and in spite of every remonstrance, Grace was condemned to have her sorrows intruded upon by the visits of a half dozen strangers to her, but friends of Mrs. Stevens, who were actuated by curiosity, or led by real commiseration, to attempt to console the poor orphan, who was thus left destitute under such peculiar circumstances.

Among those whose well-meant but fruitless endeavours to administer comfort by the usual commonplace condolences on such a subject, was a sister of Mrs. Stevens, whom Grace had once or twice seen in the house, during the first part of their residence there.

Mrs. Freeman, as she was called, was a lady's maid by profession, and, having, in the course of her various services, picked up considerable knowledge of the world, and rather superior manners, was by no means an unpleasant companion, on ordinary occasions.

She possessed too, that strong letter of recommendation, a handsome face, and good, though rather vulgar person : and though, in reality far inferior in real good intentions to her sister, who, as far as she was capable of discriminating, always kept the straight path in great matters, though in small ones, she, too, could sometimes conveniently wink, and step a few paces out of it.

Thus, *par exemple*, her lodgers might have safely trusted her with their money, their clothes, or any other valuables, but it was by no means the same case with their tea-chests, bread, butter, wine, everything in short, that could pay toll without being likely to be detected. In like manner, Grace was perfectly safe in her hands, as far as regarded the little she possessed ; but she had no scruples in adding to the bill for mourning, though the poor girl in the gratitude and generosity of her heart, had desired her to purchase for herself what she considered necessary, as far as the money would go.

"But, my dear, if this fifteen guineas are all you have ———"

Grace recollected Mr. Lovell's generous deposit.

"It cannot be used for a better purpose," thought the poor girl, "and without scruple or reserve, Grace put into her hands, the draft for ten pounds which he had given her.

"Ah, we shall be all right, now, my dear," said Mrs. Stevens, her eyes sparkling with pleasure; "my husband can advance you the money, and then, after the funeral, you can go and get it from the bank, for it's made payable only to you. Ah, poor dear Mr. Lovell, I daresay he foresaw how soon you would want it."

But, to return to Mrs. Freeman : of all those who administered, or at least, attempted to administer to Grace's comfort and consolation, under her bereavement, there was not one who was welcome to her but Mrs. Freeman, who, with more tact than any of them, avoided all commonplace compliments and condolence and sought, only by kind and comparatively delicate attentions, to lead her to look forward with hope, and to forget that she was alone in the world.

There was nothing, either, in her manner, of that air of patronage and condescension which sometimes made Grace shrink from Mrs. Stevens' officious kindnesses. Mrs. Freeman was all humility without obsequiousness ; she seemed to consider herself the obliged party, in sharing Grace's otherwise solitary apartments, and assisting in making her "customary suit of solemn black," observing that having recently left her situation she should else, have been under the necessity of seeking a lodging, and putting up with accommodations and society not very pleasant to her, who had been all her life used to the superior manners of ladies, though in the humble station of their attendant.

By degrees, Grace, who had recoiled from the proposal, that Mrs. Freeman should sleep and remain with her till the funeral, and, but that she felt too grateful to Mrs. Stevens, would have decidedly rejected it, became not only reconciled to the presence of a stranger, but thankful for having gained a friend much more congenial than any of those whose officious services were sometimes so repulsive to her feelings, that she was obliged to recal to her remembrance that her motives must be kind and disinterested, to enable her to bear with them.

Mrs. Freeman's advice was always given with gentleness and deference her compassion and sympathy was expressed rather by looks and tears, than set words and phrases, and she encouraged rather the measures by which Grace soothed her sorrows, instead of violently opposing, and declaring that she would kill herself with grief, and do no good to the poor dear departed, as was the common phrase of those who sometimes surprised Grace weeping over the pale features which were soon to be taken from her for ever.

"I, too, have lost every one that I loved, Miss Woodford," sighed Mrs. Freeman; "and I know how useless it is to try by words to stifle natural feelings. Time is the only soother of grief; and besides, as the poet says : —

'The grief that does not speak,
Whispers the o'er fraught heart, and bids it break.

It was into Mrs. Freeman's arms that Grace, after her return from the mournful ceremony which consigned her mother to the cold grave, threw herself, to vent that burst of irrepressible grief which broke from her heart, at returning to her now desolate rooms. It was Mrs. Freman's care which had removed every vestige, during her absence, which could administer to her grief, by reminding her of her she had for ever lost;

"You will not leave me, dear Mrs. Freeman?" said Grace, when those who had attended to "show respect" to the deceased had withdrawn, and Mrs. Stevens was beginning to busy herself in, to use her own expression, setting all to rights.

"Leave you!" returned Mrs. Freeman, the tears glistening in her eyes. "Oh, no, Miss Woodford, certainly not, now; and if it was in my power to say so, never. But, at least, for this week I shall, with your kind permission, defer my departnre."

Grace's looks rather than words proved how welcome was this kindness.

The week passed away, and Mrs. Stevens still deferred her departure; but she would no longer consent to be a burden on " dear Grace."

She had not been very careful, she acknowledged, or she might have had it in her power, perhaps, to have indulged the first wish of her her heart, by remaining with Grace for the rest of her life. But still she was not unprovided for on emergency; and if Grace would allow her to pay a joint share of their expenses, she would still defer her intention of taking a new situation.

Grace was now become so habituated to the society of this gentle and insinuating woman, that she would willingly have made any sacrifice to have retained her; but she felt doubly grateful for the kindness which thus conferred an obligation without seeming to consider it as such.

Time, as Mrs. Freeman had truly said, is the only soother of sorrow. That which Grace now felt for the loss of her mother was not diminished, but it was softened into melancholy remembrance and regret, and even those were sometimes lessened by the contemplation of the difficulties which seemed to threaten her.

Mrs. Somerford's busy season had now passed over, her most whimsical and best customers had taken their flight to other scenes of gaiety and fashion, and consequently Grace began daily to find that she had less demand for her services.

At last, Mrs. Freeman—who had been Grace's constant messenger, because she could not bear, as she said, to see Grace demean herself, by trudging backwards and forwards to wait upon people who ought to be waiting upon her—returned with the disheartening intelligence that Mrs. Somerford had no more occasion for Miss Woodford, nor would be likely to want her for two or three months.

"Cheer up my dear girl; I have told you the worst, because I hate myself to be deceived by people deluding one with false hope," said Mrs. Freeman, "and there is no occasion to despair. Come, put on your bonnet, and we will go to your pensioners, or rather Mr. Lovell's pensioners, you have never been yet to see them, and it will do you good—not only the walk, but to see how contented and comfortable people can be that have no ideas or wishes beyond those of the most complete ignorance. "Who knows, besides," she added, assuming a livelier tone, "but some good luck may turn up for us, which cannot be expected, while we sit looking at one another? We may find a letter, perhaps, from your friend, Mr. Lovell, when we return. Come, I have a presentiment that something will happen, to compensate for this piece of ill-fortune."

Grace complied, though she was far from feeling that buoyancy of spirit which seemed to animate her friend; and, for the first time since her mother's funeral, she left the house which had been to her the scene of so many miseries.

"Laws! is it possible you are going out? Well, to be sure, I am glad Susan has persuaded you at last. To be sure, how well you do look in black; and that is the most becomingist bonnet that ever was made. Well, if somebody as I know was to see you——well, well, I won't say who I mean, but you need not frown so."

Such were Mrs. Stevens's parting exclamations as Grace quitted the threshold.

"What does that silly sister of mine mean?" demanded Mrs. Freeman, when they had proceeded a few paces. "I know she is a famous hand at match making. Has she been attempting to try her skill with you?"

"No—not exactly," returned Grace, with some confusion.

"Well, I will not be intrusive, dear, if the subject is painful to you; but I hope she did not act so as to hurt your feelings."

"I should be very ungrateful if I was to attribute any blame to Mrs. Stevens," observed Grace, "but I will tell you the whole affair, lest you should think it more serious than it was."

As briefly as possible, Grace, recounted the circumstances attending her introduced to Sir George, suppressing only his name; but what was her surprise and confusion, when, in the midst of her detail, the subject of it suddenly made his appearance from a pastrycock's shop which they were passing, and without a moment's hesitation, approached them.

After a hasty, but respectful salutation to Grace, he addressed Mrs. Freeman.

"Is it possible," he observed, "that Lady Molyneux is in Bath again? I thought they were gone to the continent."

"They have, Sir George, and that is the reason I am here. I was unwilling to leave England for so long a time as they proposed to be absent and so I was compelled to leave my lady."

"Indeed! I am sorry to hear it, they will not I am sure, soon meet with one to supply your loss," he observed. "But, tell me, what was the cause of their sudden resolution to quit England."

Mrs. Freeman entered into a long detail, in which Grace could take no interest, and which she scarcely heard. She could not reasonably object to walk on, with Sir George at her side, whose whole thoughts seemed engrossed by the subject on which they were talking, and yet she felt uneasy and uncomfortable. It was so strange, too, that Mrs. Freeman should know Sir George, and that he should just at this precise moment make his appearance.

Still they continued to walk on; and Sir George, having exhausted, it appeared, the subject on which he seemed so interested, now turned to Grace.

"I scarcely know, Miss Woodford, whether, after the cruel misconstruction which your friends were pleased to put on some former transactions, I dare address you," he observed, "but I cannot resist the impulse of my feelings to assure you that whatever your opinion of me may be, I have heard with the deepest concern and sympathy of the misfortune you have sustained.

It was impossible for Grace to reply otherwise than with civility to this address, which seemed to occasion the greatest surprise to Mrs. Freeman.

"Good heavens! is it possible, my dear Grace, that it was Sir George of whom you were speaking, just now.?" she whispered so audibly that her accents reached him.

Grace replied only by a look; and they continued their walk for some minutes in silence.

Again, however, Sir George found some subject to renew his conversation with Mrs. Freeman, and they continued it until they reached the row of hovels, in which the latter pointed out the one which contained the objects of Mr. Lovell's bounty.

"We are on a visit of charity, Sir George," she observed. "Such, I know, are not totally unknown to you; but perhaps it would not be pleasant to you to enter such a place."

"Where Miss Woodford goes, I am sure I shall never shrink from," said Sir George, for the first time renewing that tone of gallantry, and the look of ardent devotion, which had, from their first meeting, distinguished him.

"Do not hinder his going in with us, dear," whispered Mrs. Freeman, "he is such a generous, humane man, that it wouldn't be justice to the poor people to keep him from seeing them."

Grace's scruples were disarmed; and without farther hesitation, she accompanied her companion into the house, followed by the baronet.

There was a family of seven children, all rosy, clean, and happy, though so ragged that they were literally half naked; and the efforts of the poor mother, as she dragged first one little urchin, and then another, up from the low stools on which they were seated, having their dinner of potatoes, with a little bit of fat bacon, to serve, as she said, for "say so"—meaning, that the name of meat would content them—her efforts to drag their sleeveless frocks over the brawny shoulders of the girls, and pull up the bit of shirt collar which served the place of the whole garment, to the boys showed that, though she did not possess the means, she understood the comforts of decency and appearance, even in her humble station.

"You must be hard put to it, my good woman, I should think, to get victuals for so many."

"Oh, no, bless you, sir; we're seldom quite without, though they are sometimes a little short; but then it's the father and I that feels it, more than they. But if I had my health and strength as I used to have we should do very well; though, thank God, I've no right to complain; for since I have had the rheumatiz, and have not been able to help myself, I've had a power of friends that I never had before."

"This is really quite a lesson, Miss Woodford," said Sir George, apparently deeply affected at the cheerful resignation of the poor creature who could thus draw good from evil. "You must allow me to be on your list of friends, my good woman," he added, putting a guinea into her hand; and then, as if to avoid her thanks, he walked hastily away, observing that he should have the pleasure he hoped, of meeting Miss Woodford again, either upon that or a similar occasion.

"This can never be the libertine he has been represented," thought Grace, as she walked slowly by the side of Mrs. Freeman to their lodgings; "surely Mr. Lovell must have been mistaken."

"How long have you known Sir George, my dear?" demanded her companion. "How odd it is that I never heard you mention his name!"

"It would have been still more odd if I had," returned Grace; "for I assure you, I have no title to claim him as an acquaintance, having only accidentally seen him in your sister's room."

Mrs. Freeman seemed quite satisfied with this explanation, and the subject dropped.

Within a very short time, however, again the baronet's name was introduced, and then Mrs. Freeman contrived to throw in some strong praises of his liberality, the kindness of his disposition, and his extreme sensibility.

Again and again the subject was renewed, although every time apparently totally undesignedly on the part of Mrs. Freeman; but it was so natural, in speaking of acts of kindness and humanity, to praise one who had performed more within her certain knowledge than any other person she could mention.

Such was Mrs. Freeman's reply, when Grace, somewhat struck with the warmth of her eulogies, now ventured to observe, smilingly, that it seemed the baronet had secured her (Mrs. Freeman's) good report.

"He is a great favourite, too, of Lady Molyneux," she continued: "and if it were only for that reason I should respect him."

Lady Molyneux was Mrs. Freeman's model for anything that was pure, elegant, and refined, and Grace had herself learned from hearing her ladyship's opinions, and precepts and example quoted as an ornament to her rank and sex, to consider her as, indeed, a most amiable and estimable woman.

And if Sir George was really a professed and notorious libertine, as Mr. Lovell had represented him, could it be possible that Lady Molyneux would not only afford him her countenance, but that he should have been the constant associate of her sons and daughters! Oh, no, it was quite impossible; Mr. Lovell must either have misrepresented him, or have been misled respecting him by some caluminous reports.

"It does not strike me that you particularly admire the baronet, my dear," observed Mrs. Freeman, laughing. "And yet, it is rather surprising, because I certainly think there is a great similarity between you and him, in many respects; and, indeed, I will confess the truth, my love, that while you and he were speaking to each other, it struck me that if you were in the same sphere of life you would be just cut out for each other. I am mistaken too," she added, with a sly look, "if the same thought, or something very like it, did not come into Sir George's head; and who knows, after all, Grace, whether I may not yet have the pleasure of wishing you joy, as Lady ———? Love has done many more strange things than to bestow title and fortune on one who seems born to adorn it. But I am, perhaps, talking very foolishly," she added, in a graver tone, "though I know my dear Grace will forgive an error which is solely occasioned by my regard for her."

It would have been very unnatural if Grace had indeed felt any serious displeasure at observations so flattering, and yet so delicate; and while she truly, and with sincerity disclaimed all ambitious views, she also ingenuously acknowledged that she had especial motives for distrusting Sir George, and therefore totally declining his attentions.

By degrees Mrs. Freeman drew from her the whole history of the baronet's introduction, his munificent present, and Mr. Lovell's remarks, and her consequent rejection of it.

Mrs. Freeman listened as attentively as if she had never heard a word of the story before.

"I cannot pretend to say what this Mr. Lovell's motives might be for such false aspersions, my dear, or whether he had himself been deceived by some enemy of Sir George's," she observed, "but this I am bold to affirm, that there never was a more false, scandalous, and malicious charge ever uttered ; and besides, what should this man know of Sir George, who never went into any company, and knew nothing about what was passing in the world, except what he saw from walking about the streets of a morning before anybody else was out of their beds, or gaping through the Venetian blinds at the opposite neighbours, half the day, as my sister tells me he did. And, indeed, to tell you the truth, Grace, I have had more than a hint, and I firmly believe it true too, that this Mr. Lovell himself is a man of no very excellent character, though my sister worships him because he pays her well ; but giving away money, Miss Woodford, is a very poor proof of goodness, if people don't show it in other ways, and really I never heard——"

"Oh, indeed, you are mistaken," interrupted Grace with warmth. "Mr. Lovell is—though harsh and austere in his manners—one of the most humane, kind-hearted men in the world ; he may have been in error with respect to Sir George, but I am sure he would not designedly injure a worm."

Mrs. Freeman smiled significantly.

"You know but little of the world, my dear," she replied, "and it is almost a pity that you should be taught how deceitful appearances are, though as to Mr. Lovell, I really don't know what he may have assumed towards you, for his own purposes, no doubt, but——"

"I cannot bear to hear you speak so again," interrupted Grace ; "indeed, indeed you wrong him ; Mr. Lovell is ——"

"My dear Grace, I know better than you do what he is, but I have my reasons for not telling you at present all I *do* know ; but now let me ask you a question or two, and you will see, how much you overrate Mr. Lovell's merits. He attended your poor mother, you say, with the greatest assiduity, prescribed, paid for her medicine, and administered it ; granted he did so, he might mean well, but the real fact is, that it is his hobby to act the physician, though, as Doctor Jahourdin said to me one day, that he never knew a case where Mr. Lovell had been beforehand with him, that the patient recovered. How, indeed, could he know anything about diseases, as the doctor said he had had no regular education ; indeed, to tell you the truth, Grace, though it is painful to me to say it, I think my sister was very wrong—very wrong, indeed, not to call in a proper medical man. As to you, my dear, you cannot be supposed to have experience enough to know anything about it, and of course thought everything was right and correct, but had I been here, then I assure you I should not have been satisfied with leaving poor Mrs. Woodford to the care of Mr. Lovell, whose blunders, Dr. Jahourdin told me, were quite notorious."

"Good heavens," ejaculated Grace, whose distress at these observations was only equalled by her surprise, "I thought Mr. Lovell was totally unknown in Bath, and you speak of him——"

"He is, to use the vulgar proverb, my dear, better known than trusted at least, as far as his medical skill goes; the truth is, Grace, he is a very strange, out-of-the-way eccentric man, and his being worth a considerable deal of money, gives him the power to indulge all his whims though they often cost other people very dear ; but we won't say any more about him ; you will see him in his true colours some day, if you ever see him indeed, for perhaps, before this time he's red hot in some other chase, and has forgotten you and all belonging to you."

There was something in the manner in which this last observation was made that struck Grace, forcibly, that Mrs. Freeman had, indeed, some hidden and powerful reasons for her evidently contemptuous opinion of Mr. Lovell ; and yet Grace could not be brought to believe that there was in reality any foundation for that contempt. She recalled to herself every act, every circumstance in which Mr. Lovell had been engaged and all alike confirmed her belief that though he was, as her companion had observed, a strange eccentric character, he was nevertheless humane, considerate, and benevolent.

One circumstance only tended to confirm Mrs. Freeman's opinion of him, that he had been influenced by caprice, and was now, to use her expression, red hot in some other pursuit, and that was his total silence towards her, Grace, ever since she had written to him, according to the directions he had given her, to announce her mother's death, and the non-performance of the promise he had made respecting providing an asylum for poor Joseph.

Grace, however, was, before many hours had passed, compelled to relinquish this last evidence of Mr. Lovell's inconsistency, by the arrival of a person deputed to take charge of the lad.

Heavily as Grace had felt the burthen of maintaining this helpless being, and still heavier as her anticipations were every hour becoming, as to the future, it was not without considerable pain that she beheld the moment arrive which was to separate her from the last link that connected her with Llan————. The poor fellow was himself most obstreporous, at first, in his opposition to the measure. He would not leave her. No; he protested in his own significant mode of expression, that he would die there at her feet; he did not want food, he wanted nothing but to die there. Grace's patient expostulation and explanation, as far as it was possible to make him comprehend it, that he was going only to acquire the means of enabling him to provide for her, as well as himself, at last succeeded; he at length understood that he was going to learn to work like the carpenters, and tailors, and shoemakers, whom he was used to watch with so much curiosity, and such a desire to imitate, and that he would be able to get money like them, and that then there need no longer be a necessity of shortening their meals, and going without supper, which, though he had submitted to, upon Grace's mild explanation to him, that it was necessary, he had yet evidently felt as a bitter privation.

His eyes now, indeed, sparkled with delight, as he at length comprehended all that was intended by his removal, and though, when the moment arrived that he was to quit her with his new companion, he became overwhelmed with grief, and left the house, drowned in tears, yet it was to the last moment, his constant reiteration, by his expressive signs, that he would come back to get money for her, and to live and die with her.

"What ! but benevolence, the purest benevolence, could have influeneed Mr. Lovell in this case?" said Grace, exultingly to her friend, Mrs. Freeman.

She smiled significantly.

"Time shows all things," she replied; "besides, this has cost him nothing, as I said before, but a little money that he does not well know how to dispose of; and he is paid well for it by appearing a great man; and what, perhaps, is of still more consequence in his eyes, securing your good opinion and gratitude."

"For which I do not verily believe, he cares one farthing," said Grace; "at least, this I am sure, that he has ever repressed every expression of it; but we shall agree, I see, on this point, and, as you have more than once said, I must leave it to time to bring you round to my opinion.

"You are vexed, my dear girl," returned Mrs. Freeman; "and yet, why should I not be equally displeased, that you continue still to doubt and suspect a person whom I have much more reason to esteem and respect than you have Mr. Lovell? I saw to-day, when I told you that I had met Sir George, and that he had inquired with kindness and solicitude after you, that you looked rather displeased than gratified; and yet, I am very sure that Sir George holds you in much greater respect and estimation, than Mr. Lovell has done."

The repetition of these and a thousand similar insinuations, the apparent delicacy and reserve of Sir George's manners, when again and again he (accidentally, of course), crossed their path, when Mrs. Freeman and Grace were walking, at length had their effect. Grace became thoroughly convinced of what she had been from the first inclined to believe, that the baronet had indeed been misrepresented and calumniated, and the cold reserve and distance of her manners towards him gradually yielded to increasing familiarity and confidence.

Sir George was now the friend who was to be consulted on all occasions, his opinion was received as decisive, both by her and her friend; the sense of impropeiety which had at first made Grace shrink from his society and wish that he less frequently fell in their way, was gradually forgotten, in the pleasure of conversing with one so well-informed, so intelligent, and so vivacious, and there was at length scarcely a day passed in which some portion of it was not spent in his company.

It was true that Grace sometimes felt some compunctious visitings of that prudence which she now seemed in a fair way of totally neglecting, when, after a long ramble, or an interesting conversation, in which she had totally lost sight of the distance between them, they had come suddenly upon some of Sir George's acquaintance; and she had beheld the free and bold glances with which the males had regarded her, and the averted and disdainful glances of the females; but on these occasions Mrs. Freeman was always her kind counsellor and consoler.

"Why should you heed the looks or opinions of a set of thoughtless, insipid triflers," she would reply, "when you are conscious, not only of doing what is strictly right, but that you are as far superior to the generality of them as the sun is to the little stars that twinkle around him? Besides, my dear, if you knew as much of these people as I do, you would think their disdain, nine times out of ten, a compliment. For instance, there was that painted, withered old piece of mortality, as Harry Molyneux used to call her, Lady Araminta Thomson, that passed us this morning, and gave me, as well as you, such a stare, as if you would put us quite out of countenance. Lord, my dear, if I was to tell you what things I have heard of her! Why, nothing but Sir Thomas Thomson, her husband's death—which by-the-bye, was a very sudden and mysterious one—saved her from being divorced at the age of forty-five; and ever since that she has been dressing and painting and flirting at every young man that came in her way, and it is actually whispered, is at last reduced to make love to her footman, and it is expected, will go to church with him; so that you see, my dear, how foolish you were to let her looks at you and Sir George give you a moment's uneasiness. The real fact is that she has been trying, in vain, to entrap Sir George into a noose, and it is nothing but sheer envy and disappointment that made her try to mortify us. For my part, I was pleased at the opportunity of plaguing her; I shouldn't at all wonder to hear that she has gone home, and either hung herself, or married John Trot in despair."

Grace had now become too much accustomed to Mrs. Freeman's tone of raillery and sarcasm, whenever she spoke of people she disliked, to give implicit belief to all she chose to say of that lady; but though she did not actually believe it in its fullest extent, it removed the sting of that expressive contemptuous look which Lady Araminta had bestowed on her and her companion, and she forgot again the resolution which she had at the moment formed, that she would not again be seen the companion of Sir George in the walks.

CHAPTER XXVI.

Virtue itself 'scapes not calamitous strokes;
The canker galls the infants of the spring,
Too oft before their buttons be disclosed;
And in the morn and liquid dew of youth,
Contagious blastments are most imminent.—SHAKESPEARE.

LIGHTLY and gaily as Grace's time seemed now, for the most part, to pass, there were hours when bitter reflection and remembrance would still intrude. She was still without employment, and every day added to the debt of obligation which she had contracted towards Mrs. Freeman, who continued to force upon her acceptance more even than what Grace considered it proper that she should expend, even had she possessed a much better prospect of being able to repay it, which, of course, it was fully understood between them both she was to do whenever it should be in her power.

It was true that Mrs. Freeman's apparent thoughtlessness and habits of self-indulgence often led Grace into expenses which she would not have incurred, had she been left alone, and could have exercised her own judgment and discretion. But, how could she object to paying for an extravagant repast at a fruiterer's or a pastrycook's when the money had but a few hours before, perhaps, been given to her by her companion? Or how to decline to invite the latter to share her dinners, her tea, or provide supper for her, when, but for her, she (Grace) would actually have been without those meals; and when, too, Mrs. Freeman declared, as she often did, that from her sister's sordid disposition and irritable temper, she never sat down without reluctance, and always rose without enjoyment, from her (Mrs. Stevens') table.

Totally unwittingly, and without, indeed, being able to assign the slighest reason for it, Grace found that Mrs. Steven's manners had undergone a total change towards her.

She had, in accordance with a hint from Mrs. Freeman, regularly paid her rent from the funds which the latter furnished; but, though the landlady could not be said to be actually uncivil to her when they met, every Monday morning, on this occasion—and at no other time was there now any intercourse between them—Grace felt uneasy, and mortified and humiliated, at the pert tone in which the former would inquire whether she (Grace) had got her work back yet; and her significant mode of remarking, that it was well some people could live as well without work as with it;

for her part she was obliged to work hard for what she got, and could hardly make a living after all.

These, and numerous insinuations of similar import, at length rendered Grace's situation so unpleasant that she could no longer keep silence on the subject to her friend and adviser, to whom, from motives of delicacy, she had hitherto refrained from mentioning this grievance. But Mrs. Freeman's surprising her, in tears, after one of her hebdomadal visits to Mrs. Stevens' little parlour, when the latter had been more than usually caustic and severe upon her weak-spirited lodger, at length led to a thorough explanation between them.

"I have long been wanting, my dear girl, to tell you, that I am myself wretchedly uncomfortable here," observed Mrs. Freeman. "My sister, to tell you the truth, is of such a miserable disposition that she is jealous and envious of our friendship, and would do everything in her power, I know, to break it. We have constant disputes about you ; and her not having heard, for these seven weeks, from Mr. Lovell, whose rent is now in arrear, has made her quite unbearable : in short, but for you I should have long ago quitted the house in which I met nothing but sneers and impertinence ; for my brother-in-law's jeers and laughs are almost as bad as her sourness. But I cannot leave you, my dear Grace, till I see you settled in some way. And indeed, I will confess that I am not quite disinterested in this, for I know, I am sure, that an event, which you won't let me speak of will yet take place, and then I know dearest Grace's heart too well to doubt that she will forget her faithiul though humble friend."

Grace's tears redoubled. "I cannot deceive or mislead you, my dear Mrs. Freeman," she replied. "I cannot. certainly, pretend to be unconscious that Sir George regards me with a—a——"

That he loves you ardently—loves you, adores you, Grace," interrupted Mrs. Freeman, hastily. "It is impossible you can mistake that, I am sure. You know I have said all along that you would be Lady —— I have told you that he is a man so much superior to common prejudices that he would think nothing of what other men regard as a barrier between you."

Grace smiled mournfully. "I was not thinking of what, as you say, might justly be considered as barriers between us, but of what I know to be an insuperable one."

"And what is that, Grace ?" demanded Mrs. Freeman hastily.

"My own wayward heart," said Grace, blushing deeply ; "or rather my having no heart to give," she added, in a faltering tone.

"Nonsense, my dear girl! I will not believe that story," replied Mrs. Freeman. "You in love!—so deeply in love as to refuse a baronet with three thousand a year? But, now, do tell me, for I am dying to hear who is this peerless swain who has made such a lasting and incurable wound that rank and wealth, and the adoration of a handsome, elegant, man cannot cure it? Where does he hide himself, and by what magical charm does he keep alive his influence with you? For I have been here three months, and during that time I am sure you cannot have seen or heard from him. But I suppose the fact is you have exchanged vows, and they are to remain unshaken by time, absence, or death. Come now, confess the truth, Grace ; have you broken a sixpence between you, and do you wear it, with the bit of blue ribbon he bought you at the fair, next your heart? Nay, never bend that frowning brow on me. I do not mean to say you were ever guilty of such childish ceremonies in reality ; but I would lay my life that the chain which binds you to this nameles swain is equally frivolous ; for he cannot be deserving of you, who can, for so long——"

THE PRIDE OF THE VILLAGE;

OR,

THE FARMER'S DAUGHTERS.

THE IMPERTINENT WAITER.

CHAPTER XXVI.—(CONTINUED.)

"You are mistaken," interrupted Grace, eagerly; "he is worthy. But I will tell you all our sad history; and then you shall judge whether it is likely that I can think of——"

"Sir George and three thousand a year," interrupted Mrs. Freeman, laughing; "but go on, my dear, I am attention."

Grace began with diffidence: she described the early attachment between Belgrave Mansel and herself,, her father's fostering approval and encouragement of it, and the tragic events which had totally overthrown all her hopes of happiness—everything, in fact, in her brief but eventful history, was

15

told without reserve : and Mrs. Freeman's tears flowed plentifully over the tragic tale.

"But, after all this, Grace, dear Grace," she observed—"though I acknowledge it was hard to be separated when your hearts were so united, I still remain true to the interests of Sir George, and, you must allow me to add, your own interest. I am not one who laughs at the tender ties of a first affection, and thinks it is to be broken without pain or remorse ; but I am convinced, Grace, that your romantic disposition, and the tenderness of your heart, have led you to magnify the merits and attractions of this young man, in proportion to his misfortunes. But, even supposing he is all you say and think he is, my dear, how slight is the chance that you will ever meet him again ? Besides, Grace, if you did but know as well as I do the little probability that a man will retain his constancy towards a female, however amiable and estimable, when he is absent for years, months, or even weeks,—for I have known weeks even eradicate a passion so violent that——."

"I would pledge my existence upon Belgrave's faith," interrupted Grace warmly.

"Well, well, we will not dispute it," rejoined Mrs. Freeman hastily. "Put on your bonnet, and dry your eyes, for I want you to go out with me, that we may have some sober counsel together upon another subject."

This subject proved to be the annoyances of which both complained from Mrs. Stevens' conduct, and which had originated this conversation.

Mrs. Freeman, indeed, had a proposal to make, to which, as usual, she soon, by her persuasive mode of putting the case, even though it appeared at first repulsive, she eventually brought Grace to agree. This was, that they should, without any intimation or explanation of their motives, leave the house, and retire to a little cottage, about a mile from the city, which belonged, Mrs. Freeman said, to a near relation of hers, and which had been offered her free of rent.

It was so contrary to Grace's disposition to act with duplicity, or more properly speaking, to act clandestinely, that it cost Mrs. Freeman a long hour's oratory, eloquent as she was on subjects in which she was interested, to reconcile her to the measure ; but Grace, when she had once given her consent to it, became even more anxious than her friend that it should be speedily put in execution.

So irksome, indeed, was it to her to meet Mrs. Stevens, under the consciousness that she (Grace) was going to act in a manner that the latter would feel she had a right to complain of, that she would infinitely have preferred, had it been possible, never to have returned to the house again, and her feelings more resembled those of a condemned culprit than anything else, when her landlady herself opened the door to them on their return.

To make the matter still worse, Mrs. Stevens was in the humour to be gracious. Grace's downcast and agitated look, and the hurried manner in which she attempted to pass her, excited the good woman's interest and curiosity ; and she detained her, by putting her hand, with an air of familiar kindness, on her (Grace's) arm, as the latter was hastily following Mrs. Freeman upstairs.

"What a hurry you are always in, now, Miss Woodford," she observed, "surely you have enough of my sister's company all day and night, sometimes to bestow a few minutes on an old friend."

Grace murmured a confused and indistinct apology.

"It's no compliment to tell you so," continued Mrs. Stevens, " but I can't help noticing that you don't look well to-day. Your long walks don't seem, indeed, much to agree with you; for, I've noticed, two or three times that you've come home looking much worse, and more out of *sperrits*, than you was when you went out. But come into the parlour, it's my birth-day, and you must have a glass of my own gooseberry wine, I've just tapped a bottle, and very good it is, I assure you. Now, I won't be refused, you know, so don't put on that no-thank-ye face, or else I shall be affronted, I assure you."

Grace could no longer decline the unusually friendly invitation; she ventured, indeed, to hint that it would be better to include Mrs. Freeman, who lingered half way up the stairs, listening, and waiting for her to join her; but Mrs. Stevens hastily and snappishly put a negative on the proposal.

"My sister has got no such good will towards me that I should ask her to drink my health," she observed. "Besides, it's very odd that I can't have a minute's conversation with you, but Susan must be lugged into it. She may wish you well, and I daresay she does; but she can't wish you better than I do, and that you ought to know, Miss Grace, though you seem to have forgot it lately."

It cost Grace a most painful effort to contradict this assertion, and assure Mrs. Stevens that she had never doubted her friendly feelings; but she saw it was expected she should do so, and she had not courage to disappoint her companion, or to avow that she had, indeed, for some time past, learnt to regard her rather as an enemy than a friend.

The gooseberry wine was, as the maker of it declared so good, that it tempted her to add a second and a third glass to the one which she said she had taken before; and, in proportion, as Mrs. Stevens became more elevated, her professions of friendliness and kind intentions towards Grace became warmer.

"You think, I dare say," she observed "that because I'm too busy and got too much to think of, to run up and down to you, or spend all my time with you, as my sister does, that I don't care anything about you; but you're quite mistaken, I assure you. I pass many a hour, when I ought to be asleep in my bed, in thinking and contriving what can be done for you; and I assure you, too, that when I'm fretting and stewing about Mr. Lovell's unaccountable silence and neglect, it's more on your account than my own; because I'am pretty sure I shall get my money some time or other. And, indeed, as you know, I've no reason to think otherwise, but that there is in the large trunk he's left behind him that would pay me double and double: he told me to be careful of it, for that there were articles of great value in it; and I am sure I never found any reason to doubt his word. So you see ,my dear, if I'm a bit cross and fidgetty about him sometimes, it can't be on my own account half so much as yours."

Grace was unable to contradict this, though the assertion gave her more pain than pleasure; for it seemed to convict her of ingratitude and render the act she meditated, in quitting Mrs. Stevens' ho se, one of the vilest treachery.

Mrs. Freeman's shrewd and penetrating look instantly detected the cause of Grace's uneasiness, when the latter, at last got away from her too obliging landlady, who was just now as prodigal of her kindness and favours as she had latterly been the reverse.

"You surely are not silly enough to be imposed upon to think my sister's professions really sincere, my dear Grace?" she demanded, when the latter, in reply to her questions acknowledged the feelings which Mrs. Stevens' unexpected kindness had produced in her bosom.

"What motive can she have for attempting to impose on me?" returned Grace.

Mrs. Freeman laughed.

"Do you not know, my dear, that an extra glass or two makes my sister very sentimental? If you had not happened to come in the way just now, she would have found some one else to lavish her extraordinary kindness upon. I have actually seen her embrace poor Becky, in her kindness, one evening; and you know, as well as I do, how much sincerity there could be in that. Indeed, as the poor girl said, she dreaded to see her missus so loving, for she was sure to be ten times more cross and dissatisfied next morning. I should be sorry to see you mortified, Grace," continued Mrs. Freeman; "but if you are still inclined to believe in my sister's professions, I would certainly advise you to make trial of them, to-morrow morning by requesting of her some trivial favour: you would soon be convinced that all her liberality and kindness vanishes, as the spirit of her gooseberry wine evaporates."

Grace, however, was spared the proposed trial, for Mrs. Freeman took especial care that during the day she should have no opportunity of encountering her sister, who, it appeared, had herself no disposition to oppose Mrs. Freeman's intended removal, which by accident she discovered, without, however, suspecting, as it appeared, that Grace had any concern in it, or intended to share it.

The real fact was, that Mrs. Freeman had contrived to impress her sister with a belief that she had at length procured a situation in a family similar to that she had before held; and Mrs. Stevens at once felt rejoiced, that Susan, as she called her, was once more getting into the way of making money again, and that she would thus be relieved of the presence of one whom, for many reasons, she disliked being her inmate.

Unsuspected and unobserved, Grace's trunk was carried out, together with her friend's, to the coach, which the latter had sent for.

"You may as well see me to my new home, Grace," said she, contriving that Mrs. Stevens should hear her; "the ride will do you good, and it will not be far for you to walk back."

Grace made no reply; her heart recoiled from the deceit she was practising, but in obedience to Mrs. Freeman's instructions, her bonnet and shawl were hastily thrown on, and in a few minutes she was in the coach, and out of the sight of the house which had been the scene of so many misfortunes and sufferings to her.

To Grace's surprise, instead of proceeding at once to the cottage which was to be their future residence, the coach drew up to the door of a house at a very short distance from the place they had quitted.

"Will you forgive me, dearest Grace, if I acknowledge I have practised a deception on you?" said Mrs. Freeman as soon as they were alone in the little parlour to which they had been shown. "Nay, do not look so alarmed," she continued, "for it is not yet too late to recede, if you refuse your consent to my plans. I have, it is true, ventured to deceive you so far, because I feared that had I told the whole truth that I am going to London, instead of remaining in this neighbourhood, your timid nature would have induced you to have shrunk from the risk of accompanying me."

"To London!" repeated Grace with consternation; "my dear Mrs. Freeman, what should you—what can I possibly do in London?"

"Everything, my dear, that you cannot do here," replied Mrs. Freeman; you will there be able to turn your industry and talents to good advantage, and those, with my experience and knowledge of the world, and a few respectable connections which I can boast of, will soon set us above the frowns of the world; but, as I said before, Grace, it is not yet too late for you to recede; if you dislike this plan, it will be easy for you to return to my sister and lay all the blame on me; I do not care what she says or thinks of me."

To London—it was a formidable undertaking—she would then be a hundred miles farther off dear Llan——; and, besides, Maria, her poor Maria, should she come back and not find her there————Oh, no, she could not— she dare not run that risk; and she turned to Mrs. Freeman to express her dissent, but the look she met was so earnest, so imploring, that her resolution failed her, and she remained in silent perplexity, unable to come to a resolution how she should decide.

"Dearest Grace, can I have any motives but for your interest?" said Mrs. Freeman, in her most insinuating tone of voice; "but I will not attempt to influence you. I am sorry, heartily sorry, I have so far tried to bias you, for your look reproaches me."

"Oh, no, no, you mistake; indeed you do. How can I reproach you—how can I feel otherwise than grateful to you?" exclaimed Grace; "but it is such a long way from——"

"From whom, dear?" said her companion, observing her hesitation. "There can be no place now that you can consider your home more than another. You have none either in Bath or Wales that you can reckon upon as friends; and, besides, if, as I trust and believe, you are prosperous in London, it will be easy for you to renew your intercourse with them there as here. It would cost you very little more to go from London than from here to Llan——and a few miles in travelling can make but little difference to you, and I—but I am wasting time, dearest Grace, and doing, too, what I did not wish to do, trying to persuade you."

Grace again tried seriously and calmly to run over in her own mind the various motives, both for and against the step Mrs. Freeman proposed; but her thoughts were all a chaos, the project had come so suddenly upon her, she was so totally unprepared for a serious consideration of what she would but a few moments before have considered totally impracticable, that she still wavered and hesitated without being able to adduce a single argument either for or against, except that which forced itself upon her by the recollection that her purse did not contain a third part of the sum which she reckoned would be necessary for her travelling expenses.

"How can I possibly think of going with you," she observed, "without the means of paying even——"

"If that is the only objection, dearest Grace," replied Mrs. Freeman, "set your heart at rest, for I will confess that, relying, perhaps, too sanguinely on your attachment to me, I have actually paid your coach hire; and, see, they are already putting the luggage into the coach. You must decide, therefore, my dear girl, immediately, for in ten minutes more we must be either separated—perhaps for ever—or our interests have become one, and inseparable."

Grace could no longer hesitate.

"I will go with you," she exclaimed, grasping Mrs. Freeman's hand.

"There spoke my own dear Grace! Oh, how happy you have made me! Oh, yes, I knew you would not desert me, that you would see my little stratagem in its true light, as only arising from my attachment to you; but, stay, Grace, there is a person by whom I can send a message by to my sister, for I should not like to leave her in suspense as to what has become of us both."

Mrs. Freeman flew out of the room as she spoke, and the moment after Grace beheld her in conversation with a man, whose eyes were directed with a look of earnest curiosity towards the window at which she was seated.

In another minute he disappeared, and Mrs. Freeman, returning to the room, with a flutter of exultation and triumph, exclaimed—

"Now, Grace, the coach is ready, dear."

CHAPTER XXVII.

"It is all the counsel that we two have shared;
    *   *   the hours that we have spent.
    *   *   *   *   *
    *   *   O! and is all forgot?"

SHAKESPEARE.

A PASSIONATE admirer of the beauties of nature, and powerfully impressed with the striking contrast of the cultivated scenery which now surrounded her to the wild and rude charms of her native hills, Grace soon forgot all unpleasant reflections in their contemplation. Mrs. Freeman was all kindness and attention to the inexperienced traveller. There was only one passenger besides themselves, an elderly man, who, muffled up in great coat, Welsh wig, and flannel stockings, seemed totally absorbed in his own contemplations, and, at length, gave audible notice that he took no interest in their discussion by covering his face with his handkerchief, and snoring in the corner into which he had settled himself on his first entrance into the coach, as if determined to make himself extremely comfortable, without any regard to, or even appearing to heed, that he had any fellow-passengers.

Grace was, therefore, totally unrestrained in her observations and comments, except that she delivered them in a tone so soft that it could not interrupt the slumbers of their companion, and Mrs. Freeman did her best towards keeping up her interest in the passing scene by pointing out the remarkable places, naming the different gentlemen's seats they passed, and relating anecdotes connected with their owners.

"You have travelled this road often, then," observed Grace.

"Yes; so often, my dear, that I know every mile of it as well as I do the streets and squares in the west end of London. Ah, Grace, there will be the sights and wonders for you to see, such shops—such magnificent shops—and dresses, and company, and promenades! Oh! Bath is nothing to it."

Grace's thoughts were in a moment abstracted from the present scene; she was recalling to her memory her first impressions when she entered Bath, the despair she had felt at the prospect of living perpetually in such a crowd of people, and enclosed in among so many houses, and her inability to comprehend or to share the delight which her mother and Maria appeared to feel in the exchange, which to her was a source of so much regret.

The recollection brought with it a train of melancholy thoughts, and banished the expression of surprise which she was about to give utterance to at the enthusiastic tone in which Mrs. Freeman spoke of the metropolis, though she had always professed the most extreme weariness and dislike of crowded cities and their accompaniments, empty show, and parade, and luxury, and noise, and extravagance.

"You must not look so grave, dearest, or I shall begin to think that you already repent accompanying me," observed Mrs. Freeman, with her usual tenderness; "but sure I am, Grace, that I have done the very best for your interest, and that before long you and I both shall have reason to congratulate ourselves on having ventured on this step. But a truce to all moralising; we stop here to dinner, and my appetite is too keen to admit of my talking."

Their sleepy companion now began to give signs of returning animation, his handkerchief was consigned to his pocket, his wig drawn still lower over his eyes, his immense travelling shawl brought higher over his chin, and due attention bestowed upon the other parts of his accoutrements.

"I wonder whether this dummy dines with us, or whether he will be as unsociable at his meals as he has hitherto appeared," whispered Mrs. Freeman, as she leaned her head together with Grace, who was seated opposite to her, out of the coach window.

Grace, ten minutes before, would have thought it a matter of very little consequence which he did; but within these ten minutes her thoughts of him had undergone a considerable revolution; for once she had accidentally encountered his eyes, and had felt them so overpowering, so totally unlike what she should have expected from his age and infirmities and seeming apathy, that she was absolutely startled; but she had been, if possible, still more startled by, the moment after, detecting Mrs. Freeman frowning at him, as if to repress any similar manifestation of his——what should she call it? not admiration, for that word would not express what his eyes conveyed.

"I don't half like that old man, my dear," said her companion, when they were alone in the room to which they were shown, and in which the cloth, &c., were already prepared for dinner. "I saw he quite confused you with his stare; but I don't think he'll do it again, for I gave him a look which he seemed to understand."

Had Grace known more of the world than she did, or had she been prone to suspicion, or could by any possibility have attached suspicion to her warm-hearted and affectionate friend, she would certainly have thought, if not said, that the old man and Mrs. Freeman understood each other much more readily than strangers usually do, between whom not a word had passed; for their fellow-traveller's grunting, wheezing observation of "Beg pardon, ladies, I hope I don't disturb you," when he first entered the coach had neither received, or seemed to expect to receive, a reply from either of them. But, the innocent, unsuspecting girl found in Mrs. Freeman's explanation a perfect solution of the riddle that for the last few minutes had tormented her, and she felt still more gratitude to the kind friend who had been thus roused from her usual timidity in her defence.

Though but a young traveller, Grace's experience of the exorbitant charges at the inns at which they had stopped when she had journeyed with her mother from Llan—— to Bath, had sufficiently enlightened her on the subject to know that the dinner of fowls, ham, tarts, &c., which was now set before them was much more expensive than the limited finances of her companion would allow, and hurt and vexed at the idea that it was on her account that Mrs. Freeman had incurred this extravagant expense, she ventured to express her regret it should have been thought necessary.

"'Take the good the gods provide you,' as the poet says, my dear," replied Mrs. Freeman, laughing. "Don't you remember the line? I don't know who wrote it, but I recollect it's in the 'Speaker' that we all learnt in at school, and I believe it's almost all I do remember about it; but it's quite a maxim with me, I assure you, never to stand hesitating about consequences, but to enjoy life, whenever I've the opportunity. And, indeed, Grace, after all, what is the use of standing shilly-shallying, 'and making faces at trifles? We've got but a few years to live, and why shouldn't we enjoy them as much as we can?"

Grace could not deny the wisdom of this observation : yet there was something so flippant in its delivery— something that seemed so unlike the gentle, reflective, sentimental, and decorous Mrs. Freeman, and that appeared to insinuate so much more than the precise words conveyed that she involuntarily shrank from continuing the subject, and, with a feeling of indefinable distrust and dissatisfaction, took her place at the table in silence.

"I beg your pardon, ladies, said the innkeeper, who himself waited on them, as he placed one of the dishes on the table, "but the deaf gentleman that came by the same coach with you made a mistake, and did not order any dinner for himself, thinking that the coach company all dined together. It's too late, now, to provide him any ; but if you would have the goodness to allow him to dine with you——"

"Upon my word, sir, it is an intrusion I don't approve of. I am not fond of associating with strangers," said Mrs. Freeman, with a great deal of assumed dignity. "But, however, if the person is really likely to go without a dinner—Grace, my dear, I think we must admit him?"

Grace, of course, could not dissent ; and in a few moments, the host introduced the stranger, observing at the same time—

"He needn't be any incumbrance to you, ladies, for he's as deaf as a post ; and I've been obliged to bawl till I'm hoarse, to make him understand how matters stood."

During the whole time of dinner, the stranger's attention seemed entirely absorbed in the good things which were placed before him, and to which he did ample justice, Mrs. Freeman assiduously helping, and, at the same time, indulging many arch and free remarks on the excellence of his appetite, and the *goût* with which he relished his dinner.

Grace, indeed, sometimes felt no slight embarrassment at the liberties in which her friend indulged herself, when they were left alone with the old man ; and she could not help sometimes, raising her eyes, with a look of fearful investigation, to his countenance, to be certain that he really was incapable of hearing and comprehending the remarks which, she thought, would have better fallen from any one's lips than those of a delicate female.

The traveller, however, still ate on, without seeming to be conscious that he was the subject of those arch smiles and grimaces which Mrs. Freeman so liberally bestowed upon him; and, at the conclusion of their repast, and after hastily swallowing a glass of wine from the bottle which the waiter, evidently by his previous direction, had set before him, bowed and departed, without having uttered a single word from his first entrance.

"The gentleman begs you will take a glass of wine, ladies," said the innkeeper, re-entering the room. "The bill is all settled, and the coach will be ready in ten minutes."

"Mrs. Freeman expressed some surprise and some reluctance at being thus indebted to a stranger ; but the man remarked, with a significant smile, which brought a deep crimson into Grace's cheek, that he was sure the obligation lay on the other side, and withdrew, leaving them with the decanter and glasses before them.

"Come, Grace, we may as well profit by the old fellow's liberality as leave it to the waiter," said Mrs. Freeman, filling the glasses. "I hope," she continued, "that your scruples about extra expense are now removed ;

and, to tell you the truth, I had a kind of presentiment, when I ordered the dinner, that such would be the case; for I have always been particularly lucky in travelling, and hardly ever paid a shilling for anything I've had on the road."

Grace felt still more dissatisfied. Could this be Mrs. Freeman, whom she had looked up to as a model of propriety of behaviour, and possessing a delicacy and refinement of ideas far, infinitely far, beyond what might reasonably be expected for one of her confined education and subordinate situation in life?

"Now, don't look so serious, Gracy," rejoined her companion. "You think, I see, that I am wrong in accepting these favours from a stranger; but, my dear, when you have seen as much of the world as I have, you will see the matter in a very different light. And after all what matters it what he thinks of our eating a dinner or drinking a bottle of wine at his expense? In a few hours we shall part: we go west; he, in all probability, due east; for he looks like an old carcass-butcher in Whitecapel, or a substantial sugar-baker in Thames-street, or Ratcliff-highway—places that your delicate little feet will never visit. Besides, I would lay twopence that, with all his gallantry, he has got some fat, old, burly woman, at home, that calls him husband; and, perhaps, a whole brood of gawky sons and daughters, or even grandchildren. I'm sure he looks old enough to have as many as old Methusaleh; so there's no great danger, even if he was to meet us in our promenades, of his claiming acquaintance with two smart young women like you and me."

It was impossible for Grace, whatever were her real sensations, to refrain from smiling at the arch and *naive* tone which so well became her gay companion; yet, even while she, in compliance with her repeated and pressing solicitation, at length accepted the glass of wine the former had poured out, she felt that it was not consistent with her own sense of right, and that whatever might be her real character—that which she had formerly appeared in, or her present gay, light, and accommodating one—she must possess considerable artifice to be able thus to appear so totally distinct at one time from another.

It was a source of increased dissatisfaction, too, to Grace, that, before they quitted the dining-parlour, her friend had actually finished all the wine that had been left in the decanter.

Grace herself had resolutely refused to taste a single drop more than one glass.

"Well, I don't get Madeira every day," observed Mrs. Freeman; "and as I know it can't hurt me, I shan't leave a drop for those that come after. Do, Grace, be persuaded, only one little glass more."

Grace, however, was positive in her refusal, and she rejoiced as much at her own resolution, as she felt ashamed of her companion's self-indulgence, when she beheld the significant glance with which the stranger surveyed the flushed cheeks of the latter, and then turned his inquisition upon herself.

Never, perhaps, in her life, had Grace assumed so proud, so cold, and so haughty a look as at that moment. She felt, indeed, in reality, humiliated, but she felt it also necessary to let this mysterious and penetrating old man know that she knew how to respect herself, and that she was not to be compromised by the imprudence of her companion.

A very short time elapsed before Mrs. Freeman's hearty dinner and indulgence afterwards had the effect of quieting her somewhat unruly vivacity, she fell into a profound sleep, and the stranger, again drawing himself up into his corner, followed her example.

Grace, however, felt no inclination for repose, for the first time in her life she felt the misery of self-reproach. She had felt conscious from the moment that she had yielded to Mrs. Freeman's proposal to leave her home clandestinely that it was ¡wrong, yet she had continued to surrender up her own judgment to this woman—nay, she was still doing so, though now more than half convinced that Mrs. Freeman was far from being a proper person with whom to associate herself, far less to rely implicitly upon as a director and guide. It was now, however, too late to recede, and Grace, as she acknowledged to herself that it was so, became still more miserable and depressed, as the distance between her and her late home rapidly increased.

During the remainder of their journey little occurred to withdraw Grace's attention from the harassing and disquieting thoughts which had taken possession of her mind. All, indeed, which she now beheld tended to confirm her worst fears, for at the next place they stopped at Mrs. Freeman recognised in the waiter an old acquaintance, and the twenty minutes that they remained there seemed lengthened to hours by Grace's impatience to get away from a scene so revolting to her ideas of delicacy and female decorum as was now presented to her.

It was not merely that Mrs. Freeman threw aside all reserve, and behaved towards her quondam acquaintance with a levity and freedom so totally at variance with her former manners, that Grace would have found it difficult to recognise in her the same person that she once appeared; but it was evident from the waiter's recurrence to former transactions, his low, impudent winks and inuendoes, and disgusting personal familiarities whenever he entered the room, that his former knowledge of Mrs. Freeman had been such as led him to regard her with no feelings approaching to respect. Towards herself, even, his looks and manners were most offensive; and Grace looked anxiously towards the door of the room, before which she had seen their deaf coach companion pass and repass several times after they entered the room, with a feeling that even his presence would be a protection.

"You're a devilish pretty girl," said the impertinent waiter, as she turned away from his intrusive looks. "What situation are you going to seek in Lunnun, my dear? for I suppose it's your first appearance there in any character, as the playbills say; I can tell that by the pretty rose pink that flushes your cheek at being stared at; but you'll soon get rid of that in Lunnun, won't she, Susan?"

Recalled, apparently, to more sobriety of feeling by this observation, Mrs. Freeman resumed her usual sedateness of look and manner, as she replied—

"That young lady is not going to seek a situation, I can assure you, Richard, and if I thought London likely to banish tne modesty that is so becoming at her age, I should be very sorry to have been the means of taking her there."

"Modesty!" repeated the man, with a sneering laugh, "modesty, and Sue Freeman's companion! I like that."

Mrs. Freeman frowned.

"It seems very plain, at any rate, that you have long dismissed all pretensions to modesty or even decency of behaviour, or you would not have made such an impudent and unjust remark," she observed.

"Psha, nonsense! What is the use of trying to play the hypocrite with me?" returned the man. "This young lady, I dare say————"

"The coach is ready, ladies," said a female servant, hastily putting the head-into the room; "and you, Mr. Dick, I wonder at your impudence, to stand prating there when you ought to be————"

Grace did not wait to hear the rest of this remonstrance, nor did she even, as she had hitherto done, regulate her movements by her companion's, for without even looking to see whether the latter followed her, she instantly obeyed the welcome summons, and was seated in the coach before either of her former companions.

The saucy waiter, in spite of his fellow servant's reproof, accompanied Mrs. Freeman to the coach door.

"How I wish I was going along with you, Sue," he observed. "Do you remember when you and I went down from Lunnun to Brighton together? You could blush then, almost as pretty as your companion there."

Grace turned from his impertinence, and beheld the eyes of their deaf companion peering over the handkerchief in which the lower part of his face was muffled, as if watching the effect of the man's insolent remarks upon her.

"I have surely seen those eyes before," thought Grace, almost starting as they encountered the keen glance, which, however, was immediately withdrawn as with apparent apathy and inattention; the stranger occupied himself in buttoning himself up to the chin, drawing his large gouty stockings which were rolled above his knee still higher, and although seeming intent only on making comfortable arrangements for the remainder of the journey.

"The fellow is grown quite a puppy," said Mrs. Freeman, as she drew in her head from the adieus of the waiter, who continued to talk to her until the coach drove on. "He was a footman, my dear, in the family that I first lived with," she continued, addressing Grace in a tone of apology; "and as he was then quite a raw country boy, and I a simple inexperienced girl, and were besides, both from the same part of the country, we naturally clung to on another, and were almost like brother and sister, as I may say. Richard, indeed, I believe would fain have looked upon me in a more tender light, but I never gave him any encouragement, and all he said now, is nothing but mere impudence and rhodomontade."

Grace made no reply to this attempt at apology or explanation, for she felt convinced that whatever might have been the origin of her companion's acquaintance with this man, he had certainly during it lost all respect for her, if he had ever felt any, and she therefore felt no inclination to discuss his present conduct.

CHAPTER XXVIII.

The face was young still, but its happy look
Was gone; the cheek had lost it colour, and
The lips its smile;—the light that once had played
Like sunshine in those eyes, was quenched and dim,
For tears had wasted it; her long dark hair
Floating upon her forehead, in loose waves,
Unbraided; and upon her pale thin hand
Her hair was bent, as if in pain;—no trace
Was left of that sweet gaiety which once
Seemed as if grief could darken not—as care
Would pass and leave behind no memory.
                                        —L. E. L.

At the White Horse Cellar they alighted, a hackney coach was called, and the deaf gentleman with more solicitude and gallantry than he had before shown, superintended the placing their luggage in the coach, handed them both into it, and waited until Mrs. Freeman, having directed the coachman to drive to No. ——, Crawford-street, Marylebone, bade him adieu.

"Now then, dear Grace, let me welcome you to London, and I trust, to wealth and happiness," said Mrs. Freeman, in her most fascinating tone, as she threw herself on a sofa, in a smartly furnished apartment, on the first floor of the house, at which she alighted, and when, it appeared—from the greeting of the female, who received them at the door, and immediately ushered them up stairs, they were expected guests.

Grace sighed deeply, but made no reply.

"You do not appear satisfied, my dear girl," resumed her companion, after looking at her for some time as if scrutinizing the thoughts which were passing in the poor girl's mind. "Does not this place answer your expectation? and she glanced round the room with an air of conscious satisfaction, which was totally at variance with her question.

"A much more humble home would satisfy my expectations," returned Grace, in a desponding tone; "and I will confess the truth. I have been thinking, that a less expensive one would be far more suitable to our finances."

"Excuse me, Miss Woodford," returned Mrs. Freeman. "I cannot but consider that you ought to allow me to be the best judge of this matter; we have come here, you know; dear Grace," she continued, resuming her sprightliness, "to seek our fortunes, and if you knew as much of the world as I do, you would know that there's nothing to be done without appearance and show. Do you suppose, if we were to take a garret, such a beautiful apartment for instance as the one you left behind you at Bath—do you think, I say, that it would be likely we should have many lady customers climb up to us, or whether anybody would think very highly of the fashions we should exhibit in our windows?" I forgot, though, it would not be very easy to make that exhibition, though we might, to be sure, suspend a dashing cap, or bonnet, or turban, at the end of a long pole, from the parapet, as the dyers do their goods. Well, you are determined not to laugh, I see, and so, to be as serious as yourself, Grace, I must, once, for all, assure you that if you think I will consent to live in the hugger-mugger way we did at Mrs. Stevens', you are quite mistaken. Nothing venture, nothing have, is a good old proverb, and I'm determined to act upon it."

Grace was completely silenced by these remarks; she felt, indeed, that what Mrs. Freeman asserted had hitherto been confirmed by her own observation, for certainly, it had been most painfully forced upon her, that show and confidence almost uniformly triumphed over modest, unassuming merit. Still, however, she could not feel satisfied how Mrs. Freeman's plans were to be accomplished. She had heard repeatedly from the latter, within the course of a few weeks, that her resources were nearly exhausted: she (Mrs. Freeman) had even hinted that unless something turned up to her advantage she should be obliged soon to dispose of some of her superfluous articles of finery, such as ear-rings, rings, necklaces, &c., of which, indeed, she possessed what —considering the station she had always held in life, appeared to Grace a surprising variety. Yet, now, though their journey to London must have cost her a considerable sum, and there certainly could be no immediate prospect of a supply, she seemed perfectly at her ease, and, indeed, not to give the slightest consideration to what she was accustomed to style the ways and means.

The first day of their residence in London was of course devoted to rest from the fatigues of their journey. but on the second morning Grace, anxious to lose no time in commencing that course of industry which she felt could alone enable her to triumph over the difficulties of her situation, ventured at breakfast to hint to her companion that it would be expedient to commence work without further delay.

Mrs. Freeman smiled.

" You are a strange girl, Grace," she observed; "I don't believe there's another in the world who would immediately after their arrival in London be content to sit down to work without having seen anything of the lions, as they call the sights ; however, you may set your mind at rest, for there are a little thousand of things to be done before we can go decidedly to work.   In the first place we must have cards printed and distributed and a brass plate, with our name for the front door, that's quite indispensable—Freeman and Woodford, or Woodford and Freeman, two good-looking dashing names enough ; they will sound well enough, though there's nothing like French names for bringing fashionable customers; and then, there's our stock to buy.   We must have some stock, you know, to work up; but, Lord, it's time enough to bother our brains about that ; we'll go first and have a look about us, and see what revolutions have taken place since last I saw London ; and I must go among my friends, too, and see how many of them are living, and how many of them are disposed to give me a helping hand in my new undertaking.   I shall be able then to calculate my strength better, when I know what I have got to depend upon ; and we must have a turn, too, among the milliners' shops, and see what they are doing ; or else, perhaps, our Bath fashions will prove a month or two behind the London ones." Grace could not, of course, object to this, as it was, in fact, but another means of forwarding her project than that which she had herself proposed, and she certainly was by no means opposed to the promised pleasure of seeing some of the splendours of the metropolis, of which she had heard so much. It was, however, with considerable chagrin she learned from her companion that it was too early yet, by some hours, to think of going out.

"I don't know, indeed, what I was thinking of," observed Mrs. Freeman, yawning, " to let you entice me out of bed at this unseasonable hour.   Why, my dear girl, the very housemaids are not yet stirring, nor the shop boys taken down their shutters in any of the fashionable streets.   We should not meet a soul worth meeting before one or two o'clock ; but, however, to indulge your impatience, which is very natural, we'll for once be unfashionable enough to get out an hour or two earlier, so you may hold yourself in readiness by eleven o'clock.   Let me see," and she looked at her watch " It's only half-past eight now ; I don't know how you'll contrive to kill time till then, especially as I want to stop to see an old friend of mine that lives a few doors up the street, but I won't stay long."

Grace requested she would not hurry herself on her account, and wrapping herself up in a shawl, and drawing Grace's straw bonnet over her nightcap, she shuffled away, not even troubling herself to exchange her slippers for shoes.

Grace felt surprised at this, but she had seen so much within the last two or three days in Mrs. Freeman's conduct that was new and surprising to her to allow her to dwell long upon so comparatively trifling an inconsistency as her setting off in such a hurry to visit her friends, after saying, a few moments before, that not a creature above the rank of a housemaid would be out of their beds at that early hour.

For the first hour of her absence Grace remained alone, seated at the window, sometimes so absorbed in thought of the past, or anticipation of the difficulties of the future as to forget the novelty of her present situation ; while occasionally her attention, on the contrary, would be so forcibly arrested by the busy scene which the street now presented, that in spite of melancholy regret, and uneasy foreboding, she could not help being surprised and interested by the passing scene.

From this occupation she was at length roused by the entrance of the landlady of the house, whom she had only seen casually on her first arrival, she having been called from home, as Grace understood from the servant girl who waited, to attend some relative who was supposed to be at the point of death, and from attending upon whom, it appeared that she had only that morning returned.

Towards this woman Grace felt no very great prepossession, at the moment she had first beheld her ; for, in addition to a very coarse and masculine set of features, and a corpulent, unwieldy person, Mrs. Jennings, as she was called, was also excessively dirty and slatternly while her manners were a mixture of cringing servility and insolent familiarity, which appeared to Grace much more repellent than absolute rudeness.

" So, my dear, you're all alone by yourself, as the Irishman says," she observed, as she entered the room.

Grace bowed, in silent acquiescence.

" Well, and how do you like Lunnun ?" continued Mrs. Jennings, throwing herself into a chair, immediately opposite to Grace, who shrank back almost in alarm, as she beheld the flushed face and unsteady eye of her visitant, and smelt the hot steam of spirituous liquor which issued from her lips.

" I can scarcely answer your question, madam," Grace returned, " having as yet seen little more of London than is to be seen from this window."

" And no bad sight of it, either, miss, I can assure you, observed Mrs. Jennings. " This is a wery ginteel street, and nothing to be seen in it that can give any offence, even if people are more ginteel than they seem to be."

" I did not mean to insinuate anything," commenced Grace, mildly.

" Insinivate ! No, ma'am, I should think not," interrupted Mrs. Jennings, with violence. " I'd defy you, or any other paltry little country miss, to insinivate anything against the character of my house ; for there arn't a house in Lunnun more orderly behaved, or more quiet than mine. I never takes nobody in but what's proper and well-behaved, and though I say it, I've had ladies live in this very 'partment, that rides in their *carridges*, now, with their livery sarvants behind them."

" I dare say, madam, it is very possible," observed Grace, who found she was expected to say something in reply to this elegant effusion, and yet dreaded to add, by any untoward remark, to the irritation which the woman seemed to feel.

" Possable !" the virago repeated. " Who axed you whether it was possable or unpossable, either ? Lord bless me ! I'm come to a pretty pass, indeed, when such bits o' pale-faced country hawbucks as you sets yourselves up to talk about possables, in my house, and you're a beauty, too, in some people's opinion ! Well, there's no 'counting for people's taste ; but, as I said to Mrs. Freeman, whin I first see'd you————"

The sudden entrance of the last mentioned person, prevented the conclusion of the sentence.

" Why, what the devil have you been doing, Sue, to go out that figure ?" exclaimed the woman, transferring, at once, all her attention from Grace, to her friend. " What a guy you do look !" she continued, " I say, if a certain party could see you this figure, he wouldn't say there wasn't a prettier little vixen in————"

"Nonsense, Mrs. Jennings; it's years ago since that was said of me," interrupted Mrs. Freeman, giving her a significant look to be cautious, which did not escape Grace's observation, confused and alarmed as she had been at Mrs. Jennings's vituperation.

"I am a very different person now to what I was then," she continued, "and have more serious things to think of than my looks. I've been out now upon business, I assure you. But come down stairs; I've something in the parlour that I want to show you."

Again Grace detected the significant wink with which Mrs. Freeman enforced her observation, and which was a sufficient corroboration, had there been any wanting, of the perfect understanding which existed between her and her landlady.

Mrs. Jennings muttered something which Grace did not understand, but which seemed to have a relation to the late colloquy between them, from the sarcastic expression of her maudlin eye, which was still fixed on Grace's expressive features.

"Don't be a fool," murmured Mrs. Freeman, as, with pretended playfulness, but evidently real anxiety to get her out of the room, she gently pushed Mrs. Jennings before her into the passage.

"Merciful goodness! to what I have exposed myself by my ill-placed confidence!" ejaculated Grace, resuming her seat, from which she had risen in alarm, at the moment when Mrs. Jennings had, in the exuberance of her wrath, drawn her own chair violently forward, and placing her hands on her knees, pushed her face almost close into the mild retreating one of her gentle opponent. "What shall I do?—where shall I go?—what will become of me?" continued the poor girl, wringing her hands, as the discordant tones of the landlady, in apparent anger with Mrs. Freeman, whose voice was exalted also beyond its usual pitch, reached her from the parlour beneath.

Long after the hour appointed for their excursion Grace continued alone and ruminating upon what had passed. The very thought of remaining in a house subject to the unprovoked insults of such a woman as Mrs. Jennings, was of itself sufficiently horrible; but still more so, when to this was added the fact that Mrs. Freeman seemed perfectly *au fait* in such affairs, and evidently felt no other annoyance than that which arose from her (Grace's) observation of the scene she had witnessed—

"Yes!" exclaimed the latter, in continuation: "It is but too plain that I have been grossly deceived, and that I have fallen into the hands of an artful, unprincipled woman; for what else can Mrs. Freeman be, to be the associate of such a creature as this woman? And yet," she thought, "Mrs. Freeman can have no interested motives in inducing me to become her companion. It was always in her power—at least I have always had reason to believe so—to secure herself a good maintenance by her own exertions. Let me not, therefore, be ungrateful to her, because she is not exactly what my sanguine fancy believed her. It is, perhaps, my ignorance of the class of people, with whom, as a servant, she has probably been unwillingly associated, and to whom custom has reconciled her, that makes them appear thus repellent and disgusting to me. And, yet, Heaven forbid I should ever become accustomed to such manners, such looks, such habits, as distinguish this woman! Alas! how different—how different from those————" She burst into tears, as the recollection of her peaceful home, of the friends and companions of her youth, rushed upon her mind; and was followed by the distressing conviction that seemed to arise from her present situation and prospects, that she was separated from them for ever.

"Come, my dear, I suppose you are quite tired of waiting for me, and thought I had quite forgotten all about our walk," exclaimed Mrs. Freeman, bursting into the room, with all her usual cheerfulness and alacrity of manner.

Had Grace told the truth, she would have acknowledged that the intended walk, and all connected with it, had been by her totally forgotten for the last half-hour.

"I am afraid that foolish old woman downstairs frightened you this morning, my dear," observed Mrs. Freeman, as she hastened to dress herself for the intended excursion. "But you need not be afraid, she means no harm, and is as good a creature as ever lived, only she is sometimes apt to take a little drop too much; and, indeed, there's every excuse for her just now, for she has been sitting up all night with a person that died this morning, and after all her trouble she finds that she won't get so much as a suit of mourning, for the widow has come this morning from the country, and taken possession of everything."

Grace could not at all understand how this was an excuse for a woman disgracing herself, or how it was likely Mrs. Jennings could have formed any extraordinary expectations of benefitting by a person who had, it appeared, connections to whom all of right belonged; but she did not venture to make any other observation than to express a hope that she should "never again be exposed to such undeserved insult, or witness manners so revolting and disgusting in a female."

"She is a foolish, ignorant old woman, Grace, certainly," she observed, "but she could have no intention of deliberately insulting you; you will know her better by-and-bye. I used to be like you, frightened at her once, when she got into her tantrums, but I don't care a farthing for her now, and and that is the reason she never attacks me."

The subject was dropped; for Grace, though she thought, did not give utterance to those thoughts, that no time would, she was sure, accustom her to meet her with composure, or submit without reluctance to such manners as she had that morning beheld.

With infinite difficulty, and not until after long disputing on the subject, Grace was allowed, by her dissatisfied companion, to follow the dictates of her own judgment in equipping herself for their projected excursion. Mrs. Freeman, indeed, was evidently seriously vexed that she could not prevail on her companion to follow her example in arraying herself in the most striking manner she could possibly devise, but in spite of all her assumption of knowing best what was suitable to London, and of the necessity there was of appearing fashionable and attractive themselves, if they expected to be thought capable of directing the taste of others, Grace was not to be convinced that it was either suitable or becoming to load herself with finery, or to be conspicuous by wearing all the colours of the rainbow, in flowers, ribbons, &c.

"Well, I declare, after all, Grace, I do believe you know best what sets you off to advantage," observed the former, when having at length, as it appeared, conquered the ill-humour which her companion's opposition to her mandates had created, she turned round to look at her as they crossed Oxford-street to Bond-street; "certainly that simple cottage bonnet is very becoming to your face, though I do still wish you would have had the pink ribbon and roses, instead of that plain white satin, which is so very childish; and that quaker-coloured silk, too, though it looks well upon you, is quite old-fashioned."

THE PRIDE OF THE VILLAGE;

OR,

THE FARMER'S DAUGHTERS.

SURPRISE OF GRACE.

CHAPTER XXV1II.—(CONTINUED).

Grace smiled, but she made no reply, for at that moment her eye rested
upon a face and person, which even at the distance of some hundred yards
or more she was convinced was familiar to her. Before, however, she could
utter an observation to her companion, or decidedly and satisfactorily ascertain the fact, the gentleman turned into a shop on the opposite side of
the street to that on which they were walking, and Grace's eager glance
into the shop as she passed at that distance, was baffled by several ladies
coming out, and pausing in the door to converse.

"Did you see anybody you knew there, Grace?" demanded Mrs. Freeman, whose quick eye had instantly discovered the change in her countenance.

"I thought—I am almost sure it was—and yet it was very strange that he should avoid me, for whether it was he or not, I am certain the eyes of the person were fixed on me, I saw him—I am almost sure I saw him start, as he looked first at you and then at me."

"Well, but who was it, child?" demanded Mrs. Freeman, impatiently.

"Mr. Lovell, you know whom I mean; Mrs. Stevens' lodger," replied Grace, her eyes still turned towards the shop, in the hope that the person she spoke of——

Mrs. Freeman's countenance betrayed evident confusion.

"Good gracious! do come along, I'm sure I don't want to meet him, of all the people in the world," she exclaimed.

"And why not?" demanded Grace, in surprise. "I would give the world almost to speak to him," she continued, looking back over her shoulder, as her companion hurried her onwards. At that moment she saw Mr. Lovell come out of the shop, and saw, too, distinctly, that his eyes followed her and her companion, while his usually stern countenance assumed a still sterner look, and told her plainly that his avoiding her did not arise from chance or accident, but that he deliberately shunned speaking to her.

"What can I have done to excite his displeasure?" she observed to Mrs. Freeman, as they proceeded on their walk.

"What does it matter whether he is displeased or no, the old savage!" returned the latter; "I can't think, for my part, Grace, how you can make him of such importance as to bestow a thought upon him; I have always told you he was either mad, or much worse, and I hope you'll believe me now. Pray don't keep looking back at him; what will people think of us?"

Thus reprimanded, Grace at once relinquished all hope of renewing her friendship with one whom, in spite of all Mrs. Freeman could say, and in spite even of her own experience, which certainly proved him inconsistent and capricious, she could not help regarding with feelings of respect.

During the remainder of their walk Grace was silent and abstracted; it was in vain her companion pointed out to her the splendour of the shops and carriages, or named to her different gay and fashionable people as they passed, whom she either recognised or pretended so to do. Grace's thoughts were far from London, or its sights and inhabitants. The appearance of Mr. Lovell had most forcibly recalled to her recollection all that he had promised, all that he had left her, determined, as it appeared, to perform. He had promised to leave no means untried to restore to her, and to snatch from ruin, her unhappy sister. Could it be possible that he had been insincere in those professions, or had he failed in the attempt? Grace would have given worlds to know whether he had seen Maria, to hear from him what was the actual situation of that unfortunate victim of folly, for even should it realise all her worst fears, anything was better than suspense.

"I declare, Grace, it's quite a bore to walk with you," exclaimed Mrs. Freeman, peevishly. "Three times have I asked you a question, without getting a word of answer, and you look so wild and miserable, that people are actually staring in your face with curiosity, wondering what such a woe-be-gone—— Lord, Grace, brighten up, do, there's a dear girl, do you see who that is on horseback there, talking to a lady in that carriage? Come, I've found out an old acquaintance, as well as you, and one, too, that, I'll be bound for it, won't shun us, or look black at us, as your Mr. Lovell did just now."

Sir George, for it was him whom Mrs. Freeman thus pointed out, did not indeed look displeased at this *rencontre*, nor did he apparently shun them, for he affected to be so deeply engaged in conversation, as not to see them, though a slight hesitation in the midst of the speech he was making, and an additional brightening of his florid complexion, would have betrayed to one even less observant than Grace, that he was not ignorant they were near him.

But it was not only the conviction that he saw and recognised them that rushed into Grace's mind at the moment she beheld him; a thousand minute circumstances which she had at the time noted, and then tried to believe accidental—tried to believe herself blameable in misinterpreting—for which she had even blushed at her injustice, now forcibly rushed into her mind, to confirm the suspicion that there was a mutual understauding between Mrs. Freeman and Sir George, and that their meeting now in London was not purely accidental.

Without a moment's hesitation, she turned her piercing eye upon the face of her companion.

"You expected this," she observed; "but what motive induced you to be so silent on the subject?" Mrs. Freeman looked for a moment abashed, but she speedily recovered her self-possession.

"Expected!" she repeated, "that is rather a curious observation, Miss Woodford. Certainly I knew, and so might you too, if you had taken the trouble to listen to Sir George's observations the two or three last times we saw him, that he was soon going to London; but as to any expectation of meeting him here to-day, I beg leave to deny it. What was it you meant tó insinuate, Grace, by that observation?" she continued, after some moments' silence, during which Grace, though daunted by her manner, was still revolving in her mind all that could confirm or lessen her suspicions.

"I meant to insinuate what I said," returned the latter calmly; "that you knew Sir George was coming to London, and were prepared to meet him; and I still do not retract what I said."

Again Mrs. Freeman looked confused; but the moment after she burst into a loud laugh.

"I see it is no use to attempt to deceive you, Grace, and so I may as well acknowledge the fact. My views in coming up to London have been very different to those of commencing milliner; but not a word of this, if you love me, before Sir George, who I see has turned his horse's head this way, and will overtake us in a few minutes. I must play my cards cautiously, Grace, but yet I hope, before many weeks are past, you will have to wish me joy as Lady ———."

Totally thrown off her guard by this seeming confidence, Grace's whole fabric of surmises and suspicions—founded on Sir George's professions towards herself, and the late conviction that had broken upon her mind, that Mrs. Freeman was far from being the correct, disinterested and kind-hearted woman she had appeared to her—all fell at once to the ground. Every circumstance that had appeared to her, Mrs. Freeman's new-born assumption, her recklessness of expense, her self-indulgence, and, above all, the glaring change in her style of dress, from extreme neatness and propriety to the most flaunting and showiest attire that she could make up—all was now accounted for, and Grace, in the simplicity of her heart, sighed at her own injustice in having attributed worse motives to her companion than she really deserved. Not that she, for one moment, believed that there existed any solid foundations for Mrs. Freeman's assertions; on the contrary, she was convinced that Sir George had never entertained a thought of the kind towards her companion; but Grace believed that vanity had misled her into believing what she wished to be true, and that she really deceived herself with the hope of bringing about the event of which she spoke so confidently.

As she had said, before they reached Piccadilly Sir George overtook them, and, flinging the reins of his horse to his servant, alighted, and instantly accosted them.

"I could scarcely believe my eyes, when first I saw you," he observed. "How long have you been in town? and where are you staying? It is Miss Woodford's first visit to London—is it not? We must show her all the sights. I shall be delighted to accompany you anywhere. Where are you going this morning? because I am quite disengaged, and will feel proud to become your cicerone."

All this was uttered with so much volubility, that there was neither room nor necessity for an answer to any of his questions except the last.

"We are not going anywhere particularly," said Mrs. Freeman, with one of her prettiest, most demure looks and tones.

"Oh, then we will go to Somerset House." It is the first day of the exhibition. Miss Woodford is a great admirer of pictures, I know, and all the world will be there."

Grace had no time to say she knew nothing about pictures, and had no wish to mingle with all the world; she had no time, indeed, to reflect upon the manifest impropriety of two females in their situation in life being ushered about to public places by a young, gay man of fortune and title; for the hackney-coach to which he had given a signal, in an instant was at the side of the pavement; the step was down, Mrs. Freeman seated, and without another word of explanation, Sir George turned to offer her (Grace) his hand to get in.

A conviction that all this was wrong and imprudent, however, sent the deep colour into Grace's cheeks, and occasioned her, for one moment, to hesitate; but there was no alternative. She could not, strange as she was to the streets and ways of London, say she would rather walk home alone, and accordingly she obeyed Mrs. Freeman's impatient—

"Come, Miss Woodford; what are you waiting for?" and was the next moment seated by her side.

Sir George was so full of his self-congratulation on his own good fortune in meeting with them, and his anticipations of the pleasure he should take in initiating Miss Woodford into the enjoyments and gaities of a London life, that it was some time before either of his companions could find an opportunity of uttering more than a simple negative or affirmative to all his numerous questions and observations. Grace, however, had time to remark, that though his attentions were divided between them, and though he certainly spoke more of herself, and more to her, possibly than to Mrs. Freeman, there were certain looks and smiles passing, which seemed to confirm the idea of a more intimate acquaintance between Sir George and her companion than Grace had hitherto observed.

"Well, and what sort of a journey had you up to London?" he at length inquired. "I wish I had known you were coming; for I certainly should not have trusted you to have come up alone."

"Grace will not give you credit for that assertion, Sir George," said Mrs. Freeman, smiling; "she has taken it into her head that you and I are quite *d'accord* on this occasion, and that our meeting to-day ——— You cannot, indeed, believe half the flattering things she has said to me, on your account."

She looked down as she concluded the sentence, as if overcome with timidity at what she had said, and Sir George, who appeared evidently embarrassed, and unable to take the hint she had given him, was, for a moment, completely posed what to say.

"It is no use attempting to deceive you, Sir George," resumed the lady, after a few minutes' silence. I have been compelled to acknowledge to my friend, Miss Woodford, the attachment between yourself and me, and the circumstance that compel us, at the present time, to be secret; and now, having, I trust, removed all restraint between us, I will tell you that we had a very humdrum sort of a journey, and not a single companion but a deaf old fellow, who paid, it seems, for two places (it was the four-inside coach,) that he might have room, I suppose, to stretch his long legs and snore, as he did, most musically, two-thirds and seven-eighths of the way."

"Indeed," said Sir George, laughing, Mrs. Freeman's lively sally having apparently given him time to recollect and perfectly recover his composure; "I ought to be very thankful, I suspect, to the deaf old fellow, for a stage coach affords such facilities of making acquaintance : I have myself known two elopements, and several most interesting love affairs, all attributable to stage coach adventures."

"You would not, I hope, infer that Grace was in any danger," said Mrs. Freeman, significantly; "as to me, it would be doing yourself great injustice, indeed—" and she looked at him with peculiar meaning in her eyes—"if you could suppose a stage coach acquaintance, or any other acquaintance, could for a moment withdraw my——"

"You are really too good, too kind, too condescending," said Sir George, interrupting her.

Grace looked hastily in his eyes.

If the tone of his voice was equivocal, and it certainly was so, or Grace would not have ventured to look at him at that moment, certainly the expression of his countenance was not so; for so far was it from corresponding with the words he uttered, that Grace thought Mrs. Freeman must indeed be blind, if she did not see that he was absolutely laughing at her.

There was nothing, however, in the latter's manner, that could induce the belief that she saw this; on the contrary, her expressions became every moment more and more unrestrained. She even hinted at the event, which she acknowledged she had confided to Grace, as being likely soon to take place; and, as if deprecating his anger at her incautiousness, added hastily—

"It was necessary, my dear Sir George, that I should be candid with Grace, because she very naturally would have objected to our associating with you, or admitting you as a visitor, under any other circumstances; but now, all our scruples are removed, and I may venture, without fear, to ask you to our humble apartments."

Sir George bowed in silence; to any impartial observer, it would have been at once evident that he was playing an irksome part in this affair; but Grace was now thrown completely off her guard. It was true, she still suspected, and indeed firmly believed, that Mrs. Freeman deceived herself, and was deceived by him, if Sir George, in reality, made her believe that he intended to marry her; but that there was any more deep deceit hidden under all these pretences never once occurred to her mind.

All the world, as Sir George had said, were at the exhibition; that is there was an immense crowd of all sorts and descriptions; and Grace, half-frightened, and half-amused, for a while, forgot all uneasy sensations in the novelty of the scene around her.

CHAPTER XXIX.

Go—go—'tis vain to curse—
  'Tis weakness to upbraid thee;
Hate cannot wish thee worse,
  Than guilt and shame have made thee!—MOORE.

FULLY established, now, upon the most unrestrained terms of intimacy, Sir George was scarcely ever absent from Crawford-street, and even Grace's unbelief began to give way, when she witnessed the constant assiduity and anxiety for their comfort and accommodation which he manifested.

At home and abroad, too, he was, during the first week of their residence in London, their constant companion; and Grace, thoroughly deceived by the manners and confidence which appeared to exist between Mrs. Freeman and him, was at length lulled into the belief that the latter had really superseded her in his affection; and that in despite of all that seemed to oppose such a disproportionate union, the pert, flippant, half-educated, self-sufficient lady's maid, for such, and no more, Mrs. Freeman certainly was, although the possession of considerable shrewdness, and the capability of successfully imitating the manners of her mistresses, had enabled her, for a short time, to appear superior to her station—would be merged in the lady of fortune, and title and fashion.

There were moments, indeed, that it could not fail to occur to Grace that it depended on herself alone to overturn in a moment the fabric which Mrs. Freeman seemed to think stood upon so secure a foundation. Moments in which Sir George betrayed, not only coldness and indifference towards Mrs. Freeman, but that he, without apparent design or intention, contrived to insinuate that nothing but the hopelessness of his love for her had induced him to transfer his attentions to another.

Mrs. Freeman was, or affected to be, blind and deaf to all this—she seemed to consider all his attentions to Grace, as arising out of his regard for her; and when the latter once, in the openness of her heart, and stimulated by some recent observation, which, in her opinion amounted to complete treachery on the part of Sir George, ventured to insinuate a doubt of his sincerity towards her friend, the latter completely disarmed her, by saying with archness, and at the same time patting the fair cheek which was glowing with confusion at what its possessor had said—

"And so the pretty child thinks that it could even now rival me if it would? Well, I acknowledge it is very likely that you are right, Grace, and to tell you the truth, Grace, I have more than half suspected it for some time. Indeed, I feel that it would be excessive vanity on my part to suppose that my feeble attractions could have entirely effaced your image from his heart; for—I may say it now, without offence, Grace—I know that from the first Sir George did adore you, and that had you listened to his suit he never would have bestowed a thought on me. Nay, I will go further than that, Grace, I will acknowledge to you that I believe, in my heart, that he deceives himself now, in thinking that he can be happy with me; and I will confess to you, also, that I am far from feeling certain that I can be happy with him. But, what is to be done, Grace? On the one side, stands poverty, obscurity—all that is horrible and to be dreaded; and on the other, wealth and distinction."

Grace was at once silenced and dismayed at this candid confession. How cruelly and unjustly had she accused her friend of levity and vanity and want of proper principle. How delicately had the latter now stated her situation, without once letting a word drop from her lips which could be construed into that which Grace nevertheless felt to be the fact—that, for her own unfortunate circumstances, and her (Mrs. Freeman's) having so identified herself with her, the latter would, in all probability, never have been placed in a situation in which her feelings and interest were so evidently at variance with each other.

Towards Sir George, too, Grace felt differently than she had for some time past, whom she had looked upon as a heartless unprincipled deceiver. It was not in human nature—not in woman's nature, at least—not to feel some kindness towards one whom she believed to be, in secret, so devotedly attached to herself as Mrs. Freeman had represented Sir George to be: and though she certainly gave him no reason to think that she regarded him in any other light than she had always done, as a friend, she almost unconsciously assumed a more familiar confiding tone, and shrank less from him than she had hitherto done.

Three weeks passed away in this security, and Grace, though melancholy forebodings would sometimes rush unbidden into her mind, and the most heartfelt regrets for the past steal unconsciously over her gayest moments, had yet become more familiarised to, and entered with more zest into, the gay life into which she was introduced by her companions, than she could ever have believed it possible she could.

The hurry of diversion and amusement in which they lived left her scarcely time for sober reflection, and prevented her dwelling, as probably she otherwise would have done, on several inconsistencies in both Mrs. Freeman's conduct and that of Sir George, which would otherwise have excited suspicion, and become the subject of her serious investigation.

That Mrs. Freeman should feel the most perfect confidence in her (Grace's) intentions and principles was certainly, she felt, nothing but her due; but it certainly argued worse than indifference towards Sir George, if she believed him, as she had said, devotedly attached in his heart, to leave him hour after hour, with the object of his affection, which she constantly did under the most frivolous pretences.

Often, too, on some trifling plea Grace was made Sir George's sole companion, either in his walks or drives, for his curricle was now constantly at the service of the ladies; and Grace, though with secret uneasiness, and a conviction in her inward heart that she could not conquer, though she stifled it, was persuaded to take her seat in it as the companion of the future lady——

Soon, however, it became evident to her that Sir George was much better pleased when Grace alone accompanied him; and though she at first hesitated to do so, by degrees her scruples were silenced.

The sense of propriety, and the necessity of suiting her appearance to her finances and situation in life, which had at first, in spite of all Mrs. Freeman's ridicule and persuasions, kept Grace within the strictest bounds as to her dress, was now, too, almost imperceptibly done away with. "It would be disgracing Sir George to appear with him otherwise than as dressed suitably to his rank," was Mrs. Freeman's mode of reasoning; and though Grace and she differed greatly as to the style of dress that was becoming to rank and fashion, the former could not refuse to wear the handsome presents for which she was equally with her friend indebted to Sir George's munificence; and consequently she now appeared dressed in a style quite, as Mrs. Freeman declared, suitable to the dashing vehicle which daily conveyed her through all the fashionable rides, to the admiration, as Sir George very often observed, of one sex, and the envy of the other.

"How I wish you were a horsewoman, Susan," observed the baronet, as he lolled over his breakfast one morning, discussing their plans for the day my friend, Colonel Roche, has got the prettiest creature to dispose of that ever eyes beheld. It has always carried a lady, and he would not sell it for any other purpose. He offered it to me quite a quite a bargain; but as you can't ride——"

"Don't be too sure of that," returned Mrs. Freeman; at least I am not too old to learn; and if it will please you, I will begin taking lessons to-morrow, and in the meantime Grace will ride the animal, if you will buy it for me."

"That will be just the thing," returned Sir George, starting up. "I will go directly and see Roche about it; I shall catch him in bed now, and so make sure of the bargain, for I know there are two women of my acquaintance who want it; and if it was only to disappoint them——"

"Really the women are much obliged to you," said Mrs. Freeman as he quitted the room. But come, Grace, you must go and pull out your riding habit from the bottom of your trunk. I recollect with what a sigh you deposited it there, observing that you should never, you supposed, want it again. You see how little you can foresee what is to happen. Proud enough, I recollect you told me, you felt when first you made your appearance in your habit, after being used to ride in a great stuff petticoat, or what-do-you-call-'em, like the farmer's wives that we used to see come jolting along the road to Bath. But you little thought then how much more reason you would have to be so; for I venture to say, and so I know Sir George thinks, that there won't be a horsewoman in the parks to-day that can vie with you."

It was one of Grace's weak points, to be doatingly fond of being on horse-back. Her father had himself taught her to ride; he had been proud to see her manage with ease, and sit with elegance, the most spirited animal he possessed; he had himself given orders for the riding habit of which Mrs. Freeman now spoke; and the last time that he had ever left his own house, was to ride with her to the nearest market town. It was with a mixture, therefore, of gratification and regret, that she obeyed her friend's injunctions: the habit was taken out of its retreat, and hung to the fire, lest it should be damp; the beaver hat was brushed and put into shape, as well as time and skill would allow; and before Sir George's voice was heard on the stairs, Grace was ready, and waiting to accompany him.

An expression of pleasurable surprise was visible in the countenance of the baronet, as he surveyed her particularly neat and symmetrical, figure, which certainly appeared to more advantage in this dress than any other.

"This is a pleasure I scarcely anticipated," he observed. "I was not aware that you were so well prepared for an excursion,; and I have, therefore, sent Joe to my tailor's, to desire him to come and measure you and Susan for habits; however, she can see him, and give her orders, and you can——"

Grace would have protested against unnecessary expense, but Mrs. Freeman's observation was decisive.

"Your habit will do very well for a make-shift child," she observed; "but, after all, it's old fashioned, and so not another word."

"Come to the window, Grace, and see what a pretty creature it is," said Sir George, passing his arm around her slender waist, and leading her, as he spoke, to the window, beneath which a servant in livery was walking the animal in question, while another held Sir George's horse and his own up and down.

It was indeed, a beautiful creature, and Grace did not withhold her praise from it; while Mrs. Freeman, peeping over her shoulder, lavished upon it her usual phrases of sweet, lovely, elegant, &c., &c.

But Grace saw more in the street to excite her observation, than the horse only.

There were several persons on the pavement, who seemed to have been actuated by curiosity, or admiration of the animals, to stop; and among them Grace beheld a person, who, though evidently disguised, and bearing an appearance totally different, as to outward circumstances, to what she had formerly beheld, she could not doubt her knowledge of.

It was William Mansel, who, wrapped in an old great coat, his beard unshaven, his feet in slippers, and altogether his appearance betokening the greatest poverty and neglect, stood, with a melancholy air, and seeming abstraction from all around him, gazing at the horses.

Grace's heart beat almost to suffocation; and her countenance underwent so rapid a change, that Mrs. Freeman, in alarm, exclaimed—

"Good heavens, Sir George! she is fainting, throw open the window, let her have air."

The noise which attended his compliance with this request, instantly drew the attention of the bystanders, and among the rest, William himself raised his eyes to the window.

For a moment a ray of pleasure lighted up his countenance, but the next instant it faded, and with a look of deep contempt, he turned his head aside, and walked away.

Grace had almost immediately recovered herself, and regardless of what her companions might think, was on the very point of beckoning him to come upstairs, when she was astonished and disappointed to the utmost, by the manner he assumed, and with a look of consternation, she turned to Mrs. Freeman.

"Good heavens! he will not speak to me. He is going, and I shall never, perhaps see him again!" she exclaimed.

"Upon my word, Grace, I don't think that is much to be lamented, if we may judge by his appearance," said Mrs. Freeman, sharply. "I confess you startled me so at your agitation, that I didn't know what to do or to say, or I should certainly have objected at once to your claiming acquaintance with such a ragamuffin."

At any other time, Grace would certainly have resented with spirit such an expression, and such a dictatorial tone, as Mrs. Freeman had thought proper to assume; but her spirits were now completely sunk, and with a burst of tears, she replied—

"Were he ten times more desolate in appearance, I would not hesitate to claim William Mansel as my dearest friend, though it seems he disdains to own me as such. What can I have done to deserve the manner in which he treated me?

"Really, Miss Woodford, I am quite surprised that you should attach so much importance to this fellow," observed Sir George, in an angry tone, after whispering for some moments with Mrs. Freeman. "If, indeed, he had been a relative, but——"

Grace's look of astonishment and displeasure at the authoritative manner he assumed, interrupted his speech, and induced him suddenly to vary it.

"Pardon me, dear Grace," he continued, "but I am hurt to see you thus grieve for one who is evidently unworthy that you should bestow a thought upon him. I know not what this young man may have been, or in what light he may have appeared to you; but certainly, if appearances are to be trusted, he is now a very unfit person to renew your acquaintance with. What could indeed be expected of a man who was evidently intoxicated at this time of day in the public streets, and whom I saw, though you did not, familarly join company at the corner of the street, with two of the lowest and most abandoned women."

Grace certainly had not seen this, but she had seen Sir George lean out of the window, for some moments after she had withdrawn, and she could not for a moment entertain the idea that the baronet would assert what was not true.

"Intoxicated ! if that was correct, that did indeed account for what was otherwise inexplicable ; but how fallen, how utterly changed must be William Mansel in mind, as well as in appearance, if it were true."

"And to whom, to what can I attribute this dreadful change," thought Grace ; "but to—— Alas ! alas ! Maria, is it then so that you have drawn down ruin on one who so tenderly loved you ?"

Her reverie was interrupted.

"Sir George will be dreadfully disappointed, if you do not go with him, Grace," said Mrs. Freeman, in a low voice. "I should be very sorry, on more accounts than one, that you should offend him just now. Do, there's a dear girl, try to compose yourself, and tell him that you will go in spite of what has happened,"

Before Grace could, however, command herself to appear composed, Sir George, who had been leaning out of the window, talking to his groom, advanced to her.

"I presume Miss Woodford is too much engrossed by her regret for her former acquaintance, to bestow a thought on such an insignificant personage as myself," he observed, in a tone of excessive pique ; and then, after a short pause, he added, reassuming his usual mild insinuating manner. "Must I send away the horses, Grace. I do not wish to force you, dear girl ; but, indeed, I do think, that air and exercise, and change of scene, will do you more good, just now, than brooding over vain regrets and useless recollections."

Unfit as she was to engage in any pleasure, Grace knew not how to refuse the pressing entreaties with which Mrs. Freeman seconded this observation, and in a few minutes her tears dried up, and, an assumed smile concealing the anguish of her heart, she was seated on the beautiful animal which seemed proud of its burthen.

The day was fine, the park crowded with fashionables, and Grace, as they cantered along the ring, felt her cheeks glow at the observation their appearance excited, while Sir George, though he affected to be only solicitous for her pleasure and comfort, evidently felt not a little elated and gratified at the praises and expressions of admiration which from time to time reached his ear, on his fair companion's appearance and horsemanship, as well as the animal she rode.

Repeatedly was she joined by gentlemen who by their looks, and in some instances, by words, expressed their desire of knowing something more of the fair and modest girl, who shrank with confusion from their earnest gaze ; but Sir George was determinedly blind and deaf to their hints and their curiosity, and though several found opportunities of addressing a few words of compliment to her, under the pretext of examining Sir George's new purchase, the baronet contrived effectually to elude all their attempts at a further introduction to his charge.

It could but, however, occur to Grace that all this apparent kindness and courtesy to her was entirely confined to the male part of Sir George's acquaintance, and that the ladies seemed, on the contrary, disposed to view her with sentiments of a very opposite nature. More than once, indeed, she drew back with a feeling of surprise, and almost consternation, at the looks of pointed scorn with which her casual glance was returned by some young and handsome females, whom she immediately recollected, as the same with whom Sir George was conversing on the morning when she had first recognised him in Bond-street; while scarcely less appalling or less inexplicable was the look of pity and sorrow which beamed from the dark eyes of a matron who now accompanied them, and to whom, it was plain, by her earnest bending from the window of the carriage, as for the second time Grace and her companion passed them in the circle, the former had been especially pointed out.

Grace felt as if fascinated by those dark expressive eyes; again and again she sought them out, but they were now bent on Sir George with an expression very different to what they had worn before, for they now betrayed resentment and severe reproof.

"Who is that lady?" was just hovering on Grace's lips; but its utterance was prevented, by her observing that Sir George had totally averted his head, and effected to be busily engaged in examining a new carriage, with most extravagantly gorgeous liveries, which was passing; but the moment the lady, who was seated in it beheld the baronet, she pulled the string.

"So you wanted to sneak past, did you," she observed, addressing the latter; "but it wouldn't do, I want to wish you joy of your bargain there," to the animal Grace rode. "Fred told me you had bought it of him; but now, if you don't want to commit deliberate murder, take that poor girl off its back directly, for there isn't such another vicious devil in England, she spilt me twice, the last time I rode her."

"You!" said Sir George, in a tone of derision. "You surely don't mean that as any proof of the animal's viciousness, because she wouldn't keep such a rider as you on her back."

"Why, you saucy varlet, do you mean to say I can't ride? Do you know I was out with the hounds every day last season at Melton?" said the lady.

"Indeed you do surprise me now," observed Sir George: "not that you went out, but that you ever came back again. Good morning."

"Stop a moment, I have some news to tell you," vociferated the lady.

Sir George reined in his horse, and Grace, though she had proceeded a few paces, was yet within reach of their conversation.

"First of all tell me who is that pretty girl who sits so well on that mare; she makes me almost regret I have parted with her," demanded the lady, looking at Grace. "It's very odd," she continued, "I could never make her obey the hand as she does."

"Grace is an excellent horseman," said the baronet, with conscious pride in his looks.

"Grace, Grace, what an apposite name," repeated the lady; but who is she—who are her friends, they can have but little grace, I think, to trust her with such an ungracious wretch as you."

"Nonsense; what were the news you were going to tell me? Do make haste, for I can't stay here all day," returned Sir George, very unceremoniously.

"Well then, your uncle is in town, came on purpose to make his will, and other pretty little arrangements, which———"

"In town!" repeated Sir George, "and I not know it. Tell me Clara, have you seen him? Does he know I am here? What did he say, tell me all, there's a dear girl."

"Oh, yes, I am a dear girl, now; you can be civil enough to answer your own purposes; but it would serve you right were I to leave you to burst in ignorance; however, I am too goodnatured, as you well know, and so I'll tell you at once the whole story. It's just six weeks ago, I think, that a note was delivered to my right honourable papa, as we sat at breakfast; I saw his colour change, he seemed surprised and agitated, and without the slightest apology to me, for running away, just as I had condescended to sweeten his chocolate with my own fair hands, off he marched with the servant. Well, I waited and waited, till the chocolate was cold, and then I poured it into the slop basin, and prepared to make a fresh cup.

"Who knows after all, I thought to myself as I held the sugar suspended in the tongs, whether he'll come back in time to drink this before it's it's spoiled; he can't surely condemn me, as he has often done, for inordinate curiosity if I just try to learn what probability there is of his coming. 'Where is your master?' I inquired of the servant who answered the bell.

"'In the library, madam.'

"'In the library? surely he has forgotten that he has not breakfasted.'

"'I beg your pardon, madam, I ought to have let you know before; he is breakfasting with the gentleman in the library.'

"You may be sure I did ring a pretty peal in Thomas's ears for his carelessness in keeping me waiting so long without my breakfast.

"'And, pray, who is this person with whom your master is breakfasting in the library?' I inquired, with seeming carelessness. My gracious papa particularly objects, you know, to my making inquiries of his servants as to his private proceedings—afraid, I suppose, that I should discover some of the State secrets which he confides to his *valet de chambre*, or be shocked at the intelligence that his last new *chère amie* has——"

"For shame, Clara! how you talk," interrupted Sir George. "Do, pray, let the old gentleman's amours rest in obscurity, and proceed at once to my uncle. Was it he who was closetted with my father?"

"I won't tell you a word more if you don't let me go on in my own way," said Clara, assuming a pretty pouting look and tone. "You don't suppose that my father is so bad a politician as to suffer me to make a thorough discovery at once of his secret? No, no; all I could learn of Thomas was that the stranger was a tall, surly-looking old gentleman, who refused to give any name when he sent up the note.

"'I told him,' said Thomas, 'that I was ordered not to take in any notes or letters, without knowing who they came from, because master and my young lady had been so often taken in to open begging letters.

"'Mine is not a begging letter, you puppy!" said the old gentleman, grasping his bamboo, as if he would knock me down, if I hesitated any longer. 'And if it was,' he roared after me, 'it's your master's duty and your lady's, too, to read every letter sent them, and then treat the writers according to their deserts, and not reject them all in a lump.

"If I'd a grain of sense, as you well know I have not," continued Clara, "I should instantly have set this impudent stranger down for my uncle, the earl; for, though I had never seen him since I was ten years old, I had a perfect recollection of the lecture he preached me then, about my frippery and trumpery, as he called the beautiful lace frock, white satin slip, and splendid suite of pearls, in which my poor mother had decked me, to go to her Majesty Queen Charlotte's juvenile fête, at Frogmore; and how he brought tears into my eyes, as much by the grasp of his powerful hand, as he held me fast between his knees, as with the eloquent picture he drew of the naked and hungry children who might be clothed and fed out of my superfluities, and I enjoy no less pleasure, admiration and distinction. Fine stuff, you know, cousin George, but I knew no better then than to take all for granted that he said, and cried for an hour because mamma wouldn't let me pull of all my finery and sell it to clothe and feed naked beggars and their brats.

"I went to the ball, but the old stern earl's face and voice and the description he had given of some starving family that he had just come from that morning in some dirty hole or nook, where nobody but himself that had any regard for themselves, as my father observed, would have ventuerd, haunted me all the evening, and spoilt the harmony of the music and the taste of the dainties with which we were regaled.

"My uncle went abroad the very next week, and I never saw him from that time to this; but though I forgot his lesson, or learned to know better than to practise it——"

"That is false, Clara," interrupted Sir George; "you have faults enough, but insensibility to your fellow-creatures is not one of them."

"It is well you qualified that compliment," returned Clara, "or I should have been proud, indeed, of the only one my dear and well-beloved cousin ever thought proper to pay me; but à propos de brebis, retournons à nos moutons. I had forgot for the moment all about the tall, surly old gentleman, and therefore did not find out it was he whom Thomas so graphically described, and it was all in vain that in my own pretty little, undesigning, roundabout way I tried to get out of my politic and crafty papa who it was and what was the important business which had kept him five hours shut up in the library. So far, however, I got upon the right scent, as they say at Melton, that I learned my hopeful cousin George was in some way concerned in the affair; for my father abruptly observed, the moment we were alone after dinner—

" 'So, Clara, that precious rascal, George, is in London, I find; though he has not condescended to let me know it, and, indeed, acts altogether as if there was no such person in existence. But, it's no wonder; I'm a very insignificant person, no doubt. The Right Honourable Harvey Fitz-Harvey, one of his gracious Majesty's commissioners——' "

" ' Dear papa,' said I, in my silly way, ' I dare say George does not know of your new dignity: let me write to him how highly the King has honoured you, and I'll be bound he will hasten to show you all manner of respect: for, with all his faults, George, you know, is the very reverse of disloyal, and honours, I am sure, even the very shadow——" '

" ' You think yourself, I dare say, a very facetious young lady. Miss Clara,' said my dignified papa; ' but, really, I see nothing in this affair to joke about: Sir George, I hear, has already deserted Lady Albina Mandeville; so that the three thousand pounds damages he paid for that pretty affair, and the risking his own life in his encounter with her brother, and wounding the poor young man so that he will be an invalid for life, has all been to gratify——' "

" 'Don't you know, papa,' said I, very wisely and sententiously,—— Nay, George, you shall listen to me; I have not told you half——' "

"I have heard quite enough of your rhodomontade, Clara. I ought to have known that you only detained me, to gratify your malice."

Clara burst into a loud "Ha! ha! ha!" as he put spurs to his horse, and rode off.

"Shall I tell your uncle I have seen you?" she called out, putting her head out of the carriage window.

"You may tell him you have seen the devil, if you like," muttered Sir George, between his closed teeth, as he rode up close to Grace's side, and endeavoured apparently to read in her countenance how much of this conversation had reached her ear, and what impression it had made on her;

but the investigation was anything but satisfactory to him, for her embarrassed look and total silence betrayed, as plainly as words could have done, the nature of her reflections.

"I hope you do not give any credit to what you may have heard my rattling cousin Clara say, Miss Woodford," he observed; "because I assure you there is not a word of truth in all she uttered. You may judge yourself indeed, how little what she says is to be depended upon by what she asserted as to the cause of her parting with the horse you ride on; for the fact is, she can scarcely sit a horse without being tied on. You, who ride so beautifully would die of laughter to see Clara's awkward figure. She was vexed, as you might observe, to see the animal the property of one who showed it off to such advantage; and my rallying her induced her to invent one of those malicious tales for which she is famous."

Grace, however, was not to be so easily deceived, even by the cool indifferent tone, and the insidious smile with which her companion uttered assertions.

She had happened to have a full view of his countenance, as his cousin had uttered her remarks respecting Lady Albina Mandeville; and she had seen confusion and shame, which even his bold and resolute effrontery could not wholly conquer, striving for the mastery. Besides, was it probable a female—a young, and, by her situation in life, a respectable female, could have invented such a revolting tale? It was bad enough, indelicate enough, or rather more than enough, to have recurred to it, and uttered her remarks with so much levity as this young lady had done, but it was utterly incredible that any female could invent such a tale; and during the remainder of their ride, Grace's thoughts were divided between the unhappy lady whom Sir George had deserted, as his cousin had phrased it, and the still more unhappy one who, according to Grace's belief, was destined to be the next victim.

And yet there were moments even now, when she could not help indulging suspicions that Mrs. Freeman was acting a part—that she did not in reality believe Sir George intended to marry her, though, for some reason, she judged it expedient to pretend to believe it.

Grace, indeed, was completely puzzled, and often very unhappy, at what was passing before her, without her being able to comprehend it; but she was now, at least, at no loss to comprehend Sir George, when, after paying her some well-merited compliments on her horsemanship, he observed—

"It will be time enough to buy Susan a horse, when she has learned to manage it; and therefore I must request you will consider this as your own, Miss Woodford."

Grace, without a moment's hesitation, refused the present.

"You forget, Sir George," she observed, "that you actually gave it to Mrs. Freeman—I beg your pardon, Susan, I should have called her, for I believe you do not like to hear her called by that name."

Sir George burst into an ironical laugh.

"Indeed, Grace, it is very indifferent to me what she is called," he observed; "though I have certainly preferred calling her Susan, because it was the name she was called by when she lived in my mother's service, and therefore I am most accustomed to it."

Grace looked grave and thoughtful; there was an expression of more than indifference, of contempt, in his manner, which she could not mistake, and which she felt at once gave a complete contradiction to all that her companion had asserted respecting Sir George's real devotion to her, although there was nothing in his manner which could prove it.

A long silence ensued : Sir George looked earnestly in her face, for some moments, and then observed——

"You and I have long been playing at cross purposes, Grace ; yet, I think, you have all along suspected that I have been forced, by other people's manœuvres and artful devices, into assuming a character which has sat all along very ill on me, and which, at this moment, I have determined to drop for ever. Tell me, now, candidly, Grace, have you ever believed that it was possible I could have any serious intentions towards such a woman as your companion, Susan, or Mrs. Freeman, as you call her ?"

"It would not become me to doubt it, sir," returned Grace. "But, be that as it may, I have no ambition to become your confidant."

"Phsa ! my dear girl, let us deal plainly," he observed ; "you must have seen, for women are never blind upon such subjects, that I am devotedly, passionately, fervently attached to you, that I in reality adore you, and that I have foolishly been led into a labyrinth by that artful woman, who persuaded me that you would at once take alarm if I professed my love, and flattered my vanity that you would find me irresistible upon a nearer acquaintance, and forgive the stratagem for the sake of the passion which prompted it. From day to day, and week to week, however, she has persuaded me to delay, though I've been as miserable as any poor dog could be, at the deceitful game I've been obliged to carry on. It's no easy thing, Grace, to pretend to make love to a woman you hate and despise, and that too before the very face of the only woman you can like or love," he continued, in a hurried tone ; "for I swear to you, my dear girl, that you are the only woman I ever saw in my life that I really did—"

"You may spare your protestations, sir," said Grace, interrupting him, and endeavouring to conceal, under the assumption of coldness and indifference, the terror and alarm she really felt at the discovery of the deep-laid and treacherous plot which had been laid against her. "It is a matter of perfect indifference to me, I assure you, in what light you regard me ; but I beg to be distinctly understood, that this conversation puts an end to all communication between you and me. I will deal frankly with you, Sir George, more frankly, indeed, than your deceptive conduct towards me deserves, and tell you at once, that even were you sincere, and did really mean all you profess, there is an insurmountable barrier between us. Mrs. Freeman could have told you, and ought to have told you, that my heart, my affections, my faith, were given to another long before I beheld you, and that from those engagements no temptation on earth could make me swerve."

Completely disconcerted by the course she had taken, his vanity mortified, and his consequence piqued by her cold indifference and composure, Sir George for some time scarcely uttered a word as he rode homewards by her side, beyond an indistinct and unconnected murmur at his hard fate and a complaint of Mrs. Freeman's insincerity in having led him to believe that she (Grace) was wholly disengaged, and that it was mere timidity, and a fear of acting contrary to the rule of prudence, that induced her to keep her reserve and distance towards him.

To all this Grace turned a deaf ear. Her mind, in fact, and thoughts were in a complete state of tumult, for she saw—she believed she saw—to its fullest extent, the dilemma in which she was involved. and she was now revolving, with the deepest anxiety, the means by which she should free herself from all connection with the base, unprincipled woman in whom it had been her misfortune to place such implicit trust.

She was in a strange place, without a friend, and without money, for, though living in what she considered luxury and extravagance, she had never since her arrival in London been in possession of five shillings. The clothes which she had brought up with her. she was well aware, were worth but little, even if she knew how to dispose of them, and of the articles presented to her since her arrival, and which, she was aware, were all purchased at the cost of Sir George, she was resolutely determined not to retain a vestige.

"Oh, no, no, it would be acting as mean and dishonourable as themselves," she murmured, while the deepest crimson suffused her pale cheeks at the thought. "No! I will prove to them how little they knew me, if they thought I was to be purchased by their gewgaws, or deceived by them into ———"

She turned involuntarily her eyes upon Sir George as she spoke, and beheld his eyes fixed upon her with a look of intense scrutiny.

"You despise me, I see, Grace," he observed; "yet if you could but see my heart this moment—if you could but know how ardently, how devotedly ———"

"I cannot listen to this language, sir," Grace interrupted, with decision, "but there is one means by which you can confer a great obligation on me. and prove, indeed, that you are sincere in your regret for the unworthy deception in which you have joined."

"Name it, Grace, anything, everything that man can do—all that I possess ———"

"No, no—no farther obligations," said Grace, with energy; "I'm already oppressed, cruelly oppressed, with those I have so unconsciously incurred. for I now see—at least, if I may believe what you have asserted—that it is me, instead of Mrs. Freeman, who ———"

"Name it not, Grace; would to heaven that the sacrifice of my whole fortune could convince you of my sincerity, of my devotion; but I see you bear even the offer of my services with impatience, and yet just now you said it was in my power to oblige you."

"It is, and at very little expense," returned Grace; "for all I ask of you is to conceal for the present—for a few days at most, but probably only for a few hours—the explanation that has taken place between us. Suffer Mrs. Freeman to believe that I am still deceived until I think proper to acknow-ledge that I am no longer so."

"I will give you my word and honour, that I will be guided solely by your wishes, however painful it may be to dissimulate longer with that woman," returned Sir George; "but tell me, Grace, for as a friend you must allow me to inquire, though you will not suffer me to interest myself as a lover, what end do you propose by this? and what are your final intentions? I feel, indeed," he continued, observing her hesitate, "that it is my duty to see that no evil arises to you from your connection with Mrs. Freeman, since I cannot but avow that it has been through my influence that connection was formed, or, at least, cultivated to such an extent as it has been; for be assured, dearest girl, that unless she had some object in view to accomplish that woman would never have endured for an hour the society of one whose every word and action were a reproof to her. There have been times, indeed, Grace, when, even with all her artifice, she could not deceive you, unsuspicious as you are and have been. I know that within a few short hours of your quitting Bath she so far threw off the painful restraints of decency of manners that you were alarmed and shocked, and, I believe, tempted sorely to repent having trusted your destiny so far in her hands as———"

THE PRIDE OF THE VILLAGE;

OR,

THE FARMER'S DAUGHTERS.

THE SURPRISE OF SIR GEORGE AT MEETING LADY ALBINA.

CHAPTER XXX.

"She felt her dream of happiness was gone;
  But hope, still lingering, shed its heavenly ray,
Like the fair star that in the waters shone—
  Still bright, though they were gliding fast away."

"You are right, indeed, perfectly right," said Grace, with earnestness; "but how was it possible that you should know all this?"

"Oh! the deaf old man could see, if he could not hear," he replied, with a significant smile.

17

Grace was again completely astonished.

"How have I been deceived," she exclaimed; but did Mrs. Freeman know that person ———"

"Know it, yes, certainly, my dear girl, though she was not aware that my motive for assuming the disguise, was, in reality, distrust of her. I knew that she would not hesitate for a moment to betray my interest, if she thought it would advance her own, and therefore, in addition to the delight I experienced at being an unsuspected observer of all your actions and gazing unrestrainedly ———"

"You—you—Sir George, it could not possibly be you, who ———"

"It was me, indeed, Grace. Do you suppose I would delegate to any individual on the face of the earth, the supreme pleasure of guarding you from all danger of insult, as well as of enjoying your society for so many hours? You slept, too, Grace, and during that sleep, I had the supreme felicity of taking Mrs. Freeman's place by your side. It was with difficulty, indeed, Grace, that I then preserved my disguise; but let it plead with you, as a proof of my real esteem and regard for you, that I contented myself with silently supporting you, and thought it luxury enough for so undeserving a mortal as myself, to feel your sweet cheek laid on my shoulder, and inhale ———"

A sudden pause, much to Grace's satisfaction, relieved her from hearing the conclusion of this speech, which she had been prevented effectually interrupting by the surprise, the confusion, and resentment, she felt at the discovery he had made.

Surprised, vexed, and angry as she felt, however, all those emotions were for a moment suspended, as at the sudden pause he made in his extravagant rapture, she involuntarily turned her eyes upon his face and beheld the change that had taken place in his countenance, from which every vestige of colour had fled, as he bent his earnest look on a travelling chariot, which at a very slow pace was advancing towards them.

"It cannot be, and yet it certainly is," he murmured, apparently totally unconscious of Grace's observation, or that her quick eye instinctively followed the direction of his.

A lady was seated, or rather was reclining in that carriage, for she seemed totally unequal to the task of supporting herself, and was propped up with pillows, while the front and side glasses were all let down to give her air by her attendant, who was seated by her side, and regarded her pallid face with evident alarm and interest.

Grace had never in her life seen anything to compare with the beauty of that face, though it was the beauty rather of a statute than a living being, the complexion vying in colour and transparency with the purest marble, while the jet black tresses that were crossed on the high forehead, seemed, by the contrast, to render the paleness of that beautiful face but the more striking. The eyes were closed, and Grace almost thought, as she gazed, that they were closed for ever, and that the fair statue was indeed as insensible to the cares and griefs of this world as she appeared, but that an exclamation from her attendant, who had casually turned her eyes on Sir George, as they drew near, suddenly aroused her she lifted the heavy lids that seemed a moment before to have been weighed down in death-like slumber, and a loud shriek as Sir George desperately urged his horse on to pass the carriage, told that she had recognized the unfeeling destroyer of her peace, who, trying to veil his consternation and dismay from Grace, dashed on at a pace that soon brought them to the door of the house in Crawford-street, at the window of which Grace beheld with secret disgust and abhorrence the treacherous Freeman awaiting with smiles their return.

It needed no words to explain to Grace that in the strikingly beautiful but evidently wretched and dying female whom she had thus transiently seen, she beheld the unhappy woman whose disgrace and desertion she had overheard spoken of with so much apparent apathy and levity by Sir George's relative; and though, as we have before said, not a word was uttered by Sir George which could betray anything like an acknowledgment of the fact, Grace beheld, with a feeling of satisfaction, the effect that this interview had had upon him.

Never, indeed, had she seen Sir George so totally subdued, so unable to disguise his agitation, or to veil his feelings under the mask of levity and nonchalance, which though he had tried to do, was soon dropped, and he sat silent and abstracted on the sofa on which he had thrown himself on his first entrance into the room.

"What is the matter with you, Sir George?" said Mrs. Freeman, after having twice spoken to him without having received an answer. "You look as strange and startled as if you had seen a ghost. If it wasn't broad daylight, I should swear you had been frightened; and, I declare, there's quite a cold perspiration on your forehead. What——"

"Nonsense!" interrupted Sir George, throwing off her hand, which she had placed on his forehead, with violence. "I wish you would not annoy me by your ridiculous remarks and conjectures."

"Well, upon my word, sir, you are really very polite; but you need not have bruised my hand so, against the sofa," said the lady with great anger.

"I didn't want to bruise your hand," he returned; "but I wish you would mind your own affairs, and not trouble yourself about mine."

"Really! Indeed, this is a curious change!" she began, in a high tone.

"Don't make a fool of yourself," he uttered, in an expressive whisper, which, though apparently intended only for her own ear, was sufficiently audible to be distinctly heard by Grace. "I am not in the humour," he continued, "for trifling. Who do you think I saw in Piccadilly, just now?"

"I don't know, indeed. But, whoever it was, you needn't be spiteful to me; I couldn't help it."

"You couldn't help my seeing her, certainly; but, perhaps, if it had not been for you and your artful schemes————"

"Bah! Now I know who you mean," interrupted Mrs. Freeman. "It is not the first time you have said that, but you know better; you know very well it was your own planning, and that I only did as you bid me."

"She is dying, however, between us; that can't be denied," observed Sir George.

"Dying! Who? Lady Albina? I thought you said just now, you saw her in Piccadilly?" exclaimed Mrs. Freeman.

"So I did," returned the baronet! "but so altered!—so horribly altered! I did not mind her letters, for I know you women are very fond of death and the grave, and all the rest of it, if they are disappointed; and——but it's plain she did not exaggerate. I would give ten thousand pounds, at this moment," he added, starting up, and beginning to pace the room with a hurried step—"yes, that I would, if I could only see her look as she once looked. And that scream too! I shall never get it out of my ears!"

"What nonsense you are talking," said Mrs. Freeman in a tone of remonstrance, and darting at the same time, a look at Grace, as if to discover whether the latter was attending to what was passing.

Grace, however, appeared lost in a deep reverie ; and though her countenance betrayed that the subject of her reflections was anything but pleasant, it was impossible to be certain that it was in any way connected with what Sir George had inadvertently said.

"I never saw a man so nervous as you are," continued Mrs. Freeman, after a short pause, significantly winking at the baronet. "Why should you fret yourself about what you can't help ? After all, perhaps, there's no danger of Lady Albina's dying; for, I recollect, when I lived with her, three years ago, Mr. Mandeville and all her relations took it in their heads she was going to die, because she looked so pale and thin, and lost her appetite ; and yet she got as well and hearty again as ever."

"She will never get well and hearty again, now," said Sir George, in a desponding tone.

"Well, and if she don't, I suppose you needn't break your heart about it ?" returned Mrs. Freeman. "I own it's a melancholy thing to see a fine young woman cut off in the spring of life. But, perhaps there's less to regret about Lady Albina than most. She lived very unhappy, I know, with old Mandeville ; and they ought to blame themselves most who made such a match. At any rate," she added with peculiar significance, "it would be very foolish of you, who have nothing to do with it, to fret yourself——"

"It won't do," said Sir George, in a low tone ; "she," nodding his head at Grace, "knows all about it. We met that malicious devil my cousin Clara, in the park, and she took care to tell all about Albina."

"What an unfortunate wretch I am," he continued, again resuming his walk. "And there's my uncle the earl come to town, too, and has heard some fine stories about me, it seems. I wish I was dead !" he added, with vehemence, catching up his hat, and flying out of the room.

For some moments Mrs. Freeman remained totally silent, as if resolving in her own mind what part she should take, but at length she broke into a forced laugh.

"Well, I always thought the man a fool," she observed, "but he proves himself a worse one than I expected. Now, would you believe it, Grace ? this lady Albina that he is making all this fuss about, and, I dare say, thinks is dying of love for him, and penitence, and so forth, was notorious long before she ever saw him, and had two or three liaisons as the French say, though she had only been married four or five years. For my part," she continued, "I'm sure I thought it the worst day's work I ever did, when I engaged myself to her ; for it was a miracle almost that saved my name from being brought forward in the trial, by which her old husband got a few thousand pounds out of poor Sir George's pocket, and got a divorce from his wife into the bargain : and if I had been brought forward in such a disgraceful affair it would have been quite the ruin of me, you know, my dear."

Grace could scarcely conceal her contempt and disgust at this vile hypocrisy and assumption ; but she felt that it would be bad policy to let Mrs. Freeman discover her feelings, until she (Grace) had formed some plan to withdraw herself entirely from the hateful connexion, and she therefore merely replied with as much indifference as she could possibly assume.

"You lived, then, with this lady, at the time she eloped with Sir George ?"

"Lord, yes, my dear. I wonder I never told you the story before," replied Mrs. Freeman ; "and yet I don't know why I should, for I always hated to think of it. He was completely duped, for he thought it, would settle his reputation as a man of gallantry, and be a fine feather in his cap among his gay companions; but instead of that he found he was only laughed at, for it was well known Lady Albina would have run away haf a dozen times before, if she could have persuaded any rich fool into running away with her. As to her dying, it would be all very pretty if she could persuade him into marrying her, now she's at liberty again; I fancy he'd find that her dying fit would soon go off, when once she had him fast."

"You would alter your opinion, I think, if you were to see her," said Grace, who inwardly shuddered at the levity and cruelty of these observations.

Mrs. Freeman's pretended smiles vanished at the earnestness with which Grace spoke.

"Why, you don't really think —————— but, Lord, what nonsense! If she was really dying, you know, she could not be out and about," she observed.

"She was in a travelling carriage, which, from its appearance, had come a long way," returned Grace, "and, I confess, the thought struck me directly that she was come up to London to die with her friends. Poor creature!" and Grace sighed from the bottom of her heart.

For a time Mrs. Freeman's effrontery seemed to forsake her, and it seemed as if she was in some measure conscience-stricken at hearing that her victim was really in the state Sir George had represented. But this feeling was but transitory, and a few extra glasses of wine after dinner, a luxury which she now regularly partook of at Sir George's expense, restored her to her usual spirits.

It was in vain, however, that Grace endeavoured to veil from her keen and shrewd observation that she was unusually low-spirited and thoughtful.

"One would think, my dear Grace, positively, that you were in love with Sir George, and took the discovery of his wickedness to heart," she observed. "But, Lord, my dear, even if it was so, if you knew as much of the world as I do————"

"Heaven forbid!" ejaculated Grace, involuntarily; "at least, that I should ever know so much of the world to be able to look upon such subjects as these as mere matters of course, as it seems you do."

"You are quite right," said Mrs. Freeman, laughing; "in fact," she added, after a few moments' pause, "I will own to you, Grace, that ————"

"Excuse me, let us drop the subject," interrupted Grace; "I cannot speak of it without seeing so forcibly before my eyes that beautiful woman dying, evidently, a victim——"

"Bah! For goodness sake, Grace, don't horrify one with your descriptions," interrupted Mrs. Freeman. "But where the deuce is Sir George?" she continued, suddenly seeming to recollect herself; "it's past nine by my watch, and he was to have been here by seven to take us to Drury Lane to see the new comedy."

"I do not wonder that he has forgotten his engagement." said Grace. "I should think his feelings would not suit much with comedy to-night."

"Feelings!" returned Mrs. Freeman, with a bitter sneer; "there's few people in the world besides yourself, I suspect, Grace, that would give Sir George credit for such a feeling."

"Indeed!" returned Grace, with quickness; I have heard you hold very different doctrines."

"Ah, that was when I wanted to recommend him to your favour, Grace, she replied, laughing; "but, though I tried to deceive you for your own good, mind, I was never deceived; I knew all along that there is not a more heartless, selfish libertine than he is."

"Is it possible," said Grace. who saw that she was now completely off her guard, "that with this opinion, you could wish to make a husband of him?"

"To be sure it is possible, Grace, very possible," she replied. "It is not him I want; I want his fortune, his title, and above all, I want to have the opportunity of treading on the necks of some of his proud family, and that I shall have, if I become his wife."

There was so much earnestness, such an evident impress of truth in what she had last uttered, that Grace was startled and confounded. How could she reconcile this with what Sir George had acknowledged to her—that there was no reality in his pretended addresses, and that she (Mrs. Freeman) had herself planned the deception, to aid his views towards herself.

For some minutes she sat silently revolving these considerations in her mind, while Mrs. Freeman, with her eyes fixed on hers, appeared to be endeavouring to read her thoughts.

Suddenly, however, the recollection of the latter reverted to Sir George's protracted absence.

"I hope he is not going to make a a greater fool of himself than ever," she muttered. "If, after all, he should be drawn in by Lady Albina's pretended———"

"Do not say pretended," said Grace, warmly. "I assure you you are mistaken, the poor lady is really dying."

"Well, then, if she is really dying," returned Mrs. Freeman, in a tone of extreme levity, "I can have no reason to fear her rivalling me."

"What can all this mean?" thought Grace, as, wishing to drop the painful subject, she arose to seek a book which Sir George had that morning lent her.

"Sit still, can't you, Grace? I don't like to be left alone, you know, especially just now, when I am so vexed and low-spirited; I could cut my throat."

Grace reseated herself; and Mrs. Freeman evidently unable to dismiss the train of thoughts from her mind which Sir George's absence, coupled with his having met Lady Albina in the morning, had excited, commenced questioning her minutely as to all that passed.

"Pshaw! stuff! all art! She always was so sentimental and theatrical," she exclaimed, as Grace, wishing, if possible, to awaken something like remorse in her mind, painted in the most forcible language she could command, Lady Albina's appearance and distracted manner. All that the lady whom Sir George had designated his cousin Clara, was repeated, too, as far as Grace cold recollect; and the interest with which she evidently entered into the detail, and the regret she expressed that Sir George was on such bad terms with his uncle, confirmed Grace in the belief that, whatever might be Sir George's views or intentions, she (Mrs. Freeman) certainly indulged the belief that she should become his wife.

The evening passed away, and no Sir George, and Mrs. Freeman evidently began to grow very uneasy, while Grace, on the contrary, hailed his absence as a good omen, believing that it was occasioned by repentance on his part, for the misery he had brought on the unhappy Lady Albina. The usual hour arrived for his visit in the morning; never since their residence there had he neglected calling before noon; but now one, two, three o'clock struck, without his making his appearance, and the woman of the house, who, herself, waited on them, entered to lay the cloth for their dinner.

"This is something uncommon, aint it?" she observed, addressing Mrs. Freeman, in her usual tone of familiarity. "Very uncommon," she repeated, with still stronger emphasis, "for you to be so many hours without a visit from your beau."

"I am beginning to think so, too," replied Mrs. Freeman with a significant look: "but I shall wait quietly to-morrow, and then, if he does not come, I shall soon let him know I am not to be trifled with."

"I wouldn't be too hasty, though," returned her landlady, "you know you've hooked him safe enough, so you needn't mind giving him a little line, he must come to land at last."

Mrs. Freeman forced a laugh, but it was very evident that it was not from her heart.

Grace had, as was her constant custom, turned entirely away from this woman, with whom she had been, from her first entrance into the house, completely disgusted, both from her manners, and the habits of intemperance to which she was addicted, but the understanding which seemed to exist between Mrs. Freeman and her, and the singularity of her last observation, induced her now, involuntarily, to turn her eyes upon her.

"Ah, you may look, my young lady," observed the woman, in a saucy tone, and evidently misconceiving the cause of Grace's look. "I dare say you think that it's very impudent of me to be giving my advice, but——"

"Pooh! nonsense, Mrs. Hodgson, Miss Woodford was thinking no such thing, I am sure," said Mrs. Freeman, hastily interfering, and evidently alarmed at the disposition her hostess showed to be qarrelsome.

"*Miss* Woodford!" returned Mrs. Hodgson, with a sneer; "*miss* all she can't catch, I s'pose, like me. I say, Sukey, it will be up with her *miss-ship*, as well as your ladyship, if Sir George is off."

"How can you talk such nonsense, Mrs. Hodgson?" observed Mrs. Freeman, who was evidently alarmed at the tone the former assumed.

"Well, it may be nonsense, or it may not," she replied, "but I know I shall be very to see him come, for I begin to think, if he shouldn't come at all, I should have but a poor look out for——"

"Good gracious! how ridiculous you are," interrupted Mrs. Freeman. "Hark, there's a knock at the door. Do go, there's good creature, for I'll be be bound it's a message from him."

Mrs. Hodgson left the room, muttering, and Mrs. Freeman, turning to Grace, observed that it was plain the old woman had been taking a drop too much.

"But I know her good heart," she continued, by way of apology, "and I am sure she is as anxious for my welfare, as if I was her own daughter."

"It is a strange way of showing it," said Grace, coldly; "and why am I always chosen to be the——"

"Nonsense, my dear, you should never take notice of what she says," replied Mrs. Freeman; "but hush here she comes, there is something, then, a letter, or message, or——"

"There's nothing for you," said Mrs. Hodgson, significantly, as she re-entered the room; "but here's a letter for Miss Woodford; I thought she'd got no acquaintances in London, but it seems to the contrary."

Mrs. Freeman rudely snatched it out of the woman's hand, as she reached it to Grace, who was too much startled and surprised by tho unexpected circumstance to be able to prevent her.

"It's Sir George's hand, I'll swear," she exclaimed. "What can all this mean? Do, pray Grace, open it, and let us know what all this is about."

Grace took the letter.

"I will open it presently," she said in low voice, and giving a significant look towards their hostess, who stood, wiping a beer glass with the corner of her dirty apron, and evidently waiting for the communication of the epistle.

"Oh, you mean that I'm to go ma'am, I s'pose," she observed; "I can take your hint, but——"

"Do, there's a good creature, to oblige me," said Mrs. Freeman, in a coaxing tone; "I'll come down to you in a minute," she added, "and then ——"

The rest was whispered, but it might as well have been spoken aloud, for Mrs. Hodgson immediately replied to it as if it were no secret.

"I don't want none of your treats," she observed; "if I wants a glass of liquor, or a bottle of wine either, I can afford to pay for it, without being under any obligation to you; but all I want now is to know what I've got to trust to. You know very well that I shouldn't have let you my lodgin's, and found you in coals and candles, and got up your washin' if I hadn't believed that Sir George was to pay all; but you've deceived me from beginning to end. First, you told me in your letter that the lodgin's was for a young lady that Sir George had got away from her friends, and that you was to be her companion; and then you no sooner comes here than you alter your tune, and pretends that you've got Sir George into such a string that he can't help but marry you, or come down with a handsome sum of money to get rid of you; and then, oh dear, I musn't say this, and I must do that, and I musn't come up stairs when there's anybody there but your own two selves, to have a comfortable glass, and a bit of talk about old times, because Miss Woodford is so timid, and don't know nothing about life, and——"

"This is really too bad, Mrs. Hodgson," screamed Mrs. Freeman, at the top of her voice, having vainly tried, in a quieter tone, to interrupt her animadversions; "and after all, what occasion is there for all this show off? You will be paid your money, and I suppose that is all you expect."

"It's all I want, and it's what I will have too," muttered Mrs. Hodgson, whose violence seemed suddenly curbed by Mrs. Freeman's decision of manner. "I'll know, however, before many hours are gone over my head, what I've got to trust to," she added, as she left the room.

Grace had, during all this contention, held the letter which had given rise to it unopened in her hand; and, indeed, had almost forgotten her anxiety to know what Sir George could address her for, in her surprise and indignation at Mrs. Freeman's deliberate scheme of perfidy, first towards herself, and secondly towards Sir George; and she turned now with a shudder of disgust, from the caressing tones in which the latter said :—

"Come, dear, never mind what this foolish woman has said; let us see what is in the letter."

With hands trembling with agitation, Grace broke the seal, and a bank note dropped into her lap, which Mrs. Freeman instantly seized.

Ten pounds!" she exclaimed; "and to you! What is the meaning of this, Grace? why don't you read what he says?"

"You can read it yourself," returned Grace, "but first let me tell you, that I am already decided to take the step it recommends."

"To enable Miss Woodford to return to her friends in the country," was all that was written in the envelope. Mrs. Freeman read it aloud, with astonishment and rage flashing in her eyes.

"And you mean to do as this recommends?" she observed, fixing her eyes full on Grace, who, though trembling with terror, replied with firmness.

"Certainly I do. You must feel, Mrs. Freeman, that my remaining here can benefit neither you nor me; and you must also be aware —"

"And this money," interrupted Mrs. Freeman, holding up the bank note between her thumb and finger with a malicious smile, "is to pay your expenses back?"

"Part of it only I shall want," returned Grace, "the rest, of course, I shall consider yours in part payment of ——"

"You are very generous, indeed, " interrupted Mrs. Freeman, in a tone of derision, but still affecting perfect coolness, though her eyes betrayed the fury she could scarcely control. "Well then," she continued, folding the note, and placing it in her purse, "I will, with your permission, keep this, till I have made out the account of what I have advanced for you, at different times, as well as for your board and lodging since you have been here, and then we shall see what ——"

"I have understood from you, repeatedly," said Grace in faltering tone, "that Sir George had defrayed all our expenses, both on the journey hither, and since we have been here; and mortifying as it has been and still is to me, to be indebted to him, it would be ——"

"Quiet your scruples, my dear, you neither have been, nor shall be under obligations to any one but me," interrupted Mrs. Freeman, again smiling with that look of fiendish malice which Grace had two or three times before seen disfigure her naturally pretty features. "Sir George and I will settle our accounts together, when you and I have done with ours."

Grace's heart sank; she saw immediately that she had suffered the means of escape from the power of her unprincipled companion, to slip out of her hands, when she allowed her to take possession of the note, and for a moment she suffered despair to overcome that coolness which she had hitherto managed to keep up in appearance.

"Heaven help me!" she exclaimed, bursting into tears and clasping her hands. "I am little calculated, I feel, to contend with you, Mrs. Freeman; but I trust you are fully convinced, now, that it can be no advantage to you for me to remain here; and surely, you will not, after having been the means of bringing me here, refuse me the means of returning."

"And what would be the use of returning, Grace?" said Mrs. Freeman, with calmness; you have no friends, now, to fly to, and ——"

"But, I could return to the occupation I quitted, in Bath, which is now, as I heard you observe, a day or two ago, again in the height of the season," said the poor girl eagerly. "I should have an advantage, too, in coming from London, for Mrs. Somerford, the milliner who employed me before, told me several times, that a few months in London would be a great benefit to me, and——"

"Yes, but she did not mean that you were to spend them in showing off at the theatres, and all the fashionable places, with a gay young baronet," interrupted Mrs. Freeman. "And I will tell you candidly, at once, Grace, that it was well known in whose society you quitted Bath; and, that therefore, if you were to go back to-morrow, you would only be looked upon, as the discarded mistress of——"

"Merciful God! how have I been deceived, ruined and betrayed !' exclaimed Grace, starting up in an agony of passion and terror. "Where shall I now go, to avoid disgrace, and endeavour to get a living? Oh, my mother! my poor mistaken mother ! how little did you foresee the ruin, the utter destruction, you were bringing on the heads of your poor children, when you brought them from their peaceful homes, and——'

"If you will have the condescension to sit down, and quietly listen to me, a few moments, Miss Woodford," said Mrs. Freeman, after gazing at her, for some time, in silence ; "and if you will, for once in your life, lay aside all the romantic nonsense which you seem to think mighty becoming, but which you will find won't do at all for a girl who has got a living to get in the world, I will soon convince you that I am not quite such a hard-hearted, base wretch as you seem to think me ; and that though I don't lay claim to any of your high-flown virtue, I have no wish to bring ruin and destruction on you, as you call it, but only simply mean to do as the world does, take care of myself first, and then help other people to take care of themselves."

Grace almost mechancially obeyed her ; she reseated herself, hastily dried the tears from her eye, and without uttering a word, awaited what her companion chose to say, in further explanation of her assertions.

"I am going to say, Grace," commenced the latter, avoiding Grace's earnest gaze, which was intently fixed on her—"I will not for a moment pretend that I am either sorry or ashamed at the part I have acted towards you : for I meant nothing but your good and Sir George's too when I consented to his plans. In the first instance, I believed what he said, that he really did love you more than any other woman he ever beheld. I don't pretend to say, mind, that he ever held out to me the idea of marrying you ; but I always considered him a weak fool that any sensible woman that knew her own interest could make what she liked : and I thought you, with your innocence and straightforwardness, and all the rest of your good qualities, which I don't deny you possess, though it's little good, seemingly, they do you, or ever will anybody while the world is as it is.—— There don't interrupt me child ; you'll find it all out, some day or the other, though I shall not take the trouble, now, to convince you which of us is right. However, as I was saying, I thought with my management and your fascination together, we might have succeeded in drawing him in to marry you ; and that would have been quite enough to satisfy me : and I won't deny it, I thought, too, the worst come to the worst, you would be better off as his mistress, with a good settlement on you for life, which I know he was willing to make you, than wearing your eyes out, and slaving your life away, in making bonnets and caps in a garret. It was with these thoughts that I consented to forward his plans by bringing you up to London; but I soon found that your obstinacy would spoil all. I told him that nothing but time, and assiduous attention on his part, could succeed with you ; and I flattered the fool too—what he was very willing to believe, from his former success with our weak sex—that no woman could in the end resist his generosity, his fine person, and all his various accomplishments ; but that unless he was very cautious, you would, from your inexperience, and the prejudices of your bringing up, take alarm as to his intentions, and fly off at once. In short, I persuaded him to pretend to play the lover to me and thus——"

"I am aware of all this, Mrs. Freeman." interrupted Grace, whose indignation and disgust at this shameless avowal of treachery and profligacy could with difficulty be concealed. "Sir George himself," she continued, "in our last interview, confessed to me all that you have now repeated ; but it is to the future I must look. the past cannot be recalled."

"Sir George himself told you all this, did he?" repeated Mrs. Freeman with amazement. "Then you, too, it appears, with all your seeming purity, and artlessness, and innocence, can have your schemes and your concealments, and your mystery! How little did I suspect this! Then you, after all, madam, I suppose, are the cause of his absence? you have persuaded him that——"

"You wrong me, indeed you do," interrupted Grace, terrified at her violence. "I know nothing of his intention, persuaded him to nothing; and, indeed, from the moment he made the disclosure I never thought about him or any subject than how to return to my former humble situation without giving you offence."

Mrs. Freeman remained silent for some minutes; she seemed, indeed, totally thrown out of all her calculations by Grace's ingenuous admissions and the inferences she drew from them.

"And what did he say of me, then, pray?" she at length demanded; "joined with you, I suppose, in denouncing me as everything that was horrible and——"

"No, no, indeed," interrupted Grace, anxious to moderate the rising fury which Mrs. Freeman's countenance betrayed was swelling in her breast. "He blamed himself more than you," continued the trembling girl, "but confessed that he was quite tired of the deception he had so long practised."

"And avowed his intention of putting an end to it at once?" said her companion.

"Oh, no, he did not say say so, indeed; on the contrary I had reasons to believe—I thought that—he would postpone until—until——"

"Until what, Miss Woodford? Why do you not speak out at once? You, who are all candour, all ingenousness, what is it that ties your tongue now?

"Nothing that ought to do so, certainly," said Grace, summoning up all her courage; "for I do not know why I should be afraid of acknowledging that he only delayed all explanation at my request until I could resolve upon some plan of quitting you."

Mrs. Freeman smiled.

"There has been fine plotting and counter-plotting here, it seems, though I little suspected your wise little head whould be employed in scheming to circumvent me; but we'll let all that pass now. There can be no longer any doubt that Sir George is off, and all I have to do is to devise means of making the best I can of the affair; and now I will tell you, Grace, without the smallest reserve or beating about the bush, what I expect of you. You have shown, indeed, that you have some little talent for scheming, in spite of your pretensions to open dealing and sincerity; and, therefore, I have more hopes of your perfect concurrence in my plans than I should have had some half-hour ago. Well, you are all impatience, I see, to know what those schemes are, and so I'll tell you. You have been now for some time a daily and hourly witness of Sir George's addresses to me. You know it was he that persuaded me to come up to London, with a view of becoming his wife, as he repeatedly promised, in your presence, to make me. You know that he ordered dresses for the ceremony for me and for yourself, as bridesmaid—hush! don't interrupt me—and that in Bath he prevented my taking a most respectable situation with an invalid lady going out to India, declaring that he could not, and would not, exist without me; and that he likewise took you from your occupation, in which you were making a respectable living, promising to make a handsome provision for you as companion to his wife—me, myself," she added, nodding at

Grace with a look of the most inconceivable boldness and effrontery. "In short, Grace, you must give me your most unreserved aid in establishing my claims upon him, which I do not fear to do; not to the extent of forcing him to become my husband, for that I'm afraid there is little chance of my doing, but of forcing him to buy them off at a rate which will pay me handsomely for the time and trouble I have spent in making a fool of him."

For some moments Grace sat staring at her in silent amazement, after she had concluded this explanation, which the latter had several times in vain endeavoured to interrupt.

Could she (Mrs. Freeman) be serious—could she ever hope for success in such a nefarious plot, which appeared to Grace nothing short of a deliberate scheme of robbery—and, above all, could she expect that she (Grace) would really aid her and perjure herself by giving utterance to the horrible falsehoods which she had planned?

"You see, Grace," resumed Mrs. Freeman, who either did not, or would not, see the consternation and astonishment which almost paralysed her intended victim. "You see I am perfectly undisguised with you. I do not affect any mystery or disguise as to what I aim at, nor pretend to gloss over my intentions with any plausible nonsense, though I might prove to you, if I chose to take the trouble, that all I am doing is perfectly justifiable and only a proper retribution for——but no matter, I shall say nothing about that now, but all I do want is to show you that I mean to act honourably towards you and place everything in its proper light, and so I'll tell you at once what I propose to do is, if you act up to the plan I shall lay down, is to bind myself to give you a fourth of whatever I get from him. Stop, Grace, hear me out, and then make your objections if you think proper. I say, whether I get more or less, and I don't reckon, I assure you, upon taking less than a thousand pounds—a quarter of which, I reckon, will pretty well help you forward in the world. And now I'll frankly show you what will be the consequences of your refusal—you heard what the old woman below said respecting the money that's due to her. The fact is, Grace, I have had the money from him at different times to pay her, but I've got demands upon me that neither he nor you know anything about, and without settling them, at least in part, I couldn't have shown my face here, so that I was compelled to let her account run on and use the money for my own private concerns. Now, I'll tell you candidly, she is prepared to go through thick and thin with me and you to establish my claims on Sir George; but if there's any shrinking back on either your part or mine, and she fancies that she shall lose her money, and the twenty pounds extra that I have promised her, she will have no mercy, and we may expect, both of us, to be lodged in a prison, for, of course, she'll make you answerable as well as me."

"God of mercy!" exclaimed Grace, clasping her hands, "look down and rescue me! Oh, that I were in my grave—that I had died with my poor mother—that I had——

"Fool! idiot! canting hypocrite!" exclaimed Mrs. Freeman, giving loose to all the natural violence of her temper, as she read in Grace's impassioned exclamations, the abhorrence her propositions had raised in her upright and ingenuous mind! But Grace was now insensible to the reproaches and abuse which were showered on her defenceless head, for, overcome with terror and agony, she had fainted, and the next moment she was lying at the feet of the wretch whose machinations had involved her in such a laybrinth of misery.

CHAPTER XXXI.

"If it feed nothing else, it
Will feed my revenge."

—SHAKESPEARE.

CRUEL, unfeeling, and unprincipled as Mrs. Freeman had shown herself, she could not remain utterly insensible to the heartrending supplications for mercy, and agonised exclamations of terror which broke from Grace's lips, when she awoke from the death-like swoon which had for a time steeped her senses in forgetfulness; but though the artful, treacherous woman, who had been the primary cause of her present sufferings, could not, as she said, endure to stand by her bedside and behold the piteous looks, and listen to the agonised expressions which, in spite of all her attempts to be calm, and to endeavour to devise some reasonable plan to escape from her enemies, she could not repress, there was one who could behold the scene unmoved, who could even take a seeming pleasure in triumphing over the unsuspicious girl, whom very ignorance of evil and utter inexperience in the crooked ways in which they had been accustomed to tread, had thrown into their power.

This fiendish wretch was Mrs. Hodgson, the woman of the house, she whom Mrs. Freeman had been used to eulogise as a good-hearted, well-meaning, friendly creature, whose only faults, that of a bad temper and violent language, arose from having, in consequence of misfortune, contracted habits of intemperance.

Grace, indeed, could never—had never admitted that there could be any plea strong enough to excuse such habits; she had even beheld the woman with a feeling of horror and detestation which scarcely allowed her to treat her with civility; and the latter, as if secretly conscious of Grace's feelings towards her, had seized every opportunity of showing that the dislike was mutual.

Hitherto, however, Mrs. Freeman's interposition and representations had kept her virulence within bounds; but now those restraints were removed, and with undisguised malignity she exulted over the sufferings of the unhappy girl.

"There's a great deal, to be sure, to make all this fuss about," she observed, as she assisted Mrs. Freeman to undress her victim and place her in her bed. "A great deal to cry and lament about; but I think it's me that's got the greatest cause, for here you've been leading the life of a lady, always dressed up, walking about to take your pleasure, and going to plays, and exhibitions, and shows of every kind, while your betters have been slaving at home for you, washing, and scouring, and cooking, and spending my money, too, into the bargain, to keep up your fine ladyship. Ah, you may groan and you may sigh, but I say that it is me that ought to cry out, and not you; for how do I know that I shall ever get my money back again? Howsomever, I tell you this plump and plain, that I won't be the only sufferer; if I don't get my money I can't pay my debts. I know what'll be the consequence; I must go to jail, but I shan't go there alone, that I am determined."

"Oh, God! what will become of me? what shall I do? Oh, take all I have in the world, and let me go. I will beg my way home. Home, home, I have got no home now!" exclaimed the distracted girl; "but somebody there will surely have compassion on me—they will save me from going to prison."

"Ah! fine talking; compassion, indeed! where's your compassion for me, I should like to know?" returned Mrs. Hodgson. "You are terribly frightened for your own fine bones, but you'd think it nothing for a woman like me, that's lived forty years a housekeeper, and paid rent and taxes to be dragged off to finish my old days in a jail."

"Oh, no, no, indeed," said Grace, shuddering, "I would not wish to see the worst wretch that ever breathed condemned to such a fate. Oh, if I could—if I could——"

"If you could—you know very well that you can, and what's more that you shall, too. I've a notion, indeed, of such fine feelings, that won't let people stretch a point to sarve their fellow-creatures—such a friend, too, as Sukey has been to you. Why you knows very well that she took you out of a garret to set you up for a lady, and then, if you wouldn't stretch a point, as I said before, to sarve her, what can you call yourself but an ungrateful sarpent that turns upon the hand that feeds you? But I won't say no more to you now, only this, as I have said afore, that you never had no right to come and set yourself down here to live in idleness at my expense, a poor widder that's got nobody to look arter her but herself, and so I'll have my money afore you quits this house, or else you quits it to go to one where they'll clap the blacksmith's darter upon you, and then you'll know the difference between flaunting about——Laws, I'm coming, Sukey, you needn't keep bawling so; I've only been telling the gal the plain truth—and so I'll leave you now, Miss What's-your-name, to think upon it, and make up your mind. There's nobody here that wants to hurt you, the house your'e in's a respectable house, whatever you may think to the contrary; but you may leave it, and go to a better if you can find it, only pay me my demand."

"But, my good woman," commenced Grace, who, during this long harangue had begun to recover something like calmness, and to recollect that the frantic despair to which she had for a time yielded was not likely to have any effect on one so hardened and callous as her present persecutor.

"Good woman!" repeated Mrs. Hodgson, turning fiercely round upon the frightened girl. "Good woman, indeed—and pray, ma'am Bounce, who do you think your'e talking to? or who do you fancy yourself that you can't speak in a little more civiler terms than that? I'd have you to know that my name's Dixon, and moreover, I've got a handle to my name, and that it becomes such chits as you to remember it."

"I beg your pardon," returned Grace, mildly; "Mrs. Dixon, then; but I always thought you were called Hodgson."

"Well, Dixon or Hodgson, I s'pose it makes no difference to you; howsomever, I'm most oftenest called Hodgson," she replied, with evident confusion, and lowering her voice, as if conscious she had betrayed herself in making use of a different name. "You can say what you've got to say, I s'pose."

"All I have to say," resumed Grace, in the same meek and humble tone, "is, that I never imposed upon you; it would be cruel of you to make me suffer for another's fault. I came here, or rather, I should say, I was brought here, under the belief that——"

"Oh, aye—yes, I daresay, no doubt, you are a very innocent young lady, and meant to be very honest; but, however, I'll take care you shall be honest, for if I can't have it in meal I'll have it in malt," and, so saying, Mrs. Hodgson quitted the room, leaving Grace to brood, even to madness, over the wretched situation in which she found herself placed.

Nothing in all the catalogue of evils which Grace had in her melancholy moments sometimes anticipated since her discovery of Mrs. Freeman's real character—nothing half so dreadful to her imagination as a prison ever had been contemplated. It appeared to her the climax of all human misery; and yet, amidst all the horrors of this horrible anticipation, Grace never for one moment allowed herself to dwell upon the possibility of escaping it by consenting to lend herself to the nefarious and dishonest scheme which Mrs. Freeman had planned to enrich herself.

Hour after hour she lay trying to devise some means of escaping from the clutches of her enemies, and avoid the fate with which she was threatened; yet where could she fly, without the means of securing shelter for a single night—without knowing one person in the world-wide metroplis whom she could claim as a friend?

Yes; there was one, could she but again behold him. Oh! how ardently now did she wish that she had spoken to William Mansel—that she had claimed his protection. Poor and miserable as he looked, she would now give worlds to behold him, to have some one whom she could confide in—to whom she could turn without fear or suspicion for counsel and consolation.

"And is it possible, even now," she suddenly thought, "that I may see him again; he may even now be not far from me; he knows where I am, though I cannot find him; and surely, surely, he will not, cannot mean to renonnce me without even one word, let him think what he will; and, oh! too surely does my heart tell me what were the thoughts which induced him to hurry away with such contempt and anger in his looks; yet he will—oh, yes, I know he will make an effort again to see, to speak to me, and then——"

Then, in the single circumstance of having one human being sincerely interested in her welfare—one on whom she could rely for honest counsel and sincere services, Grace now fancied she beheld the certain means of relief from all her troubles. To gain time seemed now all that was necessary, and for that important purpose she saw clearly her only plan would be to dissemble with Mrs. Freeman and her vile coadjutor.

It was such a hateful task to assume even a concurrence in such schemes; but Grace saw no other method of escaping the machinations of the artful wretches into whose power she had fallen, and she therefore resolved to suppress all outward appearance of repugnance, and suffer them to believe that she had become a convert to their plans.

It was not till late the following day, however, that she was called upon for any exercise of her new talent of deception. During the whole night Mrs. Freeman remained absent from her bed, hitherto shared with Grace, and the latter was left undisturbed to her own reflections.

But that she occasionally heard the sound of voices raised high in earnest parley, and more than once Mrs. Freeman's well-known tones were plainly distinguishable among the speakers Grace, indeed, would have been inclined to think that her unprincipled companion had left the house; but all doubts on that head were removed, when, several hours after daybreak, she heard her and Mrs. Hodgson come up stairs together and enter the room adjoining.

Much as Grace would, under any other circumstances, have detested any attempt to listen to a conversation, she could not now resist her strong anxiety to learn what had been the motives of this midnight consultation, for such she supposed had been the purpose of these two confederates in iniquity remaining up until such an unseasonable hour. But, to her great disappointment and surprise, not a word occurred during their conversation —if such it could be called, which consisted of nothing but disjointed remarks, exclamations, and expressions of weariness—which had the slightest allusion to the events of the day. On the contrary, she learned, to her infinite astonishment, that cards had been the occupation of those hours which she (Grace) had imagined had been devoted to settling their plans of proceeding; and that they had not been alone she soon also learned by Mrs. Freeman's observations respecting the modes of play and the good or bad luck of their respective companions as well as of themselves.

Not a word was breathed which showed that they even recollected that there was such a person as Grace in the world; and the latter, scarcely knowing whether she should regard this seeming indifference and forgetfulness as a good or bad omen for her, softly closed the door, which she had partly opened, and stole back to her bed again.

In a few minuts Mrs. Freeman entered the room. She did not speak to Grace, but the latter could not help being struck with the ill effects which her night's orgies had had upon the countenance and whole appearance of her pseudo friend.

From her conversation with Mrs. Hodgson, Grace had learned that she had been considerably a loser by their night's occupation. She had heard her in no measured terms at one moment execrating her own ill-luck, and at the next expressing her belief that she had been cheated by some of her companions; and Grace now shuddered, as she traced in her pale and haggard countenance the effects of the violent passions which had been excited in her mind by the vicissitudes of play.

During the whole time that she was preparing for bed Mrs. Freeman continued to give utterance to expressions of dissatisfaction.

"What a cursed fool I must be to let them persuade me into playing with them!" she muttered. "I ought to have known very well that they intended to fleece me; and that old devil, too, she was in it—I know she was, or she would not have been so liberal with her brandy. I'll be even with them all one day or other, or my name isn't Sue Freeman. Gracious, what a wretch I look!" she continued, stopping before the glass. "After all, there's nothing like the country and early hours to preserve one's good looks: I'm sure nobody would believe I was the same creature, that knew me at Bath."

Grace involuntarily sighed.

"Ah, you may sigh, Miss Woodford," observed Mrs. Freeman, "but I've got more reason to sigh than you."

Grace was not disposed to dispute this assertion; she was, indeed desirous of shunning, if possible, all conversation for the present; and Mrs. Freeman, who was evidently overcome with lassitude, the effects of her night's dissipation, was soon asleep, though, even in her restless, uneasy slumbers, the consequences of violent excitation and intemperance pursued her, and for many hours she continued at intervals to groan and utter exclamations which betrayed how dearly the votaries of vice purchase their shortlived enjoyments.

To Grace's extreme chagrin and surprise, she beheld a stranger seated at the breakfast-table, the morning after, or rather the middle of the day, for it was already past noon when Mrs. Freeman arose, and she had very unceremoniously indicated to her (Grace) that it would be as well that she should remain where she was until they both went down together.

Grace had not ventured to make any remark upon this implied restriction, for she feared to provoke a discussion on the subject, which she most ardently wished to avoid; but now it occurred to her, when she beheld a person sitting at the table whom she had never seen before, that it was to prevent her from entering into any details to this man, that Mrs. Freeman had been so anxious to keep her with her; and she (Grace) now earnestly sought to read in the stranger's countenance whether there was aught to warrant her to hope that she might make a friend of him.

THE PRIDE OF THE VILLAGE;

OR,

THE FARMER'S DAUGHTERS.

LORD FREDERICK'S SURPRISE AT HEARING OF THE ARRIVAL OF THE EARL.

CHAPTER XXXI.—(Continued).

He was not bad-looking, on the contrary he was what most people would have pronounced decidedly at once a very good-looking man; for he was tall, well-made, fair, and at first sight might have been said to possess an open countenance. How many are there in the world of whom the same observation is made merely because they have the advantage of a good ruddy complexion and a broad round face!

Grace herself saw nothing at the first glance in Mr. O'Brien's face but hilarity and good humonr; but he turned his eyes upon her after a cordial and familiar salutation to Mrs. Freeman, and, though she knew not why, she she knew there was no hope of aid in that quarter.

Mr. O'Brien was evidently an expected guest; and it was equally evident from the conversation that ensued between him and Mrs. Freeman that they had long been upon terms of confidence and familiarity. Grace was, indeed, astonished to find from his observations that he was perfectly acquainted with the whole affair between Mrs. Freeman and Sir George ; and that she herself, though she had never even heard his name mentioned before, seemed perfectly well known to him, and was addressed, whenever he had occasion to speak to her, with a tone of insinuating kindness, blended at the same time with a look and air of conscious superiority which seemed intended to impress her with a full conviction of her own insignificance and his vast consequence.

There was a something in his expression of the epithet " my dear," which he used indiscriminately to herself and Mrs. Freeman, that was particularly offensive to Grace; but all minor causes of repugnance and dislike were soon merged in utter abhorrence and contempt of the man, when, after prefacing his observations by informing Grace that he had the honour of being a member of the law, or, in other words, a solicitor, he proceeded to tell her that it would be necessary she should be perfectly prepared for what would be required from her, most probably, in a very short time—namely, to assist her kind friend and protectress in forcing that rascally weather-cock, Sir George ————

Grace interrupted him

" I have heard already, from Mrs. Freeman, sir, all that is requisite on that subject," she observed, " and it will be time enough when I am called upon for my testimony ————"

She paused, and looked down in confusion, for Mr. O'Brien's great insolent eyes were fixed upon hers, and in them she read his detection of her attempted equivocation.

He was too well versed, too experienced a practitioner, in the crooked ways of deceit, not to be always on the watch to detect it. How, then, could it be expected that Grace could for a moment deceive him?

" And so, then, you are quite prepared, are ye, darlin'?" he demanded, with an insulting laugh. " Well, by the powers, I'm glad to hear it, for your own sake; for I was led to believe that your memory was very treacherous, and that you couldn't remember all that you ought and must recollect for your friend, my client's sake. But sure it was all wrong, and I shall not have to bring to your mind all that I want : so come, now, I'll just take a bit of paper and a pen and ink, and we'll put down all that you do remember, and you shall sign your hand to it, and then, you know, my dear, there's no fear of it slipping out of your memory again."

Grace was, now, indeed, completely caught; she could not utter a word, could not devise a shadow of excuse for refusing this. She did, indeed after some moments of silence, during which some most significant looks passed. between Mrs. Freeman and her law adviser, as he called himself—she did murmur some sort of an observation that there was no necessity for this; and then added, summoning up more courage, but at the same time speaking in a tone of emphasis which could leave still less doubt than before, as to her real feeling, that there could be no fear of her ever forgetting what Mrs. Freeman had told her on the subject.

" Yes, my dear; but it's not what Mrs. Freeman has told you," observed Mr. O'Brien, again laughing in her face with that peculiar air of scornful derision which had before daunted and confused her. " I do not want to know what Mrs. Freeman has said, but what you are prepared to say and swear Sir George Beaumont has said, and whatever else you know that can prove his intention to marry our friend there, your protectress and my client."

"Then not one word have I to say, sir, which can advance your scheme," said Grace in a tone of firm resolution, all her fears and horrid anticipations totally forgotten, or, at least, appearing of comparatively trifling import compared to the disgrace, the guilt, the irrevocable degradation of becoming an actor in this iniquitous scheme. "No, sir," she continued, "I would rather die than thus deliberately sign what I know to be utterly false. I have never from Sir George's lips heard one word which would indicate that he regarded Mrs. Freeman in the light of an intended wife. I have never believed, even when she herself positively asserted it, that such were his attentions. I know now, both from her own admission and his exposure of the whole system of deception, that neither one or the other ever for a moment contemplated the possibility of such an union; and I should be base, indeed, if I could become your instrument in such a plan of robbery. Mrs. Freeman, I know, from my hitherto easy credulity and confidence in her, thinks that I am to be moulded to her purposes, but——"

She paused, and burst into tears. The spirit which had at first prompted her thus to defy them, and had sustained her till this moment, now quailed before the cool, malicious, sarcastic smile with which both Mrs. Freeman and her friend listened to her.

"Well, have you concluded, my dear?" demanded the former, "because Mr. O'Brien and I are all attention."

"When Miss Woodford has quite finished her very pretty compliments to you and I, my dear," added Mr. O'Brien, "I've a small bit of paper, here in my pocket-book, which I'll just hand over to her, for her perusal;" and, suiting the action to the word, he thrust into her hand a paper, which she saw, at the first glance, was a demand, signed Terence O'Brien, for twenty-four pounds; for twelve weeks' board and lodging, due to Alice Hodgson, and for which he was instructed, he observed, to proceed against her, according to law, unless it was immediately settled.

"It's very accommodating, you must allow," observed Mr. O'Brien, "that I should not only take the trouble of delivering my own letter to you, but of receiving your answer, my dear : so come, now, just let me know if you please, whether you are inclined to pay my client, Mrs. Hodgson, without farther trouble, or whether I shall be under the disagreeable necessity of——"

"You may spare your taunts, sir," interrupted Grace, drying her tears and assuming an air of calmness, which was strangely at variance with the expression of her deathly pale features. "You, of course," she continued, "are fully acquainted with my utter inability to pay this unjust demand. You cannot suppose either, but that I am quite aware of your purpose in making it; but I here solemnly assure you that my mind is irrevocably made up on the subject. You may send me to prison, and I may die there ; for God help me, I have little chance of ever being released, since I have not a friend in the world, who ——"

"Do not be quite so hasty, young woman, in your assertions," said a voice behind her, which made Grace start from her seat. It was her eccentric friend, Mr. Lovell, who now stood surveying the whole group.

"Oh, save me! save me! dear, dear, good sir, save me!" exclaimed Grace, her assumed calmness all in a moment vanishing, while, in a tumult of mingled hope and agitation, she flew to him and grasped his arm.

"Save you, child! from what?" said Mr. Lovell, with great coolness, and keeping his eye fixed on Mr. O'Brien, who seemed quite at a loss how to take this intrusion of one whom he considered a perfect stranger, and looked doubtingly to Mrs. Freeman, as if waiting to take his cue from her. "What danger can there possibly be to threaten you in the company of such very respectable people as these—in this very respectable house, too, and at noon-day?"

The old gentleman had still preserved the cool, equal tone in which he had at first addressed Grace; but there was either something in the expression of his countenance or the inflection of his voice which betrayed a very different feeling to what his words expressed; and Mrs. Freeman's bold, confident eye sank before him, while she in vain tried to utter a word of explanation of the singular appeal Grace had made to him for protection or her equally energetic action, as she now stood clinging to his arm.

A few minutes' consideration, however, seemed to have convinced Mr. O'Brien that there could be no reason to fear a plain, almost shabbily dressed old man; and he therefore walked up to him, with an air of affected politeness, though at the same time, a certain degree of swagger, which seemed to say, if you are insensible to fair means, old fellow, I shall try what rough ones will do, in stopping your farther interference.

"I beg your pardon, sir," he commenced, with a smile. "I am very sure you are too wise to take any notice of what this foolish girl says. It is, in fact, a mere family concern; but my client, there, Mrs. Freeman, has found it necessary to require my presence, finding the young lady quite refractory and unwilling to listen to the advice of her friends. You will excuse me, therefore, sir, if I request you will leave her to our management."

"Certainly, sir; nothing can be more reasonable," returned Mr. Lovell, with the same imperturbable serenity of manner. "But you will allow me, first if you please, to inquire of this young woman, Grace Woodford, I think her name is—she was so called, at least, before she assumed the character of a young lady, and became the protége of yourself and that lady," bowing to Mrs. Freeman, with mock respect—"I say, if it will be perfectly agreeable to you, I should like to inquire of this young woman what could be her motives for the violent panic she appeared in when I entered, and what kind of protection she so earnestly required of me."

"I ask you to save me from ruin! disgrace! despair! death!" said Grace, clasping her hands, with a most impassioned gesture. "I have been cruelly, treacherously deceived; and now look here!" and she placed the paper which Mr. O'Brien had given her in Mr. Lovell's hands. "Look! I am threatened with a prison because I will not consent to their vile purposes."

"Don't go for to take my character away, miss, if you please," said Mrs. Hodgson, who had entered unobserved during the preceding speech. "I am sure you can't go for to say as how I ever purposed any vile doings to you; all I wanted, and all I axed for, was my money, and nobody can say that, that isn't my right."

"You shall have your right, good woman," said Mr. Lovell. "I told you when I entered your house that I came from Sir George Beaumont with full power to settle all demands upon him."

"Yes, sir, but I did'nt think then that the friends, as you called them, that you've left standing in my passage were constables. What, I should like to know, will the neighbours think to see such things? My house has always borne the best of characters, so far as a poor lone woman, that's got nothing else to depend upon for a bit of bread, has been able to manage it. I'll defy parish officers or churchwardens to say as there ever was a riot or a rumpus kicked up in it since I've had it; because, for why, whenever my ladies——"

"There, there, my good woman; there's nobody who impeaches the immaculate character of your house, and if I have injured it by bringing my honest friends below I am ready to make you amends; but the fact is they came on a very different errend to that which you imagine. My nephew, Sir George Beaumont, has been led to believe, by some information which he received only last night, that you had been deceived into giving shelter here to a discarded footman of his, one Timothy Donovan, who has robbed him to a considerable amount, and who, besides, richly deserves the gallows for his ingratitude and treachery to his too indulgent master. I am glad to see, however, that the information is false, and that you have nobody here but such very respectable people as my old acquaintance here, Mrs. Freeman—I won't presume *now* to call her Sukey—and this gentleman, Mr.———may I crave the favour of your name, sir?" and again he bowed with mock ceremony to Mr. O'Brien, whose consummate assurance had sustained him, and enabled him to keep up an air of consequence and indifference until the mention of the robbery and Mr. Lovell's consequent remarks on the character of the offender whom the latter sought, when, in spite of every exertion, his countenance betrayed every symptom of confusion and terror, and with difficulty he had evidently kept himself from sinking into the chair, which he had been before twirling by his thumb and finger, with an assumption of perfect ease and nonchalance.

"My name—my name is O'Brien, sir, Terence O'Brien, sir. I am—I am a solicitor, sir; that note," and he began to resume something like courage again as he glanced at the note, which Mr. Lovell still held open in his hand, though he had not read it; "that note," repeated the *soi-divant* Mr. O'Brien, "will tell you who and what I am."

Mr. Lovell's eyes glanced to the bottom of the note which he held in his hand.

"Oh, I see," he observed; "a professional gentleman, and——"

"Yes, sir," interrupted O'Brien eagerly, and assuming at the same time a significant smile. "Really, I am quite ashamed of the part I have been drawn in to play here; I had not an idea, I assure you, of the character which it seems the house bears. Really, to a young man, and one just married, too, it is a serious thing to be even seen in such a place; but, I trust, sir, I may rely on your honour not to mention that you saw me here. Those fellows, too, below may probably know me in the way of business, and——"

"It is highly probable, indeed, sir," interrupted Mr. Lovell; "but it is time to put an end to this farce, Mr. Donovan. You, it seems, have a more treacherous memory than I have, or you would have recollected that your person had been seen often enough by the Earl of Melverley not to recognize at once the ungrateful vagabond who has so ungratefully returned his too easy master's confidence in him."

"Good God!—the earl!—then I am indeed ruined!" exclaimed the *soi-devant* Mr. O'Brien. Oh, my lord! my lord!———" and he would have dropped on his knees but that the earl sternly prevented him.

"Your supplications are in vain, rascal!" he exclaimed." "Were it even possible that such a breach of confidence as you committed could be pardoned, your conduct towards this poor, defenceless girl, your joining with that base, unprincipled woman"—looking at Mrs. Freeman—"though I do not exactly comprehend your purposes, still this very evidence to which you just now referred with so much effrontery, would be sufficient to———"

"Oh, no; do not think of his conduct towards me," interrupted Grace, who at the first mention of the supposed Mr. Lovell's rank had endeavoured to retreat from him in confusion at the liberty which she had taken, but was witheld by his kindly taking her hand and retaining it in his. "Do not let what he has done to me stand between him and mercy. He was but acting as the instrument of others, and—and—and there has been no harm done to anyone; the scheme is now altogether at an end," and she looked at Mrs. Freeman.

"You do not know what you are talking about, child," said the earl "Ransom! Woollett! step up here!" he continued, calling loudly down the stairs.

The men were in the room in a minute, and in another instant the *soi-divant* Mr. O'Brien was hurried from the presence of the earl and the trembling Grace, who, in spite of her conviction that he was totally undeserving of lenity, could not behold the despair which had usurped the place of his former bold effrontery, without joining her supplications to Mrs. Freeman's, who now fell on her knees to implore him to have compassion on the unfortunate man.

"Is he your husband, woman?" demanded the earl, sternly. "Mind do not prevaricate; give me a plain answer to my question, and the means of proving your veracity."

"He is not," she replied, hiding her face, "but he is the father of my two children; and—and we were to have been—we should have been married in a few days; the banns have been published and———"

"Yo may think yourself very fortunate that you have escaped," said the earl, gravely. "What could have been his motives, now, for wishing to make you his wife, I cannot imagine; but I suspect they were of a piece with his other conduct, for certainly the father of your two children ought to have found a time and opportunity long before this to have made their mother his wife, had he been influenced either by justice or affection. I suppose, therefore, that there was some advantage proposed by this intended marriage? Well, I do no not ask you; neither for yourself, I confess, would it concern me one jot to know; but for the sake of your friends. Your sister, I know, is a decent woman, and I have been indebted to her for much attention and civility, when she knew me only as Mr. Lovell, and therefore, if you choose to go back to her—— Do not interrupt me; my nephew, Sir George, has at last opened his eyes to the consequences of the guilty course he has so long pursued; he has acknowledged to me every transaction in which you have been his wretched instrument, and with proper feeling, he wishes to give you means and opportunity to redeem, or at least to repent, your past crimes."

"To-morrow morning, if life is spared to her so long, he will become the husband of Lady Albina Mandeville. It is his wish, not hers, for she is past all reparation; but he wishes to prove to the world that he considers her worthy to be his wife. I tell you this because I hope you have still good feeling enough to rejoice that he has at last done an act of justice; and yet, when I look at this poor girl," turning to Grace, "and behold in her another destined victim—good Heavens———"

"I never intended any harm to Grace," said Mrs. Freeman; she "knows best, and can explain what my motives were for bringing her up to London. I meant only to make her the means of forcing Sir George to do what he had over and over again promised me—to make a proper provision for me. I was first seduced by his promises," she continued with great agitation;

'he promised to make my fortune, if I promoted his interests with Lady Albina, and it was but right that——"

CHAPTER XXXII.
" The seeming truth which cunning time puts on
To entrap the wisest."

SHAKESPEARE.

It had been very evident, during the whole of this scene, that the Earl of Melverly, for such it appeared was the title which Grace's friend was distinguished by—was disposed, in spite of the sternness of his look and manner, to show mercy, and to judge with lenity, if it were possible, consistent with justice. O'Brien's own admission had convicted him, and Mrs. Freeman's imprudence, now defeated all the interest which he was inclined to feel towards her; for in the attempts to vindicate herself at Sir George's expense, she betrayed much more connection with the affairs of the latter, than the earl—who, it appeared, was the uncle of whom his cousin Clara had spoken, in Grace's hearing—had previously suspected; but her avowal, which—with a want of tact most unusual to her —she boldly made, that the purpose for which she had trepanned Grace into coming up to London was to draw Sir George into her own net, while she pretended to favour his designs upon the latter, completed her condemnation in his eyes. That such a being should have dared to entertain a thought of coupling her name with his nephew's, of appearing before the world as claiming him for her affianced husband, would have been quite sufficient to have chilled every feeling of compassion towards her in the heart of the old nobleman, in whose bosom family pride held a distinguished station; but when to this was added the certainty from her own avowal, that she had woven this web of artifice only from the mercenary motives of enriching herself at the expense of her dupe, his indignation and contempt towards her knew no bounds, and Grace, just as she was compelled to acknowledge his reproaches and observations on her, Mrs. Freeman's conduct, could not help compassionating her bitter humiliation.

" It would be but strict justice," he concluded, " to leave you to the consequences of your infamous conduct; but, as I have said before, that for the sake of your friends I will assist you. I will fulfil my promise. There," he continued, drawing out his purse, " is sufficient to enable you to discharge your debt in this house, and to go down to your sister—"

" That I shall certainly never do," interrupted Mrs. Freeman hastily. " If that is to be a condition, my lord, I——"

" I make no conditions " said the earl contemptuously ; " act as you please, but never let me be troubled by hearing of you again, unless it is to hear that you have seen the error of your ways, and have returned to your proper station in society. You are young enough, yet, to work for your living, as you ought to do. And now, Grace Woodford, what are your wishes?" he continued, turning to the latter. " You, I hope, are not corrupted so much by the life you have lately led, as to consider yourself placed above labour."

" Oh no, indeed, indeed sir—my lord," returned Grace, " I have no pretension, no wishes, but to be enabled honestly——"

" Well, well, we shall see what is to be done," he interrupted: " but are you willing to go at once with me to the person with whom I shall place you?"

"This instant! my lord!" exclaimed Grace.   "Oh, I shall be but too happy."

"Well then put on your bonnet, Mrs. Freeman will, I dare say, do me the favour to pack up your clothes, and I will send a man for them in an hour."

Mrs. Freeman could not, of course, object to this arrangement, though she looked as if she would willingly have thrown some impediment, had it been in her power, in the way of Grace's thus suddenly leaving her.

In a few minutes she followed the latter, who had ran hastily up stairs to make some slight changes in her dress.

"You will of course, Grace, let me know, when you are settled, where I can see you?" she observed, in one of her most insinuating tones; "you must, I am sure, be convinced, that whatever I may have done in other respects, I have never meant anything but good towards you. As to what passed this morning, it was not my scheme, I assure you, and I was very sorry to see it carried so far, though it was only meant to frighten you. Do, dear Grace, say that you forgive me, and promise that you will let me know where you are?   It will be in your power, perhaps, to save poor O'Brien, for Sir George——"

"I cannot promise anything without Mr. Lovell—that is, the earl's permission," interrupted Grace, who instantly took alarm at the thought of being in any manner compromised with the detestable O'Brien. "If he will allow me," she added, "I shall always be ready to serve you as far as lays in my power."

"You may spare your promises," returned Mrs. Freeman, angrily, "for I see how far your friendship goes. I am fallen now, and you think you are rising, and therefore are quite right not to run the smallest risk to rescue me from ruin. With all your disinterestedness, therefore, Miss Woodford, it is very plain, after all, you are only like the rest of the world, bent on serving yourself, and caring little what becomes of such unfortunate creatures as me."

A flood of tears enforced this complaint, and Grace's susceptible heart instantly melted. In spite of her late experience of the unprincipled conduct of her whom she had once called her friend, and of the short interval that had passed since the latter had beheld her (Grace's) tears and agony, not only without pity, but with triumph, the tender-hearted girl could not help deeply sympathising with the unfortunate woman, and she was about to give her the desired assurance when the appearance of Mrs. Hodgson, who suddenly entered the room, recalled her to sober reflection on the consequence of enthralling herself by giving the required assurance; and whilst the landlady was whispering in Mrs. Freemans's ear, the cause of her hasty appearance, Grace seized the opportunity of making her escape, and rejoining her protector.

How did she congratulate herself that she had done so, when, the moment they were in the street, (for he waited not for their return, but instantly quitted the house, followed by the delighted, yet greatly agitated Grace), he turned to her and said—

"And now Grace, I trust you have taken your leave for ever of that unprincipal, dangerous woman. May your experience in this case prevent you ever being again deceived by specious appearance, and let it prove to you that straightforward sincerity will almost always defeat the plans of deeplaid artifice. For a time, indeed, this wretched woman succeeded in involving you in her schemes; for even in my eyes she had succeeded in making you appear as infamous as herself. You start Grace, but I will tell you, that I have had information of all your movements, from the time I left you at

Bath; I was unwilling, indeed to give credit, in its full extent, to the tale which reached me, of your having openly become the companion of my nephew's vice; but when you remained silent to my letters, requiring an explanation I had heard———"

"I never received such a letter, sir," said Grace, hastily; "indeed, indeed, if I had———"

"So, so, so," interrupted the earl. "Then, I suppose, you never got the money either that I enclosed for you."

"Not a sixpence, my lord," returned Grace, "I never had even a suspicion that———"

"What! did it never occur to you that it was very unlikely after what I had said that I should entirely neglect you? It seems, Grace, that you are as ready to condemn as you are to credit upon mere appearances, and to sit down contented in both cases, without making a single effort to prove whether your belief is right or wrong."

"I was not easily contented, my lord, in this instance at least," returned Grace with modest spirit, though the tears started into her eyes at the harshness of his reproof. "I never did believe," she continued, "that your lordship's silence to me arose from your having forgotten that there was one whom you had authorised to consider you as a friend; but what means had I of ascertaining that———"

"A great many, you simpleton," interrupted Lord Melverly in a tone of kindness. "A mere inquiry at the post-office would have ascertained that I had written to you; but we will say no more on that head, for this is the place where I purpose for the present you shall remain."

"Is your mistress at home, Peggy?" demanded the earl of a slipshod, dirty-looking servant girl, who replied to his single knock at the door of a small house in the Edgeware-road. The girl, who appeared frightened and confounded at discovering who was the evidently unexpected visitor to their mistress, replied only by muttering something about being all in her dirty work, and the place not being fit to be seen; and then, having led the way to the parlour, which fully corroborated her assertions that it was all at sixes and sevens, though she did not explain why it should be so, she closed the door and left them, while she went to announce the visitors to her mistress.

"This is strange," said the earl, looking round him with an air of dissatisfaction. "I did not expect, at this time of day—but it will all be explained, I daresay, when she comes."

He walked to the window, through which he stood gazing, apparently absorbed in thought; while Grace, in spite of the agitation and anxiety she felt from the singularity of her introduction into the house, had full leisure and opportunity to take a survey of all around her.

The room was scantily furnished, but there was an evident disposition to show and parade in its inhabitants; for the walls were covered with gaudy, ill-designed and worse executed pictures, in water colours, with frames of black and gold paper, which were in most cases deserting their intended service, and hanging in ragged strips from them, while, in other cases, the pictures themselves were suspended by one corner only, the pins which had originally fastened them having either fallen from their places, or been withdrawn to answer more useful purposes. On the mantel-piece, some dirty plaster figures were mingled with still dirtier artificial flowers; two glass lustres, deprived of all their drops; what had once been a paper basket, with moss, &c., &c., but was now a shapeless mass of rubbish; and a variety of heterogenous articles, which were all clothed in the same livery of dust and smoke. The carpet was covered with shreds of muslin, threads, and crumbs of bread ; on the table stood the tea things, which appeared to have been used for breakfast ; and, on the top of a cupboard, which served the office of sideboard, was heaped together, in strange confusion, dirty plates, knives, forks, and glasses, with two or three children's bonnets and tippets, and some ragged dog's-eared, ragged school-books thrown upon them.

A full ten minutes was occupied in this survey. The earl's countenance betrayed strong impatience : he seized the fine bow of scarlet ribbon, and gold paper, which represented the bell-pull, but it came off in his hand ; and throwing it from him with anger, he was in the act of opening the door to summon Peggy by some other means, when the lady of the house entered, and with a gentleness and grace that were quite irresistable, apologised for her having unavoidably kept her visitors waiting.

"But the fact is," she continued, "that I have quite a sick house at present. My two youngest girls are laid up with the measles, Lavinia is so hoarse she cannot speak, and Clarendon has met with an accident that has made him quite frightful to look at, though the doctor tells me there is nothing serious to be alarmed at, and that his face will not be disfigured, though it will be a long time before the swelling and blackness goes off. As to mysef, I declare, what with fright and anxiety, and constant attendance upon them all, I am half dead. And this, I hope, will plead my excuse with you, my lord."

" A mother's cares and anxieties are a sufficient excuse for anything, Mrs. Burton," said the earl, in a tone of kindness. "Perhaps," he added, after a moment's pause, " I ought to make an apology for bringing you an additional trouble, at the present moment ; but the fact is, in the first place, I cannot well do without you, and in the second, I am inclined to believe, from what I know of my young friend here," looking at Grace, " that her residence with you will be mutually beneficial : she is, I can answer, from personal knowledge, a most excellent nurse."

Mrs. Burton, who had, at her first entrance, saluted Grace, with extraordinary—indeed, with what the latter felt rather oppressive ceremony and and respect, now darted a look of keen inquiry, towards her, while, with evident surprise, confusion, and uncertainty, as to what she was to understand of her new visitor, she observed, that she should feel very honoured and happy, in——

"The fact is, there is no question of honour or happiness in it, my good lady," interrupted the earl, with his usual bluntness ; "I understood from your letter, when you removed hither, that you intended to try to augment your income, and extend your society, by taking two or three female boarders."

" Certainly, my lord," returned Mrs. Burton, colouring ; and I am most truly grateful to your lordship for having afforded me the means of ——"

"Phsa ! phsa ! I do not want this ; you know how I hate it," interrupted Lord Melverly ; "let us leave all this out of the question, and perfectly understand each other. I am desirous of placing this young woman in your house, and under your care, for an indeterminate time ; I cannot say how long or how short, but I wish to know if you are willing to accept the charge, it will not be a very arduous one, for she is quiet and well-disposed, and will rather lessen than add to the cares of your family. However, we will set that aside ; I am willing to pay for her board, at the rate, whatever it may be, that you intended to require from a perfect stranger, of whose good qualities you would know nothing."

Mrs. Burton's looks cleared ; she should refer it entirely to her generous benefactor; she said, how was it possible she could name money to him, to whom she was indebted for all that ——"

"Well, well, well, we will settle this another time," interrupted the earl, impatiently: "in the mean time, there is something," handing her a cheque, which he had been writing at the table, ''to prevent your feeling embarrassed by the unexpected addition to your family, as well as to pay the doctor's bill; send him off, by all means, as soon as you can, for I shall have little hopes of you all, while you encourage his visits; by-the-bye, what pretty piece of mischief has your son been about, to get on the sick list?"

Mrs. Burton murmured—"something of boyish frolic—animal spirits—gunpowder—inexperience—an explosion and a fright," to which, however, much to her satisfaction, as she was evidently desirous of evading all further explanation, the earl paid little attention, for his eyes were rivetted on Grace's countenance with an air of deep reflection.

"You are sadly altered, child," he observed, after a considerable pause, "your London life has not, I think, improved your looks; but you must take care of yourself now you have got into good air, a quiet house, and will of course keep regular hours, and that will soon bring you round again; I shall not see you, perhaps, for some days, for I have a world of business on my hands, but when I do come, I have much to talk over with you."

A hard pressure of the hand accompanied this speech, and observing, "You will have your clothes sent here by and bye, Grace," he departed.

The moment the front door, to which Mrs. Burton herself conducted him was closed upon the earl, Grace was startled and confounded by the racket of half a dozen feet scampering up the kitchen stairs; and before Mrs. Burton could reach the end of the passage to prevent them, the whole family burst into the parlour, with a noise and celerity which agreed very little with their mamma's previous representation of them as invalids. The two youngest, indeed, from their dirty cotton nightcaps without border, and the bits of flannel round their necks, gave indication that they had but recently recovered from the disease their mother had named; the boy, a tall gawkey lad of fourteen, with the front of his red hair, his eye-brows, and eye-lashes singed close to the roots, his nose enormously swelled, and the black particles of gunpowder which had settled in that and his cheeks, added to the dirt which both his hands and face seemed engrained, giving him a most awful grim and forbidding appearance. Another, sturdy, thick boy, who was endeavouring to fight his way into the room, from which the elder seemed as resolutely bent to expel him, completed the interesting group, who were all pell-mell fairly into the middle of the room, before they discovered that Grace was quietly sitting by the window.

"What is the meaning of this, Clarendon? Granville, I'm ashamed of you both; go out of the room, instantly. Louisa, George, I shall have you both laid up again. Where is Lavinia? what is the reason she has allowed you to——"

"Law, how can I help it ma', I was up stairs putting on my new merino, and that Peggy wouldn't come and button it," answered a shrill voice from the stairs, and in another instant, a rather pretty, but awkward looking girl, of about the same age as Grace, made her appearance, with her sky-blue merino hanging loose on her shoulders, her flaxen hair all in disorder, and bearing evident marks of habitual neglect, and her countenance betraying the greatest disappointment at not having been able to complete her toilette before the earl's departure.

Equally unprepared, it seemed, as her brothers and sisters, for the presence of a stranger, she shrank back abashed at beholding Grace, who, observing that Mrs. Burton, totally inattentive to her daughter's appearance, was totally abstracted from everything but the contemplation of her own image in the cracked pier glass between the two windows, instantly arose and offered her services to fasten the gown, which, with abundance of awkward confusion, was accepted by Miss Lavinia.

"Oh, there's no occasion at all for your putting on that dress to-day" exclaimed Mrs. Burton, turning sharply round upon her daughter. "I know very well it won't be fit to seen by night, for you've dirtied all your pinafores, and————"

"Pinafores, indeed!" returned Livinia, in a saucy tone; "but I'm sure I shan't pull it off now; I suppose you are going to keep yours on, and why shouldn't I?"

A long contest ensued between the mother and daughter, in which neither appeared to very great advantage; the eldest boy, the elegant Clarendon, turned round to foment a further disturbance by advising the two younger girls to insist upon their right, to have on their new frocks, if Miss Viny, the *soubriquet* for Lavinia, kept on hers; while the young gentleman rejoicing in the patrician appellation of Granville, added to the confusion by pulling an unfortunate cat—which had followed them into the room—by the tail, and forcing it to join its discordant notes to the war of voices.

Never had Grace beheld such a revolting scene: it was evident that Mrs. Burton, though denouncing all sorts of punishments and privations against her unruly children, possessed neither authority or influence over them; and Grace was heartily rejoiced when, seeming suddenly to recollect what an ungracious appearance this spuabble must have to her new inmate, Mrs. Burton observed—

"You will, most probably, like to go to your own room for a few minutes, Miss—— I beg your pardon, I have forgotten the name, by which Lord Melverly introduced you."

Lord Melverly, had not, in fact, thought it necessary to go through the usual ceremony of introduction.

"My name is Grace Woodford," replied the latter with her usual modest simplicity.

"Grace, Grace—what a comical name," tittered the eldest boy, which was replied to, on the part of his sister Viny, as he called her, by a violent slap in the face, the return to which she avoided by dexterously shutting the parlour door, before Grace was well out of the room, and thus nearly jamming her in the door way, she having undertaken to show her new associate to her room, which Grace found rather superior to the rest of the house, it having been furnished expressly, it appeared, for a lady, who had only kept possession of it a week.

"All through our children," said the communicative Miss Viny, "who couldn't be kept from making a great uproar with a great dog that they had picked up in the streets."

Grace subsequently discovered, from the same unsolicited authority, that the accident under which Master Clarendon was still suffering, was owing to his inordinate propensity to torment the animals which were unfortunete enough to come under his dominion, he having made a squib or cracker, as he called it, and fastened it to the tale of the monkey, which had been for some time his engine of torment to the whole family.

"He never thought about the monkey in his fright jumping up on the kitchen table, amongst all the loose gunpowder," continued Miss Viny;

" and it was lucky nobody was standing by it but him, or goodness knows where the mischief might have ended. However, there was one good came of it, for Jacko darted right through the kitchen window, and we've never seen him since."

With these and similar tales of her brothers and sisters, whose faults the young lady seemed by no means disposed to soften in her narration, Grace was entertained during the half hour which she remained in her room. Rejoiced, indeed, would she have been to have been left alone for that brief time; but Miss Burton was evidently determined to improve to the utmost her acquaintanceship, and it was in vain that the former gently hinted that perhaps her mother had occasion for her, or assured her that she was accustomed to do without assistance in the slight improvement she wished to make in her appearance before dinner.

Miss Viny wouldn't take the hint; she was full of admiration of the make of Grace's dress, of the length, thickness, and natural glossiness and curl of her hair; and before they quitted the bedroom she had confined to Grace's keeping two important secrets—one that . she was desperately in love with a clergyman that preached at some chapel which she always went to on Sunday evenings, and the other that her mother wanted to keep her under, and make her appear a child, because she fancied that she was herself quite young and handsome.

"Only think of that," whispered Miss Viny, as they returned to the parlour together. "I know she thinks she'll get another husband; but law, who'd have her, with five children."

"Not with such children," thought Grace, who had felt at once shocked and disgusted at this communication.

She could not, indeed, but be struck with the fact that Mrs. Burton's appearance betokened a much greater attention and care than was displayed in anything else; and certainly, in point of personal charms, she had a manifest superiority in all but youth; for she was really a fine woman, while the utmost her daughters could lay claim to was a fair complexion and pleasing features.

There had been some pains taken during Grace's absence to render the appearance of the parlour somewhat more inviting: the absence of the two boys had been purchased by money given to buy a pair of stilts a-piece, with which they had walked off to the park.

"I hope they won't come back," added the thoughtless mother, "till we've' dined; for really, Miss Woodford, two great boys like them are enough to worry one into the grave."

"Ah, it's all your own fault," observed her complaisant daughter. "You know very well that Lord Melverly, when my father died, would have put them both to school, and then we should have been rid of them; but you fancied you could do better with the money that would have been paid for their board, and send them to a day-school, and the consequence is that they are both growing up now two of the ignorantest, rudest cubs that ever were born."

"You are a cruel, unfeeling girl, Lavinia, to make such observations. You well know that I could not bring myself to part with Clarendon, who is the very image of his poor father; and as to Granville, of course it would have been very unjust and cruel of me to have sent him away alone."

During the whole of dinner, which Mrs. Burton apologized for being scanty and plain, having intended, she said, to dine out herself, and, therefore, not being provided to entertain a visitor, a constant series of small bickerings were kept up between mother and daughter; but these were all thrown into the shade when, at the conclusion of their meal, the boisterous voices of the boys and their sisters who, it appeared, had also been the companions of their brothers' excursion, were heard in the passage.

Clarendon had a hundred tales to tell of the impudence and ill-behaviour of Granville, who in his turn vociferated that Clarendon had been nearly taken up by the police for running after and frightening some ladies. It appeared, also, that between them they had contrived to break a pane of glass in a jeweller's window, and that they had both been for some time held in durance vile by the shopkeeper, who intended to have sent to their mother, but that the two little girls' cries and screams for their brothers had induced some ladies to interfere, and they had been released on giving the direction where they were to be found.

The noise, the mutual abuse, the cool insolence of the eldest boy in reply to his mother's reproaches, and the equally saucy, but more passionate vindication of himself by his brother—the two girls' contradictory statements, the one inclining to the side of Granville, and the other, having been won by the promise of a penny, to state the case favourably to her eldest brother—together with Miss Burton's sarcastic observations on the course her brothers were pursuing, and Mrs. Burton's pathetic lamentations that her children were killing her by inches, that no mother so kind, so attentive, so exemplary, in fact, as she was, ever existed, or was ever so ungratefully repaid—joined with all parties' frequent references to Grace as umpire, and their determinate vociferation in telling their own stories in their own way—formed altogether a scene of uproar and confusion from which she would willingly have escaped; but it was too early to retire to bed, and to be compelled to listen to Miss Viny's conversation, who, she saw plainly, would be her companion, in spite of everything that she could do to the contrary, was even worse than the Babel of sounds which now deafened her.

In the midst of all, however, a loud knock at the street-door caused a sudden diversion.

" Who can that be ?" was ejaculated by every mouth.

" The officers, may be, come to take you up for your pretty tricks," said Mrs. Burton.

Master Clarendon, as he was called, betrayed unequivocal symptoms of fright.

" They can't have traced us, sure !" he exclaimed; I gave him a wrong address."

" Are you not ashamed of yourself?" said Mrs. Burton. " So you are not content with doing all the mischief you can, but you tell a falsehood to avoid the consequence of it."

" There's a man down stairs, ma'am, says——"

Peggy could not finish the sentence for the chorus of frightened exclamations this occasioned, but at last it was explained.

It was the man whom the earl had employed to bring Grace's clothes from her late residence, and every other subject was forgotten in the curiosity which this circumstance excited.

In vain Grace turned a deaf ear to the hints that were given by both mother and daughter that it would be advisable for her to open the trunks and see that all was safe—in vain she declared that she was quite satisfied that all was precisely as she had left them. Their importunities were irresistible, and in a few mements she had the mortification of seeing all her gowns, caps, ribbons, and all the et ceteras of her wardrobe in the hands of the whole party: the boys actually dragging the different articles from their sisters; one strutting about with poor Grace's best shawl thrown over his dirty jacket and a lace cap on his head, while the other had arrayed himself in a delicate blue silk frock and a lace veil.

It was alike useless for Mrs. Burton to raise her voice in loud reprehension, or for Grace mildly to remonstrate; the young gentlemen were too much accustomed to consult only their own will and pleasure to pay the slightest attention to what their mother said; and it was not until a fracture had been made in the veil, the dress torn out of the plaits, and the lace cap thrown under the fire, that the united force of Mrs. Burton and her daughter compelled her to restore the spoils and eject them from the room, at the door of which, however, they continued to hammer and kick during the whole time the investigation which the mother and daughter now seriously commenced, was going on.

So much to their taste did Miss Viny and her mamma, indeed, find the contents of Grace's wardrobe, that it was with infinite regret, apparently, that they relinquished the objects of their admiration, after trying them all on, admiring their own appearance in them, and giving vent to their regrets that their circumstances did not allow of their purchasing similar articles.

So forcibly and pathetically was this lamentation uttered, in one or two instances, that Grace, to whom it seemed strange that any person could place their happiness in such trifles, actually felt herself compelled to beg their acceptance of the articles they so greatly admired; but she soon found that the possession of one only increased their appetite for the others, and she was at length compelled to close lids of the trunks to prevent her being literally stripped.

"However can it be that the earl is so deceived as to think these people amiable and deserving?" was Grace's first reflection, when, to her infinite satisfaction, she was at last left alone in her bedroom, having rather peremptorily declared to Miss Lavinia, who volunteered to become her bedfellow, and then to help her to undress, that she preferred sleeping alone, and always undressed herself without assistance. There was one consolation, however, that suggested itself, his lordship had not placed her there as a permanent residence; on the contrary, he had spoken of it merely as a place of refuge until he could form some decisive plan for her, and most earnestly did she hope and pray that it would not be many days before that was done.

The second day of her residence at Mrs. Burton's was but a repetition of the first. The same unbearable boisterousness and tormenting mischief on the part of the children, and the same rapacious meanness and covetousness on the part of the mother and her daughter. Grace was sick to death, too, of the endless disputes between the latter; and she was wearired when they could find an interval from their incessant bickerings with the importunate curiosity with which they sought to ascertain every circumstance of her history, and especially by what means she had become known to the Earl of Melverley.

Mild and meek as Grace usually was, and conscious, too, as she was that there was nothing in the history of her first introduction to the earl that need be concealed, there was something to her so repulsive in the inquisitive and sly cunning with which Mrs. Burton continued to put her questions that the former resolved not to satisfy her, and she therefore briefly replied that the earl had known her mother, and had since her death kindly interested himself in her welfare.

"Dear me, how very good of him! And so you are quite dependent on his lordship?" said Mrs. Burton, fixing her large blue eyes with peculiar significance.

"I did not say so, madam," returned Grace, with spirit. "I have another dependence, one which, until some untoward circumstances have thrown me into embarrassments; I have found sufficient for all my wants, and which I hope to regain again.

"Oh, dear, I'm sure I beg your pardon, Miss Woodford, and indeed I'm very glad, for your own sake, to hear it; for really it would be a sad thing for a young woman like you to be dependent upon the whims and fancies of anybody. I'm sure I feel it deeply," and she sighed, "for nobody has got a more independent spirit than I have; but then, with such a family as I am burdened with, what can I do?"

Grace neither wished nor attempted to answer this question, and Mrs. Burton, finding that her guest was not disposed to be more communicative, and that her own pretended frankness failed to elicit a like feeling in the part of the former, returned for the twentieth time to a discussion with her daughter, as to the most becoming shape of a new turban which she intended to made of the materials Grace had given her.

"Law, Viny, what a dash we should cut in the dress boxes!" was Mrs. Burton's sudden exclamation, as she placed the turban on her daughter's head, to see the effect of it. "You would look very well in that clear muslin Miss Woodford has given you and the wreath of flowers, and I could wear my shot silk very well by candlelight. If we could but manage it for once, to get off without the boys knowing anything about it; it's so long since I have been at the play in proper style."

Lavinia was ready to go to the play at any sacrifice; she even condescended to assure her mother that she looked beautiful in her turban. She would be content to live on bread and butter for a month, to save the money it would cost, (Mrs. Burton had, for some reason or other, it appeared, said nothing of the cheque the earl had given her); and last, and not least, apparently in the mother's estimation, it would be so easy to cheat the boys, by pretending they were going out on business with Miss Woodford.

It was in vain Grace protested against being a party to this arrangement; in vain she declared that she had particular reasons for declining to go to the theatre, at present. Mrs. Burton and her daughter would take no denial; they had set their minds on going, but the former declared she would not give a farthing to see a play, without she had a companion whom she could talk to; and really, Lavinia, in spite of all the pains she had taken with her, was so ignorant, that she dreaded to hear her open her lips to make a remark; while Miss Lavinia, with equal complaisance, declared that she would as soon stop at home, as go humdrumming with only ma'.

Wearied with contending, Grace, at last, was obliged to give up the point; she agreed to go, but again she made a stand, that they should choose a less conspicuous part of the house than the dress boxes.

"Oh, dear no, that would be taking all the gilt off the gingerbread," Mrs. Burton delicately observed, adding—

"What would be the use of our going dressed, to hide ourselves in the back rows? No, no, if we do go, let us go like ourselves. We'll have a coach between us, it won't cost more than a shilling a piece."

Again Miss Lavinia's boisterous exclamations of delight, drowned all Grace's objections; never had anything half so delightful been proposed, for once her mother and her were quite *d'accord*, and as there was no time to be lost, an early tea was proposed to supersede dinner; and Miss Lavinia, with no small degree of triumph, undertook to break the ice to "the boys," that mamma and her were going out with Miss Woodford, to a place they couldn't go to.

THE PRIDE OF THE VILLAGE;

OR,

THE FARMER'S DAUGHTERS.

ATTEMPTED SUICIDE OF MARIA.

CHAPTER XXXII (Continued).

In an instant the whole party, the elegant and amiable Clarendon, and the polished Granville, and the two little whining, weak-eyed sisters, were all in one cry, like a pack of hounds, surrounding their mother with vociferous expostulations against the injustice of leaving them at home, and taking Miss Viny out with her.

Long and fearful was the contest, and from time to time was it even prolonged beyond its natural termination, in a compromise that they should have an apple pudding for supper, and two pence a piece to do as they liked with—by some sly hint, or apparently undesigned taunt levelled at Clarendon, by the exulting Lavinia, to which he replied, by sundry threats of how he would requite her in a few years, when he grew to man's estate, and became, as he dutifully observed, her "mother's master, let alone hers."

All was, however, at last peacefully accommodated by the additional privilege granted to them, that the whole party should go to fetch a coach off the stand, and ride it up to the door.

The coach was brought ; Mrs. Burton and Miss Lavinia looked their very best, in their second-hand-new finery, and Grace, attired with the utmost simplicity, prepared herself with patience to go through the purgatory of the evening ; but now, another difficulty arose, Clarendon had become so fascinated with the pleasure of riding on the coach-box, that he refused to descend ; he would go as far as his mother was going—nobody would notice him there, or know he belonged to them inside; and Granville, thinking that he saw symptoms of his mother's yielding to this request, as determinately sprung up behind, observing that he would go as foot boy, and he would too, if Don went. A quarter of an hour was spent in this contest; Clarendon was deaf to bribes or threats, and his brother equally resolute to rise or fall with him : and Miss Lavinia, who had made one or two efforts to drag him from his elevated station, by the heels, had received sundry marks of his dirty nailed shoes on her fair arms and shoulders, having narrowly escaped, as she declared, having her front teeth kicked out, when the question was suddenly brought to a close by one of the little girls seeing, or pretending to see, the tradesman whose window they had broken the day before, coming with two other men, on the opposite side of the way.

Without waiting an instant to ascertain whether it was indeed the enemy, Master Clarendon threw himself almost headlong from the box, and sought refuge in the kitchen. Granville, who had crouched down behind the coach, was, by a timely bribe of an additional penny, prevailed upon to follow his brother ; and Peggy, the maid, dexterously closing the street door behind her, held it fast by the knocker, in spite of the screaming and kicking of the little girls within side, until her mistress, Miss Lavinia, and Grace had made good their seats within side the coach.

"Thank heaven we are off at last !" ejaculated Mrs. Burton, with as much pathos as if she had just made her escape from some imminent peril ; "such children as mine, I believe, never were seen."

"I declare, ma'," said Miss Lavinia, who had kept her head out of the coach window, as much, apparently, for the sake of exhibiting the coronet of flowers, with which it was crowned, to the spectators, who had been assembled by the amusing contest, as to see whether they were followed—" I declare if here isn't the whole gang, coming through the thick mud after us. Oh, Lord! coachman, do drive fast, or they'll be up with us, that Clarendon's long legs are sure to ——"

Another " Oh Lord!" uttered in a loud scream, followed, and Mrs. Burton now seconded it with a vociferous command to the coachman, to stop, exclaiming at the same time, " Which of my darlings is it ?"

"It's none of your darlings," returned the tender Lavinia, in a tone of angry reproach ; " but I wish they'd all been smothered in the mud sooner than I should have lost my beautiful flowers. I do believe you fastened them on so on purpose that I should lose them, because you thought I look better than you in your peacock's tail turban."

"You may make yourself easy about the children," said Grace, who had hastily thrust her head out of the window at Miss Lavinia's exclamation, conceiving, like their really affectionate but weak mother, that they had met with some accident; "they are all safe, and have given up the chase, having been suddenly arrested by the trumpet of the showman who just now passed us."

Oh, then, all is right, and we shall have nothing more to interrupt our pleasure," observed Mrs. Burton. Come, Lavinia, cheer up, child; you look very well without your flowers, though it was shameful of that coachman that he would not stop to let us pick them up."

"Yes, I dare say you are mighty sorry," returned the sulky Lavinia. "But it would have been no use to have picked them up, because I saw that broad-wheeled waggon go right over them."

Grace's kind offer to relinquish the simple white rose which she had placed in her own hair to decorate the discontented girl at length restored peace once more, especially as both the mother and Grace joined in declaring that nothing could be more becoming to her style of beauty.

There were so few persons in London, to whom Grace was known, that she comforted herself, as she followed Mrs. Burton into the dress circle, that it was scarcely within the scale of probabilities that any one would recognise her there, or consider she was assuming a style and consequence that was not becoming her situation.

The Earl of Melverley, she had been assured positively by Mrs. Burton, never visited the theatres.

"You may be sure, my dear, I would not run the risk myself of his seeing us there," she observed; because I know what a whimsical, cross, ill-grained man he is, and that he wouldn't mind affronting us, and perhaps telling me that I had better be at home mending my children's stockings, as he did when he spied me once in the crowd at the Palace Gate, when they were all going to Court. I shall never forget it; my poor husband was alive then, and how he did laugh when I told him, though I was not very well pleased, you may be sure."

"'What are you waiting here for, my good woman?' said the earl, putting his head out of his carriage window, for he'd made the coachman stop, the moment he saw me; 'have you anything to do at Court?'

"I said, of course, 'No,' but was only waiting, like others, to see the ladies go there."

"'Psha! psha!' says he, with one of his sourest looks, knitting his brows till they met over his eyes. 'You have got plenty to look at, at home, I'm sure; you'd better go home and mend Burton's stockings, or keep the children from falling into the fire.'

"I looked, as you may suppose, very foolish," continued Mrs. Burton, "and was sneaking away when he called after me, 'Here, stop; there's something to buy barley-sugar for them; and, next time you go out, take them with you, but not in a crowd, mind; women and children have no business there."

"And how much was it he gave you?" demanded Miss Lavinia. "I'm sure it ought to have been something very handsome to make amends for such an affront."

"More than I spent in barley sugar, you may be sure," returned her mother, smiling significantly at Grace; "but come, here we are, in sight of Drury Lane, and no fear, thank goodness, of his crossing our pleasure, for I've heard Burton say that after that sad affair of Lady Melverley's eloping from him nothing on earth would ever have tempted him to go inside a playhouse, or, indeed, any other place of amusement.

Relieved thus of her greatest fear, that of being recognized and reprimanded by the stern, uncompromising old earl, Grace forgot all minor causes of dissatisfaction, such as Mrs. Burton's outrageously showy turban, which harmonized so badly with her soiled, greasy, spotted, changeable silk, or Miss Lavinia's bared shoulders, which, in spite of her mother's remonstrances, were designedly slipt out of her dress, thus completely counteracting the otherwise simple and modest appearance of her white frock, and unpretending head-dress.

The play, indeed, was well calculated to absorb all unpleasant feelings, and Grace, in her deep attention to the mystery of the scene, soon forgot not only her more insensible companions, who were totally incapable of sharing her feelings, but forgot, also, that she was surrounded by others of the same class, many of whom were far more intent upon observing their neighbours, than attentive to the performance.

They had come, as Mrs. Burton had more than once observed, very unfashionably early, and very few of the front seats were occupied; but after awhile, they began to fill, and Mrs. Burton, whether possessing the knowledge she pretended to have of the fashionable world, or only pretending to it, to impress Grace with an idea of her importance, several times interrupted the latter's earnest attention to the stage, by loudly whispering to her who were such and such individuals as they entered.

On these occasions Grace had sometimes done no more than utter a simple ' indeed;' and then, having immediately withdrawn her cursory glance, had returned to her occupation of noticing the progress of the scene.

Her companion's exclamation, however, of—

" Mercy on me! why, I declare, there's our young lord, Lord Frederick, and I never heard he was come back from France," electrified her.

" Where?—who?—where is he?" she breathlessly demanded.

" Why, there, my dear, in that box directly opposite to us. There, that's him, with the dark hair and white teeth, that's laughing so with that lady. Dear me, how very odd, I don't believe the earl knows that he's in London, for he always sets off into the country, nobody knows where, if he thinks he is likely to meet him; but, Lord! Miss Woodford, what is the matter with you? You look as pale as death, I hope you are not going to faint. Lavinia, child, lend Miss Woodford your smelling bottle."

" I declare, ma', Lord Frederick is looking at us," exclaimed Lavinia, in a tone of delight, and without paying the slightest attention to this request. " I really do believe he knows us, though, I suppose, he's rather posed, because he thinks we shouldn't be likely to be in this part of the house; he's as proud every bit, in his way, as the old earl. He does know us, though, that's plain, for he said something to that other gentleman that's standing behind the lady, and then he looked over at us. See, they are both going out of the box together, I shouldn't wonder at all if they were to come over here to speak to us," and Lavinia drew her frock still lower off her shoulder, adjusted her ringlets, and thrust her crumpled and somewhat dingy handkerchief into her reticule, in expectation of the visit.

" Don't you flatter yourself, Viny," whispered Mrs. Burton, audibly; " it was not you he was looking at; I understand now," she continued, looking significantly at Grace, " all the mystery, and I must say, I don't thank Lord Melverley at all for the compliment he has paid me; it would have been but proper, I think, that he should have told me candidly all the particulars, and left it to my judgment, whether I should receive such a person into my house; but I suppose he thinks he can do as he pleases, and I've no right to think about it."

During these observations, to which Lavinia replied by impatient exclamations of—

"Law, ma', what do you mean? If I can make out what you are talking about."

Grace had been exerting herself to the utmost to conquer the tumult that had arisen in her bosom at the sight of the seducer of her beloved sister.

Divided between the ardent desire to implore him to restore to her the lost Maria and the horror of speaking to, of hearing the voice of, him whom she looked upon with such abhorrence, she had sat motionless, meditating, or at least endeavouring to meditate, upon what would be the best plan she could pursue; and though the words of her companions had reached her ears, she had remained totally unconscious of their import, until Mrs. Burton totally changing her tone from that sympathy which she had before expressed, observed—

"I shall expect, Miss Woodford, as Lord Melverley has placed you under my care, that you will act with propriety. I'm quite sure the earl didn't expect that you'd see Lord Frederick, and so I request that if he comes you don't speak to him."

Grace looked round at her with surprise.

"Not to speak to him! Do you know, then——are you acquainted with the—the——"

"Oh, yes, I know all about it, now, interrupted Mrs. Burton, with a sarcastic sneer. "I suspected there was something that was not very creditable, and now I am quite aware of the whole story, as much as if you had told me the whole at once, as you might have done, if you had had any candour about you."

"I do not know that it was any fault, madam, that I was unwilling to speak of circumstances which were so painful to recall," replied Grace, her meek eyes filling with tears.

The box-door opened: but Lavinia's assumed, and Grace's real trepidation, were alike unnecessary; it was a stranger who entered; and after standing some few moments reconnoitring the party, whispered a few words to Mrs. Burton, which had the effect of considerably heightening her colour.

"Really, sir, I don't know what to say; it is a very odd request. I wish you'd be good enough to tell Lord Frederick that I am afraid of displeasing the earl; and he knows very well————"

The stranger whispered again; and Mrs. Burton, after a moment's hesitation, arose.

"Don't move from your seat, Lavinia, on any account, till I return; I shall not be many minutes."

"I will take charge of the young ladies," he observed, as he handed her to the box-door.

Grace rose, in great agitation.

"One word, Mrs. Burton, if you please," she faltered. "Tell him that I will forgive—that I will ever pray for him, if he will let me see my ————"

"Really, Miss Woodford, this is quite outrageous. Dear me, do recollect where you are? and besides, to want to make me a go-between in such matters—I who have always kept a respectable——"

The stranger closed the door upon her before she had finished her speech, and then sat down by Lavinia, keeping, however, his eyes fixed upon Grace, whose bosom was heaving and swelling with irrepressible emotion.

Never had Lavina in her whole life, perhaps, been so happy as at this moment. The stranger was well-dressed, good-looking, and showy; and, moreover, he appeared disposed to be on very familiar terms with her, though his attention, anyone else would have seen, was evidently fixed upon Grace, to whom he did not attempt to utter a word.

"Your mother looks remarkably well, Miss Burton," he observed, after some common-place remarks respecting the house, the performance, &c., to all of which Lavina had given assenting answers.

Lavinia looked at him with surprise.

"My mother, sir? Dear me, I didn't know you were an acquaintance of mamma's."

"Oh, yes," he replied. "And I am an old acquaintance of yours, though you don't recollect me; nor had I myself any idea when I was looking at you and your mother from the pit, that you were the same little girl I used to romp with when I brought messages to your father from my lord to take to the earl. Don't you recollect me now?"

"Lord bless me! I declare it's Mr. Harvey!" said Lavina, who was evidently greatly mortified that the supposed man of consequence was after all, only the valet of Lord Melverley, though her own father had, it appeared, held the same important station with the earl.

"Yes, it is Mr. Harvey," he replied; "and very happy, I assure you, I am, to be once more among my English friends, after so many months' banishment. Indeed, it's nearly two years since I was in a London playhouse, for before that, you know, I was in Bath."

"In Bath!" repeated Grace, turning eagerly round. "Oh, then, perhaps, you were with—with——"

"I think I have had the pleasure of seeing your face there, miss," said Mr. Harvey; "or, at least," he added, very significantly, "I have known somebody that you very strongly resemble."

"Yes, yes; you must have known. But, pray, pray, do not trifle with my anxiety; tell me is she—is my——"

"Really, I should be most happy, if I could give a satisfactory answer to your question," replied the young man, in a compassionate tone; "but all I can tell you is that that person quitted *us* in Paris so suddenly that not a trace of her could be found. We had reason, however, to think that *our* old gentleman—the earl I mean—had some hand in her flight; because there was found, on her dressing table, a direction to Mr. Lovell in London, which was the name the old gentleman, when in his eccentric fits, goes by. She had, seemingly, forgot it in her hurry; but, however, it took away a good deal of *our* uneasiness; for we thought at first that she had really put her threat into execution, of making away with herself! and Paris, as I've often thought to myself, is the worst place in the world for any one that's got such a notion as that in their head; for, Lord! the French people think nothing of suicide—it's as common as eating and drinking among them. I've seen three or four bodies taken out of the Seine in a morning and carried to La Morgue—a place, miss, where they lay them out just as they find them until some of their friends or relations come to own them; and if they don't they bury them, and hang up their clothes; so that you're sure, sooner or later, if you lose a friend in that way——"

"But my sister?" said Grace in a voice of suppressed agony.

"Oh, no; nothing of that sort, I do assure you," replied the young man, "for I went every morning for more than a week to look at the bodies that were laid there, fully expecting——but, dear me! you look very pale. Had you not better come out of this warm box into the saloon; if you should faint you can have a glass of water there."

Grace would willingly have gone anywhere to get out of her present irksome situation; for, though she did not apprehend that she should faint, she was conscious that many eyes were witnessing her uncontrollable agitation; but Lavinia, in a tone of decision, immediately objected, observing,

"Miss Woodford may do as she likes, but, for my part, I shall stay where I am till ma' comes; for I'm sure she'd say it was highly improper for us girls to go out with anybody."

"I should be the last, I'm sure, to wish you to do anything improper," observed Mr. Harvey, with a smile: "but as I think it might, perhaps, be not so pleasant for Miss Woodford to meet the party your ma' is gone to speak to, I won't press her."

Grace was therefore doomed to sustain the agony that struggled for vent in her bosom, for another ten minutes; and then Mrs. Burton's return, and her look of meaning towards her (Grace), as she entered the box, rendered it impossible for the latter any longer to keep up even the appearance of comparative calmness.

"I must go home; pray let me go home!" she exclaimed, with an hysterical sob: "I can bear this no longer."

"I was just going to propose that we should go home," said Mrs. Burton, assisting her to rise. "Lavinia, do you not see Miss Woodford is ill? Do, pray help her to put on her cloak, and bring your own shawl along with you, you can put it on as you go along."

"I'm sure I shall do no such thing," replied Miss Lavinia in her most determined tone. "I'm not going to be dragged home before the play's half over."

Mrs. Burton now began one of her usual expostulations; but Grace was now incapable of hearing it, or comprehending what was was passing, for she had fainted, and when she had recovered her recollection, she found herself in the lobby, surrounded by a crowd of people, who were all eagerly administering water, volatiles, &c., while Mrs. Burton stood bewailing, in the most pathetic terms, her dreadfully unpleasant and unprotected situation, and the misery of having an undutiful child to contend with.

"Is it of this young woman, you speak, madam?" inquired a plain, matronly-looking female, who had been particularly solicitous about Grace's recovery, having, it appeared, quitted the party with whom she had been sitting in the next box, to offer her services on seeing what had happened.

"Oh, dear, no ma'am; heaven forbid! I have quite trouble enough without that, I assure you, returned Mrs. Burton in one of her most querulous tones. "This young person is no relation of mine, and, indeed, I'm very sorry that I ever consented——"

Grace opened her eyes, and Mrs. Burton, seemingly suddenly to recollect herself, assumed a tone of kindness, and inquired if she thought she could walk now to the coach, which she had sent for.

Grace replied in the affirmative. She was, indeed, most anxious to escape from the general attention which her indisposition had created, though she felt truly grateful for the assistance that had been so readily afforded her.

"Come, then, take my arm, and we'll go," observed her companion. "As to that obstinate girl, Lavinia, I've been obliged to leave her under the care of Mr. Harvey, for she's determined not to stir a step till it's all over."

"Take my arm, my dear," said the female before mentioned, who had been listening with evident surprise to what Mrs. Burton had been saying:

"I'll see you safe into the coach, if you'll give your arm; and, indeed, I've something to say to you; I want to ask you a question or two."

Grace took the proffered arm in spite of Mrs. Burton's significant nudge of the elbow, which was intended, apparently, to admonish her not to encourage the advances of strangers; but there was something so warm, and cordial, and unpretending in the look and manner of this stranger that she felt irresistibly attracted to her, and without hesitation she accepted the proffered assistance.

"That good lady," said the stranger, as they slowly descended the stairs, "tells me that you are not her daughter, and there's something in your face that so strongly reminds me of a little girl I once knew many—many miles from here, that I could almost swear ——"

"Dear, dear Mrs. Mansel," exclaimed Grace, suddenly throwing herself into the arms of the stranger. "Oh, yes, I know—I am sure ——"

"It is Grace, then, my own little Grace, as I used to call her,' said Mrs. Mansel. "Good heavens! how strange we should meet here: I thought the very moment I saw you this evening, that I knew the countenance: and now must part, as soon almost as we have met," she continued, "and I have so much to say to you, so many questions to ask, and some things, too, to tell you, that will, I doubt not, surprise you; but where are you living, Grace? or, never mind, I will give you my direction, and to-morrow, you can come to me. There is nothing to prevent that, is there? That lady ——" looking at Mrs. Burton.

"Oh, dear, I'm sure, ma'am, I don't pretend to any authority over Miss Woodford," said Mrs. Burton, comprehending, it seemed, this appeal, "I've enough to do with my own unruly children."

Grace yet clung to the arm of her new-found friend; she too, had so many anxious questions to put, and the time of suspense seemed so immeasurably long till the morrow.

"I am much better now," she observed, with timidity: could we not send away the coach, and——"

"Good gracious! how inconsistent and ridiculous that would look, Miss Woodford, after giving people such a world of trouble!" exclaimed Mrs. Burton; "besides, I really want to get home; I'm not very easy about the children; surely to-morrow will be time enough for you to see your friend, and then your time's your own."

Grace was compelled to submit, especially as Mrs. Mansel herself seemed to think Mrs. Burton's objections quite reasonable; and having given her address in the city, her warm-hearted friend shook hands with her, and returned to her party.

"Dear me, you seem quite to have forgotten every thing else but your joy in meeting with your friend, Miss Woodford," as soon as they were seated in the coach. "I'm sure I haven't yet got over my surprise and fright at your illness, but you can guess, of course, who it was that sent for me out of the box."

"I do guess," said Grace faintly; "but I do not now want to hear anything about him; the evil he has done me is past remedy, and ——"

"He is very anxious, however, to make every amends that is in his power," interrupted her companion, eagerly.

"Amends!" repeated Grace, indignantly. "Do not, for heaven's sake, repeat that word again! are you aware, Mrs. Burton, what the injury ——"

"Oh, dear, no," interrupted the latter, in a tone of extreme affectation, "of course, Miss Woodford, it wouldn't become me as a female, and the mother of a family, to enter into any discourse upon such subjects; but I can pretty well guess what it is you allude to, and I don't want any further explanation; indeed, I'd rather not hear anything about it; however, I think it my place to advise you by all means to hear what he has got to propose, before you decide."

"Heaven forbid!" exclaimed Grace, with energy—"Heaven forbid that I should ever listen, for one moment to his proposals, if he were daring enough to make any to me."

"He is very anxious about you, however," observed Mrs. Burton, "and asked me a thousand questions; and when I told that it was the earl himself that brought you to me, and that I understood he had been a great friend to you, he seemed quite struck. He said, indeed, that it was altogether a mystery he couldn't fathom, but that he supposed you could explain it."

Their arrival in the Edgward-road, interrupted the conversation, which was growing every moment more painful and irksome to Grace. The instant the coach stopped, it was surrounded by the whole tribe of noisy urchins, who had been left at home, all equally vociferous in their questions, reproaches, &c.; and Grace, anxious to escape from a scene now doubly annoying, ran forward, intending to go instantly to her own room.

In the passage, however, which was totally dark (the servant maid, having carried out into the street, to light her mistress, the only candle, it appeared, there was in the house), she was suddenly stopped, by some one seizing with gentle violence both her arms, while a well-known voice exclaimed—

"Miss Woodford—dear Grace, how unexpected————"

"Let me go!—wretch!—monster!—let me go, do not dare to speak to me, unless you can give me back my unhappy sister!" exclaimed Grace, in an agony of surprise and horror.

"Hush! hush! listen to me, Grace. Would to God it were in my power to do so, but——"

"Then I have nothing to say to you, nothing to hear from you!" exclaimed Grace, again attempting to pass towards the stairs.

Lord Frederick Melverley, however, (for by his title, and not the name of Captain Frederick, which he had assumed for such unworthy purposes, must he henceforth be recognised), forcibly withheld her, and Grace, now surrounded by the group of urchins who had transferred from their mother to her and the stranger all their attention, and assailed by Mrs. Burton's repeated remonstrances of, "Do, pray, Miss Woodford, go into the parlour?" this is not a place to talk in. Do, for my sake, go in——" suffered herself to be led into the room.

"It is precisely with the view of ascertaining where your sister is, that I have sought this interview with you," observed Lord Frederick, as soon as the door was closed; Grace, having, however, by an irresistible gesture of entreaty and command, drawn Mrs. Burton—nothing loth to have her curiosity satisfied—into the room with her.

"Listen to me patiently, Grace," he continued: "I am not going to attempt any defence of my conduct, or to plead a penitence I do not feel."

Grace darted a look of horror and indignation towards him.

"Our modes of thinking," he resumed, "are so different, I dare say, on this subject, that you think me a wretch for saying so; but the fact is, Grace, I am as sorry and as much disposed as you are to lament what has happened, since, it has been the means of so much unhappiness to yourself and others; only I do not feel that I was so entirely the blameable person, as to take upon myself a vast degree of penitence and sorrow; but I do most sincerely lament that Maria should have been foolish enough to withdraw herself from my protection."

"It is the only source of consolation—of satisfaction, that I can feel," said Grace, fervently.

Lord Frederick proceeded, without appearing to notice her interruption, "I was in hopes when I saw you first to-night that it would be in your power to give some decisive information as to the poor girl's situation, for I naturally expected that she would immediately upon her arrival in England have sought you out; and what Mrs. Burton told me, when she came to me, of your being under the protection of the earl, my father, strengthened the supposition. Your first exclamation, now, however, leads me to conclude that Mrs. Burton was right when she assured me that, from various circumstances, she was convinced that you knew nothing of your sister; but now, tell me candidly, Grace—I ask it for her sake as well as your own, not for mine, because, if you require it, and she also would wish it, I will solemnly promise never to come voluntarily into her sight again; but I trust you will deal candidly with me, and tell me what the earl has told you respecting your sister, whether he has ever acknowledged to you that he was the means of inducing her to leave me, and if so, what——"

"Lord Melverley has never mentioned my sister's name to me since, at Bath, without knowing or suspecting his relationship to the pretended Captain Frederick, I confided to him the cruel, base conduct, which had sent a mother to a premature grave, and torn from an unhappy orphan her only consolation," observed Grace, with solemn emphasis.

"But he did not know—it was not possible he could know—that it was me of whom he spoke," returned Lord Frederick, who seemed more intent on discovering from her words some clue from which he could trace the unhappy object of their solicitude than impressed by the reproof which they conveyed. "Tell me," he continued, "dear Grace, in what manner did you become acquainted with the earl? I heard the sad tale of your mother's death," he added, before Grace could reply to his question, "at Bath, whither I naturally first directed my inquiries. Some mysterious tale, too, was told me, of your clandestinely quitting the house you had so long resided in; but I was assured that it was with a female companion only; and the woman of the house, Mrs. Stevens I think you called her, was inclined evidently to accuse you of ingratitude and deception towards her, who had been, she averred, your best friend; she declared, that you were in every other respect a miracle of industry, prudence, and virtue. Not a word was then said of your acquaintance with the earl; and yet, I am inclined to think, from the woman's manner, that——"

"To what purpose is all this, sir?" said Grace. "It is true that I am under the protection of the noble-minded earl, your father. Oh! how unlike his son, who——"

"Hush! hush! Miss Woodford," interrupted Mrs. Burton, in a low whisper, pulling her sleeve at the same time, so as forcibly to arrest Grace's attention, "that's a delicate subject," she continued, in the same significant tone, and with an important shake of her head.

"Pray, Mrs. Burton, allow the young lady to proceed," said Lord Frederick, in a peevish tone; "your interruption, I assure you," he continued, "is far more annoying than anything she can say."

"I have nothing more to say, sir," observed Grace, who did not comprehend the bye-play, but was completely thrown out of what she had intended to observe. "I feel, indeed," she added after a moment's pause, "that I am degrading myself by holding any conversation with you; and I should be still more so if I were to condescend to enter into any explanations."

"Stay, Grace, I cannot allow you to go yet," said Lord Frederick, placing his back to the door, towards which Grace had moved at the conclusion of the last sentence. "I have not yet told you the purpose for which I sought this interview, and I trust you will give me a patient hearing. Your sister, if she is not under the protection of my father—which, I own, I now begin to think she cannot be, or he would undoubtedly have satisfied your mind on the subject, though, in the rigidity of his moral principles, he might have considered it improper to bring you together again. Poor Maria, I say, must, I fear, if she is living, be suffering considerable embarrassment from the want of money. She was near, too, her confinement; and I acknowledge, Grace, it has given me many a sleepless night since her departure to think that she and my child——"

Grace burst into an hysterical fit of tears, which for some moments interrupted him; and even the cold-hearted, silly Mrs. Burton seemed moved by the agony she evidently suffered, and attempted, in the best manner she could, to console her.

"Now, what I want of you, Grace, is to obtain, without, of course, naming me to the earl—for your own sake, indeed, as well as other motives, I would advise you not to do so—but I would have you, in any way that you and Mrs. Burton can invent (my old friend here," looking at Mrs. Burton, "is, I know, fruitful in stratagem), inform the earl that it has been positively stated to you that Maria left Paris, if not with him, at least under his auspices : this, indeed, I am almost positive was the tact. Whether satisfied with having detached her from me and broken up my happiness, and considering her, in his great righteousness, as one not worthy of his care, he afterwards abandoned her; or that she, disgusted at his stern uncompromising manners, which she would, I am sure, as an erring woman, towards whom he would have neither mercy nor compassion—voluntarily left him, is what, perhaps you will learn; but at all events, Grace, you will obtain a clue, if you manage well, which will enable me——"

"Not you! oh, never! never!" exclaimed Grace, with energy. "Spare yourself the trouble of any further observations," she continued; "for be assured I would not, even to purchase my instant reunion with my sister, which is all I wish, or pray, or hope for in this world—even that, I say, I would not purchase at the expense of deception towards my noble benefactor, whose kindness and care to my unfortunate mother, far more than all his benevolence to myself, will, to the last moment of my life, be constantly remembered by me with the deepest gratitude. No, be assured, I shall tell the earl openly all that I have heard, and from whom, and——"

"Oh, good God! Miss Woodford!" interrupted Mrs. Burton, with a countenance and accent of the deepest alarm; "you would not, surely, go to ruin me and my family, by telling the earl that we were at the play, and that Lord Frederick came here ! It would be the utter ruin of me, even if it was known that I spoke to him, and——but you won't—I am sure you won't be so cruel. I have not a dependence in the world beyond the paltry sixty pounds a year, that was all poor Burton had saved in his long service ; and what's to become of me and my family, if you should go and make mischief between me and his lordship, who has allowed me nearly double that sum, and all for my good-nature, and because I was willing to serve you, as I thought, and oblige Lord Frederick ?"

Mrs. Burton's tears had begun to flow, before she had half finished this appeal, and she now sobbed with apparent terror and agitation.

Grace was agitated and distressed beyond measure ; for though she was far from comprehending the whole motives of Mrs. Burton's fears at being known to hold any correspondence with Lord Frederick, she was so far aware of the earl's disposition, which his son had truly styled stern and un-compromising in his distinction of right and wrong, not to feel that this poor weak woman would be likely to be a severe sufferer, should he discover how grossly she had swerved from his known wishes.

"You have placed me in a most unpleasant situation, sir," said Grace, after a few minutes' consideration, during which Lord Frederick had watched her expressive countenance with a look of intense interest. "There is but one course left for me to pursue," she added, in a more decisive tone ; "and that is to remain altogether silent on the subject, and await the earl's own time, if he thinks it proper at all to make the communi-tion."

"And if he does not," resumed Lord Frederick, with bitterness, you will renounce your sister, and probably consign her to poverty, misery, and des-pair."

"This is cruel ! cruel, indeed !" exclaimed Grace, with deep emo-tion. "What can I do to———" she paused, unable to finish the sen-tence.

"It wouldn't be a bit cruel, and nobody would be a bit the wiser, if you'd only do as I would recommend, Miss Woodford," said Mrs. Burton, sud-denly drying her eyes, and resuming her usual alacrity of manner, when she had something to plan, or some object in view, which was to be gained by tortuous means rather than direct advances. "There would not be one bit of difficulty in it," she continued, if you'd only tell the story as I'd have you. Why can't you say that you had been out this evening, and that you accidentally met Harvey, Lord Frederick's man, whom you'd known before, and that it was him that told you all about your sister ? You needn't then bring in my name, or Lord Frederick's at all, and yet may learn all you want to know."

"It was, in fact—in reality from that person—from Mr. Harvey, that I did hear all that has since been repeated to me," said Grace, reflecting.

A thundering knock at the door interrupted the reply Mrs. Burton was about to make ; and, in an instant, Peggy the servant rushed into the room.

"Laws, ma'am ! I forgot to tell you as how the old gentleman that brought Miss here," she exclaimed, glancing at Grace, "called before you'd hardly got clearly out of the house."

"Good heavens ! I am ruined ! What did you say ? That is him at the door, as sure as fate ! What shall I do ?"

"Laws ! I never told him nothing, only as you was just stepped out, and would be back in an hour or so, and miss had gone with you," said Peggy. "Do you think I'd be so *unprudent* as to tell him you were gone to the play ? Here he is again ; I must go and let him in ;" and away she ran, evidently impressed with a wonderful sense of her own importance.

"I can go this way," said Lord Frederick, opening the door of com-munication between the two parlours. "Grace, be careful ; you know not the wretchedness, the ruin, of which you will be the cause, if you men-tion me to the earl."

Grace had little time for reflection ; it was, indeed, totally impossible for her to assume even the outward appearance of composure before the earl entered.

"I was surprised to find you out, Grace," he observed, as he entered the room. "You have been visiting, too, I perceive ;" and he glanced his eyes from Grace's dress to Mrs. Burton's fine turban, which, in her confusion and alarm, she had forgotten would betray her, and render nugatory the tale her ready invention had planned to account for her absence from home. Ever prompt at an excuse or falsehood, however, she now assumed a ready smile, and with a simper observed that she had been to pay a wedding visit to an old schoolfellow, and Miss Woodford had been so kind as to make her a little smart for the occasion, as they were people who lived in a little style.

"And has Miss Woodford been with you?" said the earl, fixing his penetrating eyes on Grace's countenance. "I must confess, from her looks I should have expected it rather to have been a funeral than a wedding visit. What is the matter with you, child?" he continued, surveying her still more minutely; "I am certain something——"

"Yes, my lord; poor Miss Woodford has been sadly agitated," interrupted Mrs. Burton, officiously; "for we unexpectedly met at my friend's a person whom she knew—at Bath, was it not, my dear?" turning herself round, so that the earl could not observe her features, and giving Grace a look which implored her not to betray her.

"I really wish, my good woman, that you would pay your visits alone," said the earl, in a tone of evident displeasure; "but who was this person, Grace? Mrs. Burton, you will, perhaps, like to retire and change your dress," he added, evidently misinterpreting Grace's faltering and inability to reply to his question to a wish not to expose too much of the former.

Mrs. Burton was evidently unwilling to quit the room: and she was, indeed, in terror lest Grace should either voluntarily or involuntarily betray the truth, which she was so anxious to conceal; and, priding herself as she did upon her ready wit and her cleverness in getting out of scrapes, she conceived that so long as she remained near it would be in her power to remedy any blunder, as she would have called it, into which Grace might fall.

It was impossible, however, to misunderstand the earl's hint to her to leave the room, and to prolong her stay would only be to draw upon herself a more direct and angry dismissal, and, with another sidelong look, therefore, at Grace, she left them together.

"And who is this person, my dear, whose appearance has so sadly shaken you nerves?" demanded the earl as soon as the door was closed.

Grace faltered out with difficulty that it was the valet of him she had known as Captain Frederick at Bath, adding in still lower and more agitated tone that she should not have recognised the man, whom she did not remember to have seen more than once or twice, when he had brought presents from——

"Yes, yes; I understand, child," interrupted the earl: "but he, I suppose, recognised you, and it is the intelligence he had to convey to you that has agitated you so, not his appearance."

Tears were Grace's only answer to this observation.

"Poor thing!" he continued in a tone of kindness; "I am sorry that this should have happened, though it has spared me from a very unpleasant task, which, strange to say, I came this very evening prepared to fulfil."

"You know, then, my lord," said Grace, timidly, "that my sister is not with——"

"I know, my child, that she quitted him in consequence of my representations, added to the neglect she had begun to experience from him— the anguish with which she beheld him devoted to another illicit, I should rather say, in its proper terms, adulterous connection. My representation of the certain and inevitable misery that attended her remaining with him was enforced by her discovering that his injured, heart-broken, but too fond and forgiving wife, had actually arrived in Paris, and was making inquiries, which must inevitably speedily be successful, to discover his place of abode."

"The prospect of meeting Lady Frederick Melverley's eye, in your sister's present degraded state, was more than she could bear. Her seducer was absent, absorbed, as usual, in a round of heartless pleasures, as he would, I suppose, call them. She had no friend, no sympathising companion to whom she could turn for support, for she could not even make herself understood in the language of those around her. Her mother's death had made, too, a deeper impression on her than I had hoped or expected, and her thoughts naturally turned to you as her only friend. I saw the impression I had made. I had introduced myself to her as the physician who had attended her mother's death-bed, and as having been charged by you to endeavour to prevail on her to return to you and endeavour, by a life of penitence and usefulness, to compensate for the past. I saw, as I said before, that she was strongly disposed to adopt the measures I suggested. She owned, indeed, that there was but one drawback—she was without money.

"How even could she raise sufficient to pay her expenses to England—how could she voluntarily throw herself on the compassion and charity of her sister, whom I represented as industriously——But I will not hurt your feelings, Grace, by dwelling on this part of my narrative. It is sufficient to tell you that I removed all scruples on this head, and with them all obstacles to her to return to you.

"I did not hazard another interview with her," continued the earl, "for I had strong motives to wish to avoid the seducer's discovering me as the instrument of her removal. I wished, in fact, to avoid him altogether—to forget, if I could, the part he had in the affair, and look only upon her as one whom it would be a blessed thing to save from destruction; but I employed a trustworthy person to manage the whole affair, if she continued firm in her determination; and, accordingly, I had the satisfaction of hearing, on the second day after my interview with her, that she had sailed in the packet from Calais, whither my agent had conducted her.

"I wrote at that moment to you, Grace, to apprise you that I had succeeded in what I had promised to try to effect, and that you might expect to see the object of your anxiety in a few weeks at farthest. That letter, of course, you never received; and that, by-the-bye, is a point on which I must have a little talk with Mrs. Freeman. Well, my dear, to return to my story. I remained in Paris longer than I at first intended; during that time I heard nothing from your sister; but that did not much surprise me, for I imagined that she was not much accustomed to writing; indeed, she had said as much; but conceive my surprise, when I arrived in London, to find that she had never called according to the direction I had given her, and that my housekeeper, to whom I had written, directing her to take all possible care of the poor girl, had never seen or heard of such a person, except from my letter.

"From that moment to this, Grace, I have never been able to trace what became of her after she arrived in London; so far did I ascertain that she travelled by the mail from Dover, and took a hackney coach from the inn at which she stopped, at the West End of the town, but there all traces ended."

Grace had listened with deep emotion and gratitude to the benevolent earl's narration, and it was scarcely concluded before she recollected what had been told her by the valet (Harvey), respecting the directions which had been left, certainly by mistake, in Maria's bedchamber, and which had been the means of betraying the part the earl had taken in quitting France. It was the loss, probably, of that direction, which had been the sole cause that her unfortunate sister was not now under the protecting care of him who had so warmly interested himself in her fate.

"How wretched might not that fate now be, unknown and unbefriended in such a place as London!"

Grace wept bitterly as she made this remark, but the earl endeavoured to console her, by observing, that if that was the real cause of her sister's not having been heard of, he still had hopes.

"At all events," he continued, "I shall now think myself bound to set on foot inquiries which I have never yet attempted, to ascertain her situation, for I will tell you candidly, Grace, that I have till now given her up in despair, believing that she voluntarily returned to the same course of life from which I had endeavoured to rescue her; however, I shall leave no stone unturned now in my endeavours to find her out, and something flatters me that I shall be successful."

The subject which had been thus started seemed so totally to have engrossed the good earl's mind, that he uttered not a word respecting Grace's present situation, except at his departure to express a hope that Mrs. Burton made her comfortable, to which of course, she was compelled to reply in the affirmative.

"Yes," he replied, "I do not doubt she will do the best she can; but don't let her persuade you, child, to gad about among her acquaintances; they may be very good sort of people, I dare say they are, but not exactly such as you should make your companions. There, there, don't make any excuses; it's natural, at your age, to like company, and to think all gold that glitters; but still, I think you have good sense enough to take a hint, and therefore I give it."

The appearance of Mrs. Burton, who, hearing the parlour door open, came to curtsey the earl out, prevented Grace's reply to this caution, and, in fact, prevented her betraying both Mrs. Burton and herself by her answer, as she was on the point of assuring the earl, with her usual ingenuousness, that she had not been introduced to any person since her residence there, forgetting what Mrs. Burton had assigned as the cause of their evening's excursion.

"Thank goodness, he's gone," said Mrs. Burton, the moment the door was closed. "I've been upon thorns all the time, for fear that thoughtless, obstinate girl, Lavinia, should come home while he was here. And there's Lord Frederick, too, locked in the back parlour; I must go and let him out."

Grace's countenance fully expressed the indignation and disgust she felt at the meanness Lord Frederick had been guilty of, in thus remaining a listener to the conversation between her and the earl.

She did not wait, however, to let him see the contempt his conduct excited; for, determined to shun all conference with one who she so heartily detested and despised, she took the opportunity, while Mrs. Burton was engaged in going round to unlock the door, to escape to her own room; from whence neither entreaties nor persuasions—and Mrs. Burton did not spare either— could induce her to come out, or even to open the door, though the latter endeavoured to prevail by sending Peggy to assure her that Lord Frederick had quitted the house.

The narrow escape which Mrs. Burton had had from being discovered by the earl, added to her conviction, which Grace's observations had enforced, that she would not again be made a party in deceiving him, prevented any repetition of such scenes as those we have described. Lord Frederick came no more, though Mrs. Burton let no opportunity slip of assuring Grace that it was entirely owing to her firm determination not to admit him, for that he had been most pressing in his entreaties; and indeed, she gave Grace to understand, that it was a considerable loss to her that she did offend his lordship, who had ever been a very generous friend to her and her family. But, though she affected to place her self-denial entirely to her (Grace's) account the latter soon discovered that it was chiefly owing to her conviction that, in encouraging the son's visits, she should be running the risk of forfeiting the father's favour.

"It is a sad thing, Miss Woodford," she observed, "that father and son should be on such terms; but I do think there never were two people that so hated the very name of each other, as the Earl of Melverley and his son."

"That the earl should feel indignant at conduct so unlike his own, I do not wonder," returned Grace; "but as to personal animosity between them——"

"Oh, you don't know what I know," she interrupted, " or you wouldn't say so; and yet, I suppose, you have heard some part of the history?"

Grace replied in the negative; she had never even known the earl by his title, but only as Mr. Lovell, till within a short time.

"Ah, that was one of his mad freaks, as my poor husband used to say," replied Mrs. Burton. "Nobody, I believe, knew the earl better than he did; and, indeed, it was likely he should, seeing he was his confidential for near five and twenty years before this young lord was even born. Ah, the earl was a very different man, then, I've heard Burton say."

"But what was it that altered him?" demanded Grace, who saw that Mrs. Burton, expected to be asked to tell the story.

"That which alters many people, my dear; an unhappy marriage," she replied. "The earl married one of the daughters of Sir William Cople-stone: she was very poor, for Sir William had ten children; but our good earl never cared in his life about money. I've heard Burton say, many a time, that he never in life saw such a handsome couple as the earl and his lady, though the earl was a good many years older than her; for she was quite a girl, not more than sixteen or seventeen, and he was more than thirty; and Burton said his mind misgave him, when he saw her gay giddy manner from the first day of their marriage, that it would not turn out a happy match. Well, it soon showed he was right. She was mad for pleasure, and fashion, and extravagance; and the earl was just the contrary. The honeymoon was hardly over, before they quarrelled, for all he doated on her; but he would not allow her to turn off all his old servants for mere whim, because their looks were not quite agreeable to her; Burton was the only person that pleased her.

" 'How in the world, Burton,' said she, can you bear to live with such a set of frights as the earl has got here?'—that was at Melverley Hall, where they went six weeks after they were married. And then she mimicked the fat, waddling, old butler, and the prim, long-necked housekeeper; and one had got too long a nose, and another too flat a one; and so she ran on; but Burton said, though he laughed, it wasn't becoming of a lady. The earl, however, wouldn't listen to her, when she talked of turning them away, and sending to London for some better-looking ones; neither would he let her pull the old hall to pieces, as she wanted. But this was nothing to what followed , for when they came up to town for the winter, he soon found he had got more than he could manage.

THE PRIDE OF THE VILLAGE;

OR,

THE FARMER'S DAUGHTERS.

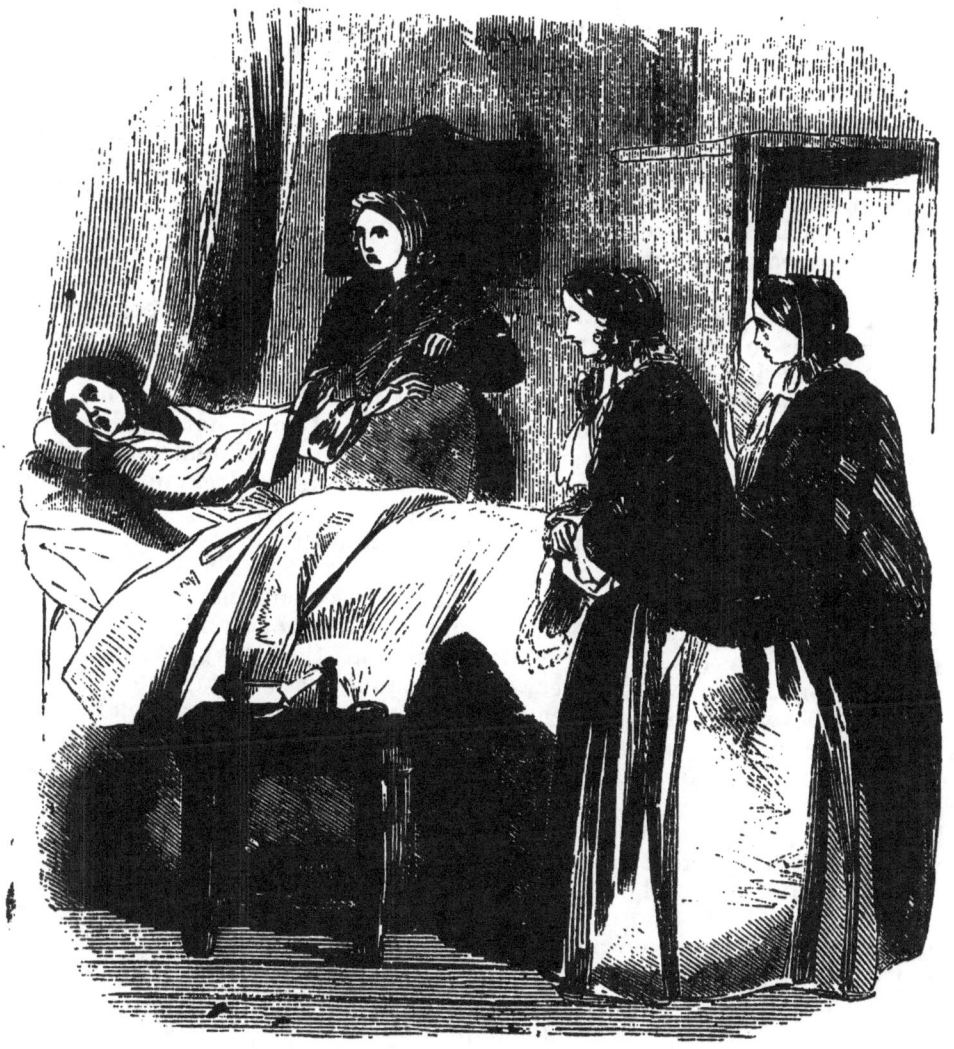

THE INVALID'S REMORSE.

CHAPTER XXXIII.

> "——even to vice
> They are not constant; changing still
> One vice, not half a minute old, for one
> Not half so old as that."
>
> SHAKESPEARE.

"It was all in vain for him to talk and look stern; she was the only person, as Burton said, that ever he knew that never seemed daunted by the earl: but she used only to laugh at his big looks, as she called them. And then she was so beautiful, and so playful, and the earl was so fond of her, that she carried it all off, let him be ever so angry; and so the house was full of company, from morning till night, and nothing was talked of but Lady Melverley's balls, and routs, and concerts, and *dejeuners*, and everything else that she could think of, to spend money. But even this the earl could have borne : but then she took to gambling, and he became outrageous, My lady set him at defiance ; and, for the rest of the winter, there was nothing but misery between them, in private : and, Burton said, if ever a man was mad, without the world suspecting it, his master was. At last came the time for going down to the hall ; and then, Burton hoped there would be a little peace between them, and that the countess would have time to think, and see her error. But, no ! for they were no sooner there, than the house was filled with her racketty sisters, and their London acquaintance ; and there was nothing but singing, and dancing, and *fetes champetres*, and acting private plays, and such like. And, indeed, when the earl was safe out, Burton said, the cards were pretty freely in play ; and often, he said, he read, in Lady Melverley's harassed countenance, the consequences of the midnight parties, when the earl thought she had been for hours in bed and asleep.

" She was in very delicate health at this time, and the earl, being very anxious for a heir to his title and estate, gave way, more than he would have done, to all her whims. She had a separate bedroom, quite away from all the rest of the house ; and many a time, Burton said, when the earl had led her to the door of her bedroom, and bade her good night, she had gone back to the riotous set in the drawing-room, and laughed at the good easy man, who was gone to his quiet bed, little dreaming how he was deceived.

" There was one visitor there that the earl particularly disliked ; he was first cousin to my lady, and a noted profligate. The earl did not know, it seems, till after their marriage, that this cousin had been a suitor to my lady ; but he was too poor to marry, over head and ears in debt, and little more than his pay as a lieutenant in the army, to keep him. Lady Coplestone, who was a very deep managing woman, soon found out what was between her daughter Eliza and young Beauchamp, as he was then called, and she manœuvred to have him sent out of the way, by getting him a captain's commission in a regiment that was stationed in Ireland.

" This broke off, it seemed, the love acquaintance, though it proved afterwards, that they kept up a correspondence, even to the very day of her marriage with the earl, and that he persuaded her to accept the earl's offer, because he said, he had no prospect of ever being able to maintain his dear Eliza, in the style she ought to be kept in.

" Well, they hadn't been married many weeks, the earl and his lady, before a rich old uncle, or some relation of his mother's died in the East Indies, and left this Captain Beauchamp all his fortune, on condition that he took the name of Paget, his name.

" You may be sure, Captain Beauchamp Paget, as he was now called, was not long before he left Ireland : he exchanged into the Guards, and then he became a constant visitor at the earl's.

" Lady Coplestone had tried hard to get him for her next daughter, Julia, and every body not in the secret thought it was Miss Julia that brought him down in the country ; and the poor girl herself thought, I believe, that she was sure of being the wife of her handsome cousin.

" The Earl could not be uncivil to him because of his connection with the family ; but he had a very bad opinion of him, and often said to Burton, that Lady Coplestone would devote her daughter to certain misery, if she married her to Beauchamp Paget, who was a heartless libertine.

"Servants, however, are generally more quick-sighted in such matters than their employers, and so it was in this case, for Burton, all along, suspected that it wasn't Miss Julia Coplestone that was the attraction, and so it proved, but I must not be beforehand with my story.

"The summer passed away, and the young heir was born; and never, I suppose, were greater rejoicings seen than upon this occasion: my lord was so delighted that he forgot every cause of complaint against her ladyship and her extravagant family. He paid all her debts that she had kept secret from him, and they were not a trifle, though he had made as handsome a settlement upon her, Burton used to say, as if she had been a duke's daughter, and brought him thousands; and he made such handsome presents to her brother and sisters; even with Captain Beauchamp Paget he was now upon friendly terms, for my lady had proposed, without his having said a word about it, to nurse the child herself, and to put off her London engagements for three or four months, that the boy might have the benefit of the country air.

"All the gay parties at the hall were, of course, broke up when my lady was confined, but it was far from dull, for Lady Coplestone and her unmarried daughters stayed to keep her company, and the earl's good spirits revived again, and he was fonder of my lady than ever, and thought, Burton used to remark, that there never was seen such a beautiful sight as the young mother and her child. Beautiful they certainly were, as far as outward beauty goes; but, as the old saying has it, 'beauty is but skin deep.'

"Well, everything went on seemingly well, though Burton said there were a good many little things that did not escape his observation, but he dared not breathe a word to the earl, for fear he should be wrong; and, indeed, it would have been a pity to have made him unhappy without a certainty; but Burton said he knew that Lady Melverley was constantly receiving letters under cover to her maid, and the maid, who was a pert, saucy, ignorant, creature, used to take such airs and liberties with her lady that nothing could account for but her being in some secret, for the countess was not a little proud and haughty to her inferiors, and would have been the last to put up with any insolence from her servants if there hadn't been some motive for it.

"The nursery maid, too, used to say that her lady often cried over the child, when she thought nobody observed her; and, altogether, Burton said, he was convinced it was a calm before a storm, and that some day or other it would come upon them in a minute.

"A whole twelvemonth, however, passed on; the boy was weaned, and the earl and countess came up to London for the winter; they had never been before since the heir was born, except for a week or two, when he was obliged to attend the House of Lords.

"Burton now fully expected it would be the same game as ever, the house filled with company from morning till night: but no, Lady Melverley seemed to have grown quite domestic, and not a single party did she give.

"The earl, of course, had his dinners now and then; but they were quite a different set to those that used to visit my lady.

"It was some time before Burton could find out what was become of Beauchamp Paget; but at last he learnt that he had gone off to Italy, leaving Miss Julia Coplestone in the lurch, and that all the family were greatly enraged against him, except my lady, who declared that she did not blame him, for that Julia had made herself quite ridiculous about him, and she did not, in her heart, believe her cousin had ever given her the slightest cause to think that he preferred her to her sisters.

"'To my single sisters, I suppose you mean,' observed Julia, spitefully.

"This was said in the earl's hearing, and the consequence was that Miss Julia was all but expelled the house from that time, not that the earl applied it to my lady particularly, for there were three of the Miss Coplestones now married, and the insult was, as he said, applicable to any of them.

"Altogether, indeed, there was a great coolness between my lady's family and her; but this might be because she lived what they called a humdrum life now, to what she had done.

"Well, the London season was almost over, and the earl, who had been a good deal fagged with public business, for he'd been appointed to some place, I forget what, then was beginning to talk of going down into the country again, and orders had been sent down to New Place, another of the earl's seats, to clean and ornament, and so on, for their reception. My lady seemed quite willing and contented to go, in public, that is to say, when the earl talked about it; but Burton said, her maid's hints, and her own low spirits told a different story in private, and still the secret letters came; and now he was more than ever convinced they were from that wretch Paget, for they were foreign letters, though the maid, when hints and jeers were thrown out among her fellow-servants, accounted for it, by saying that her brother was gone out groom with a young gentleman that was travelling on the Continent.

"'Are you quite sure it's your brother? it isn't your cousin, is it?' said the housekeeper, who had never forgotten or forgiven her ladyship's ridicule of her long neck and sallow complexion, when first she became her mistress. Burton used to say, 'Once tell a woman that she is ugly, and she is your enemy for ever, there's nothing else that a woman can't forgive;' but I'm forgetting my story.

"It was not above three weeks after this remark that the nurse, who had never seen Beauchamp Paget, began to whisper to one of the footmen, who was her sweetheart, that she never now went out airing with her lady and the child, but they were met soon after they left the carriage, which was always at the park gate, by a very handsome, tall man, who seemed very fond of the child, and always walked with them in the most retired part of the park, or Kensington Gardens.

"She often observed, too, that Lady Melverley was crying, as they walked on before her, and her lady had even condescended to tell her not to mention at home that they had met any one, and enforced the request by giving her a guinea to buy a new gown.

"Thomas, the footman, had lived too long with the earl to be easy under this secret; besides, he had been one of the servants whom her ladyship had insisted upon discharging, because she said he had two odd legs, and he had never forgotten this obligation. How little do ladies and gentlemen foresee the ill-consequences of making themselves disliked by the people about them. Well, the nurse's tale was told to Burton, but he determined to make sure before he said a word, and so, accordingly the moment my lady drove off, as usual, with the nurse and child, away went Burton, close behind them in a hackney coach, which he had ready waiting, a few doors down the street.

"I've heard him say he could'nt have felt more if it had been me he was going to watch; but he wasn't long in suspense as to who it was, for just as he was getting out of the coach at Knightsbridge Gate, who should dash past, as fast as he could go up the road, but Beauchamp Paget on horseback, with a groom behind him.

"Lady Melverley had got out of her carriage, and was walking quickly up the park with the nurse and child, so Burton saw the plan was for her gallant to leave his horse with the groom at the barracks, and then meet her.

"He kept her in his eye, and walked slowly on at some distance behind her, and sure enough it proved just exactly as he thought ; and so then, without ceremony, for he was a bold man, especially when he knew he was in the right, he quickened his pace, and got round so as to come right in front of them before they got to the gardens. They did not at first see him, for they were leading the little boy between them, and both so attentive to him that they did not observe anything else ; but the moment the little boy set eyes on Burton, of whom he was very fond, he began to pull his hands away from them and shout with all his little might to go to him.

"Burton declared, bold as he was, he was ready to sink when the lady lifted her eyes up to him. She tried to look unconcerned and smile, but she turned all manner of colours.

"' Is anything the matter, Burton ? ' she at last faltered out ; ' did the earl send you here?'

"' No, my lady,' he replied, very shortly ; ' but, shall I attend your ladyship to the carriage ?'

"He'd got the little boy in his arms by this time.

"' You will finish your walk, Eliza,' said her companion, with all the cool impudence imaginable.

"She hesitated, and then looked at Burton, whose looks betrayed, I dare say, all he felt.

"' No, I think I had better go home," she replied ; ' I have walked far enough.'

"' Well, at all events, I shall attend you to the carriage,' said Paget, still trying to face Burton down by his proud looks. ' Mr. Burton, your services are not required ; Lady Melverley is safe under my protection."

"Burton, however, still walked on, with the child in his arms ; and, before they reached the place where the carriage stood, Paget turned round to Burton ; Lady Melverley had been whispering to him for some minutes.

"Burton, I want to speak to you,' he observed ; turn back with me a few minutes ; Mrs. Nurse will take the child.'

"No, sir ; excuse me, there is nothing to learn from you which I can listen to,' said Burton ; ' my duty is to attend my lady and my master's child.'

"Burton said he should never forget the sneer that was on the wretch's face that minute.

"' Well, Mr. Burton, you know your own affairs, best,' he observed ; ' but, I suspect, you'd have been none the worse for a little more civility to me. Eliza, I shall call on the earl, in an hour or two ; and I shall certainly congratulate him on possessing the most impertinent valet, or steward, whichever Mr. Burton calls himself, I ever met with.'

"Burton said, in spite of all this bravado, he knew well that the wretch had no intention of calling ; but his mind was made up, if he did, how to act.

"Not a word passed between the countess and my husband. He handed the child into the carriage to the nurse, and then came home, melancholy enough, as he said, to think that it should be his duty to break up all his lord's happiness, by telling him what he had seen.

"Determined, however, to be very cautious, he began by observing, while the earl was dressing, being engaged out to a dinner party, that he had been much surprised at seeing Captain Beauchamp Paget had arrived from Italy.

" 'You are surprised, I suppose, Burton, that he does not come here?' said the earl, who was used to talk to Burton quite familiarly ; ' but the fact is I have taken care to let him know my doors would be closed against him.'

" Burton did not know what to say to this. He was afraid of going too far at once, and yet he knew he ought not to keep secret what he'd seen. However, before he could make up his mind, a note was brought to the earl, something of consequence, that took up all his attention ; and so Burton thought he would put off all he had got to say till his lordship should be going to bed.

" The countess was engaged that night to go with a party to Drury Lane Theatre ; and, accordingly, there would be plenty of time, Burton thought, to tell his story before she came home.

" Well, my dear, the earl came home, as usual, early from his party ; and then Burton summoned up courage to say that he hoped his lordship wouldn't take it amiss what he had done, as he only did it out of regard to his (the earl's) honour.

" So then he told all about seeing the captain with his lady, and how he had acted.

" The poor earl was thunderstruck ; for it seemed my lady had been so hypocritical as to pretend quite to approve of the earl's resolution not to invite her dissipated cousin to the house.

" ' I will not see her to-night, Burton,' said he ; ' so, if she inquires when she returns, say I have gone to bed indisposed. I will consult my pillow before I resolve how to act ; and in the meantime I trust to you, Burton, not to mention to anyone what you have seen.'

" Burton, of course promised he would not ; but he could have told the earl that it would be of little use his holding his tongue, when every servant in the house was talking of their lady's imprudence.

" Well, the earl went to bed ; and, of course, Burton didn't stay up long, for it wasn't his place to sit up for his lady. But I should have told you that Lady Melverley's maid had gone away that morning, having quarrelled, as she pretended, with her lady. And, indeed, it seemed nothing strange that her ladyship had discharged her, for such a bold, pre-suming, insolent creature could scarcely be found in London as she was ; and Burton said his only surprise was that she left without betraying any of the secrets that he knew she was trusted with ; however, that was all explained after.

" Well, to go on with my story. One of the upper housemaids had helped the countess to dress for the theatre that night, and she was ordered to sit up for her ladyship in her dressing-room.

" Poor Hannah! I shall never forget her. She told me afterwards that she tried to keep herself awake after twelve o'clock was passed—and the house was all quiet—first with one thing, and then the other; but it was all in vain. She had been very hard at work in the day, and so when she did fall asleep in the large arm-chair nothing could hardly have aroused her. Never was any poor creature more startled, she said, when she awoke, to see the sun shining through the window-curtains, and see by the timepiece on the table that it was seven o'clock, which was her usual time of getting up in the morning.

" Her first thought was that her lady had undressed herself and gone to bed without waking her; and she felt her cheeks grow as red as fire with shame and vexation, because she had fully hoped and expected that, by pleasing the countess with her cleverness and attention she should be promoted to be lady's maid herself; but after looking round her a minute, she found everything the same as it was the night before : and so then she stole on tiptoes to the bedchamber and peeped through the keyhole ; and, sure enough the bed had never been slept in. So she bustled about, and put her cap to rights, expecting every instant to hear her lady at the door ; but another half hour passed, and then she thought proper to venture downstairs, and see who was up, and hear whether any message had been received from her lady that she was not coming home, or anything. But no ; the porter had not heard a word : the carriage had been sent home from the theatre, because Lady Melverley intended to sup at her friends, and they would see her home ; and that was all he knew, for he had been asleep, too, all night, in his great leather chair, by the hall fire.

" Well, they were talking, when Burton came in the hall, being just risen ; and the moment he heard what they were talking about, his mind misgave him, as he said, that something was wrong.

" What to do he didn't know ; but just at that minute the earl's bell rung.

" ' What time did your lady return last night, Burton ?' he demanded. I never heard her ; and yet I could have sworn that I never slept the whole of the night. I have been thinking, indeed, of what you told me last night ; and I have come to the resolution that the wisest plan would be———— but what's the matter, Burton, my good fellow—you look agitated and perplexed ?'

" My lady, your lordship—my lady has not been home at all since yesterday evening.'

" Out of bed started the earl ; and, Burton said, he could scarcely stand to get his clothes.

" ' Quick, Burton ; my great coat,' were the first words he uttered.

" ' Won't your lordship be pleased to have the horses put to the carriage ?' said Burton, for he said he was frightened at the earl going out alone in the state he was in.

" ' No, no carriage,' he replied. ' And yet you are right, Burton ; you are right ; it will look better if, as God grant, there is nothing more than folly in the case.'

" Burton knew what he meant was that if she had been induced by some of her dissipated companions to stay till that time in the morning, it would save appearances to have the carriage, as if he had merely called to take her up ; but, Lord bless you ! she had never been near Mrs. Collumpton's, where she said she was going to sup ; nor had she staid with them more than half an hour at the theatre, but, under pretence of indisposition, had left them to go, as she said, home.

" Never was seen such a distressed house, Burton said, as theirs now was. The earl was at first raving ; and if it hadn't been for the constant watch Burton kept over him, and his taking care that no instruments of destruction should be left in his way, he would certainly have put an end to his life, or have done some mischief to those about him, for he was completely insane as ever any lunatic that was shut up in Bedlam.

" This lasted for nearly three weeks, and all this time not a word was heard of the countess, except that Burton ascertained that she had left London in a travelling equipage with the captain, and it was supposed they had gone to the Continent.

" At length the earl began to grow more rational and composed ; and almost the first proof he gave that he was coming to his perfect senses, was his asking to see his child—his poor deserted boy, he called him, as he wept over him.

"Burton declared he never was so hurt in his life as to see the earl shed tears; for he was such a stern man, that they seemed unnatural like to see him: however, it appeared that they did him good, for he became quite calm and composed afterwards, though he never got rid of his melancholy from that day. I never saw him smile, indeed, since; nor I don't think any one ever did, except it is a bitter kind of smile, that means anything but mirth. But, let me see, what was I telling you? Oh, about the child. Well, from that time his whole thoughts seemed fixed on the boy.

"'Thank God, he is a boy,' he used to say to Burton; 'for if it had been one of the other sex, I should have hated the child.'

"He used to sit for hours, Burton told me, watching the child and seeming to forget everything else on the face of the earth.

"All this time he would never see or correspond with her mother or sisters; for, I think, he considered they were to blaim in concealing from him so much as they had done.

"Well, at least it was discovered that Lady Melverley and her wicked companion were living together abroad—in Switzerland, I think it was; and so then the earl immediately set off after them, intending, no doubt to challenge the man who had destroyed his happiness, and brought such disgrace upon his name; but the captain, it seemed, got information of his coming, and, like a coward as he was, got out of his way.

"For five years the earl continued to travel abroad, expecting some time or other to meet with him; but so it happened, that though he was often in their very track, he never could come up with them. I suppose by this time his fiery rage got pretty cooled down, and he returned to England. I should have told you, though, that he had succeeded in getting a divorce from his lady; and now, as he told Burton, he had nothing left to occupy his thoughts but the boy, whom he had not seen all the five years he had been on the Continent, and who was now grown a fine boy, between seven and eight years old, and was under the care of a clergyman and his wife, distant relations of his lordship.

"'Never,' said Burton, 'shall I forget the earl's look when the boy, who had been taught to expect his arrival, came running down the gravel-walk in front of the house to meet him.'

"'Papa,' said the boy, holding out his hand, with a pretty, graceful attitude —'papa, you are welcome to England.'

"The earl sank back in the corner of the carriage.

"'Is this my child, Burton?' said he. 'Look at him! Does he resemble me? Tell me!' and he grasped Burton's arm with such a force as to make him ready to cry out. 'Who is that boy like?'

"'He is very like the countess—his mother, I should have said, my lord,' said Burton, though he knew very well what his lordship meant; for, he said, never in his life did he see such a striking likeness as between the boy and Captain Beauchamp: his every look and feature were his, and just the same bold confidence in his manner of carrying himself and of speaking.

"'It is false!' exclaimed the earl, with great violence. 'There is not a single trace there of the adulteress: but of him—of him —— oh, God, how have I been deceived!—how have I deceived myself! My last hope is gone!

"Burton did not dare say a word in contradiction; but he begged of the earl to recollect himself, and not suffer the clergyman and his wife, who were now coming forward to meet him, to see that he was so discomposed.

"The earl acknowledged Burton was right.

"'Yet, how can I ever look on that child without shuddering?' he exclaimed. 'And he must be the heir to my estate, too!—the spurious issue of the villain who now laughs at me, and hugs himself in the consciousness that the offspring of his guilt is —— unnatural wretch! why did she not take his child with her, and at once open my eyes to the truth, that it had no right to call me father?'

"Never, perhaps, even in the first discovery of the countess's guilt, had the earl suffered so severely as now. He never turned his eyes upon the child without betraying disgust and abborrence; and the boy, not finding himself treated with the kindness he expected, soon learned to dislike his supposed father as much as he did him.

"The earl did not remain long, however, in this miserable constraint; but having settled that the child should remain with the clergyman, Mr. Murray, he left the country again, and from that time till my poor Burton died, the son and his supposed father had never met. Burton, however, had seen him, and he declared, that there needed no other confirmation than his looks and the tone of his voice, to tell whose son he really was."

"And is the countess still living?" inquired Grace, who had listened with the deepest interest to this circumlocutory narrative.

"Yes, the captain married her after the divorce, and they lived together for some time in great splendour," returned Mrs. Burton; "and the earl was still more set against his son, as he was obliged to call him, by hearing that he was in the habit of associating with them. It had altogether, indeed, such an effect upon my lord, that it is doubtful even now whether he is perfectly in his senses. Often and often he has left home, without even a single servant—since poor Burton died, he has never trusted and confided in any one as he did him—and no living creature has known where he has gone, or what become of him, for weeks and months together; but Mrs. Beauchamp, as she is called now, is sadly fallen of late; the captain died wretchedly poor, for he was a regular gambler and the greatest profligate that ever existed; and often enough, I dare say, she has repented that she gave up title, and wealth, and character for one who, according to all accounts, never tried to make her amends for these sacrifices."

CHAPTER XXXV.

"Yet I curse thee not in sadness—
Still I feel how dear thou wert;
Oh, I could, not, e'en in madness,
Doom thee to thy just desert

"Yes, 'tis useless to upbraid thee
With thy past or present state,
What thou wast, my fancy made thee—
What thou art, I know too late."

—BYRON

NOTWITHSTANDING the Earl of Melverley's persevering and incessant endeavours to discover the retreat of the hapless Maria, three months passed over without their being rewarded with success.

During these three months Grace had remained an inmate of Mrs. Burton's, and disagreeable as that residence had in the first instance been, sh felt too grateful for the earl's kind intentions in placing her there to suffer him to think that she was not perfectly contented.

Mild and unassuming, indeed, as Grace really was, she had, by the mere exertion of good sense, and the assumption of a little spirit, succeeded in making her situation far more comfortable than it had at first promised.

The unruly boys, who had so tormented their yielding mother, and every one else they came in contact with, were, in compliance with Grace's persuasions, sent to school; the little girls, who were really good-tempered and docile, Grace took upon herself to manage and instruct. Her personal exertion and example, too, introduced comparative regularity and industry into the habits of the family, and Mrs. Burton herself acknowledged that even independent of the handsome sum which she received for her board, the earl's introduction of Miss Woodford had been a real blessing to her.

But Grace, though thus endearing herself to, and conferring happiness on all with whom she was connected, was still far from happy, or even comfortable, herself. The past still presented nothing but melancholy images, the future was shrouded in uncertainty; and even in her present situation, she felt there was nothing permanent on which she could rest, nothing but what caprice or some other motive on the part of her benefactor, might in an instant deprive her of.

Of Belgrave Mansel she had never, from the time of her leaving Bath, heard the slightest intelligence, and often, in the many solitary hours she spent in her own apartment, did she sit lost in melancholy retrospection of the events which had separated them, as it appeared, for ever, and wondering, indeed, if he were still living, whether he ever thought of her, or whether some new attachment had banished all remembrance of her from his mind.

"If I knew that he was happy," she would say, with a deep sigh, "If I could see him restored to his home, his character re-established, and his happiness secured by an union with one who knew how to value his worth, I could—yes, I think I could be content to know that he had forgotten that such a person as Grace had existed."

The flood of tears which generally followed this heroic declaration, however, proved that Grace overvalued her own resolution, and she was obliged to fly to active employment to dissipate the melancholy which these reminiscences occasioned.

From the period when she had suffered such uneasiness from the consequence of their visit to the theatre, Grace had stedfastly declined entering into any similar gaities with Mrs. Burton and her daughter; and, indeed, for a considerable period had confined herself almost entirely to the house from an apprehension of encountering Lord Frederick, whom she had so many reasons to avoid.

He had, however, now again quitted London, for Harvey, who had diligently cultivated his acquaintance with Miss Lavinia from the time he had met her at the theatre, had taken his leave, and did not expect to return, he said, until the following summer.

Relieved, therefore, of all fear on that head, Grace occasionally indulged herself and her two little grateful pupils with a ramble in Hyde Park, at those hours when it is considered unfashionable, and therefore, was nearly empty.

On one of these occasions she had suffered the children to run on a considerable distance before her, and was herself carelessly sauntering along, when they came running back, both in one breath entreating her to give them some halfpence, of which they had made her the treasurer, that they might relieve a poor woman with a little baby in her arms, who was sitting on the grass, and looked so thin and pale, they said, that they were sure she wanted relief very badly.

Pleased to find that her lessons, inculcating pity and benevolence, had not been unheeded by the children, Grace readily gave them what they required, and adding to it sixpence of her own, suffered them to scamper off with it, to carry it to the poor creature, whom she could just discern sitting in a disconsolate attitude some distance from the path.

She does not look as if she sat there to beg, thought Grace, for there are few who would see her even there; and with some slight apprehension that the children might, in their chraitable zeal, perhaps, hurt the feelings of the woman, who, though poor and dejected, might be above receiving alms, she hurried her pace to overtake them.

It was too late, however, for she saw them both approach the object of their compassion, to whom they timidly offered their little alms.

Grace saw her start and raise her eyes as if to thank them, and then clasping her child closer to her breast, she seemed to give way to a burst of agony.

"The poor woman *is* crying so, Miss Woodford," said Louisa, the elder, as they turned back to meet her; "and she couldn't speak a word when we gave her the money. Oh, poor thing, I am so sorry for her; and the baby is so thin and pale."

"Hush! hush!" said Grace, for they were now close to her, and she feared their remarks might distress the poor creature, whom she approached and addressed with the utmost gentleness.

Scarcely, however, had she uttered the first words of the inquiry she was about to make, when the young woman started and uttered a faint scream.

"Grace—Maria—my sister—my poor sister," broke simultaneously from them, and in an instant they were locked in each other's arms, for Grace had instantly thrown herself down by her sister, who was unable, from weakness and agitation, to rise.

It was long before either of them could give utterance to a coherent sentence; but the frightened looks of the two little Burtons and the curious stare and observations of several persons who had stopped to look at, without comprehending, the affecting scene at length recalled Grace to something like composure, and reminded her of the necessity of making an effort to remove her sister at once from her present situation.

"You must come home with me, dear Maria," she whispered. "It is not very far; you can lean on me, and——"

"I will carry the baby. Do let me carry it, Miss Woodford? I will be very careful," exclaimed both the little girls in a breath.

Grace placed the infant in the arms of the eldest girl, and then endeavoured to lift her sister from the ground.

"I cannot go, Grace, till William comes," said Maria, seeming suddenly to recollect herself. "He has promised to come here to me and——"

"William!—what William? Who do you mean, my dear Maria?" demanded Grace, who from her sister's look and manner believed that her mind was wandering.

"I mean William Mansell," she replied, looking down. "Oh, Grace," and she burst into tears, "how hard it is for me to be depending on one I used so cruelly, even for a morsel of bread; and yet but for him I must have perished, and my poor child, too; and now I'm afraid even that last stay is gone, for poor William has exhausted everything, and since yesterday neither he or I have had anything to eat."

Grace clasped her hands in agony.

"What shall I do?" she exclaimed. "You will, indeed, perish if you remain here long? Where is William gone, and why did he leave you here?"

"Because I had no place to go to," returned the poor girl, in a disconsolate tone. "They would not suffer me to sleep in the room he had taken for me last night, because he could not get money to pay them for the last week, and we have walked about all night, until I am so weary that I felt as if I could lay down and die here after he had left me. I do not know where he has gone," she continued, looking wildly round her; "but he told me he would bring me relief if it cost him his life. Ah!" she exclaimed, uttering a faint scream of joy, "there he comes; look how he is hurrying, though he is ill, and so weak that he can scarcely walk."

Grace looked in the direction her sister's eyes had taken, and all doubts of her sanity vanished, for it was, indeed, William Mansell, who, with breathless haste, and with the deepest anxiety and eagerness imprinted on his countenance, was making towards her.

"I have brought you nourishment, Maria!" he exclaimed, sinking down quite exhausted on the grass by her side, and at the same time producing a small loaf and bottle.

"This is wine," he continued, eagerly holding it to her lips. "I thought that would revive you more than anything else."

"But you want it yourself, William. How dreadfully pale you look. Oh, you are killing yourself, and for me, too—for one so unworthy of your kindness ————" And Maria leant upon his shoulder and sobbed bitterly.

"No, no; I am well—quite well. Eat, pray eat, Maria. Oh! how long the time has seemed since I left you, and what dreadful thoughts have come into my mind!" exclaimed William.

At this moment he raised his eyes casually to Grace, who, unable to speak, had been attentively regarding this affecting scene.

Until then he appeared totally unconscious that any one was present but the object of his intense anxiety, but at the sight of Grace's pale and agitated features a flush of deep crimson suffused his brow.

"I did not expect to meet you here," he observed, with peculiar emphasis, turning away at the same time with a look of cold contempt, and again holding the bottle to Maria's lips, with an earnest entreaty not to spare it, for it would do her good.

"Take it, Maria, that you may gain strength to leave this humiliating scene," he continued, in a lower voice. "I have got sufficient to enable you to return to your lodging, for the present, at least, and we will trust in God for the future; he has not deserted us in this, our bitterest extremity, and——"

"William, dear William, what is this misunderstanding on your part towards me?" interrupted Grace, at last regaining power to speak, as she saw him, after wrapping the thin shawl which had fallen off her sister's shoulders, preparing to assist her to rise.

"Misunderstanding!" he repeated, turning round and fixing his eyes upon her with sternness. "No, Grace, there is no misunderstanding; you could not have misunderstood the motive of application to you—you could not, dare not for a moment suppose that it was for myself I appealed to your humanity. No, not to save my existence would I have consented to accept from your hands—— Well, well, it is no matter now, she for whose sake I stooped to solicit from you——"

"You are condemning me without reason, William," interrupted Grace ; never, until this moment, have I heard of your applying to me ; but this is not a place to enter into explanations. Is it far to the place you spoke of ?—will it not be better that you should go home with me? You can have no great inducement, I suspect, to return to a habitation where you have been treated with such barbarity."

"Maria, of course, can do as she pleases," he returned, coldly ; "and, indeed, I should, perhaps, be doing wrong to advise her not to accept your invitation."

"But you will come, too, William?" said Maria, anxiously.

"Certainly not, Maria. I am not yet fallen so low, that I can consent to become a mere dependent on your sister's——"

"Not upon me, William?" hastily interrupted Grace, unconscious of the harsh term with which he was about to conclude the sentence. "I am, indeed," she added, "at this moment, a dependent myself upon the charity of one—the most noble and liberal of all created beings—one who will be as much rejoiced at this meeting as I am. When I tell you, Maria, that it is the Earl of Melverley, the same person to whom you were indebted for——"

"The Earl of Melverley !" repeated William. "That was not the person under whose protection—to use the phrase which, I suppose, will suit your ears the best, though I should give a different name to the connection : but certainly that was not the title ; it was a Sir George somebody with whom I saw you in——"

"Good heavens ! how cruelly have you misconstrued my situation !" interrupted Grace, bursting into tears. "And you, too, above all, William, from whom I should have expected the utmost candour and charity !"

"I judged only from what I was told, and from what I saw," returned William, hastily ; "but even allowing—which God grant—that your situation was misrepresented, and that you are free from blame on that head, what excuse, what plea can you offer for your cruel indifference to your sister's situation, your unfeeling repulse to my frenzied application to you on her behalf, at a moment when she needed every kindness and attention ? I have thought of that moment, Grace, till my blood has run cold, and my head turned dizzy, to think that a life of guilty splendour and indulgence could have so hardened a heart, which I used to think the kindest and gentlest that nature ever formed. But, why should I wonder at anything, when I feel how altered I am myself ?" he added, in a tone of bitterness.

"You are indeed altered, William," returned Grace with mildness. "Strangely altered you must be, when you could thus implicity believe all you have said respecting me, without having seen me, and heard from my own lips that I was become the worthless wretch you represent me. Nothing less than that, William,—nothing but your own avowal would have convinced me you was base, and vile, and heartless ; and I should have thought that you would not have condemned me without equally undeniable evidence. But we will say no more of that, now ; I shall be easily able to convince you that you have wronged me, hereafter ; at present, let us be thinking of getting to some place of shelter : that is, if you still believe my home to be one which it would be disgraceful to you or my sister to enter."

"I will believe that it is not, Grace : in spite of my own senses, I will believe you," said William, after gazing earnestly in her face for a few seconds, as if he knew he could read, in that eloquent countenance, the heart of which it was the index.

"It is for your own sake, rather than mine, I wish you to do so," replied Grace, with calmness, as she passed her arm around her sister's waist ; and leaning on William on the other side, Maria commenced her slow journey to the gate of the park, from which Grace had recollected they could take an hackney coach for the remainder of the way.

CHAPTER XXXVI.

"———— ——————— Upon her cheek
The story lived ; you may plainly read
The burning characters : shrinking shame was there—
Beseeching looks—painful humility ;
And from her face was gone—hope, save when she
Glanced in petitioning beauty to the skies
Seeking relief or pardon."
                                        BARRY CORNWALL.

IT was many hours after this meeting, before either Grace or her sister had acquired sufficient calmness to enter into a particular account of what had passed during their separation from each other.

The death of her mother, which Maria had heard of, of course, from the earl, whom she had known, however, only by the name of Lovell, and as the medical attendant upon her during her last illness, seemed now fresh revived by their meeting ; and Maria, with bitter tears, bewailed her fate, in having been absent at the awful period.

It was in vain that Grace assured her over and over again, that her mother had never spoken of her but with the kindest affection. Conscious how little she had deserved it, the poor girl could not believe but that the mother whom she had so deceived must have thought of her with aversion, and spoke of her with detestation.

It needed but little, however, on the part of Grace, to convince William that she had been most grossly misrepresented ; but her feelings could scarcely be described when she learnt that, previous to her having seen him at the window, William had discovered her residence, having met her and Mrs. Freeman in the street, and followed them home.

"Conscious that my appearance was not such as could confer any credit on females dressed as you were," he continued, sighing heavily, "I did not attempt to speak to you ; and, I will confess to you, too, Grace, that I was not much prepossessed in favour of your companion. The house too, into which I traced you, was, I thought, dubious ; and the result of my inquiries in the neigbourhood confirmed that impression.

"I was told that the woman who kept the house was of infamous character ; but that, having been threatened by her neighbours with punishment, she had become lately more cautious, and now kept her house comparatively decent and quiet.

" ' She has got, however, one of her old lodgers back again, I see,' observed the man from whom I learnt this ; ' and they have got too, with them, I see, a pretty-looking, innocent girl, who, I suppose, they have trepanned into their snares.'

"I need not tell you Grace, how my heart bled at this account ; but while I was talking, a gentleman in a curricle, with two grooms, drove up to the door of your residence, which was immediately opposite the little shop in which I was standing.

"'That is the gentleman who is the present supporter of the house, I believe,' observed the man; 'at least, I do not see any other visitor there, thought I do not know which of the ladies is under his protection, as they call it, for he takes them both out with him: for myself, I should naturally judge it is the young one, only my wife will have it that he is the same person that used to be here three years ago, with the eldest.'

"'And so it is,' observed the wife, who had heard our conversation, and now came out of the little back room. 'I'll take my oath,' she continued, 'that it is the same: he is a Sir George somebody, and came to a great fortune about that time. But for all that, though, I've heard from the woman that chares in the house, and came in here yesterday for hearthstone and some other things, that it is the young one that is the favourite, and he has brought her up from Bath, where they say she has got very respectable friends.'

"How could I doubt after this, Grace? I left the place with a heavy heart, but I dared not tell Maria what I had learned; for, in the midst of all her own sorrows, it had been a constant subject of comfort and consolation to her, that she knew Grace, whatever might be the difficulties of her circumstances, would never have any cause to reproach herself, or to feel that she had deserved to suffer.

"How often, indeed, had she reproached herself with not having listened to Grace's advice, with not having followed Grace's example; but to return to my story.

"Within a few days of my having seen you, Maria was taken ill; she had previously given birth to that poor child."

William cast down his eyes, and for a moment was unable to continue his narrative.

"The difficulties and privations she had at that time suffered had greatly weakened her, and she now was seized with fever, which for some time appeared likely to close the scene of her troubles.

"It was with difficulty I had been enabled to struggle on till this time, but I had now exhausted, as I believed, every resource; and, alas! I found that with the means of paying for it, had vanished all the compassion and sympathy which those persons among whom we had been thrown had hitherto affected towards us.

"Hour after hour I sat by her bedside, without the means of alleviating her sufferings. One kind creature, indeed, there was in the house, who took charge of the child, and suffered it to share the nourishment of her own little one; but she was nearly as poor as ourselves, or, at least she had nothing to spare from her own family.

"It was in consequence of her repeated inquiries whether my———— whether Maria had no female relations living in London, that I at last formed the desperate resolution of applying to you, and making known her situation.

"I wrote a hurried, incoherent note, in which I merely stated that your sister was ill, probably dying, and in great distress; and adding to it her address, I sent the person I have mentioned to the house at which I had seen you: but imagine my feelings when she returned, and, putting five shillings in my hand, told me that the lady to whom the note was addressed had read it, and said she was very sorry, but that the person had brought all her troubles on herself, and that was all she (Miss Woodford) could do for her.

"And could you, did you for a moment believe that it was in my nature to act so?" observed Grace, in a tone of gentle reproach.

"I take shame to myself that I did believe it," returned William;

"but oh, Grace! how can you wonder that I should believe anything, after all I have suffered, all that I have seen!"

"There was a time," he continued, rising and walking across the room with vehement agitation, "that I would have staked my existence on your sister's purity and truth. Even when she treated me with scorn and cruelty, I attributed all to the evil councils and advice of her mother. I believed her own heart to be well disposed, and free from guile as an infant's; and yet, you see, she deceived that mother and me! Oh, me! how has she ruined, destroyed me for ever!"

"Do not say so, William," said Grace, soothingly; "you have pardoned her; she has repented, bitterly repented for her errors, and ——"

"Yes, she has repented, because their consequences have proved so different to what she anticipated," he exclaimed, turning with a look of almost fierceness upon Grace; and then, hiding his face with his hands, burst into tears.

"Grace," he resumed, after a few moments' silence, "I am a miserable, unhappy wretch! I cannot exist without your sister, and yet with her I am wretched; for never can I forget that she voluntarily deserted me, that she has been ——"

"Hush! she will hear you," interrupted Grace. Maria was sleeping, overcome with fatigue and exhaustion, on a temporary bed which Mrs. Burton, with ready kindness, had made up on some chairs in the back parlour.

"Ah, she knows but so well what are my feelings," returned William, sighing deeply; "but what were we speaking of, Grace? Oh, I know but I have little more to say on that subject, it was your supposed cruelty and apathy towards your sister; but tell me, Grace, what could be the motive of that woman preventing my letter reaching you, as it is now evident she did?"

Grace replied by as briefly as possible detailing the circumstances of her connection with Mrs. Freeman, and the manner in which the latter had previously acted in intercepting the letters which had been addressed to her (Grace) from the earl.

"Probably," she continued, "she was fearful that if I saw my sister, her unwarrantable conduct might be discovered; and, at all events, I suppose she was anxious to keep me entirely in her power. But now, William, that this matter is perfectly explained, for I am sure you do not doubt me, and if you do you will not when you see my kind benefactor, and hear from him——"

William would have spoken, but she gently prevented him.

"Well, well, we will say no more on that head, now, William; what I am anxious to hear is, by what means you and Maria met, and how, indeed, you came to be in London at all."

"I will tell you then, candidly, Grace, the whole story," he replied. "You cannot but believe that I was distracted, when I first learned you had quitted Llan——; for some time, indeed, I was totally unable to attend to business; but the remonstrances of my uncle Meredith, and the jeers of my companions, who could have but little sympathy with my feelings, at length roused me. I tried to forget her, and sometimes, too, I tried to believe that some unforeseen circumstance would restore her to me again, and that we should be happy together. In this manner six months passed away. I got well, as to health, though my mind was still wretched and unsettled, and at the end of that time it became worse, for my uncle, having given up all hopes of seeing Belgrave return, had become very anxious that I should marry, and settle in the farm.

THE PRIDE OF THE VILLAGE;

OR,

THE FARMER'S DAUGHTERS.

THE DEATH OF MARIA.

CHAPTER XXXVI.

"'It was no use,' he said, 'to think of managing the farm without a wife;' and then he would point out a two or three of our associates who, he considered, would make good wives, and were suitable for me.

"Our disputes on this head became at last serious, for he suspected all along what were my real feelings; and I need not tell you, Grace, that there were other motives besides your sister's conduct to me that made him set his face against any connection with your family.

"So serious at last did our disputes on this subject become that he declared, unless I gave him a solemn promise that I never would make Maria my wife, he would alter his will, and leave every farthing of property to strangers, rather than I should have it.

"I need not tell you that I refused, and from that time, though I still continued to manage the farm for him, I felt that I was looked upon with, none of his former affection and kindness. His temper, never very good, too, became sourer and sourer; and the house, which once used to be the abode of peace and comfort, became hateful to me.

"I could not, however, find it in my heart to leave him; he had been a parent to me and my brother; and now, to leave him in his old age, comparatively too impoverished—for circumstances which I need not now stop to explain had greatly altered his situation in the world—would, I thought be the height of cruelty and ingratitude.

"We continued thus to drag on a miserable life together, when my poor uncle was suddenly snatched from the world by an attack of the complaint by which he had been for some time threatened.

"From the first moment of his seizure he was speechless, and only at intervals sensible of his situation; but at those intervals all his kindly feelings and affection for me resumed their force; and full well I comprehend the signs by which he endeavoured to render intelligible his wish to reverse what—in a moment of anger and revenge for what he considered my obstinacy—he had done; but it was too late, he never recovered sufficiently to be able to explain his intentions to the satisfaction of others, and I found myself at his death the possessor of no more than fifty pounds, with an expressed desire that I should be allowed to retain the management of the farm, at a stipulated salary, so long as I continued single.

"The property, itself, was left in trust for my brother, should he ever return to claim it, and should he not, after his death, was devised to build alms-houses.

"I felt very little sorrow as this, Grace, for just at that period, the intelligence reached me that she, for whom I had incurred the forfeiture, and for whom I would not have hesitated to forfeit my life, had placed an insurmountable barrier between us by her own act, and had condemned herself to everlasting misery and disgrace.

"Scarcely had I met this shock, and before I could resolve how to act, a letter was put into my hands, which had been addressed to my uncle, and was now given to me, as his representative. I have that letter here, Grace." He produced it from his pocket-book.

It was, as he had said, addressed to Meredith, and was as follows:—

"SIR,

       "About six weeks ago I was crossing by a packet from Calais, having been to Paris upon business. There was a young female on board who attracted a good deal of notice, not only because she was remarkably pretty, but because she seemed to be in a great deal of trouble, and was constantly crying.

"I own I was very anxious to find out who or what she was, and what was the matter with her; and I did so far succeed as to learn that she was a native of my own dear birthplace, Llan——. It is so long since I left it, that I dare say you've quite forgotten me.

"However, I have not forgotten Llan——, nor Mr. Meredith, who more than once stood my friend, when I was striving to make everybody my enemies by foolishness. You will remember now, perhaps, a wild young chap, by name Tom Richards, who some thirty years ago used to be the torment of the village, and ——but, however, I'm not going to write my own history now, and so I'll say no more on that subject, but return to the young woman, of whom I made inquiries of several people that I had left behind me when I quitted Llan——; and among the rest I mentioned

your name, and was surprised to see her change colour and look greatly
agitated, as she replied that she knew you very well, and that the last time
she saw you you were very ill with the gout, but she had heard since that
you were better.

"I saw she was very unwilling that I should ask her any more questions; and, indeed, she contrived just then to be very sea sick, and that
lasted till we landed, so that I had no farther opportunity of speaking to
her; and as she didn't go straight on to London, as I was obliged to do, but
staid behind at Dover for a day or two, as I understood, I lost sight of her
altogether, which I was very sorry for, as I felt greatly interested in her,
and couldn't help fancying she was somehow connected with you, though I
know you are, like myself, a bachelor, for I had asked her that question.
She couldn't be your daughter, therefore; and all the way as I jolted along
on the coach to London, I kept trying to conjecture what tie there could be
between you.

"Business, however, and a crowd of fresh faces, soon put her out of my
mind; and I'd forgotten her althogether, when last week, strolling along the
bank of the Serpentine, I saw a young woman on the opposite side hastily
pull off her bonnet and shawl and throw them on the grass; and then, putting
her hands over her eyes, she jumped into the water.

"I'm a very poor swimmer myself; but, however, I threw off my clothes
as fast as I could, calling out all the time for help; and, indeed, it was well
I did, for I was soon out of my depth myself, and should have stood a chance
of being drowned within a few minutes, but luckily there were two or three
men within hearing who could swim, and in a few minutes, the poor girl
and I were both on dry land again. She was quite insensible however;
but the moment I got sight of her features, I recollected them to be the same
that had struck me on board the Dover boat. It would not, indeed, be very
easy for any one to forget them that had once seen them; for I think they
are about the handsomest I ever met with, and I've seen some pretty faces,
too, in my time.

"I was now doubly rejoiced that I had been the means of preserving her
for, though she was apparently lifeless, I did not despair of her being
brought to life again: and accordingly I followed, as soon as I could get
my clothes on, to the place to which they conveyed her, and soon had the
pleasure of seeing her perfectly restored to life, though, not as it appears
to her senses, for she was in a state of complete delirium; and the
doctor there declared she was in a raging fever, and, as the best plan that
could be adopted, he sent her to St. George's Hospital, where she still is,
and where I have visited her every day, without being able to learn from
her any farther particulars than I knew before, except that her name was
Maria; her surname she has in all her ravings avoiding mentioning. She
has, however, used expressions which have made the people about her to
conclude that she has clandestinely quitted her friends: her mother and
sister she has frequently spoken of, and accused herself of having broken
their hearts.

"It seems, too, that she is in the way to produce a living witness of her
shame, should she survive this disorder, which seems now probable, as the
doctor consider she has passed the crisis, though she is so low and weak that
she appears to me more likely to die than recover.

"It is a mournful situation to see such a beautiful young creature in; and
it is still more mournful to think that, if she recovers, she will be totally
destitute.

"'I have no friends—no home!' has been her repeated exclamation.
'The world has all deserted me, and why should I wish to live?' Now, I

need not tell Mr. Meredith that Tom Richards's heart is bigger than his pocket? and, indeed, my old friend, I never so much regretted as I do now that I had not been prudent and careful, and have made myself a home that I could take this poor worried lamb to, where she could eat of my bread, and drink of my cup, and be unto me a daughter; but thanks to my own folly, I am only a poor, invalided soldier, with half a crown a day to live upon.

"The thought struck me this morning, however, that though I can do little to help her, you may have it in your power : at all events, you will in all probability know who she is, and whether she has any friends who can or will assist her. To help your recognition of her, if you are at all puzzled, I subjoin a description of her person. Rather above the middling height, and remarkably elegant person. Very fair, regular Grecian features, fine teeth, large blue eyes, and the greatest profusion of glossy flaxen hair I ever saw in my life.

"I believe now I have said all my dear sir, that I need say, except that I hope you are reaping the reward of a prudent and virtuous life in a green old age, and the means of making it comfortable, and awaiting with anxiety your answer.—I remain, yours truly,

"Address to me,   "THOMAS RICHARDS.
"7, Pollard Row, Knightsbridge."

Tears, terror, and gratitude, to the kind-hearted writer. detained Grace long over this epistle, but at length she returned it to William, who immediately resumed his narrative.

"I leave you to imagine, Grace, what were the feelings with which I read this letter. There appeared to me but one course to be pursued, and that very night I was on my road to London.

"I had no difficulty in finding the friendly Richards, he was just going to pay his usual visit to the unfortunate object of his benevolence, and after a very short explanation he consented to my accompanying him, assuring me at the same time that she was considered quite out of danger.

"It was with difficulty I bridled my impatience, and consented to wait on the landing place while he prepared her for my visit, and he represented how fatal might be the effect of any sudden surprise on her weak frame, and I suffered him to proceed his own way.

"The bed which she occupied was close to the door ; and oh, how my heart throbbed, when in a few minutes, I heard her well-known voice repeat my name in a tone of agitation and surprise.

"'Oh! no, no, no,' she added, 'do not let him come, not for the world I would not see him. Oh! how he must despise and hate me!'

"I did not waite for the preconcerted signal when I heard these words, but flew to her bedside, and a very few minutes convinced her, Grace, that even with all her errors, and all her cruelty to me, she was still dear to me as the vital drops that warm my heart.

"A long explanation followed; she had, it appeared, taken the first opportunity of quitting her villanous seducer ; but you know that part of her story, it seems, and, therefore, I need not repeat it. On her arrival in London she discovered that she had left behind her the address of the benevolent man who had furnished her with the means of quitting France, and who had promised to befriend her when she arrived in London.

"She was now completely alone, and uncertain what course to pursue. There was a woman in the coach with her, who represented herself as the wife of a mate of a vessel which had just sailed from the Downs. She had been down, she said, to see him off, and was now returning to her family and home, which was at the East-end of London.

"She appeared a matronly, friendly woman, was very chatty and inquisitive, and strongly pressed Maria to go home with her for a day or two, observing, that now her husband was gone, she should have a spare bed, as her daughter always slept with her when he was away.

"Maria, however, who was still unconscious that she had lost the important direction to Mr. Lovell's housekeeper, but believed she had locked it in her trunk, which she could not get at, civilly declined her invitation; observing, that her friends resided at quite the opposite end of the town, all that she retained in her memory being, that Mr. Lovell's house was situated in one of the square at the West-end.

"They therefore parted when the coach arrived at its final destination, Mrs. Clarke, as she called herself, giving Maria a written direction to her residence, and the unsuspicious girl promising to take the first opportunity of visiting her.

"Thrown totally out of her intentions by the discovery that she had lost the address, Maria was for some hours totally at a lost how to act, or where to go, when suddenly the recollection of her late friendly companion rushed into her mind, and she resolved on the following morning, to go there and see if she could make any arrangement with her, or at least to get her advice.

"With some difficulty the coachman whom she employed found the obscure street in the Commercial-road, in which Mrs. Clarke's residence was situated; and when it was at length found, Maria felt disappointed and surprised at the appearance of the house, which was low and mean; but she was still more suprised and disappointed, when she beheld the dirty, slatternly-looking figure who appeared in answer to the summons at the door, and in whom she with difficulty recognised her late smart and somewhat fashionable companion of the stage coach.

"Mrs. Clarke, however, was all cordially and kindness, the coach was dismissed, Maria's trunk brought in-doors, and Mrs. Clarke bustled about to put every thing to rights, as she said, observing, by way of excuse for the confusion, dirt, and litter that disfigured the room, that they had a bit of jollification last night on her coming home, and had all laid abed very late; indeed, her son and daughter were not yet up, but she should go and call them.

"Maria had not before heard this son mentioned, but in a short time a young man and woman made their appearance, and she was introduced to them as the young lady whom Mrs. Clarke had mentioned as her fellow traveller.

"From the moment your sister saw the man whom they called Neil she felt a dislike of him; but the feeling did not seem natural, as he paid her in his rude way a great deal of attention, and assured her that he had been quite anxious to see her.

"'Yes, and what's still better,' observed Mrs. Clarke, 'Mrs. Woodford is come to stop with us for the present, at least; art't you my dear?'

"'If you will be so good as to accommodate me with a room until I can discover my friends,' observed Maria.

"The young woman said nothing, Maria observed, but seemed to view her with a great deal of curiosity during the breakfast, which they sat over till nearly noon.

"Unsuspicious and inexperienced as Maria was, she began to grow uneasy, and fearful that she had acted rashly and hastily in thus entrusting herself to strangers. The man was evidently a blustering, ignorant, licentious fellow; his whole conversation was of dogs, horses, and fights, intermingled with oaths and inuendoes scarcely decent. The young woman, who was called Amelia, sat apparently half stupid and vacant : and Mrs. Clarke herself declared that she should not be right for two or three days.

" It was not until several hints to that purpose, that Maria succeeded in getting to the room which she was to consider as her own so long as she chose, and for which she agreed to pay seven shillings a week, a sum which she felt was infinitely more than it was worth though Mrs Clarke seemed to make it a great favour that she let her have it at that price.

" Day after day passed on, and Maria was still in the same situation ; nor could she, indeed, devise any means by which she could either discover Mr. Lovell's residence, or let him know hers ; her money was fast diminishing, and she was rendered still more wretched and unhappy by the discoveries she daily made of the character of the people among whom she had been so unhappily thrown.

" The woman, Mrs. Clarke, she discovered, made a living by selling either smuggled goods, or what she pretended to be such. The son's occupation appeared still more equivocal, for he sometimes lay abed all day, and was out all night, and at others was away for two or three days together ; and the daughter, Maria at length discovered, was almost constantly in a state of stupifaction, from the effects of cordials, without which she could not, she said, exist.

" At times nothing was thought of but mirth and jollity ; and Maria, in spite of all objections, and her pleas of ill health and low spirits, was then dragged from the room, to share in scenes which were totally repugnant to her disposition ; and these jollifications, as Mrs. Clarke expressly called them, were sure to be succeeded by quarrels and mutual abuse, during which Maria was unwillingly a witness to accussations and recriminations which made her tremble and shudder. But the worst of it all was (and here William rose, and began to pace the room with great agitation), that the rascal of a son dared to insult her with his violent passion for her ; and she was in constant fear of him, whenever his mother was out of the way, for the daughter was a mere cypher, and could afford her no protection.

" In this manner passed six miserable weeks, and then a run of ill luck, as she called it, reduced the woman Clarke to great necessities. All the little money that Maria had treasured up to provide for her coming confinement was borrowed from her, and then her clothes were taken to raise money, until she was completely destitute of everything except what she had on.

" This, however, proved only the commencement of the woman's difficulties ; for she was arrested for debts, and taken to prison ; and, the following day, an execution was put into the house, which swept away all the goods, and Maria was left without a bed to sleep on, or the means of even procuring a night's lodging or a meal.

" It was at this juncture that the wretch Neil, as he was called, chose to increase her misery by his insulting passion. He returned home, after an absence of nearly a week : and, without expressing the least sorrow for his mother or his miserable sister, he called Maria aside, and, showing her a handful of money, pressed her to leave the house with him, and share the loding he would provide.

" I need not say she spurned him and his offer : the monster, exasperated at her undisguised abhorrence, loaded her with insult and abuse, and she was compelled to fly to her room, and lock herself in, to avoid his violence.

" All that day and the next night, she sat on the bare floor, without food or covering, except the old shawl, which had been left her only because nothing could be raised upon it.

"She felt dreadfully ill from the united effects of terror and suffering, but her old thoughts were upon one subject, that of getting beyond the reach of the villian, who had attempted to take such an advantage of her unprotected situation.

"He had passed the night smoking and drinking in one of the lower rooms, in which an old chair or two had been left, as not being worth taking away: and towards morning, his occasional snatches of low songs, and his burst of abuse and threats of vengeance towards her, had all subsided into profound silence. She ventured to open her door and listen, and his hard breathing convinced her he was asleep. This was the opportunity she had so anxiously waited for, and with cautious steps she stole down stairs. The front door was locked, and he had taken the key away; for he had sworn the most bitter oaths that there he would stay till hunger brought down what he called her squeamishness, and she should be glad to humble herself to him: but he had forgotten to secure the window of the front room, and with trembling hands she unclosed the sash, and got into the street.

"It was not yet daylight; there was a mizzling rain and a cold raw breeze; but she thought of nothing but to get as far out of the reach of the monster as she could, and she continued to walk on without any reflection whither she was going, or what was to become of her.

"The day had nearly broke, the sun shone out in splendour, and then she found herself in one of the squares, which, from its appearance, she knew must be in quite a different quarter of the town, to that which she had quitted.

"Exhausted from long fasting, the want of rest, and the speed with which she had walked, or rather run, she sat down for a few moments on the steps of one of the mansions, but she was almost immediately ordered in an authoritative manner to move, by a watchman, who observed, she musn't sit there.

"Terrified at his brutal tone, the poor girl arose and crawled a few paces farther, and then, totally overcome, she again sank down.

"The watchman had now gone on his regular beat, and she fortunately, as she said, escaped his notice; but she had not sat long before the sound of voices laughing and conversing was heard approaching. They came nearer, and distinctly, too distinctly, she recognized accents which —— I cannot name him, Grace, his name would blister my lips, but it was he to whom she owed all the misery she was now suffering.

"Breathless and speechless she hid her face in her hands, and he passed close to her, humming an air which she had often heard him sing, and leaning upon the arm of a companion.

"So close did they pass, that his cloak brushed her, yet she did not speak, she felt as if her heart would burst, for the tone of levity, the careless song, and his being at that hour returning from some scene of dissipation, all told her that no regret for her fate ever for a moment marred his happiness, and she thought she would rather die where she sat, than appealed to his pity, or suffer him to see to what extremity she was reduced.

"They passed on again, she heard his light laugh ring in the air; she fancied even, that it was occasioned by some remark of his companion, at her expense, for she felt convinced that they had noticed her sitting in that forlorn and wretched plight, though they could not suspect who she was; the thought made her desperate, and gave her strength to rise and hurry, though with tottering limbs, away in a direction opposite to that which they had taken.

"From that moment she had but a confused remembrance of what had occurred; she recollects only being urged on from place to place by questions which she would not answer, or observations which she only partly comprehended, and which she yet strove, until at last the green fields, as she supposed the Park to be, seemed to offer her a refuge, and she wandered on to that spot where she was first beheld by Richards.

"I have already told you the rest; and now, to return to the moment when I beheld her in the hospital.

"It was long before I could prevail on her to look up to listen to me or to reply to my anxious inquiries, by any other than bitter lamentations and condemnation of herself; but I at length succeeded, she became more composed, and I had the satisfaction of hearing her acknowledge, before I left her, that she was now happier than she had felt for many, many months. She could die now, contented, she said, since I had forgiven her.

"I soon convinced her, however, that it would be for my happiness that she should try to live and get well; and she did get rapidly better, and as soon as she could safely be removed, I conducted her to a lodging which I had taken for her.

"The child was born a few weeks after; but alas! Grace, we managed but badly, and there were so many expenses to contend with, that we soon began to feel the approaches of poverty.

"I tried in every way I could think or devise to get employment, there was nothing I would have shrunk from to be able to keep her from feeling want; but alas! I had neither friends or recommendation. The kind-hearted Richards was the only person whom I knew in London, and he was powerless to assist me, except with advice.

"I need not distress you by telling you how we rapidly sank lower and lower; and then, too, I had, for a time at least, lost Richards' friendship; he had opposed, strongly opposed, the idea of my marriage with your sister; and when we were married——"

"Oh! thank heaven you have then ——" Grace burst into tears of joy and thankfulness, she had not dared before utter the question which she was dying to hear answered.

William sighed heavily.

"Yès, Grace, we are married; I loved her too ardently, too sincerely to expose her to farther——but—but let me say no more on this subject, the world will laugh at me, will despise me—she herself, perhaps despises me—there are moments when I despise myself; and yet, could I see the woman I so truly loved——Oh! Grace, you cannot conceive—you can never know what struggles, what misery I have endured; but she is my wife."

"And she will live to reward you, William, by a life of devoted tenderness and affection," said Grace, earnestly.

"No, Grace, I shall die to prove my gratitude to him," said a voice.

It was Maria who spoke, and before William could reply, she continued.

"It is useless to deny it, William, you have repented ever since that you did make me your wife, and I can only pray to heaven that you may soon be released from your wretched burthen. I own I have wished to live, for the sake of this poor innocent," and she pressed her child closer to her bosom, and burst into tears; "but now that it has got some one to care for it, for Grace, I know, will never desert it, I care not how soon my misery is at an end. You will be yourself again then, William—you will forget me and all the sorrow and uneasiness I have occasioned you. I well know that it is impossible we could ever be happy together. I know that the time would soon come when you would repent and reproach me."

"Reproach !" repeated William angrily.

"Yes ! reproach !" reiterated Maria. "I do not say, indeed, that your words ever reproached me, William, but your looks, your conduct has been the bitterest of reproaches. You know well what I mean," she continued, with significance. "You cannot deny that your conduct, since we have been together, has not been such as it would have been had we married under different circumstances."

"I do not deny it, Maria" he returned moodily; "I have acted wrong, but there are times when I cannot bear the weight of my reflections, when life itself seems hateful to me, and I have tried to drown thought and remembrance for a time in dissipation; but I deny that I have ever repented that I made you my wife; I would give the whole world, were it at my disposal, to restore you to—to what you were when I first loved you; but as you are, Maria, yes, as you are, your are dearer to me than all the world beside."

Maria did not reply, but she continued to weep, and Grace felt almost angry with her, as she thought she could trace a degree of petulance and resentment in her observations, which she considered unwarranted.

It was plain, indeed, that there were much deeper sources of misery and despondency between this unhapy pair, than the difficulties of their situation; and Grace beheld with pain how little effect the cheering prospect—when she attempted to hold out to them, of being enabled, by the Earl of Melverley's power and interest, of being placed in some way of providing for themselves—had in removing the gloom and despondency of both their manners and looks.

By the kindly aid and exertions of Mrs. Burton, a decent lodging was procured at a house nearly opposite, for William Mansell and his wife, and thither Grace accompanied them, as soon as Maria was sufficiently recovered to walk so far.

"A night's rest will, I trust, greatly improve you both," she observed. "And I will be with you early, and we will breakfast together, and the earl—I know I shall see him to-morrow, for he has not been since Monday, and he never stays many days away; and oh, how glad, how rejoiced he will be, to learn that I have found you."

Maria sighed heavily.

"You are a dear good girl, Grace," she observed; "you always were; and I always was a trouble and a burthen to you : but it will not be for long now."

"No, it will not," returned Grace, making an effort to suppress her tears and affecting to mistake her sister's meaning. "You will have no occasion to be troublesome to me, if you ever were, when you get into the country again, and strong and hearty as I know you will be."

Maria was about to say something in the same gloomy strain in which she constantly spoke, but Grace hastily repeated her "good night," and hastened out of the room.

"Do you think my sister is really so ill as she believes herself? or do you think with me that rest and good nourishment will restore her?" demanded Grace of William, who insisted upon seeing her home.

"I have not heard her complain of any disease except the mind," he replied, with a deep sigh; "and grief does not easily kill : I know that, Grace, by sad experience."

"We shall see, however, to-morrow," rejoined Grace, who thought it best not to notice his last observation; "and if she does not appear better, I shall be anxious that she shall have medical attendance."

"Who can minister to a mind diseased?" replied William, in the same gloomy tone which had never, from her (Grace's) first meeting with him left him.

"The diseases of my sister's mind are, I trust, not incurable," returned Grace. "Kindness and forbearance on the part of others, and consciousness of endeavouring to do her duty, and prove her conviction of her former folly, cannot fail to restore her to peace and——"

"I have never been unkind to her," interrupted William, hastily: "she wrongs me if she says so. It is true I have sometimes acted foolishly, and obtained a few hours' forgetfulness of the misery that haunts me at the price of——but I do not know that I have any right to accuse myself of unkindness, though, perhaps, under the effects of liquor, I may sometimes have made remarks that were not pleasant to her, and have spent, perhaps, more money than our situation warranted: but I cannot help it now."

"No, you can only resolve to avoid it in future," said Grace, with emphasis.

William did not reply to this observation, nor did he again speak until he bade her adieu for the night; and Grace felt as she replied to him that as much as she pitied and sympathised with him, her confidence in him was greatly shaken even by his own avowal.

CHAPTER XXXVII.

"I am not mad, I would to Heaven I were,
    For then 'tis like I could forget myself;
Oh, if I could, what grief should I forget!"

SHAKESPEARE.

It proved that Grace was not mistaken in her anticipations of a visit from the earl, for she had but just returned from her morning visit to her sister, when his carriage stopped at the door. With the greatest interest he listened to her narration of her meeting with her sister, but, contrary to her expectations, he expressed no desire to see either Maria or her husband."

"I am afraid they have not increased their chance of happiness by their reunion," he observed: "however, we must do all we can for them, Grace. There is some money for present expenses; and as the young man has been brought up, you say, to farming life, I will consult with my steward what can be done to re-establish him in a way of maintaining himself and his wife and family; for a family, I suppose, he is likely to have."

Without waiting to hear another word, he hurried away; and Grace with a joyful heart hastened to impart to her sister the realization of her expectations from the earl.

"And where is William, dear Maria?" she demanded, after she had repeated all the earl had said. "I am in hopes this intelligence will cheer his spirits as well as yours."

"William has gone out," returned Maria, with a sigh. "It is seldom, indeed, Grace," she added, after a moment's pause—"very seldom that William stays long with me."

"It can scarcely be expected that he can confine himself to a room," observed Grace, who felt unwilling to encourage in her sister the tone of querulousness which she thought she had observed.

"If he had any proper way of passing his time," returned Maria, "I should not object to it: but it is no use to attempt to disguise it, Grace; the company William keeps is only such as will bring him to ruin. You know not, indeed," she continued, "how dreadful he is altered, Grace. The moment he has money he flies off, and I never see him again until it is all gone, and he is quite intoxicated; and then, oh, what bitter things he will utter, and yet pretending all the while to love me."

Grace was shocked and grieved at this confirmation of the suspicions she had formed from William's own avowal; but she was still more so when her sister proceeded to relate circumstances which proved that her husband was indeed devoted to habits which must inevitably entail misery and ruin on himself and all connected with him.

"Even now," continued Maria, "he has taken a part of the trifle you gave me, under pretence of paying what he borrowed yesterday, to get the wine and bread he brought into the park. It may be so, to be sure; but if that is the case I know very well that he will not return sober, for never—when he knew that he had left me without common necessaries—has he returned to me so long as the means of intoxication could be procured. And, oh, how have I trembled for fear of what he might be led to do in such circumstances—frenzied with liquor, and urged by the want and misery which stared him in the face at home, and his utter despair of ever retrieving himself."

"And if the earl should hear this?" thought Grace. "And if he should not hear of it, and William should abuse his bounty, what will he think of me for misrepresenting him as I have done to him—as one of the best and kindest and most upright beings that ever existed!"

"But he will mend his conduct when he is again settled, and when he has a clear prospect before him and is occupied; and in the country, too, he will be out of the reach of temptation," said Grace."

"For his own sake, I hope it will prove so," returned Maria; "but I shall never see it."

It was in vain that Grace tried to move her despondency and cheer her with the prospect of being again reinstated in comfort and happiness: she sank lower and lower, and before Grace left her that evening the latter was compelled to acknowledge to herself that the turn of fortune had come too late.

It was nearly midnight when Grace left her unhappy sister, and William was not then returned. To Maria this was evidently no new occurrence, nor did it appear very greatly to affect her; but Grace was at once shocked and indignant at the confirmation it gave of his confirmed habits of intemperance and dissipation.

"There is only one hope," she incessantly repeated to herself: "he must leave London immediately; every hour of his stay increases the mischief."

With this hope, and with a prayer on her lips for her sister, Grace fell into a profound sleep.

How long it had lasted she knew not, but she was awakened by an incessant knocking at the front door; and the instant she jumped out of bed the strong glare of light which dazzled her eyes told her, before she heard the cries of fire and the rattles of the watchmen, what was the matter.

Her first impulse was to fly and awaken Mrs. Burton and the other inmates in the house, supposing that they were in imminent danger; but a second glance convinced her that it was farther removed than she had imagined. She threw up the sash, and all her fears were in an an instant confirmed; it was in the house in which she had but a few hours before beheld her sister enjoying more tranquility and comfort than had for some time fallen to her lot.

Grace did not scream or faint; but she stood motionless, with arms extended, and eyes that seemed starting from their sockets, gazing on the devouring flames that were now pouring from every window in the house.

Again the knocking at the door below was repeated, but Grace neither heard nor regarded it until a voice that seemed to her as if it was issuing from the grave called upon her by name.

"Grace!—dear Grace!—for the love of heaven come down and admit us!" it exclaimed-

In another instant Grace was at the door. It was no dream, it was her sister, whom she beheld in the arms of, not William, but his long-lost brother, Belgrave Mansel!

"She has fainted, dear Grace! let us take her in-doors, !" he exclaimed.

Maria opened her eyes.

"My child! my child!" she exclaimed. "Let me go! my child will be——"

"It is safe, Maria! it is safe!" exclaimed Belgrave.

There was a choking in his voice which contradicted his words, and as Grace's eyes met his he turned them away with a look of agony which confirmed her suspicions.

"Where is William, your brother, Belgrave—where?"

Belgrave raised his hand to her as a signal of silence, while his countenance became still more ghastly, and Maria uttered a shriek of agony.

"He has perished, Grace, and I—I——" She relapsed into a fainting fit, and in that state she was conveyed to Grace's bed, Mrs. Burton and her family being now roused by the noise and confusion, and all eager to assist the wretched sufferer.

For many hours Maria continued happily insensible to the horrid occurrence which had rendered her a widow and childless, and during that period Grace had learned from Belgrave all that he knew respecting it.

He had some days before arrived in London in search, at once, of the object of his youthful affection and his unhappy brother, and had only that evening gained a clue to trace the latter to one of the haunts of vice and folly which he frequented.

"I found him, Grace," he continued, "but in such a state of mad intoxication that I could scarcely make him comprehend anything I said to him. At last, however, I succeeded in getting from him his place of abode, and I learned, too, that Maria was with him, and that you were near her.

"Rendered, as I thought, supremely happy by this information, I next attempted to persuade him to let me accompany him home, and after some difficulty succeeded in getting him into the coach that was waiting for me.

"The woman of the house was up, waiting his arrival, and with a look of reproach she informed him that his wife was much worse than she was this morning, and that her sister had been with her till past twelve o'clock; she added that she believed the poor young woman was fast asleep now, and advised him to go up quietly that he might not disturb her. He took the candle from her hand with a look half stupid, half sullen, and I heard the key turn in the chamber door.

"For some minutes I remained in conversation with the woman, whom I rewarded for her civility: she told me that she considered the poor young woman to be in a rapid decline, and that she was afraid her husband was not very kind to her. I begged she would pay her every attention, and

This was uttered by a tall, elderly, emaciated man, who stood on one side of the coffin, with folded arms, contemplating the once lovely form of the hapless Maria Woodford; while opposite to him was Belgrave Mansell, his eyes also fixed on the pallid face of the corpse, but his thoughts wandering, and his ear intently listening to every sound that proceeded from the ajacent chamber.

It need scarcely be said that chamber was Grace Woodford's. Three days had passed since the death of her sister, yet Grace had not yet recovered sufficiently from the shock to be able to converse with Belgrave. Twice only had he been admitted to see her, and then the thoughts and remembrances that rushed into her mind so completely overpowered the little fortitude and resolution she had acquired, that she was incapable of attending to or making any communication to him.

Mrs. Burton, however, had reported her better and more composed that morning, and Belgrave had just sent in a request, not only to see her, but to introduce to her an old friend, in the person of Sir Walter Fitz-Geffrey.

Yes, it was indeed Sir Walter, who now appeared as the friend and companion of Belgrave Mansell, and who, while awaiting admission to Grace, thus apostrophised the remains of her unfortunate sister.

Sir Walter! The title had made a great impression on Mrs. Burton, and she hurried away to Grace to inform her of the honour done her by the baronet's request.

Prepared as she was by the knowledge that Sir Walter was still in existence, Grace could not but feel startled and surprised at the announcement of his name. How many painful, agonising recollections did it bring to her mind! To Sir Walter's first appearance, indeed, in the peaceful village of Llan————, she migh attribute all the misfortunes that had subsequently befallen her; and, under this impression, she was about to utter an excuse for not seeing him, when Mrs. Burton added—

"The young gentleman, Mr. Mansell, is with him; and he desired me, in a whisper, to tell you that he hoped, for his sake as well as your own, that you will not refuse to admit Sir Walter."

For Belgrave's sake what was there she would not have endured? And, accordingly, struggling to repress the agitation which shook her whole frame, she requested Mrs. Burton to show them in.

Sir Walter's manner was kind and friendly; and the way in which he alluded to her and Belgrave during the course of conversation set Grace's mind entirely at rest with respect to his motives in wishing to see her. Sir Walter, indeed, seemed to have totally forgotten the circumstances of his own addresses to her, which had been the source of so much uneasiness, and the cause of such unfeeling persecution towards her on the part of her mother; and to look upon her interests and those of Belgrave as inseparably united, and of himself as a friend deeply interested in their welfare.

The perfect ease, indeed, which characterised his manner towards her, and the respect with which he was treated by Belgrave, soon rendered her visitor much more acceptable to her than he had ever been, but still more did her heart warm to him, though her eyes streamed with tears when he spoke of the recent loss she had sustained with a sympathy and kindness which she had little expected from him.

He had, indeed, he avowed, sought an interview with her for the purpose of consulting her as to her wishes respecting the last resting-place of her unfortunate sister; and Grace could almost have fallen at his feet and worshipped him when he observed that it appeared to him that it was natural she should not like the thought of burying her in London, which, it was probable, she never might visit again.

"I have been consulting, therefore," he continued, "with Belgrave, and he agrees with me that if you could bear the journey, the most preferable plan would be for us all to travel with the funeral down to Llan———, and there let the poor girl be laid with her father."

Grace could not speak her thankfulness—her gratitude—for this arrangement. She was above the pretence even of affecting to demur on account of her inability to defray its expenses; for she was well aware that Sir Walter must, through Belgrave, be perfectly acquainted with her circumstances, and had, therefore, made up his mind to pay the charges, which would necessarily be very heavy, before he had mentioned the subject.

There was only one thought that pressed heavily on her mind with respect to the proposed journey. Sir Walter had said that it would be necessary to prepare herself to commence it on the following evening at farthest; and how could she decide upon taking so important a step without the concurrence of the Earl of Melverley—of the noble and disinterested benefactor to whom she owed so deep a debt of gratitude. She had not seen the earl since the hour of her sister's death, nor did she know, even if she dared take the liberty, where to send to him.

As if, however, it was ordained that at last every obstacle should be removed to what she felt was the only measure that could restore her to anything like peace—a return to the dear, peaceful spot where she had passed her childhood—a letter from the earl was put into her hand by Mrs. Burton at the very moment that she was timidly communicating to Sir Walter and Belgrave her difficulty, and was as follows :—

"DEAR CHILD,

"I shall not see you for some months—perhaps years; I know not, indeed, that I shall ever revisit England. If I do, you shall be among the first I shall seek; but whether I do or not, whether I live or die, I have taken care that you shall be out of the reach of want. The enclosed is one half of the sum I have settled upon you, to be received yearly; the next payment will be due this day six months. And now I leave you to your own prudence, only suggesting that your income will keep you better in the country —say your own native place, for instance—than in London. The person who brings this will settle all demands with Mrs. Burton, so that you are free to act as you like. Your address, whithersoever you go, you will, of course, leave with the banker from whom you are to receive your money, and whose address I subjoin. And now, dear child, farewell. Continue to be what you have been, and I need not wish you happinness—that will follow, of course, though the follies or crimes of others may for a time cloud it. Think of me always as your friend, "MELVERLEY."

The enclosure was a bank note of fifty pounds; and Grace's heart swelled with gratitude and conscious pride that she had been thought worthy of such a friend as she put both letter and enclosure into Belgrave's hand.

He handed them, after perusing them, to Sir Walter.

"This must be returned, Grace," observed the latter; "the heiress of Walter Fitz-Geffrey must no longer be indebted to any one. You look surprised; but it is only an act of justice on my part that I should compensate you, as far as it lies in my power, for all the evil of which I have been the cause to you."

THE PRIDE OF THE VILLAGE;

OR,

THE FARMER'S DAUGHTERS.

SIR WALTER RECOGNISES HIS SON.

CHAPTER XXXVIII.

" The grave is an altar, whereon the heart proffers
    Its feverish pleasures, its troubles, its woes :
Stern, silent, and cold, the dark sanctuary offers
    Its gloomy return of unbroken repose.

How much of the sorrow that life may inherit,
    That early departure to slumber may save ;
The hope that drags onward the world-weary spirit
    Rests but when its fever is quench'd in the grave."

                                 L. E. L.

Grace, grateful as she felt, and endeavoured to express herself to Sir Walter, inwardly sighed at the conviction that seemed to press heavily on her mind. How insufficient was wealth, now that she had lost all those with whom to share it would have been, indeed, happiness. Not all, Belgrave's expressive eyes seemed to say; and Grace felt a blush suffuse her pallid cheek as a thousand thoughts connected with that look rushed into her mind.

Belgrave withdrew his eyes. It seemed as if he had read her thoughts, and confessed that this was not the time to press his claims; and Sir Walter, after a few moments' silence, returned to the details of their proposed melancholy journey.

Belgrave would have stopped him, but Sir Walter, in a low voice, observed—

" She will be better able to bear it hereafter by accustoming her to hear and to speak of what cannot be avoided, and then she will, in the inevitable bustle of preparation, gain strength and calmness. Half the evils of our existence would be reduced to mere shadows if we had but the courage to look them in the face.

Sir Walter was right. Before the hour appointed for the commencement of their journey Grace had acquired a calmness and composure which surprised all around her; but it was sadly shaken when at length the necesssity was announced to her of taking a last look at the remains of her lamented Maria, previous to the coffin being closed for ever and deposited in its outer leaden covering.

Belgrave, however, was with her, and mingled his tears with her's, and Sir Walter's observations on the selfishness and inefficiency of sorrowing so deeply for one whose removal from a scene of, to her, hopeless misery and vain regret were so true, though common-place, that Grace felt it would look like obstinacy and ingratitude to him not to make every effort to conquer the outward demonstrations of grief; and when the coach was announced as waiting her tears were dried and her voice and manner calm.

The parting with Mrs. Burton, to whom, with all her faults, Grace felt deeply indebted, would have been much more painful than it was but that that lady had eagerly accepted an invitation from Sir Walter, to pass two or three months, together with as many of her family as she chose to bring, at Llan—— in the following spring; and as this invitation was accompanied by a handsome present to defray expenses, and as the good lady evidently reckoned upon other probable results from her powers of captivation, when she should have a fair field to exert them in, she was in such high spirits as scarcely to be able to assume the necessary gravity for such a mournful occasion as the present.

Sir Walter had chosen the hour of dusk to commence their journey, that Grace might see as little as possible at first, and become gradually accustomed to the sombre and gloomy appearance of the coach in which they travelled, the hearse, &c.; and with a thoughtfulness and kind consideration for her feelings that she once thought him incapable of, he had decided on going through Oxford, Gloucester, &c., instead of the Bath and Bristol road, that Grace might not be reminded of the melancholy events which had attended her residence in the former city, in which her mother had found a grave far from all her family and connections.

It was a long and tedious journey at the pace they travelled; yet, in spite of all the mournful and depressing circumstances attending it, Grace seemed from the hour they left London, to feel the reviving influence of the pure fresh air, and Belgrave observed with ecstacy the colour return to her fair cheek and a gentle and patient resignation to the will of heaven, succeed to the agonising and expressive grief, which the loss of, as she emphatically said, not only her sister, but the last, the only human being with whom she could claim kindred, had occasioned.

The tolling of the funeral bell had excited the greatest curiosity and surprise among the inhabitants of the village of Llan——. They were returning in the evening from their rustic labours, when its mournful and unexpected sound reached their ears; but the questions which each asked of the other, were soon answered by the man who had been sent forward to make the necessary arrangements for the funeral, and though it was long after dark before the mournful cavalcade arrived at its final destination, the village green was crowded with those who were actuated, either by curiosity, or a better motive, anxiety to behold the last of the once happy family which had flourished among them.

Grace's fortitude had all given way at the first mournful sound of the well-known bell, and her sobs were audible as she was lifted out of the coach by Belgrave, and carried into the inn, where they were to remain until after the funeral, and till the necessary arrangements could be made, by Sir Walter, for a different habitation; but the sympathy which her grief excited, was soon banished by a more pleasurable sensation among those who recognised, not only Belgrave Mansell, but with him, and evidently on the most friendly terms, the very person whose supposed murder had created such horror, and loaded him with suspicion.

Scarcely, indeed, could the joy and surprise of his appearance be kept within the bounds that the melancholy occasion on which he appeared before them demanded; and when the corpse had been conveyed to the church, where it was to remain for the night, and a short time had been allowed for necessary refreshment, Belgrave was compelled to yield to the reiterated requests that were sent to him, in the name of first one, and then another of his old acquaintances and associates, to come among them, if but for a few minutes, that they might assure him how much they rejoiced in his return.

But how came you to go away so strangely? and how is it that we see the very person with you, that you were accused of murdering? were the questions that were pressed on him on all sides.

Belgrave did not then answer them. It was too long a story, he observed, to be told now, but at a future time, the anxiety of his friends was satisfied by a full relation of all that had happened to him, from the moment he quitted Mrs. Woodford's presence, by her desire, for ever; we may as well now give the narration in his own words, premising that they were addressed to Grace, who, it may be reasonably supposed, was not the least anxious of those who required an explanation of the seeming mystery.

CHAPTER XXXIX.

"But bear with me: indeed, you'll find me useful
Upon your pilgrimage. But come, pronounce
Where shall we now be errant?
          Where the world
Is thickest, that I may behold it in
Its workings."   BYRON.

"I WILL not now, my dear Grace," observed Belgrave, "dwell upon the feelings of rage and despair with which I quitted the farm, after hearing myself accused insolence and presumption in daring to aspire to the honoer, of your hand; but so it was, that I walked away in the direction of my homu in a paroxysm, as I verily now believe, of madness. Before I reached my uncle's, however, I resolved to return and make another effort to persuade you to listen to my prayer, of uniting your fate with mine, in defiance of the cruel mandate that had pronounced our separation. I did return as you know. You refused to see me, and again I rushed from the spot, a thousand desperate thoughts coming into my mind, but one at last becoming the fixed and settled purpose of my soul to leave for ever the scene where all my happiness had been wrecked.

"Revolving this project in my mind, and the means of carrying it into execution, I threw myself along, on the grass, under the large oak, in the path though the wood, where you and I have often sat; but I had not lain a minute before I was started by the murmuring sound of voices approaching, I did not wish to be seen in my then state of mind, and I therefore retreated behind the tree, till the persons should have passed. To my suprise, they proved to be the French valet of Sir Walter, his butler, a tall dark man, of rather genteel appearance, whom I did not know; and to my great discomfiture, they sat down on a grassy bank, at a little distance from my hiding-place. I did not attend to, nor did I wish to hear their conversation, my thoughts were in fact, fully absorbed by my own concerns, yet, from time to time some words reached me, which betrayed that the strange man was complaining bitterly of the treatment he had received from Sir Walter Fitz-Geffrey, and vowing revenge against him, in which the two faithful servants, who were both evidently intoxicated, seemed to confirm him. I had heard that Sir Walter was very tyrannical with his servants, and, therefore, should not have felt surprised at the epithets they bestowed on him, if I had thought about it, which I did not, from the pressure, as I have already said, of more momentous concerns. Somthing I afterwards recollected hearing, respecting a large sum of money, and also, that the dark man declared he had that very hour refused him a guinea.

"They separated, at last, to my great satisfaction; the dark man pursuing the path through the wood, while Sir Walter's two servants crossed into the fields, to get home, as it appeared, the shortest way.

"At any other time, I should have been struck with these appearances as suspicious, probably, but I was now too engrossed with self; and I returned to my station under the tree, where, I dare say, I had been a quarter of an hour, when Sir Walter himself passed me, on horseback, taking the same path that the dark stranger had previously done. In the gloom of approaching darkness, he did not observe me; and as I had no inclination to make myself known, I remained stationary till he had passed; and then, having just made up my mind as to how I should act, I arose, intending to go home, at once, and make the necessary arrangements for my departure, when I was startled by hearing a loud cry of 'Help! murder!' which I was convinced came from Sir Walter, who was scarcely out of sight. In an instant the dark stranger's threats rushed into my mind: and, without a moment's hesitation, I tore up a large hedgestake, which providentially caught my eye, and rushed to the spot; at which I arrived just in time to see Sir Walter extended on the ground, his horse galloping off mad with fright in an opposite direction, and the tall, dark stranger holding Sir Walter down with one hand, while other essayed to reach a pistol, which I afterwards learnt Sir Walter had struck from his hand with the butt end of his riding whip, at the moment he presented it.

"Neither of them saw my approach; there was not an instant to le lost;

and at the very moment the wretch's hand was on the pistol, I felled him to the earth with the rude weapon I carried. He lay extended, senseless and helpless, while I raised Sir Walter, who seemed scarcely to believe it possible that I was the means of rescuing him from the death which he had considered inevitable. I secured the pistol; and then I would have proceeded to make sure of the man, who was beginning to recover from the stunning efforts of the blow I had given him, but I was prevented by Sir Walter.

" 'No, no,'' he exclaimed; 'he is punished sufficiently; for he knows that not only has he failed in his present attempt, but that every future hope from me is lost. I told you to-day,' he continued, addressing the half-conscious man, 'that I had made a provision for you in my will, and that I would still continue to pay to you the annuity you have received from me ever since I discovered that you were unworthy of becoming my heir, as I once intended: both these promises I now retract; and this, giving him a pocket-book, 'is the last you will ever receive from me. And now let me advise you to make the best of your way out of this country; for if you linger here, depend upon it, for my own safety, I will have you apprehended, both on account of your recent violence, and some former affairs which you are aware of.' "

" The baffled ruffian uttered not a word; but he regarded both me and Sir Walter with a scowl such as I never saw on the face of any human being, and rising with difficulty, walked slowy away.

" It was not for me to question the wisdom of Sir Walter's decision; and, indeed, to tell the truth, I thought very little about it, for my attention was occupied by himself; for he was looking so ghastly, that I thought he would faint, as he stood looking after the man from whose ruffian attack he had had so narrow an escape. I offered him my arm, and he took it, and continued leaning on me until the man was out of sight.

" ' You have saved my life,' he observed, turning to me ; 'tell me in what way I can prove my gratitude.'

" I scarcely know what I replied; but whatever it was, I am aware it was cold and repulsive, for I had all along looked upon him as the cause, in a great measure, of your mother's rejection of me· Sir Walter seemed hurt and disappointed, and I—it is not in my nature to be insensible to proferred kindness—endeavoured to counteract what I had said by my attention to him. Suddenly I recollected that I ought to acquaint him with the circumstance of his two servants' coalitition with his intended assassin. He was thunderstruck, and evidently terrified; and then, Grace, he confided to me the secret of his connection with the dark stranger. He was Sir Walter's son; his mother was a woman of colour, possessing all the fiery passions of the sultry clime in which she was born, and her son inherited, as Sir Walter said, all her worst qualities. He had given him education, had destined him to be his heir; but long before he had arrived at years of maturity, his vices had assumed such dominion over him, that the father's heart became hardened towards him, and he sent him to a distance from him. He had, it appeared, from time to time made the most unconscionable demands upon Sir Walter, and latterly had been denied, which had, of course, driven him to this desperate step; but up to the present day he had still believed that he should be Sir Walter's heir, and the two unworthy servants were probably of the same pinion, and hoped to find in his prodigality and extravagance more indulgence for the same vices in themselves than they now did from Sir Walter. This, however, is mere conjecture; the only certainty was, that they were colleagued against their master with his unworthy relative, and this circumstance seemed to make a deep impression on Sir Walter."

" ' My life is not safe with the wretches,' he observed ; ' I will not return home, to-night, but leave them to suppose their wretched associate's plan has succeeded, and see how they will act, and then made up my mind what I shall do. I cannot take any open measure against them without including him, and that I would fain villain as he is, avoid."

" I confess I felt very little interest in Sir Walter's future proceedings. I was satisfied with having rendered him so essential a service, but I cared nothing more about him further : my mind was fully occupied with my recent cruel disappointment, and my determination to quit the scene of it for ever ; and I scarcely heeded what he said to me, except stiffly to decline his proffered services by way of reward. Two or three times, indeed, it did strike me that he might exert his interest with your mother successfully in my favour ; but I will tell the truth, Grace, my pride revolted from owing even your hand to such a source, and I remained silent. Little did I then suspect, what I afterwards learned, that he had within the very hour purchased your mother consent to make you his wife, and was then on his way to my uncle's, to pay, as I might say, the purchase money. He had forgotten it himself—forgotten everything but the recent attack on him, and his escape ; and as I walked on at his request with him to the confines of the wood, he was wholly occupied in discussing with himself how he should act. I left him, when I considered him in safety, in the high road, from whence he could, you know, either proceed home, or take the coach, which would pass in half an hour to Bristol, which he seemed to say he thought he should do, and there finally resolve how he should act. I have since learned that he did so ; but the blow he had received from his intended assassin was more serious than he had apprehended, and that, with the agitation and terror he had suffered, operated so violently on his constitution, that before many hours were past, he was insensible, from a concussion of the brain, from the effects of which he did not recover for months. During the weakness and nervousness that this occasioned, he formed the strange resolution of quitting England, leaving all except his banker in Lodon in uncertainty of his fate ; and the latter he bound to secrecy. Little did either he or I suspect the interpretation that was put upon our simultaneous disappearance.

" And now to return to my own story. I wandered about the whole of that night in the neighbourhood of the farm ; I saw and heard much of what passed in consequence of Sir Walter's disappearance, and beheld his two faithless servants at your gate venting their hypocritical lamentations ; but I had promised Sir Walter not to divulge what I had witnessed, and therefore left matters to take their course. Disappointed in the hope of once more beholding you, and taking a last leave of you, I returned to my uncle's, and taking what I considered necessary, quitted Llan——, as I believed, for ever, and took the road to London. It would be useless now, dear Grace, to enter into a detail of all I suffered in my efforts to procure the means of subsistence. I was too proud to write to my uncle, though every day that I stayed in London, brought me nearer and nearer to the verge of famine. At last I saw an advertisement in the paper, which I found on the table of a little coffee-house, where I took the only meal I could allow myself during the day ; it was for a young man to undertake the management of a small farm beyond Bath, and as I knew that I possessed the necessary qualifications, I instantly applied at the address mentioned in London. My appearance and account of myself were satisfactoy and I was engaged and requested to proceed without delay to the place. At this moment I possessed but two shillings in the world, but I was afraid to own my poverty, lest it should operate to my disadvantage with my employer. I therefore commenced my journey on foot, but the weather was hot and I was weak, and I made such slow progress, that when I arrived at the farm, I was informed that they had given me up, supposing I had changed my mind, and had engaged another person. The disappointment, the exertion I had made, and the privations I had suffered, combined to overwhelm me.

"I walked back again to Bath, seven miles, and then sunk quite exhausted, a fever followed, and but for the charity of one individual I must have perished."

A long explanation here followed from Grace, by which Belgrave learned that Mr. Lovell, to whom he had been so deeply indebted, and her noble benefactor, the Earl of Melverley, were one and the same person, and Belgrave then proceeded.

"My generous friend did not leave his work half done," he continued, "for when I recovered, he inquired minutely into my circumstances and future prospects. I told him so much of the truth as was necessary, adding, that I should write to some friends, who, I hoped, would pay my passage to America, where, I did not doubt, I should be able to turn my farming knowledge to good account. He seemed to approve of the plan, but observed, 'that dependance on relations was precarious; there,' he added, putting two ten-pound notes into my hand, 'is what will enable you to carry your scheme into execution without delay.' Before I could utter a word he was gone, and conceiving I should best fulfil his intentions by so doing, within a few hours I departed for Bristol, where I expected to get a passage to New York.

"During all this time, by some strange fatality, as it appears, I had never heard a word of what passing at Llan——, and that I escaped the search that was making for me is astonishing, for I never disguised my name, or where I came from; but so it was, I was standing on the Back, as it is called, at Bristol, looking anxiously at different vessels, when some one put their hand on my shoulder. It was Sir Walter; and much as I was prejudiced against him, the sight of a familiar face, at this moment, was a cordial to my heart. He was more than friendly to me. I went with him to his hotel. He, like me, was just recovered from a dangerous illness, and, as I have said before, his intention, like mine, was to leave England. Neither of us was fully explanatory on the motives which actuated this resolve, but Sir Walter again pressed his offers of service on me, and I candidly told him my views. He persuaded me to put off till the morrow looking for a ship, and on the morrow he made me an offer of becoming his travelling companion in his intended tour on the Continent. The offer was too advantageous to be refused; I learnt every hour to know him better, for though he has faults they are more of his head than his heart; and to be brief, we left England the following week together, and could I have forgotten you, Grace, I should have had nothing to regret. I am not going to give you a history of our travels, but I must relate one strange event which occurred, and which, in fact, put an end to them. We were residing at the Villa de Campagna in the Papal States, the neighbourhood of which was kept in continual alarm by the reports that were circulated of the marauding incursions of a band of ruffians, who had taken up their residence in a ruinous old château about five miles from our residence, and, what interested us more than anything else in the stories that used to form the regular accompaniment to our breakfast table was, that the leader of the banditti was said to be an Englishman. The nearest habitation to ours was tenanted by a widow lady of Irish extraction, a rigid Catholic, who had married a Count of the Most Holy Roman Empire, and her two pretty daughters, Florence and Alina, whom she intended for nuns, were consequently kept in a state of the strictest seclusion, but of whom Sir Walter had sometimes caught a distant glance over the high hedge that separated our domains. They were very charitable, however, and none applied at their door in vain. One summer's evening, it appeared, the two daughters were amusing themselves in the garden with their guitar, the faint notes of which we had often heard twanging in the distance. 'Hush!' exclaimed Florence, 'there are footsteps approaching that are not of our household.' And so there were, for almost directly appeared a man, limping with seeming difficulty, who told them a pitiful story of having been plundered and ill-treated by the banditti, that he had fled for his life, and had been so terrified that he had climbed the hedge into the garden instead of making his way round to the gate. The tale was belived, he was taken into the house and attended to with great care, and as he pretended to be a stranger in the country—a fact which his imperfect knowledge of the language attested—he was invited to stay until perfectly recovered. What it was occurred to raise suspicion I cannot accurately tell you; but so it was, that the elder daughter Florence mistrusted the truth of his story, and more especially were her suspicions roused when she discovered that he declined retiring to bed, but preferred remaining in the kitchen, where he had supped, under the pretext of the sooner commencing his journey in the morning. Fearful of alarming her mother and sister, she communicated her suspicions only, after they had retired to rest for the night, to the old priest, who was the director of the household. He agreed with her that there could be no harm in taking precautions, and accordingly they proceeded together to the kitchen. where their guest, who had drank rather freely during the evening, was stationed. Cautiously she opened the door; he did not move, and, leaving the old priest to keep guard, she stole into the room. The stranger still remained motionless. She bent over him, and ascertained, beyond doubt, that he slept; but she observed at the same time that a drawn sword was in his hand, and a pair of pistols peeping from beneath his doublet. This was enough, for he had said he was totally unarmed when he encountered the banditti. Their whole household consisted but of two aged men and some women servants, and without a moment's hesitation, Florence flew across the garden, climbed the hedge, and made known to Sir Walter and I, who were still up, the predicament in which they were placed. There could be no doubt that the stranger was an associate of the banditti, who meditated admitting his fellows very quietly, when all were at rest; and we lost not a moment in rousing our servants, and quietly followed the heroic Florence across the garden to the spot where the robber was still sleeping.

"It was at first proposed that we should keep watch, and let him carry his plan into execution, and thus entrap more of the band into our power; but we were imperfectly armed, and could not place implicit confidence in our forces, and therefore thought it best to upset the whole of it at once, by taking the culprit into custody, and rousing the authorities of the neighbouring village. For this purpose, Sir Walter, myself, and the others behind us, entered the kitchen; but the moment we did so the object of our suspicion started up. The light which was burning beside him on the table fell full upon the face of Sir Walter, who stood as if transfixed in astonishment, while the stranger, with a dreadful oath, sprung to the other side of the room. 'It is useless to resist,' I exclaimed; 'your time is come—surrender, or I fire.'

"He uttered some indistinct exclamation, drew a pistol from his bosom, and took aim at Sir Walter; but I rushed between them and struck his arm down, the pistol going off and wounding me slightly in the side.

"It seemed that we were not a moment too soon, for instantly, upon the discharge of the pistol, three or four men rushed into the kitchen from the court yard; but we were too strong a party for them to attack, armed as we all were and prepared to receive them, and they fled with more precipitation than they had entered, leaving their chief in our hands, for two of our servants had seized him the moment he fired, and now held him firmly in their grasp. Sir Walter was sinking with terror and surprise. He had instantly recognized the voice of his depraved son, though it would have been difficult in the foreign dress he wore, and disguised as he was by immense whiskers and mustachios, together with his naturally dark skin, to have supposed him to be other than a native of the country. I saw there was a hard struggle in the unhappy father's mind, whether he should interpose to save the culprit from the fate that awaited him at the hands of justice. For myself I had no hesitation as to the part I should take, for I knew how sanguinary would be the punishment of his crime if he were delivered over to the law, and, wretch as he was, I determined to save him. There were none present who comprehended the relationship between Sir Walter and he but myself, and recommending the former in a whisper not to interfere, I desired the servants to bring away their prisoner to our residence, where, I observed to the ladies, there were better means than in their house of securing him till morning, when he would be delivered over to the proper authorities. They were very glad to get rid of such a dangerous inmate, and Sir Walter, understanding my hints, that I would take upon myself the responsibility of his wretched son's escape, agreed to my proposal, that he should remain with one servant to guard the ladies, lest the banditti should return. Up to the moment of our leaving the house our prisoner had been cool and sullen, expressing his feelings towards Sir Walter only by a malignant smile; but when we got into the open air and the clear moonlight, and he found he was being hurried away he knew not whither, for we had not let him hear our conference, he became violent, and attempted to shake off the two strong fellows who held him on either side. There were five of us, however, though I was scarcely to be reckoned upon, for I was getting very faint from loss of blood, having concealed from everyone that I was wounded while I remained in the house. We had to go a considerable round to the front of Sir Walter's residence, for we could not take our prisoner across the barriers between the gardens, though we had made that our way in going; and just as we arrived in sight of the gate I fancied I espied a figure gliding along under the shade of some trees on the opposite side of the road. It was not my object to let the prisoner escape to return to his companions; on the contrary, I intended to make conditions with him, being fully assured that Sir Walter would ratify anything I proposed. As may be supposed, therefore, I was anxious to avoid any collision with the bandits, though, from the cowardly manner in which they had taken flight, I did not think they were much to be feared. I kept my eye, however, on the suspicious spot, and stepped forward in advance of the prisoner and his guards to prevent their making a rush to rescue him; but my caution was fruitless, for at every instant the snap of firearms was heard, and the next our prisoner lay a corpse at my feet, a ball having passed through his body. I at first thought it was intended for me, but I was soon convinced by those around me that I was mistaken : his companions had shot him because they could not depend upon his not betraying them. Dreadful as was this termination of the wretched being's career of guilt, I confess, after the ffrst shock, I looked upon it as an event rather to be thankful for than to deplore, nor did Sir Walter think otherwise.

" ' It is the first time,' he observed, ' that I have breathed freely and with the consciousness of safety from the moment that he first threatened me when I refused to accede to his demands, for well I know what he threatened he would sooner or later perform, and this it was that made me so long a wanderer, in the hope of eluding him.'

" By the aid of money, which in that country can do anything, the affair was all hushed up, the body received Christian burial, without its being known beyond our own household in what manner he came by his death ; and Sir Walter having, as he observed, no longer any reason to fear, resolved to return to England and settle for the rest of his life at Llan——. Up to this moment, Grace, he and I had never come to a direct explanation, but my declining to accompany him to Llan—— brought it about ; and what was my astonishment when he confessed that you, and not Maria, were the object of his attachment, if it could be so called. I have very little more to add, dear Grace ; Sir Walter was pleased to think that his obligations to me for having, as he said, twice preserved his life, called for return on his part, which I considered far beyond my deserts or expectations. In fact, he rendered me independent, and, in addition, assured me that it was his intention to secure your mother's consent to our immediate marriage by engaging to make you the heiress of his fortune. Full of hope and expectation, I accompanied him to England, and after one day's rest only in London we were on the point of setting off for Llan——, when I accidentally encountered Tom Lewis, whom you must recollect at Llan——, and from him I learnt that which filled me with bitter disappointment, sorrow, and alarm, and put a stop to our journey. I learnt, too, at the same time, how shamefully and cruelly I had been aspersed ; but I knew that the time was not far distant when I should be able triumphantly to prove my innocence, and I did not, therefore, attempt to vindicate myself to him. The rest you know, dearest, or at least all that is necessary for y u to know, for it would interest oou very little to detail in what manner I was enabled to trace my unfortunate brother, and eventually one still dearer, my own, my beloved Grace."

CHAPTER XL.

" She is young ;
But her heart's youth is gone, and innocence,
And peace, and soft and gentle thoughts have fled,
A heart, the sanctuary of unhallowed fires,
That love has led to guilt."

ANON.

ON the evening following the arrival of the mournful cortége, all that remained of the Pride of the Village was consigned to its last resting-place, by the side of her father, in the humble, unostentatious churchyard of Llan—— and few among the numbers who were present were there who did not sympathise with the bereaved orphan who, the last of her race, now gazed, with eyes blinded with tears and a heart throbbing with agonising recollections of the past, into the dreary abode which was so soon to shroud from her for ever the last of her kindred. Few, however, regarded her with more pity and kind commiseration than an old, plainly-dressed, and weather-beaten man who leaned against one of the buttresses of the church, which partly concealed him from the thronging crowd, but did not intercept his view of her face or witnessing the whole of the impressive ceremony. Motionless he remained until it was ended, and Grace, supported by Sir Walter and Belgrave, left the ground, and then slowly he returned to the inn at which he had arrived but the hour previous.

It was the Earl of Melverley who thus unostentatiously did honour by his presence, not to the departed, for she, in his eyes, was but a weak, misled girl, whose exquisite beauty, like the wings of the gaudy butterfly, had only served as a lure to the destroyer; but it was Grace, the simple-minded, dutiful, kind, affectionate Grace, who had had influence enough over his cynical and austere mind to induce him to turn aside twenty miles from his direct journey to be assured that she was in as fair a way to eventual happiness as Mrs. Burton had represented. Circumstances unlooked for had recalled him to London on the very day that Grace and her companions left it, and he resolved once more to see the gentle girl whose virtues had almost made him acknowledge that women could be what he had once dreamed they were, and had been so rudely awakened; but Grace was gone hours before, and from Mrs. Burton he listened somewhat impatiently to the tale she told of his protegé's future prospects, and then resolved with his own eyes to judge whether the picture she drew of the person on whom Grace's future happiness would in all probability depend was a true likeness.

The earl's surprise was great when he recognised in Belgrave the young man in whom he had been so deeply interested nearly two years before in Bath. In the curiosity and somewhat better feeling which this discovery excited he found a temporary relief from the thoughts and recollections that "preyed upon his heart and gnawed his vitals;" but though his heart, seared as it was with suffering, still owned so far kindred with humanity as to rejoice in the prospect of happiness which awaited these creatures of his bounty, he shrank from the acknowledgments and expressions of their gratitude; nor was it until long after that Belgrave and Grace knew how highly they had been honoured.

Months passed away before the grief that had saddened Grace's young heart and brow was so far subdued that Belgrave Mansell dared venture to claim from her the reward of his constancy and long suffering; and perhaps he would even yet have deferred the fond request but that he was made painfully aware that there were those (probably envying her good fortune) who began to speak doubtingly of her situation, and wonder, after all, whether it really was his intention to marry her at a risk, or whether he wouldn't be prudent enough to wait till Sir Walter died and she really did get his money, for that there was many a slip between the cup and the lip was well known.

Too candid and sincere to affect a reluctance she did not feel, and deny her hand where she had long since acknowledged to have given her heart, Grace readily yielded her consent to become the wife of Belgrave as soon as the customary time for wearing mourning had expired. Yet, intensely happy as they were in each other's affection, and smiling and unclouded as were their worldly prospects, even at the altar the memory of the past threw a shade of pensiveness over the fair face of the bride and the handsome, manly features the bridegroom.

> " They wore a joy somewhat subdued
> With shadows from another mood ;
> They gave the young, the lost, the fair
> Tears that the happy well may spare."

If not the gayest in spirit, however, in outward show seldom had been so showy a wedding in Llan——— as that of Belgrave and Grace. It had been her wish that the marriage should be as private and unostentatious as had been the current of her life; but this did not suit Sir Walter's ideas. She must be married as became his heiress; and, accordingly, a handsome carriage for the bride and bridegroom was provided, Sir Walter himself following in his own and giving her away at the altar.

Belgrave had at first taken possession of the farm which had been his uncle's and afterwards his unfortunate brother's, who had deeply mortgaged it, and which encumbrance Belgrave paid off. Grace, to prevent any ill-natured observations, had remained as a boarder with the widow of the late clergyman, who still inhabited the rectory; but Sir Walter was already tired of living alone in his splendid mansion of Belle Retraite, of which he had at once taken possession, and for a time had found sufficient occupation in renovating, new modelling, and furnishing it. But when that was over he sighed for constant society, and right happy was he when the marriage of his two adopted children—for in that character he now considered them both—supplied this want, it being settled that the new-married pair were henceforth to reside with him.

"At least until your family becomes so large," he observed, with a smile, " that you are either compelled to take a larger house or turn me out of this to make room for them."

But, to return to the wedding—that most important and interesting event in human life. It had at first been proposed by Sir Walter to give a splendid entertainment, and send cards to all the gentry round, but Grace's influence prevailed over this intention. She wanted time, she said, and instruction to enable her to play the part of hostess of such a mansion with propriety; and though both Sir Walter and Belgrave warmly asserted and believed that she possessed a " native elegance and ease beyond the reach of art," she was too diffident and modest to believe that this was other than the effect of their partiality. She did not, however, make the same objection to the treat which Sir Walter, on a slight hint from Belgrave, proposed to give to all who were not above joining in a merry dance on the village green and partaking of the substantial old English fare—roast turkey and chine, sirloins of beef, legs of mutton, and all the suitable appendages of pies and puddings, with plenty of ale and cider; and she took especial care that the cottages of those who were prevented by age or infirmity from joining in the festive scene should be to the full partakers of its comforts. Among those, old Alice, her youthful friend, was particularly recommended to the care of the steward; and a couple of bottles of good old wine, and a large piece of wedding-cake added to the portion assigned her, which was rendered still more acceptable by a kind note, in Grace's own handwriting, hoping that she would enjoy it.

" Heaven bless her !" exclaimed the old woman, wiping away the tears that dimmed her spectacles. " Heaven bless her sweet face! How often have I heard people admiring her sister, and passing over Grace as if she was nobody; but I always did her justice."

Dressed in a beautiful blonde dress, over white satin, her hair, neck, and arms encircled with strings of the purest and most costly pearls, the gift of Sir Walter, her cheeks glowing with modesty, and her eyes glittering through tears of happiness, Grace certainly looked very lovely as, with Belgrave and Sir Walter on either hand, she walked through the assembled ranks, many of whom were her former associates, and very few of whom were not her friends, and received their congratulations. But she was most happy when this ceremony, which she had submitted to in compliance with Sir Walter's wish, was over, and she escaped from the overwhelming gaze and scrutiny of so many eyes.

Grace's first care, when she became possessed of the means, by Sir Walter settling a handsome dowry for her sole use and benefit at her marriage, was to seek out and reward all those who had shown kindness to her in adversity even the humble Becky, Mrs. Stevens's servant, shared with her mistress in the handsome present which was sent to Bath on the occasion of Mr. Belgrave Mansell's marriage; while Jane, whose good-natured exertions had been the means of introducing Grace to Mrs. Somerford, and thus enabled her to prevent her mother's feeling the actual pressure of want, was rendered supremely proud and happy by being sent for to fill the important office of upper housemaid in the establishment at Belle Retraite. The old servants of her lamented father, too, were all sharers in her bounty, especially the simple, well-meaning Sally, who had recently married one of her former fellow servants, and was now rendered happy and independent for life, by the gift of a cottage and garden by her former favourites, Belgrave and Grace. But none, perhaps, more intensely felt the blessing of Grace's well-deserved prosperity than poor Joe, the dumb boy, who, having recived the full benefit of instruction in the noble institution in which he had been placed by the Earl of Melverley, was, at the request of her who had been from infancy his firm friend, sent down to Llan——, without being made acquainted whither he was going, or whom he was to see. To describe his transports would be impossible, when he beheld his young benefactress, and by degrees comprehended the change of fortune that had attended her, and that he was henceforth to remain with her, having been rendered capable by instruction of acting as under gardener. He laughed, cried, and laughed again, in a breath; but that which gratified Grace most was, that when his first wild transports were over, she found he had been rendered capable of giving a more rational proof of his gratitude in well and neatly-written thanks for all her kindness, and a promise to deserve it by future good conduct; a promise which was kept to the letter.

By Belgrave's directions, a plain, handsome monument was placed over the grave of Mrs. Woodford, in the burial-ground at Bath; and the first excursion which Grace took with her happy husband from Llan——, six months after their marriage, was to visit this spot.

On this occasion, Mrs. Mansell did not fail to call on those who had any claim on her remembrance; and among them Mrs. Stevens, from whom, worldly and avaricious as she was, as much kindness had been shown to the former as her nature had been capable of. That she was received with a profusion of compliments and expressions of satisfaction at her good fortune, may be easily conceived; but Grace waited impatiently for an opportunity of asking her a question, which she was very desirous of having answered.

"Your sister, Mrs. Freeman," she inquired; "have you heard of her lately?"

"Ah, Miss Grace—I beg your pardon—Mrs. Mansell, I should have said," she replied, bursting into tears—"I have had a world of trouble about

Susan; but she always was a disgrace to me and my family. But, however, I don't think it will be for long, now; for she is dying by inches in the infirmary; and hard enough it is on me to find her in all she wants there. And, indeed, I have often thought of writing to you, because I know you are so kind and good; but when I mentioned it to her, I thought she would have gone into fits, for she said you was the last person on earth that she could have anything to hope from."

All remembrance of Mrs. Freeman's faults were instantly banished from Grace's gentle bosom at hearing this, and she directly put a handsome sum of money into Mrs. Stevens's hand, for the purpose of supplying her unfortunate sister with every comfort.

"Tell her, too, from me," she observed, "that if she would not object to my visiting her, I will stay another day in Bath for that purpose. I have not forgotten with what kindness she soothed me, and bore with my complainings, when my poor mother's death left me desolate and alone in the world."

Grace had just retired from the dinner-table at the hotel at which she and her husband were staying, when she was informed a person wished to speak to her, and in a few moments Mr. Stevens entered the room.

"My poor sister, Mrs. Mansell!" she exclaimed, bursting into tears, "she is dying, and she says she should die happier if she could hear from your own lips————"

Grace lost not a moment in attending her, and in a few minutes they entered together the ward of the infirmary which contained the wretched victim of vice.

The wretched woman stretched out her worn hand in reply to Grace's gentle soothing, but in vain she tried for some moments to utter a word.

"I am dying, Grace," she at last articulated. "Oh! it is hard to die! so young, too, and with the fears, the horrid fears that there is an hereafter, where, where——Oh! save me! save me!" she uttered, with frantic vehemence, "I will strive—I will repent—I will try to make amends—Ah, it will not go; there—there—there is the same horrid form, it threatens me—save me! save me!"

She sank back fainting and exhausted on the pillow, and Grace—her eyes streaming with tears—awaited with anxiety the moment when she should revive sufficiently to listen to the words of comfort with which she would fain have spoken peace to her departing spirit; but it was in vain, it had been the last effort of expiring nature which had prompted that tremendous struggle; the countenance grew more and more livid, the features more rigid and contracted, and the fixed glazed eyes confirmed what the nurse whispered, in compassionate accents, that all was over.

———————

YEARS have passed, and the memory of the unrighteous is forgotten, while Grace, loving and beloved, has lived to look upon all that troubled her as only a painful dream which has passed away, leaving in its place the certainty of substantial happiness which arises from a steady perseverance in well-doing, surrounded with a rising, beautiful, and united family and encompassed on all sides with the enduring effects of her benevolence and care for her fellow-creatures, there is little fear that, when she closes her career of usefulness she shall soon be forgotten; while the plain marble tablet that records simply the day of her birth and of her death, and the fond remembrances that still exist in the memory of Grace and Belgrave is all that remains of the Pride of the Village.

www.ingramcontent.com/pod-product-compliance
Lightning Source LLC
Chambersburg PA
CBHW080724020726
47503CB00010B/2780